THE HO

After taking a Mo...
Elizabeth James t...
worked with chil...
ran a bookshop with her husband, but since 1987
has been writing full time.

Acclaim for *Claudia and Amy*

'This is a book you won't put down. I loved it'
Denise Robertson

'Vivid, utterly absorbing – a beautiful and extraordinary book'
Cynthia Harrod-Eagles

'An appealing story about two radically different women'
Lisa Appignanesi

'Brilliantly drawn characters'
Elizabeth Elgin

By the same author

CLAUDIA AND AMY

ELIZABETH JAMES

The House Above the Sea

HarperCollins*Publishers*

This novel is entirely a work of fiction.
The names, characters and incidents portrayed
in it are the work of the author's imagination.
Any resemblance to actual persons, living or dead,
events or localities is entirely coincidental.

HarperCollins*Publishers*
77–85 Fulham Palace Road,
Hammersmith, London w6 8jb

This paperback edition 1999
1 3 5 7 9 8 6 4 2

First published in Great Britain by
HarperCollins*Publishers* 1999

A catalogue record for this book
is available from the British Library

ISBN 0 00 649940 6

Typeset in Ehrhardt
by Palimpsest Book Production Limited,
Polmont, Stirlingshire
Printed and bound in Great Britain by
Caledonian International Book Manufacturing Ltd, Glasgow

THANKS

To Rachel Hore, Susan Opie and Sarah Molloy for extreme patience and forbearance.

To Vivienne Furtwängler, Llinos Merks, David Thomas, Olwen Powell for invaluable large and small items of background information.

To Sandy and David, Angus, Viv, Angela and Alan, Judith, Sue H and Sue P, who were good friends through bad times. And to my wonderful family.

Prologue
May 1986

❀❀❀

'Not in the churchyard,' Odile had insisted. 'It would be a lie. He never went to church.'

A long, long time ago, and probably frivolously, Jerome had expressed a desire for his ashes to be buried in the little graveyard above Plas Felix. For nearly nine years Olivier's had lain there, in a shady corner, beneath a stone plaque. But Odile was adamant. The house itself, she decided, was the place her husband had loved best in all the world, and his ashes must be scattered there, on the wind. In her eyes, death had transformed Jerome from oppressor to lifelong companion, guardian angel, and she wept for him piteously. There was no resisting her grief.

'I won't come with you,' she told her children. 'I couldn't bear it. This is something I'm asking you to do for me.' She included Kate quite naturally in the mission.

Pascal collected his father's ashes from the crematorium. The woman who released them to him asked suspiciously what he intended to do with them. He had the impression that there were all manner of rules and regulations she was just dying to invoke.

'Goodness knows.' He shrugged, deliberately vague. 'We'll have to have a family confab first . . .'

Obituaries in the up-market dailies had spoken of a brilliant mind, a certain naïve vanity, an ill-advised populism that led him to spread himself too widely and too thin . . . A redemption, ultimately, through tragedy and good works. A number of bereaved parents whom Jerome had helped wrote gratefully of his patience and persistence, the generous way he gave of his time. To Kate his funeral seemed a social ritual for the benefit of elderly and ageing ex-colleagues, rather than an expression of the family's personal grief.

I

The unfolding nuclear disaster at Chernobyl furnished an unnerving backdrop to the days of mourning, the sickly sense of poison loosed on the world, seeping and dripping in the moist air.

In accordance with Odile's wishes, her three children – Beatrice, Pascal and Nelly – plus Kate, drove down to Wales with Jerome's ashes. They used Pascal's car, taking turns to drive.

A half-hysterical gaiety seized them as they put space between themselves and the death-permeated atmosphere of grieving and condolence, funeral arrangements, form-filling, legal correspondence – as if they were children bunking off school. Their nerves were frayed and frazzled by the last few days and the tension emerged in black humour, dour honesty. Never before had Kate felt so absolutely and unquestionably part of the family.

'We're all of us fucked up in one way or another,' Nelly declared cheerfully. 'Now he's dead, can we put the blame on Pa?'

'Lives of quiet desperation,' Beatrice murmured.

'He has to be the ultimate emasculating father.' Pascal sat in the rear, pale and impassive behind expensive-looking tinted glasses. 'Successful, exuberant, no self-doubts, a guilt-free adulterer . . .'

'A life tailor-made for his convenience,' Beatrice chimed in. 'Domesticated wifey to pander to his every need . . . Until she turned.'

'Yeah, the bastard,' Nelly said. 'But he *was* my big, lovely dad.'

'Look at Odile now.' Kate pulled out into the fast lane, enjoying the power of Pascal's Volvo. 'It seems literally years since she last said an amiable word about Jerome. But suddenly it's as if he was St Francis and Albert Einstein rolled into one.'

As the car sped westward she was ambushed by a sudden vivid sense of the world as it had felt to her thirty years ago – more – when she'd first set eyes on the Felix family.

PART 1

The Fifties

Chapter One
1955

❧❦❧

'They're nice people, Kate. They're warm and easy-going. Jerome says the kids are all dying to meet you . . .'

Ellis Stephens turned his harassed attention from the tea-chest he was packing to his fourteen-year-old daughter standing in the doorway. His voice sounded echoey in the dismantled bedroom.

'They don't know me from Adam!' Kate was angry, exasperated. Her father must see how his glib lie insulted her intelligence. 'I'm just some stranger who's being dumped on them. Some nobody!' She was shouting now, though she'd vowed to keep calm this time.

'For God's sake! Do you have to be so bloody bolshy and obstructive all the time? Can't you see I've got enough on my plate?'

When her mother had first died – almost six months ago now – Ellis had been endlessly gentle, endlessly concerned. But, finally, it was clear he considered that Kate had indulged her grief for long enough. He had a new job waiting for him in an American college. A new life. The upheaval of selling up the family home, sorting out his affairs this side of the Atlantic had taken its toll of his patience. He was increasingly irritated with Kate's moods, her sulks and tears. It was time for her to pull her socks up.

'Let me come with you.' Even Kate was repelled by the pleading in her voice, repetitive and scratchy as a worn gramophone record.

'You can't. And that's that. We've got nowhere to live over there. I'll have all manner of arrangements to make . . .' Ellis reverted to the staleness of his own litany. His brown eyes took on the glazed, withdrawing look that left her stranded, thrashing

5

uselessly, totally alone. 'You'll be joining me soon enough, once everything's settled.'

Kate stood staring at the bare lino, its grey and red pattern blurred by the effortless tears that welled from her eyes.

The bombshell had landed a month or so back, after one of Ellis's lunches with Jerome Felix – the two had been friends since they were at Cambridge together. For as long as Kate could remember her father had spoken his name with a special irrepressible smile. Because Jerome was famous – in demand on radio shows like *Any Questions* and the *Brains Trust*. 'The philosopher with the common touch', the papers called him. Kate had never met the man – he was someone Ellis kept to himself, saw for drinks or lunches, as if his wife and daughter would not be equal to such exalted company. But she'd seen him on television once or twice. Jerome had a small, clipped beard that didn't disguise the rounded baby-face beneath and, when he talked, he seemed to mock his own cleverness with a private, mischievous smirk.

'Jerome's been offering you a home for the summer, Kate,' Ellis had announced, breezing in the door after their lunch, expansive with the beer and the good company. But he spoke with an unconvincing casualness that showed he anticipated trouble. 'At their place on the Welsh coast, with the whole family. It'll solve everything . . . You'll be taken care of while I go on ahead and get things moving over there . . .'

Ellis had stayed with the Felixes once, a couple of years ago, after a seminar in Bangor. He'd come back raving about the size and situation of his friend's house.

'The kids are a bit wild, though.'

There were four of them, apparently, and they'd stayed up until midnight, wandering in and out of the room where the adults sat talking, constantly interrupting their conversation. Ellis hated that sort of thing and it didn't happen in the Stephens family. Kate could remember the quiet glow she'd enjoyed at her own implied superiority.

And now her father was proposing to loose her among this undisciplined horde. Kate had been speechless at first.

6

'You don't mean it,' she said, after a long, incredulous silence.

Ellis frowned and shrugged defensively. 'Of course I mean it . . . It's the perfect solution . . . You'll like them, Kate. They're fun.'

She was devastated by her father's bad faith. The wildness he'd deplored transformed on an instant into 'fun'. And, apart from that, how could he think she was in a mood for anything of the sort, when each night she lay clenched with misery, and woke to the despairing knowledge that she would never see her mother again.

'I can't . . .'

'Don't be silly, Kate.' He'd become irritated. 'It's time you started to look outward and get on with your life.'

For a month they repeated this dialogue, reached the same stalemate. Only Ellis — being an adult — prevailed. While Kate felt herself powerless and altogether betrayed.

Soon after six in the morning on the first day of the school summer holidays, Ellis unlocked his black Morris Minor, ready for the drive to North Wales.

Sliding into the passenger seat, Kate felt as if she'd swallowed a tennis ball-sized lump of granite. While Ellis arranged her two suitcases, her wellingtons and her tennis racket in the boot, she stared at the unremarkable house of grey-brown brick in Stapleton Road, Camberwell Green, that had been her home for the last seven years. Dark, under a whitish-gold, watercoloury sky, it looked identical to the two houses that flanked it, identical to the whole row of houses. But, for Kate, the building was imbued with the shadowy domestic warmth of their particular lives — her own and her parents'. And here she was leaving it — so casually, it barely seemed possible — forever. Those empty rooms held the last ghostly traces of her mother's aura. Kate gazed helplessly at the blank windowpanes.

As Ellis sat down beside her, she saw him glance up, following the direction of her eyes. But he made no comment and Kate guessed he was scared of unleashing in her a rush of the inconvenient emotion he was trying so resolutely to avoid.

'Ready?' he asked in a neutral tone of voice.

Kate nodded and, as the car pulled away, she gazed stolidly ahead of her.

It was a morning of raw, weak sunshine, alternating with periods when the sky turned a deep dramatic blue-grey and the grass and trees shone yellow-green. Once they'd left London behind and were bowling along roads with fields on either side, through unknown villages and hamlets, Kate began to feel a little better.

She and Ellis hardly spoke. And as usual, when there was nothing specially pressing to think about, pictures of Rose, her mother, drifted into Kate's mind. There was one particular portrait – the first she'd ever stuck into her white Woolworths photo-album – that had become imprinted on her brain like a flesh-and-blood memory. It showed Rose as she really was – her fine, straight dark hair worn in a child's bob, the fringe shading eyes that were alert like a bird's. She looked puckish, observant and deeply unsure of herself.

'You're like sisters,' a neighbour used to gush. After she'd gone, Kate and Rose would pull faces at one another, disowning the cliché. Yet Kate remembered the two of them strolling down Oxford Street last summer, arm-in-arm, up in town to buy a new dress for Kate, have lunch in Selfridges, then go to the pictures. And Rose's pleasure in the day to come had been as gleeful as Kate's own, as if the seriousness of being an adult had somehow passed her by.

She and Rose seemed always in cahoots, Ellis the odd man out, grown-up and vaguely disapproving. His attitude made Rose nervous and eager to please, but sometimes she would be seized by a fit of giddy playfulness. Kate recalled her imitating the telly puppet, Muffin the Mule, in a grotesque, stiff-legged dance that was spot-on, poetry in motion. Kate had laughed delightedly. Ellis gave a stage-sigh, rolling his eyes jokily heavenwards. But you could sense the irritation that bubbled below the surface of his pretend-tolerance.

A lot of the time he seemed to lump his wife and daughter together, with the unspoken implication that they were infantile beings whom, by the sweat of his brow, it was his lot to feed, clothe and house. So perhaps when the neighbour compared them to sisters she had not been so wide of the mark.

8

'Penny for your thoughts.' Suddenly, awkwardly, Ellis broke the silence between them.

'I'm thinking about Mum,' Kate said defiantly, knowing the admission would spark his impatience.

'I wish you'd –' Abruptly he checked himself.

'What? Forget her?' She turned towards him. 'It's easy for you. You'd gone off her anyway. You picked on her. She got on your nerves!'

Kate had never said anything so shocking before. Her voice seemed to ring in the close confines of the car, sounding offensive and spiteful. Ellis didn't reply, but she could see how shaken he was.

Around lunch-time Ellis stopped the car alongside a lake. He'd planned for them to eat their sandwiches here. They were in Wales by this time, in wild mountain country so spectacular that they'd marvelled at it together, breaking the tense hush that had prevailed ever since Kate had rounded on him with such hostile passion.

She slid out of her seat. 'I'm going down to look at the water.'

He gestured at the mountains and the dark surface of the lake. 'Jerome said to be sure and have our picnic here. It *is* glorious, isn't it . . .'

Kate didn't reply. He watched her go, upright and somehow disdainful, experiencing an ache of love for her lanky figure. The gingham dress she was wearing had grown too short, revealing far too much of her coltish legs. She'd shot up since last year when Rose must have bought it for her. He would give Odile, Jerome's wife, some money, ask her to take Kate shopping and buy her some suitable new clothes. Since Rose died, Kate's black hair had grown to shoulder-length, hanging in rat's-tails that Ellis found oddly touching. Rose used to keep her daughter's hair tidily clipped to chin level. Watching her stoop to dabble her hands in the shallows of the lake, Ellis thought – as he'd thought before – that his child looked waif-like and vaguely neglected.

He poured himself some tea from the Thermos. Privately Ellis had hoped the journey to Wales would be in the nature of a day out, what with the novelty of the scenery, the alfresco lunch. Instead he was forced to confirm what had grown increasingly clear to him over the last months – that, without Rose to bridge the gap between them, he and Kate were becoming near-strangers.

In the days when his wife was alive, the three of them used to sing in the car, Ellis in his operatic tenor vein, Rose doing Alma Cogan, Kate giggling and joining in with an outrageous spoof French accent. Such joint high spirits seemed almost unimaginable now.

He was still shaky from the harsh accusation Kate had flung at him in the car. Outwardly he'd ignored it. In all conscience he could not refute it. He *had* become weary of his wife's fey childishness. Even her moments of wild gaiety, which he'd once found so adorable, had come to grate. When she did her mad, inspired dances, or aped some comedian – with uncanny skill, he had to admit – Ellis experienced the blooming of an annoyance he couldn't hide.

Rose had always been fragile but, in the face of his increasing impatience, she'd become timid and apologetic, her bright bird's eyes hurt and mistrustful. The process saddened him, but also – Ellis couldn't deny it – afforded him a cruel, furtive pleasure. Somehow, though, he'd deluded himself that Kate was a child, too young to notice their covert manoeuvring. The thought that she'd been observing them all along was deeply disconcerting.

How ironic it was that Rose had died in a car crash. Her Riley had collided with a lorry – God knows how – in the Walworth Road. One thing his wife had been was a first-rate driver. Vastly more adroit than he. Sitting beside her while she chauffeured them round London, absorbed and oblivious of his attention, Ellis could almost recapture the easy tenderness he'd felt when, as a young student, he'd first fallen in love with her.

He drained the last dregs of his tea from the plastic picnic mug. 'Kate!' he called. 'Your sandwiches are getting cold.'

It was a feeble joke and she didn't acknowledge it. But his daughter turned away from the water's edge and began to walk slowly towards him. With a love he found almost impossible to express, Ellis eyed her adolescent skinniness, the scowling ungraciousness of her expression. When this summer was over and they were carving out a life for themselves in the States, he clung to the hope that a new closeness could develop between them. Ellis took heart. There was time enough for things to mend.

Chapter Two

❦❦❦

Ellis signalled, slowed, and pulled abruptly on to the offside grass verge. He rolled down his window, stuck his head out and pointed. 'That's the place, Kate . . . Look.'

She peered, craning her neck. To their right a field fell steeply away, its greenness dotted with the dirty white of grazing sheep. At the far end the slope flattened out. Some scrubby bushes marked the boundary, and beyond them she could see the long outline of a mauvish roof with chimneys and gables standing out against the misty blue of sky or sea – it was hard to tell which. Kate stared with misgiving. The place seemed big and isolated like an institution of some sort – an old folk's home or an orphanage.

'Well, say something . . .' There was a hectoring quality to her father's joviality.

Kate shrugged. 'Say what?' Ellis was leaving her here against her will – he couldn't, surely, expect her to enthuse.

'Oh . . .' His exasperation bubbled to the surface. Savagely he revved the car-engine. 'Just carry on the way you are, Kate! Don't even try . . .' Ellis ran out of steam, pulled sharply out on to the road again.

Fifty yards further on a pair of stone gateposts flanked the entrance to a lane that veered off to the right. Her father took the turning and began to follow it slowly and cautiously. The surface was rough and ready, though the worst of the ruts had been levelled with a layer of stone chippings. A rocky wall, about five feet high and overgrown with ivy and brambles, ran alongside the path.

Suddenly, ahead of them, a figure jumped out from behind a thicket of weeds and capered into the middle of the road. It was a girl about Kate's age, grinning and waving her arms, signalling them to stop.

Ellis braked and glided to a halt. The stranger bounced up to them. She wore plimsolls and pink shorts, a rose-coloured sleeveless top. Kate had a quick impression of long narrow eyes, a shaggy fringe, a wide smile.

The girl bent down so her face was on a level with Ellis's window, which was still open. 'Hello, Ellis,' she said breezily. 'Do you remember me? I'm Nelly.'

This must be one of the 'wild' children. Kate was impressed by her casual familiarity. Her father had always been sarcastic about brats who addressed their elders by their Christian names.

But he replied pleasantly enough, 'Hello, Nelly. Are you going to hop in?'

The girl opened the rear door and slid into the back seat. Kate glanced over her shoulder, acknowledging her presence. She was disconcerted by the newcomer's self-possession, her look of health and vitality. Nelly had slim, tanned arms and legs, thick hair encompassing all shades of blonde from mousey honey to a sun-bleached near-white.

'May I introduce my daughter Kate,' Ellis announced, with a formality that Kate found embarrassing.

Nelly leaned forward between the two front seats. Her smile took on an amused, mischievous edge. 'Hello, Kate. I've been waiting out there for nearly an hour for you to come. I wanted to be the first to see you.'

'Hello,' Kate mumbled.

She couldn't suppress a twinge of gratification at Nelly's frank declaration, but struggled to maintain the aggrieved, aloof air with which she'd punished Ellis throughout the journey.

The car continued on down the lane, eventually reaching a high wall, a tall gateway. A faded sign, professionally lettered, blue on white, read Plas Tan-yr-Allt. Kate guessed it to be the name of the house. Underneath, in shaky letters, using bright pink paint that looked like nail varnish, someone had printed the words Plas Felix.

'Plas Felix. That's what Dad always calls the house,' Nelly explained. 'Well, we all do . . . And one day me and Olivier got some paint and wrote it on the sign. Dad was cross at first, but now it feels as if it's always been there . . .'

Beyond the gateway, they found themselves in a tarred courtyard and in front of them was the huge house Kate and Ellis had viewed from a distance.

'This is our little grey home in the west,' Nelly said. There was something in her voice – not an accent as much as a musical rise and fall – that Kate thought of as peculiarly Welsh.

The building was not particularly attractive. It looked sturdily built, was rendered in sandy brown plaster, and had lots of windows. Those downstairs were tall, the ones on the first floor smaller and narrower. At roof level three gables jutted, each with its own central window.

'Come upstairs with me,' Nelly urged Kate. 'I'll show you your room right away.'

'Yes, go on Kate.' Ellis latched on to Nelly's eagerness.

The house door – a massive oaken affair – stood open and Nelly led Kate, via a narrow vestibule, into a large hall that smelt strongly of wax polish and had the warm, enclosed feel of sunshine striking through glass. Straight ahead of them was an imposing staircase, carpeted in jade green, with a carved brown wooden balustrade.

'Up here.' Nelly ran up the stairs two at a time. At the top was a long corridor extending in both direction. She turned right, carried on to the last door, which she pushed open.

Kate followed in her slipstream, unwilling but bemused and helpless. Under the circumstances it was impossible to maintain the show of passive resistance with which she'd comforted herself all day. In any case, she had the impression that Nelly, blithely involved in her own vivacious performance, would simply not have noticed.

'This is your pied-à-terre,' she announced, standing aside to allow Kate to enter first.

The room was impressive, large and white, with the mellow, sun-warmed late afternoon glow Kate had noticed downstairs, only

14

here it was lighter, brighter. She crossed straight to the window and mentally caught her breath. Outside – beyond a long, sloping field that appeared to end in a steep drop – the sea extended, calm and glittering, blending in the distance, almost imperceptibly, with the thin blue of the sky. Kate experienced a dazzled soaring of the spirits.

Impulsively she turned to Nelly. 'Fancy having *this* outside your bedroom window.'

Nelly shrugged. 'I'm used to it. It just seems natural.'

She paced the room, drawing Kate's attention to its various amenities. A bed, at least four feet wide, covered with a red and blue striped blanket. A white wardrobe. A multi-coloured, plaited rag-rug which – so Nelly informed her – Jerome had brought back from a lecture tour in New England. A table with a blue and white tiled top, above which three startling pastel studies of science-fiction monsters had been fixed to the wall with drawing-pins.

'Olivier did those for you. My little brother. He's mad keen on drawing and those are what he does at the moment. A little while ago it was dragons and griffons and things.'

Kate examined it all with a growing sense of surprise and appreciation that dented the hard, protective shell with which she surrounded herself. The room had been prepared with thought-fulness, even gusto, as if, far from an inconvenient nonentity who'd been foisted on them, the family saw her in the light of a welcome guest. And – disloyal thought – it was so much bigger and brighter than her bedroom at home with its dreary view over grey, undistinguished Stapleton Road.

'This is lovely.' Kate's voice sounded sad and hollow, but Nelly seemed not to notice.

She pointed out a door in the left-hand wall, between the bed and the wardrobe.

'See this.' She flung it open. 'Look, Kate, it leads through into my room.'

Kate peered through the opening, catching a brief glimpse of floor-to-ceiling shelves crammed with books, stuffed toys, brightly coloured boxes full of assorted junk, before the door was closed again.

'We'll be able to have fun in the dorm . . .' Nelly's grin was somehow unfocused, as if fuelled by its own momentum. 'Midnight feasts and schoolgirl confidences.'

Kate gave a crooked smile in reply to what she perceived as Nelly's irony. Privately she thought the girl affected, a show-off. All the same, she couldn't help being intrigued by the melodic timbre of her voice, her narrow, excitable eyes. Hot eyes. Kate envied the luxuriance of her hair, the way she looked in her top and shorts, so sharp and modern. Kate was ruefully aware of her own childish frock, too short and badly cut. Even more than that, Nelly made her conscious of how low she was in spirits. Kate felt dead and Nelly was so buoyantly alive.

'Come and meet the others,' she enthused.

'OK.'

With a resigned sinking of the heart, Kate allowed herself to be led back downstairs.

Odile, Jerome's Swiss-French wife, sat at the head of the long family table. She made Kate think of a ballet dancer, the way her dark hair was swept back into a low chignon. Her eyes were long and narrow, like Nelly's. In front of her was a large rectangular dish of something hot with melted cheese on top, which she was serving with a large spoon.

'Lasagna, Kate?'

'Please.'

Kate nodded composedly, concealing the fact that she had not the faintest idea what lasagna was. It seemed vital to her not to let the Stephens family down. She only hoped she'd be able to eat whatever it was with the same appearance of sang-froid, without heaving or gagging ignominiously.

While passing the plate Odile gave an encouraging smile, as if she understood that Kate felt out of her depth. On first acquaintance Odile was the one, out of all of them, with whom she felt safe. There was something quiet and still about her that contrasted

16

reassuringly with Nelly's exuberance, Jerome's clever-dick smile. Her movements were unhurried. She wore a scoop-necked grey dress, mid calf-length, with a loose waistline and a gathered skirt that fell in graceful folds like the garments you saw in medieval paintings.

Kate felt intimidated by the two elder children, Beatrice and Pascal, both extravagantly good-looking, casually self-assured. Both had Odile's long, slanting eyes. Only Olivier – at twelve the baby of the family – had the round, grey-green eyes of his father.

Jerome sat at the foot of the table, portly and bearded in a black polo-necked sweater that was tight on him. Close by stood two uncorked bottles of red wine.

He turned to Pascal. 'Do the honours with the liquor, won't you, old man.'

The way he said 'old man' was sort of satirical, Kate thought, like Harry Lime in the *Third Man* film.

Pascal got to his feet and began to dispense the wine, starting with Ellis. Covertly Kate admired the easy negligence with which he leaned and poured. On his spare, broad-shouldered frame the blue shirt and pale khaki trousers hung loose and elegant. His dark hair fell in lax curls across his forehead.

Olivier was allowed half a glass of wine, Nelly two-thirds. Both clamoured that they'd been given short measure. Pascal made a show of knocking their heads together. Reaching her, he cocked one eyebrow enquiringly, offering the bottle, his smile oblique and careless.

'No, thank you.' She shook her head, looked down again at her plate. Rose and Ellis had always disapproved of children being offered alcohol. Kate had never touched wine, but didn't like the smell. And anyway the lasagna was risk enough to take for one evening.

'You sure?' His tone was matter-of-fact, equal-to-equal, his voice deep as a man's.

'It's all right, Kate,' Ellis put in, hastily disowning his own injunction.

'No, really.' She smiled shyly up at Pascal.

17

'Sea green. Incorruptible,' Jerome intoned mysteriously. It was clearly a joke of some sort, but Kate didn't get it.

Cautiously she took her first forkful of lasagna. On furtive inspection it had proved to consist mainly of minced meat, with bits of bacon and vegetable in it – nothing too strange or alarming. Experimentally Kate chewed it. At once her taste-buds were flooded with a flavour that was deep and rich and concentrated, quite unlike anything Rose had ever cooked. She took another forkful. It tasted even better. There was a sort of sauce mixed in with it and some flat, chewy stuff. But it was all really rather nice. Kate's relief was private, but profound.

They were eating in a large downstairs room with French windows open on to a terrace, a sort of platform on which the house was built and which raised it above the field Kate had seen from upstairs. From here the view of the sea was more restricted. The broad, grassy slope dominated the foreground, occupied now by ten or a dozen peaceful-looking horses, ambling to and fro and cropping the grass.

Jerome saw her looking. 'They're not our beasts,' he explained. 'They belong to the local riding-school. I let them graze here and in gratitude they turn a blind eye to my unruly sprogs riding them bare-backed when the fancy takes them.'

'Pa likes to live in his own cosy version of the truth.' Beatrice, the eldest of the Felix children, addressed the table in general. 'In actual fact, every time I see George Beynon he moans about Nelly and Olivier taking liberties . . .'

Jerome seemed amused by his daughter's challenge. 'And we turn a blind ear to his carping.'

'It's easy for you,' Beatrice replied tartly. 'Sitting in your ivory tower while he picks on Ma and me.'

Kate thought her awe-inspiring. So engagingly petulant, with such long, silky brown hair, such clear skin, her neck so straight and slender. She wore black cotton trousers and a black knitted top, off-the-shoulder, like a film star. The sort of outfit Rose would have pronounced 'unsuitable', though anyone could see Beatrice looked wonderful in it.

18

Jerome laughed at her provocation. He sat leaning on one elbow in an attitude of convivial relaxation, using just a fork to eat his lasagna and washing it down with liberal gulps of red wine.

He turned his attention to Ellis. 'What's the latest on your move then, old man? Everything sorted out at last?'

'Not a bit of it.' Ellis spread his hands in mock despair. 'We've got nowhere to live. I've got no curriculum. No one answers my letters. I've sold all the furniture. The rest of my worldly goods are in store – they insisted on re-packing all the tea-chests at my expense . . .' He gave a wry, appealing smile. 'What with one thing and another, everything than *can* go wrong, has.'

For Jerome's benefit, Kate noticed sourly, her father made light of his tribulations, when for the last month or so he'd been like a bear with a sore head.

'Never mind. Trust us to keep the sprog entertained while you disentangle your problems, free as air.' Jerome threw Kate a conspiratorial glance which she ignored.

From a table near the door Odile fetched two large pottery bowls. Kate eyed them discreetly. One held a jumble of unfamiliar leaves topped with small cubes of smelly blue cheese and slices of what looked like raw mushroom. In the other, large chunks of ripe, misshapen tomatoes glistened with an oily dressing which reeked of some kind of pungent seasoning. It all looked aggressively hearty and aromatic. Kate decided to pass.

Odile placed the bowls on the table, deftly tossed the green leaves with a wooden spoon and fork. In her sculptural grey dress she seemed the embodiment of domestic savoir-faire. 'Please don't be concerned about your daughter, Ellis,' she said in her formal, accented English. 'She will be part of the family, just like one of our own.'

The prospect struck Kate as unlikely. Still, she was warmed by the woman's kind words.

As soon as they could, Beatrice and Pascal excused themselves from the communal table and returned to their own mysterious concerns. Kate thought them the most glamorous creatures she had ever met and could not begin to imagine what their private world would be like.

Beatrice claimed she had to work on her dissertation. Kate wrote essays and compositions at school, but the word 'dissertation' implied a level of academic sophistication which, combined with the seventeen-year-old's enviable good looks, she found wonderfully impressive.

'Don't wait up for me.' Languidly Pascal pronounced his own exit-line. He was sixteen – only two years older than Kate herself – yet his manner had an amused self-confidence she would never attain in a hundred years.

'Jerome and I will drink coffee on the terrace with your father, Kate.' Odile stacked plates and cutlery. 'You can join us with pleasure – or Nelly and Olivier could show you the beach . . .'

'Kate's not a great coffee-drinker,' Ellis put in discouragingly.

Kate hated the thought of being dragged around by the younger children like some cumbersome parcel, and would have preferred to sit unobtrusively with the adults. But her father's remark made a visit to the beach a *fait accompli*.

However Nelly and Olivier seemed willing enough to lead her across the field below the house, past the grazing horses, to a stile in the far corner. Beyond that a rough path wound steeply downward, almost swallowed in places by ferns and gorse.

Olivier touched her elbow. 'Watch your step down here, Kate. You don't want to turn your ankle.'

She found his solicitude sweet and surprising in a boy. On first acquaintance, Olivier seemed nothing like the traditional pestilential younger brother. There was something rather angelic about him with his long eyelashes and tousled blond hair, his trusting smile. He had an unprotected 'niceness', as if in all his life no one had ever bullied or been unkind to him. But he made her laugh too, leaping in and out of the gorse bushes with the improbable suppleness of a young monkey, squawking ruefully when he missed his footing and scratched his bare brown legs.

Nelly walked in silence, as if her earlier fizz had evaporated and gone flat. The beach, when they reached it, was pebbly, the tide high. The sun was beginning to set and there was a mistiness in the air. The shore was deserted apart from two figures fifty yards or so off to the left.

'Robert! Gwyn!' Explosively Nelly came to life.

The boys turned and approached them. They were evidently school friends and the two Felix children began to converse in a seemingly random mixture of English and Welsh.

Kate was forgotten, but content to be so. As the others joshed and jostled their way along the seashore, she lagged behind, gazing at the horizon glowing cream and gold with the setting sun, the hazy pink streaks in the sky above it. She was soothed by the rhythmic, repetitive swish of the sea on pebbles. Kate savoured the fragile peace of this moment of remission. Tomorrow her father would be gone and she would be left alone to flounder in this alien, challenging world where she could never hope to belong.

Kate slept like a log and woke to her unfamiliar bedroom. The room's red curtains filtered the morning light, making the space seem intimate. She would have been happy to drowse indefinitely in the wide, comfortable bed, nervous of abandoning her quiet and privacy to confront the terrifying vitality of the Felix family home.

One thing, though, was hers to enjoy without anxiety. Kate sat upright, slid her legs over the edge of the bed, her feet encountering the nubbly, plaited surface of the rag rug. She crossed to the window and lifted a corner of the curtain, drank in the sight of the sea spread out before her – a restless, metallic grey-blue – beneath a clear sky dotted with a few small, silver-edged summer clouds.

But her attention was diverted by something closer to the house, a figure in the field below, riding a grey and white horse without saddle or bridle. A girl wearing something loose and pink, her bare legs straddling the creature's rounded flanks, fair hair bouncing against her shoulders. It was Nelly, Kate realized, hunched low over the horse's neck as it cantered towards the further end of the field. Close to the stile she kicked her unshod feet into the animal's

21

side. It wheeled and slowed a little as it started on the uphill pull towards the house.

Nearing the terrace, Nelly shifted her position so that she sat side-saddle for a moment or two, her right knee crooked against the animal's neck. Then, in one graceful, vigorous movement, she slid from the creature's back to land upright in the rough grass. The light garment she was wearing fell into position, hung softly from shoulder to mid calf. It was her nightdress, Kate realized.

She stared silently as Nelly made her airy way towards the terrace and disappeared from view. Kate found herself rapt and shaken. She felt like a prince in a story catching a tantalizing first glimpse of the damsel he'll move heaven and earth to marry. If she were a boy, Kate thought, she'd be in love. Maybe, in a sudden, secret sort of way, she was.

The family ate breakfast on the terrace. Odile had set out the ingredients on the dining-table inside the French windows. People helped themselves, then carried plates and cups outside into the air. There was coffee, milk, butter, honey, yoghurt, a big bowl of strawberries, and what looked like fresh-baked rolls.

Neither Beatrice nor Pascal were up yet, so Odile informed her. Through a window Kate saw Nelly, cross-legged in her pink nightdress, hands cupped round a mug of coffee. The grey and white horse stood in the field below. The animal's head was level with the edge of the terrace and Olivier, dressed but still barefoot, lay full length, petting the animal's muzzle while he munched on a buttered roll.

'Take lots of strawberries, Kate,' Odile told her. 'I grow them myself. We've eaten them since a month already and we're quite blasé . . .'

This morning she was unmade up, her long hair caught casually back in a black ribbon. She had on trousers, a man's striped shirt worn loose over them. Kate had the impression she'd been up for hours.

Jerome, on the other hand, lounged in a deck chair wearing a knee-length towelling dressing-gown, hairy white legs crossed in front of him. Kate could see him through the open French window as she filled her plate. Draining his coffee, taking a healthy bite out of a roll dripping with honey, he radiated the same unruffled air of wellbeing she had noticed the previous night.

'If it weren't for your august presence, Ellis –' Jerome was exclaiming boisterously as Kate emerged on to the terrace with a dish of strawberries and a glass of milk – 'I usually avoid this barbaric time of day like the plague!'

Her father stood close by, cradling his coffee. He was washed and shaved, wore slacks and an open-necked shirt, had the jumpy air of someone eager to be on his way. 'You rarely surfaced before midday, I remember . . . back in the old days,' Ellis confirmed with a crooked, congratulatory smile. 'I was well and truly gutted when you got your First.'

He noticed Kate. 'Sleep well, darling?' His tone briskly affectionate.

'Fine thanks.'

'This is such a glorious spot.' Ellis addressed Jerome, but gazed voluptuously out at the horizon, as tenderly hazy as a watercolour wash. 'What a place to spend the summer!' He turned to Kate. 'Think of me, darling, straining to wring some sense out of the administrative powers-that-be, trying to spot a potential home among a jumble of identical suburban boxes, all on my tod in darkest America . . .'

The inevitable thought flickered through Kate's mind that it was her father's choice to be on his own. But this morning she was too bereft to dwell on grievances. Sitting on a folded rug, eating her strawberries with her fingers, she stared silently, concentrating on his features before they vanished from her sight.

She'd always thought he had a marvellous face. Not pink or pudgy like some of her friends' fathers. Not round and boneless like Jerome's. He had plenty of hair too, yellow-brown and healthy looking. He wasn't film-star handsome but sometimes Rose, when she was feeling expansive, used to reminisce about her courting days and how girlfriends said her Ellis had such an 'interesting' look. Taken one by one, all his features were striking, from the

23

luminous eyes – whisky-coloured he sometimes joked – to the narrow, slightly hooked nose, cleft chin, lips full but not fleshy, not too red, precisely modelled.

In a half-repentant flash, Kate recalled how kind he'd been just after Rose died, how he'd sat by her bed each night for two whole weeks so she wouldn't have to fall asleep on her own. He'd rested his hand on her shoulder so, even with her eyes shut, she could feel his presence . . .

'Time I was getting along.' Her father's energetic pronouncement betrayed an edge of apprehension. But for now he ignored Kate, turning first to his hosts. 'Jerome . . . Odile . . . I can't thank you enough. Your hospitality goes way beyond the call of duty . . .'

Jerome stood up and shook Ellis warmly by the hand, clasping his elbow for added emphasis. Odile kissed him on both cheeks. Each assured him of Kate's continued wellbeing. Ellis said goodbye to Nelly and Olivier, left amiable messages for the other two.

'Kate, walk me to the car.'

Like an automaton she rose to her feet. She felt stiff-legged and unnatural re-entering the French windows, accompanying her father through the sunlit house and out of the main door, his hand resting – self-consciously somehow – in the nape of her neck.

Reaching the car, he turned to face her. 'You'll be all right you know, Kate. You'll settle down. Odile knows you're still a bit . . . weepy.'

Her pride protested at the adjective. It belittled her grief and anger, made them sound weak and vaporous. But there was no point in arguing the toss. Ellis had won anyway.

Bending to kiss her, he scanned her face. She was pleased to see that his eyes were troubled. She would hide her own emotion, withhold her love. That was the only weapon she had left.

'See you in September, darling.' He kissed her on the lips.

'Goodbye,' she said tightly. 'Have a good journey.'

Kate watched the squat black shape of the car containing her father getting smaller as it trundled slowly down the lane. Its departure signified the withdrawal of all familiarity. The brief satisfaction she'd enjoyed in snubbing Ellis turned to smoke as the Morris disappeared from view.

Chapter Three

✧✦✧✦✧

'Have a Spangle. Here, Kate, catch!' Nelly threw her a sweet. Kate stuck out one hand and casually plucked it from the air. Nelly admired that. She was a rotten catch herself.

'Flash!' Robert Williams was impressed too. He spoke in English so Kate would understand. Nelly liked him for that. Gwyn and Ros, another classmate, spoke Welsh all the time, as if to exclude her. Robert lay back in the sand, arms folded behind his head, bare-chested, brown hair, wet from the sea, flopping in his eyes. He looked sexy like that, Nelly thought. It wasn't the same when he was in school, in his uniform.

Ros got hold of his foot and started tickling him. She was a skinny, gingery kid, always touching the boys, always attracting their attention like some irritating, buzzing fly. As if she knew they wouldn't look at her otherwise.

'Get off.' Lazily Robert kicked sand at her and Ros scudded some back in his direction. In a sense she'd got what she wanted.

Gwyn started doing his handstands again. The boy was obsessed, couldn't leave them alone. Ros watched him, cheering or jeering according to his success or failure. Nelly liked the way his arm muscles went taut, his torso stretched out, the ribcage prominent. But Gwyn was too curly-haired and rosy-cheeked for her taste.

In her plain, black regulation school swimsuit, Kate sat a touch apart, making patterns in the sand with some pebbles she'd picked up. Silent as usual. And yet currently she interested Nelly more than the other three put together. Kate's arrival had reminded her of a fantasy she used to have as a child. She'd invented a twin sister, sort of another self really, someone she could say anything to and never feel embarrassed or ashamed. Beatrice had always been too

26

sharp and clever, made her feel like a little kid. But the imaginary sister was on Nelly's side. She'd been ten or eleven before the fancy gradually faded from her mind. And now, when she'd way outgrown such infantile make-believe, more or less forgotten about the whole thing, it was as if the fates had suddenly decided to make her childhood dream come true.

'She doesn't say much, your friend, does she?' Ros said out of the blue, distracted for a moment from her ogling of Gwyn. She'd made the selfsame remark God knows how many times in the last week.

'So what?' Nelly replied sharply in English. She switched to Welsh. 'Change the record, Ros. That one seems to have got stuck in the same groove.'

Robert sniggered and Ros went red. She got up and joined Gwyn in his acrobatics. Her legs shone in the sun, pinky-white. Ros never went brown. She wobbled and screamed, giggled at herself, collapsed in a heap, bringing Gwyn down on top of her. He lay sprawled across her body, then began to tickle her. She wriggled and shrieked. Nelly watched blank-faced, knowing that if she chose to lift her little finger both boys' attention would revert in an instant to herself. Knowing that Ros knew it too.

Nelly crawled across to where Kate was sitting. She picked up a handful of pebbles and began to add to the pattern the girl was making in the sand. Kate glanced up at her, neither welcoming nor rejecting. Nelly was intrigued by her scowly face and lank dark hair. There was something deprived about her, something rather romantic, stemming no doubt from the fact that her mother had died. Sometimes Nelly deplored her own prosaic look of health and high spirits.

Robert joined them. They collected further pebbles. The pattern grew. They became involved in the process and Kate joined in their chat about what should go where. As they worked, the 'twin' idea came back to Nelly. Stupid as it was, she couldn't seem to shake it off.

A couple of days ago Nelly had asked Kate if she had a boyfriend back in London.

'I don't know any boys,' Kate had answered, ungracious but somehow perfectly self-sufficient, without evasion or apology. Kate's very sullenness attracted her, so unlike Ros's fidgety attention-seeking.

Nelly saw Kate as difficult, her reserve a challenge. The desire grew, insidiously compelling, to involve her in some sort of secret intimacy. Nelly was used to getting other kids to do as she wanted. Some loved to be bossed, grateful to be noticed on any terms. Kate wasn't like that. She would have to be wooed, charmed. But Nelly knew she could do it.

Gwyn and Ros drifted across to examine Kate's whirly pebble design. Their own flirtatious scuffling had played itself out. They began to trace the loops and arabesques of the pattern with their feet, as if it were a maze.

'Baggsy!' Abruptly Nelly made a dive for the surfboards. They were primitive things, mere slabs of wood rounded at one end. But there were only two of them and you had to grab.

'Come on, Kate. Let's you and I have another swim.'

A sudden brilliant smile lit up Kate's dour face. She stepped towards Nelly and accepted the proffered surfboard. The two of them ran across the wide stretch of gleaming sand towards the long, low crescent sweep of the sea.

'Kate,' Jerome called, as she passed by the open kitchen door. 'Take this cuppa out to Odile, will you?'

His wife was outside tending her little acre, so he said, pointing her towards a gateway in a low wall to the left of the terrace. Kate followed his instructions and emerged into a part of the property she hadn't yet discovered.

A large rectangle of rich, dark, friable earth was crisscrossed with row upon tidy row of flourishing vegetables, flanked on either side with a long line of fruit bushes. At the far end a long, low building with a slate roof and thick stone walls seemed to serve as a shed and windbreak. The sheltered, cultivated enclosure contrasted strikingly with the rolling landscape surrounding it and the boundlessness of the sea below.

To the right of the patch Odile, in espadrilles and a brown

cotton dress, was picking blackcurrants. She glanced up as Kate approached and gave a pleased smile. 'This is kind, Kate. I'm dying of thirst.'

'Jerome made it.' Kate felt it necessary to give credit where credit was due.

'You want to sit down for a while?'

In the shelter of the outbuilding there was a wooden bench that faced back towards the house. Kate took her place beside Odile, who sipped her tea with satisfaction.

'It must be strange for you to be here,' she commented after some moments of silence. 'I have the impression that your father finds my children . . . not very disciplined.'

Embarrassed, Kate sidestepped the remark. 'It's strange living in such a huge place.'

'You should have seen it when we found it,' Odile said. 'With holes in the roof, broken windows . . .'

'Honestly?' Kate was surprised, had never thought to picture the building as other than it was now.

Odile explained that she and Jerome had first come across their home while on holiday in the Lleyn Peninsula during the summer immediately after the war. The weather was gloomy and, looking for a place to picnic, they'd turned off the road towards the sea. And there was the house, clearly empty, ramshackle, neglected.

'We ate our picnic on the terrace and then it started to rain. We climbed in by a broken window. The children adored the naughtiness of it. For them the house was an enormous playground. Jerome and I explored every corner . . .' Odile smiled at the memory. 'We dreamed that it belonged to us.'

At once, and irrevocably, Jerome was determined to make the dream come true.

'If Jerome really wants something, he has to have it.' Odile's expression was enigmatic.

The first problem was to discover who owned it. By making enquiries locally he found out that the house used to be the country home of a Lancashire cotton king called Oakwood. In the thirties he decided he preferred Capri and sold up. The place had been run as

29

a hotel for a few years, but never thrived. The hotelier had been killed in action. The house belonged to his wife, who'd remarried and now lived in Sheffield. She couldn't be bothered with the effort needed to render it habitable. The price she named was extremely reasonable.

At the time Jerome was an obscure lecturer, still some years away from fame and fortune. Low as the price was, it was way beyond his means. All the same he put the family's London home on the market.

'You must have been terribly keen,' Kate remarked.

Odile rocked her hand from side to side in a gesture of equivocation. 'I was scared. But I was seduced by the dream and Jerome swept me along.'

They were still way short of the sum needed. During the war Jerome had worked in Intelligence. He approached an old buddy, aristocratic and well-heeled, cajoled and bullied the man into offering a loan, making promises he'd no means of keeping.

Odile turned to Kate, her expression dour, but admiring. 'He was quite without scruples.'

The first winter was the coldest in living memory and it was hell. The holes in the roof were only partially blocked off by inadequate tarpaulins. Birds flew into the second-floor rooms and had to be shooed out. A lot of the time Jerome was away in London, teaching. Odile and the children lived in one room. She felt like a refugee. Beatrice was desperately unhappy at leaving her friends behind, hated being forced to learn Welsh. At her new school she was teased and bullied . . .

But when the fifties dawned Jerome started making a name for himself with his books, his radio and television appearances. To everyone's surprise he was able to pay back the debt with time to spare. By then the building was structurally sound and Odile began the process of throwing out the floral carpets and chintz curtains and decorating the place to her own taste.

Briefly she raised her eyes to the house. 'My blood is in the bricks of that place.'

'But it was worth it in the end, wasn't it?'

Odile gave an unsentimental shrug. 'Who can say?'

It wasn't the reply Kate had expected to hear.

The bright sunlight flickered like a faulty film as the bus passed under a canopy of overhanging trees on the coast road towards Caernarfon. The oscillating light–dark contrast enchanted Kate. She'd started drinking coffee at breakfast-time and noticed how it sharpened her mood, lent her an alertness, a new intensity in viewing the world.

She was filled this morning with a quietly churning euphoria that half scared her. She'd not felt anything like it for so long. The sunshine set the scene, but mostly it was due to the unimaginable freedom of a whole day out with just Nelly, with cash to buy their lunch, and a generous proportion of the clothes-money that Ellis had paid over to Odile. No doubt he'd envisaged a supervised visit to some suitable local outfitter, as in Rose's day. Instead, with a recklessness that took Kate's breath away, Odile had entrusted it to herself and Nelly, left the choice up to them.

'We'll get you a bra,' Nelly had said at once. 'And about time too.'

Kate nodded agreement, though she would probably have been too embarrassed to mention it herself. She admired the two neat half-moons of Nelly's breasts beneath her blouses and sweaters and longed for her own to look so stylishly lifted and restrained.

'I used to sew all Nelly's clothes when she was a little girl,' Odile told Kate with a sidelong glance at her daughter. 'But now she only wants to wear flashy rubbish, ready made, badly finished . . .' It was clearly a long-running complaint that had metamorphosed into a family joke.

Nelly had just grinned and linked her arm through Kate's in a way that made her feel warm inside. 'We'll have a marvellous time. We'll get you a wide skirt like my red one, a black top . . . a pair of ballerinas, some shorts . . . a new swimsuit – you'll be able to get rid of all your girlie little frocks for good.'

Odile frowned. 'Nelly, that isn't polite.'

But, disloyal as it was to Rose, Kate agreed. She couldn't wait to start looking like Nelly . . . She'd already borrowed an outgrown pair of her white shorts, which she wore with a shirt of Olivier's, the sleeves rolled really high . . . And she'd seen that Nelly's friends looked at her in quite a different way.

'There's a place in town where they sell rolls and frothy coffee. We'll go there once we've got you an outfit.' In the seat beside her, Nelly looked blank and enigmatic in black sunglasses with white rims.

'OK.' Kate was happy to go along with anything she suggested. The day ahead seemed to fizz with potential. Everything she saw through the bus window pleased her – hillsides with sheep, stone walls overgrown with ivy and vigorous weeds, bright pink roses spilling over cottage fences, the sea viewed hazily here and there through trees and over walls. Even the tall, rather grimly Welsh houses that lined the road in places shone in the sun with a certain mellow charm.

She'd had a long letter that morning from Jess, her best friend back in London, a pale girl with heavy, languid features, a precocious acid cynicism. Apparently her family had relatives to stay from Rochdale and, in her stylish, spidery black handwriting, Jess cut the northerners wittily down to size.

Under normal circumstances Kate would have treasured such a letter, but today it had struck her as smug, nit-picking, ill-natured, a missive from a narrower and more grudging world. A dingy world, so it seemed to her, when here, this morning, all was lightness and brightness.

Kate found it hard to credit the open-hearted welcome offered her by the Felix family.

'I wouldn't trust her further than I could throw her.' That had been one of Rose's catch-phrases for as long as Kate could remember.

Here, in this unfamiliar household, her mother's suspiciousness stayed with her. A small, hard nugget of fear and mistrust was with her all the time. And yet it was so tempting to accept at face value the easy affection of Nelly and Olivier and Odile, even though she'd done nothing to deserve it. In the evening Kate had started to

drink the small measure of wine the younger children were allowed.
She noticed how it warmed her inside, made her laugh, made her
free and easy, so she stopped wondering all the time whether they
really liked her or whether one of these days she would discover
that their niceness was just a polite and handy front.

Yesterday evening she and Nelly, Olivier and a friend of his called
Evan, who was staying the night, had played a wild, cheating game
of Monopoly upstairs on the second floor, in one of the bare rooms
under the roof that were used mainly for storage. It had a sloping
ceiling, from which a naked light bulb hung suspended by a length
of flex. They'd spread out some spare blankets and eiderdowns,
lain on their stomachs in a circle. The contest had gone on until
after midnight, when they called it a draw because everyone was
stealing from the bank and sneaking free hotels.

Kate had lost herself in the game, laughed so much that, for
the four hours or so it lasted, she'd completely forgotten her dead
mother and her absent father, the fact that she'd been dumped
against her will in a strange house. It had been hilarious, but
afterwards, alone in her room, she'd looked at the vivid, vulnerable
photograph of Rose and cried.

There were other pleasures to be had in the Felix household. She
was beginning to acquire a taste for Odile's aromatic, unfamiliar
food – pasta dishes with all kinds of sauces, rich casseroles and
herby salads, vegetables Kate had never seen before, home-grown
in the kitchen garden.

Garlic was something Kate had only ever heard mentioned with
distaste, something rank and foreign, a source of bad breath and
social embarrassment. But Odile served it chopped on hunks of
bread with herbs and melted butter. Kate had tried it suspiciously,
found it was one of the most delicious things she'd ever tasted.

Jerome had laughed. 'She's a greedy-guts like us. A sybarite.'
Kate had glowed inwardly at his approval.

For years, like everyone, Rose had been hampered by shortages
and rationing. Even so, her daughter was forced to acknowledge,
she'd been a timid cook. Kate had always regarded meals as a
sort of ritual, a discipline almost, marking the stages of the day.

Now she saw they could be a source of discovery and sensuous enjoyment.

At a bus-stop two women in floral dresses and peep-toe shoes got on with four young children. They joked flirtatiously with the conductor as he struggled to help them with an intractable pushchair. The scene was amiable and inconsequential. For months now Kate had shrunk from high spirits and boisterous banter. Today they seemed just an amusing part of the whole sunny morning.

Nelly pointed at a crossroads up ahead. 'See that? That's where Pascal was knocked off his bike two years ago, by an old fart in an ancient rattle-trap. He was about ninety with spectacles an inch thick . . .'

'Was Pascal hurt?'

'A bit. Cut his head open. He's still got a bit of a scar. The old buffer was disqualified. Blind as a bat he was.' From behind the blackness of her sunglasses Nelly gave a mischievous smile.

Kate admitted inside herself that she was interested in everything that had to do with Pascal. She'd never seen a boy she thought so . . . It was hard to find a word. Her school friends would say he was smashing but that sounded giggly, stupid. Kate felt all eyes when she saw him, felt something like a sudden intake of breath. He was streamlined. He was perfect. He had wide shoulders, long legs, skinny hips. In the evening, when he drank wine, his eyes took on a dark, glittery look. He had a smile that was easy and friendly, but sort of . . . as if he was laughing at the whole world.

Yesterday he'd sat smoking on the terrace, leaning back in his seat, legs crossed, feet resting on another chair, beautifully relaxed as a cat. She'd watched him, pretending to leaf through a magazine. He'd framed his hands round his eyes so they formed a square and looked out to sea. Photography was his passion, but he was constantly frustrated by lack of cash.

'Work for it. Get a holiday job.' Jerome was amiably callous.

And a look would flicker across Pascal's face, quirk the corners of his mouth – an expression she found irresistible, quick and deprecating – while his eyes mocked his own idleness.

Yesterday he'd been smoking a cigarette that smelt different, strong and somehow decadent, wafting on a little breeze. She knew it was French. Some friend of Jerome's had been to Paris and brought them back for Pascal. Jerome didn't mind him smoking. He favoured little black cigars himself.

Pascal had looked across at where Kate sat with her magazine. Lazily he held up the packet, blue and black with a dancing woman on it.

'Gitanes,' he said, in a tone that showed he thought them something special. 'Want a puff, Kate?' He offered her the cigarette.

She took it gingerly, inhaled cautiously, got a mouthful of acrid smoke.

'Nice?' he asked.

'Not really.'

He laughed. Kate was enchanted. She was nothing, no one, an unworthy, embarrassed, ill-dressed urban bumpkin. Why did he bother to take notice of her?

In her different way, Beatrice too was an object of awed fascination. She was so effortlessly elegant with her straight shiny hair and even tan and, at the same time, so cool and studious, ambitious to get to Oxford and do philosophy, of all things, always deep in a book or absorbed in some delicate, detailed still-life drawing of jugs, vases or miraculously transparent bottles, with professional-looking highlights and cross-hatching.

Yet Beatrice too treated her with easy acceptance, offered her sweets, showed her the drawings she did, posted a letter for her once and, in her mock-feud with Jerome at meal-times, included Kate in her exasperated, eye-rolling sideways glances.

The bus was rumbling now through the unbeautiful outskirts of Caernarfon. Soon Nelly nudged her, pointing vaguely past some lugubrious grey buildings. 'We're here almost. The bus station's just over there, look . . . I'm itching to get started on blowing your cash.'

Nelly led Kate to Annabel Davis in the town centre. They had a great laugh, trying on loads of clothes. Though the trip wasn't for her benefit, Nelly couldn't resist stripping down to her bra and

35

knickers too and putting on a taffeta dress with a low sweetheart neckline and a watered silk sash, which she clearly had no intention of buying. The saleslady hovered uncomfortably then drifted away. She must have gone to talk to the manageress because a large woman with dyed black hair and a navy blue dress bustled into the changing-room and stood sourly by, arms folded, while they examined themselves self-consciously in the long mirror. Her disapproval only made the expedition seem that much more amusing.

Kate purchased a skirt, then Nelly took her to the underwear department of Lewis's in search of brassieres. In the coffin-like changing cubicle Kate insisted on trying them on over her dress. Like Superman, she claimed. They giggled wildly and once again the department supervisor made it plain that she would prefer them to move on.

Passing through the jewellery department, Kate bought them each a pair of clip-on hoop earrings. In Junior Miss they found shorts and blue jeans, summer sweaters, another skirt, a pair of black ballerina slippers. Given their spending power, the smart blonde saleslady treated them with brisk affability.

'That combination will take you anywhere,' she assured Kate with a suave air of professional expertise. 'Dress the sweaters up for evening with a little scarf at the neck.'

Kate nodded, her expression wide-eyed and earnest. Once round the corner they spluttered with renewed laughter.

For lunch they went to a coffee bar, ordered cappuccino and flaky cakes with shredded coconut on top.

Kate looked wonderfully different, Nelly thought proudly, in a blue and white striped sweater and rolled jeans, the gold hoop earrings glinting through her dark hair.

'We're getting to look like sisters,' she said. The notion of them as twins coiled through her thoughts continuously.

Kate smiled and turned pink. 'It was fun this morning,' she said.

'You look smashing . . . Did your ma use to buy your clothes?' Nelly hoped it was OK to mention her dead mother.

'Yes.' Kate hesitated. 'Well . . . her tastes weren't really mine.'

'Your dad'll get a shock when he sees you.'

She pulled a face, self-deprecating, sort of hurt. 'Then he shouldn't have left me here.'

'Didn't you want to be left?'

'Not really.' Kate stared into her coffee-cup.

'Do you hate it here?'

'No.' She glanced up and shrugged. One corner of her mouth was smiling. 'Actually, it's quite a bit better than I thought.'

Chapter Four

❈❈❈❈❈

It was nine o'clock. The light was fading fast but the summer air was soft and warm. On the terrace behind the house Kate and Olivier carried on hitting a tennis ball to one another with a pair of cheap kids' bats.

They co-operated, neither attempting to score off the other. There was a ping-pong table down in the rough-hewn cellar and there Kate played to win – usually successfully – against all members of the family. But out here what they wanted was to keep the momentum going. The point was the activity itself, the unhurried trajectory of the ball, its blunt, satisfying impact against the bat.

'That's twenty without stopping,' Olivier called.

In the dusk his brown limbs, the tanned angel's face, looked dark against the white of his shirt, the faded beige of his shorts, his sun-bleached hair. Most twelve-year-old boys would run a mile rather than play with a girl, but Olivier mixed easily with either sex.

'Let's see if we can make it to forty,' Kate replied.

She was touched by Olivier, the sweet-natured Benjamin of the family, and cherished by all of them for that reason. Most of the day he hung around the house or the beach below with a gang of local boys. Wide open and seemingly without malice, he struck Kate as a likely candidate for bullying and boyish cruelty. Yet Olivier seemed immune, getting by less on strength than on . . . lovability, if that was a word.

Jerome sat reading in the open French window, a glass of red wine at his elbow, beneath the harlequin glow of a Tiffany lamp. Brahms piano music welled, clear and passionate, from the radio.

Nelly was still for once, sitting near him on the floor, propped on a cushion, her eyes vague and dreamy.

Horses grazed peacefully in the field below. The sky was a luminous deep blue. The sea could be sensed rather than seen, though far out a lighthouse twinkled elusively in the dusk. In the gathering twilight Kate and Olivier continued to bat the ball back and forth, back and forth.

In Kate's room around midnight she and Nelly lolled on the bed reading a shared copy of *Picturegoer* magazine. Being awake this late had a wayward feel for Kate. Rose had always insisted she was in bed by ten, but the Felix parents made no rules as regards the correct time for sleep.

Together Kate and Nelly mused over a portrait of the hot new American actor, James Dean. In the picture he slouched and gazed at the camera so that his full lower lip drooped in a wonderfully sulky way, while his eyes looked hurt and confused. Neither had seen his film yet, but they longed to.

Nelly grinned. 'He can put his boots under my bed any night of the week.' It was an expression she'd adopted in relation to any male fantasy figure that caught her eye. 'What d'you think, Kate?'

'He's all right.'

He wasn't a patch on Pascal, she thought, his eyes self-pitying somehow, where Pascal's were gloriously sardonic. But she couldn't say that out loud.

'You're a picky one, that's for sure.'

They returned to the crossword, but by now Kate was too tired to raise much interest.

Before Nelly disappeared through the communicating door that led to her own room she gave Kate a big hug, hooking one arm round her neck and kissing her on the lips. 'Sleep tight, darling – have lots of nice, juicy dreams.'

Kate could imagine her friend Jess back in London looking askance, rolling up her eyes, at this extravagant show of affection. A little while ago Kate herself would have felt the same. But now she loved to be called Nelly's special friend – her sister even. The girl's exuberance made her glow inside, thawing out the frost that had numbed her feelings for so long. In contrast, Kate's goodnight sounded dry and reserved, but she knew from experience that Nelly didn't need an equal response. Her high spirits were sufficient unto themselves.

Before switching out the light, Kate glanced round the room that was beginning to feel like home. A new picture was pinned up above the tiled table across from the bed, a swirly pastel portrait of James Mason that Olivier had done for her after she told him *The Prisoner of Zenda* was her favourite film.

Her bed was a lot more comfortable than the two-foot six job she'd had in Camberwell, but then her bedroom had been far too small for anything so roomy. Kate curled up under the striped blanket, between the smooth, cool sheets. Increasingly at the end of the day she had a sense of wellbeing, memories that made her smile.

She recalled Nelly that morning on the beach, taking off her scuffed white plimsoll and threatening Robert Williams with it, after he laughed when she fell on her bottom in a rock-pool.

'Smell it, you bastard!' she'd yelled at him and shoved the shoe in his face, while he fell back laughing helplessly and kicking his legs in the air.

Kate had grinned at their roughhousing, laughed along with Ros, who was getting a lot friendlier nowadays.

Last night Nelly had told her that she'd necked one evening on the beach with Robert. 'He touched my breasts and I touched his willy,' she confided with a half smile.

Kate was agog. 'Will you do it again?'

'No.' Nelly shrugged and shook her head. 'Not for a long time anyway. He'll get to expect it all the time and I don't want to be like Ros. She's always doing that sort of thing just so the boys'll take notice of her.'

The confession reinforced the sense Kate had of inhabiting – however temporarily – a freer, bolder world than her own. And, as August drew towards a close, she understood that, against all expectation, she had fallen in love with that world.

She adored the house, its smell, its spacious, welcoming feel, the sweep of field behind it, the bracken and gorse scramble down to the beach. She never tired of the miraculous view from her window of the sea in all its moods and the changing sky.

And, in differing ways, she was in love with every one of the family's members – with Jerome's foxy, good-natured smile, Odile's exotic domesticity. From a distance she worshipped the thoroughbred glamour of Pascal and Beatrice. She loved Olivier's sweetness and, most of all, the way Nelly had claimed her as a sister. It gave her a warm, wanted feeling – like when people used to say she and Rose were like sisters.

Kate's longing for her mother was beginning to recede into the background – emerging at times to ambush her with a clutch of misery – but less often now that her mind and body were absorbed by new activities, new people.

Kate remembered Rose once showing her a magazine photograph of a shrine some old lady kept in her bedroom to the memory of Rudolf Valentino. Massed portraits of the star hung above a small polished table full of artificial flowers and candles that flickered softly in the gloom. Sometimes her feelings for Rose seemed like that, burning secretly in her heart as if in a darkened room while, increasingly, Kate was outside playing in the sun.

In the Stephens household the word 'hospitality' had always had the force of a threat. They rarely had visitors, mostly just family, and there were few enough of them – both Ellis and Rose were only children. But occasionally Ellis would announce it was about time they gave a dinner-party to repay whatever sparse invitations had come their way in the last months. He talked about 'owing' hospitality. Rose would go into a panic and leaf despairingly through her cookery book with its garish colour plates of Baked Alaska and yukky-looking vegetables in aspic jelly. She'd grit her teeth and plan the whole thing like a military campaign, then sigh with relief when it was all over for another year or so.

The Felix attitude was in complete contrast. Odile never gave dinner-parties and yet there was a constant stream of visitors to the house – friends of the children sleeping over or dropping in for meals, friends of Jerome and Odile, who turned up, stayed a few days, then motored off again.

No fuss was made over their arrival. Annie, who did the cleaning, would make up a bed but, apart from that, life went on as usual. Jerome worked in his study during the day, Odile did her vegetable garden or her upholstery or her sewing as always. And at mealtimes guests shared whatever she happened to be cooking for the family.

And yet the house was a hundred times more welcoming than Kate's home in Stapleton Road had ever been. After dinner the adults would sit and chat, get merry, over a couple of bottles of wine in the long, light living-room or on the terrace. The young people were free to do their own thing or join in the conversation if the fancy took them. It was all delightfully relaxed and natural, and a revelation to Kate.

By and large, involved as she was with Nelly and her friends, Kate took little notice of the grown-ups who came and went. Most seemed perfectly likeable, specially in the evening, flushed with wine and laughter. On one occasion she realized that a fattish, curly-haired man Jerome called Dobbsy was the journalist Reginald Dobbs whose progressive views Ellis often quoted. She watched him for a while, rather impressed, then went up to the empty rooms at the top of the house to play records with Nelly and Ros.

But towards the end of August the Felix family had a visitor who was altogether different. He was French, for a start, and noticeably younger than the general run of their guests. Kate wasn't good at guessing adults' ages, but she and Nelly put him at thirty or so. He was skinny and rather small, with brown hair that was short at the sides, a bit longer on top, and brushed up and away from his high forehead. He wore a black shirt and nearly black trousers and smoked the kind of strong cigarettes that Pascal raved about. His face was boyish but quite crinkled. He wasn't handsome, not at all, but awfully appealing in an almost monkeyish way.

He wasn't a family friend – a mutual acquaintance had given him Jerome's name and address. There was something bemused in his manner as if he felt vaguely out of his depth in this foreign setting.

42

At the same time he was courteous and eager to please. But beneath his polite smile Kate sensed the crackle of something sharp, even mocking. And his eyes were shrewd. There was a sense that he was watching and storing impressions in an analytical, unsentimental fashion, which he probably was because he was a writer.

His name was David Lacoste and he was over for the publication of the English language edition of his first novel. After doing the obligatory round of interviews he'd decided to take off and see something of the country, follow up some contacts.

Via Odile the Felixes had strong European connections. The family generally combined a visit to her relatives in Lausanne with a stay in Paris. They had friends all over France as well as in Austria and Italy.

Pascal, in particular, was a keen Francophile. Odile's brother sent him a continuous supply of French magazines so he could keep himself informed on books, films and personalities.

'Lacoste's novel stirred up quite a storm in France,' he told the rest of them over dinner the evening before the writer's arrival. 'Blacklisted by the Vatican and all that . . . It's about disaffected post-war youth drinking Scotch and having affairs all over the place, and it's mixed up somehow with the war in Indo-China . . . Lots of sex and violence and bad language . . .' He passed on the information with an air of detachment, but Kate didn't miss the excitement bubbling beneath his nonchalance.

The advance publicity was titillating and Kate noticed that, during the three days or so of Lacoste's stay, the household buzzed with a heightened verve, as if his presence made life more interesting. And yet his behaviour was perfectly conventional. He relaxed on the terrace, reading and smoking, walked down to the beach occasionally, sat drinking in the evening with Jerome and Odile and generally radiated amicable goodwill.

Jerome made a show of getting out good wines for the Frenchman, showing him the labels, getting him to taste them and comment. With an edge of self-mockery he addressed his guest as '*mon vieux*', and talked to him in fluent, confident, atrociously accented French.

43

'I'm no expert in wine . . .' Lacoste protested, gesturing with one of his host's slim black cigars and wearing his bemused, attractive smile. But he was clearly tickled by Jerome's genial attention.

Kate heard him in the kitchen one morning talking vehemently to Odile in French. She was struck by how different they both sounded speaking their own language – no longer hesitant but intimidatingly voluble and assertive. Their conversation was unintelligible to her, then she caught the word '*Algérie*' and guessed they were talking politics.

Kate was carrying a pile of breakfast crockery to the kitchen for washing-up. Entering, she felt an intruder, was taken aback by Lacoste's look of amused challenge, Odile's flushed animation. Kate laid the dishes on the table. Instead of exclaiming, as she usually did, at Kate's consideration and helpfulness, Odile merely glanced at her with eyes that were vague and preoccupied.

For the occasion of Lacoste's visit, Pascal made sure his allowance stretched to a couple of reels of film. Diffident at first, he took general snaps of the Frenchman at dinner with the family or chatting on the terrace with Jerome and Odile.

'*Vous permettez?*' Finally he plucked up courage to ask the visitor to pose on his own.

'Oh . . .' To Kate's surprise Lacoste gave an embarrassed shrug, flashed a quick, self-deprecating smile.

He seemed ill-at-ease, posing in a spoof strong-man attitude, then – eyes shaded – gazing out to sea like a Victorian explorer. Later he lit a cigarette and relaxed, staring into the lens half smiling, half defiant.

'Beatrice, come.' In self-defence he pulled the girl towards him. He grinned at Pascal. 'Your sister is prettier.'

Next to him on the slatted garden seat Beatrice faced the camera, pretending to smoke his cigarette, inscrutable, poised and ravishing. Kate watched him watching her with a sharp, speculative interest that disturbed and excited her. Nelly rated him almost as sexy as James Dean.

On the last day of his visit Kate and Nelly were on the beach below the house with Robert Williams and his friend Gwyn. The

44

weather was cool and breezy, but they decided to swim anyway, stripping down to their swimsuits and paddling into the shallow waves. Combined with the keen wind, the sea felt freezing. They stopped short, up to their knees in cold water, daring one another to wade further out into the choppy grey brine.

They began to splash and scream – Nelly had a particularly overwrought scream and she gave it full rein, culminating in a kind of strangulated yodel. The others began to imitate her, their voices ringing out in wild discord.

Suddenly they became aware of Lacoste standing further up the beach, watching them with an amused smile.

'*Bon courage*,' he called, waving them on. '*Allez y*!'

They grinned stupidly, unable to think of any reply, mortified at being caught out in their infantile high jinks by this sophisticated foreigner.

'*Merci*,' Robert answered feebly.

Lacoste raised a hand in amiable greeting and started back up the rough path towards the house.

They gathered to say goodbye in the small, tarred courtyard by the front door, where Lacoste had parked the little car he'd borrowed from friends in London. There was something ecstatic in their farewells, Kate thought, as if the Frenchman had spent much longer with them than a mere three days, as if they'd all shared some deep and meaningful experience. In fact, as far as she could see, his stay had been uneventful. But Lacoste's aura was such that to be liked and accepted by him seemed enormously gratifying.

Even Pascal and Beatrice, who normally slept for half the morning, had dragged themselves from their respective beds to see him off, and stood in their dressing-gowns blinking with exaggerated bleariness in the bright early sun.

Lacoste laughed at their bedraggled air, clapped Pascal on the shoulder, kissed Beatrice on both cheeks, then held her at arms' length, looking at her with a mocking, flirtatious insistence. 'So beautiful so early in the morning!'

He turned to the younger ones. 'Nelly. Kate. Olivier,' his voice

45

caressing. The Frenchman enclosed the three of them simultaneously in a huge bear-hug, rocked them teasingly from side to side.

Odile stood by, wearing one of the scoop-necked, loose-waisted dresses she made herself, this one in olive green and black. She hadn't pinned her hair up yet and it hung on her shoulders, thick and dark, with streaks of grey. Lacoste took her hand and kissed it in a gesture that was flamboyant and, at the same time, boyishly appealing. He held her hand to his heart and addressed her in a French too rapid for Kate to catch, while Odile laughed, looking young and pretty.

To Jerome he presented a copy of the British edition of his novel. It was called *A Damning Verdict*. The jacket was sandy yellow with the title and author's name in big scrawly black writing.

Jerome grinned, genial and expansive. '*Merci mille fois, mon brave*,' he said in his lumbering French accent.

They embraced. Kate was impressed. She'd never known men to do any such thing.

'*Au revoir tous.*'

Lacoste stepped into his car and started the engine. They waved madly until he was out of sight. When his car disappeared round a bend in the lane they were left with a sense of anti-climax.

'Did he sign the book?' Olivier asked.

They all crowded round Jerome. He read out the dedication slowly, translating as he went. 'To my friend, Jerome, and Odile, his discreet and charming companion. And . . .' Jerome paused with his sly smile '. . . to the most seductive family it has been my happiness to meet.'

Listening, Kate approved heartily of the Frenchman's sentiments. She could not have put it better herself.

Chapter Five

❈❈❈❈❈

'Your mother had an amazing face.' Pascal stared at the portrait of Rose in Kate's photograph album, considered it in silence for some moments. 'She looks almost like a child . . . Sort of thin-skinned. As if everything she felt showed through in her eyes . . .'

'Yes . . . Well, she was a bit like that.'

Kate was astonished by Pascal's perspicacity, his perception of Rose's particular quality, and his appraisal had the effect of reawakening her appreciation of Rose's specialness.

At the same time she was almost embarrassed at having captured Pascal's attention so decisively. Via her cheap and nasty photo album, of all things, with its white fake-leather cover, mock-croc finish. It had been lying on the table in her room when Pascal spied it through the open doorway.

'May I?'

Obsessed as he was with photography, however mundane, Pascal had picked it up and started turning the pages, immediately rapt. He examined each snap in turn, really looked at them, as if they mattered.

He grinned at a picture of Kate, aged nine, dressed as a tree-sprite for a school play, facing the camera with a cool, ungracious stare. 'I thought fairies were supposed to simper.'

'Not when they're being photographed by some nitwit from the *South London Press*.'

He laughed. 'Oh, I see . . . a publicity still.'

Pascal flipped over to a snap of her chum Jess sitting on a swing, eyes narrowed, humorously truculent. 'Who's that?'

'Just a friend.' Kate was aware she sounded dismissive. Disloyal even. Under Pascal's hard, handsome scrutiny, Jess appeared pasty and frumpish. She owed her former best friend a letter, Kate recalled. Jess seemed far away, part of a staider, stodgier life.

Handing the album back to her, Pascal remarked casually, 'Considering you've lived fourteen whole years, there aren't very many of these.'

'We had loads more at home. But in this book I only want pictures I really like a lot.'

The thought seemed to impress him. Later that day he asked if she'd be interested in sorting through a box of his own photographs – his spares, as it were. If any caught her eye she was welcome to take them to add to her own select hoard.

Kate was quietly overwhelmed by his offer. Pascal brought a big box-file to her room. It was brimful with snaps. She settled on the floor, took out thirty or so and spread them out on the plaited rug. Some of them were of people she didn't know. Others were pictures of buildings taken from strange angles so that they appeared to taper abruptly to a point in the sky. Kate recognized the Arc de Triomphe and the Eiffel Tower, but none of the others.

Kate pushed these aside and reached greedily into the box again. What she really wanted was to wallow in Felix family photographs, to glimpse all its members frozen in private moments, in earlier incarnations, in the years before they'd existed for her.

Her curiosity was more than satisfied. Pascal must have been given a camera quite young, at eight or so, because there were pictures of Nelly at around six years old, Olivier at four, Beatrice looking scrubbed and childish in plaits and an unflattering padded, belted raincoat. Jerome, beardless in shirt and shorts, with his eternal benign smile and small, dark cigar. Odile, radiantly beautiful in a swimsuit, her hair waist-length, holding hands with little Olivier, bizarrely dressed in a satin tailcoat and a paper top hat. Nelly again, aged eleven or so, hanging by her legs from the branch of a tree. Beatrice at fourteen, posing vampishly with a martini glass and a cigarette-holder, barefoot, a feather boa hanging from her shoulders.

'Anything strike you?'

Pascal wandered in again and joined her on the floor. Intent and critical, he began to pore over the snaps that lay spread around, half ravished, half appalled by his own youthful efforts. He seemed very keen to be represented in Kate's album. She could have been tempted by at least twenty of the snaps, but didn't want to seem a grasping eager beaver.

In the event, Kate chose just two photographs. One was a close-up of Nelly on the grey riding-school horse – Pascal must have taken it from the terrace. She was laughing and saying something to him, a mocking expression in her long, narrow eyes, while the wind whipped her hair – strands of it straggled across her cheeks and neck. The other snap was only a week old and showed David Lacoste and Beatrice side by side on a slatted bench seat. Intent but expressionless, Lacoste was looking at Beatrice while she held his cigarette to her pouted lips. Both, Kate thought, appeared the very embodiment of contemporary chic, both strangely inscrutable.

She held up the prints. 'Can I have these?'

'Yes.' Pascal stared hard at the snaps as if attempting to see them through Kate's eyes. He looked up. 'Only two?'

Among the photographs in the box-file she'd come across one of Pascal himself. It seemed recent and in it he wore an expression she saw as characteristic – gazing through half-closed lids, smiling but quizzical and somehow impatient. It was him to the life. She would have loved to have it, but wouldn't reveal herself by asking.

'Two's fine.' Kate grinned. 'Can't lower my standards.'

'You're a hard woman.' She adored the way he said that.

That evening she stuck the photos in. With glue. Kate liked to think of her album as permanent, and if you used those little corner mounts they dried out and came unstuck.

Afterwards, in bed, she began to leaf through the whole book, but stayed staring at a picture of Ellis leaning on the rail of a Thames pleasure boat. Rose had snapped him last summer, the day they went to Hampton Court. Her parents had had a quarrel the night before and the trip appeared threatened. But they made it up in time and the two of them seemed really fond of each other that day. It was sunny. They had tea in a cottagey café with a garden and Ellis bought them all double strawberries and cream. Remembering, Kate felt close to tears and had a sudden raw longing to be with him.

Ellis wrote every week. His letters were frustratingly short, as if he couldn't be bothered to elaborate on the nuts and bolts of his settling in. Kate would have loved him to dwell on his first impressions of Coningsburgh – of America in general – to paint vivid word pictures, but he gave the impression of being in a constant hurry, which he probably was. Ever since she could remember, Ellis had claimed to be a rotten correspondent, almost boasted of it, so she had no real right to be disappointed.

He didn't seem particularly struck with whatever it was he'd found. Kate was surprised by his refusal even to fake any kind of enthusiasm. He was having trouble finding a suitable house and seemed unwilling to compromise in any way. He said he was lonely. He said he was missing her. She was pleased and felt kindly towards him, regretting once more the sulkiness of her farewell.

By the fifth letter he sounded quite markedly more optimistic. He'd made a friend, Bill, met a colleague called Fay. They were taking him out, showing him around, helping him with the house situation. Their know-how made a huge difference, Ellis said. He hoped to have good news in the near future. He didn't say he missed her and Kate felt disproportionately hurt by the omission.

And then he wrote to say he'd found a place – Ellis sounded jubilant. A house with a front porch and shady trees in the back garden. He'd fallen in love with it and knew Kate would too. The one drawback was that it wouldn't fall vacant until the new year.

Then came the bombshell. Ellis thought that, if the Felixes were agreeable, the best thing would be for Kate to remain in Wales until that time. He'd enclosed a separate letter for Jerome and Odile, explaining the situation.

She handed the sealed envelope to Jerome, then went outside, scrambled down to the beach below the house. Wandering along the sand, she picked up all the flat stones she could find and skimmed them, marvelling at their swift, improbable, ricocheting flight across the still water. Her mind felt empty and blank.

'We'd love to have you stay, Kate,' Odile reassured when, an hour or so later, Kate returned to the house. 'It's cosy here in winter, you know.'

But Kate noticed she looked searchingly at her as if anxious to gauge how Ellis's abrupt change of plan would affect his daughter.

Kate wasn't actually sure. Some days she felt sad, some days she felt angry. Sometimes, oddly, her pride was hurt, as if it were plain for all to see that Ellis wasn't bothered about her, that he could do perfectly well without her. At other times the anticipation of staying on and going to school with Nelly was like secret gold, reflecting its warm, burnished lustre on the months to come.

Odile worked steadily, digging her main-crop potatoes. She'd planted a huge number this year. The magnitude of the task ahead was soothing. Odile knew from experience that the exertion, the fresh autumnal air, her absorption in the job would eventually produce a mood of calm elation, combined with a wonderful physical lassitude.

Suddenly she noticed her husband standing beside her. 'Jerome!' Startled, she clapped a hand to her heart. 'You horrible man! Don't creep about like that.'

He grinned with mock innocence, enjoying her disarray. In his hands were two cups of pale, scented tea. Odile would have preferred something plain and strong, but Jerome liked to potter with recherché blends during breaks in his writing. She took her cup. He put his free arm around her, kissed her ear. He was shorter than she but solid. Odile leaned against him for a moment, savouring that solidity. She no longer desired him – perhaps she never really had – but his presence, his sheer bulk, was perpetually reassuring.

'Good to have the kids back at school?'

She shrugged. 'At this age it doesn't make so much difference. They're no real trouble. Not physically. Mentally, that's another thing.'

'I don't know why you worry about them.'

51

He never did. Odile marvelled at his sang-froid. Or was it, basically, just indifference?

She shrugged. 'It's quite natural to worry.'

'It's a self-induced state of mind.'

She didn't reply. It was a difference they no longer bothered to discuss except in the most ritual fashion. As she sipped her thin tea, Odile looked out to sea. Simultaneously she was conscious of her wellington-shod feet in the dark, friable earth she cultivated with such dedication. Sometimes it seemed . . . puzzling . . . improbable, that she should find herself in this beautiful, alien place, that in some way she belonged here.

'Did you read Ellis's letter?' Jerome asked.

Odile pulled a face. She wasn't particularly keen on Ellis. This morning a second letter had arrived, fulsome and apologetic, expanding on the initial *fait accompli*, and containing a handsome cheque.

Jerome laughed. He was amused by Odile's antipathy to his friend, but it made no difference to his own attitude. Ellis was an old mate. If anything, Jerome seemed rather to admire his coup, as he secretly approved most self-serving gestures.

'Kate does not say very much but this thing was so sudden . . . And after she lost her mother. He should consider her feelings more.'

'She'll get over it,' Jerome said comfortably.

'Maybe yes, maybe no. You don't know, Jerome.'

'She looks a lot happier since she came here.'

'This is true.' Odile drained her cup and gave it back to him. 'And now we must both work.'

'I love your peasant soul.'

It was a joke and yet, at the same time, it expressed what Jerome had decided he believed – that Odile's satisfaction in cultivating her vegetable garden harked back to some peasant ancestry, was tied in somehow with her Swiss-ness.

She'd stopped arguing with him about it. In fact Odile's upbringing had been entirely urban – a second-floor flat, shops and restaurants. The possibility of growing her own food had been a

52

discovery Odile had made herself, a break with the past if anything, even an unwitting rebellion against her parents' bourgeois comfort, Jerome's growing affluence.

But Jerome's obstinate view of her in this respect tied in with other vague, sentimental illusions he insisted on harbouring as regards his wife, one of which had led to Kate's coming to stay in the first place.

'Odile loves kids,' Jerome claimed to friends and acquaintances. 'The more the merrier.'

It was a wild simplification but, where human beings were concerned, that was the way Jerome's mind worked.

True, she'd adored her four babies, still did, but it was Jerome who'd wanted to carry on, have a fifth, a sixth – 'We've got this huge house to fill' – Odile who put her foot down and called a halt. But these facts had done nothing to dislodge the pat phrase, 'the more the merrier', from his mind.

'But you love kids,' he protested when, in the first place, Odile had raged about her husband's cavalier offer to his friend, Ellis.

'Understand this!' she screamed at him. 'I don't have this stupendous, extraordinary love for children. It exists only in your imbecile imagination.'

The fury and exasperation had died down. Odile had gone along with Jerome's invitation and she did like Kate. Partly because her spiky, intense young presence had its own appeal. Partly because it had become so clear that Kate was smitten with *them*. With the whole family.

It was gratifying to see her laugh, watch her become less guarded day by day. She'd been such a waif when she arrived, so pale and mute and resentful that Odile's heart had sunk. Now Kate's increasing bounce did them all credit, while her obvious admiration was like a mirror, reflecting back a pleasing self-image.

Odile glanced up for a moment from her newly dug row of fresh-skinned pink potatoes. Jerome was just re-entering the house through the open French window. She watched him go. The black polo-neck he wore made his head appear hunched on his stocky shoulders. From this distance her view of him was coolly appraising.

Sometimes, even now, it surprised her to think that this was the man of her life.

She used to fall in love rather easily, used to be thought beautiful. She'd had better-looking suitors by far. But ever since the summer of '36 when they first met – in the Deux Magots in Paris, Odile was doing a desultory summer painting course – Jerome had commandeered her existence. He was never intimidated by her beauty, but desired her more . . . aggressively than anyone she had ever known. Odile simply didn't have the fight to resist him. She'd lurched into marriage on a wave of something that had, perhaps, less to do with love than sheer passivity.

Just before they left for school in the morning, at around twenty past eight, someone had to take a cup of coffee up to Jerome, still snoozing in bed with the radio on.

'It's gross when you go in,' Nelly giggled. 'The room smells of a mixture of eau-de-cologne and farts.'

Officially all four children took turns. In reality they squabbled, traded, claimed to be in a tearing hurry. Mostly Nelly and Olivier capitulated.

One morning Beatrice and Nelly argued in the hall for fully five minutes while the clock ticked inexorably on towards leaving time.

Beatrice, her voice and manner serenely hectoring, was the irresistible force to Nelly's immovable object.

'Get lost, Bea. Who do you think you are? You haven't done it for at least two weeks . . .'

'I'll go,' Kate exclaimed. 'Or we'll all miss the bus.'

She grabbed the cup off the kitchen table, carried it in haste up the wide flight of stairs, knocked on the door of the parental bedroom.

'Come!'

She entered, was greeted with a blast of the warm, fetid air Nelly had described. Jerome was sitting up in bed reading, plump white chest and shoulders bare, half-moon reading glasses perched halfway down his nose. He didn't look up.

'Here's your coffee.' She placed it hurriedly on the bedside table.

At the sound of her voice, he turned, raising the spectacles to his forehead, grinning with the novelty of having her minister to him.

'Kate . . . Well, you really are one of us now – taking your turn in the coffee-run . . . Thank you.' Returning casually to his book.

The very insignificance of the exchange delighted her, gave her a sudden vivid sense of belonging, sang in her heart as she ran back downstairs to join the others.

Kate had been surprised to realize that Jerome was opposed to the whole idea of public schools. His voice was so plummy that she'd taken him for the product of one or other of them. In fact he came from Streatham, she discovered, where his father worked as a postman. He'd achieved his academic success thanks to the basic state system and had always been determined that his children would go the same route.

The school was in nearby Porth Lleian. Each day they walked to the top of the lane, so that the bus could pick them up from the road. The autumn was cool and dull. The air had a wet, earthy smell. It felt strange to Kate to stand waiting in the damp green shadow of a mountain, while her eyes rested on the distant hazy whitish void of the sea.

At first it was a shock to see the Felix offspring in uniform. Up to now she'd known them as free spirits, but the donning of blazers, ties and sensible shoes, flannels or serge skirts, demonstrated that they were bound by the same petty restrictions as the rest of humanity. The boys had their hair cut. The girls tied theirs neatly back with black petersham ribbon.

'It's all right for you,' Nelly grumbled. 'You don't have to walk around in all this lumpish stuff.' Since she was only there for one term, Kate was excused the wearing of uniform.

Her previous school, the Sybil Dane Academy, had been girls only. This one was mixed. The experience of learning Maths, French, History and the rest alongside boys seemed outlandish at first, not quite real. The staff were different too. At Kate's school the mistresses had seemed somehow a race apart, eccentric misfits. You couldn't imagine them living and breathing outside the chalk-smelling classrooms and sombre corridors where they reigned. Here, the teachers of both sexes were recognizable human beings who seemed to want to be liked. Some were young. They made jokes and their clothes were relatively up-to-date.

The Felixes had spoken Welsh all their lives and had no difficulty in following lessons. Kate was one of four English-speakers in her year who sat together, had lessons explained to them separately, took Welsh language lessons in the lunch-hour.

In class, Kate found, Nelly was a personality, recognized and indulged as such by pupils and staff alike. Her style was madcap, saucy. She understood and embraced her role.

'*Yes*, Nelly?'

When she put up her hand the teachers had a particular way of responding – wary, amused, anticipating some kind of a cheeky challenge.

English lessons were taught in the English language. During the first lesson in that subject Nelly quizzed the male teacher. 'Cross your heart, sir, aren't you bored when you go and see a Shakespeare play . . . if you're really, really honest with yourself?'

Kate had been amazed. At Sybil Dane such a question would have been viewed as heresy, punished with icy hauteur, not to mention detention or lines. But middle-aged, ginger-haired Mr Probert grinned as if Nelly had said simply what he would have expected.

'It may be you'll grow out of your philistinism with time, Nelly,' he replied mildly. 'Or maybe you'll remain in a state of arrested development . . . To the properly mature, Shakespeare is not boring.'

'Sir, sir –' The other kids hissed and heckled. It was all very good-natured, but to Kate awesomely irreverent.

All the Felix children attracted attention because their father was a television personality, because they were English and self-confident and lived in a large, locally prominent house. Of all of them it was Beatrice, with her aloof reserve, who became a target for sporadic envy and spite. On the whole, the boys and Nelly were accepted and liked because they mixed easily and didn't put on airs. Kate was privately aware that her own stock was raised by their reflected notoriety. Her position as honorary sibling lent her a curiosity-value she would otherwise have lacked.

But in her own right Kate possessed skills that stood her in good stead in the rough and tumble of school life. She was agile and good at athletics, gymnastics and, better still, blessed with outstanding ball sense. They were abilities she'd always had and took for granted, but she knew from experience that they could buy a certain prestige.

'Into the team with you, girl, right away, before we lose you,' Jenny Widdecombe, the fleshy, flashing-eyed games mistress exclaimed after Kate's first netball session.

Going on court she seemed to enter a new state of consciousness and concentration. Instinct took over and rarely failed her. She became alert and nippy, knowing exactly where to position herself for each pass, able to judge the height and placing of the ball for a goal. The team's season began successfully and Kate was exhilarated at this opportunity to prove herself. This was something for which she wasn't indebted to the Felix family, a talent of her own.

Some evenings and weekends she and her team-mates travelled long distances by coach to far-flung fixtures. On occasion they doubled with the rugby team and Kate was told that Tim David, the fly half, fancied her. He was a lean, dark boy, the strong, silent type and neither had much to say to the other. But one evening on the way home from their respective matches he sat next to her and put his arm resolutely round her shoulders. His breath had a sweetish smell. He French-kissed her most of the way home. She let him – it was the fashion – but felt strangely detached throughout. Next day the skin round her mouth was disgustingly rough and dry. Her classmates seemed far more excited by the interlude than Kate herself.

Nelly was ecstatic. 'He looks quite a bit like Montgomery Clift,' she enthused.

'I don't see it.'

'You old grump – Ros is mad about him.'

'Surprise surprise.'

Kate found her imagination far more closely engaged by Pascal's relationship with a girl named Bronwen Percy. Bronwen was in Pascal's class, a willowy creature with delicate wild rose features, her fine blonde hair permed into curls that were quite miraculously consistent, seemed unaltered by wind or weather. Kate envied the girl's bandbox perfection passionately. At weekends Bronwen often dropped by. She and Pascal would disappear upstairs to his room and close the door. What did they do in there? Kate's private preoccupation with the question disturbed her like a shameful secret.

One Saturday Bronwen was due to be picked up by her father around seven o'clock, just as the Felixes were about to sit down for their evening meal.

She addressed Odile. 'Thank you for having me, Mrs Felix.' She had a light, breathy little voice. A drippy voice, so Nelly always said.

'We'll see you again soon.' As ever, Odile was reassuring and kind. Pascal left the dining-room to see his girlfriend off.

'Thank you for having me, Mrs Felix,' Beatrice parroted in a cruel imitation of Bronwen's baby tones. She sat at the table, chin in hand, long eyes narrowed, sceptical, sly.

Nelly, Olivier and Kate choked with appreciative laughter. It did Kate good to hear Bronwen debunked. When Pascal returned the atmosphere was still tight and giggly, he couldn't help but sense it.

'What's up?' he asked.

Provocatively Beatrice remarked, as if continuing a conversation started in his absence, 'You see, Pascal likes them vacuous . . .'

He shrugged, seeming unfazed, took his place at the table, passed his plate up to Odile for a helping of lamb casserole. 'So what?' Pascal said. 'So what if Bron's not got much between the ears . . . She looks just like a Botticelli.'

The statement impressed Kate. It stuck in her mind. In bed at night she recaptured the tone of his voice as he said it, recalled the

58

look on his face. She couldn't decide what she felt about his words, but they held a strange power for her. It was as if, for Pascal, the fact of Bronwen's beauty answered everything.

Kate pondered on the thought, which seemed somehow to tie in with Pascal's fascination with her photograph album, with his own snaps . . . with the indefinable chic of David Lacoste . . .

A few days later, walking along the first-floor corridor, she passed Pascal's room. The door stood open. Inside Pascal was kissing Bronwen with slow application. One hand was round her waist, the other flat against the blue cotton of her skirt, against her belly, fingers curving into the cleft between her thighs. The sudden vision of them together like that burned hot and bright into her brain.

They must have heard the soft sound of her footsteps. Pascal turned his head sharply.

'Oh, hello, Kate.' He sounded relieved and grinned at her, embarrassed, but brazen too.

Bronwen's expression remained blank, like a photograph advertising cosmetics.

'Hello,' Kate muttered. Ashamed she passed by, an unwitting voyeur, feeling squat and graceless as a troll.

Chapter Six

❁❁❁❁❁

As the academic year got under way Jerome began to divide his time between Plas Felix and a small pied-à-terre in Bloomsbury. He was attached to Imperial College, London, so had teaching and lecturing obligations. He used his sojourns in the capital to slot in radio and television work, returning home every fortnight for a long weekend.

Though he was far from being a heavy father, there was a sense of lightness and liberation in the air during his absence. They had their meals in the kitchen at the large table with a top thick as a butcher's block. Strings of onions and garlic, bunches of dried herbs hung overhead. Coarsely woven russet curtains and frosted amber lampshades made the light look warm and mellow. Odile served food straight from the pan. The radio was left on. There was a cosy, slumming feel to mealtimes.

Jerome's study was on the first floor, next to his and Odile's bedroom. Kate had never been in there – officially the children were barred.

But one Thursday – Odile's Gardening Club night – Nelly suggested, 'Come and have a peek . . . While the cat's away . . .'

Curious, Kate entered the secret chamber. Not that there was anything particularly remarkable to see – just a lot of bookshelves, a big desk, a homely patchwork of faded oriental rugs covering the scuffed floorboards. Her attention was caught by a portrait on the desk of Odile as a young woman, her dark hair centrally parted and worn in a thirties plaited coronet, terribly like Beatrice was now, except that her eyes had a demure, submissive look.

Next to it stood a rack in dark, carved wood, holding a number of books.

Nelly ran her hands lightly along their spines. 'This is all the stuff he's written.'

Most looked heavy, dull and nondescript, not unlike the three history textbooks Ellis had had published. But four volumes, side by side, had the shiny brown and white laminated covers of the popular 'Who is . . .' series, featured as students' aids in all good bookshops. Jerome's titles were Socrates, Voltaire, Hegel and Karl Marx. Next to them stood a book called *The Dark Spirit*, an opulent-looking production in a glossy black dust-jacket, then what seemed to be a companion volume, in crimson, entitled *Season in Valhalla*, which Kate recognized because Ellis used to have a copy.

'Look at this, Kate.'

Nelly stood by a green baize notice board, attached to the wall behind Jerome's desk. She was pointing to one of the newspaper and magazine clippings that were pinned up there. Kate moved closer, peered and grinned. It was a Giles cartoon showing Jerome talking on the television, his bearded baby face and mocking smile immediately recognizable. He was being watched by a proletarian couple seated foursquare in matching easy chairs, the man in cap, vest and braces, a glass of beer in one hand, his wife wearing a hairnet, a floral overall and check carpet slippers.

'We are all of us philosophers, by right of birth . . .' Jerome was saying in the caption, while the couple beamed their agreement.

'Good, eh?' Nelly patted the cutting proudly.

Kate's eyes moved sideways to a review from the *Telegraph* of *The Dark Spirit*, deriding Jerome as an implacable vulgarizer with a burning, self-imposed mission to reduce the whole of Western thought to the language of the public bar or the working men's club . . . Above it in green ink Nelly had written 'sour grapes', Olivier had added 'pompous prick' and Jerome had scrawled 'Thank you, my children'.

'We'd better be going,' Nelly said. 'If Beatrice sees us she's bound to rat, and Ma regards keeping us out of Dad's study as some kind of a sacred trust . . .'

She crossed to the door and switched out the light so the room was illuminated only by the glow from the corridor outside. Kate hesitated a moment before following. Like her own, the room had the additional ingredient of a living landscape, framed in the rectangle of the window, visible now the study was in darkness.

Jerome's room was on the opposite side of the house. Instead of sea, it looked out on the black shape of the mountain flanking the road and the sky above, streaked grey and deep gunmetal with clouds that masked the silver disc of the moon. For a moment she drank in the potent combination – the warm, workaday comfort of the interior, the cold silence of the landscape outside.

'Come on, Kate,' Nelly urged.

They went out, closing the door quietly behind them, tiptoed along the corridor to Nelly's room, bright and messy – a jumble of clothes and film magazines on the floor, shelves full of junk she couldn't bear to throw away, old kids' books, stuffed toys, shells and pebbles from the beach. And again there was the contrast of the night sky outside, the dark emptiness that was the sea.

Kate crossed to the window but her mind was not on the view. Instead she was overwhelmed by the thought that living with her father wouldn't be like this, it wouldn't have the richness, the laughter and companionship.

'I don't want to leave,' she said suddenly to Nelly. 'I love it here.'

'I know.' At once Nelly stood beside her, hooked an arm round Kate's neck, kissed her cheek. 'It isn't fair. I'm going to hate it when you're gone.'

'It's not the same for you . . . You'll still be here. This is where you belong.'

'You belong too, darling,' Nelly soothed.

But she didn't, Kate thought, however much she longed to. However much she loved them all. However much they loved her. And that was the difference.

After that night Kate had the helpless awareness, dogging everything she did, of time running out. She and Nelly had a passion for the season's hit record – Bill Haley's 'Rock Around the Clock'. They used to go up to the bare top floor of the house and play it over and over, dance along to its heavy, insistent beat. And all the time Kate kept thinking that she wouldn't be here much longer.

The night term ended she and Nelly went down to the beach with Robert Williams and Tim David, lit a fire and tried to cook potatoes. Nelly sneaked a bottle of red wine from the cellar.

The potatoes burned their mouths, were black outside and raw in the middle. But it didn't matter. The flames flickered startling orange in the cold darkness, lighting up their faces, heating their skin. The sky was filled with stars and the sea swished against the shore. And Kate was possessed by a soaring sense of the wonder and the joy of life.

Nelly and Robert began to kiss and cuddle. The wine and the surroundings made Kate feel more receptive towards Tim. His relentless, thorough kisses seemed less tiresome than usual.

'Will you write to me, Kate?' he whispered. He did look handsome in the firelight.

'All right.' Her voice was intimate, almost soundless. The thought of having a boyfriend on the far side of the Atlantic seemed suddenly rather romantic.

The next few days were a welter of Christmas preparations. Jerome was home by now and full of expansive good cheer. Since Kate's days among them were numbered he chose her to go along with him and help him select the family Christmas tree.

'Looking forward to seeing your dad again?' he asked affably as they drove towards a local farm.

'Yes.' Her tone was hollow and unconvincing.

'You don't sound very sure,' he laughed. But Jerome wasn't one to probe the recesses of the human heart, and he let the subject drop.

They picked out a bushy ten-footer. Jerome had to open the sun roof to get it into the car. That evening they all helped decorate it with silver balls and red fairy-lights. The tree stood by the French windows, bright and festive against the black sky outside. It would stay there until Twelfth Night, but by then Kate would be gone.

Pascal scoffed at it nowadays as sentimental hypocrisy, Odile's custom of attending the Christmas midnight service at the nearby little church of St Stephen's.

'Oh, Pascal!' She just shrugged. 'I do it for me and I do it for the grandparents. Nobody forces you to come.'

Jerome never came either, in spite of the fact that he'd once said he wanted to be buried in the churchyard here.

Olivier had always enjoyed the ritual. It started Christmas off, it was traditional. He hated the way Pascal tried to spoil things, putting everything under the microscope, so scornful and superior. He liked the dark outside, the sharp smell of the fir branches used to decorate the church, the candles burning in the wall-brackets, casting a pale cosy light over the small congregation.

The vicar, Grumpy Griffiths, was talking to them in Welsh about the true meaning of Christmas. Along the pew from Olivier all three of his grandparents sat looking attentive and intelligent, though they obviously couldn't understand a word.

He loved his Felix grandparents. They were little and smiley and never bad-tempered. Olivier couldn't help knowing that he was their favourite. Grand-mère was different – rather scary with her harsh voice, her smart whitish-mauve hair, her black clothes and silver jewellery, her disapproval.

Just before they came out tonight she'd snapped at him, 'Olivier, you will clean your shoes, no?'

'Yes, do it, Olivier.' With her mother Odile took the line of least resistance.

Beatrice was Grand-mère's favourite because she was clean and tidy and always had her nose in a book. In particular Grand-mère liked her long, shiny hair. At least once a day she rearranged it with her knobbly fingers and commented admiringly, '*Belle chevelure.*'

'*Belle chevelure*' had become the season's secret catch-phrase, repeated sotto voce to muffled giggles. Even Beatrice joined in the bubbly, silent laughter.

Kate sat next to him. Olivier nudged her. Not for any particular reason, just to make contact. She turned towards him with a grin. He liked the way she looked – her white skin and beige-coloured lips, straight eyebrows, the darkness of her eyes.

'Be specially nice to Kate over Christmas,' Odile had said to him the other day.

'I always am,' he protested.

According to Nelly, Kate didn't want to go and join her father. She'd rather stay here. Olivier didn't blame her. He'd thought Ellis Stephens a bit of a prick. Anyone could see Kate was better off with them. His own home was warm and cosy. It made him sad to think of her having to go away into the cold outside world.

Odile wouldn't let him say bad things about Ellis. But with Beatrice she was more open. 'He couldn't wait to . . . dump her and simplify his life,' Olivier had overheard her saying. 'Then he lets her down again just like that. And now he tells Jerome he's got some sort of a girlfriend . . .' When she was indignant Odile's French accent sounded sweet and funny. But she and Beatrice had clammed up when they saw him standing in the doorway.

Olivier had noticed that Kate seemed rather quiet the last few days. And she seemed to be looking at everything really hard, as if she wanted to remember it all. But perhaps he was imagining that.

Grumpy Griffiths announced the final hymn. Olivier sang along at the top of his voice to impress the grandparents with his knowledge of Welsh. Then there was a prayer and then it was time to go out into the frosty, starry night. They had to hang around for a while for Odile to wish the neighbours Happy Christmas and for the neighbours to pay their respects to the grandparents. Then they started on the half-mile walk home, along the road and down the lane.

Grand-mère went arm-in-arm with Odile. He could hear her telling some long story in her strident French. Grandma and Grandpa Felix walked behind. They and Grand-mère never found much to say to one another. It could have been awkward only Jerome closed his eyes to any kind of tension.

'He just glides through it all,' Beatrice had marvelled the other day, 'As if he's walking on water. And he ends up carrying Grand-mère and everyone else along with him.'

After church they always had mince pies and ginger wine before

65

they went to bed in the early hours of Christmas morning. Surprisingly Grand-mère approved of mince pies, though she always tasted them suspiciously before nodding and telling Odile, '*C'est bon.*'

Nelly walked along the road singing 'It Came upon the Midnight Clear' in a loud, trembly soprano. She obviously thought she sounded great.

Olivier drew alongside her. 'Are you an angel, young woman?' he mocked.

Nelly clouted him in the ribs without missing a note. Pretending to stagger, Olivier collided with Kate.

'*Belle chevelure,*' he murmured to her in Grand-mère's wondering tones. Kate laughed, but she looked sad too.

Chapter Seven
1956

❈❈❈❈❈

'This is it – home sweet home. At long last.'

The garage door rumbled shut. Ellis picked up Kate's suitcase and carried it up the three steps that led to the porch. It was dark, but a lantern above the front door threw a circle of cold light, revealing a section of the house's façade – timbered, white-painted – and its open wooden porch, fading away in the snow beyond.

Her father took off his thick, clumsy gloves, fumbled with his bunch of keys, opened up and stood aside to let her pass.

'Welcome, sweetheart.'

Fuddled with tiredness, Kate entered a hallway. She was greeted by a welcome blast of warm, dry air. Ellis followed her and switched on the light. She blinked at the sudden harsh brightness.

He pushed at a door to her right. 'The living-room.'

She went in. The room was plain and tidy, a stranger's room with nothing familiar in it. With blank, exhausted eyes Kate took in a rectangular black sofa with spindly legs, three chairs in pale, curved, shiny wood, padded in kingfisher blue, a 'free-form' coffee table. They looked 'contemporary', the sort of thing you saw in magazines. On the wall was a large oil landscape of pines in snow. It hung above a rough stone fireplace with a glowing stove. Kate stared, feeling nothing.

'What do you think?'

'It's nice,' she said dutifully.

Ellis seemed changed. Bigger, ruddier, wearing clothes she'd never seen – a thick plaid jacket, a woollen hat, heavy-soled shoes. It was hard to feel he belonged to her in any way.

'Are you hungry?' he asked.

She shook her head. 'No. Just tired.'

'I think you should get straight to bed. We'll talk in the morning. There's so much I want to show you.'

Her room was small and plain, holding just a wardrobe and a single divan bed, a small, empty bookcase. But the bed was covered with a patchwork quilt – red and black stars on a white background. On it was laid out a warm, red, long-sleeved nightdress. From the way Ellis looked at her it was clear he expected her to exclaim.

Eventually he prompted. 'A friend chose the quilt for you. And the nightdress . . . Fay. You know . . . I've mentioned her in my letters.' The way he spoke – with a studied negligence – awoke in her a sort of uneasy, unspecified suspicion.

Kate shrugged. 'It's nice,' she said again and could tell Ellis was disappointed by her lack of enthusiasm.

'I'll leave you now, sweetheart. Get some rest . . . Sleep as long as you like.' He bent and kissed her cheek. 'I'm so glad you're here at last.'

She gave a small smile. 'Good night, Dad.'

When Kate had seen Ellis's face among the crowds at the airport, she'd experienced a surge of real pleasure. Yet, almost immediately, the old buried sense of grievance resurfaced. He was too cock-a-hoop with himself and his life. Kate couldn't bring herself to be nice to him, it seemed, for even five minutes. She could never quite decide whether or not her resentment was justified.

'Good night, Kate.' He left, closing the door.

Tired as she was, Kate did not fall immediately into sleep, but lay curled in the red nightdress, beneath the handsome quilt, feeling nothing, neither happy nor sad. Then by and by her mind drifted inevitably back to her goodbyes with the Felix family.

Nelly, never one to miss an opportunity for drama, had sobbed and clung to her, the way she had the day James Dean died. Olivier just lifted his hand in a curt little wave but, to Kate's surprise, his round, grey-green eyes had brimmed with sudden tears.

'We're your family too, you know,' Odile said as she embraced her. 'You can always call on us.' It was as if she thought Kate might be in some kind of need.

68

Beatrice and Pascal were in their dressing-gowns, hair still tousled from bed. With a wry, teasing smile Beatrice had handed Kate a small package wrapped in Christmas paper. Pascal had placed a satirical-fatherly kiss on her forehead. For a moment Kate breathed in the acrid scent of his body. Hours afterwards it was as if the brief touch of his lips remained imprinted on her skin.

She travelled with Jerome – he had to be back in London anyway. For the first hour or so of the long car journey Kate snivelled quietly. Jerome left her to it. Then she pulled herself together, dried her eyes. After a bit she reached for Beatrice's gift, peeled off the green and red wrapping paper.

'Oh, my God.' It was a 'housewife', a small sewing set in a compact tan leather case – Beatrice's Christmas present from Grand-mère, a source at the time of muffled laughter and ribaldry. 'Look what she's done –' Kate showed Jerome – 'she's given it to me!'

Inside, Beatrice had tucked a square of white card with the words, 'No traveller should be without one'.

'The hussy.' Jerome grinned, amused, then he added, 'Poor old Antoinette – she never did have much of a clue with presents.'

That night Kate slept on a dusty maroon velvet chaise-longue in Jerome's small flat in Bedford Square. The following day he put her on the bus to the airport.

When Kate awoke the room was bright. Daylight pierced white rep curtains she'd barely noticed the previous night. She lay for a while collecting her thoughts, then got out of bed and crossed to the window.

Outside the sky was blue. A shiny black ribbon of road showed between banks of clean white snow. A line of pleasant-looking white frame houses stretched away on either side of the street. As Kate watched a woman came out of the home opposite. She wore a red coat and a red and yellow knitted cap, got into a red car and drove away. To Kate it seemed a land of primary colours, bright and improbable as a Christmas card.

Feeling hungry, she padded downstairs. Voices came from behind

69

the door at the far end of the ground-floor corridor. Her conscious mind had hardly registered the fact before she reached for the door handle.

Ellis was sitting at a red Formica-topped kitchen table. Opposite him sat a woman. They were smoking and drinking coffee in an atmosphere of ease and animation. The tableau lasted just a split second before they turned, startled, to face Kate.

'Kate! You're awake. I didn't hear you come down.' Ellis sounded flustered.

Kate stood and stared. Her eyes were heavy. She felt stupid.

'This is Fay,' her father announced hastily. 'Fay, meet my daughter, Kate.'

'Hi, Kate.' The woman smiled, serene and friendly.

'Hello.'

'Fay's a colleague of mine, Kate . . . I've mentioned her in my letters . . . Without her I doubt I'd have survived the first weeks . . .' He threw the woman a jokey sideways glance.

'Oh, come on now, Ellis . . .' Her disclaimer held an edge of playful irony.

She was young with wavy fair hair that dipped over one eye. Her face was round and pretty, the jawline full. She had blue eyes, a neat little nose, smiling red lips, looked healthy, happy and wholesome. Fay was almost plump, but wore a high-necked yellow sweater and bright plaid slacks with panache.

'Fay's the one who chose that quilt for your bedroom – and the nightgown you're wearing,' Ellis reminded.

He grinned approvingly at the woman and she smiled back. Kate felt herself the outsider of the three.

'Thank you,' Kate said.

'That nightgown looks so warm and cosy on you,' Fay enthused.

'In fact it was Fay who tipped me off about this house in the first place.' Ellis continued with his eager endorsement.

'Would you like some coffee, Kate?' Fay reached for the silver percolator.

'She doesn't drink coffee,' Ellis said.

'I do now.'

70

'Oho – the Felixes leading you into bad ways . . .'

'Good ways,' Kate said.

Fay laughed. 'That's telling him!' She pointed to a brown paper bag standing on the table. 'I brought us some bear claws.'

Kate was mystified.

Fay dipped into the bag and held up a sticky pastry. 'Bear claws . . . They're one of my vices.'

'The least of your vices.' Again Ellis smiled at her, as if his words had a significance only they could understand. Fay gave him an amused sidelong glance. Once more Kate felt an intruder, rather as if she'd come in halfway through a play whose plot was unknown to her.

That afternoon Ellis and Fay showed her round Coningsburgh. The centre was simple and attractive, the buildings grouped round an area of snow-covered grass known as The Green.

There was a white church with a domed bell-tower, a big meeting house – Dutch-barn style, so Fay informed her – painted rusty pink, a historic tavern in blue clapboard with white shutters and diamond-pane windows, which now housed the town bookstore.

Chestnut Street was the shopping centre. Here the white clapboard buildings had plate-glass frontages, and all appeared to be thriving. Bernhard Street contained most of the handsome big houses. On the corner stood a statue of James Bernhard, the town's former benefactor. He looked tall and grave, with an Abraham Lincoln beard.

Already Ellis seemed to know quite a lot of people. He greeted several with a casual 'Hi', stopped and talked to several more. All seemed breezy and friendly, spoke amiably to Kate. In these surroundings Ellis appeared larger than life, more expansive than he'd ever been back home. Kate felt strange and unreal, knew she'd never remember the faces of Ellis's acquaintances, let alone their names. Fay chatted brightly to her, either ignoring or not noticing Kate's confusion.

They went to see Bernhard College, a little way out of town, consisting of four large white modern buildings grouped round a

71

central campus. They visited Ellis's office in the History Faculty and one of the lecture-halls. It all looked very prosperous, smelt of cleanliness and central heating.

'It's a good place to work,' Fay said. She was in Ellis's department, had taught here for just a year before he came.

'It's an excellent place,' Ellis agreed. And again they smiled at each other in a way that excluded Kate.

They had burgers, fries and chocolate milk shakes at a place called the Dutchman's Kitchen. It all tasted fine, but Ellis and Fay seemed to assume that Kate would see these foods as positively ambrosial. Six months ago she knew she would. Since then she'd acquired a liking for Odile's gutsy, garlicky fare and resisted the idea of these two adults taking her taste for granted. For no definable reason Kate felt suddenly close to tears and longed to be alone with her father.

In fact Fay left them soon after. She had grading to do, she said. Kate and Ellis went home. The house seemed impersonal, like premises rented for a holiday.

'You must be free and easy here,' Ellis said. 'Raid the fridge if you're hungry, all that sort of thing.'

'I'm fine.'

Back in the old days, when he and Rose were a couple, she was never allowed to eat between meals.

He flicked on the television and they watched the last ten minutes of Lucille Ball in silence. Then he flicked it off again.

After a moment or two Ellis asked, 'Do you like what you've seen of Coningsburgh so far?'

'Yes. It's pretty. And well kept.'

'What do you think of Fay?' He spoke with the same assumed nonchalance she'd noticed the previous night, but Kate had the impression that her reply was of breathless interest to him.

'Nice.'

Ellis stared at her for a moment, as if hoping for more. Then he said with feeling, 'I think she's a wonderful person.'

Listening, Kate felt her heart gripped by a strong, painful emotion she couldn't name. No reply seemed possible.

Her father pointed to the canvas that hung above the rustic stone fireplace. 'Fay did that.'

She glanced up at it. The painting seemed quite good, with a pinkish sheen on the snow, the dark pine branches spiking away from the trunks at lifelike angles.

'She's so good at everything she does,' Ellis continued fervently. 'And at the same time so warm and full of vitality.'

Kate experienced his praise of Fay as criticism of herself. So cold and so withdrawn.

'I like this town. *And* this country. I really think we can make a new life here.' His voice held a quiet intensity. 'A good life.'

She was stricken. It was as if his old life – the one he'd shared with her and Rose – had been worthless, something he was heartily glad to shake off. As if Rose was someone of whom he was finally free. And as if now, here, in this far more congenial environment, it might at last be possible for Ellis to become the person he'd always wanted to be.

Kate understood, with a kind of amazed clarity, that her father was in love. With bouncy, friendly, American Fay. The idea was too bizarre to contemplate.

He looked at her, as if refocusing his attention from an inner to an outer world. 'I do hope you're going to be happy here, my sweet.'

In Kate's mind, suddenly, her father's words had the ring of a threat.

Chapter Eight

◄○►◄○►

Ellis had been hired – for two years initially and at an appreciable boost in salary – to breathe new life into the History Faculty of Bernhard College. Her father's goal was to transcend small-town limitations and aim at excellence, find the right balance between rigour and adventurousness. The challenge, Kate could see, absorbed him fully.

Chatting to Fay at the kitchen table, hammering out questions of curriculum and presentation, the kindling and maintaining of student enthusiasm, her father's 'interesting' hawkish face and amber eyes would shine with fire and determination.

At times like these Kate would watch him with fascinated pride. But always it was in discussion with Fay that the transformation took place – she was in on his schemes, all in favour of his vigorous new broom. Her round, smiling face would take on an impressive seriousness as together they argued and planned.

Sadly Kate saw that in conversation with herself Ellis lost his animation and had difficulty thinking up things to say, falling back on dutiful enquiries about homework and what she'd done at school, domestic chores and arrangements.

Kate herself was no better. She longed to be easy and fluent like Fay, but took refuge in shrugs and scowls. Deep down she felt inadequate, unable to hold her father's attention for more than a desultory second or two. Had it always been like this? Kate wasn't sure. Rose had always been there as a buffer.

It was actually much easier when Fay was with them. Her warm personality was like a lubricant, oiling the rusty wheels of their communication. All the same, Kate had mixed feelings about her being there so much of the time. She felt suspicious, as if Ellis was trying to foist a new mother on her, a younger, brighter, more presentable model.

Ellis liked to delegate to her some of the mother-and-daughter things Kate and Rose used to do together. Soon after she arrived Fay took Kate shopping for boots, ski-pants and a thick coat.

'These are cute.' She recalled Fay, who favoured plaids and bright extrovert colours, holding up a pair of red and blue checkered trousers.

Kate had rolled her eyes. 'Ugh. Kindergarten style!'

'Oh my!' Fay shook her head over Kate's choice of blacks and greys, a grouchy protest against the primary colours that surrounded her. 'You're going to look like the school vampire!'

In her heart of hearts Kate was touched by Fay's kindness, but it had the effect of making her all the more surly and ungracious.

She began to dream of Rose, night after night. And always her mother seemed to be left behind in some way – missing a train, or stuck on top of a cliff while Kate and Ellis walked unconcernedly on the beach below. Once she dreamed someone was tapping out a desperate message on her bedroom window. Drawing the curtains, she could see only darkness but knew Rose was out there somewhere.

Then Kate would wake with a simmering sense of hostility towards her father as if, somehow, he had engineered Rose's death so he'd be free to live life as he pleased. In the dark, discouraging early-morning hours the fancy seemed real and damning, and Kate was forced to remind herself that it wasn't, it was just a dream. Yet the hostility would linger on, fogging her day like a hanging, heavy vapour.

Ellis and Fay had a record by someone called Tom Lehrer. It was considered risqué and un-American and had to be privately distributed – the man mocked the Army and the Boy Scouts, sang songs about missile testing and drug dealing. They played it often, chuckling companionably at its daring. Kate hated the man's smug, smart-arse tones.

One evening in February all three of them were gathered round the wood-burning stove in the living-room. Fay and Ellis sat at opposite ends of the sofa, she marking assignments, he reading. Kate lay on the floor doing her homework. There were cups of hot chocolate, Tom Lehrer on the phonograph.

The cosy warmth was hateful to Kate. It was built on Rose's death. She lay quietly, working through a page of mathematical problems while, inside, a churning tide of black bile swamped her stomach and her head. She wanted to scream. She wanted to smash her fist down on the turn-table, stop Tom Lehrer once and for all in his self-satisfied tracks.

Ellis looked up from his book and sighed with pleasure. 'It's perfect –' he spread his arms in a vague, all-encompassing gesture – 'everything . . . It's the classic long winter evening by the fire.'

Fay turned to smile at him, ironic but pleased.

'I'm going to bed.' Brusquely Kate stood up and crossed to the door. If she'd stayed she would have harangued him like an incoherent fishwife and choked ignominiously on her tears.

As the days passed Kate felt as if the black bitterness inside her was growing. It bubbled corrosively in her guts, until the secret rancour became the most real thing in her life. In contrast the outside world seemed highly coloured and two-dimensional like a stage set. The façade of Coningsburgh High School, where Ellis dropped her off each day, made her think of a backcloth. It was a pleasant red-brick building – post-war, but designed on traditional lines, with a bell-tower, three rows of mullioned windows, a flight of steps up to a wide, colonnaded entrance.

Each morning Kate screwed up her courage before entering the large, well-heated concourse with its polished wood-block floor. She was intimidated by the rowdy hustle and bustle of the place. In their bright sweaters and heavy shoes, her fellow pupils appeared almost ruthlessly exuberant. Their breezy confidence, like Fay's, seemed bred in the bone. She found it daunting – Kate's own upbringing had been of the 'seen but not heard' variety.

The high school kids who jostled and joshed their way to class looked to her like extras from *Rebel Without a Cause*. She was the only one who didn't know her lines, didn't know how to behave and stuck out like a sore thumb. She felt gawky and stiff, out of her depth. She felt alone and miserable.

Some of her classmates were friendly, only they seemed to see her as representing a land of thatched cottages, beefeaters, bowlers and umbrellas, and to be uninterested in any other view.

On the first day Debbie Van Hage – who was little and blond and wore fluffy angora sweaters – had asked Kate if she knew the Queen.

'Of course not,' Kate answered, bemused, and Mickey Neville had imitated her English accent, and everyone laughed.

Kate went red. She felt stupid, but despised their shallow laughter. All the same, after that, she became self-conscious about the way she talked.

Some of the teachers seemed to think that, because she was British, she would be especially clever.

'Kate . . . You tell us.'

Mr Kennedy, who taught English, with his grey moustache and tweedy jacket, would turn to her when answers weren't forthcoming, with an expectant smile, taking for granted that she could instruct the rest in the finer points of grammar.

She *did* know the answers – the Sybil Dane Academy had been hot on such things – but wanted no part of the swottish image he wished on her. Kate began to shrug and plead ignorance, but denying what she knew made her feel even more of a misfit.

A girl called Myra Brown asked her home one night in February. Her mother was Austrian and served up the sort of aromatic casserole Odile might have cooked. Mrs Brown's English was halting – like Kate she seemed out of place, a little bit at sea.

After the meal Myra and Kate went out into the backyard. There was a basketball hoop on a pole and they took turns aiming at it with a large rubber ball. It was dark but an outside lantern fixed above the back door diffused a cold white light. It was peaceful out there and they played for almost an hour until Ellis arrived to pick Kate up. It was the best time she'd had since coming to America.

Boxed in temporarily by another parent's car, Ellis watched Kate

77

walk up the stone steps towards the entrance to Coningsburgh High. What on earth had possessed her to choose that dismal dark coat? Among the gaily dressed hordes of her fellow pupils she made him think of a spider, black and out of place. He observed her with an anxious affection that shaded into impatience.

The concern he often experienced as regards his daughter began to nibble at his mind. Ellis dismissed it with an effort of will. There was too much else for him to think about. He had a meeting with the Dean this morning, needed to put a convincing case for radical changes in the first-year curriculum, a restructuring of the whole money thing . . .

'She'll settle in. Just give her time.' Fay was always reassuring when Kate seemed out of sorts.

The Chrysler in front of him edged forward, leaving Ellis an opening. He nosed his way back into the flow of the traffic. He liked the wide roads here, the simplicity of the layout – they made him feel a halfway decent driver. Behind the wheel Fay was far more skilful and decisive than he. Just as Rose had been . . .

Thinking of Fay he smiled. Nothing seemed to faze her. She was amiably philosophical in the face of Kate's sulkiness towards herself – 'Ellis, I have nephews and nieces' – and she would roll her eyes with that tolerant, humorous look he loved.

Rose had been weak, but Fay was stable and strong. A man could be made or broken by the woman in his life. Ellis marvelled every hour of every day that Fay found him worthy of her consideration, let alone her love. They had even discussed marriage, but agreed to wait until Kate was settled.

Driving smoothly along the pleasant highway that led to Bernhard College, Ellis indulged himself by picturing Fay's compact, muscular body – a generous country girl's body, the breasts heavy but buoyant, strong, shapely thighs swelling into the firm, full arse and hips. Almost instantaneously he became hard. In bed she had a willing, but somehow innocent, energy. Like Doris Day, he teased. They'd made love on a few occasions only, discreetly, during weekends away.

'I'd be finished at Bernhard if they knew I was fucking the boss,' she laughed, sounding brassier and more experienced than she really was. And now of course there was Kate to consider.

The memory of his daughter was like a splash of cold water. She was being brattish, walking around all the time with a face as long as a fiddle, reminding him of everything he'd hated about his former life.

Here in America, Ellis had discovered in himself a desire for stability and continuity. He was forty-two and wanted to belong somewhere, be respected as a man, cultivate life-long friends, give something back to a benevolent community. With Fay as his wife he could achieve all this. They'd have kids who were strong and easy-going like her. He wouldn't let Kate scupper his dreams. If – God forbid – it came down to it, he would choose Fay.

Nelly wrote often, on big, lined foolscap sheets torn from an exercise book, her letters decorated with doodles and exclamation marks. She had a biro that wrote in three colours and she changed from one to another quite arbitrarily.

'Darling twin . . .' she always started, before launching into all the gossip she knew Kate would be avid to hear.

Beatrice had been accepted by Oxford University. Pascal had got three photographs printed in *Camera World*. He'd split with Bronwen Percy and she'd been crying in assembly the other day. Robert Williams was being boring, accusing Nelly of making eyes at some cousin of his – 'I was!!!' Nelly admitted cheerfully in brackets. Olivier was learning the guitar. The netball team had lost nine out of eleven matches since Kate left. Tim David said hello and when was she going to write . . .

Reading Nelly's outpourings, Kate lost herself in another, less problematic world where, however temporarily, she'd felt at home. The contentment stayed with her for a time afterwards, along with the recollection that she hadn't always been the sour-faced outsider she seemed over here.

'That letter looks fun.' Fay happened on Kate in the kitchen one Saturday afternoon devouring one of her friend's multi-coloured missives. 'Who wrote that?'

'My friend, Nelly.' Kate was still elated and forgot to be on her guard.

Fay started asking her about the Felixes and Kate was happy to sit at the shiny red kitchen table and chat to her about Nelly and the others, the house above the beach, her bedroom, school . . . Fay seemed interested and it was lovely to talk about them all. Then, after a while, Kate saw that Fay wore a sort of indulgent smile, as if at the unselfconscious prattlings of an infant, and she clammed up again.

It was a freezing iron-grey day halfway through March. A fresh fall of snow was forecast. With elaborate insouciance Kate sauntered up the school steps. She knew Ellis would be watching her. In the concourse she lingered unobtrusively for a minute, until her father pulled away. Then she slipped back outside and started walking down the street. Nobody challenged her.

Last night in bed the idea had come to her quite suddenly. Ellis wouldn't know – she made her own way home each evening. And even if he did find out, what punishment could he inflict? Kate rarely went anywhere or did anything she cared about. If he grounded her it would make little or no difference to her life. Ellis had the right to make her live here, but here was something *she* could do. The notion of playing truant seemed coolly rebellious, like Holden Caulfield in *Catcher in the Rye*.

Instead of her black coat she'd put on a thick blue check jacket Fay had left behind at the house. She would be more anonymous in that.

'That's a bit more like it.' Ellis had smiled at her without his usual disapproving reserve. 'It suits you, that coat.' Kate guessed he was gratified that she'd borrowed something of Fay's.

Striking off towards the west side of town where no one knew her, Kate felt calm and lawless. It was good to imagine her classmates yawning through a *Tale of Two Cities* with Mr Kennedy, taking notes on the Canadian prairies to Mrs Ladnier's sing-song dictation.

It was icy and a few flakes of fine snow drifted across her vision. After a while the streets petered out and Kate found herself walking along a dirt road between two empty fields. There was no one around except for a tiny, lone pick-up truck bumping across the far horizon. The sky was wide and purple-grey, the solitude a pleasure.

Around eleven o'clock Kate turned and retraced her steps, needing to eat early before the lunch-time rush, when there would be a greater chance of being recognized. At the Dutchman's Kitchen she had coffee and a thick burger, juicy with soft fried onions. Outside the big plate-glass window snow began to fall in earnest. When she'd eaten, Kate went to the record store and monopolized the booth, listening to Pat Boone and Frank Sinatra until the woman behind the counter turned hostile. After that she sat at the long table in the library and read magazines. *Life* was doing a feature on existentialist Paris. There was a page with photographs of literary rising stars and one of them was David Lacoste. She stared at his picture for some time, entering a kind of reverie, recapturing the particular flavour of her summer with the Felixes, while beyond the high window wet snowflakes fell, thick and silent.

When she left, the streetlights had come on, throwing a beautiful yellow glow across the fresh snow, illuminating each separate twig on the rough, bare trees. Kate trudged home with a low exhilaration in her heart. That evening she, Fay and Ellis went to the movies. Richard Burton was on in *The Robe*, a real tear-jerker. Kate and Fay cried buckets while sharing a monster carton of popcorn.

'What a pair of softies.' Afterwards Ellis teased them, seeming pleased by their feminine susceptibility. On the way home he walked between them, an affectionate arm round each of their shoulders. If only he knew, Kate thought.

Chapter Nine

❦❧❦❧

The following day, and the day after that, Kate repeated the experiment. She wrote a blow-by-blow account of her exploits to Nelly, certain her twin would approve. But, in a small town like Coningsburgh, anonymity could not last long. On the third day Ellis ran into Kate's English teacher in the bank and kind Mr Kennedy asked earnestly after his pupil's health . . .

Kate was lounging on the sofa, watching cartoons on television when her father got home. She had peeled potatoes ready for supper and sorted an untidy pile of newspapers into small, string-tied bundles, a job Ellis had been meaning to do for some days. She anticipated praise.

Instead her father marched into the living-room and switched the TV off without a word. Kate saw that the game was up. Her stomach knotted as he turned to face her, looking pale, his eyes burning.

'You've got something to tell me, I imagine.' The quiet menace in his words brought goose-bumps up on her arms, made her feel six years old again.

Kate stared at him, her eyes locking with his. It was like looking into his soul. She was hypnotized, could think of nothing to say.

'*I* thought you were at school. Jim Kennedy thought you were home in bed . . . So where *were* you?' Ellis spoke even more softly, but his voice was vibrant with righteous anger.

Kate summoned up a doomed bravado. She shrugged, with a shaky smile. 'Just walking about. In the record shop. In the library . . .'

Her words and, more damningly, the tone of her voice – thin and offensively flippant – hung in the air between them.

Clearly enraged, Ellis took a step towards her. Kate cowered, let out a whimper. He was going to hit her, shake her . . . She covered her head with her arms. At the last moment Ellis checked his aggressive lunge, but stood above her, tall and terrifying.

'I'm disgusted with you,' he said finally. He used to speak to Rose sometimes with that same cold contempt. 'You've let me down. You've let yourself down.' A pause. 'You've made me look a fool –'

'And that's what you really care about,' Kate put in.

There was a silence, prolonged, as if the assertion had hit home. Then Ellis knelt down on the floor by the sofa, brought himself down to her level. 'You're wrong,' he said gently. 'I care about *you*.'

He asked her why she'd played truant. Kate said she didn't fit in. She stood out like a sore thumb, was never going to belong. She began to cry. Ellis cuddled her, dried her tears.

'You have to be brave,' he told her softly. 'You have to keep trying.'

'I will,' Kate promised. With Ellis on her side, understanding, maybe things would improve. She felt better.

Later, though, they fell out over some homework she was doing. Kate knew she was right and Ellis knew he was. She saw him briefly roll his eyes ceilingward, as if to say 'another tantrum', and she knew that nothing had really changed.

Fay's family owned a cabin in West Virginia, just over the border from Pennsylvania. As a child she used to spend most of her holidays there.

'It's the loveliest place in the world,' she enthused. 'Primitive, I have to admit, but that's part of what I like about it – always was a girl scout at heart.'

The place would be empty over Easter and Fay suggested that the three of them drive down to spend a week or so away from the madding crowd.

Ellis tightened his lips. 'We could certainly do with a change of scene.' The simple statement bristled with buried meaning.

The drive took two days. They spent the night in a small, scruffy motel just south of the Allegheny Forest. Throughout the journey Ellis made an effort to be good-natured, so as not to sour the holiday atmosphere.

Curled on a travelling-rug on the back seat of Ellis's Pontiac, Kate watched the endless flat farmland pass by, illuminated by shrill, watery sunshine. Further north, snow was still lying in places, but here, south of Pittsburgh, the verges bloomed with early spring flowers.

'Fay?' Kate held out a packet of Wint-O-Green Lifesavers. She found their medicinal flavour weirdly addictive.

'No thanks, honey.' Fay turned and pulled a quirkish face. She had on the yellow sweater that made her complexion look pink and healthy. 'How can you eat those things?'

Kate sucked the lozenge with hammy rapture. 'They're my drug.'

They arrived in the early evening. You had to drive at a snail's pace down a mile and a half of dirt track before coming upon a simple, square, blue-painted, one-storey wooden house. Behind it was a copse of slender trees just coming into leaf, in front a stretch of pasture-land with a shallow river, a tributary of the Potomac, so Fay told them.

'Dad used to drive his truck clear through it,' she laughed. 'We kids thought that was great.'

The front door led straight into the main room of the cabin, which had a musty, enclosed smell, but seemed cared for. Apparently the family paid a woman from the trailer park five miles along the road to keep an eye on the place, to clean and get it ready when people were expected. Fay had a large family and the house was often used.

'First things first.' Fay set her cigarette lighter to a heap of paper, kindling and logs the woman had laid in the grate. The flames began to lick cheerily. She threw open the window to air the place.

The room was neat and plain, with a couple of couches draped in crochet blankets, a table and four upright wooden chairs by the window, a bookcase full of *Readers' Digest*s and *National Geographic*s. The floorboards were painted a dull rusty red, the only carpeting

84

a large hearthrug in autumnal russets and golds – a family project, so Fay claimed, handmade over years by parents and grandparents, aunts, uncles and cousins.

'When I was a kid the cabin had a dirt floor,' she told them. 'But we've gone up-market since then.'

While there was still light they explored the immediate vicinity. Fay pointed out the dogwoods blooming by the river, white violets in the copse behind the house. She seemed elated, as if sharing something that lay very close to her heart. The sky was turning dusky gold and the air seemed thin, cold and fresh.

Back inside, Fay lit a couple of frosted glass kerosene lamps – the cabin had no electricity. In the tiny kitchen she set a pan of canned tomato soup to heat over a kerosene stove. She wore a flowered apron, looked flushed and happy.

Ellis drew water from the stone well beside the house. He brought in a pile of logs, pretending to puff and pant. Fay teased that he was getting to be an old man. She emptied some Ritz crackers into a pottery bowl and made peanut butter sandwiches, sent Kate down to pick some flowering dogwood twigs to decorate the table. Fay laid a blue cotton cloth, on which she arranged the tureen of soup, the sandwiches and crackers, the twigs in a glass, red paper serviettes.

'That looks wonderful, Fay,' Ellis said feelingly.

All through the meal he ooh'd and aah'd. Kate had been lulled by the jolly camping-out atmosphere and Fay's pleasure in having them there. But suddenly her bitterness returned. All Fay had done, after all, was warm up soup. With a rush of resentment Kate remembered how her father used to belittle Rose's cooking until she began to apologize for everything she put on the table.

Afterwards Kate had a Coke. Ellis got out a bottle of bourbon from the box of groceries they'd brought and poured two generous measures for himself and Fay. It was homely by the fire, with the kerosene lamps glowing warmly in the corner.

'It's so quiet,' Ellis marvelled. 'Miles from anywhere and any*one*. Absolutely just what the doctor ordered.'

They played Scrabble for a while then Kate began to yawn. The cabin had two bedrooms, one leading into another. Fay would have the first, Kate the further one. Ellis would sleep on one of the couches, which folded down to form a spare bed.

'I'm for the apples and pears,' Kate said, although the cabin was all on one level. It was a phrase Fay found delightfully bizarre.

'Goodnight dear.' Ellis seemed pleased that she was off.

'Sweet dreams, honey.' Fay reached out and touched her cheek.

The bed reserved for Kate was wide, with a pronounced dip in the centre. By the light of a stumpy candle she saw that it was covered with a crochet blanket similar to those on the two couches in the living-room – some relative of Fay's must spend her whole life making them. There was a wardrobe and a plain wooden chair. A shelf on the end wall held a pile of children's books and what looked like a stuffed Goofy doll. Kate shivered as she undressed but, slipping between the sheets, found that Fay had placed a stone hot-water bottle in the bed . . .

Some time later Kate awoke with a jerk. She must have been dreaming but had no memory of it. The candle had burned out and the room was in total darkness. A sense of sadness, even dread, filled the sightless black void. Kate decided to go and sit by the embers of the fire, have a glass of milk and some Ritz crackers, as if sight and taste and warmth could push away her sudden fear. Fay and Ellis would be sleeping, but she would tiptoe . . .

She located the door and entered Fay's room, where a candle still burned. Kate saw that the bed was empty. So much the better if the two of them were still up . . . She lifted the latch of the living-room door and entered. The kerosene lamps cast their warm light and the fire glowed red in the hearth . . .

On the hearthrug Fay and Ellis lay full-length, engaged at first sight in some kind of a tussle. In an incredulous flash Kate saw that Ellis wore only a white singlet, Fay was naked except for her yellow sweater. He was crouched over her, between her legs, braced on his arms, moving in a strange, urgent, compulsive fashion, groaning repeatedly as if in pain. Fay arched her hips towards him, head thrown back, hair tumbled, eyes closed, mouth stretched taut, her sighs rhythmic, frantic. Kate could see one fleshy flank and one out-thrust white leg reflecting the coral of the firelight. In a split second she was flooded with amazed comprehension.

'Oh, my God!' Fay became aware of her presence and gave an anguished cry.

Ellis turned, following her gaze. 'Get out!' he roared savagely. 'Get out of here!'

Quick as a targeted animal, Kate turned and vanished.

In the dark she lay across her bed, body clenched, breath coming in hard, heavy gasps, fingers tangled in the crochet blanket. From a distance she could hear the voices of Ellis and Fay talking low and urgent, it seemed for a very long time.

Then the door to her room was opened and Ellis entered carrying a candle in a holder. Kate turned towards him. With the flickering light and shadow his finely moulded face had a sculptural gravity. Her father was fully dressed again, though barefoot, his hair slicked.

'Christ, Kate, why the hell didn't you knock?' He spoke with a sorrowful, but also an accusing vehemence that produced a hot rush of indignation in his daughter.

'It's not up to me . . . How on earth could I know . . .' Grievance rendered her incoherent. Even so, the contempt in her voice was biting and unmistakable.

'Look . . . I'm sorry you saw what you saw.' He didn't sound it. He sounded angry, rattled. And deeply embarrassed, as she was.

Kate turned away, sinking down again across the bed.

Ellis sat down beside her and touched her shoulder. 'Kate . . . love . . . This term's been . . .' He paused. 'You've been a brat. It's been disastrous. And now this.' His tone expressed exhaustion and discouragement.

Kate began to sob, the tears burning sensuously on her cheeks. She sobbed and couldn't stop, the sound rising to a crescendo, histrionic, satisfying, cleansing. Giving vent to the resentment and loneliness, the sense of failure that had writhed in her guts these last months, fed on her blood, brought her low.

Ellis laid a gentle hand in the nape of her neck. 'Kate . . . Don't . . .'

She ignored him.

His voice grew harder. 'Stop that, Kate. Pull yourself together.'

Abruptly she looked up. 'I hate it here, Dad. I hate it. Let me go home.'

'Don't be a baby.'

'The Felixes would have me.'

'That's ridiculous. You're *my* child.'

They fell silent. In the impasse Kate's statement rang with a mute and powerful logic. She saw that Ellis felt it too.

After that night the atmosphere in the lonely cabin had been hell. Fay was utterly mortified, losing at a stroke all the warm, welcoming elation of that first evening. Constantly Ellis demonstrated his solidarity with the young American, touching her shoulder, putting an arm protectively round her as if, somehow, she had been unjustly injured. His attitude seemed to place Kate vaguely in the wrong.

Next day they all went on a long hike. Then, the following morning they drove to Washington for the day, visited the White House and the Capitol and the Lincoln Memorial. Kate felt like a prisoner, handcuffed to them, forced to do everything they did.

On the third day she and Ellis argued over whose turn it was to fetch water from the well. The spat escalated into an almighty row. Fay went out on her own and left them to it.

Kate screamed that he was a bastard, that he was happier now Rose was dead. 'And you want me to act as if I'm just as happy as you are. But I'm not bloody happy . . . *She* was my mum and you're trying to foist this fake on me!'

'From the word go you've looked like Banquo's ghost, forcing your bloody misery down everyone's throats.' Ellis's light brown eyes burned with frightening intensity from his waxen face. 'You've treated Fay like shit, day in, day out, as a matter of course . . . You don't deserve anyone as good as her . . . She's made my life worth living and you've done your best to drive her away with your rudeness and your bloody moping!'

'Let me go home, then!' Kate yelled. She was trembling, couldn't stop. 'I hate the sight of you. You hate the sight of me. At the Felixes they liked me. They didn't think I was –'

'Fine! It's fine by me.'

They left the next day. The journey home was tense and wretched. Back in Coningsburgh her father made secret transatlantic phone calls. It was agreed that the Felixes would have Kate at least until she'd done her O-Levels.

Later Ellis talked as if it were a calm and rational decision they'd all arrived at together. 'We've come to the conclusion that Kate will be better off completing the current stage of her education in England,' he told friends with an air of concerned gravity. 'She'll be living with the family of a good friend of mine.'

He took the same line with Kate, for all the world as if he'd forgotten the savage insults he and she had snarled at one another, face to face, alone in Fay's isolated log cabin.

There was a scramble, then, to pack and buy plane tickets so Kate could get home for the start of the summer term. In just five days' time, Kate mused incredulously, she would be back with Nelly and Olivier and Odile . . . She had already started counting the hours.

Chapter Ten

❈❈❈

Nefyn Beach was beginning to fill up, with families mostly, this bright late-morning in August. The tide was out, exposing a long, gently curving stretch of springy golden sand. The wide sky was a tender cerulean blue, the light very clear. The headland, a mile back towards Plas Felix, stood out in sharp focus, a mottled patchwork of grass and bare rock.

As Kate and Nelly walked barefoot along the sand, their hair was whipped by a keen breeze that made the sun feel bracing rather than languorous. Over their swimsuits they wore shorts and matching tops in red, black and white stripes, bought off a market stall in Pwllheli. They hadn't even brought towels – it was good to feel unencumbered.

A couple dragged their reluctant toddler down the beach towards the glittering water. Older children – goose-fleshed but absorbed and enchanted by the waves and the wet sand – glanced at the whimpering infant with contempt.

'I used to grizzle like that,' Nelly said. 'Olivier used to sit in the shallows for hours, nude, like a little cherub with his bucket and spade . . . eating worms and live crabs most likely, happy as a sandboy. Beatrice used to tell me what a sissy I was compared to my baby brother.'

Kate flicked dark rats' tails of hair from her eyes. 'At the seaside once I got caught up in a plague of jellyfish, huge they were and *blue* . . . I've never seen anything like them before or since . . . I just *screamed*. Dad was disgusted with me . . .'

'Oh, look!' Suddenly Nelly squealed and grabbed her arm. 'There's that gorgeous bloke again, down by the boats.'

'He's not that gorgeous.'

Nelly ignored her. 'There's two of them there. That's handy.'

'Oh, Nelly.' Feebly Kate objected.

'Bet we can get talking with them.'

'They're grown-ups.'

'Doesn't matter.'

Nelly couldn't be stopped when she got an idea into her head. Generally Kate went along with her, half reluctant, half tickled to have such an audacious friend. All the same, the men looked to be in their mid twenties.

The one Nelly described as gorgeous seemed to be cleaning the side of a brown-painted sailboat with some kind of a scraping tool. But he did it in a lazy, desultory fashion, as if the occupation was just an excuse for being out on the beach in the sun. His friend made no pretence of being useful, but sat leaning back against the boat, a half-pint brown bottle dangling from his loosely clasped hands.

The friend watched them coming from some way off, then said something to his companion, who looked up from his work to observe Nelly and Kate. Kate felt foolishly self-conscious but Nelly appeared perfectly comfortable with the scrutiny. Drawing level with the two men, she fished out a packet of Polo mints from the pocket of her shorts.

'Want one?' she asked breezily.

The 'gorgeous' one grinned and took a sweet. His hair was thick and fair, falling across his forehead in a film-starry quiff. He had blue eyes and the kind of smile Kate thought of as complacent.

His friend was paler and more poetic-looking, with sandy curls and a cleft chin. He shook his head. 'Beer and Polos don't mix.'

'Oh, I don't know,' Nelly said airily. 'This your boat?' she addressed Gorgeous. She got out her sunglasses and put them on. They made you look older she'd told Kate lots of times.

'It's in the family,' he replied. 'We come down here a lot . . . What's your name?'

'I'm Nelly, and this is Kate.'

'My name's Adrian.'

'Chris,' the curly-haired friend announced shortly. Like Kate he seemed less than eager to dally.

'Nelly,' Adrian repeated. 'That sounds rather old-fashioned.'

'My real name is Eliane. My mother's French.' Nelly spoke with a regal air, Kate thought, as if she knew from experience that the information would impress.

'I thought you looked different.' Adrian smarmed on cue.

Nelly and Adrian chatted for a while, animated, flirtatious. Kate and Chris stood by, bit-players in their scene. Adrian invited the two girls out for a sail that afternoon. Nelly accepted for both of them.

'How old are you anyway?' he asked as an afterthought.

'Eighteen.' Behind the blank, dark lenses of her spectacles, fifteen-year-old Nelly lied blandly.

'And the rest.' Chris wore a sceptical grin.

'Well, we will be next month.' Winsomely Nelly admitted to her previous untruth.

'I won't be till October.' Kate added plausibility to Nelly's second line of defence.

'By the jetty then. Three o'clock.' Adrian cut short any further prevarication.

They bought Coca-Cola and sandwiches, had their lunch sitting on the pebbles at the top of the beach, people-watching, critical, irreverent.

A white dog loped past accompanied by a fat woman, her red hair mussed by the wind, eyes squinched against the brightness. A balding, skinny husband trudged alongside her.

'Imagine those two shagging,' Kate said. 'Like a stick insect on top of an elephant.'

'A sperm whale, you mean,' Nelly giggled.

A moment later they turned their attention to a boy their own age, ambling self-consciously along the beach. He wore jeans and a T-shirt, the sleeves rolled to expose unremarkable biceps, and smoked a cigarette in quick, inexpert puffs. The wind played havoc with his greased pompadour.

'Elvis Presley.' Maliciously Nelly called after him.

He turned with a truculent glare.

'Hard man,' Kate mocked. 'Ooh, scary.'

The two of them together were clearly too much to take on. The boy retreated with scowling dignity.

They grinned at one another. Nelly looked wolfish, Kate thought, with her narrow eyes, teeth gleaming against her sun-tanned skin. She sat with her knees drawn up, raised the Coke-bottle to her lips with negligent grace.

Kate reached for her own bottle, wedged in a nest of pebbles. The taste of Coca-Cola made her think of America and – even now, more than three months after her return – the thought trailed in its wake a sharp tug of pain, the ache of remembered shame.

Deeply, viscerally, Kate felt humiliated by her wretchedness in that upbeat world where all unhappiness seemed failure. She was ashamed because, as a daughter, Ellis had found her wanting – graceless, unsatisfactory. And most of all because she'd glimpsed her father transformed into a grunting stranger, frenziedly ramming his cock into a young woman's lush, spreadeagled body. Even here, half a world away, on a crowded beach in broad daylight, the image made her break out in a hot, horrified sweat.

What relief, what a wild relief it was, to be back with the Felixes, to go around with Nelly and laugh and snigger like a pair of brats. To be accepted.

She turned and touched Nelly's arm. 'We're really going to meet these men, are we?'

'Course we are. It'll be fun.'

'They're a bit old for us.' For the second time Kate voiced her doubt.

'What d'you think they're going to do? Rape us?'

For all her ambivalence, Kate knew she would fall in with Nelly's plans. Because she needed terribly to belong here. Last summer the Felixes had merely dazzled her. Now they were her salvation. After Coningsburgh, Kate knew herself to be a dull creature, unworthy of even her father's interest. Nelly was brave and reckless. Like the rest of the family she offered a camouflage, lending Kate a spurious coat of glamour and panache.

*   *   *

Lounging on a grey army blanket in the bottom of Adrian's boat, Nelly contemplated her own legs, slim and brown, gleaming here and there with tiny soft blonde hairs. She loved her legs in summer, their warm tan glowing cleanly against any colour she chose to wear.

Adrian lounged alongside her, though lounging was too luxurious a word. Nelly could feel ridges forming in her bottom from the boards beneath the blanket. Their backs were propped on a sort of padded car seat affair. Adrian's bare upper arm was wedged snugly against her own.

His eyes followed the direction of her gaze. 'Did anyone ever tell you you've got marvellous legs, Nelly?'

Nelly flashed what she took to be an enigmatic smile, but made no reply. In fact people commented on her legs all the time. Envious friends. Boys she knew. Holidaymaking lads she encountered on the beach. Men called after her in the street – 'Ooh, darling, legs!'

Grumpy Chris had elected to sail the boat, leaving his friend free to concentrate on Nelly. He sat silently in the stern, his hand on the tiller. Kate sat his end, sideways on, dark hair blowing, eyes closed, face turned up towards the summer sky. She looked absent and wonderfully disdainful. Kate rarely played the flirting game.

In a way Nelly admired her for it. She herself felt the need to show off, act bubbly and chirpy. Kate kept her dignity, Nelly thought, but *she* had more fun. Like that song. 'I'm just a girl who can't say no.' Nelly hummed it inside her head. Each day she kept a mental note of all the masculine looks and remarks that came her way, marvelling at this power she was discovering in herself. But she *did* say no. Not like Ros, who all the boys called a tart.

'Cigarette, Nelly?' Adrian fished in the pocket of his shorts. As he did so the cloth pulled taut and, with a little thrill of pride, Nelly saw he had an erection. He held a packet of Players out towards her.

'Don't mind if I do.'

As she helped herself their eyes met. His were hot and insistent. Nelly met them cheekily.

* * *

By the time they returned to the beach it was nearly seven. The wind had dropped and it seemed hotter than at midday.

'Fancy a drink, girls?' Adrian suggested.

'Not half.' Nelly was game at once.

Neither Chris nor Kate enthused, but neither did they raise any objection.

They went to the Lobster Pot. Jerome had always mocked the place as the bourgeois watering-hole of the sailing set, but Nelly nursed a secret hankering to sit in the tidy garden with its geraniums and lobelia, sipping something cooling in the sun. She asked for a crème de menthe, a drink her parents despised, though she found its rich green colour and uncompromising flavour rather bracing. Kate settled for a glass of red wine.

There was a hiccup at the bar apparently. The landlord queried the girls' ages in an ostentatious undertone. With icy self-righteousness Adrian maintained that they were both eighteen.

'Officious little toss-pot,' he said, returning with their tray of drinks.

'It *is* his job,' Chris murmured.

'Cheers!' Deftly Nelly steered the conversation away from questions of age, holding up her tulip-shaped glass of green liqueur so it caught the rays of the sinking sun, making a production of sipping it with little sighs of satisfaction. She grinned at the men. 'My father says this is a tart's drink.'

Chris raised an eloquent eyebrow, compressing his lips in a sarcastic fashion.

'Is your beer OK?' Nelly asked him with mock concern. 'You look as if you'd swigged a dose of Parazone.'

She and Adrian lit cigarettes. He pulled his chair closer and soon they were oblivious of the presence of the other two.

'You're by far the most attractive girl on the beach, you know,' Adrian flattered, tracing the line of her upper arm with his fore-finger. She made no attempt to move away. He began to explain that, with her looks and figure, she could be a mannequin or model fashions in women's magazines – swimsuits specially, he told her with a droop-lidded smile. While talking he stared into

95

her eyes while a lock of sun-bleached hair fell fetchingly forward on to his brow. Almost absently he caressed the smooth skin of her inside arm.

Nelly bubbled inwardly with pleasure. As Kate had pointed out, Adrian was a man in his twenties, a grown-up, with savoir-faire and clean-cut looks and he clearly fancied her rotten, probably hoped to take her to bed later. She knew this drink was all there could be. If he found out her real age he'd back off like a shot, but, for as long as the moment lasted, she basked in the glow of his lust, returning his looks with lazy, languorous encouragement.

She glanced across at Kate. Rather late in the day she and Chris seemed absorbed in earnest conversation. With her friend's attention otherwise engaged, Nelly decided to romanticize a little.

'Actually I've got a place booked for January at the, you know, Anna Black Modelling School in London . . .'

Adrian made admiring sounds and for a moment Nelly saw herself through his eyes – poised and pretty and nearly eighteen, set fair for a modelling career.

''Nother drink anyone?' Chris asked.

Over their second round Adrian started to tell Nelly about a love affair he'd just ended in Beddgelert where he lived and worked. The girl had marriage on her mind, he said, always hinting about rings and eyeing vacant flats. *He* wanted to fit in a whole lot more living, Adrian explained pointedly, before he was ready to settle down . . . Nelly grinned sassily, nodded understandingly.

Suddenly Kate looked round from her tête-à-tête with Chris. 'If we're catching the five past nine bus we'd better get a move on,' she remarked. 'We promised your ma we'd be home by nine thirty.'

Nelly winced at the infantile connotations of a nine-thirty curfew, the childish accountability implied. But she knew that if she dawdled Kate would simply leave without her.

'I thought we could go for a meal . . .' Adrian began. His eyes held a dawning confusion.

'Sorry, we've got to rush.' Nelly flashed him an apologetic smile. 'Thanks for the drinks and the boat ride.'

Adrian seemed not to understand. 'Can't we go on somewhere . . . You can't just leave . . .'

'I'd love to, but . . .' Through her bustle Nelly was tickled by his discomfiture.

Their exit was scrambled and undignified. At the bus stop they laughed at their own clumsiness, Adrian's mortification.

'Poor chap,' Nelly giggled. 'He's had a hard-on all afternoon.'

'Nelly, you're such a . . .' But reluctantly Kate grinned.

Later, on the bus, Nelly was curious. 'Anyway, you and Chris seemed to be getting on famously. What were you talking about?'

Kate gave her an ironic sideways glance. 'About you, a lot of the time.'

'Come on. What did he say?'

'You don't want to know.'

'Yes I do.'

Her friend pulled a face. 'Among other things he said, "Your little pal's really asking for it, isn't she . . . One of these days she's going to get herself into trouble."'

'He said that?'

Nelly raised her eyebrows, pursed her lips, contemplating the man's words. They clearly weren't meant as a compliment. But there was something about them that filled her with a perverse sense of elation.

Chapter Eleven
1957

❧❧❧

Outside the classroom window the sky brooded, dull and heavy as grey flannel. Inside the electric lights had been on all day. It was February, last lesson on Monday afternoon. Along with the other English speakers Kate had been given exercises to get on with until her turn came for tuition. An air of apathy hung over the classroom. Kate doodled in the margin of her maths book.

Miss Arnold, with her white face and nubbly brown suit, stood out front, attempting to compel the interest of her pupils in the Extensions of Pythagoras.

'Why the blank faces? We've done all this before . . .'

Kate knew enough Welsh by now to understand the teacher's irritable outburst.

Immediately, though, Miss Arnold collected herself. 'Pay attention, all of you. I'll run through these proofs just one more time . . .'

Two rows away from Kate was an empty seat, normally occupied by Nelly. This afternoon she'd been sent to stand outside the headmaster's study – for the third week running she'd failed to hand in her homework.

'I know when I'm not wanted, Miss Arnold.'

She'd exited from the classroom with good-humoured defiance, head erect, eyes bright, a luminous flush beneath her skin. Even in winter Nelly seemed to give off a kind of restless heat, a vitality that seemed halfway beyond her control.

The world was too tame for her, too slow. She was growing raggedly impatient of school, hadn't the patience to wait for teachers – or her parents – to finish speaking before sweeping their words away with her boisterous, impetuous responses.

At Christmas she'd played Audrey in the school production of

As You Like It and this had focused her energy for a while. Now, in the gloomy latter months of winter, concentration and effort seemed way beyond her, the sheer sameness of each school day well nigh unbearable.

But neither was the school best pleased with Kate. Her particular penchant was for daydreaming. Not infrequently, faced with a teacher's sudden point-blank question, she would come to with a start and realize that – goodness knows for how long – she had been perfectly oblivious to sight, sound, time, place, everything going on around her in the real world.

Even now, when she'd been home for nearly nine months, her thoughts drifted obsessively back to that time in America, an interlude that had become fixed in her memory as hateful, nightmarish, visualized in harsh, bright Technicolor, twinned with jagged black shadows.

'You're like Banquo's ghost, forcing your bloody misery down everyone's throats . . .'

Ellis and Fay were married now. A small ceremony, Ellis had written, witnessed by just a couple of friends . . . No point in disrupting your studies to come over . . . That was fine by Kate – if the truth were known she never wanted to see either of them ever again.

She clung that much more closely to the Felixes, fantasizing scenes in which they praised her, claimed her as their own, demonstrated to Ellis how highly they regarded her. Each real-life gesture of affection and approval Kate treasured, replaying them time and again in her head.

Beatrice was away at university now – she'd been home briefly at Christmas, glossy and distant, her inward eye focused on people and things her family knew nothing about. But Kate had settled back into the rhythm of her relationships with the two boys – Olivier so sunny and easy to be with, strumming endlessly, experimentally at his new guitar.

As for Pascal, her crush on him was strong as ever. And in lessons Kate indulged herself by picturing his wayward grin, the long brown eyes, so like Odile's, the way his broad shoulders narrowed into the mobile waist and hips. But she kept a tight rein on her imagination, never allowing herself to dream of kissing, being touched or held by him. In any case, he had a new girlfriend now, older than himself, a student nurse, dark and Celtic-looking, with a fascinating, sulky face.

Though he loomed so large in her world, Kate was perfectly aware that, beyond provoking a certain careless, affectionate goodwill, she barely existed for Pascal. But she'd forged a new link with him, by way of the French novels he loved to read. Out of curiosity she'd pulled from the shelves in the living-room the volume David Lacoste had presented to the Felix family, the English translation of his book. When she finished it – slightly dazed by the vehemence of language and content – Pascal told her he had a couple of Lacoste's subsequent novels in French.

'You could read them – with a dictionary. That's what I did to begin with. Still do sometimes.'

Kate was dubious but she tried. It wasn't easy but she was lured on by the seductive shades of both Pascal and Lacoste himself, shimmering in a sensuous haze at the back of her mind. Lacoste's writing was forceful and direct, quite simple really, but with strong sexual images that fired her imagination and her blood.

'Good going.' Idling at her desk in the maths class, Kate could hear the timbre of Pascal's voice, see his casual, approving grin.

In an effort to retain his interest and respect she read further novels. It got easier and the French language became linked in her mind with a vague, voluptuous reverie, the books – by Sagan, Vian, Camus – seeming imbued with a wonderful world-weary chic.

Jerome and Odile were impressed by her seeming studiousness, missing the point that, by spending countless hours dreaming over French writers, Kate was in fact neglecting homework, revision, all the mundane duties that would yield a respectable harvest of O-Levels.

'Is everyone clear about what I've just been explaining . . .' From her place at the back of the class Kate observed Miss Arnold through glazed, absent eyes, as she paced and gesticulated, wielding a long pointer, turning away from the runic characters

chalked on the blackboard to address her pupils, then turning back
again . . .

In her mind's eye Kate relived a fragment from the previous day
– Sunday morning at Plas Felix, a watery sun filtering through the
long window at the far end of the first-floor corridor, herself lolling
on the broad window-seat with her dictionary and a Boris Vian
novel. From behind the closed door of Pascal's room music drifted,
the lazy, insinuating sounds of a jazz saxophone. The air was filled
with the rich scents of garlic and thyme from the kitchen below,
as Odile began to prepare Sunday lunch. And Kate experienced a
sudden sharp moment of . . . awareness, a gut-feeling located in her
body rather than her brain, and she understood, really understood,
how fiercely she loved this family and this house.

'Kate Stephens, what did I just say?' The cold voice of Miss
Arnold pierced her abstraction. It came to Kate that the teacher
had switched to English. When? For how long?

Kate felt as if she'd been snatched from a blurry, comforting
underwater place, where miraculously she was in her element,
weightless, sinuous as a fish, up into a strident world in which
she lacked the faculties needed for survival.

'You haven't heard a word!'

'I'm sorry, I was . . .' Kate floundered.

'You and Nelly make a pair,' the teacher snapped. 'I'll waste no
more time on you. Just make damn sure you learn the theorems –
word perfect – for tomorrow's lesson, first thing.'

'Yes, Miss Arnold.'

Then, once again, she was left in peace to sink back into the
secret waters of her own daydreaming.

'You and Nelly make a pair.'

No praise had been intended. But Kate hugged the reprimand
to herself like gold. Each day she marvelled that a girl as vivid as
Nelly would claim her as sister, as best friend.

Even now, on winter nights, when the world outside was black
and forbidding, Nelly couldn't bear to sit tamely at home.

'Let's go trudging, Kate.'

And they would put on the hooded, padded jackets Odile had

brought them from Switzerland, take a torch and scramble down the rocky path below the house, fight their way along the dark, stony beach, shouting to one another above the whoosh of the wind, laughing at the wild power of the waves. And Kate loved Nelly fit to bust and knew she'd never have another friend like this ever again.

It was time for the presents and the family toast, the traditional climax to Jerome's birthday supper. They'd polished off Odile's blanquette de veau, her sublime mashed potatoes, her delicate Île Flottante, all Jerome's favourites – nursery food with a French accent, so he declared each year, tucking in with gusto.

Olivier was getting impatient. His mother was still faffing around, stacking dishes, sorting out glasses and cutlery ready for washing up. She radiated the sense that her deliberate slow care was a statement of some sort and had better not be challenged.

'Sorry, folks, but I'm going to set the ball rolling.' To Olivier's relief, Nelly jumped to her feet and gazed provocatively round the table. 'I'm going mad, Ma.' She flashed an edgy grin at Odile. 'Honestly, I think you're turning into Grand-mère.'

The remark brought a reluctant smile to Odile's lips, but still she refused to be hurried. 'I won't be long . . . Start without me if you really can't wait.'

This year, for the first time, one of the children was absent. It was the last week in April, still vacation time according to Oxford, but Beatrice was away in Paris with a couple of university friends, staying in some cheap rat-hole, so she said, and soaking up culture.

On the other hand, Kate was with them now and, in Olivier's view, she was a lot nicer and easier to get on with than his elder sister had ever been. They were joined, too, by Pascal's girlfriend, Mary, with her swaying breasts and narrow waist, about whom Olivier had hot, secret fantasies.

'Time for the loyal toast.' Nelly picked up her glass of red wine, ignoring Odile's discreetly martyred air. 'To the man we love to hate, and the man we love to love – our Dad. Raise your schooners . . . Happy forty-fifth, Pa!'

'Happy forty-fifth!' Olivier joined the chorus. From way back the toast always specified Jerome's age. They drained their glasses. Pascal had poured his wine into a transparent plastic goblet, a free gift with Odile's washing powder. He drank deep then flung it dramatically over his shoulder. Everyone laughed as it bounced and skittered along the parquet floor.

Odile, over by the sideboard took a swift and highly perfunctory swig from her wine-glass, then carried on pointedly, pointlessly sorting spoons, knives and forks into separate piles.

Jerome seemed not to notice, but sat like a bearded Buddha, wearing his usual serene, foxy and somehow imperious smile. He raised one hand in a mock blessing. 'Thank you, my children.'

'Present time!' Nelly picked up a gaily wrapped parcel from the collection on the floor over by the French windows. She placed it on the table in front of Jerome, bent to kiss his forehead where the pepper-and-salt hair was starting to recede. 'Pa, with my love.'

Smiling in anticipation – a fêted, benevolent patriarch – Jerome began to unwrap the gift. Olivier watched affectionately. He loved tradition and was quietly relieved that the ceremony was taking place at all. In the small hours of the previous night he'd heard his parents arguing in their bedroom across the corridor from his. The doors and thick walls had kept their words inaudible, though at one point Odile had exclaimed 'it's grotesque' in an overwrought shriek, before the aggrieved rumble of their row had again become unintelligible.

Olivier had almost dropped off again when he heard their door open, Odile's voice declaring, '. . . And you expect me to serve you a meal for a gastronome and smile as if nothing has happened like a good little wifey . . .'

For all his mother's distress Olivier couldn't help smiling at the mix of English idiom and Odile's French accent.

'It's up to you, my love . . .' Jerome sounded urbane as ever. 'If it makes you happy you can brood and sulk and spoil things for the children . . .'

The door closed again. Odile went downstairs for something. Olivier lay pensive for a while, then fell asleep.

But the birthday supper had taken place as usual and Olivier was glad. The row must have blown over. If he'd been Nelly – or Beatrice if she were home – he'd have been up in arms, asking questions, taking sides. But Olivier liked peace and harmony. He preferred to let sleeping dogs lie.

'*Bellissima*!' Jerome was holding up Nelly's present, an outsize glass. She'd bought some special paint and decorated it, writing cheers and *prost* and *skol* and other words in the same vein – some were even in Russian and Japanese and Hebrew scripts, painstakingly copied from a Christmas card she'd saved. Slowly, with an appreciative grin, Jerome examined the glass. He was always good to give presents to. Then he tipped his wine into the capacious container, adding another generous slug on top and taking a sizeable gulp. 'I've got the best kids in the world,' he assured Nelly. 'They actually encourage my vices.'

Talk of vices was opportune. Olivier stepped nimbly in with his own gift. He'd bought some of Jerome's favourite black cheroots. Extracting the box from its wrapping, his father looked up at him in the way that always charmed Olivier, wryly smiling as if to say you know me too well. Jerome reached up, briefly hugging the head of his youngest child to his solid, comforting shoulder.

'Mary, you go next,' Pascal said.

Mary stood up, a dark-haired young woman of twenty-one. Three years older than Pascal – Olivier was consumed with awe and envy. Her olive skin was free of make-up and she wore black, had the Left Bank style that Pascal admired. She laid a package on the table in front of Jerome.

'Mary – you shouldn't have.' He shot her a crinkled, satirical smile, but Olivier saw a momentary gleam in his eye revealing that his father found the young woman as distracting as he did.

Jerome enthused over the unremarkable desk-tidy she'd bought him and claimed a kiss. Mary offered her cheek coolly, almost sternly. Olivier was impressed. Most girls would have been smiling pinkly, out of politeness if nothing else.

Pascal joined them, standing behind Mary, encircling her thin waist with one arm, pulling her close in a way that made Olivier feel dizzy. At the same time he handed his father a photograph in a frame – Pascal pooh-poohed the wrapping of presents. It was a snap he'd taken of Jerome in brutal close-up, much enlarged. He'd been arguing one Sunday afternoon with his friend, Dobbsy, the journalist, about the previous year's Suez débâcle and Pascal had caught him making a point with uncharacteristic anger, leaning forward in his chair and stabbing the air with his cigar. Jerome was clearly half-cut, His lower lip slack, eyes narrowed with a sort of naked, bullying passion, each sag and bag of his middle-aged face starkly defined.

'God.' He stared at it, seeming half pleased and half dismayed. 'I feel like Churchill clapping eyes on the Sutherland portrait,' he told Pascal. 'But I have to admit, reluctantly –' his smile was slow and rueful – 'you're a damn good photographer.'

Kate was the last of the children to offer her present. She'd showed it to Olivier ahead of time and it was brilliant. In an art lesson at school she'd started to mould a human figure in clay and laughingly remarked to Nelly that it looked a bit like Jerome. She'd worked on the likeness and painted the figure to enhance it – reproducing Jerome's grey-flecked beard and receding hairline, the half-moon spectacles he used to read, the black polo-neck he affec- ted, even down to the dandyish black-and-white co-respondent's shoes he'd bought in New York and wore with an ironic twinkle.

Jerome looked puzzled when he first held the stocky little man- nikin up to view, then abruptly he burst out laughing.

'Kate! You hussy!' A wealth of affection in his tone. He stood up and enclosed her in a warm bear-hug. 'Though I will say it's a damn sight more flattering than Pascal's offering.'

Olivier watched Kate as she returned to her place at the table. She wasn't smiling but her face was pink with pleasure. All of them understood, without ever saying it out loud, that Jerome's appreciation meant more to Kate than it did to his own children. It was something she knew she had to earn, not hers simply by right of birth.

Odile had observed the ceremony from the sidelines, standing by the door, arms crossed, her expression enigmatic. There were moments when Olivier saw her as a separate person, not just his mother, and he did so now. She wore a dress he'd always liked in blackish wool with swirls of red and orangey-brown and her dark hair hung loose on her shoulders. It occurred to him suddenly that she looked young – and hurt, and alone.

'Your turn, Maman,' he said. Calling her *maman* was special, a private signal.

She shook her head. 'I told Jérome –' she pronounced it in the French way – 'he would have to wait a few days.'

'You can't, Ma.' Olivier was shocked. She was changing the rules.

'Yes she can.' Jerome crossed the room, holding Nelly's glass in his hand. He stood beside his wife, laying an arm about her shoulders. Odile stared straight ahead without acknowledging the gesture, but she didn't move away. In the room a sudden silence fell, perplexed and uncomfortable.

'Pa, your turn to toast us.' Nelly hastened to dispel it. Jerome's toasts to his family were always the final ingredient in his birthday ceremony.

Her father switched on his broad, familiar smile. 'I'll drink to that.'

He turned to face Odile. '*Mon amour*,' he murmured throatily. There was an element of mockery in the endearment, but Olivier saw that, like a wayward child, his father was angling for some kind of indulgence, a forgiveness. Jerome raised the outsize glass. 'Now and always, I drink to our household goddess.'

He tipped up her chin and placed a soft, slow kiss on her lips. She watched ironically through half-closed lids as he took a large swig of his wine.

Jerome waited for a second, as if for a further response, then transferred his attention swiftly to Pascal and Mary. 'To our resident existentialist and his lady . . .'

His son answered with a negligent smile, a deprecating shrug. He glanced sideways at Mary. For years Pascal had been a bit above family ritual.

Downing another slug of wine, Jerome looked across at Nelly and

Kate. 'And now the ladies, God bless 'em . . .' He lent a hammy slur to the words. When the kids were little he used to make them all laugh pretending to be pissed and the tradition died hard. Now he lifted his glass again. 'Our reprobates, our ne'er-do-wells . . .'

'Oh, Pa . . .' Nelly sighed. Kate pulled a guilty, pop-eyed face.

At the end of last term their form-master had written, warning that both girls were seriously neglecting their studies. Both had decent brains, he declared, but currently seemed intent on wasting them. For a few days there had been ructions but, basically, Jerome was cavalier. Academic success came so easily to him that he'd no particular respect for it.

Now it was Olivier's turn. Jerome's smile for him was gentle, his eyes soft. Sometimes he thought he was his father's favourite. Sometimes he thought he was Odile's favourite as well.

'To our sunbeam,' Jerome said. 'Our good angel.'

His voice was strong and full-blooded, avoiding any taint of sentimentality. The words could have been sarcastic, but Olivier knew they weren't.

His parents saw him as the uncomplicated one, the sunny one, who could cheer them up if they needed it, simply by being himself, funny and nice, the way he was. Olivier recognized and was proud of his role. Willingly he shouldered the responsibility.

The glass shade of the bedroom lamp cast lozenges of red, blue and amber light across her skin as Odile sat at the dressing-table mirror brushing her long hair. It was odd how, barring a few wrinkles, a slight heaviness beneath the chin, her face had hardly changed since she was young. In middle age Jerome's features had taken on a quality of caricature, what with the pouches below his eyes, the fleshy jowls only partly masked by his neatly clipped beard, the smile – cherubic, amiable, self-indulgent, shrewd – reflecting his attitude to life. Her own expression was composed and enigmatic, seeming designed to conceal her thoughts and feelings.

And, anyway, sometimes she wasn't sure what she *was* thinking and feeling. Jerome was all of a piece. Odile had always been much too good at appreciating all points of view. Her opinions fluctuated from one day to another, depending on her mood.

Take the children. Most of the time she regarded her three youngest with pride, as high-spirited thoroughbreds, attractive and free of . . . guilt, anxiety. Beatrice was the odd one out, scratchy and self-protective, still scarred by her sudden childhood transplantation into this new and alien community.

But there were days when this view seemed blinkered and self-deluding. When Beatrice – spiky as she was – appeared the only one of the four capable of any kind of productive effort. The other three were indulged, undisciplined brats and Odile could see no possibility of any of them ever amounting to anything in the cold, exacting outside world.

'Have a bit of faith.' Jerome just laughed at her doubts. 'They're fine. They'll *be* fine. They'll find their own paths.'

Sometimes his blithe confidence was reassuring. Other days Odile knew he'd simply made up his mind, and closed his eyes to inconvenient complexities.

She undressed and put on one of the white, round-necked cotton nightdresses she'd worn ever since she was a child. Even now Maman still sewed her a couple each year.

'It's like raping a nun,' Jerome used to say when they made love. Once or twice in the early days he'd bought her lingerie in black silk and satin. But she never felt comfortable in it and, after a while, he took the hint and stopped.

From along the corridor in Jerome's study she heard the click of the phone being replaced. A colleague had called him late. Now, annoyingly, instead of coming to bed, Odile knew he would potter unhurriedly at his desk. She was tired, but there seemed no point in turning out the light.

As she drowsed on her side of the bed, one arm covering her eyes, pictures of Jerome's birthday ceremony filled her mind. Odile was naggingly dissatisfied with her own part in the proceedings. She'd lacked the pluck simply to call the whole thing off, and her passive resistance had appeared merely peevish, got on everyone's nerves. And somehow – once again – Jerome had come out on top.

And yet, indisputably, he was the villain of the piece. Jerome had been unfaithful. Last night, on his plump white chest, she'd seen the lacerations from a set of fingernails and, more nauseatingly, two ugly, mangy mauve love-bites. She'd accused him and he'd confessed. She'd shouted. He'd remained calm. And Odile had had a weird sense of *déjà-vu*, as if she were finally acting out a scene she'd mentally rehearsed many times.

She wasn't even sure how upset she really was. After all, it had been years since she'd even halfway desired her husband. Her first reaction had been a tepid surprise at the fact that someone else apparently did. The numbness remained, but abruptly it would spiral into a suffocating heat, her blood seeming to curdle and boil at the treachery, the sheer unfairness of Jerome's behaviour.

Ever since they'd lived here, ever since he'd spent so much of his working life apart from the family, Odile had vaguely fantasized his having an affair. But somehow she'd always pictured some ugly but fascinatingly intellectual female who wore coloured stockings, offered dry sherry and lived in a cold, fusty, book-lined flat.

The reality, to Odile's eyes, was far more bizarre. Those scratches and love-bites had been administered by Janet, who cleaned Jerome's small flat in London, a hard-working divorcée with a six-year-old daughter — he always spoke of her with a mixture of admiration and patronizing amusement. Odile had no idea what the woman looked like, but she visualized dry, permed hair, a strong, squat white body, the kind of working-class body on which the sun had never shined. Did Jerome give her money? Would that make the situation better or worse? Here again, Odile could not make up her mind.

She heard his footsteps approaching along the corridor. He entered the bedroom.

'Sorry. That was Leo. He's having trouble with his publishers . . . Though why he has to ring at nearly midnight . . .'

Offended by his matter-of-factness, she made no comment.

Jerome came and sat down on her side of the bed. The mattress sagged beneath his weight.

'Odile?' In the soft, spangled light he looked searchingly at her, wore a pleading, teasing look that must have been winsome when he was a small boy. 'Let's be friends . . .'

'I don't know . . .' At this moment she felt nothing. Then again, she'd never really been any good at sulking. But no doubt she would wake in the black small hours and the boiling, angry feeling would be back.

'I'm a beast.'

'Yes, you're a beast.'

He bent to kiss her forehead. 'Thank you for my banquet.'

She shrugged and closed her eyes.

Jerome got undressed and turned out the light, climbed heavily into his side of the bed. He came close and began to caress her. Odile lay passive. Quickly, expertly he brought her to orgasm, then entered her. In a rush of sudden energy she moved to sit astride him. With a sort of methodical vehemence she began to scratch his chest with her work-blunted fingernails, wanting to hurt him, scar him. Jerome lay beneath her in the dark, sighing, growling in muted ecstasy.

Chapter Twelve

❧❧❧❧

Already Fay was pregnant, expecting a child early in December. Ellis had telephoned Kate from Coningsburgh – a thing he almost never did – to break the news, and to tell her that the two of them would be in London for a week towards the end of July. A delayed honeymoon, he explained briskly.

'I'm going to book a room for you in our hotel. We'll spend a week pretending to be tourists and showing Fay the sights . . .'

'Mmm. All right.' Kate didn't hide her lack of enthusiasm. She had absolutely no desire to spend time alone with her father and Fay, specially at the end of term when there was so much to look forward to where she was. But there was no refusing.

Ellis ignored her ungraciousness. Kate guessed he'd made a resolution to be patient. 'It seems so long since I saw you, darling. I'm looking forward to this week. We both are – Fay feels the same. She sends love . . .'

He didn't sound like her righteous, critical father. Nor was there any reminder in his tone of their acrimonious goodbyes, the savagery of the insults they'd exchanged, which, in the secret small hours of the morning, still had the power to bring her out in a sweat of rage and shame.

Kate stared out of the train window. The rhythm of the wheels made her somnolent. They'd left Wales far behind and the industrial Midlands looked dismal to her under an unseasonable grey-white sky that reflected her own gloom.

It wasn't only the prospect of spending time with Ellis and Fay that depressed her. There was a further factor. It was ten days or so since she'd finished sitting her O–Levels and Kate didn't think she'd done well. She wasn't surprised, knew she hadn't worked. Most of her teachers had predicted disaster and Kate had learned to live with the idea. Only Ellis had always had such high and demanding expectations of her, and she couldn't imagine him accepting her failure without a flurry of rows and recriminations.

Jerome was so different, so exhilaratingly casual. Kate was actually rather shocked by his laissez-faire attitude.

'Better a happy dustman than an angst-ridden academic,' he would claim provocatively when Odile anguished over Nelly's and Olivier's school reports. 'Why should you expect them all to be eggheads? Children have to find their own path and the chances are it won't be the one the school maps out for them.'

He was proud of Beatrice, but tickled by the fact that Pascal, who was expected to do well in his A-Levels, had opted not to go to university and had a job lined up for the whole of the summer in Llandudno, photographing holidaymakers on the pier. Though he'd taken the precaution too of enrolling on a Technical Photography course with the intention of slipping through the National Service net.

Before she left, Kate had mentioned her apprehension to Odile. Quicker than thinking, Odile's eyes had hardened, her lips twisted in a semi-snarl. 'What gives him the right . . . ? If your father wished for perfect results he should have seen to it himself.'

Kate was startled. Odile always spoke of Ellis with respectful neutrality and she was disconcerted by the hostility implicit in her words and manner.

Odile herself seemed to feel she'd been indiscreet. A moment later she added, 'Don't misunderstand me, Kate. I meant no criticism. But Ellis is so far away. He has to give up some of his control. He can't expect . . .' The sentence tailed off. Odile's expression became encouraging, conspiratorial. 'Anyway, wait and see. Your results could be better than you believe.'

In the last few days she had come up with a brand new project. Odile had a sudden bee in her bonnet that North Wales was a backwater and the girls needed to be exposed to a more cosmopolitan milieu. In a recent letter Grand-mère had sung the praises of an excellent school quite close to her in Lausanne, where one of her neighbours taught, attended by girls in their late teens from all over the world. It offered a thorough grounding in the French language and culture, as well as all sorts of other useful accomplishments.

Odile approached Jerome, a purposeful look in her eye. 'If they're not going to be eggheads, then why not this?' Kate grinned now at the earnest way she'd said it, as if egghead were a profession in itself. 'It will give them a certain . . . polish, and you don't have to pass examinations to get in.'

Jerome was sanguine but frankly sceptical. 'Sounds like the sort of institution that used to be called a finishing school, the kind of thing that was passé in the thirties. Maybe it's not a bad place to keep Nelly out of mischief for a year, but don't imagine she'll be qualified to earn a living when she comes out the other end.'

They were eating dinner. Absently Jerome served himself another helping of mushroom risotto. 'It won't be cheap either . . . And as for Kate – I'm not sure I can see Ellis coughing up for anything so . . . debatable.'

'You've got a mission while you're in London,' Nelly urged later. 'You've got to convince that father of yours that this is just the most marvellous idea.' She rolled her eyes, grinning fiendishly. 'Think of it, Kate . . . You and me on the loose in Lausanne for a year . . .'

In the few days since its inception Odile's plan had become essential to them. Neither Nelly nor Kate could now imagine an alternative future. The proposed year in Lausanne was the be-all and end-all. Beyond it lay nothing that they cared to imagine. Nelly knew and loved the town already. Kate saw the scheme as somehow bringing her closer to an adult Lacoste-ish, Pascal-ish fantasy world. But, like Jerome, she was pessimistic. It didn't sound the sort of idea her father would countenance for a single second.

They were all booked into the Bay Tree Family Hotel in Bloomsbury. It was a big white building that had once been a private house, with a dark blue awning over the entrance, dwarf marigolds in twin blue tubs, one each side of the front door.

The receptionist looked like a boy in his first pair of long trousers.

He telephoned up to her father's room. 'I have your daughter here in reception.'

To Kate he seemed absurd, a child-actor playing a grown-up's part, but he performed his role without a flicker of irony.

'You may go straight up,' he told her self-importantly. 'Room six. Turn right on the second floor.'

The corridor smelt of lavender polish. All along the walls, in narrow, gilded frames, hung a series of Victorian fashion-plates, women in bonnets and frilled crinolines and tiny little pointed boots. Kate felt tense, noticed the beating of her heart. It was well over a year since the hostile parting with her father. There was absolutely no gladness in her anticipation. She arrived at the right door and knocked.

'Come in.'

As Kate entered she saw that Fay was stretched out, fully dressed, on the bed, her father in the act of rising from a chair he'd pulled up close beside her. She had the familiar, fleeting sense of disrupting their unity as a couple.

'Kate!' Ellis crossed the room and took her in his arms. For a long, fervent moment he embraced her. Then, taking her by the shoulders, he removed her gently to arm's-length. 'God, you've grown.'

How robust and thriving he appeared in the flesh, how tanned and handsome. The phrase 'the prime of life' popped into Kate's head. Ellis wore a pair of casual light grey trousers, a crisp sports shirt in pale butter-yellow. His amber eyes looked clear and alert, his hair thick, well-shaped lips cleanly etched against the background of his healthy skin. Her father radiated a sort of powerful wellbeing and, in spite of everything, Kate felt her spirits rise. She took pride in the impression he gave of mental and physical buoyancy.

He seemed to feel the same about her. 'You look marvellous – so grown-up and well.'

When he'd last seen her Kate had been lost and confused. Today she taken trouble with her looks, wanting to appear insouciant, happily self-sufficient. She wore a roll-necked cotton sweater, sloppy joe style, in fashionable shocking pink. The loose top hid her collarbones, disguised her lack of bust. She'd teamed it with a wide black skirt Odile had made her, gilt bangles, hoop earrings – she saw Ellis glance at them – that gleamed through her dark shoulder-length hair in a film-starry way.

Ellis turned to Fay. 'Doesn't Kate look wonderful!'

'Straight off the cover of *Seventeen* magazine.' Fay sat up, swung her bare legs over the edge of the bed and rose to her feet. 'Hi, honey. It's good to see you.' Her voice, so it seemed to Kate, held real tenderness.

'Congratulations on the baby.' Her own words sounded dry and stiff. For no reason that could be logically stated, Kate begrudged Fay's pregnancy. Obscurely, she wished to remain Ellis's only child, for the struggle between them to be exclusive, one on one. A baby, a young child would dissipate his attention, provoke feelings that were less bitter and ambiguous.

Fay kissed her and pulled a charming, rueful face. 'Right now it's a mixed blessing. I get sick and I get tired . . .'

'She's being terribly brave,' Ellis put in. 'But she's not at her bubbling best.'

'It'll pass.' Fay waved away his concern. 'Are you thirsty, Kate? Shall I send down for some tea?'

'Yes please.'

Fay *didn't* look all that well. Where Kate and Ellis were tanned, her skin was pale, as if she'd spent the spring and summer months hiding away from the glare of the sun. There were bluish smudges beneath her eyes and her natural blonde curls appeared dry and lank. She wore a spotted smock – creased from her nap on the bed – over a white blouse with a wide, rounded collar. The clothes had a little-girl quality that made her seem younger and more vulnerable than Kate remembered.

She picked up the bedside telephone and ordered tea. It was delivered by a shy-looking girl about Kate's age. Ellis poured cups for them all. Fay perched on the bed to drink hers. Kate sat on the floor, Ellis on the curved Lloyd Loom chair.

He began to ask after the Felixes with a courteous interest that seemed studied to Kate, as if her father were pursuing a conscious strategy. She mentioned that Jerome was appearing on television in a few days' time, moonlighting on some silly quiz show, delightedly cocking a snook at the intellectual establishment.

'Jerome always was a character,' her father explained to Fay. 'Lay in bed all morning, got drunk each night, then walks away with a brilliant first . . .' For the first time Kate sensed that Jerome's glib facility rankled with Ellis.

'Sounds quite a guy,' Fay commented on cue.

'And the children? Pascal's just done his A-Levels, hasn't he? Has he got a university place?'

'He's working as a beach photographer.' Kate took pleasure in confounding her father's expectations.

Ellis looked surprised. 'But the girl's at Oxford . . .'

Almost at once, though, he seemed to forget about the Felixes. Dunking a digestive biscuit into his cup of tea, Ellis announced feelingly, 'Kate, I just can't tell you how much Fay and I are looking forward to this week. Just the three of us rubbernecking around. No timetable, no pressure. We've both been working so hard, and what with Fay's morning sickness . . . You too, Kate. *You* must have been cramming for your O-Levels for months . . .'

Kate hesitated, made sounds of vague agreement.

Ellis looked at her, his expression earnest, a sort of appeal in his eyes. 'It was bad last year. Everything went wrong. I freely admit my own part in the whole mess – Fay and I have discussed it endlessly . . .' He touched his wife's knee, glanced wryly at her. 'Both of us want to make a fresh start and we want you to help us do it.'

Kate had to admit to herself that she rather enjoyed the days that followed. The sun shone. She and Ellis showed Fay all the touristy things she just had to see, Buckingham Palace, St Paul's, the Tower, and she was impressed with it all, exhilarated to be in London – she'd never been abroad before. They ate in restaurants, bought silly souvenirs, shopped for new clothes at the summer sales. Kate remembered her father as careful with his cash, but on these expeditions he demonstrated an easy open-handedness.

All three of them were on their best behaviour and they all got on pretty well, defusing any potential moments of tension with determined goodwill, an eagerness to compromise.

'You wouldn't believe how glad we are to see you such a grown-up young lady, so happy and well,' Fay confided to Kate on the evening of the second day, as they sat together – briefly alone, Ellis had gone to the lavatory – in a homely Austrian restaurant called Hartmann's across the road from the hotel. 'It's weighed on Ellis, you know, the anger between you . . . He's thought about you, talked about you a real lot during the last year, trying to work out how and why it all fell apart . . .'

'Mmm.' Kate's response was noncommittal. She couldn't deny a small flicker of gratification at the thought of her father feeling troubled in any way about their vexed relationship, perhaps even reproaching himself for his behaviour. At the same time she suspected that Fay was probably overstating the case by way of reinforcing the general well-intentioned drive towards reconciliation.

When Ellis came back from the lavatory Kate found herself observing him for signs of the brooding self-doubt Fay had hinted at. But Ellis seemed in excellent spirits.

'I'm having such a good time,' he enthused to his daughter over a plate of schnitzel and fried potatoes.

'I am too,' she replied. Though, even as she said it, Kate knew it wasn't as simple as that.

Most of the time, down at Plas Felix, Kate had the impression that she'd 'got over' her mother's death, the memory of Rose pushed out by the day-to-day adventure of living. But the presence of Ellis and Fay resurrected old emotions, old grievances.

Even as she enjoyed the fragile truce between herself and her father, a sardonic alter ego lodged in her brain, looked out through her eyes, noticing things, making comparisons.

Shopping and sightseeing with Ellis and his replacement wife, Kate was still ambushed by feelings of disloyalty, nettled by the difference in her father's attitude. When Kate was a child Ellis had often been grumpy and grudging on days out. In her memory there was always the sense of doing things on the cheap, taking flasks and sandwiches and picnicking in uncomfortable circumstances, under umbrellas or on damp public benches with the wind in their hair. How Rose would have loved Ellis's new expansiveness, the eating out, his impulse-buying of frivolous gifts. Fay just didn't know she was born.

'Who's for apple strudel?' Ellis asked, as if he'd somehow read Kate's thoughts. He smiled at Fay beside him, briefly patted her belly. 'I bet Junior would like some of that.'

On the Thursday Kate left her father and Fay to Hampton Court, took a bus down to Camberwell to visit Jess, her old school friend. They hadn't seen one another for two whole years. Walking down the terraced back-street where Jess lived, a mere stone's throw away from the one in which she herself had grown up, Kate experienced distaste. The streets seemed cramped, the houses unlovely, the grey-brown colour of the bricks downright ugly. In her pink sweater, black skirt and earrings, Kate felt she'd moved on. She felt confident. Jess would be impressed by the change in her. Last time they'd been together Kate was still in abbreviated little girl dresses and ankle socks.

She walked up the short, tiled path to Jess's house and rang the bell. Almost at once she saw movement through the frosted glass panes in the front door.

Jess appeared in the open doorway. She grinned. 'Wotcher.'

Kate was mildly disconcerted by the laconic greeting, she'd become used to Nelly's raptures. 'Hello, stranger,' she said. 'Golly, you look different.'

Somehow it hadn't occurred to her that Jess would have changed as well. Kate's mental picture of her friend was fixed, a black-and-white photograph of a graceless fourteen-year-old on a swing. But the figure standing at the door was – as Fay might have remarked – a grown-up young lady.

Jess had never been pretty. She was pale, heavy-featured, rather dumpy. But her unremarkable looks were coupled with a stubborn streak that used to fascinate Kate. She was never actively naughty –

her schoolwork was excellent in fact – yet many of the teachers took against her, seeming to sense a scepticism, a passive resistance, a sardonic independence of mind that made them feel uncomfortable, the very things that attracted Kate to her.

Jess had always been defiantly frumpy. She was still no beauty, yet, standing there in a pale green summer dress and white high-heeled sandals, her brown hair cut and permed, small pearl earrings and pink lipstick in place, she exuded a sort of nubile bloom.

'Come on in. God, it's ages. We're by ourselves. Mum's out at work.'

Jess's father had been killed in the war. Her mother was some kind of a civil servant. Quite nice, Kate recalled, but always in a hurry, with harassed eyes behind horn-rimmed spectacles.

'We'll go and sit in the garden. There's some ginger beer in the pantry. Want a glass?'

'Why not?'

Kate followed her through the familiar long hallway. It seemed lighter than it used to be. 'You've had it decorated.'

'Mum's had the whole house done.'

In the living-room there was a new three-piece suite, cream with pink and navy flowers, matching frilled cushions. Rather upright and unyielding, Kate thought, not the sort of thing that encouraged you to lounge.

'Country Cottage range.' Jess gave a mocking grin. 'Just the thing for South London.' She pronounced the last two words in satirical, music-hall Cockney.

The house was undoubtedly brighter and fresher than Kate remembered, but it struck her as distressingly poky. Had she really spent years in a place just like it?

Two deck chairs had been set up under the shade of the apple tree in the long, narrow back garden. Kate recalled that Jess's mother used to give her bags of knobbly, wormy windfalls to take home for Rose, who always dumped them straight in the bin.

'Gosh, I feel as if I've come back to a little ... to a mini-dream world.'

'You'll be talking about li'l old England next,' Jess commented with amiable acidity. 'Like some big-headed American film star.'

The ginger beer was lukewarm. There was no fridge in Jess's household. In fact Rose had only acquired one a year or so before she died. In America and with the Felixes Kate had got used to drinking her cold drinks chilled. The brownish liquid in her glass seemed dishwatery and brackish.

But Jess sipped hers with evident enjoyment. She started talking about school, telling Kate bits and pieces about girls she used to know – how Dorothy Herbert had faked an attack of sunstroke to get out of sitting her O-Levels, how Janet Solomon had pinched Kay Piercy's boyfriend and looked like a tart nowadays. In the dappled shade of the apple tree Jess seemed fourteen again as if, in the intervening two years, nothing had changed at all.

'Oh, and you remember Nell – you know – the games teacher . . . Well . . .' Jess's grin held depths of delighted *schadenfreude*. 'You'll never believe . . . At guide camp she fell into the latrine pit – honestly! She had poo all down her legs . . .'

Kate laughed at her tales. A part of her was curious, amused. At the same time she was invaded by a kind of contempt for Jess, because she was still the same, still in the same place, nothing had happened to her. She felt a shudder of . . . dread at the thought that her own life could have stayed the way it was, so narrow and nothingy. Even the wretched months in America seemed preferable.

Following on from Jess's saga about Kay and Janet, Kate began to talk about Nelly and the ups and downs of her relationship with Robert Williams. She was aware of being motivated partly by the desire to impress Jess with the unconventionality of her adopted environment, the waywardness of her new friend.

'They've been sort of boyfriend and girlfriend for ages, but Nelly's a terrible flirt. And sometimes Robert just has to get even. He . . . went all the way with this girl called Ros on the beach one night . . .' Kate imagined Jess might be shocked by a more explicit term. '. . . And now Nelly's getting even with *him*, going with this boy from Criccieth who plays in a skiffle band . . .

Only deep, deep down she and Robert . . . Well, there's something between them that . . . They can't do without all the messing about and making each other jealous . . .' The thought had never occurred to her before.

Jess listened, her expression inscrutable. She made no comment. Kate had forgotten – Jess never ever admitted to being impressed by anything, ever.

Her friend deflected the conversation. 'What subjects are you doing for A-Level, Kate?'

'First things first. I reckon I've probably failed most of my O's.' Kate was rather pleased with the airy tone of her statement.

'I bet you haven't. You've always been one of the brainy ones.'

'I didn't work.' She gave a careless shrug. 'Nelly and I –'

Sharply Jess cut in. 'Sounds as if this Nelly person's taken over your mind. She's got you wrapped round her little finger.'

The sour observation took the wind out of Kate's sails. She stared stupidly at Jess, unable to muster a riposte.

'You're daft if you let yourself fail. There's nothing particularly hard about O-Levels . . .' Jess sounded worldly-wise. Somehow she had turned the tables, put Kate on the defensive. Jess had always had that knack, Kate recalled.

Chapter Thirteen

That evening the three of them dined once again at Hartmann's across the road. Their schnitzel was glorious, their strudel supreme. Fay bubbled with enthusiasm for Hampton Court, though she'd had a funny turn in the maze and had to sit down for half an hour.

'I don't think Junior was very impressed with all the twisting and turning.' Ellis patted Fay's hand with a rueful smile.

Kate found herself increasingly irritated by his arch references to 'Junior'. It sounded twee and false to her, and most unlike the Ellis she knew of old.

'How was Jess?' her father asked. 'You passed on my best wishes, I hope.' This comment, too, annoyed her with its insincerity. When the families had been virtual neighbours, Ellis had barely given Jess or her mother the time of day.

'She was fine – just the same.' Kate had no desire to enlarge. Jess's comment about Nelly still rankled, unsettling her with a pinprick of self-doubt. Though on the way home Kate had rationalized, putting her friend's ungraciousness down to envy and pique.

They skipped coffee. Jerome was appearing on his quiz show tonight and they didn't want to miss the start. The immaculate hotel lounge was deserted. The television set stood in one corner on a highly polished occasional table. An array of armchairs in rose-pink velours were lined up round the periphery of the room, each with its own maroon velvet cushion, perfectly plumped, forming a tidy diamond shape against every chair back. Ellis pushed three of them over towards the television.

The programme was called *Follow On*, the object being to create long strings of words, using the last syllable of one to form the beginning of the next. Kate had come across it several times while switching idly from one channel to the other. There were rules but the emphasis seemed to be on personality and a zany but controlled anarchy.

Kate was used to seeing Jerome on serious *Brains Trust* sort of programmes but it was bizarre to encounter him – looking so much himself, with that private, amused, rather sly smile – perched on one of *Follow On*'s high stools beneath a curlicued canopy, teamed with Rowena Yardley, a Rank-style starlet who figured every other week in Nelly's *Picturegoer*.

'A spiv with an Oxford accent' was how Jerome had described James Nottcutt, the show's resident compere.

As he introduced the evening's contestants Nottcutt's grin oozed insolent bonhomie. Opposing Jerome and Rowena were a middle-aged character actress with shrewd, cold eyes, and a journalist from *Punch* with a boozer's heightened complexion, obvious even in black and white. Jerome was labelled 'everyone's favourite egghead' – Kate couldn't seem to get away from that word.

When finally he turned to Rowena, Nottcutt's eyes sparkled, embracing both the studio audience and the nation's viewers with a sort of lubricious complicity. The camera cut to the young woman, displayed on her high stool, legs coquettishly crossed, hair blonde and softly curled away from her high forehead, wearing pearly stiletto-heeled shoes and a pale dress in stiffened brocade, constructed with tucks and darts to fit her hourglass figure like a shapely carapace.

'She looks scared,' Fay said.

But as Nottcutt introduced the starlet, smirkingly presenting her in the guise of a luscious, lust-provoking dunce, Rowena laughed along with everyone else at the incongruity of someone as dizzily gorgeous as she finding herself in partnership with one of the country's best-known intellectuals.

'Look at her eyes.' Fay turned to Ellis. 'There's panic in them.'

Her observations made Kate – who'd been as amused as anyone at the juxtaposition – see Rowena in a different light. Once the game got under way she noticed how constantly the young woman turned to Jerome for approval and support as if she felt out of her depth.

Jerome remained smilingly unruffled. The contest was a doddle to him and he was unfazed by the probing of the cameras and by Rowena's dependence on him. Blatantly he prompted his glamorous team-mate, while Nottcutt flaunted a smarmy tolerance. It was all in the spirit of the game. The actress and the journalist on the opposing team let slip the odd acid protest, but were clearly aware that to get upset would make them look dour and unsporting. Kate found it all hard to watch, her stomach knotting with the tensions that lay behind the inconsequential banter.

'Jerome's my friend,' Rowena announced at one point, cradling his hand against her cheek.

The words came out too loud and too fervent. There was a general awkwardness, a drawing back. Kate read dismay in the young woman's eyes at what she perceived, too late, as a gaffe, but Jerome rescued her with a casual witticism, drawing attention back to himself and away from the starlet.

In the event the opposing team, quite rightly, won. Yet it was glaringly obvious that Jerome and Rowena were the stars of the show. Kate felt proud of him and fond of him and abruptly homesick for Plas Felix.

Ellis clicked off the television and turned to Fay. 'That's my friend Jerome,' he said. 'Though quite what he's doing lending himself to that kind of drivel . . .'

Fay pulled a dubious face. 'Not if he wants to be taken seriously . . .' She too clearly had reservations as to the wisdom of Jerome's choice.

Their cool criticism triggered in Kate a hot rush of defensive anger. 'He *is* taken seriously,' she blurted, sounding more aggressive than she'd intended. 'Why shouldn't he have a bit of fun? What gives you the right to judge him?'

'It's an opinion, Kate.' For once Fay was sharp. She was flushed with an exasperation as sudden as Kate's own. 'I'm not judging the guy. "Judge" is a silly, emotive word.'

Kate was startled. She'd come to rely on Fay to soothe all aggravation. It was as if a crack had revealed itself and she was on one side, Fay and Ellis on the other. But the breach had been there all the time. Their rapprochement was a sham, mere polite pussyfooting. Truth was the rancour that ebbed and flowed in the gulf between them.

The following morning Fay felt sick and didn't come to breakfast. They were going to the theatre that evening. She didn't want to miss it and so opted to spend the morning in bed. Ellis had to pick up some books at Foyles and he suggested Kate come with him. They could have lunch somewhere afterwards. It was their last day. Tomorrow he and Fay would be flying on to Paris, Kate returning to Wales.

This morning the sun shone through a humid haze. Kate was keyed up. She hadn't yet mentioned her exam fears to Ellis and this could be her last chance to do so. Today she felt less touchy, but still convinced that the peace between her father, Fay and herself existed only at the price of unrelenting self-censorship, by dint of sweeping everything inconvenient blandly under the carpet.

'Let's have a good old English fry-up,' Ellis suggested, harking back to one of their rare moments of camaraderie. One winter's day when Rose was out they'd sizzled a greasy mountain of bacon, eggs, potatoes, mushrooms in two frying pans, pigged out companionably at the kitchen table.

Charing Cross Road was rich in snack bars. They found one called The Manchester. Behind a sort of shop-front the place was furnished with two rows of yellow and black Formica tables, a counter at the far end. Ellis ordered two mixed grills. The table-top was still wet from a recent swabbing. Two elderly men sat across the aisle from them, smoking and drinking tea, flanked by their empty egg-stained plates. They were silent and somnolent as if in the wake of a long night-shift.

'So-o-o, Kate.' Her father leaned back in his chair, smiling, expansive, linking his hands behind his head. In a well-pressed Cambridge blue shirt he radiated health and wellbeing. 'I'd say this whole trip has been pretty successful, wouldn't you?'

His use of the word 'successful' grated, as if Ellis had set himself a goal and achieved it to his own satisfaction. The goal being a truce with his bolshy daughter. Mission accomplished.

But Kate swallowed the slight irritation and smiled. 'Yes, it's been nice . . . Better than I expected,' she added tactlessly.

But if Ellis noticed her clumsiness he ignored it. He said yet again how happy he was to see her in such good spirits – the contrast with the winter before last was quite unbelievable. He quite saw that he'd been hasty in expecting her to get over Rose's death in so short a time. He'd been thinking about her future, he told her, and it seemed to him that she really ought to think now about giving America another chance, finally settling down with Fay and himself, and completing her education out there . . .

Kate barely listened, she had her own agenda. 'Listen, Dad,' she said suddenly. 'I expect to fail most of my O–Levels.'

Bizarrely the statement put her in mind of an engagement announcement, something rather public and formal.

'Number fourteen!' the woman called from behind the counter. She held two brimming plates in her hand.

It was their order. As he got to his feet, Ellis's eyes stayed on Kate, blank with startled incomprehension. Then he turned and went up to the counter, collected their plates and two sets of cutlery.

'What d'you mean?' he asked as he sat down again.

Kate shrugged. 'I mean what I just said.'

'How can you know you've failed?'

'I didn't work.' No point in evasion. 'I just know.'

There, she'd said it, got it over with. There was silence between them. Kate turned her attention to a huge mushroom oozing black juice.

It seemed to take a little time for her father to digest the sudden revelation. And all the while he chewed his way through bacon rashers, rounds of black pudding, brown-crusted potato slices, methodically dunking each forkful into the yolk of his egg. Kate felt light and relieved, as if she'd dumped a parcel that had been weighing her down all week.

'Weren't you supervised?' Ellis asked abruptly. 'Didn't the Felixes supervise your work?'

'A bit. Not much. Basically, Jerome lets his kids choose . . . He says we're not all supposed to be eggheads.' Kate trotted out the word with a flash of private amusement.

'But Beatrice . . .'

'She's academic. So's Pascal – though he's mad on photography too. Nelly isn't academic. And I don't think Olivier will be either. That's just how it is.'

Her father's lips twitched in a vexed fashion, but he made no reply. Kate sliced into her tomato – to her mind always the least enjoyable part of a mixed grill. She looked up. 'I'm certain I've passed French. Pascal's got me reading French novels . . .'

'Yes, I saw one in your room . . . Fay and I were impressed . . .' He waved the topic away. 'Look here, Kate, what you say convinces me even more strongly that you should come back to the States. You need a tighter framework than the Felixes can give you . . . I'm absolutely out of sympathy with Jerome's muddle-headed laxity.'

'No. I won't come.' She spoke with quiet finality, noticing in passing that one of the lizard-like old men at the next table was following their conversation with sleepy interest.

'Oh, Kate,' Ellis sighed. 'I get so absolutely sick and tired of your sheer, endless cussedness.' His voice had an edge of steel, but Kate guessed he wouldn't make a scene in so public a place.

'Of course – it'd be lots nicer for you if I agreed with everything you said.' She took advantage of his public reticence to press home her own side of the argument. 'Look, you keep saying how well and happy I look. Why d'you think that is? It's because I'm with the Felixes and I love being there!'

His only comment was a brief, sharp exhalation of breath expressing impatience and contempt.

'It's true. And you're well and happy too. You're happier with Fay than you ever were with Mum. I see that . . . And you're happier in America than you were in England.' She spread her hands in an emphatic gesture of appeal. 'Why don't we both stay happy where we are . . . Apart.'

On stage, in clownish make-up and a loud checkered suit, Sir Laurence Olivier cracked jokes with the hard fake bonhomie of

127

a music-hall comic. In the hot, dark, hushed auditorium Kate sat enthralled by the strength and skill with which he managed to convey the venomous self-loathing that lay behind the jovial professional mask of his character, Archie Rice.

She was in a funny state of mind, thin-skinned, her heart swelling with a confusion of powerful, nameless feelings. It had been an emotional day. Back at the hotel the peace sustained all week between Ellis and herself had finally broken down.

Ellis had returned to his dictatorial best, adamant that there was absolutely no alternative to Kate's returning with them to Coningsburgh, ready for a new and earnest blitz on her education. In the dim hotel bedroom, curtains drawn against the sultry heat outside, her father's face looked pale, yet blazed with a focused conviction so impressive it almost made her waver.

But she'd rallied in pure self-defence, would not give in to his overbearing . . . adultness. Somehow she matched Ellis's certainty with an obstinacy of her own, put forward Odile's Swiss project with a calm assertiveness that belied her anticipation of his scorn. Sure enough, he dismissed the idea with a tight-lipped impatience that made her feel a child again, conjured up disagreeable shades of the disdain with which he'd so often treated Rose. Passionately Kate had envied Nelly her indulgent parents, her easy, sunny path through life.

On stage Archie Rice received the news of his son's death in the Suez fiasco. Kate was rapt, involved, body and soul, in the character's roller-coaster ride, simultaneously terrified and elated at the prospect of a pain strong enough to break through the character's cynical shell. Tears pricked her eyes. Rose was in her mind.

During their clash Fay had for once stayed put. She hadn't had much choice. She'd lain on the bed, propped on one elbow, staring blankly at a page of her magazine. Her face looked white and rather beautiful. Her blonde hair was rumpled, her shoulders pale, fleshy and smooth beneath the straps of a pink nightgown.

'I'm your father!' Ellis had roared at one point. 'It's my place to *tell* you what to do. It's absurd I have to argue and cajole!'

In a small, clear voice Fay had demurred. 'You can't *make* Kate want to be with you . . .'

And later, when he jeered at the Swiss proposal, she commented quietly, 'It's not such a stupid idea, Ellis, and it's something she really wants to do.'

The two statements were calm and cool, like two trickles of limpid water on the self-fuelling heat of their anger. Kate's heart had filled with a quick, flooding gratitude in the same way as it soared now with the passions of the play. But Ellis had shown no signs of relenting.

Archie Rice began to moan, uttering strange, formless sounds that coalesced slowly into a blues lament, gut-wrenching, unbearable. How could he do that? With such searing conviction that you ached for his grief. Kate was filled with awe at the sheer tightrope-walking audacity of the performance.

Chapter Fourteen

✿❀✿❀✿

Halfway through August, when he got back to the States, Ellis phoned Odile and told her to go ahead – if it wasn't too late – with booking Kate into the Swiss school. Fay must have worked on him. Kate had accepted the fact that it wouldn't happen, and her happiness was like one of those fireworks that whoosh up to the sky and burst slowly in a shower of stars.

As it turned out, her O-Levels had been less disastrous than she feared. While Nelly had scraped just three passes, Kate had been successful in five subjects, including the dreaded Maths, and her French result had been outstanding. She'd been scared for a while that Ellis would have second thoughts. But perhaps Fay had convinced him that it was in all their interests for him to keep his daughter happy.

In mid September Kate and Nelly flew out to Geneva. It had been decided that they would spend a couple of days chez Grand-mère before term began. They took the train from Geneva to Lausanne. Kate had never been to Europe before and was daunted by the foreignness of everything, the sights and smells, the breezy yet vehement way people spoke. But, at the same time, there was a jolt of excitement, anticipation. She knew right away that she was going to like it here.

Grand-mère's first-floor flat was comfortable, but intimidatingly clean and tidy, the living-room stuffed with furniture in highly polished wood and rich, dark-printed plush. The place smelt of some kind of musky polish and looked out over a patch of green with benches and autumnal trees. Grand-mère greeted them in her stern-but-gracious fashion, donned an incongruous apron over her gunmetal afternoon dress and cooked them omelettes with gruyère cheese, served a salad made with the big, misshapen tomatoes that Odile favoured.

After the meal she got out the family photo albums featuring Odile as a skinny, long-legged child, Grand-mère herself looking unfeasibly young and happy, and '*mon mari*' – long dead – a slight, boyish, dapper man posing in sports jackets and breeches, or old-fashioned swimsuits with shoulder straps.

Kate and Nelly slept in Grand-mère's spare room, in a pair of high beds with white linen duvets and hard square pillows. The next day Nelly showed Kate the town. She was charmed by Lausanne, a delightful mixture of steep, narrow, cobbled streets and big, bright modern buildings, the smell of strong French cigarettes in the air, and coffee, and cooking, the people so prosperous-looking, so chic it did your heart good.

They ate a lunch of steak and salad on the terrace of a café in the lakeside district of Ouchy.

'It's all just so exactly how it should be . . .' Kate was dazzled by the bright autumn sun, the sheer fun of eating outside, the way the surface of the lake sparkled and glittered, the mountains rising up like a mirage on the far side, their tops in snow.

Their fellow diners seemed to take it all for granted, as if it were only right and proper that their days should hold such transcendental moments of leisure and pleasure.

Nelly sat munching her way methodically through the juicy steak, the over-dressed salad. Her fair hair straggled pleasingly across the shoulders of her new red sweater. She was serenely aware of the interested glances of a man at a neighbouring table, a suave-looking individual in sunglasses and Prince of Wales check.

'This is going to be the best year ever, Katie . . .' Conscious of being watched, she smiled in a coquettish, cat-like fashion. 'I can just feel it in my bones.'

To a sudden ripple of applause a curly-haired woman in black stepped on to the low dais in one corner of the terrace. She carried an accordion and, without further ado, launched into a wheezy, languorous version of 'La Vie en Rose'.

* * *

The school, Les Rosiers, was a large three-storey house with a turret at each end, hinting at aspirations to château status. The façade was painted a warm yellow-beige, the three rows of windows flanked by sage green shutters. A tidy vine meandered photogenically across the frontage. The main doorway was arched, the door heavy and studded, and framed by a pair of vigorous climbing roses, for which the school was named. As term began they were still festooned with a late flush of lax, opulent white blooms.

Grand-mère had hired a taxi to ferry the two girls and their suitcases the short distance from her flat to the school. The forecourt was a jumble of trunks, cases, cars, along with girls of every nationality, some looking lost and alone, others clinging to parents and siblings in passionate farewell.

In the entrance-hall a harassed woman with a clipboard directed a morose-looking middle-aged Italian to carry their bags up to the second-floor room they were to share, apparently, with a Brazilian girl named Barbara Richter.

The room was bright and spare, with shiny honey-brown floorboards, three beds with matching bold, 'contemporary' bedcovers in kingfisher and black, three narrow white wardrobes, a small table and three chairs, a wash-basin in a cupboard-like recess with strip lighting above the mirror.

'The atmosphere is agreeable.' Statuesque and smart in a dark coat, the lapel enlivened with a tasteful silver brooch, her mauve hair curling crisply, Grand-mère was thoroughly approving. 'You're going to be happy here.' It sounded like an order.

At four o'clock the pupils were asked to assemble in a concourse on the ground floor. It was a big, bare room, flooded with afternoon sunshine. The gloomy Italian caretaker who'd carried their bags was in the process of setting out rows of elegant stacking chairs in moulded white fibreglass.

From a low platform framed with long, shifting white curtains, the headmistress, Madame Voss, welcomed her new arrivals. She spoke briskly of the school's aims and expectations. Kate listened with half an ear. In spite of her O-Level success, she did not yet expect to understand a native French speaker, and anyway it sounded conventional stuff about the value of French culture and the necessity for application and hard work. She was far more interested in observing her companions and her surroundings.

Then came the bombshell. The school had rules, Madame Voss announced, a steelier tone entering her voice, and they were rigorously enforced. From the outset it had to be understood that she stood *in loco parentis*, responsible for a large number of *jeunes filles*, many of them away from home for the very first time. She must make it quite plain to them all that their moral and physical safety were paramount. They were not, therefore, free to come and go as they pleased. Excursions and cultural visits would be made en masse and under the supervision of the staff. Only once a week – from two until five on a Friday afternoon – were pupils permitted to go out alone . . .

The announcement was repeated in English, Spanish and German in order to make absolutely sure that no girl remained in the slightest confusion.

Kate and Nelly looked at one another with mounting anguish. Nelly's eyes rolled in horror and incredulity.

'This is disastrous,' she hissed. 'It's just awful. It's going to ruin everything!'

A little later she whispered urgently and audibly, 'We'll have to think of some way round all this . . . Grand-mère's going to have to be our alibi.'

'*S'il vous plaît, mademoiselle!*' the headmistress rapped, glaring Medusa-like in Nelly's direction.

Madame Voss, headmistress and proprietress of Les Rosiers, was tall and intimidatingly smart. Her short hair was dyed a dashing, artificial shade of pinkish auburn, the sides swept back, the top rising then swooping dynamically across her forehead. She looked to be in her late forties, her face bonily mobile, her nose aquiline, mouth wide and plum-coloured. She wore tailored suits in strong, clean greens, blues, tans – never garish, but certainly not understated.

She had a beautiful voice, clear and resonant – had trained as an actress, the story went. She could speak at normal volume and make herself heard above a hubbub of chatter. Her manner was forceful and absolutely decided. For all her talk of culture and the arts she seemed more of a businesswoman than an educator. Kate thought there was something ruthless about her, but at the same time her vibrant presence had an undeniably uplifting effect.

The pupils of Les Rosiers were scared of her, but the teachers more so. Even Madame Jobert, who taught 'culture' while slouching against her desk in an elegantly sardonic fashion, pulled a quick rueful face and straightened up when Madame Voss came sweeping into the room.

The headmistress's husband was a quite different proposition. He was tall and broad, yet his physique conveyed a clumsiness, a hangdog quality that his expensive suits could not redeem. Monsieur Voss was fresh-complexioned, quick to flush, his receding hair clipped straight across at the base of his skull and worn in a kind of bob. On the school prospectus he had several degrees attached to his name, yet there was something almost vacant about his expression and presence.

He seemed to have little function in the running of the school. The day-to-day administration was managed by his wife with fiery competence. Her husband was rumoured to have business interests of his own – he possessed two gleaming Mercedes – yet he spent an awful lot of time at Les Rosiers just hanging about, wandering round the grounds in an aimless fashion, or deep in consultation with the gardener.

Madame Voss was Lausannoise born and bred, but her husband's nationality was a matter of speculation. Barbara from Brazil, who shared a room with Kate and Nelly, said he was Latvian. Another girl claimed he was from the Ukraine.

'Bet he's a war-criminal in hiding,' Nelly claimed with slanderous glee.

'Or a fifth-columnist.' Kate wasn't too sure what the word meant, but she liked the sound of it.

He wasn't the only one whose background aroused their curiosity. Madame Weber taught French but her home town was Athens. The maids, along with Guido, the caretaker, were all from Southern Italy, where unemployment was astronomical. They sent most of their money home, saw their families for just a month a year. Though Barbara came from São Paulo her surname was German and she spoke the language like a native. Kate and Nelly fantasized that her father might be a Nazi who'd escaped with illicit gold, had plastic surgery . . . The school's cosmopolitan diversity seemed perfectly appropriate – Lausanne itself swarmed with expatriates of all kinds.

There were places in the school for fifty students – currently forty-seven were on the roll. Some were the daughters of comfortably off doctors, academics, civil servants. Others had fathers who were diplomats or politicians. A girl called Francine Civetta was apparently the child of a Hollywood actress called Sherry Clare. Neither Kate nor Nelly had heard of her, but above Francine's bed hung a glossy publicity still of a pretty, smirky woman with glossy shoulder-length hair, wearing a figure-hugging brocade dress, a fur coat draped casually round her shoulders. Francine bore little resemblance to her gorgeous parent. She was tubby and none too keen on soap and water, bit her nails down to the quick, wore sloppy joe sweaters to disguise her figure, topped with a succession of her mother's cast-off wigs.

Violetta Casals, on the other hand, struck Kate as one of nature's aristocrats. She was beautiful and imperious, with a smooth olive complexion and long chestnut hair worn in a stylishly haphazard topknot. Her sweaters and skirts were cashmere, in deep, dark colours, against which her skin glowed richly. She'd been horrified at first at having to share what she considered to be a poky little room, almost a cupboard. At home in Ecuador she was rumoured to have a whole suite to herself and a maid who slept on the floor at the foot of her bed.

Barbara Richter was a plain, hardworking girl with heavy features and hair that frizzed distressingly in spite of all her efforts. She was always writing letters to her parents and school friends back in Brazil, or simply just writing, in methodical little notebooks – French vocabulary lists, accounts of money spent, reminders of chores to be done. At bedtime her hair-curling, tooth-brushing, cleansing and moisturizing routine took forever and was never skimped.

Her unhurried thoroughness drove Nelly mad with impatience. 'One of these days I'm going to grab her rollers and her *tonique floral* crap and hurl them right through the window . . .'

But Barbara's rituals bothered Kate not at all. She thought her sweet. The young Brazilian was so unspoiled with her quick, artless smile and her helpfulness. Everything in this bright, bizarre new world seemed exotic and delightful.

In those first weeks Kate felt mellow and uncritical about everything. She enjoyed waking up in the shared bedroom, washing and dressing with Nelly and Barbara in a sort of collective sleepy trance, loved the waxy, celluloid-y smell of floor polish in the corridors, and the rich coffee aroma downstairs in the dining-room, the fatty, crumbly texture of the breakfast croissants.

And afterwards she would take her place in one of the pleasant schoolrooms, the new-looking, expensive-looking tables and chairs a rich contrast to the battered, ink-stained, graffiti-covered desks she thought of as the norm. Through the window she could see blue sky and the delicate, fluttering, yellowing leaves and bright white trunks of a group of silver birches.

During the whole of each morning the pupils studied French. They were graded according to ability and the lessons were grinding and intensive. Slow learners were drilled and grilled until they caught up. Kate and Nelly had the impression that the teachers were terrified of attracting the wrath of Madame Voss by achieving a less than one hundred per cent pass rate in the final examination that threatened like a storm cloud on the horizon. The fierce linguistic focus was supplemented by courses in French culture – brisk gallops through the realms of art, music, history, drama and poetry.

Kate was avid for her French lessons, absorbed them like a sponge. To her the language was special, had a private personal glamour. She longed to speak with the strident fluency of Odile, Grand-mère, David Lacoste. In her mind's eye she was drawing closer to Pascal's fantasy world of black-clad existentialists, Gauloises, Left Bank cafés . . .

In the afternoon she enrolled in German and typing courses. Kate felt alert and purposeful. The teachers praised her as a model pupil.

And beyond the wrought-iron gates of Les Rosiers she was agreeably aware of Lausanne, exciting yet unthreatening, so European. As Madame Voss had decreed, pupils were allowed into town only once a week, on Friday afternoons. The restrictions didn't bother Kate. She simply looked forward to the day, relished the opportunity to look round the sophisticated shops, watch the rich, smart women in the Rue de Bourg, saunter along the lakeside promenade at Ouchy, sit with Nelly on the terrace of the Café Caroline in the crisp autumn sunshine, wearing enigmatic dark glasses and drinking filter coffee. It was wonderful, it was enough. Even now Kate marvelled at the mere fact of being here, could still hardly believe her luck.

Nelly felt murderous. She lay brooding on the bright, splodgy coverlet of her bed while Kate and Barbara and a skinny African girl called Nina sat round the table reciting a speech Madame Jobert had ordered them to learn for the following day. They were involved heart and soul in the activity.

How could they care? Nelly felt betrayed by Kate, who seemed suddenly to have acquired a taste for swotting, a desire for high marks and praise. She saw herself as the big, bad wolf casting malign eyes on the three little pigs. Across the room, against the white wood of Barbara's wardrobe door, three wholesome faces smiled – her austere, bespectacled father, demure mother, fat-cheeked sister . . . Barbara was beginning to drive Nelly insane, with her blushes, her little notebooks, her pink rollers. She brought out a streak of cruelty Nelly hardly knew she had. She longed to jeer at Barbara, call her names and make her cry. But Kate stood up staunchly for the irritating girl.

To think she'd been dying to come to this place – Nelly was aghast at her own naïveté. She'd imagined some kind of a college where they'd be free to come and go as they pleased, run wild in an agreeable foreign town. And here she was trapped in a place where they treated you more like novice nuns than anything else, locked in, checked up on . . .

137

And the atmosphere was so . . . Back home at school everyone knew who she was, they knew she wasn't a boffin, but even the teachers liked her because she was cheeky and she made them laugh. Here all they were interested in was screwing as much money out of your parents as they could manage, and they had to deliver something in return . . . Madame Voss had eyes like blue flints. There was no place for a free spirit in her tight scheme of things.

At night the proximity of the town, with its bars and clubs, tortured Nelly. Life was going on out there without her. She couldn't sleep, fantasized stealing out to bright lights, music and dancing, flirtation, admiration. She was woefully short of these drugs. But they were stuck up here on the second floor and the downstairs door was bolted and double-locked.

Robert wrote often, making her nostalgic for the familiar freedoms of her life back home. Yearningly she imagined walking along a windswept night-time beach, laughing and dancing in the echoey rooms at the top of the house, teasing Robert, playing with his feelings, getting him angry and worked up, then having a glorious, emotional reunion. Airily she'd told him not to be faithful – she wouldn't be. That was a laugh in itself.

'We'll drive you home. We'll get you back in time.' The man called Jean-Yves was casually persuasive.

'Promise?' Nelly said.

'Promise.' He had a nice, reassuring grin. He was probably in his thirties, Kate thought, but attractive, with an easy manner, a thin, lively face and a small moustache.

His friend, Pierre, was taller, more Swiss and reserved, his hair beginning to recede a little. He looked a bit out of place in this young person's nightclub, the first Kate had ever been to: Le Scotch – Violetta had told them about it. She guessed the two men had taken off their wedding-rings for tonight's jaunt, but so what? It was nice sitting here in a little partitioned-off booth, talking French and sipping the sophisticated Pernod Pierre had ordered for them, and it was only for an evening.

Dim blue lights set into the wall illuminated the scene. All round them, in a haze of cigarette smoke, chic young people chatted and danced. Kate was all eyes. The atmosphere was so perfect it almost stifled the anxiety that floated in the back of her mind, the fear that they were playing truant and might get caught. They'd used Grand-mère as an alibi, been given official permission to visit until eleven, but stayed with her a mere half hour before rushing off, claiming a concert-outing. Just so long as neither Grand-mère nor the school cross-checked . . .

Meanwhile the four of them laughed at the simple-minded little joke they had going. Kate and Nelly had claimed to be adoptive sisters and now Jean-Yves was kidding them that he and Pierre were brothers.

'*Jumeaux identiques!*' He drew his smiling face up alongside Pierre's, an engaging twinkle in his eyes. Kate grinned. How funny and sweet he was.

Last week, on their afternoon in town, Kate had fallen out with Nelly, who wanted to go to a tea dance in one of the hotels, an amusement that was strictly out of bounds. Kate refused at first. The penalties for any kind of rule-breaking were very clear and it seemed madness to risk expulsion.

'I can't believe what a sickening little Goody Two-Shoes you've turned into!' Right there, on the busy Place St François, Nelly went crazy. 'I can't stand any more! I'm off my head with boredom. It's not bloody much to ask!' Nelly was screaming. Her eyes were hot with a glittery, scary anger and, to shut her up, Kate went with her to the stupid *thé dansant*.

They met three banking students from Basel, danced and chatted. Kate didn't say much. She was still shaken by Nelly's startling outburst. Perhaps Nelly was stirred up from all her shouting, because she seemed a bit strange, flushed and very pretty, but super-talkative, over-friendly. The polite young men looked uneasy and out of their depth. But the awkwardness was short-lived because she and Nelly had to go, anyway.

Tonight she wasn't like that, just sparkly and funny, setting the tone, she and Jean-Yves duetting in easy, flirtatious harmony while Kate and Pierre plodded along behind.

139

'Soft as a little lamb . . .' With jokey lechery Jean-Yves stroked the fluffy white mohair of Nelly's sweater and she laughed, tossing back her thick, fair hair with one hand, glancing sideways at him from her long, narrow eyes.

A little later it was Jean-Yves who glanced at his watch and got to his feet, announcing that it was time they made a move. Kate was surprised and impressed by his sense of responsibility. He and Pierre walked them to a nearby side street, where Pierre had parked his car.

'I adore these cars,' Nelly gushed. It was one of the new Citroëns that she and Kate agreed looked like a frog, with its long snout-like bonnet and pop-eyed headlamps. With tipsy expansiveness she traced the lines of its bodywork.

'Come and try it.' Jean-Yves pulled her into the back seat. Kate sat in front, alongside Pierre. In the rear-view mirror she glimpsed a brief flash of Nelly nestling into Jean-Yves' shoulder before the interior light was extinguished.

Kate felt drowsily, drunkenly relaxed. What bliss to be whisked home in such comfort, in such good time. Lazily she registered that Pierre was heading in the right direction, she recognized the streets.

After a couple of minutes Jean-Yves muttered something to his friend, too terse for Kate to understand. Pierre said nothing, continued driving. Kate heard a quiet, caressing laugh from Nelly, an answering murmur from Jean-Yves, guessed they were snogging in the back there. Outside they passed a group of elaborate, tall houses Kate didn't recognize. Pierre turned right up a steep, leafy lane, glided to a halt under some trees.

'Where are we?' Kate asked.

'We've got some time,' Pierre said. 'We can talk for a while.'

'No, it's too late.'

'Eleven o'clock, quarter past, half past, what's the difference?' Jean-Yves sounded brusquely impatient, quite unlike his former easy-going self.

There was no comment from Nelly. It was dark in the car, but Kate sensed that her friend and Jean-Yves were groping, fondling.

A low growl came from Jean-Yves, unequivocally lustful. A sort of restless heat seemed to radiate from behind, almost as if some wild animal were hiding there in the obscurity. Kate was anxious, embarrassed. They were going to be late. She'd no desire to start anything with Pierre.

Hesitantly he placed one arm around her shoulder. Kate ignored it, sitting stiff and bolt upright.

'Non!' A sudden protest from Nelly. '*Laisse moi . . .Laisse moi*!' The blunt vibrations of a struggle jolted Kate's backrest.

'Nelly . . .' The reproachful rumble of a male voice.

Kate turned. 'Nelly, are you OK?'

The scuffle became convulsive, violent prolonged. There was a snarl from Jean-Yves like a balked, enraged animal, then the click of a door-catch, a rush of cold night air, and Nelly was outside facing a barrage of violent, incomprehensible abuse from the man in the back of the car.

'Oh, God.' Kate felt for her own door-handle, stumbled out into the air. 'Nelly, what is it?'

Nelly was sobbing now. Kate put her arms around her, felt Nelly shudder, gasp for breath, her body taut and tense.

'Don't. Please don't . . . It's all right . . .' Cradling Nelly's head against her shoulder, at the same time drinking in the welcome cold night air, registering the clouds, the foliage of the trees sharp in the lamplight, a sliver of moon.

The car door slammed. Jean-Yves got out. He was shouting. '*Emmerdeuse*! *Allumeuse*!'

Kate stood braced but he didn't approach them, instead walked round to the passenger seat and got in. The Citroën revved and was gone, its occupants faceless now behind the dark windows.

'Where the hell are we?' Kate held Nelly tight, patting her shoulder almost automatically as she looked about her. She couldn't believe the mess they'd landed in.

Chapter Fifteen

❦❦❦❦

They got off lightly with the school, were grounded but not expelled. Grand-mère rose awesomely to the occasion, sussing out the essentials of the situation as if by instinct and lying for them. They'd been playing cards that night and had such an amusing time they'd forgotten all about the clock . . . Madame Voss went along with the story, though her hard blue eyes signalled that she didn't believe a word . . .

One cold night, three weeks later, Guido erected the screen and set out the stacking chairs for the usual Thursday evening film-show in the concourse. Blasé, elegant Madame Jobert manned the projector. It was pathetic, Nelly knew, but now she wasn't even allowed into town on a Friday, the film-show was the high-spot of her week.

True, she and Kate were still permitted to participate in collective outings to the theatre, but all they saw there were things like Molière that bored everyone silly. You could lose yourself in a film, swoon over Gérard Philipe or Yves Montand, have a good cry and go to bed feeling you'd had some kind of an experience.

Tonight she was really in luck. *War and Peace* – with French subtitles admittedly – but *in English*. The story was panoramic and utterly absorbing. And the warm, high-spirited, imperfect Rostov family made Nelly feel lonely for her own home and family. Sitting rapt in the dark, she identified passionately with Natasha, played by Audrey Hepburn, who must be the most beautiful woman in the whole world. Natasha was wayward and susceptible and got seduced by a devastating philanderer in breeches and high boots, betraying Andrei, her true love.

Nelly understood her weakness only too well, her mind filling up with images of that disastrous evening with Jean-Yves, images that made her stomach knot with a whole tangle of emotions. Sitting in the back of the car that night, in the comforting darkness, with the tang of petrol and the smell of new upholstery, it had been bliss to be kissed by him, have him fondle her legs and breasts. Though he was worlds away from Natasha's dashing Anatole, Nelly had definitely found him attractive, a grown-up man with exuberance and style . . .

But the scene had degenerated into farce. When the car stopped he changed, turned frantic and rapacious, thrust his hand between her legs, tried to force his stiff, suddenly naked cock on her with a shocking, startling force and fury . . . Nelly relived the sensations yet again with a fascinated mixture of repulsion and excitement . . .

She'd fought him off, terribly aware of Kate and Pierre only inches away, politely ignoring their scuffle. If it hadn't been for them Nelly knew she would have let him; she'd longed to give in, but at the same time something just as strong in her rebelled, and she'd shouted and struggled, looking an abject little prick-teaser, pathetic and inept.

'I wish now I'd let him do it . . .' Nelly had mused to Kate time and again since that night. The thought obsessed her.

Each time Kate rolled her eyes upward in exasperation. 'I wish you had, too, then we wouldn't have to keep talking about it . . .'

For perhaps the first time there was genuine grievance between herself and Kate. Nelly felt herself prickly and impatient with Kate's tepid good sense . . .

One day the previous week, in sudden irritation, she'd snapped, 'We didn't stand much of a chance, did we – what with you and Pierre sitting there like a couple of cardboard cut-outs . . .' Too late she heard the viciousness in her own voice.

'For God's sake, Nelly. You don't honestly expect me to drool over some balding idiot with his wedding-ring in his pocket just so's you . . .' Kate had been lost for words, but flushed with a righteous anger that frightened Nelly. She was so used to her twin's uncritical admiration.

When the film was over and the shutters opened they saw that it was snowing. The light from the room flooded out on to a fresh, feathery layer of white that covered everything in sight. A storm of flakes whirled wildly against the deep blue-black of the sky. The girls shrieked and ran to the window, exclaiming with an almost hysterical delight until Madame Jobert, who was anxious to get home, ordered them all upstairs to their respective rooms.

In the bedroom Nelly flung open the window. She and Kate leaned out, reaching for the soft flakes, breathing in great gulps of the icy air. Barbara joined them and stood, arms folded, clutching a thick brown cardigan around her. Outside all was virgin white. Even Madame Jobert's footsteps were fast disappearing under the silent, relentless fall.

'It's just like the frozen Russian wastes,' Nelly sighed.

The novelty of the snow enhanced the remembered magic of the film. The three of them stood and raved about the evening's show, in a random mixture of French and English, forgetting their differences for a while in shared enthusiasm.

Then Barbara shivered and said, '*Il fait froid*. Let's shut the window now.' She went to her wardrobe, got out her bag of rollers and began the nightly ritual of setting her hair.

A surge of irritation bubbled up in Nelly. 'I swear, if the atom bomb dropped you'd still put those stupid rollers in every night.'

Barbara looked hurt, but carried on. Then she started on her methodical cleaning and toning routine.

Suddenly Nelly experienced a rush of something like despair. What with the drama of the film, the surprise of the snow, she'd almost forgotten where she was for a while. But Barbara's pottering brought her back down to earth. She was still here, buried alive in this stifling nunnery.

'*Ferme la fenêtre*, Nelly,' Barbara begged.

Nelly ignored her, turning away, continuing to gaze out at the snow. An image from the film came to her mind – one of the boisterous young cavalry officers drinking a bottle of vodka or something, for a bet, while perched on a window-ledge high above St Petersburg ... and simultaneously Nelly remembered half a bottle of gin she had hidden among the sweaters in her wardrobe, bought out of devilment in the days when she and Kate were still allowed out, and smuggled back into the school. She'd had a couple of nips, then forgotten all about it.

'Who's for a drink?' she said.

'Oh, Nelly . . .' Barbara wavered. Her upbringing had brain-washed her into a knee-jerk disapproval of all alcohol.

'No thanks!' Kate screwed up her face and shuddered exaggeratedly. 'Not without some orange or lime or something.'

Bolshy and impatient, Nelly found the bottle, unscrewed it and took a hefty gulp, defying the objections of the other two. It *was* pretty vile, but the burning warmth put heart into her, making her feel jaunty, provocative. She crossed back to the window and straddled the ledge, then swung round so she was sitting with her legs dangling outside the building.

'Nelly, *non* . . .' came Barbara's imploring, irritating voice.

Raising the bottle, Nelly giggled. 'I'm Dolokhov. Watch me. Bet I can down the lot.' Grinning back over her shoulder she saw that Barbara had hidden her face in her hands.

'Don't be stupid,' Kate said roughly. 'Come on in. Give me the bottle.'

'I *want* to be stupid.'

'Grow up, Nelly, for goodness sake – it's dangerous.'

Nelly ignored her. It was wonderfully exhilarating sitting there, looking out on the virgin snow and swigging from her bottle. It made her feel like the person she really was, not someone squashed into submission by a pettifogging regime. The gin tasted nasty but it warmed her insides and life seemed beautiful to her, spacious, glorious . . .

'I'm free,' she said to Kate. 'I feel free.'

'For God's sake, Nelly, come on back inside.'

Nelly watched as a car crawled slowly through the tall wrought-iron gates of Les Rosiers, the acid gleam of its headlights extravagantly beautiful against the blank snow. It pulled up and two small figures got out. Monsieur and Madame Voss. Nelly stared down at them. They were like two black spiders against the expanse of white, like two spiders in a bath tub, she thought. Neither had noticed her.

Then suddenly Monsieur Voss glanced up and saw her. He grasped his wife's arm and pointed. Her gaze followed the direction of his finger. Nelly waited for them to call up, to say something, but they didn't, and soon they had vanished inside the building.

She held up the bottle. Less than half the gin remained. Nelly felt woozy and floppy. She was getting cold but had the conviction that, once she set foot back inside, this soaring sense of euphoria and detachment would evaporate into thin air and she would start weeping with hopeless, homesick self-pity.

Behind her she could hear Kate and Barbara arguing in an undertone as to whether they should fetch one of the staff. Confusingly Nelly had the impression that Barbara was against the move, Kate in favour.

'*Il n'y a rien à faire.*' Kate was suddenly decided. '*J'y vais. J'y vais.*' Nelly heard the bedroom door close.

Only moments later a second car arrived, with flashing lights that vibrated spectacularly against the snow. The police. Fuddled as she was, Nelly experienced merely a mild curiosity. She felt invisible, and was startled when one of the men called up to her – in English – telling her to hold on tight and not to move. They were here because of her, Nelly realized with vague surprise. She obeyed instructions and sat tight, resigning her fate to these new arrivals.

Soon afterwards the door opened behind her and someone came into the room.

'Mademoiselle, stay quite still.' A male voice, soothing and monotonous now, as if addressing a sleepwalker. 'Don't be afraid. You will be safe.'

The newcomer approached. Suddenly two strong arms encircled her body and she was hauled back into the room. When the arms released her Nelly sank to the floor and lay there feeling like a rag doll. She saw that the two policemen from outside were standing above her. She glimpsed Barbara's bewildered face, heard footsteps in the corridor and the energetic voice of Madame Voss.

'*Elle est ivre,*' one of the men said dispassionately. 'You are drunk, miss.'

'*Oui.*'

Nelly imagined her grin as saucy and insouciant. But suddenly she felt sick, tried to get up and get to the wash-basin, but her legs were flaccid as foam rubber. Madame Voss appeared, incongruously trim and smart in a fuchsia two-piece. Roughly she thrust a blue and white vase from a table in the corridor under Nelly's nose. Her aquiline face was a mask of disgust.

Repeatedly Nelly retched into the receptacle, too dazed to feel embarrassed. A part of her relished the absurdity of the scene. At the same time she was aware that later, tomorrow probably, there would be grave consequences.

'Nelly!' Kate pushed past the two policemen and dropped to her knees. 'Oh, God . . .' She saw the sick-bowl, and her eyes glinted with sardonic sympathy.

Nelly stretched out a limp hand towards her twin. Their eyes met in wry solidarity. Kate's pale face and lank dark hair were wonderfully familiar. How stupid that they'd quarrelled, how wrong Nelly had been to hold a grudge when Kate was the only person here who understood her.

She made an ill-judged attempt to explain to the two policemen. 'This is Kate, my best friend . . .' The two men exchanged pitying glances.

The sickness had receded. Nelly closed her eyes. The policemen lifted her on to the bed and pulled the coverlet over her. Someone closed the window.

As if from a long way off, Nelly heard the well-modulated tones of Madame Voss apologizing for her, praising and thanking the men for their prompt action, while their modest disclaimers formed a low, rumbling counterpoint. She saw them out and Nelly heard their car drive away.

'*Couchez-vous*, Barbara, Kate . . .' Soon the headmistress was back in the room.

She crossed to where Nelly lay, feeble and disgraced. Though her eyes were closed, Nelly could sense the woman's hard scrutiny.

'*Petite merdeuse,*' Madame Voss hissed.

Torpid as she was, Nelly was shocked by the headmistress's language. She was too far gone to care but understood that, at any other time, the woman's scathing, scornful tones would have turned her bowels to water.

Chapter Sixteen
1958

❦❦❦

In mid January Kate arrived back at Les Rosiers after the Christmas break. She was alone. Nelly had been expelled. Madame Voss sent for her almost immediately. Her office was cosier and chintzier than the rest of the school's décor – very *style anglais*, with an eau-de-nil carpet, button-back chairs in old rose and swagged floral curtains that combined both colours. An artificial coal fire burned in the grate and Madame Voss indicated two chairs, one each side of it. The headmistress wore a thick, boldly patterned Fair Isle sweater, above which her auburn hair was crisp and freshly coiffured as ever.

Kate guessed she wanted to talk to her about life post Nelly, and so it proved. Kate, so Madame Voss declared, had a brain and the capability for sustained work. Last term she'd been led astray by her sad susceptibility to Nelly's influence. But now there was nothing to stop her fulfilling her true potential.

The headmistress paused. '*Tu comprends*, Kate?'

'*Oui, madame.*' Kate kept her face expressionless, her voice uninflected. That way she felt no disloyalty to Nelly.

The Felix girl had been a disaster, Madame Voss continued, a lazy, hysterical, undisciplined child, of whom the school was well rid. Kate was disconcerted by the hardness in her tone. She was so used to thinking of Nelly's wilfulness as special and enviable that the headmistress's blatant dislike was like a slap in the face.

'You've been weak and easily led,' Madame Voss announced. 'Nelly Felix is no example to follow.'

Kate maintained her blank poker-face.

Both Odile and Jerome had been disappointed and angry at Nelly's ignominious return home. On the second afternoon of the holiday she remained closeted in Jerome's study with her parents for three whole hours, during which time tears, recriminations, threats and insults echoed down the corridor. Nelly had emerged, red-eyed and very quiet, and gone straight to bed.

The following morning her eyes were still swollen, her hair hanging in waif-like clumps. She and Kate sat drinking coffee at the kitchen table, while Odile stirred a large bowl full of dried fruit, chopped apple, fragrant nutmeg and rum, ready to fill the mince pies. The atmosphere was tight and silent.

Suddenly Nelly gasped 'Ma . . .' in a tragic voice that choked dramatically on the edge of tears.

Odile paused in her stirring and looked wryly at her daughter. With unruffled deliberation she set down her spoon and held her arms out to Nelly. They embraced, silent, fervent. Sitting by, Kate was embarrassed. And she was envious. For all her ease and familiarity she could never, ever belong to the Felix family in the same unqualified, inevitable fashion.

All holiday, from that morning on, Nelly had a deep, ecstatic look in her eye as if she'd come to appreciate the wonder of her own home with an abrupt and passionate intensity. Here she was free to sleep late, stay up until the small hours, come and go as she pleased, leave her room in a state of comforting chaos. Outside were fields, sea and open sky. It was the quiet season for the riding-school and the proprietors were happy for Nelly to exercise the horses, galloping along the firm, wet sand when the tide was out, returning with damp, wildly curling hair and a bloom on her cheeks that seemed unearthly in its brilliance.

She also lost her virginity to her on-off sweetheart, Robert Williams. Kate wasn't surprised. Since that night with Jean-Yves, Nelly had been like a cat on hot bricks. That Christmas the secret was between them all the time, heaving and pulsating beneath everything they did like an underground lava-flow. The mystery of it preyed on Kate's mind, an endless forbidden private film show – her two school friends, naked and panting, absurd, the way she'd seen her father and Fay, leaving her reluctantly aroused, sweaty and hot, her guts knotted in repellent excitement.

Whenever she and Nelly were alone they could talk of nothing else. Nelly's attitude to the event fluctuated disconcertingly.

'Honestly, Kate,' she would confide, 'you know how cool and in control he always looks . . . Well, in bed he goes crazy . . .' A rueful, half bashful grin. 'Gosh, I love him . . .'

At other moments she would give her cat-like smile and announce, 'Isn't it awful, I just can't wait to try it with someone else . . .'

For Kate the vacation was a time of secret anxiety. An old worry raised its ugly head – the knowledge that, compared to Nelly, she was a dull, docile creature. And, come the New Year, she would be going away to school and leaving Nelly behind. How could she ever hope to keep her special place in the Felix household warm and alive? Little by little she would become a stranger to them . . . The thought tormented her endlessly.

In late November Fay had given birth to a boy-child. He was named Richard, immediately shortened to Ricky. Ellis's Christmas card to Kate enclosed a photo of the three of them – Fay looking tired but smiling hugely as she held a round-eyed infant, Ellis gazing adoringly at both . . .

'Isn't he the most beautiful baby you ever saw?' her father wrote ecstatically.

Kate had no eye for babies. The child looked skinned and raw to her, with slack, dribbly lips. And he seemed to signal that the flimsy hold she still had on Ellis's affections was under threat as well. Some nights, lying awake in the dark, Kate had the despairing feeling that she belonged nowhere.

During the day she mostly managed to convince herself that things were OK. Though Nelly spent a lot of time with Robert, Kate and Olivier were a pair, testing the fairy lights together, fetching and decorating the tree, playing a never-ending table tennis tournament in the cold, rugged basement. Beatrice and Pascal were, as always, both friendly and remote. Kate's crush on Pascal endured strong as ever. He admired an outfit of hers – striped grey skirt, black sweater and knee-socks – as very *rive gauche* and she glowed. And for Christmas he gave her a framed print of a Braque still-life.

'It *was* Braque you said you liked, wasn't it?' her Adonis confirmed carelessly, and Kate's heart raced at his remembering her ignorant, throwaway opinion.

Every day there were plenty of happy moments when it seemed that nothing had changed, nothing would. But they alternated with flashes of hard, bright panic when Kate knew with blinding conviction that she was about to vanish, unmissed, into outer darkness.

'That creepy virgins' sanctuary,' as Nelly had taken to describing Les Rosiers, with a superior little shudder.

The sky outside the bedroom window was deepest blue-black. Inside the light was tawny and warm, echoing the amber colour of the parquet, mellowing the white of the walls. The atmosphere was studious and peaceful. Kate and Barbara sat at the table, immersed in their homework. Kate was doing her German. She'd enrolled in the course last term, and had managed to keep pace while doing the bare minimum. Now she was determined to make it a viable second language. It helped having German-speaking Barbara as room-mate. Between the two of them a sense of order reigned. They lived side by side, Kate thought ruefully, like Darby and Joan.

'We're better without Nelly,' Barbara declared often.

If Nelly were here now she would be sulking, sighing, restless, making concentration difficult, if not impossible.

'Maybe . . .' Kate had been disloyal to that extent. This term she'd discovered that she did relish the luxury of being able to work in peace without Nelly's constantly disruptive presence.

At the same time, in her heart of hearts, Kate despised her present taste for order and endeavour. Pascal's Braque print hung proudly above her bed, and into its frame Kate had tucked a photo of Nelly taken on the beach below Plas Felix – she was grinning into the camera, her hair spectacularly windswept. And sometimes, catching sight of it, Kate had the anguished sense that something wild and wonderful had been torn from her, and she was left here, bereft and reduced, lobotomized, pursuing tame, attainable goals.

Her twin wrote often. With indefatigable glee she described the latest ups and downs in the saga of her relationship with Robert.

Kate had come to feel a bit impatient with their never-ending boy-girl soap-opera. But at least her friends were living and feeling. Their very silliness seemed part of a desirable world that was lost to Kate.

Barbara looked at her watch. 'Nine o'clock. We've earned ourselves some Toblerone . . .' With a smile, she got up and crossed to her wardrobe.

'Oh, for heaven's sake!' Kate was on the point of blurting . . . but she held her tongue. Barbara's rituals could drive you bananas. At the same time she wasn't averse to a hunk or two of chocolate.

Chewing the chunky, nutty triangles, they paused companionably in their work. Kate leaned back in her chair, hands linked behind her head. She wasn't unhappy here. Her prowess in French was considered phenomenal. She came top of every test and was learning to talk with guttural vehemence like Grand-mère, with silken steeliness like Madame Voss. Now her German, too, was coming on by leaps and bounds. And this term her behaviour was exemplary. Approval warmed her from all sides, the more so because of the 'prodigal son' aspect of her story.

'Kate, your change of attitude delights me. You must never again allow yourself to be led astray.' With benevolent hauteur Madame Voss had remarked on her reform.

'*Merci, madame*,' Kate had mumbled, imagining the ghost of Nelly lurking in the corner of the headmistress's comfortable study, observing the scene with satirical eyes.

A knock came at the door. It was Rose Ladnier, an American girl, whose tall, square-jawed father played musical chairs from consulate to consulate. Rose had freckles and long, rich, curly red hair. She was the first girl Kate had ever met who wore spectacles and genuinely didn't care.

'Come on up to Violetta's room – she has some new discs . . .'

Violetta Casals' Latin-American dance records were dynamite, throbbing with intricate, irresistible drum rhythms. They were like plugging into a wider, more anarchic world, had everyone dancing crazily until made to calm down by some passing member of staff.

Kate was tempted. These sessions made her think of clomping around with Nelly and Robert and Olivier in the attic at Plas Felix.

'I'll come later – got some work to finish first.' Kate savoured an almost voluptuous sense of self-control.

Rose rolled her eyes. 'Let me out of here . . . I can't take the odour of sanctity . . .'

Madame Jobert stood out from the rest of the teachers for an air she had of disrespect. She slouched and smoked and scowled, lounged against doors and walls while teaching, gave the blatant impression that, if it were not for her monthly salary, the institution of Les Rosiers would not see her heels for dust.

This term Kate had her once a week for poetry, taught from a navy-blue anthology that claimed to contain the hundred best poems in the French language. At each lesson Madame Jobert briskly dissected a couple of these, then set her students to learn them for the following week. She was ruthless, though, in testing that this chore had been completed, and in following up any defaulters.

From January to March the girls spent each weekend in a huge brown chalet beneath Les Diablerets, a jagged little range of mountains that stood out against the sky like a row of uneven but gleaming white teeth. On Saturday they had skiing lessons on the gentle hillside slopes above the hostel, returning to eat a hearty peasant supper in the rustic dining-room with its spectacular views of the serrated mountain peaks.

They travelled down on Friday evening in a large hired coach, accompanied – on a rota basis – by two members of staff. One evening in late February Kate found herself sitting alongside Madame Jobert on the bus.

At first they didn't say much. Madame Jobert was not the kind of teacher who felt any obligation to draw her pupils out. She sat in enigmatic silence, head tilted slightly backward, eyelids lowered, so that she seemed to peer out in a sceptical, calculating manner from beneath her heavy fringe of chestnut hair. Her face, between the hanging curtains of her page-boy haircut, was thoroughly made up, with beige panstick foundation, plum lipstick, the corners of her eyes extended outward in the doe-eyed look. Her style made her appear younger than the majority of the staff but, close-to, a network of fine lines was visible beneath her eyes and round her mouth.

Kate's mind wandered. She enjoyed these weekend jaunts. Even at this early, safe stage skiing was wonderfully exhilarating and she'd always been good at sport.

Her thoughts drifted to a letter she'd had from Olivier. He was in trouble at school for laziness.

'They say I'm worse than Nelly,' he reported, seeming proud of the fact rather than otherwise.

'How is your friend Nelly?' Madame Jobert asked suddenly in French, as if she'd read her mind. Kate jumped and turned towards her. Madame Jobert sat waiting for a reply, eyebrows raised, face set in her usual uningratiating expression.

'All right,' Kate stammered. 'Better than when . . . She didn't like it here . . .' How clumsy and tactless she sounded.

'As soon as I saw Nelly, I knew she wouldn't last the term.' The teacher's voice was briskly unjudgmental.

'She likes to be out and doing things . . . She felt rather trapped here.'

'That's understandable.' A gleam of black amusement. 'She's found a new plan of action?'

'Not really,' Kate admitted. 'Not yet.'

Madame Jobert shrugged. 'We're not all made to be madly ambitious.'

The statement didn't seem to require a response. But Kate warmed to the teacher. She was the only member of staff to have mentioned Nelly with any kind of understanding.

Ellis insisted that his daughter spend the Easter break in Coningsburgh.

'I want you and Ricky to get to know one another as soon as possible,' he wrote.

For the three weeks of her stay the weather was cold and grey, alternately raining and freezing. When it froze the sky turned pewter-coloured and hard flurries of sleet rattled against the windows.

'This durn weather,' Fay sighed several times each day. 'New England can be so beautiful in spring.'

To Kate she appeared to have lost her radiant prettiness, along with the sharpness that spiced her likeable personality. She saw her stepmother with distaste as a contented, overweight cow. Fay slopped about all day in a baggy pair of Ellis's jeans and one of his check shirts, which she unbuttoned at the drop of a hat to reveal huge milky breasts, into which Ricky snuggled with indecent bliss.

The house smelt of boiling diapers and baby sick. Fay and Ellis seemed not to notice. They marvelled at everything their child did, which wasn't much.

'He'll be on the move any day now,' they declared, when he lay on the floor doing ineffectual little press-ups.

'Look at his eyes,' Ellis would cry. 'He doesn't miss a thing!'

Her father seemed rejuvenated, the spiky corners of his personality rounded and smoothed. He'd put on weight, as if with contentment. An unclouded pleasure shone from his eyes. Kate could not recall him ever looking at her with the unadulterated tenderness he bestowed on her infant half-brother.

She was bored and didn't hide the fact, read magazines all day, or studied self-righteously in her room.

Ellis was impressed with her commitment to her work. 'Maybe now really is the time to think about enrolling in college over here next year . . . Not Coningsburgh, necessarily. Maybe California, New York . . .'

Kate experienced a flash of irritation and disdain. Her father persisted in believing that one day she would come to her senses and embrace this country just as he had. She shrugged her shoulders. 'I think I feel more of a European nowadays.'

'Your daughter's becoming quite the cosmopolitan . . .' Fay chimed in, not altogether amicably, as baby Ricky suckled with noisy concentration.

*　　*　　*

As the summer term progressed it seemed inevitable that Kate would do outstandingly well in the final French examination. There was a procedure involved – students took the ferry across the lake to France, sat the examination in a school in Evian-les-Bains. The prospective ceremonial made the whole event loom that much more impressively.

The staff – apart from cynical Madame Jobert – were on tenter-hooks, feeding their charges with pre-digested revision, drilling them continually on tricky grammar points, clearly terrified of achieving results that would do them less than credit in the flinty eyes of Madame Voss.

But in spite of the tension, the summer term was perfectly pleasant, with tennis coaching, a picnic trip to the Château de Chillon, an open-air production of *Le Bourgeois Gentilhomme*. Kate, Rose and Barbara studied in the grounds behind Les Rosiers, in the shade of a large copper beech. On Fridays the town was sunny and bustling with tourists.

One day in late June Kate was lured into the Librairie Payot, a large bookshop on the Place Saint François, by a window display featuring a moody photograph of David Lacoste, along with a stack of his new novel, *Trente Ans*.

'We don't have time, Kate.' Rose was late for her tennis lesson.

'You go ahead. I'll catch a later tram.' She was curious to flick through one of the austere beige French paperbacks.

Further copies of the novel were piled on a table inside the shop. Kate picked one up and began to leaf through it. The pages were folded and uncut, but the portions of text that were visible appeared as forceful and shocking as ever. She browsed absorbedly, forgetting where she was.

'That's hardly proper reading for a well brought-up young girl,' a female voice commented.

Kate looked up. Madame Jobert was standing next to her, wearing a spotted, sleeveless summer dress and a crooked smile.

'I was being nosy. I met him once, Lacoste. He's a friend of Nelly's father.'

'Is that so?' The teacher looked briefly impressed. She held up a small stack of books. 'I'm about to pay for these . . . Would you like to go for a coffee afterwards?'

Kate was taken aback. 'If you like.'

Madame Jobert seemed amused by her ungraciousness.

Kate had never yet become inured to the seductive pleasure of taking her place on a café terrace in the sunshine. The mere act induced an instantaneous sense of leisure and wellbeing.

While they waited for their coffees to arrive Kate and the teacher talked about David Lacoste. Madame Jobert seemed to enjoy the fact that the first book Kate had ever read in French was one of his scabrous early novels.

'Madame Voss would not approve,' she commented with her sardonic smile. 'She likes her *jeunes filles* to be conveniently naïve. It makes them so much easier to handle.'

Their coffees arrived. Madame Jobert lit a cigarette. 'Well,' she said. 'Are you ready for the final grand examination?'

'I suppose so.'

The teacher looked at Kate through half-closed, black-edged lids. The way she crinkled her eyes emphasized the lines beneath them. The blue smoke of her cigarette curled away into the bright air. 'Obviously you'll do brilliantly.'

Kate shrugged, a touch embarrassed.

Madame Jobert paused for a considered, dramatically effective moment, then added, 'It's a pity the exam means absolutely nothing to anyone.'

Kate stared, not understanding.

'You'll get your certificate.' The teacher pronounced the word with ironic precision. 'Your handsome little scroll with its crest and copperplate writing . . . from the tinpot organization Madame Voss has affiliated herself to . . . Trouble is, it's not worth the paper it's written on.'

She paused again, compressing her brightly painted lips, gesturing dismissively with her hands. 'Of course, the pretty little piece of paper is perfectly sufficient for most of the dabblers at Les Rosiers. But if you've got a brain or any kind of ambition . . . I can assure you, Kate, from the point of view of qualifications, you'd have been better advised to stay in your own country, doing your own version of the bac.'

Madame Jobert said no more, concentrating on her coffee and her cigarette, allowing her words to fade away into the general buzz of conversation. Kate didn't know what to think or say. She wasn't exactly devastated. Vaguely she recalled Jerome saying something to the effect that the girls wouldn't be qualified for anything after their year was up. At the time, the fun of going abroad with Nelly was all that had mattered. But, since she'd been at Les Rosiers, the idea of the final exam had been elevated like some primitive god to be worshipped and dreaded without question.

'Do you like Lausanne?' Madame Jobert asked suddenly.

'Very much.' Kate was emphatic. She had an abrupt and vivid awareness of the present moment, of the sun burning pleasurably into her arms, the transparent cups casting both light and shadow on to the white tablecloth, the hum of conversation in a rich mix of languages, the passers-by in their summer clothes.

'Have you plans for next year?'

'Nothing definite,' Kate admitted. She felt passive and woolly. 'My father would like me to study in America, but I prefer Europe . . .'

'I have a suggestion.' By contrast, Madame Jobert sounded absolutely decided.

She drained her coffee cup and stubbed out her cigarette. 'I have two children, and . . .' she paused, a dour expression crossing her features '. . . an absent husband. At Les Rosiers I often have to work late and at weekends. The crèche I've been using charges exorbitant rates. I need a nanny . . .' Madame Jobert used the English word, fixing Kate with a basilisk stare.

'I guarantee I could get you through your French A-Level . . .' Her pronunciation of the term was outlandish. 'I would pay for your German tuition so you would pass that examination too. I'd give you time to study. The year would not be wasted.'

Kate's mind raced, her future falling into place almost faster than

159

thought. How independent and enterprising she would appear to the Felixes. How impressed Ellis would be with her initiative and organization.

'Sounds rather a good idea,' she remarked brightly.

Chapter Seventeen

❊❊❊❊

Madame Jobert – or Martine, as Kate was now instructed to call her – lived with her two children on the first floor of a square white block of flats in the residential district of Chailly. Her apartment had only two bedrooms, but she converted a small study into a room for Kate, managing to cram in a narrow bed, a small wardrobe and what looked like a child's desk. The room was cramped, but clean and bright, and Kate hung up her Braque reproduction, her photographs of the Felixes and a dutiful framed enlargement of Ellis, Fay and Ricky.

It seemed odd and uncomfortable at first, moving in with this family of strangers. Kate had little experience of children and, to begin with, seven-year-old Pierre and three-year-old Louise regarded her with suspicion and reserve, Louise particularly clinging to her mother, who had scant patience with her vapours.

'*Sois raisonnable*, Louise,' Martine ordered briskly, as she departed on the first day for work, leaving Kate alone with the two scared, hostile children.

Louise wept uncontrollably. Pierre looked worried and upset, then began to shout at his sister to stop crying. Kate stood by, feeling helpless and useless, knowing simply that, somehow or other, she had to get Pierre to school, Louise to her morning nursery. Pierre was only too keen to be delivered, donned his jacket and satchel without needing to be told. Louise had to be forced into her coat and dragged, still bawling, down the stairs and out into the street.

'Ss-h-h, Louise,' Kate hissed feebly, as she pulled the child along the pavement, feeling a brute, and hugely conspicuous.

Pierre was dropped off first. As Louise watched him go her heartrending sobs redoubled in volume and intensity. At the nursery she made a dash for the supervisor, her swollen eyes wide with misery and distress.

'*Viens, chou-chou.*' The woman gathered the shaking child into her arms, glancing towards Kate with complacent contempt.

Kate fled, filled with relief at having somehow managed to fulfil this initial chore, but only too aware that later Louise would have to be collected, manoeuvred home, fed and entertained. Sure enough, at one o'clock, the process was repeated in reverse. Louise was dragged screaming back to the flat, would eat no lunch and refused to be distracted with toys. Finally she became too tired to weep and fell asleep on the floor in the far corner of the living-room. Kate longed to let her rest, but had to rouse the child in order to go and fetch Pierre. This time Louise was quieter, but whimpered all the more piteously.

'It went well?' Martine enquired breezily on arriving home at six o'clock that evening.

'Very badly.' Gloomily Kate began to recount Louise's unhappiness, her own inability to comfort or console.

'Don't worry.' Martine cut her short. 'It's no tragedy. It's all just a question of habit. She'll soon get tired of bawling. It'll bore her after a few days. You're a perfectly amiable person. She'll come round.'

And eventually Louise *did* come round. By Thursday morning she allowed herself to be buttoned into her coat, held Kate's hand without protesting, greeted her at lunch-time with matter-of-fact acceptance rather, Kate felt, to the disappointment of the nursery supervisor.

'*A demain,*' Kate called casually, praying that Louise's new co-operativeness would last at least until they were out of earshot.

The two children were utterly unlike. Pierre was tall, fair and enormously self-contained. Each morning he got himself ready for school without forgetting anything. On his return, having completed the bits of homework he'd been set, Pierre would spend hours copying pictures of cars from newspapers and magazines, colouring them and labelling them in his tidy handwriting.

'He's the image of my husband,' Martine told Kate. 'Tall, blond and silent . . .'

She rarely referred to the children's father but on this occasion, after a reflective pause, Martine added dourly, 'Never make the mistake of confusing quietness with sincerity.'

Louise was dark and stocky with the same pageboy hairstyle as her mother. Unlike Pierre she made her presence felt at every moment of the day, asking endless questions, involving Ket, as she called her, in non-stop games of make-believe, protesting vehemently against being made to wash, dress, undress, eat, bath, get up, go to bed . . .

Pierre kept Kate at a polite distance. He was never any trouble. Louise was skittish and tactile. She hugged Kate, climbed on her knee, clambered on to her back, snuggled up for a story, smacked her petulantly when displeased, then felt sorry and kissed the same spot. After a couple of weeks Kate felt thoroughly at home with the child. But of Pierre she remained wary.

Martine Jobert hated Les Rosiers and Madame Voss with a deep and abiding passion. One Sunday morning, not long after Kate's arrival, over coffee and croissants in her tiny, tidy kitchenette, she railed sourly against her employer.

'With that phoney voice of hers the parents think she's graciousness personified, but the one and only thing that counts for her is money.'

The headmistress exploited her live-in staff quite ruthlessly, Martine explained, paying them peanuts and allowing them almost no free time. She made deals with local stores, getting a kick-back when she directed her pupils to buy their books, stationery or sports equipment from them at specially inflated prices. She charged the parents top rates for cheap block theatre bookings, reduced rail fares, cut-price tennis and ski coaching . . .

'The woman can't bear to do anything without feeling she's somehow getting some nifty little financial fillip . . . And as for that husband of hers, if you ever shake hands with him count your fingers afterwards . . .'

Kate was agog at hearing these august beings so unceremoniously debunked. Still wearing her long scarlet housecoat, Martine leaned back in her plastic kitchen chair, drew dourly on her filter-tipped Marlborough. 'Don't be fooled by his vacant look. Casimir Voss is sharp as knives . . .'

He was involved, so she claimed, in all sorts of louche international financial deals, had been since before the war ended. He'd an array of secret bank accounts under a variety of names – the school was just a lucrative front for his real business . . .

'If only,' Martine mused, apparently changing tack, 'I'd gained some decent professional qualifications . . .'

Her youth, she hinted, had been frittered away in short-sighted fun and frivolity. If she'd only buckled down back then, she'd have a proper steady career now in the state school system, with paid holidays and a guaranteed pension. As it was, she had to scrabble for a patchwork of bitty, insecure jobs in unregulated establishments like Les Rosiers, and a couple of other similar schools, as well as slotting in private home French lessons for the pampered wives of a shifting population of Iranian and Greek businessmen . . .

Nelly, she suggested, was in danger of travelling a similar route, but if Martine had anything to do with it, Kate would not make the same mistake. With her arrival the teacher had gained peace of mind for a year on the childcare front. In return – it was almost a threat – Kate would take home A-Levels in German and French.

Two evenings a week Kate was dispatched to German language classes. Another night a colleague of Martine's came to the flat to teach her the appropriate German literary texts. Martine took charge of the French literature side.

'For God's sake, don't waste the time when Louise is away at the nursery. Use it to study. You can always do a bit of dusting and vacuuming while she's at home with you . . .'

In Martine's eyes children were to be minded rather than amused. It was Kate's idea to take Louise to the park, or set out paper and paints at home. Her employer required no such optional extras.

By mid October Kate was well ensconced in her new routine. Without being over-stretched, she was always busy, had some immediate goal in mind at every moment of the day. The children were congenial, Martine a fair and egalitarian employer. Kate became friendly with a couple of other au pairs she encountered in the park with their charges. At German class she met a Spanish accounting student called Salvador.

Kate was boosted, too, by the general approval of family and friends. Her elders, particularly, seemed terribly impressed by her supposed initiative, saw the job as somehow glamorous.

Fay wrote, 'In the last year or two you seem really to have decided what you want and gone all out to get it. You really are a determined young lady – your father's very proud of you . . .'

In her letters Odile never failed to remark on how tickled the whole family was at Kate's cleverness in landing such a timely position in such lovely surroundings. In contrast she was anxious about Nelly, who flitted from one 'silly' job to another and seemed to have no idea what she wanted to do with her life. 'Jerome just smiles, of course, and says it's all good experience . . .' Kate marvelled anew at such fatherly indulgence.

A letter from 'home' – from Nelly or Olivier or Odile – always made her day. Kate was fine out here just so long as it could be demonstrated that she still had her place in the charmed world of Plas Felix.

Every month or so she paid a dutiful visit to Grand-mère and made stilted conversation over a cup of coffee in her dark, highly polished living-room.

'Nelly is so wild,' the old woman would complain each time in her emphatic, rasping tones. 'If only my grand-daughter could be reasonable like you.'

In a funny way, this final accolade always had the effect of making Kate feel glum.

One evening in early December Kate came home from her German class to find the lights dimmed in the living-room and Martine curled on the sofa watching television. She was in her stockinged feet, a sign of being off-duty. She never took her shoes off until the children were in bed.

Kate's employer had confided that she would be forty in January and was none too happy at the prospect. But, in the light of a small table lamp, she looked young and smooth-skinned, her hair just brushing her shoulders. Though her chin, thrust forward to rest on one hand, gave her a belligerent air.

In front of her, on the low coffee table, stood a glass and a half-empty bottle of red wine.

'How was Diego?' Martine asked, without taking her eyes off the screen. She made a point every time of getting his name wrong.

'Salvador.' Kate's unemphatic correction was also part of the ritual. 'Fine, I suppose . . . I beat him in the test.'

'So I should hope.'

Kate stood and watched the film for a moment. It looked thirties. A man in a hat was swearing love to a radiant woman with blonde hair set in little rows of curls.

'Don't believe a word he says,' Martine heckled the heroine. She turned to Kate. 'I'm indulging myself. Help yourself to wine if you want . . .'

Kate fetched a glass and decided to watch the rest of the film with Martine. She enjoyed it. The actors seemed old-fashioned and solemnly ridiculous. It was fun to harangue them, gee up the decent but naïve hero, insult the oily lounge lizard who made a play for the girl, shake their heads over the heroine's wide-eyed waverings.

By the time it ended happily, in a long, lingering embrace – for which the hero finally removed his hat – the wine was all gone.

'Why do they always end films when the couple get together, when the real story begins,' Martine grumbled. 'Too depressing, I suppose.'

'Not always,' Kate challenged casually.

'Always.' Martine was tipsily adamant. 'How many happily married couples do you know?'

Kate thought. 'Not my parents, that's for sure . . . But my father and his new wife.'

'They've not been married five minutes.'

Kate was going to cite Jerome and Odile. But something stopped her – she wasn't sure what, just a feeling. She'd always taken it for granted that they were happy, but suddenly the claim seemed an over-simplification.

In an abrupt lurch Martine rose up from the sofa and crossed to a small bureau she used for writing letters and preparing lessons. She stooped and pulled at the bottom drawer. It was tightly packed and difficult to open, but after some heaving and re-arranging Martine managed to retrieve a large, framed photograph.

She thrust it under Kate's nose. 'This is my husband. Victor.'

Surprised, Kate took the portrait and examined it. The man had a Scandinavian look about him, was undeniably handsome, with a long skull and short fair hair. He wore something dark that threw his strong features into artful relief. His eyes looked steady and calm, his lips firmly modelled – a bit like Ellis's, it occurred to Kate. His chin tapered then squared off, was attractively cleft.

'He's good-looking.'

'Yes. The bastard.'

Kate knew only that Victor currently worked for the United Nations in New York. And that Martine wanted a divorce and financial support for the children. His lawyer was obstructing her case with infuriating delaying tactics. Martine must either force herself to be patient, or go quite mad.

'What's he like?' Her employer hardly ever mentioned her husband. Kate was curious, but prepared for a rebuff.

'What's he like?' Martine mused, clearly not put out by the enquiry. A half-smile formed on her lips. 'He's plausible, very plausible . . . He's quiet and he seems shy. And you feel he's got to be handled gently and drawn out and not frightened off . . . And you feel you're giving him the confidence to be himself, his wonderful self, and you're the only one can do it . . . And you fall in love.'

In the hush and the lamplight her words had an imposing gravity. Martine shrugged, her expression hardening. 'We had eight beautiful years in Brussels. He was working for a fancy new international organization – Administrative Techniques, it was called. They had swanky premises and he earned good money, and I gave half-baked little French lessons to housewives . . . We went to parties and I had lots of new clothes and went to the hairdresser twice a week, and we had holidays . . . And later I found that most of that time he'd had other women . . . And now I look back on that golden age with sheer horror . . . How could I be so happy and such a fool?'

As she spoke, Martine ran her fingers through her hair. The fringe stood up in spikes. Beneath one eye was a blotch of smudged eye-liner.

A silence. Then she spoke again, sounding brittle and intense. 'What you don't understand about him is that, underneath that seductive diffidence, he's solid . . . dense as a rock, doesn't need you, doesn't need anyone . . . And there'll always be another woman who imagines she's protecting him and drawing him out – there'll be one with him right now . . . right now.'

For some moments Kate was silenced, then she asked tepidly, 'Do the children miss him?'

'Not Louise. I left Victor three months after she was born. I think Pierre does. He adored his father.' She gave a shrug, a defensive grimace. 'But I really can't allow myself to think about whether Pierre is or isn't psychologically injured for life. I'm too busy just trying to stay afloat.'

Martine stretched, yawned. 'I'm going to bed. Not that I'll sleep. I'm too wound up now.' A quick, half-hearted, mischievous grin. 'Poor Kate. If you're not careful, I'll make you cynical before your time.'

When she woke the next morning at half past six, Kate got up to make herself a coffee. Tiptoeing down the hall in her night-dress, she noticed that the living-room light was on. Perhaps, after their minor booze-up, she and Martine had forgotten to turn it off.

In the doorway she reached up to flick the switch, then noticed that Pierre was in the room. He'd found the photograph of his father which Martine had neglected to put away. Sitting on the sofa in his striped flannel pyjamas, a wayward crest of blond hair sticking up on the crown of his head, Pierre gazed intently at the portrait. His expression, as ever, gave nothing away.

Then, suddenly, he lifted the framed photograph to the level of his face, laid his lips to Victor's and kissed them. Kate turned and crept silently away.

Chapter Eighteen
1959

❈❈❈❈❈

The following summer was fabulously hot. They sweltered in Martine's small flat, though the windows were kept open all the time and the curtains closed, the fierce luminous glare of the sun showing only in narrow slits and long, blinding spears of light.

To Kate there was something intense and magical about the eternal relentless sunshine that was there before they woke and lasted until night. It was pointless trying to put the children to bed until they were well and truly exhausted.

Each morning Kate made a jug of real lemonade – according to Odile's recipe – and put it to chill in Martine's little fridge, ready for the evening when they all sat out on the balcony that faced the setting sun. Pierre, in his bathing trunks, played long, silent, complicated games with his toy cars. Louise had an assortment of containers and plastic dolls, and a large bowl of water in which she splashed and poured and dunked, chatting to herself contentedly for hours. Martine did her marking or read a magazine.

With a book on her lap, Kate revised desultorily, but felt she was gilding the lily. She'd been so well-prepared and, with Martine's bullying, had studied so hard that she couldn't fail. A lot of the time she spent watching the summery pedestrians in the street below, or the customers in the café across the way.

Kate felt coiled inside. This examination was the final hurdle. For the last two years she had buckled down, embraced the forces of order and hard work. The time would come when she had to make proper plans for a career, for the rest of her life. But just now she was almost within grasp of the bubbling sense of a hazy, delightful freedom that was somehow tied in with the gold of summer and the prospect of returning – altered, wordly-wise – to the promised land of Plas Felix.

Martine liked to leave the television on, talking to itself, in the twilight room, even when they were all outside on the balcony. She wasn't sure why its flicker and sound had such a calming effect on her. Nor quite why she was in need of the reassurance.

Passing through the living-room on her way from the kitchen, she glanced at the animated screen and saw a face that seemed familiar to her. At first Martine couldn't place the man, then it came to her . . .

She put her head round the long, blue-green curtain and out into the light, where Kate – wearing shorts and a bra – sat sunning herself with the children.

'Kate,' she said. 'Friend of yours on the *télé*.'

Kate turned with a look of amused scepticism. 'Oh yes . . . who?'

'Come and see.'

The children, too, were intrigued, stopped what they were doing and stepped through the shadowy curtain. Kate peered at the screen, then shrieked, 'No! Oh, my God!'

It was David Lacoste, being interviewed by a carefully coiffured middle-aged female presenter. She was badgering him somewhat on the profanity and nihilism of his work, but signalling simultaneously that she was really no threat. Wearing a bemused and courteous smile, Lacoste was defending himself. Although, Martine reflected, the atmosphere of jumpy flirtation was far more potent than anything either had to say. Lacoste wore the uniform of the intellectual, a dark polo-necked sweater. With his boyish but ravaged face she found him attractive. And it was clear from Kate's parted lips, her pink-cheeked, animated attention, that she did too.

'Idiotic woman!' Kate muttered as the hot-eyed speakerine returned insistently to the fray.

The kid was so pretty nowadays, Martine thought. She'd urged Kate to have her hair cut more often – not to wait until it hung in long, lank rats' tails – so that now her dark locks looked thick and shiny and swung when she turned her head. And Kate herself was choosing plainer clothes in subtler colours. There was one particular outfit – a loose-knit gold top over a cream pleated skirt – in which the child looked quite lovely.

And, clearly, Kate sensed that she did. It was obvious the girl was ready to move on. Martine was touched by her restlessness, envied her, in sudden waves of nostalgia for the kid she herself had been once. But nowadays she saw life through dark-lensed spectacles, and she knew that, in the world she was so eager to discover, Kate's naïve vanity would be punished, her trust betrayed, her heart broken.

'One thing I refuse to do is lie . . .' David Lacoste was declaring – rather pompously, Martine thought. The camera cut to the interviewer nodding respectfully.

'They film those nods later,' Martine said. 'Then they slot them in. Victor told me.'

Kate pulled a quick 'fancy that' sort of face. How sad it was that she had to leave. Recently, shamefacedly, Martine caught herself thinking that all the time. When it came down to it, she, Martine, was supposed to be the adult, mature and in control. So it wasn't appropriate that she should feel these twinges of near-panic when she contemplated Kate's impending departure.

Her presence made all the difference to the family dynamic, made them seem *more* of a family, not some left-over little group of rejects. Martine had always known she wasn't the maternal type. But with Kate around she found it easier to act wise and humorous and easy-going. Take her away and once more the kids would seem scratchy and demanding, and she would be irritable and anxious, easily riled. She'd get bogged down again in her all-consuming anger against Victor, and in the never-ending stalemate of her divorce.

She was working on finding a replacement. Alma Braks, a rosy-cheeked, capable girl from Holland, seemed the most likely candidate, but it wouldn't be the same.

'Go with the truth, the way it is. Leave it rough and inconclusive. Never rearrange it to fit in with your own preconceived agenda. Then your work will be truly honest.' From the way the camera was moving in on Lacoste's earnest face, Martine gathered that the interview had reached its conclusion.

'David Lacoste, thank you.' The woman's smooth tones spoke of a job well done.

'What a scream.' Kate flicked off the television, grinned at Martine, then turned to Louise. 'I hope your babies haven't drowned out there in that bath of water.'

Both children were tickled at the thought. 'Let's go and see.'

Martine was left alone in the darkened living-room.

'Oh, yes, they have!' she heard Louise exclaim, and smiled to herself.

'It's not too late.' Kate's voice was loud and merry. 'I think we can still rescue them.'

From this point, on the train journey to Geneva, you could see terraced vineyards descending in orderly ranks down the hillside. Through the opposite window, the surface of the lake was a smooth, translucent azure blue. It was not quite seven in the morning. Drowsily Kate leaned back on the slatted third-class seat, drinking in the landscape through half-closed eyes. Today was her final examination and, in a couple of weeks, she would be gone.

Kate rummaged in the bag beside her. She had a letter from Nelly to re-read. Every week or so she received a scrawled, excitable, amazingly frank communication from her friend. Kate could never decide whether Nelly's ramblings were directed at her personally – as soulmate and twin – or whether she regarded the distance between them as a warrant to pour out all the incriminating thoughts she kept hidden from the folks at home.

This summer, apart from swimming, surfing and sailing, Nelly had a waitressing job in a new seafood pub/restaurant on the coast. The place was a magnet for the young bloods of the sailing set as – reading between the lines – was Nelly herself.

'Two chaps had a fight over me at a party last week,' she exulted. 'A waste of time, though, because I wasn't interested in either of them. I was busy getting off with Mac, who's from London and twenty-five. Honestly, Kate, I think I'm becoming "promiscuous" – that wonderful hissy word we used to giggle at. Well, I bet if I got in the newspapers now, they'd call me promiscuous. It's quite easy when you know how . . .'

Not so long ago Kate had seen a re-run of a notorious Bardot film, in which the heroine was predatory as a man, selecting and seducing her sexual partners quite brazenly, scandalizing the local bourgeois with their tight lips and disapproving glances. And ever since she had somehow visualized Nelly in the part.

Kate had her own favourite, had seen a couple of films with Jeanne Moreau in the leading role, who wasn't beautiful exactly but had this enviable, offbeat glamour that made you dream of being that way too. David Lacoste had it as well – she'd been seduced by him all over again the other week on television. Kate hoped that, after two years here, some smidgen of this elusive quality might have rubbed off on her, so that when at last she got back to Plas Felix her siblings would notice and approve the difference in her.

'Can't believe I'll be seeing you in two little weeks,' Nelly wrote. 'Actually, I don't even believe you exist any more!!! You're a mythical beast. Come home, darling twin, and prove you're flesh and blood . . .'

The openness of Nelly's appeal filled Kate with a glow of pleasure. She drowsed in the somnolent warmth of the morning sun, gazing absently at the passing scenery, hugging to herself like secret gold the prospect of her return home.

At half past nine at night the air was still stuffy and warm. Kate felt half incredulous. In a few minutes she would get on a train – just take a step – and be whisked away for good from this hospitable town that for the last two years had been her home.

'Kate's going to sleep on the train,' Louise told Pierre yet again. 'In a proper bed.' The idea charmed her.

The child had on her best dress – pink with broderie anglaise daisies – in honour of seeing Kate off. In the harsh artificial light, against the hard grey of the platform, she looked tiny and ethereal, reminding Kate of a picture of Tinkerbell in a book she'd once had. And this would probably be the last sight she ever had of the kid she'd washed and dressed, comforted and scolded and kissed goodnight, day in, day out, for nearly a year.

Pierre stood by, keeping a certain dignified distance. As ever, he seemed to have all the cares of the world on his skinny little shoulders. Looking now at his grave, achingly young face, Kate longed to give him a protective, enveloping hug, but knew he would be horrified at any such demonstration.

Martine fussed around, buying magazines and chocolate, double-checking Kate's reservation, her auburn-rinsed bob bouncing busily. She looked chic and enigmatic in a black linen shift and sunglasses, though outside it was getting dark.

The train glided in alongside the platform. Kate's heart lurched with a sort of dread at the prospect of tearing herself away. Martine was already striding down the platform on the lookout for Kate's carriage.

'The letter G – Quick, there we are.'

With ostentatious efficiency she marshalled Kate to her place, laid brisk claim to the window seat, requisitioned a passing male to hoist the girl's suitcase on to the luggage rack.

'Where's the bed?' Louise asked.

Kate tapped the back-rest. 'In there. They let it down when it's bed-time.'

Louise looked disappointed.

Back on the platform Kate shook Pierre by the hand. 'Goodbye, sweetheart. Look after Maman and Louise.'

The exhortation, Kate reflected, only served to reinforce the poor kid's over-developed sense of responsibility, but it was all she could think of to say. He nodded, his eyes wide and serious, and she couldn't resist placing a swift peck on the top of his spiky head.

His sister launched herself at Kate, who swung the child up into her arms. Louise kissed her with lips touchingly pursed. Then she wrapped her legs tightly round Kate's waist. 'I won't let you go. You'll have to take me with you.'

Laughingly Kate tried to disentangle her, but Louise would not be dislodged.

'Don't be silly, Louise,' Martine said sharply, and at once the child's boisterousness subsided.

Martine enclosed Kate in an emotional bear-hug, clung to her for a long, intense moment. Kate was moved and impressed by the vehemence of her embrace. When they separated she saw Martine slip a finger up behind her dark glasses to wipe away a tear. Kate had never ever seen Martine cry. At the same time, with a rueful smile, her employer signalled her own sentimental foolishness.

'We're going to miss you terribly,' she said. 'Don't forget us.'

'Never.' Emphatically Kate shook her head. 'Never.'

From the train window she waved frantically until Martine, Louise and Pierre were tiny dots in the distance, until finally she couldn't see them at all. It was awful, unbelievable that you could lose people so easily, people with whom you'd lived on intimate terms, who in a funny sort of way you loved. She went back to her seat and flicked through Martine's magazines, but abstractedly, her mind still filled with the receding little figures standing waving on the platform.

Then the steward came to sort out the couchettes and Kate went and stood in the corridor for a while, staring out at the nearly dark landscape. And gradually the pictures of Martine and the children began to be replaced by flashes of Nelly, Olivier and Pascal, smiles, open arms, the familiar, longed-for house above the sea.

Chapter Nineteen

◈◈◈◈

'There she is!'

Kate heard a shriek and tried to collect her wits – she had hardly slept for two days. Then she saw Nelly rushing towards her.

In the neon dazzle her appearance had a hallucinatory quality. She looked silvery and larger than life. Her blonde hair – longer and unrulier than it used to be – seemed to Kate to have a Medusa-like vitality of its own. Nelly wore a white shirt, knotted to expose her midriff, and brief white shorts, against which her legs appeared very bare and very long. Her face was a caricature, a broad, broad grin and slits for eyes. Her presence conveyed a startling, heightened animation. With blue darkness surrounding the harshly lit platform Nelly seemed somehow on stage.

'Katie! Katie!' She hurtled into Kate's arms, full of animal vigour and warmth. 'Welcome home!'

On the train Kate had felt hollow-headed, dirty, gritty, had half-dreaded this meeting. But, as she embraced Nelly, her spirits soared irresistibly, intoxicated by her friend's exuberance, her reference to home. 'It's *brilliant* to see you,' Kate said fervently. 'It's like a dream come to life.'

Gradually she became aware of someone standing behind Nelly, a young male figure, with fair hair spiking almost down to his well-defined eyebrows. His dark, striped shirt revealed powerful shoulders. With a sudden shock of recognition she saw that it was Olivier.

His face was thinner, making his cheekbones appear more prominent and this, in turn, lent his eyes an almond slant. His mouth relaxed into an unassuming half-smile. He was beautiful and he was almost a man, with a light stubble on his upper lip and precisely moulded chin.

'Olivier . . . ? God, you're so grown-up. I almost didn't know you.' She was shy, a little tongue-tied, as if with someone new.

An amused, diffident gleam. 'Likewise . . . Hi, stranger.' He bent and kissed her lightly on the lips. She smelt beer on his breath.

Nelly butted in. 'This is Mac.'

The man she presented was tall and personable, with an open smile and thick, straight hair. He wore a white polo shirt, the two buttons left open. Even in this lurid, unnatural light Kate could see that his complexion glowed with outdoor health.

'Hello, Kate.' He was well-spoken and radiated general affability. 'Well, shall we make tracks?' He picked up Kate's suitcase, jerked his head towards the stairs.

Kate, Nelly and Olivier followed him towards the exit.

'Mac's driving us – in his Jag . . . He's not a filthy plutocrat,' Nelly emphasized, 'just good at doing things up.'

'It's a 36 saloon, three and a half litre.' Mac said.

'That doesn't mean a whole lot to me,' Kate confessed.

'You're a philistine, like Nelly,' he reproved, sounding like an uncle joshing a flighty niece. Kate recalled Nelly mentioning that he was twenty-five.

Nelly sat in the back with Kate, her smooth, bare legs crossed, illuminated in fits and starts by neon streetlights and passing headlamps. The car's interior smelled of warm leather. Its head-lights swept the familiar road from Bangor.

'You know we've got the house to ourselves,' Nelly said.

Kate nodded. Odile had written that Beatrice was off in Greece, Jerome had an American lecture tour and she would be going with him.

'While the cat's away . . .' Nelly flashed her a saucy side-ways grin.

'She's being a bad girl,' Mac put in.

'Shut up, Mac.' She aimed a kick at the back of the driver's seat. 'He reckons he disapproves. But it doesn't stop him staying the night when the fancy takes him.'

'The fancy always takes me.'

Privately Kate would have preferred normality, was mildly alarmed at the prospect of such freedom. Olivier was silent and she wondered how he felt.

As they drove along, Nelly relayed local gossip, with Olivier slipping in the odd amplification or contradiction. It seemed no time at all before Mac turned off the main road and down the dark, narrow lane that led to Plas Felix.

He parked in the small courtyard, which was illuminated by the lights that shone warmly from the entrance hall. As soon as Kate set foot inside she was enveloped by the particular, indescribable scent of the house. And this, in turn, revived a familiar response – a diffuse mixture of wonder and gratitude that, in a sense and to a degree accepted by the whole family, she belonged here.

'There's some wine in the kitchen.' Nelly led the way. Kate followed, dazed.

She was exhausted, had slept hardly at all the previous night, anticipating her arrival here. And now Kate was flooded with quiet relief at the realization that, after a whole year's absence, she could return and, quite naturally, resume her allotted place.

The kitchen was as she remembered it, with its huge, heavy table, coarsely woven curtains, its hanging bunches of herbs and strings of garlic. Though Odile would never have countenanced the overflowing sinkful of dirty crockery. A large half-empty bottle of rough, red wine stood on the table. Nelly poured four big measures.

'Here's to your homecoming, beloved sis.' She raised her glass. Olivier and Mac followed suit.

'Gosh, I feel like a zombie.' Blearily Kate took a swig of her own wine. 'But a happy one.'

'We're having a party next week,' Olivier told her. 'So you've timed your arrival pretty well right.'

'Wonderful.' Kate roused herself to enthuse.

As she sat, half-somnolent, round the table with the others, there seemed a fanciful, faraway quality to her surroundings. Opposite her, with the dark wine staining his lips, Olivier resembled some handsome young Bacchante in one of the florid nymphs-and-satyrs paintings they'd studied in History of Art at Les Rosiers. All he needed was a wreath of vine leaves round his temples.

Mac and Nelly began to discuss whether they would borrow pub glasses for the party or use Odile's own. Between sips of wine Kate felt herself drifting away.

Then suddenly her eyes flicked open and she became aware that someone else had entered the kitchen. It was Pascal, bare-chested, barefoot, in jeans, his dark hair hanging in his eyes.

'Mary wants a drink of water . . .' He stopped short. 'Kate! Hi, stranger.' Unconsciously echoing his brother's words.

Pascal exuded an odd aura of lazy, sensuous elation. He bent and kissed the nape of Kate's neck. As he moved she caught a drift of some sweaty, gamey odour and guessed he'd just made love.

He examined her. 'You look different.'

'She looks French,' Olivier said.

'Yes . . . Maybe that's it.' Pascal crossed to the sink and filled a glass with water, simultaneously addressing Kate over his shoulder. 'Have you seen *Les Tricheurs*? Have you seen *Les Amants*?'

'Yes, I've seen them.' Both films had raised little eddies of scandal.

'What about *Le Beau Serge*?'

'Seen that too.'

He smiled at her approvingly. 'I knew you would've . . . What did you think?'

'Good . . . Different.'

Pascal turned towards the door with his glass of water. 'Let's talk tomorrow. I want to hear all about it.'

Kate basked in his casual approbation. The habit was still ingrained.

Kate didn't wake until nearly midday and, even then, she drowsed for half an hour or so, luxuriating in the knowledge that nothing was expected of her. The sun shone in through the red curtains of her room, turning everything ruddy. She got up and crossed to the window, anticipating her first view of the sloping field and the sea beyond.

Lifting the corner of one of the curtains, Kate caught her breath. Outside was so different, the field bleached straw colour, almost white in the wake of the long, hot summer, the sea and sky gaudy as a Mediterranean postcard. The landscape, usually gentle and moist, was baked and hard-edged, with deep, black shadows alongside walls and hedges. It was like looking out at a place she didn't know, full of unfamiliar threats and attractions.

Kate rifled her suitcase for some shorts, found a creased check shirt, and tied it as Nelly had done in a knot below her breasts. She went downstairs, slipped outside. The air was gloriously hot and dry on her skin. She sat dangling her legs over the edge of the terrace, gazing towards the sea.

Someone came out through the French windows. Kate glanced over her shoulder. It was Olivier. He sat down beside her.

'Good to be back?' he asked. 'Or does it seem ever so tame?'

'Tame's the last thing . . . I feel as if "Good to be Back" is zinging through my veins.'

He made no comment. The silence between them was easy, Kate thought, as if they'd picked up where they left off. Yet, at the same time, there was this sense that things had . . . not changed exactly, but somehow shifted, were brighter and more dangerous, had connotations that she hadn't learned to understand.

'Only . . .' Kate hesitated, 'it all seems a bit different. And you're different. Specially you. It's as if this whole place had been plonked down in a different country . . . but not a real country . . .' She shrugged and gave a crooked grin. 'This sounds stupid. I can't explain . . .'

Olivier grinned back, perfectly at ease with her incoherence. 'We've had brush fires,' he said, as if in an oblique way confirming her impression. 'Quite a few. Sometimes you see the smoke on the hills . . .'

In the harsh sunlight the change in him was even more evident. But at the same time it was easier to see the boy she remembered, the boy with the sweet smile, who liked everyone and took it for granted that everyone liked him.

Though his body – in shorts, the striped shirt from last night, but hanging open – was heavier, hairier, more muscular. He was the age Pascal had been, Kate realized, when she first came here.

'Where's Nelly?' she asked.

'Still in bed. With Mac.' His expression gave nothing away. Kate wondered again how he felt.

Pascal had been serious when he told Kate that they must talk about the films she'd seen. That very afternoon, down on the beach, as they strolled ankle-deep in water that was almost tepid, he quizzed her, coaxing out details of plot and camera-work, snippets of dialogue she was hardly aware of remembering, as if she were in possession of some fabulous secret.

For a year he'd been working in a photographic studio in Bangor, doing portraits of babies, bridal couples, graduating students. He was taking a break now, but next month he would be starting a job Jerome had wangled for him as dogsbody with a BBC camera-team.

'I can't wait to get to London,' he said vehemently. 'And have a chance to see some decent films.'

Kate was quietly bucked by his implied envy of her own cultural advantages.

But he had all the theory, read *Les Cahiers du Cinéma*, kept talking about the New Wave. *La Nouvelle Vague* – Kate knew the expression, but had never taken much notice of it. Now suddenly, in Pascal's mouth, it acquired a potency and a significance that was at one with the whole new charged atmosphere of Plas Felix.

Pascal spoke with authority. 'Those films see things the way people our age really see them, without the clichéd story-telling. You can do anything you like . . .'

'I think they're great too.' How inept she sounded, Kate thought, and how toadying. But Pascal seemed pleased by her enthusiasm.

'I've been filming all summer,' he told her. 'Just round the house and the beach . . . Some of the footage isn't bad.'

'I'd really like to see it some time.'

Kate had been dubious as to how it would be at Plas Felix in the absence of Odile and Jerome. It took her less than twenty-four hours to decide that it was delightful, and the days that followed only served to confirm that impression.

From getting up – never before midday – until bedtime, in the wee, small hours, everything was free and easy. She didn't have to do anything special, could do just as she liked. And the hot, bright sun accentuated the glorious indulgence of it.

People, young people, came and went all the time. Nelly, Olivier and Mac had part-time jobs – Nelly as a waitress, Olivier in a nearby garage, Mac at the boat-club giving sailing lessons. They disappeared for their allotted stints of duty and, on their return, usually trailed two or three friends, locals or holidaymakers, who stayed for just a coffee and a cigarette, or lingered on into the evening, even overnight.

Kate chatted to whoever was around. Or else she parked herself on the terrace in the sun and read her way through a great stack of *Cahiers du Cinéma* that Pascal had lent her. Once he came and filmed her as she did so, from weird angles, zooming in on the name of the magazine. Kate felt shy, but made herself act cool and blasé, resisting the temptation to hide her face or mug to the camera.

'Nice, nice . . .' Pascal crouched beside her with his camera artfully tilted, and she felt like a character from a New Wave film herself.

Pascal was as lazy as she was, lounging around reading and smoking and listening to music, disappearing into his bedroom for hours with Mary, his nurse girlfriend, when she was off-duty.

Mac tinkered endlessly with his car. Kate could never understand why, since it seemed to run perfectly well. In fact she wasn't too struck with Nelly's new flame. His smile was too ready and his pleasant, full-blooded voice sounded somehow contrived.

'He's always teasing Nelly about how young and naughty she is.' Olivier felt much the same about him. 'I keep wanting to tell him to change the record.'

'What's happened to Robert?' Kate asked.

'Been doing his A-Levels. He's been rather out of circulation . . .

In fact, Nelly's been playing the field all summer. Before Mac there was someone called Tony, and before that a Morgan . . .'

'She tells me all about it in her letters.'

'Robert goes to university next month and Mac won't be here all that much longer. In winter he's a skiing courier . . .' Olivier grinned sardonically. 'Wouldn't you know it?'

All the same, Mac's car was useful for fetching crates of beer. Or fish and chips at any hour of the day or night. Food was currently an optional extra at Plas Felix. Sometimes there was bread in the house and sometimes not. Quite often there were crisps, bought along with cigarettes and beer. Nelly and Olivier downed snacks at work, on the run. Some days Kate walked into Nefyn to buy chocolate. The hit or miss attitude to eating struck Kate as just another picturesque aspect of the whole regime.

For her, for all of them, the beach below the house was an ever-present extension to the house and grounds. You could go down there any time to be alone, to cool off, walk in the lapping shallows or swim in the long, flat, mild waves.

But this summer it was at night that the small bay really came into its own. The Felix kids, their friends and acquaintances, used it as an unofficial meeting place. 'It's our youth club,' Nelly joked, 'except we can drink and smoke and snog if we like, and there's no one to say us nay.' Some of the people who gathered there were visitors, on the Lleyn for only a week or so. Others Kate knew from way back. Ros came sometimes and one night Tim David was there, the boy who fancied Kate way back when she was fourteen.

It was perfect down there in the warm August darkness, half circled by the protecting cliffs, the air soft and balmy, with the waves swishing on the shingle and the sky huge, starry, velvety. They lit bonfires and brought down battery radios tuned to crackly Luxembourg, drank beer, chatted and laughed and scuffled and flirted in the flickering firelight.

Pascal was wild to film these nightly gatherings with their shifting, erratic cast of characters. The firelight was magic he said, but volatile and short-lived. Sometimes he bullied some of the others into building three bonfires at once so that, for ten or fifteen minutes, the mercurial orange light was fierce as day, contrasting violently with the black emptiness beyond.

'What are you,' friends moaned when he produced his cine-camera yet again, 'a bloody voyeur?'

Pascal agreed good-naturedly that he was a man obsessed. 'The light's so different every time. And I *do* it differently too . . .'

Up in his room he had ten or twelve reels of film, unprocessed, planned to have it all developed at once, then cut it up and re-splice it, add a soundtrack . . .

'Summer of fifty-nine. *Cinéma-vérité* . . .' It was as if, already, he saw his name in *Cahiers du Cinéma*.

One night, in the small hours, just Kate, Olivier, Nelly and Mac were left on the beach, lounging half-somnolent by the embers of the fire. The moon was bright, reflecting little silver shimmers in the dark ripple of the waves.

Nelly lay with her head in Mac's lap. She sat up, yawned and stretched. 'I'm for bed.' Then, shaking back her hair, 'But first I'm for a swim.'

She got to her feet and, in a smooth movement, pulled her white T-shirt off over her head, then unhooked her bra, stepped out of her shorts and knickers, the process swift and dramatically effective.

In the dimness her body was a long, pale smudge with mysterious shadows and silvery highlights. She flashed a saucy smile at all of them, then turned and began to pick her way down the beach.

Mac stood up, eager, excited, took off his shorts and shirt. Inescapably, Kate's eye was drawn to the dark patch of his pubic hair, the shadowy stiffening penis. He saw her looking and grinned.

'Sexy cow! Wait for me!' Mac yelled as he capered across the shingle. At the water's edge he caught up with Nelly, caught her by the waist as they paddled into the sea, screaming and laughing as the water got deeper.

Kate was left with Olivier, feeling both embarrassed and not embarrassed at the same time. She was tired and wine had taken the edge off any anxiety she might have felt. But her brain worked independently on the problem of what to do next. To strip off and swim could appear, so it seemed to Kate, a sad aping of Nelly. But not to might seem timid and repressed. And by putting off her decision until Olivier had made his own quite clear, she was in danger of looking even more of a copycat.

She stood up. 'A midnight swim . . . Sounds mighty romantic.'

Kate tugged at her clothes, not meeting Olivier's eye. Soon she too was naked, with the night air wafting pleasantly across her damp skin. She set off down the beach, entered the water quickly and quietly. Soon it was waist-deep and she started to swim.

'Here's Kate!' Nelly sounded pleased, welcoming.

'Over here!' Mac waved energetically.

Kate waved back but carried on swimming, keeping well away from where the two of them were splashing and frolicking in flirtatious horseplay. Kate concentrated on the slow, steady movement of her arms and legs. The cool water caressed her body. She could keep on like this for ever, in the moonlight, her mind empty and peaceful, the water deep and dark below her, the shouts and laughter from Nelly and Mac reaching her as if from far away. She swam and kept on swimming out towards the silver horizon until – after she had no idea how long – a prick of fear began to nag at the vastness and depth of the water all round her. Then Kate turned round and struck out back towards the shore. She saw that, a long way off, Olivier too had braved the waves.

'Bloody Olympic type,' Mac said admiringly, when finally she rejoined the others by the almost dead fire. He was still naked. Nelly had on his shirt. Olivier had donned his shorts and shirt again.

Hastily Kate slipped into her own clothes, not stopping to shake the sand out of them, eager to hide her body.

'You coming back to the house?' Olivier asked.

'Yes.'

'Night,' Nelly said breezily. Neither she nor Mac showed any sign of accompanying them.

The first bit of the cliff path was a scramble. Olivier went first, then leaned down and offered Kate a helping hand. When at last they got to the bit where you could walk two abreast, he kept hold of her hand and they trudged up the steep path together, silent with their own thoughts, maintaining a mute solidarity in face of the daunting sexuality of Nelly and Mac.

Chapter Twenty

❀❀❀

Ten days or so after Kate's arrival, in the hard, mellow heat of the late afternoon, a car drew up in the little courtyard by the house. Kate and Nelly heard it and peered out of an overlooking window. Below stood a dusty Citroën Deux Chevaux. They were intrigued. You barely saw them in Britain.

A male figure stepped out. He appeared slight, medium-young, wore dark, casual clothes. His hair was short and brushed back off his forehead. They stared perplexed for a moment or two.

Then Kate twigged. 'Oh, my God, it's David Lacoste.'

The realization was accompanied by an odd sinking of the heart. She was so at ease in this carefree new world. Lacoste would be an intruder, an adult, a difficult, anxiety-inducing presence, a speck of grit in their cosy private oyster.

'Oh, my God, oh my God. It *is* him!' With girlish hysteria Nelly hid her head in Kate's shoulder.

Lacoste looked about him, unaware of being observed. Kate felt too shy to call from the window. But the next moment Pascal was in the courtyard, explaining, presumably, that his parents were away and that they were on their own. The writer appeared sanguine and, from Pascal's gestures, Kate guessed he was inviting the newcomer in.

A little while later, after they'd checked the mirror and brushed their hair, Kate and Nelly went downstairs. Pascal had taken Lacoste through to the terrace and given him a beer. They were both smoking Gitanes. A squashed, near-empty packet lay on the bench alongside the writer. No doubt Pascal was already launched on an intense analysis of the new French cinema.

The writer must have heard the two girls' footsteps because he turned away from his tête-à-tête to watch them approach. Kate was overcome by a wave of self-consciousness. She and Nelly had been kids, more or less, on Lacoste's last visit and here they both were, all grown up. He would be duty-bound to exclaim at the change in them. Nelly walked towards him with smiling aplomb. Kate gritted her teeth.

'What have we?' Lacoste exclaimed on cue. 'Two beautiful bronzed young women!' He stood up to greet them.

Kate was both disappointed and relieved to see his eye settle firmly on Nelly.

He stayed overnight and, the following day, showed no sign of moving on, seeming indifferent to the absence of Jerome and Odile. His presence was embarrassing to Kate, the dormant crush that dated back to his previous visit flaring abruptly into a violent physical reaction – a heat that swept through her at the sound of his voice, a racing of the pulse.

She hated herself for it. He'd never been handsome and his hairline was starting to recede. But he was clearly oblivious to these disadvantages. There was a calm assurance about him, an amused stillness, the instinctive conviction that he had nothing to prove. And, of course, Kate had read his books with their cynicism, their casual lewdness . . .

On him the dark cotton trousers, the loose, thin, navy sweater he wore had a pared-down chic. There was a formidable sharp knowingness in his brown eyes that contrasted intriguingly with the naïve, halting charm of his imperfect English.

Lacoste was clearly taken with the atmosphere of the house. 'It's *anarchie* . . . It's perfect . . . It's . . .' A bemused shrug '. . . Just *anarchie* . . .' He pronounced the word in the French way, gave a quirkish smile at his lack of linguistic skill. 'No rules. No boss. And everyone is happy.'

His viewpoint lent glamour to something that had seemed merely accidental. It lent significance, as if they were conducting some kind of experiment in living. And the illusion came again to Kate, came all the more strongly, that all of them were acting in a New Wave film.

189

But David – as he told them to call him – didn't really fit in. He was too old and too famous. He was a bit like an anthropologist, studying but not belonging to a strange tribe. Ignoring the group dynamic, he would focus on just one person at a time, exclusively, intensely.

For all of the first evening he engaged Pascal in animated film-talk – David was a big fan of all kinds of cinema and personally acquainted with several of Pascal's heroes. As night came down the two of them remained out on the terrace, smoking and chatting, quiet and companionable in the warm electric glow that shone from the lighted house. Pascal appeared dazed and star-struck.

Next day David spent a couple of hours out in the little courtyard with Mac, apparently talking cars, peering alternately into the engine of Jag and Citroën, Lacoste grinning in a way that seemed to mock both his own ignorance and Mac's expertise. When finally they came back into the house he was laughing and clapping Mac on the shoulder.

With Olivier and a couple of his friends art was the topic of discussion. He'd examined some of the sploshy Pollock-inspired paintings Olivier was currently churning out – executed in children's poster paints – at least a couple every day. As she passed through the room Kate heard David telling the overawed teenagers about a friend of his who painted with stiff household brushes and some kind of cement-like stuff. The writer stumbled winsomely and gestured wryly with his hands as he tried to express the image in comprehensible English.

In each case David left the objects of his attention disarmed by his un-stuffy charm and dazzled by his flattering interest in their thoughts and opinions.

Mysteriously, with Nelly, the chemistry did not gel. David approached her on the beach at night. They conversed for a while, absorbed and separate, then appeared to be sharing some private joke. But, after a while, the momentum between them seemed to peter out and they drifted apart.

Kate watched them covertly, jealously. She was avid to know

what had taken place between them. Later, casually, she asked Nelly what she and David had been talking about.

'Nothing really.' Nelly was vague. 'Only it was a bit funny – I felt as if he was talking to himself, not me . . .'

To Kate's relief he made no move to strike up a relationship with her. She couldn't have coped, she'd have blushed violently, become tongue-tied, made a fool of herself. All the same she was disappointed. Why didn't he want to know her better? Could he see so clearly that she was different from the thoroughbred Felixes? Kate felt humiliated by his neglect.

On the following evening they had the party that had been planned ever since Kate arrived home. Already a couple of dates had been set, but neither had worked out.

Mac ferried crates of beer and cheap Spanish Sauternes. Nelly was working that night but would be back later. In the early evening Kate, Pascal and Mary, Olivier and his friend Eddy cleared away the furniture, put red bulbs in all the downstairs lights, sliced cheese and French bread, set out twiglets and cheese footballs. It was still hot, a gorgeous blue and gold summery evening. They broached the warm, sweet wine.

At once Pascal spat a mouthful across the terrace. 'Tastes like Turkish Delight.' He disappeared to fetch himself a bottle of beer.

'It needs a little something.' Olivier added sugar to his own and Kate's glass. They drank it with giggly bravado.

Mary put 'Living Doll' on the turntable, a record she was mad about just now, ignoring Pascal's disdain. She and Kate and Olivier began to dance. David Lacoste had gone out somewhere on his own. Free of the oppressive allure of his presence, Kate felt light and happy. She wore her black bikini top over narrow black trousers, a white lacy shirt of Nelly's hanging loose and open. Her freshly washed black hair brushed her shoulders as she moved in time to the music.

'You look the bee's knees,' Olivier told her.

'Better than the cat's pyjamas.'

191

Friends began to arrive and soon the terrace was dotted with girls in summer dresses, boys in light shirts, people Kate knew, either well or a little. It was shading slowly towards dusk. The air was still warm. There was a buzz of chatter, eddies of laughter, the aromatic drift of cigarette smoke, a sense of sharpness, a feeling of ease. In the background, music played, undemanding and danceable.

Kate was approached by Robert Williams, Nelly's former boyfriend. He looked grown-up and filled out, self-sufficient and handsome with his tanned face and the lock of straight, sun-bleached hair flopping diagonally across his forehead.

They danced. Kate was exhilarated by his familiarity, his good looks, the happiness spreading inside her like a burst of silent, slow-motion fireworks.

Robert seemed sunny and serene, so she ventured to tease him about his relationship with Nelly.

'I see the off-season's come round again.'

'Yet again. Yeah.' He gave a smile that managed to be both sheepish and defiant. 'Only we're linked – we're sort of . . . on elastic. However far away she goes – or I do – we stay joined. And every so often the elastic pings and we come staggering back together again.'

Kate was touched by his faith. As they came together in the dance she kissed him lightly on the cheek.

Later in the evening she felt thirsty and walked along to the kitchen to get herself some water. Entering the room, thinking herself alone, she was surprised to encounter David Lacoste, standing with his back to the table and drinking from a tumbler. Kate caught the sickly-sophisticated aroma of Scotch. David had changed for the party, she noticed. He wore a handsome shirt of Madras cotton in sombre stripes of olive and dull gold.

Both were taken aback at the sudden meeting. Under normal circumstances her reaction would have been one of embarrassment, even panic. But, elated as she was with the party mood, Kate remained easy and unruffled as she opened Odile's wall-cupboard, extracted a mug, crossed to the tap and filled it with water.

'*J'ai soif.*' Unthinkingly she spoke in French.

'Have some of this.' Jokingly he held out his whisky-glass. David, too, spoke French. 'I've a secret store . . . That wine is completely undrinkable.'

'It does the business. Lifts the spirits . . .' It felt good to rediscover her ease with his language.

'Induces instant nausea . . .'

Kate laughed, took a sip of her water.

'You look charming.' He made the remark dispassionately, his gaze steady and neutral. 'And I must say I'm open-mouthed at your skill with French.'

'It's probably my only skill. But I love speaking it.' In her present loose state of mind Kate felt able to take his compliments in her stride. But she was exhilarated by the writer's unexpected attention. Could it be that her turn had come at last?

Olivier danced with his arms wrapped round Megan, from his class, his body pressed against hers. But the larger part of his attention was otherwise engaged. Over her shoulder, as if through the wrong end of a telescope, Olivier's eyes were fixed on the corner by the French window where Kate stood talking to David Lacoste.

He had mixed feelings about the Frenchman. When he was with you, you couldn't help feeling chuffed and rather proud because he seemed really interested in what you had to say. He was famous, but he didn't act it. Just friendly and rather bumbling, struggling with his English and pulling long faces when he couldn't find the word he wanted. But Olivier didn't like the way he'd cornered Kate. He was too old to chat her up. And speaking French like he was, the writer seemed smoother. You could tell he was a lech.

But Kate seemed fascinated by everything he said, and full of her own opinions too, torrents of French pouring out of her. She looked so sweet, pink and sort of glowing, and she obviously fancied the bastard rotten. But somehow Kate kept that small edge of reserve as if, as well as fancying Lacoste, she was laughing at him too.

Ever since she came back from Switzerland Olivier had a new feeling for Kate – she was less of a sister, more her own person.

193

She'd got on fine without the Felixes for nearly two years. Olivier watched her now, a lot. He'd always liked how she looked, but living abroad had made her sharper and more stylish.

And he couldn't put out of his mind her nakedness that night on the beach, so sudden and unexpected, changing the way he saw her for ever. She'd walked up the beach from the sea, her body narrow and elegant, slick with water, striped white across her breasts and hips, triangular bush of hair casually, unthinkably exposed. She'd been ill at ease, Olivier could see, but hid it with a kind of demure composure. The memory came to him time and again, rousing him, making him hard. Like now, as he danced with Megan. Olivier eased his body a little away from hers.

Kate and David Lacoste made to go outside through the French windows. As she passed in front of him, David's hand brushed against Kate's bare, tanned midriff. Olivier closed his mind to the lurch of envy that jolted him. He laid his lips in the crook of Megan's soft shoulder. She snuggled her full breasts up against him as they danced.

As they walked across the rough, sloping field David Lacoste took her hand. Kate was mesmerized, couldn't believe this was happening. She and David were out alone under the wide, cobalt sky, breathing in the soft air, while the buzz of the party receded behind them. The dark shapes of horses still grazed in the near-dark.

Kate's legs felt weak and drained, they carried her automatically. She had no will of her own. And all the time she and David continued to talk, talk about his books.

He was so gratified that she'd read his novels and had opinions on them, which she could express in fluent, easy French. Back in the house, deep in conversation, Kate had all but forgotten the party going on all round them, the dancing and the drinking. And David's whole being had become animated. He'd held her gaze with a live, keen interest that – she couldn't help thinking – was quite different from the way he looked at any of the others.

They reached the steep little scramble that led down to the beach.

David kept going, as if as a matter of course, and with her hand in his, Kate too started down the path.

'You know,' David said suddenly, 'I'm touched by you all . . . you kids together in this big old house . . .'

Kate loved his saying that, but shrugged a disclaimer. 'We're just kids whose parents are on holiday.'

'And . . .' He turned to her. 'I find touching, too, your relationship to this family . . .'

'I love them,' she said simply.

'And your father, your real father?'

'I don't know. I feel rejected by him. But, for all I know, he might feel the same about me.'

David gave a low, caressing laugh. He stopped in mid path and pulled Kate towards him. He kissed her, several times, with a teasing tenderness, cupping her face in his two hands. Kate felt as if her heart might burst.

'*Viens.*' Gently he took her hand again, led her further down the slope. Dazed and obedient, Kate followed. Fleetingly, distantly, she sensed a breath of danger, glimpsed some point of no return. But nothing in the world could have made her pull back.

David returned to his former topic. 'All of you kids make me feel wistful . . . You remind me how it was to be young.'

'But you don't seem old,' Kate exclaimed. She thought immediately how naïve and toadying she sounded, but once again David laughed as if she'd said something sweet and clever.

He scrambled ahead of her on the last steep section, lifted her down from waist-high. As he did so, Kate was acutely aware of the wiry tension in his muscles.

They stood contemplating the calm sea. The tide was almost in. Far out, in the dark, hazy blue, the lighthouse twinkled on and off. David's arm was round her shoulder.

'Sublime.' He indicated the sweep of the seascape. 'Don't you think so, little Kate?'

'Yes . . . Yes it is.' Her voice sounded young, weak, and she wished she could think of something more inspired to say.

They wandered along the beach. David held her by the waist.

Once or twice his hand brushed across her buttocks. The casual intimacy made her stomach knot with excitement. They came to a spot where the pebbles gave way to coarse sand. David stopped and kissed her again.

'Kate,' he said in a low, husky tone. He stroked her hair. 'It's like a blackbird's wing . . . Kate, little blackbird.'

Some deep reserve of scepticism found the endearment ridiculous. But the caressing vibration of his voice made her feel as if she were melting. Faintly Kate could smell the worldliness of Scotch on his breath. Blankly, brazenly she kissed him back.

'*Viens.*' He pulled her down to the ground beside him, kissed her and murmured husky flattery, caressed her breasts through the material of her brassiere. He laid one leg across her, shifted so his body lay half on top of hers. Kate felt the bulge of his erection. It was for her, because of her. She was awed.

After a while he slid one hand between her thighs. Kate stiffened. No one had ever touched her there. She tried to move away. He was persistent. She pushed at his hand.

'You're not going to be a little prick-teaser are you?' There was a new hardness to his tone, a menace.

Kate said nothing. She knew – from the boys at school, from everyone, since forever – that a prick-teaser was one of the worst things you could be. And in a sudden cold flash she recalled the women in David's books who fucked so confidently and made no bones about it. How he would despise her schoolgirlish fears and hesitations.

He was unfastening the waistband of her trousers and dumbly Kate let him. He slipped his hand down inside them, inside her pants. Kate lay passive, let him touch her, let him stroke her. Nelly had told her about this. It was embarrassing, but dizzying. The sensations he stirred up made her gasp. She let out a kind of sob.

'Take these off,' David murmured, pulling at her trousers.

Kate obeyed and he too undressed himself, spread his fine shirt for them to lie on. She was abashed. His erect penis looked grotesquely large beside the slender pallor of his body. It was sort of ugly, except that words like ugly and beautiful no longer meant quite the same. He guided her hand to his cock. She caressed it experimentally, inexpertly.

'Are you a virgin?'

Kate nodded with a wry, apologetic smile.

'Not for much longer.' A flash of black humour.

His fingers probed briefly between her legs then, positioning his cock, David began to force an entry with long, insistent strokes, gradually wearing down her body's resistance. At a certain moment he broke off and fiddled with what Kate presumed to be a French letter. Then he was inside, pushing deeper, deeper.

'You feel me?' he asked throatily.

'Yes.'

Another thrust. 'You feel me?'

'Yes.' What else could she say?

'You feel me?'

'Yes.' The litany was becoming absurd.

She prayed for him to keep quiet and just do it. With a coiled, fascinated curiosity Kate observed David's mounting frenzy, his closed, almost agonized face, the groaning, wracking spasms of his release; she lay numbly incredulous beneath his sprawled, spent body.

After a few moments he stirred and rolled off, lay alongside her propped on one elbow. He gave a sort of inward smile and said, 'You've just lost your virginity to the writer David Lacoste . . . There's something to tell your grandchildren.'

Kate was ruffled by a breath of displeasure. She thought he sounded smug and self-important. Though, admittedly, as she lay spreadeagled beneath his labouring body, similar thoughts had pulsated through her own head.

Her reservations receded as they made their way back to the house. David was sweet and attentive, concerned for her welfare.

'How does it feel to be a woman?' His grin was playfully ironic, but also tender.

'It makes your legs tired,' Kate replied as they toiled up the steep

197

path. She was pleased with the flippancy of her response, thought she sounded like a female in one of his books.

David laughed and gave her an affectionate hug. '*Petite farceuse.*'

The joke cut through any potential tension and they began to chat again, trivially, inconseqentially. Kate asked his opinion of the Felixes.

'You like Pascal? You like Olivier?'

He praised them with unforced warmth.

'And Nelly?' Kate was almost reluctant to ask. Nelly was so attractive, so magnetic. She was scared of finding that David thought so too.

To her surprise he gave a dubious shrug, turned down the corners of his mouth. 'She's too mad for me. Too overwrought.' Adding hastily. 'Of course, I barely know her . . .'

There was a silence, as Kate digested the thought.

'You're not offended?'

Kate shook her head. Another time she might have been. But tonight too many other emotions fought for her attention.

At the house nobody seemed to notice their arrival. In the dimly lit living-room couples were dancing to one of Pascal's Miles Davis records. The music set a loose, languorous mood.

'Ah.' With pleasure David recognized the sound. He pulled her to him. 'Dance, Kate?'

He enfolded her in his arms. One hand lay heavy and sensuous in the nape of her neck. David's body was warm against hers, warm and familiar. They'd made love. The thought filled her with awe. From a doorway Kate noticed Olivier watching them and smiled at him. He turned his head away.

David kissed her. 'Little blackbird,' he murmured.

This time the pet-name disarmed and pleased her. As they danced, Kate laid her head against his shoulder. She felt as if she were in love.

Chapter Twenty-One

❈❈❈❈❈

The following morning Kate padded downstairs around eleven. She'd got to bed at four and barely slept, her mind seething with images of David – his smiles and gestures, the way he'd touched her, his nakedness . . . They were with her still as she reached the hall. The sun cast its usual sharp, bright rectangles across the green carpet. Kate felt heavy-eyed but suffused with a kind of shivering languor.

From the kitchen she heard sounds of someone washing up. Entering the room, she was confused at first. The woman standing at the sink, her back towards Kate, was not familiar. She was barefoot and wore a blue-green dress. Long silky hair straggled down her back. Kate stared, then recognition dawned.

'Beatrice!'

Startled, she turned. 'Kate! You made me jump . . . I thought everyone was dead to the world.'

'When did you get back?'

'Early this morning. A friend drove me down overnight.' Ruefully Beatrice indicated the dirty glasses and ashtrays on the draining board. 'I couldn't believe my eyes. There was stuff everywhere. What a cliché . . . Wild parties the moment the aged P's turn their backs.'

'You didn't have to . . .'

'I was possessed by a demon of energy.'

Beatrice was deeply bronzed by the Greek sun, her hair streaked with long, bleached strands, but it looked dirty and unkempt. Her dress was creased and, beneath the tan, she appeared drawn and tired. Clearly she'd been travelling for some days. But in spite of all this the elder Felix daughter still radiated her own effortless glamour.

'Congratulations on your degree, by the way.'

199

Beatrice pulled a face. 'A Second sounds so mediocre and worthy. A First or a Fourth would have been a lot more stylish . . . But enough of me!' She crossed to where Kate was standing and embraced her warmly. 'It's *good* to see you . . . It seems ages . . . And you look different. What is it? Have you lost weight?' She grinned. 'Or fallen in love?'

It was clear that Beatrice was happy to be home and her exhilaration made her seem less aloof, more approachable. All the same Kate wasn't ready to confide the wonders of the previous night.

Flippantly she hedged. 'With Odile away there's never any food in the house.'

'What about *your* exams?' it occurred to Beatrice.

'My . . . ?' In the last couple of weeks they'd all but vanished from Kate's mind. Hazily she groped for the meaning of Beatrice's enquiry. 'Oh . . . I haven't heard yet.'

'They're bound to be brilliant . . . Kate, I've made some coffee. Let's drink it on the terrace.'

Afterwards Kate helped Beatrice to finish the clearing-up. And then, on her own, she walked down to the beach. Today the familiar setting was imbued with a new aura, an altered significance. The shining, lapping water, the azure sky seemed more beautiful than ever before.

In her bra and shorts Kate paddled for a while, then swam with slow, lazy strokes, still in a kind of sensuous trance.

Last night, in the upstairs corridor, before wishing her goodnight, David had tilted her chin and looked searchingly into her eyes.

'You're all right?' he asked. 'You're sure?'

Kate had smiled and given a saucy nod, to show he need have no worries on her account. She took things in her stride, was no wilting flower. At the same time his concern intoxicated her and she was only too aware of the abject adoration and gratitude that must be shining from her eyes.

He'd kissed her, simply, sweetly. '*Dors bien*.'

As he disappeared down the corridor, her heart had ached with loss.

* * *

Walking back across the field, Kate became aware that two figures were sitting together on the terrace. Coming closer, she saw that they were Beatrice and David. He was smoking. They were chattering and laughing. How absolutely right they looked in one another's company.

Her insides gave a great involuntary lurch, releasing a pain that overwhelmed her with its strength and suddenness. The reaction was quite beyond her control. Feebly she scrabbled to regain a sense of balance. What did she expect? Their tête-à-tête was perfectly natural. All of them were living under the same roof. But far stronger than any such reasoning was the abrupt and horrified gut-certainty that Beatrice and David formed a far more convincing twosome than she and David ever would or could.

As she drew near they smiled and waved. She waved back with as much insouciance as she could muster.

'You've been swimming,' Beatrice said, as Kate reached the terrace. 'The energy of the girl!' She wore inscrutable sunglasses, had pulled her skirt up to mid thigh, exposing her legs to the sun.

'Come. Sit with us.' David patted the space next to him on the bench. Kate saw, or imagined, bland treachery in the casual invitation.

'In a minute.' Her smile felt fixed as a carnival mask. She went inside. The cool of the house was soothing to her shaken spirit. Upstairs she sat on her bed, silent and shocked, as if she'd been granted a vision of things to come.

After a while Kate told herself she'd over-reacted, stupidly, childishly, pulled herself together, manufactured a mood of artificial calm. She washed her face, brushed her hair, put on a clean dress and went downstairs. No one was around, except for Olivier, idly strumming his guitar.

He looked up. 'Did you know Beatrice was back?'

'Yes, I saw her . . . She cleared up all the party stuff.'

'Amazing. Beatrice has never been one of life's great manual workers.'

Kate grinned, warming to his uncomplicated beauty, his unthreatening familiarity, in the wake of last night's brush with the unknown.

After playing a few desultory chords, Olivier said, 'Beatrice and David have gone out in the car. To the shops. Beatrice left her toothbrush on some Greek island and . . .'

'Mmm.' Kate crossed to the window and gazed out, hoping she looked preoccupied and unconcerned. The pain in her heart had leapt again like a sudden flame. She forced it to subside to a simmering ache.

'There's a letter for you,' Olivier remembered.

To her conscious mind the words were meaningless. But automatically Kate trailed into the hall. An envelope lay on the dark, polished table-top.

It was her exam results. She had Distinctions in both French and German. Kate felt as if the news concerned someone else. She didn't bother to tell Olivier.

There was a fair crowd down on the beach that night, but it didn't include either David or Beatrice. It was Nelly's night off and Kate sat with her and Mac, sharing a bottle of warm, sweet wine left over from the party. All three of them were tired. Nelly and Mac bickered gently. Kate joined in, faking amusement, involvement. Her head ached with the effort. She thought her voice sounded cracked, but no one else seemed to notice.

They went back to the house around eleven for an early night. As they crossed the dark field a faint sound of music floated towards them from the house.

'Mozart. How civilized,' Nelly mocked.

'It's divine . . . Listen.' Kate was captivated by the buoyant drift of melody. 'You've got no soul, Nelly.'

'She's an out-and-out philistine.' Mac grabbed Nelly by the scruff of the neck.

They climbed the low, stone steps up to the terrace. Illuminated by amber lamplight, David sat on the floor next to the open French window, listening to a piano sonata. Beatrice lay with her head in his lap, apparently asleep, her long hair pleasingly tumbled. He smoothed it reverently off her forehead and temples. As they approached he gazed vaguely at them, as if from far away.

Upstairs in the bathroom Kate was violently sick. Then, annihilated, she slunk to bed and slept like the dead until the following midday, finally surfacing to fresh contractions of misery and humiliation, aching to run from the whole embarrassing mess. She had an airline ticket to New York for the following week and had dreaded leaving. But suddenly escape to another continent appeared a liberation, infinitely desirable.

But she couldn't get away, not yet. Kate lay in bed with her knees drawn up, dreading the day ahead. Wounded as she was, she couldn't bear the thought of confiding her predicament to anyone else. Somehow or other she had to save face. All that was open to her was to act as blasé as she could, as if to demonstrate that the encounter had been as meaningless to her as it clearly was to David. She must be like one of the hard-headed female characters in his books, however unconvincing her performance.

As it happened, the pretence was not immediately needed. Beatrice and David had gone out for the day. She had the information from Pascal who was sitting on the living-room floor, head in hands, absorbed in studying a set of black-and-white photo-portraits spread out on the floor in front of him.

'Thank God,' Pascal added. 'I'm getting bored with having him around.'

'Really?' Kate was cheered, intrigued. 'I thought he was a hero of yours.'

'I dunno . . . When you scrape off the top layer, the silver plating . . .'

She sat down on a chair nearby, made a show of scanning the photographs, agog for him to say more.

'Basically the man's a tosser.'

'In what way?'

'He lights up like a little flashlight when he talks to you.' There was a bitter vehemence in Pascal's voice. 'But actually he's not listening to a thing you say. He's only listening to himself, admiring his own smoothy charm.'

Beneath the animosity Pascal sounded hurt, Kate thought. He sounded like she felt. And she wondered what could have taken place between them.

'Anyway,' Pascal continued. 'He's too old to be hanging round here, sniffing round you and Beatrice.'

Kate felt herself flush, but she said nothing. Though Pascal's words were like balm to her soul.

Instead she pointed to a picture of Olivier. 'That's nice . . . He looks like a pop star. And I like that one of Nelly. I've seen that expression on her face.'

'She looks like I've just insulted her and she's on her high horse. Which was exactly what did happen.' He glanced at Kate with a flicker of amusement. 'Have you still got that photo album of yours – the white one, with about ten hand-picked photos in it?'

'Course I have.' She grinned. 'I'll have it till I'm old and grey.' She was touched that he'd remembered.

'D'you want those two pix? You can only have them if you'll put them in your album . . . It's like being hung in the most exclusive gallery.'

'OK –' Kate picked them up – 'it's a deal.' Her heart swelled with gratitude. Not for the photographs, but for Pascal's timely debunking of David Lacoste.

The conversation alerted Kate to a change in the dynamic of the house. In the eyes of all but Beatrice, David had outstayed his welcome. Olivier obviously thought so. Nelly thought so. Even Mac, though not generally sensitive to atmosphere, clearly felt the same.

Not that David or Beatrice noticed anything. They were far too wrapped up in one another. They were inseparable, coming and going in their own time, scuffling and laughing like a pair of kids, sunning themselves on the terrace, photographing one another, buying food and cooking up private meals in the kitchen, drinking whisky from David's secret store, even dressing alike – Beatrice plundering David's wardrobe for dark, stark sweaters and sombre striped shirts. Then they would lock themselves away in Beatrice's bedroom for hours at a time. From behind the closed door strains of Charlie Parker would waft, and Gregorian chant, and muffled whoops of laughter, followed by long, eloquent silences.

Abruptly David and Beatrice became the enviable, self-absorbed hub of the household, reducing the rest of them to peripheral status. The outsiders retaliated with ill-natured mutterings and eye-rolling glances.

One stifling afternoon deep mauve clouds gathered above the sea, seeming to signal the end of the extraordinary heat-wave. David and Beatrice sat together in a corner of the living-room. David was holding forth on the subject of a fellow writer, a friend of his, who'd written a subtly atmospheric novel set against the French defeat in Indo-China. The book had been filmed, so David claimed, to produce a crass and shallow piece of blood and thunder. He spoke with melodious fluency, methodically ticking off the differences between the original and film versions.

Outside on the terrace Pascal and Kate watched the boiling clouds and listened with companionable scepticism to David's omniscient tones.

Pascal nudged Kate. 'How can she stand him pontificating like that?'

Big drops of rain began to splatter on to the terrace. They stretched out their hands and tilted their faces up to the downpour.

'I'm ready for this,' Kate said. 'All that heat was getting sort of one-dimensional.' She was pleased with Pascal's throwaway comment, but didn't trust herself to respond.

'Actually,' Pascal continued, 'all Frogs pontificate, given half a chance. Have you noticed that?'

In this atmosphere it was not too hard for Kate to bounce back from her brief infatuation with David Lacoste. Her show of indifference became almost real. Mentally she could almost write the experience off, no actual harm done. Except that her pride lay shrivelled like a soft, wrinkled, deflated balloon. And, alone in her room, she blushed and burned, remembering the doggy devotion that had shone from her eyes on the night of the party.

* * *

Three days later Beatrice and David left for London. As it happened, at the time of their departure, only Kate and Olivier were in the house.

The hot spell seemed to have broken for good. Already hints of greenness had crept back into the straw-coloured grass of the field.

Olivier waved the couple off. Kate skulked upstairs, watching their leave-taking from a first-floor window.

As he stood by the Citroën in the drizzle, she heard David say, 'Where's Kate?' And then, addressing Olivier. 'Give a kiss to little Kate from me.'

'Kate! Goodbye, Kate!' Beatrice shouted vaguely up at the house.

When they'd gone she came downstairs. Olivier planted a kiss on her cheek. 'That's from David.'

'Huh.' Kate was unimpressed. 'That's H-U-H.'

'So that's how you pronounce it.'

Outside the rain began to come down in earnest, soaking deep into the parched field, bouncing off the smooth stone surface of the terrace.

Olivier stood at the window. 'There's a cowboy film where it starts to rain at the end, and the sharecroppers stand outside their shack and mingle their thankful tears with the rain . . .'

'Weather like this reminds me of an evening after I'd come back from America first time. And you and me and Nelly and Robert played Monopoly up in one of the top rooms . . . It was all dark outside and the rain was hammering against the windows and we were all wrapped up in blankets and eiderdowns . . .'

'I remember that night.'

On an impulse Kate suggested, 'D'you fancy a game of Monopoly now?'

They found the board and shook out the musty-smelling eiderdowns, spread them out on the bare wooden floor. While setting up the board they continued to chat idly. In the empty room their voices had an echoey ring. The unshaded light-bulb filled the room with yellow light, made the sky outside look heavy and dark.

'You'll be in New England next week with the autumn leaves drifting by your window . . .'

Kate screwed up her face. 'Fay's pregnant again. And Ricky's toddling and saying cute things. Dad'll be in heaven . . .' She gave a crooked smile. 'And I'll be like a spare prick at a knocking-shop wedding.' It was an expression of Olivier's whose bluntness appealed to her. He smiled sympathetically.

Kate threw the dice mechanically, but her heart was not in the game. Her mind dwelled wretchedly on the image of David and Beatrice, so jaunty and compatible, disappearing in David's amiably scruffy Citroën, its bonnet and mudguards streaked with dust and rain.

As if reading her mind, Olivier suddenly said, 'I wish Beatrice hadn't gone off with that . . . She can be a pain in the arse, but she's basically straight. Too straight for him.'

'She's twenty-one,' Kate replied stiffly. 'So she's supposed to be able to take care of herself.'

'Anyway.' Olivier gave her a searching look. 'How do *you* feel about it? You seemed pretty pally with him at the party . . .'

'Not really.'

'Oh, come on. You disappeared for ages. I was watching.'

Kate fell silent. The rattle of the dice sounded loud and dry. With a rush of nostalgia she relived the feel of that night on the beach, the incredulous floating wonder, a swelling sense that at last her life had begun. In her mind she'd denied and belittled the experience. But it was the best she'd ever had. Tears welled behind her eyes. She threw the dice and peered through a blur at the number.

'Six.' A tear plopped on to the Monopoly board. With a forefinger she rubbed it in.

'Kate . . . Hey, Kate, I'm sorry, I . . .' Olivier's voice was low with concern and contrition. She dashed away the tears, tried to smile a reassurance, but failed.

'You mustn't cry.'

How sweet he sounded. She was stricken by his sweetness when the world seemed full of treachery. Kate began to weep in silent earnest, while the rain gusted noisily against the windows. Olivier's hand was on her shoulder, shaking her gently.

'Don't cry, Kate.' His face was earnest and young. He seemed beautiful as an angel.

'Did he fuck you?' The question came, hoarsely intimate, while, nakedly, his grey-green eyes held hers.

Kate nodded. She cleared her throat. 'Yes.' She wanted to add some explanation, but wasn't sure what.

He leaned towards her and she felt his lips on hers, cool and gentle. His kisses were like a child's, wanting to comfort. She was heartened by his kindness and, in gratitude, began to kiss him back. After a while Olivier pulled her down alongside him on the faded eiderdown. They lay tightly enclosed in one another's arms and, later, by a mutual instinct, pulled the other quilt across to cover them.

'Don't cry for him,' Olivier whispered. 'He's not worth it.'

It was so snug lying there, close and cocooned. Kate couldn't remember feeling so safe and cherished in her life before. She wanted to feel like this for ever. But the muscular bulk of Olivier's body was sexy too and it came to Kate that – courtesy of David Lacoste – she had this new knowledge, and it seemed a shame not to use it. Olivier's kisses were changing, becoming more lover-like. Now his hands crept under her shirt and found her breasts, his leg insinuated itself between hers. She felt equal to the situation, in control even, not timid and overwhelmed as with David. Piece by piece they shed their clothes and lay skin to skin, enveloped by the worn, downy coverlets. Olivier was wildly aroused, his penis hard, distended in the same way David's had been, exciting and disconcerting her – for years she'd thought of him as a mere boy. He entered her in a long, melting push, gasped incredulously with each new thrust. But it wasn't long before he climaxed with a groan of unbearable pleasure, and lay spent across Kate's prone body while she stroked his tousled hair.

'Sorry – I was too quick,' he murmured. 'I've never done it before, not all the way.'

'Ssh.' She didn't want to speak. Just to lie there, safe and warm, and watch the darkening sky and listen to the rain pattering against the windows, on and on.

PART 2

❦❦❦

The Sixties

Chapter Twenty-Two
1963

❦❦❦

'Have a brandy with your coffee, Kate,' Jerome urged.

'I shouldn't. I've got work to do when I get home.'

'It'll sharpen your wits up a treat. Believe me. I know what I'm talking about.'

Kate relented. 'Just a small one.' She could rarely resist when pressed by one or other of the Felixes.

It was a warm July evening in Soho. The door to the Gay Hussar stood open on to the street. Inside, the restaurant was full, the air thick and warm, the tables crowded, convivial. Jerome's presence caused the usual small buzz. Kate had seen fellow diners casting covert glances, whispering discreetly to their companions.

'That's my girl. Indulge me.' Jerome smiled approvingly, his benevolent, bearded baby-face flushed with the wine they'd already consumed. 'One of the few pleasures left to us oldies is treating our kids to slap-up meals they couldn't otherwise afford . . . Pascal? How's about you?'

'A Calvados. A double – in view of what you've just said.'

'Olivier?'

'Orange juice.'

'Come on, old man. You're letting the side down.'

'I'm thirsty. But if you twist my arm I'll have a Slivovitz chaser.'

'Consider your arm twisted.' Jerome beamed up at the austere waiter in his rimless spectacles, taking for granted that the man must share in his own patriarchal pride and pleasure. 'Got that? And a Kümmel for me, if you please.'

At this point in his career Jerome had become something of a national institution, a telly-pundit, good for a fresh, pithy, debunking quote on anything topical, from US foreign policy to the current – breathlessly unfolding – Profumo sex-and-politics drama.

He was happy, too, to shed his dignity and take part, with gusto, in down-market quiz and game shows. In fact, for Jerome, this kind of frivolity had become an article of faith, in the face of critics who felt that an academic ought to confine himself to paths of sobriety and decorum.

'I detest the kind of bigot who thinks we should all stand for one thing and one thing only,' he explained in an interview with the *Observer*. 'Human beings are rich and contradictory . . . We feel, we think, we work. But we play as well. We laugh and we're silly. We need our candyfloss. Why on earth should so-called intellectuals have to pretend they're any different?'

If he alienated a number of his fellow academics, students in general adored him, specially after his bemused and cherubic guest-appearance on the late-night satire show, *TW3*. In fact Jerome no longer did a great deal of teaching. His TV appearances paid better, along with foreign lecture tours and journalism – the chunks of comment and analysis he wrote on anything that caught his imagination, for *Punch*, *Private Eye*, the Sunday newspapers, the political weeklies, even – to his glee – *Esquire* and *Playboy*.

When it came out – via an article in *Vogue* – that Jerome's elder daughter lived in France as the lover of writer David Lacoste, the information, by association, boosted his legend, provoking, among contemporaries and rivals, a ripple of titillated interest, along with taunts of a grudging 'they-all-piss-in-the-same-pot' variety.

A couple of months ago he'd had a new book published – a slim volume entitled *A-Morality*, which argued for the public acknowl-edgement of a more robust and open, a less mealy-mouthed code of conduct, reflecting the way people really were.

'A farrago of truisms. Guaranteed not a new idea in it.' In private Jerome affected a dismissive flippancy. 'I dashed the thing off in a couple of weeks flat to meet a deadline . . .'

It was the kind of work which – despite its stylish green and black jacket, its punning title – would normally have sunk without trace.

But, with Jerome's high profile and his notorious irreverence, the book attracted a little flurry of controversy.

It was condemned by some clerics, fiercely defended by others, notably the Bishop of Woolwich. A prominent ex-colleague of Jerome's accused him of aspiring to be a kind of pop-academic agony uncle and condemned his lack of intellectual rigour.

In a wry refutation Jerome pooh-poohed the man's concept of intellectual rigour – 'That sterile tit the British love to suck, though it offers neither pleasure nor nourishment.'

The 'agony uncle' jibe and Jerome's riposte were absorbed into his media persona, seeming set fair to be trotted out in the introductory spiel to his television appearances for ever and ever amen.

When the liqueurs and the coffee arrived Kate sat back to enjoy – consciously – the final few minutes of the meal. She had several pages of a technical translation to complete when she got home and knew she'd be lucky to get to bed at all that night. In fact she had already refused to go to the pictures that evening with Jess, her old school friend, pleading pressure of work. But when, out of the blue, Jerome rang to invite her to dine with himself and the boys, Kate had accepted with alacrity. She adored these evenings, with their warmth and laughter, their perennial reassurance that, even after several years of independent living, she was still accounted one of the family.

Jerome raised his glass. 'Cheers, lads.' Then, turning to Kate: 'Cheers, little worker-bee.'

'Don't remind me.'

'I love to think of you hunched over your desk in the wee small hours, by the lurid light of your Anglepoise lamp . . . It restores my faith in the younger generation.'

'I don't do it for pleasure.'

Sometimes Kate felt wounded by Jerome's representation of her as a plodding eager beaver – it came perilously close to the unflattering secret image she harboured of herself. But tonight the wine and good cheer had put her beyond the reach of that particular angst.

Jerome addressed his younger son. 'How long d'you reckon this new thing of yours is going to last, then?'

Currently Olivier was 'helping out' – his euphemism for work – in a friend's new wine bar in Chiswick.

He gave his amiable smile. 'Who knows? Till my attention span runs out or I get a better offer.'

Twenty-year-old Olivier dandled his liqueur-glass loosely between his fingers. He looked tanned and handsome in a button-down shirt of tiny yellow checks. His hair, shorter than it used to be, spiked across his forehead in the style of a Roman sculpture. The expression on his face was one of good-natured impudence, like a favoured schoolboy who knows his cheek will be indulged.

His father grinned. 'I won't hold my breath, then.'

Jerome was diverted, even impressed by the succession of casual jobs through which his son earned his erratic living. It seemed Olivier had the happy knack of bumping into people with amusing projects on the go. In the last year or so he'd helped out as cocktail waiter, landscape gardener, dry-stone waller, bass guitar player in a short-lived backing band.

Now both were based in London, he and Kate saw one another casually but consistently. Olivier made friends easily and liked his friends to know each other. In the amorphousness of London he provided a sort of social pool for Kate to paddle in. Since that afternoon four years ago they'd never again been lovers. But, on some wordless level, the incident had deepened their relationship.

'It's a nice place.' Kate had eaten there with a boyfriend a few weeks back. 'That onion soup is ace. But why do those little bistro-ey places always put so much shredded red cabbage in the salad?'

'Visual appeal. And most people leave it, so you can use it again.'

Olivier smiled innocently, Kate sceptically.

'How's the ravishing Amanda?' Jerome asked Pascal.

'Swanning in Greece with her parents, lucky bitch.'

'One of the perks of working for your pa.'

Arriving in London in the autumn of 1959, Pascal had split with his long-time girlfriend, Mary. Since then he'd had a string of replacements who, to Kate, appeared always of a type. Extravagantly beautiful, but silent and enigmatic, seeming passively to invite, not warmth or friendship, but worship.

Amanda, who worked nominally as a secretary in her father's tile-importing firm, was no exception. Tiny and pale-skinned, with a cloud of baby-blonde hair and an unnerving doll-like stare, she wore fluffy sweaters and suits in pastel tweed. At parties she sat on the edge of the action, remote and absolutely self-sufficient, though she danced when required to with a kind of childlike gravity. In conversation she was not precisely rude, but oddly slumberous. While admiring her porcelain perfection, Kate could never think of anything to say to her.

'She's been asked to do some modelling,' Pascal recalled. 'For one of those firms that do sheepskin jackets and lambswool twinsets.'

Jerome nodded. 'Sounds right up her street.'

It fascinated Kate how the brothers differed in their taste in women. For all Olivier's own beauty his girlfriends were chosen for niceness and approachability rather than looks. Pascal seemed always to be seeking a muse.

Pascal pulled a face. 'Those catalogues are such crap . . . flat colours, badly printed . . . And they'll reduce Amanda to some perky, permed English Rose. She deserves better.' He grinned. 'Now if *I* did the Hargreaves brochure she'd look like the Dietrich of the beagling set . . .'

Kate laughed. 'And twinsets would become a sign of decadence.'

He gave a crooked, amused smile and downed the rest of his Calvados. Pascal had the dark, glittery look in his eyes that he got when he drank alcohol and his hair was nicely ruffled. He wore a cream shirt, loosened at the neck, and a narrow blue and grey striped tie. On the back of his chair hung a handsome jacket, tailored in blue-grey cotton. Since earning a little money he'd become quite dandified.

Kate had not lost the quiet crush she'd had on the elder Felix brother ever since the age of fourteen. But it was a familiar presence and brought no suffering – she had never allowed herself to dream of any kind of romance. She saw less of him than of Olivier, but they shared a love of French films and, every so often, they got together to check out the latest Godard, Truffaut or Chabrol.

Pascal didn't talk much about his work. Kate knew he'd risen from 'glorified tea-boy' – his description – to what he satirically termed a 'roving cameraman'. A lot of the time he drove round with a team in a BBC van filming local news.

But, since they'd been in London, she'd come to view him rather differently. Back at Plas Felix he'd seemed a sort of aesthetic loafer with his endless moody photographs and self-conscious fragments of home-movie. Now she seemed to detect a hard-headed quality in him, had begun to see that he was cannier and more ambitious than any of them had guessed. And, fancifully, Kate suspected that even his earlier, studenty, apparently dilettante-ish jobs, had probably been part of some private, guarded master plan.

This week he'd been filming, outside the Old Bailey, the fascinating comings and goings of the protagonists in the Stephen Ward trial. Pascal and Olivier had a long-running dispute going as to who was the most fanciable – Christine Keeler or Mandy Rice-Davies. They resumed their bickering again now. Pascal was all for Christine. Olivier favoured Mandy's sassy pink-and-white prettiness.

Kate drained her coffee, summoned up all her strength of will. She must get home and tackle that blasted translation.

Olivier put a hand on her arm. 'Before you go let me tell you this stupid Profumo joke I heard yesterday . . .'

'I really ought to go . . .'

But in the face of Olivier's appeal her resolution faltered. Kate was putty in the hands of any one of the Felixes, and knew it. She settled back in her seat to listen to his story.

Around quarter to five the following morning Kate rolled the final page of her German translation out of the typewriter. It was a patent specification for some printing gadget – she was a bit rocky on picturing the actual working detail.

'Don't worry,' the firm's manager was sanguine. 'Just give us as literal and stylish a translation as you can. Our specialists can brush up the technical terms.'

She must be doing something right because, for the last six months or so, Holland & Conrad Patent Agents had been sending her a constant stream of work, so much it was sometimes difficult for her to keep up.

'Mr Holland's delighted with you,' his friendly, rouged secretary said each time she dropped off a new batch of translations. 'He's never found anyone so sharp and so reliable.'

Kate's reaction to the praise was ambiguous. A part of her was pleased by this tribute to her professionalism. At the same time there was a scepticism that saw such conscientiousness as irredeemably dull.

The translation was due in at ten o'clock. She'd have to leave home by nine to be sure . . . That left her time for a few hours' sleep. But it would be pointless to leap into bed right away, with her mind still racing and a mega-dose of caffeine zinging in her veins. Kate knew from experience that she must force herself to relax for at least fifteen minutes, maybe down a slug of that soporific cough medicine she had left over from the winter, to counteract all the coffee she'd drunk.

It felt chilly and she set a match to the gas in the beige-tiled fireplace, turned off the light and lay down on top of the red and blue striped blanket she'd brought from her bed at Plas Felix. Her furnished room, on the second floor of a tall yellow-brick house in Randolph Avenue, Maida Vale, was large and high-ceilinged. Sometimes she loved its shabby-elegant spaciousness, specially when spring sun shone in through the long sash-windows. And now, in the warm, quavery light of the gas fire, her domain appeared both mysterious and cosy.

But there were long, grey winter afternoons when the fusty furnishings – the beige mantelpiece, beige on beige loose-covers, the scuffed brown carpet with its pink and green Art-Deco roses – would seem to conjure up shades of all the lonely, rootless tenants who'd occupied this room over the years. And the ceiling seemed to rise above her like a vault and, working alone at her desk in the corner, Kate would feel like some tiny, insignificant insect, quite alone in the world. She would be unable to shake the feeling until evening came and she got dressed up, went out to be with other people, talked too much, drank too much, until she felt human again.

Now she closed her eyes and deliberately slowed her breathing, pursuing sleep, focusing her mind on the pleasure of the previous evening's meal, the warm sense of belonging.

In a drawer in her desk lay the latest photograph of her father and Fay and their two lively blond children – Ricky and three-year-old Justine. Kate had hidden it away, unable to bear the ecstatic, almost fearful look of happiness that shone from Ellis's eyes.

She hadn't visited Coningsburgh in almost two years and rarely wrote. To Kate her father's domestic contentment had become more rather than less of an affront. It was almost worse now Ellis had a daughter. She carried with her a mental image from her last visit. It had been evening. Justine was teething and wouldn't settle. Ellis had sat nursing the distressed baby, murmuring to her and stroking her wispy hair until gradually she calmed down, her eyelids fluttered and she began fitfully to doze. Then Ellis had smiled across at Fay – a smile of perfect intimacy and satisfaction – while he sat still and quiet so as not to disturb the sleeping child. And Kate had watched with a mixture of enchantment and cold bitterness.

Kate willed the memory away. She turned on to her other side, pummelled and re-positioned the pillow. As her mind drifted it occurred to her that she must be careful not to mention last night's meal to Jess, not after she'd turned down her invitation to the pictures.

Jess, who was now teaching history at a large comprehensive in Islington, lived a short tube-ride away. They saw a lot of each other. Sometimes they went out, but mostly they dropped by one another's bedsits, drank coffee, watched television, moaned about their jobs and their love-lives. Jess hadn't changed. She was dumpy and dowdy, wore cardigans and shirtwaist dresses, white wedgie sling-backs, styled her hair in a kind of brown puffball, was not someone Kate felt she had to live up to in any way.

Yet an evening with her in front of the telly was highly enjoyable. Jess was sarcastic and sharp-tongued, impossible to impress. This summer they'd had particular fun watching government ministers squirm under the daily ration of new and ever more scandalous Profumo revelations, jeering at their well-bred confusion, their huffing moral indignation. With Jess, Kate was totally at ease, never troubled by the secret sneaking feeling that she wasn't quite good enough.

And yet she'd never introduced her old school friend to Olivier or Pascal. Deep down, Kate acknowledged, she was ashamed of Jess. As if she let the side down. As if being friends with her said something less than flattering about Kate herself.

Chapter Twenty-Three

❧❧❧❧

Duncan Mitchell had moved into the room above hers in early January during the big freeze. She used to bump into him from time to time on her way to the bathroom or lavatory situated on a sort of mezzanine between her floor and his.

In those days, even indoors, he was always dressed in a thick speckled sweater and a black donkey jacket, Kate in an outsize Aran sweater that belonged to Olivier and trousers tucked into grey mountaineering socks. They used to grin at one another in a long-suffering fashion, compare notes on their efforts to keep warm. Later, when the taps froze, they would go downstairs together with their buckets to beard the grumpy old Polish couple in the basement flat who still had water but resented sharing it with the ragtag and bobtail from upstairs.

Each time she encountered him and exchanged a few words, Kate would mentally be trying to decide whether or not she thought him good-looking. Mitchell was tall, broad-shouldered, but lean and gangling. His face was striking, strongly moulded, with wide cheekbones and deep-set dark blue eyes. His lips were full but shapely, his skin rather pitted. His thick fair hair stood up in a long crew-cut.

The was something unworldly about him, she decided. He lacked some quality that was hard to define. Gloss perhaps. Savoir-faire. Attributes both Pascal and Olivier possessed in abundance. On a bad day he made her think of a raw country-boy newly arrived in the big city. Which he was. On good days – in his black sweater and jeans – she could see something romantic about him, could imagine him as a starving artist in a garret. Later she found out that he was that too, in a manner of speaking, because he was trying to write.

Hearing him moving about upstairs during the daytime, Kate had at first assumed that he was out of work. About a month passed before she found out that Duncan had taken an evening job in a launderette, in order to leave the days free for working on his novel.

They began to meet up every so often for coffee or tea. Kate found out that he was about her age – just a few months older – and that, up to now, he'd lived in a small village in Norfolk, where his parents owned a newsagents. Duncan had gone to grammar school and, ever since the age of twelve, he'd had the scribbling bug, as his parents put it. He left school at eighteen and since then had done casual and seasonal work – turkey plucking, potato picking, a spot of gardening or decorating for neighbours – in order to buy himself tracts of free time to concentrate on his writing.

His parents got impatient and nagged him to get started on a proper career. He was wasting his education, going nowhere. Duncan argued that his professional ambitions were perfectly clear-cut and, as long as he paid his way – which he did – they were no one's business but his own. His parents were equally convinced that their eldest son was living in Cloud-Cuckoo-Land and it was time he got up off his arse and got to grips with the real world. Their differences blew up into an angry row in the shop on Christmas Eve.

'We had to keep breaking off, though, to serve people,' Duncan recalled. 'And plaster phoney grins across our faces, and wish them a Happy Christmas.'

He'd left home after the festivities, as the first snows of the long winter began to fall. The extreme weather lent his early days in the capital a kind of drama. Duncan felt like the hero of a Russian novel. He loved his lonely, independent life, only wished he'd made the break years ago.

'Don't you ever feel isolated? Don't you get days when the walls seem to close in on you?'

He shrugged. 'I can always go to the pub.'

The reply was flip and noncommittal. But the more she got to know him, the more Kate understood that her neighbour actually was remarkably self-sufficient. Though he appeared to take pleasure in talking to her, and to the motley, multi-national mix of working people and students who frequented his launderette, they were incidental to his main preoccupation. Every day Duncan thanked his stars for the fact that he'd managed to assemble the perfect conditions for concentrated, unhurried work on his novel and the handful of short stories he had in progress. Kate was perplexed by his single-mindedness.

Generally speaking, the inmates of the house came and went anonymously – you knew their names from the letters on the long table in the entrance-hall. Kate found she enjoyed having a real neighbour. It was useful too. Duncan did her shopping when she was laid up with the flu, and she returned the compliment. He took her sheets and towels to work with him and delivered them back to her, clean and dry. She let him watch football on her television.

Kate had a bee in her bonnet about rearranging her room as if, in so doing, she might stumble on a plan that would disguise the essential dowdiness of the décor. Duncan viewed her quest with good-natured scepticism, but put his strong back and arms at her disposal.

They began to eat lunch together every few days. Duncan always offered the same. Ham sandwiches and tea served in big blue-and-white striped mugs. He was probably the only person she knew in London who hadn't switched at least to Nescafé, if not the real thing.

'Don't you ever eat any vegetables?' she asked him one day.

He had a humorous way of narrowing his eyes. 'Not if I can help it.'

Kate provided real coffee, French cheeses, and Greek bread from the shop in Kilburn High Road. Always salad or fruit, or both. Duncan ate dutifully but without enthusiasm. They laughed companionably at the differences between them. He mocked her poncey French food. Kate jeered at his conservatism.

'I'm educating you,' she told him. 'Widening your horizons.'

'Foreign muck.' Obligingly, Duncan played up to his own caricature.

She looked forward to their lunch-time meetings. They talked easily and frankly about everything, from books and records to work, or their uneasy relationships with their respective parents. Kate felt no need to put on airs, to tell anything but the truth. Duncan meant little to her. Deep down there was an element of condescension in her attitude towards him. In his company she never bothered to change out of the ancient sweaters and jeans she wore to work in, left her hair droopy and untitivated. And she was similarly unguarded in her conversation.

But on one point a defensiveness remained. No matter how animated and absorbing their dialogue, Kate always made sure that it was she who called a halt to the tête-à-tête.

She would glance at her watch, pull a mournful face. 'Time I got back to the grind.' Some ingrained snobbishness could not accept the thought that Duncan might dismiss *her*.

One Friday lunch-time in May Duncan told her he had the evening off. 'D'you fancy coming down the pub later tonight . . . if you're not doing anything?'

They had never *been* anywhere together. The novelty of it appealed to Kate. And she wasn't doing anything.

'Why not? Nine o'clockish?'

She decided to surprise him, put on a dress, took trouble with her hair, made up her face. Rather to her surprise, Kate had discovered that she had a deft hand with eye-liner, could elongate her lids with accuracy and dash.

'It's the hand-eye co-ordination.' Nelly claimed that her skill was somehow tied in with being good at table tennis.

When she opened the door to him, Duncan mimed a dazzled double-take. Though, a moment later, in the downstairs hall, he told her. 'That stuff on your eyes makes you look like Tweetie-Pie.' A teasing sideways glance that Kate found engaging.

'I see myself more as Wile E. Coyote.'

The Prince Rupert was a crowded barn of a place, with bare floorboards and huge mirrors engraved with borders of ferns, dark polished tables and a mismatched auction sale collection of chairs.

The clientele was multi-cultural with a preponderance of Irish. On his way to the bar Duncan greeted a number of fellow customers. Launderette regulars, so he told Kate.

She wanted to go Dutch – he earned considerably less than she did – but Duncan wouldn't hear of it. 'And don't go nursing half a pint of shandy all evening. I want you to enjoy yourself.'

As a compromise Kate opted for cheap red wine, poured from a litre bottle and served by the glass. They pushed their way to the far corner of the room and, after a while, a couple at a nearby table vacated their seats. Duncan pounced and they took possession of the chairs and an area of table. In these new surroundings there was a certain diffidence between them, but soon enough they relaxed into the pattern of their lunch-time sessions.

Somehow they got round to discussing their favourite film stars. As a boy Duncan had seen the film of *Ivanhoe* and fallen in love with Elizabeth Taylor as Rebecca, the beautiful, wronged Jewess.

'I collected all the little model knights that tied in with the film . . . Front de Boeuf, Brian de Bois-Guilbert and the rest. Luckily I couldn't get a Rebecca figure. Otherwise I swear I'd have had some sort of weird sexual fetish about it . . .'

As he told the tale, with a self-mocking smile, the rustic East Anglian tones in his voice became more pronounced. Kate was tickled by the reminiscence.

'For me it was James Mason in *The Prisoner of Zenda*, leaping out of the window in his tight breeches and riding boots . . .'

Later Duncan had gone on to more sophisticated things. He'd conceived an enthusiasm for the films of Ingmar Bergman, which had not been easy to satisfy in Norfolk. Now, in London, he was catching up with everything he'd missed. His new passion was for Harriet Andersson, the voluptuous heroine of *Summer with Monika*.

'I adore Jean-Paul Belmondo. *A Bout de Souffle* is my favourite movie ever – I've seen it five times.'

'But what about real life?' There was a sharp, but subdued interest in his eyes. 'Have you ever found anyone to compare to Jean-Paul or James?'

'Yes . . .' She thought of Pascal, David Lacoste. 'But that doesn't guarantee they see me in the same way.'

'Aaah.'

'I've had my flings. But so far I've never met . . . well, Mr Right, for want of a better word.'

Duncan nodded towards her glass. 'Another of those?'

'Yes please.'

'What about you?' Kate asked, when he returned with the fresh drinks. 'Have you met anyone who matches up to your idols?'

He sat down, took a swig of his beer. 'Maybe I get too easily carried away . . . There are times when I see perfection in the most unlikely people.'

'Such as who?'

A couple of years ago, Duncan told her, he'd done some decorating in the house of a neighbour, a married woman around forty with kids at secondary school.

'She seduced me. I'd never have dared . . . I was doing her bedroom and the mattress was stacked against the wall. We used to lay it down on the bare floorboards and make love in this completely empty room, with the smell of paint and turps . . .' He narrowed his eyes in the way he had when laughing at himself. 'She had dyed blonde hair with the black roots showing. She used to wear a roll-on and when she took it off there were red welts all across her flesh . . . But at the time I saw her as this complete sex goddess . . .'

'She sounds divine.'

Kate felt suddenly hot, not quite in control. The remark disguised a rush of susceptibility stirred up by Duncan's words. Their talks, up to now, had been general, neutral. Kate had never noticed any provocation or flirtation in his manner, and wasn't sure whether she was imagining it now . . .

To disguise her awkwardness she began to recount her experience with David Lacoste. As she spoke Kate marvelled at the way time had taken care of her annihilating sense of betrayal. Now, four years on, she felt able to present the episode as a story against herself, to hold her pain flippantly at arm's-length. And, of course, there

225

was the name-dropping aspect of the story . . . Duncan was duly impressed.

While she talked Kate watched him. It was as if her perception of him was somehow shifting. As if he were becoming more real to her and, at the same time, more mysterious. Duncan seemed less the boy upstairs, whose presence she took for granted, whose lack of polish she could mentally patronize. She was suddenly aware of him as his own person.

Maybe it was the wine, or the change of setting . . . but in the pearly glow of the lamp above his head, against the background of the dark shirt he was wearing, Duncan's odd, unusual looks – the broad cheekbones, coarse skin, thick fair hair – took on a style and an authority of their own.

As they left the pub it crossed Duncan's mind to put his arm round Kate's waist and establish some sort of physical contact, the way he would have done if she'd been a girl from back home. But he had a suspicion that the gesture would seem clumsy to her, the lumbering overture of a country bumpkin.

'It's gone chilly,' she said and shivered. Over that figure-hugging green dress she had on just her little leather jacket.

'Have my sweater,' Duncan offered. Like the hero in a romantic film, he reflected. Then the girl always looked adorably fragile in the outsize garment.

Kate gave him an amused glance. 'I'll manage, thanks . . . We're hardly in the wilds of Alaska.'

In the cold, white glare of the street-lamps she tapped along on her high-heeled shoes, elegant and very upright. Tonight – with her hair puffed out somehow and those fashion-model black lines swooping across her eyelids – Kate seemed like someone else. A chic, merciless town girl who could have no possible interest in a skint provincial with a deadbeat job, for all he was a potential literary genius.

He felt easier with her the way she usually was, pale and unmade-up, with her hair hanging anyhow. But even then Duncan found himself rather awed by Kate's years abroad, the two intensive years of professional training, her proficiency at her job. And then there was her relationship with Jerome Felix and family . . . It wasn't that Duncan particularly admired the man – he'd always been put off by Felix's self-satisfied smile – just that he himself had never met anyone famous in his life. And now it turned out she'd had some kind of a fling with David Lacoste of all people . . .

But, in spite of all this, as he loped along beside her, Duncan's heart was racing with a wild kind of hope. He had fantasized, of course, about his alluring fellow tenant. But, inviting her for a drink, he'd had no further expectations, he'd meant just that. And yet – amazingly – in the pub Duncan had had the flattering impression that Kate's cool, dark eyes were looking at him in a new way, that her smile held an edge of something he recognized but couldn't quite name – a reluctant excitement, a half-embarrassed provocation. He kept blundering on, harping on women and sex like some bloody pervert, just to keep that tantalizing look on her face. And it seemed to him that she kept crossing and uncrossing her legs, and the swish of nylon made his mouth go dry, and he'd been that close to reaching out and running his hands down their slim, silky length.

'Can I tempt you to a nice late-night cuppa?' God. How obvious could you get? He might as well ask her up to see his etchings.

'OK.' She was amiable, enigmatic, and no doubt cynically aware of the breathless speculation that filled his mind.

They reached home. He followed her upstairs, his heart in his mouth, mesmerized by the tight swing of her hips. She carried on up, past her own door, to his room on the top floor. He unlocked the door and switched on the light. Kate stepped inside.

Duncan screwed up his courage. As he bent to kiss her she wore an odd, defensive little smile. He laid his lips to hers – he'd always noticed and liked their paleness and their smoothness. They were cool from the night air. She made him feel strong and warm. Kate made no move to pull away. With one hand he smoothed her hair, caressed the back of her neck, then pulled her body closer. She let him. Duncan hardly dared believe the evidence of his senses. Could this sophisticated, desirable female really be so accommodating? He

227

slipped his tongue into her mouth, pressed his groin to hers. Still she made no objection.

Though, after a minute or two, Kate stepped back. 'Can't we sit down or something? Take off our coats?'

Nervously he offered. 'I'll put the kettle on.'

She looked at him mockingly, through half-closed lids. 'I shouldn't bother.'

228

Chapter Twenty-Four

❦❦❦

After that night everything was changed between them. Kate and Duncan were an item, a twosome, up and down the stairs between their respective rooms several times each day, sharing gossip, sharing food, sharing a newspaper, familiar with the minutiae of one another's lives. Though their working hours remained separate and inviolable, the couple slept together almost every night. For Kate the anticipation added a sense of excitement to even the most routine of her days.

Almost always they used Kate's room, which was less spartan than Duncan's, the bed a little wider. Kate would undress by the pale light of the small lamp on her desk. Then she would cross the room and join Duncan beneath the sheet. He would smile and make a soft growling sound and gather her against him, envelop her with his long, wiry body and she would be safe and warm.

'I don't half love you,' he would whisper. And the slow stirring of sexual excitement would begin to tingle through her veins and nerve-endings.

Sex with Duncan was like a private, infinitely absorbing, slowly evolving experiment that spilled over into everything else in her life. As she queued in the bank, or stood crushed in the underground rush-hour, or wrestled with some dry technical translation, her mind would fill with pictures. Duncan's hands on her breasts and between her legs, his powerful body crouched above or braced beneath her, his tongue hot and probing. She would recall the closed intensity of his face, the words that jerked from him in the convulsions of passion, revisit her own soft, deep, wet arousal. Her body had changed, seemed vibrant, always ready. She'd never felt like this before. It was as if, at last, she'd been initiated into some fabulous secret.

After they had made love she would drowse luxuriously in Duncan's heavy warmth. In the near-darkness she could picture rather than see his tousled hair and cheekbones, the face expressionless in repose. Kate had never quite decided whether she thought him handsome but his strange, striking looks triggered an irresistible sexual response. She loved the intimacy of the early morning, loved to see him naked in her room, making tea or catching up on yesterday's paper.

At other times Kate saw a sort of mystery in him, liked to surprise him at his typewriter, so that he looked up at her with eyes absorbed and glazed, as if staring blindly from some faraway place. He was secretive about his writing and never showed it to anyone. But one day, when he was out buying groceries, she'd sneaked a look at the manuscript of his novel and been almost disconcerted by the self-sufficient world he'd created out of his own head.

'It was like looking at the submerged bit of an iceberg.' Kate confessed her snooping on the phone to Jess.

She had introduced Duncan to her friend. They took to one another, and some Sunday evenings the three of them would take in the double horror bill at the local fleapit, and afterwards buy chips from the van parked by Warwick Avenue underground station.

'Are you in love with him, then?' Jess asked one evening as she sat marking exercise books in Kate's room while the television flickered in the corner.

Kate was frying eggs on her Baby Belling. For a second or two she concentrated on flipping them over without breaking their yolks. 'Honestly, Jess, I'm not sure. Sometimes I simply ache with adoration . . . And then I'll be put off by some stupid little thing . . .'

The truth was that she harboured reservations, though she knew them to be shallow and unworthy. Sometimes Duncan seemed just too much of a country clodhopper. There was a sweater he wore, knitted by his mother, that Kate just hated – it was battleship grey, too short and too tight, highlighting the thick bones of his wrists, showing his midriff whenever he moved, making him look like Smike in *Nicholas Nickleby*. Then there was the habit he had of eating a whole packet of ginger nuts, dunked in cup after cup of tea. And again, when he visited his family, he would have his hair trimmed up at the local barber's, and the man all but scalped him round the neck and ears and it would be a fortnight or more before he looked presentable again. Small things in themselves but carrying, for Kate, the taint of a fatal provinciality.

Kate knew she was a snob, but couldn't help it. And this was the reason she'd never introduced Duncan to Pascal or to Olivier's crowd. She simply couldn't bear the thought of being tarred, in their eyes, with the same unfashionable brush.

In the early days, unguardedly, Kate talked a lot to Duncan about the Felixes, about their kindness and hospitality, how much she loved their welcoming house. She'd showed him photographs and told anecdotes she thought would amuse him about Nelly and Jerome, rattled on about Pascal's home-movies.

Then, one stifling July evening, the two of them sat drinking tepid beer at the Prince Rupert. They felt sticky and lethargic and began to fantasize about cold things – chilled wine, mountain streams, blocks of silvery blue ice . . . Eagerly Kate started to tell the story of Nelly at Les Rosiers, drinking gin on the windowsill above the freshly fallen snow.

'Can't you change the record, Kate?' Duncan remarked mildly. 'I've actually heard that story at least three times before . . .'

Kate felt her face flush, with surprise initially, but then with an angry heat – the comment made her sound a garrulous nitwit. Haughtily she shrugged her shoulders. 'So sorry to bore you.'

'It's just that, well, you *do* rather put the Felixes on a pedestal.'

'I talk about them, if that's what you mean. They're my family, for God's sake.'

'I just get a bit tired of having them rammed down my throat . . .'

'You talk enough about your boring family.'

'Not half so much and not in the same way . . . I don't act as if the sun shines out of their backsides.'

Kate gave a small, dismissive laugh. 'Well, they're just petty shopkeepers, after all.'

A moment of hostile silence, in which the aftertaste of her words lingered sourly.

Up till then Duncan had striven to keep his tone neutral, tactful. Now his voice held a cutting vehemence. 'They don't pretend to be anything else . . . And anyway, what's so great about that smirking little Cheshire cat of a Jerome?'

In a rush of fury Kate propelled the contents of her glass in Duncan's direction. With savage satisfaction she saw him wince, but the glass was almost empty and the meagre dregs splattered harmlessly across the dark table-top.

'I hate you!' Blindly she scrambled to her feet, turned to leave. Her legs felt weak and trembly, but she kept going and they carried her across the crowded stretch of floor and through the door.

Outside the air was suffocating. Kate was shocked and shaken by the insult to Jerome. Her scalp prickled. Thin rivulets of sweat ran down her body from beneath her arms. She wondered if Duncan would run after her, but he didn't. Back in her room she felt depressed and blushed to recall the snobby little remark she'd made about *his* parents.

Later a knock came at her door. Duncan stood outside, his blue eyes contrite. 'I'm sorry,' he said. 'I was out of order.'

He looked honest and unpretentious, highly attractive with his summer tan. Kate had never been any good at sulking. 'You were,' she said. 'But I was too.'

They went to bed and made love. The sultry weather, the heightened adrenalin, made Kate feel incredibly sexy. Afterwards, as they lay close, Duncan confessed, 'To be honest, I'm jealous of them . . . the Felixes. I want you to love me as much as you love them and I don't think you ever will.'

'But I do,' she whispered, and meant it, in the euphoric after-glow of sex.

But, from then on, both were aware of the Felixes as an issue between them, a subject to be skirted and avoided. Kate mentioned them only in passing, Duncan responded with cool courtesy. It seemed easier that way. Only, deep down, Kate was ill at ease with the embargo. It was like living in two separate worlds, denying one to the other. It couldn't go on for ever.

In early August Nelly wrote to Kate, informing her that she was getting married the following month. As usual the letter was spiced with a copious sprinkling of exclamation marks.

'Robert's the lucky man, in case you were in any doubt!! Be absolutely sure to keep that weekend free!!! We're having a party afterwards, so bring a friend if you want to! Robert sends love . . .'

The announcement came as a complete surprise. For the last four years Nelly had continued in her role as local femme fatale, while waitressing in a country club housed in a big white mansion on a headland overlooking the sea. In letters, over all that time, she had prattled indiscriminately about Mark and Michel and Paul and Ianto, and others too numerous to recall. Robert had been away at university for three of those years, studying for his law degree. Their decision to wed struck Kate as somehow arbitrary, even perverse, specially as Nelly had added, 'PS I'm not pregnant!! I hope you believe me – nobody else does.'

Kate's relationship with her twin had altered. At this distance she was no longer enmeshed in the intricacies of Nelly's day-to-day adventures, an admiring, biddable satellite. In fact, for ages now, Kate had viewed her friend's relentless succession of men with a kind of weary indulgence. She'd come to terms with the fact that she herself would never aspire to the hedonism she used to envy so in Nelly.

But they wrote often and, whenever Kate had the time and money, she travelled down to Wales to visit her friend and drink in the nourishing atmosphere of the Felix family home. A couple of times a year Nelly came up to the big city to see Kate and her brothers, and explore their exciting new playground.

And, whatever doubts Kate harboured at a distance, in the flesh she was still dazzled by her twin, ravished by the vividness of her beauty – the long hot eyes, wayward smile, wild hair, brilliant complexion. Always Kate found herself caught up in Nelly's exuberance,

233

drawn into her laughter and gossip. You couldn't resist. Nelly was a force of nature.

'Bring a friend,' she had written, and it seemed to Kate than an opportunity had been created. Nelly's letter was a catalyst, shaking her out of her inertia. Here, dropped into her lap, was the chance to bring her two worlds together, introduce Duncan to the Felixes, and they to him, for better or for worse . . .Kate was determined to grit her teeth, bite the bullet. It had to be done. Surely, with a little goodwill on all sides, everything would turn out just fine.

Duncan sat halfway down the long Felix family dining table. The room they were in was huge. The house was huge. And outside horses grazed in the setting sun. He felt entirely out of place.

They were eating some kind of stew with small whole onions in it, which he pushed discreetly to the edge of his plate. The meat was in a rich gravy that had a tang of something like unseasoned wood. The potatoes were recognizable as potatoes, but flecked with little bits of what looked like pine needles. Quietly, steadily, he was managing to demolish the unfamiliar fare, but knew his unease made him look glum and disapproving. He was drinking too fast in an attempt to relax.

'Pascal, old man, fill Duncan's glass,' came the full-blooded tones of Jerome, his host. 'Then pass the bottle down to me.'

It felt unreal, sitting at table with this famous face, a face Duncan had casually insulted for years, each time he saw it on the box. In the flesh the man looked more . . . just more human. More vulnerable somehow.

Pascal held the bottle aloft and raised his eyebrows. There was an arrogant assurance about him that put Duncan's back up.

He nodded. 'Yes, I will, thanks.'

At first sight he preferred Olivier, whom he'd studied with a particular covert interest, knowing that once upon a time, years ago, he'd fucked Kate. The younger Felix brother was disconcertingly handsome, but seemed friendly, and the girl he had with him was cuddly and unthreatening.

'You can fill my glass too, if you please.' Pointedly Nelly addressed Pascal.

She was as Kate had described her, scatty and wildly pretty. The sort of girl who had a constant humid, excitable flush to her skin. Juicy, attractive, but somehow exhausting. The moment they arrived she'd taken Kate to one side and he heard them giggling madly.

'Nelly,' Odile demurred, 'don't forget tomorrow . . . Don't give yourself a hangover for your wedding day.'

'Maman, you know I don't get hangovers.' Nelly seized the bottle from her brother and topped up her glass, before walking down to the foot of the table to refill Jerome's. As his daughter bent over him, he smiled up at her with pleasure and pride. And for a second Duncan softened towards him.

The man didn't deserve his wife, though. Duncan was much taken with Odile's calm, classic beauty – her slanting eyes and smoothed-back hair, the olive skin that glowed warmly against a scoop-necked dress the colour of pale sand. She'd welcomed him kindly in her fluent but adorably accented English. And now, as he sat at table, an image flared briefly in his brain – himself in bed alongside a golden, naked Odile, worshipfully kissing her breasts while she lay back with her tranquil smile.

'Duncan.' Suddenly she spoke his name. He blushed. 'Would you like some more of the casserole?'

'No, I'm fine thanks.' How flat he sounded, how lacking in style.

'More for me, please!' Kate held up her plate like Oliver Twist. She sighed yearningly. 'Gosh, I miss your cooking.'

'You are thin, Kate. Do you eat enough?' Odile spooned more stew on to the proffered dish.

'I eat fine – ask Duncan. I'm always forcing him to dine on charcuterie and stinky cheese. Salad too . . . He's an egg-and-chip man at heart.'

'This is true?' Odile returned her grave attention to him.

Duncan felt himself blushing again. 'Well, that's the sort of thing I was brought up on.'

235

He cursed the sheepish tone in his voice. In private he never let himself be cowed by Kate's food snobbery.

'Everyone loves egg and chips,' Jerome soothed, with his annoying smile.

'When did *you* last eat them?' Nelly mocked.

'You don't know what I get up to in London by myself.'

'Whenever I see you you're at Wheeler's or the Gay Hussar,' Pascal put in.

'Was that a cherry cake I spied on the kitchen table?' Kate asked Odile.

'Of course.' Odile smiled. 'You know I always make one when you come home.'

'Wonderfuller and wonderfuller.' Duncan had never seen Kate so straightforward happy as she was here with the Felixes. He begrudged it.

'You can eat a cherry cake, Duncan, I'm sure.' Odile was trying to be nice, but her kindness cast him in the role of finicky brat.

'I should think so.' He aimed at light-hearted irony, but succeeded in sounding merely ungracious. A heartbeat of puzzled silence greeted his reply.

'What're you wearing tomorrow, Kate?' Nelly asked.

'A kind of shift. A bit twenties.' A quick grin. 'And a cloche hat . . . if I dare.'

'You've got to!' Nelly enthused. 'I'm dying to see it.'

'I even stuck some artificial flowers round the brim.' Kate gave a saucy smile, her cheeks pink. How sweet she was. Duncan's heart swelled with a mixture of anxiety and love.

After the meal Jerome lit a black cheroot and disappeared upstairs to his study. Pascal set out in the family car to meet his girlfriend from the station. Kate and Nelly and Olivier adjourned to the kitchen to help Odile with food for the following day. At a loose end, Duncan took his unfinished glass of wine out on to the terrace. The solitude soothed his soul. He took deep breaths of the fresh, fragrant air. The sky was dusky blue and the rough, rolling field sloped away to a misty infinity. Far off, on both sides the dim hulks of headlands loomed above the sea and a lighthouse twinkled in the distance. How free and spacious it all was. No wonder Kate loved it here.

'Catching a breath of fresh air?'

Rosie, Olivier's girlfriend, stepped up beside him – a wholesome, roly-poly sort of young woman in a sugar-pink dress, with flicked-up blonde hair.

He turned and smiled, acknowledging her presence, nodded towards the landscape in general. 'Beautiful, isn't it?'

'Isn't it divine,' she agreed fervently.

Silence. They stood side by side, gazing out at the scenery, a touch awkward.

Then Rosie said, 'They're such a fabulous family, aren't they?'

She spoke with an unforced goodwill that made Duncan ashamed of his own rancour.

'Yes . . . they're nice.' His voice had a hollow ring.

Why couldn't he simply accept the family the way Rosie did, as agreeable, lively, welcoming? Duncan knew the answer straight off, without stopping to think. It was because, in his eyes, the Felixes were rivals – for Kate's attention and love. And he had the helpless certainty that all the odds were stacked in their favour. How could he hope to compete with this big, beautiful house, the telly-star father, the mother with her European sophistication, this brood of handsome, high-spirited siblings who took their own advantages so casually for granted?

'I think it's lovely the way they've sort of adopted Kate,' Rosie continued. 'You can see she genuinely is like one of the family.' She gave a mischievous giggle. 'In fact, Olivier says she's much nicer than his real big sister, Beatrice . . .'

'I'm going inside to top up my drink,' Duncan interrupted, rather brusquely. 'Can I get *you* anything?'

Later on everyone sat round in the enormous living-room and Jerome offered liqueurs. It was cosy, Duncan had to admit, with one door of the French windows open on to field and sky, and candles burning in two tall, branched holders. Duncan sat in one of the squashy armchairs and Kate curled on a cushion at his feet.

237

She leaned against him and he touched her hair, caressing the curve of her neck.

Jerome asked him about his writing and Duncan answered his host's questions but, as the words left his mouth, he ceased to believe in them. As a rule he never allowed himself to doubt his future but tonight his plans sounded, even to his own ears, like the self-deluding dreams of some cloddish Walter Mitty.

His lack of conviction must have showed, because the subject was quickly changed. Jerome seemed far more at ease as Duncan described his job at the launderette, tickled by his account of the drunks he had to chuck out and the prostitute, Rona, who used her weekly laundry session as an opportunity for drumming up trade.

But, after that, the Felixes and Kate began reminiscing and of course Duncan had no idea what they were talking about. To begin with, Kate explained everything, trying to coax Duncan into the fun. But, after a while, she gave up. Amanda, Pascal's pretty, doll-like girlfriend, was out of it too, but seemed indifferent to the fact, as if silence were her chosen element. Rosie asked eager questions, squeaked with amusement, appeared as delighted with their stories as the Felixes themselves. Duncan had drunk an awful lot of booze and it seemed to have made him morose rather than lively.

They were all waiting for Beatrice to arrive, along with Odile's brother and his family. They'd flown in from Paris earlier in the day and were driving down in a hired car. Their absence lent an edgy, open-ended feeling to the evening. Odile was clearly anxious.

Abruptly Pascal announced, 'Amanda's all in. I reckon we'll be heading bed-wards.' As if at a pre-arranged signal they both rose smartly to their feet.

Duncan seized his chance. 'I think I'll turn in as well.'

He hoped Kate would come with him, but she smiled up at him from her cushion and said, 'You don't mind, do you . . . I think I'll hang on for a little while. Beatrice can't be long.'

Arriving that afternoon Duncan had been amazed, even slightly shocked, to discover that the Felix kids were permitted to sleep with their respective lovers under the parental roof. Undressing

238

upstairs in Kate's white-painted bedroom, he felt alone and vaguely depressed. He hadn't particularly wanted to come to the wedding, but Kate had persuaded him. He viewed the visit as a sort of test. And, as he climbed into bed, Duncan was gloomily convinced that he was failing miserably.

His life at present held two precious, private pockets of magic. One was the sheer joy of creating pictures, characters, worlds out of words. The other was the intoxication of sex with Kate. The naked complicity of it. The heady power he apparently possessed to dismantle her coolness and her cleverness, reduce her to a state of fevered lust. He needed that now, he needed her, to exorcize his social clumsiness, to restore his sense of himself.

He tossed and turned and finally slept. Duncan had no idea how much time had passed when the blanket lifted and the mattress dipped as Kate slid into bed beside him.

She felt cold. He wrapped himself around her. She purred with his warmth, but when his hand slid down across her belly and between her legs, she moved to evade him.

'No . . . I'm tired.'

'Please, Kate.' He pressed himself against her.

'It's gone three . . . I'm not wearing my diaphragm.'

'I'll be careful.'

'No, Duncan.'

She turned away from him and soon he heard her breathing, soft and regular. He lay on his back in the darkness, alone with his throbbing; spurned erection.

Chapter Twenty-Five

❦❦❦

Nelly lay in bed, hands laced behind her head, staring at the ceiling. By the filtered light in her room she could see her wedding dress hanging on the wardrobe door, long and white with cobwebby sleeves and yoke. It made her think of a christening robe, the sort of ceremonial garment that bore no relation to real life.

Sometimes she panicked at the thought that Robert had made her choose. When he proposed to her that day on the beach she could have said yes or no. He'd posed the question with a sort of take-it-or-leave-it finality. Something made her accept, but it could have gone either way, and here she was faced with the unlikely reality of her own wedding. By lunch-time she would be Robert's wife.

When it came down to it, she'd said yes because she couldn't face losing him. Since forever she'd taken for granted his presence in her life. Robert understood her. He knew all about her and still seemed to think she was wonderful. She was like a kite, bobbing and shifting and turning with every little breeze and, though she flaunted the fact, it scared her. But it was all right because Robert kept her tied to the ground. If he wasn't there she would go careering away into dizzy space. Robert said if she turned him down, he'd go, he'd find someone else. Nelly couldn't bear that, the thought of her rock, her anchor, her very own, passing into the hands of some stranger.

A muted knock came on the door that led through to Kate's bedroom.

Nelly sat up. 'Come in.'

Kate wore her old Viyella dressing-gown – it still hung in her wardrobe after all this time. Her hair was tangled and uncombed. She squinted to demonstrate to Nelly how bleary she felt. 'How you feeling?'

'Unreal . . . Scared . . . Give me a hug.'

They clung together. Tears welled behind Nelly's eyes. 'I feel as if I'm saying goodbye.'

'You can still pull out, you know.'

'Not a bit of it.' Nelly disentangled herself. 'I like to entertain regrets, but another part is simply raring to go.'

Kate sat down on the bed, grinned through her dark rats' tails. 'I feel like a handmaiden come to minister to the Queen of the May . . . Where are your curlers and the lotion?'

Nelly sat down in front of the dressing-table mirror. Kate began to wind her hair up in outsize rollers.

'What's the time?' Nelly asked.

'Quarter past eight-ish.'

'Duncan awake?'

'No, he's still dead to the world.'

Nelly mused on Kate's new boyfriend. He was prickly, the way Kate had been when she first came to stay with them. He looked sort of *deep* . . . Nelly gravitated to more extrovert men. But Duncan intrigued her.

'I don't think he liked us very much,' she said to Kate.

She surprised a tiny flicker of hurt in Kate's eyes, quickly superseded by a nonchalant smile.

'I'm sure he adored you all.'

The morning was a blur, the house in purposeful pandemonium, what with people arriving and the huge buffet to set out. Kate rushed up and down stairs, helping Odile with the food, then painting Nelly's eyes, brushing out her hair, trying to find time to sort out her own hair and make-up, exhilarated to be so much a part of the family on this very special day. The sun shone and everyone looked smart and unfamiliar in their wedding clothes.

Kate happened to be in the hall with a party of newly arrived guests when Nelly came from her room down the wide staircase. Everyone turned and stared. It was like a scene from a film.

Her dress was lovely, in ivory-coloured, gossamer-thin Swiss cotton, the peachiness of her shoulders and breasts glowing demurely through the lace yolk and sleeves. Like a southern belle she carried the white, wide-brimmed hat she was to wear and its ribbons trailed to the carpet. Her hair bounced on her shoulders in loose waves. Her wide grin and sassy eyes sparkled through the smooth surface of her make-up. Some tension, some intensity inside Nelly seemed to light her up from within so that her presence dazzled with a heightened radiance.

The small group in the hall below responded with a figurative intake of breath, collective oohs and aahs.

'Bellissima!' Dobbsy, Jerome's old journalist friend, raised his arms in triumphant appreciation.

Reaching the ground floor, Nelly stopped and spun slowly round, arms outstretched, to show her dress. The movement was light and playful, the filmy skirt and petticoat billowed, her hair rose and fell. Kate had never seen her twin look more beautiful. The twirl was greeted by a burst of clapping.

Hearing it, Olivier came through from the dining-room, still polishing a wine-glass with a linen cloth, ushering Jerome's mother in front of him, a tiny white-haired widow in an old lady's navy-and-white crêpe dress.

'Grandma.' Nelly stooped to enfold her twiggy frame, enfolding her, lifting her clean off her feet.

'You tinker!' In her pale, powdered face the old woman's eyes sparkled with the fun of it. As Nelly set her down she laughed like a child. 'Silly girl,' she chided happily. 'You'll muss that lovely dress.'

The guests began to proceed in a straggly line up the lane and towards the church, Odile's mind was occupied with smoked salmon and tarragon chicken, pâtés and salad dressings. 'For God's sake, woman,' Jerome had urged, 'get a caterer in.' But she was too much of a perfectionist to offer food that had been prepared with a cold eye to portions and profits.

'This bridal procession is like something out of a Jean Renoir film,' Beatrice said, walking beside her mother in a narrow cream checked suit with an elegant droopy collar – 'Emmanuelle Khanh,' she explained to all who admired it. Her dark hair was centrally parted and drawn back into a black bow. She looked flawlessly Parisian. Odile felt a little in awe of her.

'So sad Grand-mère can't be here.' Her mother was laid up in Lausanne with her hip. Secretly Odile was relieved. Without her autocratic presence everything flowed more smoothly. 'But she's thrilled to tell all her cronies that Nelly's marrying a young lawyer. It's so suitable. I think she can't quite believe it.'

Beatrice raised an eyebrow. 'I think none of us can quite believe it.'

Odile wasn't sure what she thought. Sometimes, guiltily, she pitied Robert, taking on a desperado like Nelly.

Jerome just laughed, sanguine as ever. 'He's got his heart's desire. The rest is up to him.'

But there were times, like today – seeing her in that fairy-tale frock, so carelessly, stunningly lovely, a nymph, a free spirit – when Odile knew she would never think any man good enough for her daughter.

It was one of those perfect September days of sharp, light sunshine.

Kate was charmed by the ragged line of guests in their wedding finery strolling up the lane and along the road to the church. How festive it felt to have her own place among them. Not counting birthdays and Christmases, this was the first real rite of passage she had shared with the Felix family.

Kate was bucked, too, by the acclaim that had greeted her wedding outfit. Her dress was cheap – a waistless, knee-length shift in Madras cotton, dark olive green with narrow stripes of dusky pink. To go with it she'd bought an olive straw cloche that cost twice as much. Kate had pinned a spray of artificial poppies to the hat-band that echoed the grey-pink in her dress. Her shoes were buttoned and pointed and she'd painted them with olive shoe-dye. She felt trim, a little giddy, like a twenties flapper.

Jerome claimed that Kate looked like Clara Bow, his childhood goddess. 'M'dear,' he joshed, 'you've made an old man feel young again.'

Odile pronounced her adorable. Nelly let out a piercing wolf-whistle. The boys joked about the Charleston and the Black Bottom. Even super-stylish Beatrice praised her ensemble. Kate felt elated and ready for a wonderful day. Only one thing jarred her golden happiness – the presence of Duncan walking beside her, silent and morose.

She saw now that it had been a mistake to bring him. She should have introduced him on some less distracting occasion – perhaps over a meal with Jerome and the boys – when she had the time and the inclination to smooth his path, oil the wheels of communication. Not this weekend, not today, when all of her heart and mind was otherwise engaged.

At this moment he seemed a dead weight, a drag on her soaring pleasure in the whole dynamic of Nelly's wedding. Ever since he got up he'd seemed grouchy and somehow disapproving. And right now – wearing his only suit, a relic of his sixth-form years, too tight and badly cut – he didn't even seem fanciable.

'It's a lovely church,' Kate told him, to break the stiff silence between them. 'It's really old and it's got a leper's window . . . You know, where they could peep in and get their fix of religion without infecting anybody . . .'

'Oh, yes,' he replied, with an ironic, feigned interest. The tone of his voice jeered at her half-hearted overture.

She looked coldly at him, annoyed by his unhelpfulness. But he wasn't going to spoil her day. She wouldn't let him. He could stew in his own ill will. She would go her own way, enjoy herself, just as if he wasn't there.

When they arrived at the church Robert was already there, along with his ma and pa and his two toothy little sisters in their blue bridesmaids' dresses, and all the guests that lived locally. Olivier found it deeply disconcerting to see a boy he'd grown up with, right from primary school, decked out as a bridegroom and seeming so at ease with the idea. What was going on in Robert's mind? Olivier couldn't begin to imagine.

He laid a hand on Robert's shoulder. 'Don't forget, man, it's still not too late to pull out,' he joked in Welsh.

Robert grinned, with his freshly cut hair and crisp, dark suit. He nodded towards his sisters. 'Can't disappoint the kids, can I?'

But it was clear he'd no doubts, no second thoughts. None at all. To Olivier his certainty was incomprehensible.

No matter how sunny the day outside, the air within the church was always chill, as if you were entering a place where warmth and pleasure didn't count. Olivier was happy to be sitting next to Rosie whose cuddlesome body exuded a constant low heat. He moved closer, put his arm around her. She smiled, looking pretty, but matronly somehow, in a petally hat and a greenish dress with a frilly collar.

In the pew in front of them Kate sat, very upright, very separate from this boyfriend she'd produced out of the blue. Olivier acknowledged, secretly, that he was vaguely affronted by the fellow's presence. In fact by his very existence. It wasn't that he was jealous, exactly. He'd always been happy for Kate to take up with friends, friends of friends, chaps he introduced her to. But none of them had been important enough to bring to a family wedding.

Kate looked different today. Not quite natural. A bit too dolled up. But Olivier saw through her disguise. She was like a Bisto kid in her mother's hat and shoes. As with Robert, he was sharply aware of the girl she used to be, and still was underneath it all. Olivier was quietly gratified to observe that she was far more interested in being part of Nelly's day, part of a family occasion, than in paying attention to the boyfriend. He looked vaguely pissed off, as if he felt and resented her neglect.

All at once Delia Hughes struck up a wheezy march on the church harmonium, her Clarks sandals working hard on the plush-faced pedals. The vicar, Grumpy Griffiths, led the way down the narrow aisle, followed by Nelly, Jerome and the little bridesmaids.

'Your sister looks absolutely stunning,' Rosie whispered fervently. She was so nice and uncomplicated, seemed to possess no streak of envy or malice.

He smiled at her. 'You do too,' he lied.

As Nelly and his father drew level, Jerome cast his younger son a swift sidelong glance, a grimace that mocked the patriarchal role he was playing. It made him look like a kid and Olivier felt a surge of tenderness.

The austere stone interior was decorated with boughs of mountain ash hung with red berries from the thicket in the churchyard – Odile had an aversion to simpering arrangements from the florist. To Olivier the branches had a primitive, superstitious aura that made the church seem, more than ever, the setting for some outlandish fertility rite without the remotest relevance to real life.

What made people want to do it? To join the straitjacket fellowship of the married? The urge was incomprehensible to Olivier. And why Nelly, of all people, who'd always flaunted her wildness? Why, come to that, a decent, straightforward bloke like Robert? What possessed them suddenly to call on Grumpy Griffiths to declare them legitimate when, since forever, the man had been a joke, with the hairs in his ears, the way he seemed always to be squinting down at the bristles that sprouted from his nose. And why did everyone act so jolly about the whole thing? Olivier shivered in the chilly air. As far as he was concerned, all this social rejoicing covered something alien and nightmarish.

Kate and Nelly sat with their legs dangling over the edge of the terrace. They'd taken off their shoes and stockings. Nelly had hitched her wedding dress to mid thigh. Each held a glass of champagne, recently refilled by Olivier who was acting as wine-waiter while Pascal committed the occasion to celluloid.

'I thought old Grumpy was never going to stop,' Nelly giggled, 'with his "true significance of marriage" address to the nation . . .' Her cheeks were flushed, her eyes slitty and laughing. 'Considering only half the congregation understand Welsh, you'd think he might've settled for the abridged version . . .'

'When you think about it, it's a bit cheeky of him to crack on like he's got the big secret. I mean, does an obscure Welsh country vicar have a hotline to God?'

'You only have to look at him and Sybil . . .'

Kate grinned. 'Point taken . . . They've got the secret, all right.'

'When d'you think they last had it off?'

'Some time in the early forties, perhaps.'

They spluttered with laughter. The joke seemed exquisite. To Kate the day was exquisite. Sitting here with Nelly in the sun, in her favourite place in all the world, the champagne sparkling in her bloodstream. Behind them, from the French windows, the record-player thrummed with the new Beatles record. Two college friends of Robert's circled one another in a fluid, tipsy dance. Red-haired Ros jigged with her two-year-old daughter. The little girl, in her pink dress and frilled bloomers, let out an ecstatic, hiccuping laugh.

The guests had spread out across the sunlit field, lounging in small groups with their food and drink. Kate half closed her eyes, squinting at the light shirts and dresses against the blurred green of the grass. Then she held up her glass to see the sun twinkle through the blond bubbles.

'I'm happy,' she said. 'Are you?'

Nelly looked up at the wide blue sky, studded with tiny fresh white clouds. She tucked her legs against her body, circled them with her arms. 'I feel like water bubbling up a plughole, if that could happen. Swirling and swirling upward . . .'

'Mmm.' Kate pondered her words. They giggled.

In the distance Kate saw Duncan sitting with Robert on the grass. They seemed to have plenty to say to one another. No need to worry about him. She watched Beatrice, deep in conversation with an academic friend of Jerome's. She'd taken off her jacket to reveal a sleeveless crêpe top the warm mid-brown of autumn leaves.

'Beatrice looks so sophisticated.' She had a job in a Parisian art gallery. Kate was awed.

Nelly mused for a moment. 'Why didn't that bastard Lacoste come to my wedding . . .' Then, abruptly, she leaned forward and called out, 'Hey, Mac!'

A tall man was walking up the field towards them. He grinned and waved, broke away from his female companion. Nelly's boyfriend from the summer Kate came back from Switzerland.

'Long time no see!' His greeting embraced them both, but at

once he turned to Nelly. 'So someone's made an honest woman of you at last.'

'At last!' She was indignant. 'I'm practically a child bride.'

'But old in experience.'

Kate recalled that, back then, he'd always harped on Nelly's precocious sexuality. Mac must be thirty now, or almost. He'd thickened, coarsened, though he still had the outdoorsy look Kate remembered, his ruddy complexion heightened by alcohol. Today, in his suit and tie, she thought he looked like a boozy travelling salesman.

With clumsy high spirits he caught hold of one of Nelly's bare feet, tucked over the edge of the terrace. She didn't resist him, but let her shapely tanned foot – the nails pink-painted – lie in his large hand. Briefly, with a light caressing movement, the other hand stroked her smooth shin. He looked up at her, his eyes discreetly insolent.

'Kiss my foot, you dog,' she said suddenly.

With theatrical fervour he took her foot in both hands and laid his lips against her instep. As he did so Nelly sat back in an attitude of mocking languor. Mac began to lick the arch of her foot, glancing up with a kind of brazen complicity.

'Even your feet taste good.'

Then he growled and pretended to take a bite from her big toe. Nelly squealed with a mixture of shock and delight. People turned to stare.

'You bastard!' She kicked out at Mac and almost sent him sprawling.

Kate noticed Mac's woman friend watching their horse-play, blank-faced behind dark glasses. Then Robert arrived.

'Saint Robert!' Nelly called. 'Saint Robert! Save me from this slavering beast!'

He grinned, looking like a handsome head prefect, clear skin glowing against the white of his shirt, the fringe of thick honey-coloured hair falling slantwise across his brow. He stepped up to the terrace and took Nelly by the waist. They smiled into one another's eyes, open as children. He lifted her down on to the rough grass.

'My hero.' She lifted her arms to circle his neck. He bent to give her a long kiss. They clung together, the very model of a young bridal couple. There were claps, a few whistles. Pascal was on the scene with his cine-camera.

Watching, Kate was moved. It was as if, for a moment, all the misgiving and the head-shaking that surrounded their marriage were put to shame in the light of this candid evidence of a love that had somehow survived the bumpiest of rides.

With a twinge of guilt her thoughts turned to Duncan. Her eyes scanned the scene in front of her. There was no sign of him.

'Where did Duncan go?' she asked Robert.

'Thataway.' He nodded towards the far end of the field. 'Maybe he's gone for a stroll on the beach.'

Barefoot, Kate set off towards the stile in the far corner. As she negotiated the path, the sea spread and lapped below her, a calm, dark greeny-blue, studded with the twinkling reflections of the sun.

Far along the flat, shining stretch of sand she saw a lone figure and recognized Duncan's thick crew-cut. His shoes and socks lay at the foot of the path. As Kate stepped on to the beach, he turned, and started to walk back the way he'd come. She waited, then strolled towards him.

His shirt hung open and untucked. His hair was ruffled, his fair, coarse skin flushed a little by sun and wind. In the bright light his eyes looked clear and pale, their expression elusive. The two of them stood face to face.

'I didn't know where you'd got to,' she said.

Simply and naturally they stepped into one another's arms. The action triggered a replay in Kate's mind of the embrace between Nelly and Robert. A truce was called. But they had grievances, both of them, and it solved nothing.

Around six o'clock Nelly and Robert left, in his third-hand Riley, with tin cans tied to the bumper and a sign on the boot saying 'Passion Wagon'. Nelly threw her bouquet – of small red roses from the hedge alongside Odile's vegetable garden – to Ros, in the hope that Andy from the village, the father of her little girl, would do the decent thing and marry her. The newly-weds were catching the overnight ferry to Ireland. As they waved their way off down the lane, all smiles, Kate was seized with a sudden sharp pang of loss.

Their departure was a signal for some of the older guests to leave. But the younger ones hung around the terrace in small groups, talking and drinking, occasionally dancing, unwilling to call it a day, while the sun went down and the sky filled with long streaks of rose and dusky blue. Then they started to hunt for stray glasses, abandoned by guests around the house and grounds. It turned into a game, boisterous and competitive.

As Kate returned her haul to the terrace, it seemed suddenly to have got a whole lot darker. Shouts and laughter rang out from further down the field, as some of the others searched with torches for fresh booty. From the house she heard the scratchy sound of one of Jerome's jazz 78's.

Peering in the lighted French window, she was confronted by the sight of Jerome and Odile dancing a slow and stately jive.

Jerome had changed out of his wedding clothes into a loose Hawaiian shirt. In one hand he held a tall glass of what looked like gin and tonic. Odile had kicked off her shoes and her thick, dark, grey-streaked hair hung to her shoulders. She looked young and light-hearted. As they moved to the music, they smiled and talked.

Odile said something to Jerome that Kate didn't catch, her expression quirkish and amused. He burst out laughing. Kate wasn't sure she'd ever seen them like this before – thinking themselves alone, relating purely to one another. She rattled the glasses she was carrying, to announce her presence, before entering the room.

'Still partying, eh?' she remarked, for something to say.

'We try . . .' Jerome gestured with vague expansiveness, slopping his drink a little in the process. 'Tell us, Kate. You're not going to up and marry, are you, and leave your old foster ma and pa lonely . . . ?'

'Not in the foreseeable future,' she replied, sounding far more vehement than she'd intended.

* * *

Duncan sat and stared out of the train window, baked and drowsy in the hard brightness of the afternoon sun. Kate sat across from him, looking weary after her weekend. She flicked though a magazine pinched from Nelly's bedroom. She crossed her bare legs, tangled her fingers in her limp, dark hair.

Last night at least she'd let him fuck her, made no excuses about tiredness or contraception. But something had been missing. Kate was subdued. Their lovemaking had not brought him the usual rush of power and exhilaration, the conviction that, with his cock, he could cure any and all of the differences that arose between them.

Straight afterwards they fell asleep, but he had come awake in the small hours with a sense of panic, the feeling that something indefinable had happened to sabotage their relationship. In the bustle of packing, leave-taking, Duncan told himself that he'd been imagining things. But, now again, the doubt returned.

Kate leaned forward to show him a picture in her magazine, of a woman wearing what looked like a black leather balaclava, teamed with a leather tunic, leather leggings and long boots. 'This is what we're all going to be wearing this winter, so they say.'

He was reassured by her good humour. 'I could see you in that.'

Kate closed the magazine and laid it on the seat beside her. Like Duncan she began to watch the passing scenery, the early autumn gardens, blooming with mauve and gold flowers, the trees heavy with fruit.

'I love the autumn,' Kate said. 'When it's sunny like this.' A silence. Then she sighed, 'And I loved this weekend . . . Even if they get divorced next week, yesterday was perfect – I'll never forget it.'

He said nothing. And, clearly, silence amounted to criticism. Duncan was only too glad that the weekend was behind him. He felt as if he'd been away for far longer than just two days. He yearned to resume his own life – his life with Kate – and have it proved to him that his doom-laden imaginings were groundless.

The visit had brought home to him how passionately Kate was involved with her adopted family. In the beginning she used to talk about them, endlessly, maddeningly. His protest had called a halt to that. And he had been lulled into the presumptuous illusion that his presence in her world had partially displaced them.

'Say something, then,' she challenged.

'Say what?'

'Anything.' She spread her hands. 'Thank-you-for-a-lovely-time.' She parroted a child's dutiful manners.

'Thank-you-for-a-lovely-time.'

Another silence. Separately they watched the world go by. A sense of danger in the air.

'You didn't like them, did you?' she accused.

'Don't be daft.'

'Did you?'

He shrugged. 'They were OK. They were fine . . . I didn't *love* them.'

'That was obvious.'

With fake innocence he asked, 'What d'you mean?'

'I mean you seemed hostile the whole weekend. As if you thought them all futile and you didn't want to be there.'

The gauntlet was thrown down and Duncan could decide to appease or attack. Appeasement came hard to him.

'And you spent the whole two days acting as if *you* didn't want me to be there.'

She gave a can-you-be-surprised-at-it sort of shrug, to which he didn't rise. Kate picked up her magazine again, and thumbed it distractedly.

Then she looked up again. 'Listen, Duncan, I love them, the Felixes – they're the most important people in my life. They took me in . . . They . . . I couldn't love anyone who . . .' Her eyes were naked and truthful. 'I wanted you to like them. I wanted so much for them to like you . . .'

He was stricken by her use of the past tense, as if both of them knew that her wishes had come to nothing. It made him cold, sarcastic. 'Sorry I didn't do you credit . . .'

She turned to gaze out of the window again. '*You* said it. Not me.'

252

Chapter Twenty-Six

❧❧❧

'Look,' Kate said when they got back to Randolph Avenue, 'I think it'd be better if we didn't see each other for a bit. I feel mixed up. I need to sort out my feelings . . .'

He'd pictured her saying it many times since, standing outside the door of her room, still holding her weekend bag. She'd looked washed-out, waif-like, with beige shadows under her eyes, her hair hanging in rats' tails. In the dimness of the landing her unpainted lips were terribly alluring. In a mental flash he imagined kissing them, holding her, making everything all right.

Instead he shrugged. 'OK, if that's what you want.'

He'd turned away with an air of indifference and climbed the stairs to his room, praying for her to say something else, to call him back. But she hadn't.

The following days were numb and unreal. Each evening he turned up at the launderette and did what he was supposed to. But at closing time Duncan found he had almost no memory of the hours that had gone before. He lived inside his own head, replaying ad nauseam scenes from the wedding, the journey home, and Kate's final, casual bombshell. These images were underscored with dark, private, pornographic clips of Kate, sweet and sexual, that kept his body in an almost constant, futile state of arousal.

During the hours he'd set aside for writing, Duncan sat, stomach clenched, head aching, the pictures coming between him and the blank sheet of paper he'd rolled so briskly into his typewriter, commanding his attention, ousting the increasingly shadowy claims of the novel he was supposed to be finishing.

His moods fluctuated wildly. At lot of the time he sat hating himself, hating the upbringing, the temperament that remained coldly suspicious of people like the Felixes, rich and privileged and carelessly charming. Show-offs, his mother would have said. Phoneys, his father might have added. And Duncan knew he was imbued with the same prejudices, his hackles raised by the easiness of their lives, their concern with style and food and wine . . .

After a while his thoughts would change and he'd feel a surge of savage anger against Kate for choosing them and not him, aligning herself with people who didn't value him, leaving him to sink or swim . . . But then again he would mellow and have a flash of how it must feel to be Kate, let down by her father, her mother dead, belonging and yet not belonging to this substitute family . . .

In bed at night, fuddled by the whisky he'd bought to help him sleep, Duncan fantasized knocking on Kate's door, throwing himself on her mercy, abject and repentant, imagined her cool arms round his neck, the healing intimacy of her naked body. More often he visualized himself simply walking in on her in the dark, climbing into her bed, crushing her beneath him and taking her by force. He conjured up her struggles, her anger, then the grateful, lascivious surrender . . .

In his mind he wrote letters to her, some scathing, some humble. Mentally he polished and improved them. But he never wrote them down, would never send one. At times when he considered himself sane, Duncan's consolation lay in the fact that Kate was ignorant of his turmoil. For all she knew, he'd simply, calmly put their affair behind him. Some primitive male bravado could not allow a woman to understand the strength of her hold over him.

One day Duncan sat down at his typewriter and, in a single vehement session, he wrote an account of the wedding, a sort of rough and ready short story, caricaturing all concerned with spiteful malice, presenting himself as the biggest buffoon of the lot – a lumbering, snarling dancing bear, the grouchy mask concealing a total lack of savoir-faire, the craven yearning to be accepted and admired by the hosts he so derided.

He wondered whether, down in her room, Kate could hear the headlong clatter of his typing. He would have liked her to, but probably she wasn't there. She was out most of the time nowadays. He had no idea where she went.

All that autumn her room gave Kate the horrors. She couldn't bear to sit home, but took to going out each morning, decamping with her translations to the London Library or the British Museum, and working in studious anonymity. At lunch-time she nipped out for a sandwich. The routine made her feel a part of the human race, not a solitary, home-based lost soul. It meant she had to type her translations up later – at home or on the agency's spare typewriter – but, to Kate, that seemed a price worth paying.

Her life with Duncan, Kate decided, had been almost domestic. She'd been lazy, not got out half enough in the evenings, lost touch with Olivier's set.

'Everyone's still here . . .' he reassured her on the telephone '. . . just waiting for you to come and mingle . . . There's a party this Saturday on a barge – there'll be plenty of people you know.'

'Lovely. Can't wait.'

Kate's spirits soared in gratitude. Olivier could always be relied on for some handy fun. She went out and bought a striking new dress – quartered black and white like a flag – and a pair of knee-high boots.

At the party she got drunk and went home with someone called Kelly. Sleeping with him she felt desolate and missed Duncan. Kelly was smug and unimaginative, and his bed looked as if the sheets hadn't been changed in a long while. Still, it didn't matter. He was just a step in her rehabilitation. Sunday morning they met up with some friends of his for late breakfast in a little back-street caff.

Kate's going out, her keeping busy, was aimed as much at the shadowy presence of Duncan as at her own wellbeing. She couldn't bear it to be thought that she was drooping around at home at a loose end. She wondered how he was feeling. Was he suffering at all? Kate had no way of knowing. Abruptly he'd become opaque to her. Bumping into one another, on the stairs or on the way to the bathroom, they said hello, but crouched behind an invisible wall of cagey neutrality.

Staying out became an end in itself, an obsession almost. She aimed never, ever to be home before midnight. One night, sitting with Kelly and two Australian friends of his in some dismal after-hours drinking club, Kate found herself watching the fancy gilt clock on the wall, determined not to leave before one in the morning, though her eyelids were drooping and the bragging conversation of the men echoed scratchily inside her head. This is crazy, she thought, but sat tight with her glass of warm beer until the big hand limped painfully round to the vertical position.

Some nights her friend Jess quite literally threw her out. 'It's all right for you. You can doze over your pad and pencils in the Reading Room. I've got to face 5F at the crack of dawn.'

If Kate wasn't dog-tired before she got to bed, she would lie in the dark, aching for the feel of Duncan's body, aching to be fondled, and for the particular intimate heat of skin on skin. At such times her notion to split with him seemed perverse and inexplicable . . . If only he would knock on the door now, right now.

One evening in November, coming home to change before meeting Olivier, Kelly and some others at the Marquee, Kate switched on the television and saw with incredulity that President Kennedy had been assassinated – shot dead, in daylight, on the open street. She sat for some minutes, staring stupidly at the black and white flicker, not really taking in the urgent commentary of presenters and experts. Assassination was such a . . . historical word, a banana-republic sort of word and yet . . . In a mental flash she pictured her father and Fay gazing at one another in shocked incomprehension.

Then, on an impulse, Kate ran upstairs and knocked on Duncan's door. He wasn't there. She was half inclined to rush round to the launderette and marvel with him at the momentous news but, on reflection, pride and reticence regained the upper hand. Instead, she walked down to the pay-phone in the hall and telephoned Jess.

At Christmas she went home to Plas Felix. Apart from Beatrice, everyone was there, including Grand-mère and Nelly and Robert.

'Your boyfriend didn't seem to like us much,' Jerome teased on the very night she arrived. True or false, the dictum had entered into family folklore.

'Doesn't matter, she's dumped him anyway,' Olivier put in.

And, throughout the holiday, Kate was relieved that Duncan wasn't there with her. Her loyalties were not divided. She didn't have to defend him or act as go-between.

In January, just about a year after they'd first met, she ran into him on the stairs in company with a pretty, long-haired, arty-looking young woman in a grey duffle-coat.

'Off out?' Duncan asked, with impersonal benevolence.

'Just to the pictures.' She was meeting Pascal.

Outside it was dark and cold. A misty drizzle filled the air. Walking towards the underground station Kate felt like the Flying Dutchman, doomed to walk the night-time streets forever. Which was stupid because she'd been chuffed as anything when Pascal phoned to say the two of them *must* go and see the new Godard together, the moment it was released.

Lighted windows on either side made her think of gas fires and record-players, bedsitter cosiness. With a perverse, nostalgic envy she pictured Duncan and the strange young woman drinking tea together from his stripey half-pint mugs.

Chapter Twenty-Seven
1964–5

❧❧❧

Kate pressed the door bell and waited, breathing in great gulps of the light, lovely scent of a big mauve lilac bush that bloomed in the small front garden next door. It almost drowned out the stale smell of dustbin that would otherwise have predominated in the basement area in which she stood.

A skinny, smiley blond man came to the door. Kate was caught off balance. She was expecting Pascal.

'Hi, you must be Kate.' He had a transatlantic accent of some kind. He peered up at the golden evening sky. 'What a fabulous day it's been. Is winter really over d'you think . . . My name's Greg, by the way. I'm Pascal's new lodger.'

As Kate followed him down the cramped corridor that led to Pascal's kitchen, she was struck by the narrowness of his hips in jeans with a Levi flash on the pocket, like her own. Greg assured her that Pascal wouldn't be long. He was round the corner shopping for wine, picking up fish and chips.

They sat down at the red Formica-topped table. She was mildly put out by his presence. Pascal had a new projector and he'd invited Kate and Olivier round to his Notting Hill basement for a nostalgic evening watching home-movies. She'd looked forward to a cosy private wallow.

But Greg was easy and engaging. He'd only recently moved in with Pascal and made Kate laugh talking about the shit-hole he'd just vacated, the oven inches thick in grease which he'd never had the guts to tackle, the dear little mice he used to catch by hand and release into the wild until it dawned on him that there was an endless supply and he'd better find some less labour-intensive way of dealing with them.

'When I first arrived the kitchen cupboard was filled with unwashed milk bottles, and in one of them I found a pair of mouse corpses mouldering quietly into sludge.'

As he told the story Greg wore an irresistible inward smile, while his very blue eyes held hers with laughing complicity. His amusement was contagious. It made her want to respond with the absurd story of Jess's Camden Town ghost, the one that smelled of rotting apples and used to rearrange her lesson notes and hide her Nescafé tin . . . She was in full flow when Pascal got back with the wine and a hot, bulky parcel of fish and chips.

'You've introduced yourselves then.'

'You kidding?' Greg got out the corkscrew and went to work on a bottle of red. 'Already we know things about each other we've never told anyone else.'

A couple of minutes later Olivier arrived and the four of them sat round on the red kitchen chairs, eating fish and chips off the thick, chipped white plates that came with the flat, drinking wine from unmatched tumblers.

Olivier nodded towards two large photographs tacked to the cork board above the fridge. 'That your new bird, then, Pascal?'

The pictures showed a dark-haired woman, all cheekbones and doe eyes and sulky lips, pouting over her shoulder in a rain-swept street.

Pascal examined them briefly, with a gleam of complacency. 'Yes, that's Sofia. She's Israeli.'

'Damnably sultry.' Olivier grinned. 'What happened to Amanda?'

'We drifted . . . Ultimately I found her a touch vapid.'

'Ultimately? I thought that *was* the attraction.'

Pascal sipped his wine, refusing to rise to Olivier's provocation. 'I've never denied rating stupid-and-beautiful over ugly-and-clever.'

'Shallow bugger.' Olivier turned to Kate. 'I bet you'd put brains above beauty any day.'

'Don't be so sure.' She speared a crispy-looking chip on her fork. 'Anyway, I'm no authority. My taste in men is notoriously deluded.'

Kate spoke playfully. She felt happy. It was spring. She had wine and the best of company, a brand-new pair of Levis, a chic skinny sweater. At this very moment all was right with the world.

Olivier appealed to Greg. 'What about you? Beauty or brains?'

The new lodger pulled a quirkish face. 'Beauty's too much responsibility for me . . . It's like dating a woman with really large breasts . . .' He grinned. 'You feel pressurized to keep admiring them, mentioning them, leering at them . . . I guess I'd rather have cute than beautiful – and small tits.'

Pascal laughed. 'You're in, Kate.'

Later they adjourned to Pascal's room. He blacked out the windows with army-surplus blankets and rigged up a screen. Kate bagged the big, padded armchair. Olivier and Greg sat on the floor at her feet. Pascal set the projector running.

The first picture to appear on the screen – rather wobbly as Pascal adjusted the focus – was Kate, lounging on the terrace, back in the hot summer of '59, reading Pascal's *Cahiers du Cinéma*. She wore shorts, a black top and black sunglasses. How tanned she was. How young she looked. The camera angled round her, creating a series of pleasing skewed images, then zoomed in on the magazine until the words *Cahiers du Cinéma* filled the screen.

The pictures brought back to Kate, sharp and clear, the way she'd felt that day. Flattered, embarrassed, but determined to hide the fact. She recalled the sun on her limbs, the breeze that ruffled her hair, cooling her scalp, her elation at being back with the Felixes.

'Too cool.' Greg turned to crane up at her. 'You treated that nosy cameraman with the contempt he deserved.'

The camera panned across the field – Olivier and Kate exclaimed at the pale straw colour of the frazzled grass – and returned to the house. Its familiar lines were etched on Kate's heart.

Greg whistled at the size of it. 'You live there, Pascal? I'm sick with envy.'

Suddenly flames filled the screen. Bonfires in the dark. The beach below the house that summer. Familiar figures capering for the camera, lit up by the fierce, flickering coral light.

'There's Megan!' Olivier said. 'And Eddy. And look, Kate,

260

there's that kid down from Birmingham who reckoned he was the spitting image of Gene Vincent.'

There was a deal of beach footage. It was bliss for Kate to relive that time, to see Nelly wild-haired and grinning, scuffling with Mac, boyish Olivier swigging beer from the bottle. Ros dancing drunkenly as the waves lapped round her ankles. Kate herself, in a bikini top and shorts, laughing and kicking water at Pascal filming her. She was overwhelmed with a secret pleasure at being a part of it all. And it was fun explaining things to Greg, who seemed intrigued and curious.

Suddenly it was daytime again. David Lacoste stepped from his Deux Chevaux, smoking a Gitane, raising one eyebrow at the camera. Looking a touch self-conscious, Kate thought, but undeniably seductive.

For Greg's benefit, Pascal explained who he was, adding cheekily, 'He and Kate were like that for a while . . . weren't you, Kate?'

'Yes, for my sins.' She was amused and not displeased by Pascal's good-natured innuendo, the anguish of the episode lost in time. 'Before Beatrice swept him off his feet.'

'Let's have something more recent.' Pascal changed the reel.

It was last summer, Nelly's wedding. The ragged procession to the church. Candid shots, filmed at the reception, of family and guests, waving and grinning or coyly turning away, playing the drunk or gazing into the camera lens with emphatic composure. Nelly and Robert locked in an embrace then, separating, seeming to grin at the unlikeliness of the whole carnival, like two kids in fancy dress. Then came a panoramic shot of the guests, gathered to toast the bridal couple. Kate's eye was drawn to Duncan, but his face gave nothing away. Neither Pascal nor Olivier remarked on his presence. For them, clearly, he had passed into history.

The first thing Kate noticed about Greg Dillard was the way he seemed always to be amused, amiably and without malice, at the world in general. The inward laughter showed through in his slightly prominent blue eyes, in the habitually bemused expression on his skinny face. It made him easy to be with. He simply shrugged away all tension, all awkwardness, all potential conflict, with his good-natured smile, his air of infinite tolerance.

He was Canadian. At twenty-four, a year older than Kate. And, so he informed her on their first date, a perpetual student.

'It's the ideal way of life . . . The moment I begin one course I'm on the trail of the next, researching grants and scholarships and things . . . I'll carry on like this until I'm ninety if I can swing it.'

At present he was at the London School of Economics – 'on a Moody scholarship', he told her, pulling an appropriately long face.

But he went on to explain that the late Rufus Moody had been a mine-owner with a social conscience, who'd left a seemingly bottomless bequest for the furthering of travel and study among succeeding generations of young citizens of Sudbury, his home town. 'All power to the man, though he keeps us on a tight budget.'

Greg was medium-tall and wirily built, with mousy blond hair, cropped short. His face was lively and pared-to-the-bone thin. He wasn't handsome but had an impish quality that people were drawn to. Left to himself, he wore a sort of uniform consisting of jeans and a grey sweatshirt – he had several of each – that looked washed-out, sun-bleached.

'Can I call you?' he'd asked at the end of that first evening at Pascal's.

'That'd be nice.' Expansive with wine and company, Kate had not played hard to get.

Greg took life effortlessly. He took it as it came. And, once they started seeing one another regularly, he seemed to bestow the same ease on Kate. She was never beset by the reservations, the no-go areas that had hedged her about during her time with Duncan.

With Greg, for the first time, she discovered the pleasure of being an established couple. It meant never having to go to the pictures by yourself. It meant foursomes – trying out the pretentious new Italian Restaurant in Westbourne Grove with Pascal and his Sofia. It meant going to Olivier's parties simply to have fun, without the ambiguous pressure of being a single woman on the loose.

In July Kate and Greg spent a long, hot, lazy weekend at Plas Felix. In carefree contrast to Duncan, Greg relaxed immediately into the rhythm of the household, helping Odile to make a huge salade niçoise, flirting tongue-in-cheek with Nelly, drinking brandy and smoking skinny black cheroots on the terrace with Jerome and Robert after dinner . . . At midnight Kate and Greg went skinny dipping with Nelly and Robert and it seemed the most natural thing in the world. Throughout the visit Kate felt blessed, as if all the strands of her life had meshed to form a harmonious and enviable whole.

'I like your young man,' Odile commented, as she and Kate made a contemplative tour of the vegetable garden. 'And Jerome thinks he's good for you . . . You look so well and pretty.'

'He's a bit of all right,' Nelly enthused, kissing Kate goodbye on the station platform. 'You've hit the jackpot this time.'

Kate glowed with the general approval. And, on the journey home, Greg raved about the Felixes and their hospitality, the house, the setting, the whole weekend.

Kate spent less time than ever in her own digs now. At weekends she decamped to Greg's, lock, stock and barrel. It was a bonus too, seeing so much of Pascal. And Sofia, though moody, could be good company. Sometimes she and Pascal had great noisy, volatile rows – you could imagine yourself in an Italian movie. But Greg usually got them laughing again with some silly joke, the unruffled conviction he radiated that nothing was really serious.

One Sunday night in September, returning home to Randolph Avenue, Kate saw that Duncan's door stood open. Going up to investigate, she found that all his belongings had been removed from the sparsely furnished room. He must have moved out. He hadn't warned her he was going, had left no forwarding address. And though she'd paid almost no mind to him in the last months – caught up as she was in the exhilaration of her affair with Greg – Kate was hurt by the way he had vanished, just like that, without saying goodbye.

If she'd only known he was going, maybe they could have salvaged a sentimental farewell, parted with a nostalgic, no-hard-feelings sort of hug, stayed friends, stayed in touch, looked one another up every so often. That would have been nice.

Greg backed her against the wall of her room and raised her skirt, exposing her suspenders, knickers, the tops of her fashionably lacy stockings. He groaned lustfully at the sight.

'We're late already . . .'

'So?' Ignoring her half-hearted protest, he slipped his hand between her thighs, began to rouse her with an insistent, practised hand. Kate arched towards him, abandoning any thought of resistance.

She closed her eyes but could picture his face, closed and somehow ruthless, a fevered, glittering look in his eyes. Greg's everyday manner was so amiably loose and relaxed that his passion startled and impressed her. It came suddenly, as if some alien force had entered his whipcord body, compulsive, driving him.

'Oh, Katie, you're so . . .' He completed the sentence with an expressive, lewd, guttural sound.

She was weak and wet with arousal. Greg unzipped his jeans. His penis reared dark and assertive. He guided it into her, began to thrust with an air of ecstatic relief, like a bucking horse loosed into an open field.

Kate felt her own orgasm approaching, taking hold, convulsing her with sensations of piercing, edgy pleasure. Greg lunged harder, groaning, his hands gripping her buttocks, pulling her on to him. His climax came hard and fast in a final frenzied thrusting. He clung to her, kissed her over and over. 'You're so perfect, baby . . .'

Disengaging herself was anti-climactic. Her room looked prosaic under the bright electric light. Kate pulled down her skirt, went downstairs to the bathroom to wash. Times like this there was a breath of nostalgia – diffuse as smoke – for the way it had been with Duncan. Making love in warm, blind comfort at the dead of night. The way she felt afterwards, drowning in delicious languor.

Greg's attitude to sex was different. He was invigorated by it. Tonight he saw it as an appetizer for the evening to come. Tonight Kate had felt obscurely oppressed by his advances. They were going out to a party – she was dressed and made-up, ready. Only she didn't want to be seen as the kind of woman who worried about her hair getting mussed. She'd played it Greg's way and, admittedly, she'd enjoyed it. His hot, hard lust had a way of infecting her. But now she felt let down. And they *were* late and her dress was creased.

Greg loved to make love in impromptu, even risky situations. In the park at night. In the car he sometimes borrowed from a fellow student. In his room, with Pascal and Sofia, and maybe others, talking and laughing a few feet away, beyond the communicating door. Many times, most times, Kate was aroused by his recklessness . . .

In the bathroom she washed between her legs, brushed her hair and touched up her make-up. Returning back upstairs, she found her ill humour had partly evaporated.

They managed to hail a taxi. From the window Kate stared out at the October night sky, a dark, dramatic claret colour. It was election night and she'd voted for the first time earlier that day. Almost everyone she knew was hoping for a Labour victory. No one her age could recall anything other than the Tories in power. What with the Profumo affair, the jibes of *TW3* and *Private Eye*, they'd become a laughing stock. It was high time for a change.

She and Greg had agreed to call for Jess and Jess's boyfriend, Bill, before going on to Olivier's to wait and watch the results as they came in on television.

'They'll wonder where we've got to,' Kate said.

'They'll guess.' Greg was nonchalant. He lounged sideways on the back seat of the cab, one hand resting on Kate's thigh.

Times had changed. Kate no longer kept her friend Jess in a box, hidden away from the august gaze of the Felix brothers. She was out in the open now, acknowledged, included quite naturally in casual invitations. And Kate blushed to recall her own snobbery.

It was Greg, again, who'd worked the magic. He was easy with everyone. Everyone liked him. He could never have understood Kate's private embargo as regards her friend. With Bill – Jess's big, booming, long-haired history teacher – they formed another amiable foursome.

'Come to my place on Sunday – I'm cooking brunch,' he'd urged them back in the summer term.

They'd come – and met Pascal and Sofia, and they'd all had a perfectly nice time. And Pascal hadn't appeared to think any the less of Kate for her rather schoolmarmish friend. And soon enough Jess and Bill had met Olivier and become one of the shifting crowd of friends and acquaintances he kept swirling around him like a juggler with his clubs. And, again, Kate marvelled at the way Greg – with his infinite good nature – had unified and simplified her life.

'What sort of a time d'you call this?' Jess greeted them with cheerful belligerence.

She'd changed her hair recently and wore it in a Vidal Sassoon bob. But even now, in a Mary Quant shift and up-to-the-minute Courrèges-type boots, she remained her sturdy, earthbound self.

'Sorry,' Kate said.

'We got waylaid,' Greg explained innocently.

Jess gave him a sceptical glance.

The taxi was crowded now, mainly due to the presence of Bill, who was six-foot four and long-legged, with the beginnings of a paunch lapping over the waistband of his jeans. He had a big, boyish face and his limp brown hair straggled down to the collar of his jacket.

'Who did you vote for, Bill?' Kate asked. 'If it's not top secret.'

'Spoiled my paper.' Bill was a Marxist, though a lazy one, who dreamed of – rather than working towards – revolution.

Currently Olivier lived in Muswell Hill, in a huge bare flat with five other people. But Olivier's arrangements were always temporary affairs. His page in Kate's address book was a series of crossings-out and scribbled alterations, bearing witness to his zigzagging progress through a haphazard selection of the postal districts that fell within the ring formed by the North and South Circular Roads.

The cavernous flat was crowded, the lights heavily shaded. It was like entering some smoky underworld. In the big, shared living-room the television was on and had already attracted a crowd, though so far the menu consisted of waffle rather than hard results. People danced in the broad hallway and spilled over into an adjacent bedroom.

Advancing through the press, Kate encountered a sprinkling of familiar faces, but it was some time before she spotted Olivier, sitting on the floor in a corner of the living-room, talking to a red-haired woman. Both were smoking. Kate tapped him on the shoulder. He glanced up, pale in the dim light, heartbreakingly beautiful with his spiked fringe and long eyelashes, his air of sweetness. But there was something glazed about him. He offered her a puff of his thin hand-rolled cigarette.

'It's hash,' he said. 'Tom gets it. Try it.'

She was dubious. 'What'll it do to me?'

'Only one way to find out.'

She took several tentative drags of the cigarette. Nothing dramatic happened. She discerned, perhaps, a kind of muffled wellbeing, but it was hard to separate it from the effects of the rough red wine she was drinking.

In the L-shaped bedroom off the hall Kate came across Pascal, Sofia, and Sofia's friend, Lisa, trying out the snappy line-dance Pascal had seen and loved in the new Godard film. Kate joined them and so, after a bit, did Bill.

'You won't get me making a prat of myself.' Jess opted to skulk on the sidelines. But she took charge of the music, stopping and starting a Supremes track as required.

Kate noticed Greg lounging in the doorway with his crooked smile, chatting to a man she didn't know. When the dance was finished Kate walked over to them.

'Exhibitionist.' Greg's eyes were laughing. He drew her affectionately to his side and kissed her cheek. He presented her to his companion. 'This is Kate . . . my girl.'

Kate was charmed by the easy tenderness in his voice, and secretly proud to be so publicly claimed by this popular and desirable man.

Quite soon the results began to come thick and fast. Almost everyone adjourned to the living-room. The television was turned up and each new Labour victory greeted with whoops and cheers.

At this stage it seemed a potential landslide. Kate was infected by the euphoria. The old farts would be swept away. A new, forward-looking regime would take control. Greg was as involved as she was. He boggled constantly at the aristocratic old buffers who held power.

There was a lull in the flow of results and the man with the swingometer embarked on an ebullient analysis of the situation. Kate and Greg wandered out into the scrubby garden. They stood hand in hand looking up at the fading moon and at the black outlines of the trees. To Kate they appeared extravagantly beautiful.

'I smoked a bit of Olivier's hash cigarette,' she said. 'I'm not sure if I feel any different or not.'

'You danced pretty,' Greg replied.

Kate suspected him of mockery and shot him a sceptical glance. But the look on his face was impressively serious. In a sudden, silent rush of feeling he turned and took her in his arms, kissed her over and over, softly, sweetly. She was moved by his sincerity, his fervour.

'I don't want to lose you,' Greg whispered. 'I want you to come with me. Wherever I fetch up next. I want to marry you.'

Kate was incredulous. She was used to his lightheartedness and his sudden urgent lust. But this earnestness was something new. She gazed at him, struck dumb.

'Kate, say something,' he begged, a hint of laughter returning. 'Let me off the –'

'Do you mean it?'

His grin mocked both Kate and himself. 'No, I was just kidding . . .' He rolled up his eyes in disbelief. 'Yes, I mean it. I mean it. What d'you say?'

Kate felt as if, far off, she'd glimpsed a tiny point of light, which – as she assimilated and considered his words – came closer, opened up, grew larger, brighter. What Greg proposed seemed the most delicious of options. To marry him, go somewhere with him . . . not even to know where. The adventurous haziness of the prospect was seductive, delightful . . .

Dawn was beginning to break, the sky lightening. Kate hugged herself, shivering a little with the cold, with wonderment. She smiled into Greg's blue eyes. 'It sounds a brilliant idea.'

'Does that mean yes?'

'Yes.'

The election turned out not to be the projected landslide. But Labour did win and, in the months that followed, there was a honeymoon feeling in the air that seemed somehow tied in with fashion and pop music, Britain's surprising new image as chic and avant-garde.

And that atmosphere was reflected in Kate's own personal life. The sense that she'd come in from the wilderness, from a kind of drifting, that her life was delightfully mapped out. She'd found her man. He was sexy and amusing and everyone liked him. All her problems were solved. She belonged.

Just occasionally, in the lonely small hours, Kate would lie awake, clenched and sweating. She'd entrusted her happiness to Greg. He thought her this beautiful, clever, uncomplicated girl. But Kate knew the shadowy double that crouched inside her. A needy, contemptible wraith with no home to call her own. A creature Greg had never met. But, next morning, her terrors would have shrunk to manageable size. She'd feel OK and trust the luck that had brought her this far.

'Pray God the blessed Rufus Moody doesn't let me down . . .'

Among others, Greg had applied to the Institut des Sciences Politiques in Paris. His mother was French-speaking, Greg pretty well bilingual. He'd been accepted subject to financial viability. In April he received the news that the Moody Foundation agreed, provisionally, to cough up. Unless he flunked his final economics exams, they were home and dry.

Kate wrote nothing to Ellis of all this. She had the suspicion that, if they knew, he and Fay would want to take charge, to hijack the wedding, as if in compensation for their own selfish happiness, their sense of guilt, hers of grievance and neglect. They might decide to make the trip to England and turn the ceremony into some big production that had nothing whatsoever to do with her and Greg . . . That wasn't going to happen. She would break the news to them only when it was too late for them to do anything about it.

'We'll make it quick and easy. Just a few friends.' Greg's parents were too tied up with their central-heating business to take time out. And, anyway, he was one of four and his elder sister was getting married that summer as well.

'Just the Felixes and Jess,' Kate agreed.

They got married at Kilburn registry office one bright, blustery Saturday morning in June. Jerome and Odile were there, *in loco parentis*. Nelly – radiantly, chubbily pregnant in a striped chiffon dress – came on her own. Robert was working all the hours God sent on some long-running inheritance suit. Olivier, fragile and hungover, hid behind a pair of wraparound sunglasses. Jess and Bill toted twin Whiteley's carrier bags containing the sheets and pillow-cases they'd bought as presents. Sofia looked film-star exotic in a pale crochet dress worn over a flesh-coloured body-stocking. Pascal switched deftly between his two roles as ring-bearer cum provider of taxis, and official photographer.

The ceremony was short and to the point, and afterwards they all journeyed by cab to Soho, where Jerome presided over a long, drunken lunch at the Gay Hussar. Then Kate and Greg caught the overnight sleeper to Paris, where they allowed themselves a week's honeymoon before they started looking for somewhere to live.

Chapter Twenty-Eight
1966

❁❁❁

'For God's sake, Kate, have another of these pastries. I don't want to be left with a plateful of these fattening things.'

Beatrice held out a dish containing three elegant confections of fruit and crème patissière.

Kate was full but she took another, simply because they were there and delicious and expensive.

For their regular Wednesday afternoon tea-date Beatrice always provided posh cakes, but never ate more than half a one herself, though she drank cup after cup of Earl Grey tea and smoked almost continuously.

'Well, how was it last Saturday . . . the party?' They saw one another so regularly now that Beatrice was up to date with Kate's social life.

'Excellent . . . Good fun.' Kate's reply was bland, though she had a mental flash of Greg fucking her, upright, in someone's darkened bedroom. Living dangerously as usual. But knowing that, if they had been discovered, the reaction would have been amused, approving. Nobody would have been shocked. 'We got home at six in the morning and slept all day Sunday . . . Except we went out for a bite of supper at the Pendule in the evening. It was a bit of a lost weekend . . . What did you do?'

'Oh . . . cleared up some things at the gallery Saturday morning. Did some shopping, read a book. Saw David in the evening . . .'

'Did you go out anywhere?'

'No. We stayed in. David was tired.' Her attitude, though not precisely cagey, didn't encourage further questioning.

She leaned back in her smart armchair, upholstered in some tastefully coarse gunmetal grey material with a slight sheen on it.

Beatrice drew on her cigarette and crossed her slim legs in smooth greyish stockings. Tights were taking over but Beatrice never wore them. 'David detests them,' she'd explained, more than once. Her dress was in charcoal wool, soft in texture, but short and trimly cut. Her glossy hair was centrally parted and drawn severely back.

She looked exquisite and her room was exquisite, with walls of a strong grey-blue, grey-blue curtains, the simple, elegant but comfortable gunmetal chairs, tinted mirrors engraved with a fluid border of stylized leaves and flowers, the subdued colouring enlivened by a bowl of cream-coloured hyacinths, cream cushions in textured silk, hand-embroidered with abstract designs in coral and dark grey. Everything in her comfortable little flat seemed chosen with discrimination, deliberation.

'Amazing happenings . . . You wouldn't believe . . .' Animatedly Beatrice began to relate the continuing saga of a juicy art-fraud involving some startlingly big and reputable names. Kate listened with half an ear. In itself the story was mildly intriguing, but the characters meant nothing to her.

When she and Greg first arrived in Paris, Kate had been shy about contacting Beatrice – she had always been a touch awed by the elder Felix daughter's self-sufficiency and savoir-faire. But Beatrice had greeted them with enthusiasm and warmth.

Greg and Kate had found a studio flat at the top of a tall house in a little side street off the Boulevard Raspail. By way of housewarming Beatrice had bought them a set of hand-painted Art-Deco plates. Kate stood them up on a high shelf opposite the window where they radiated a kind of raffish glamour that was in keeping with the glorious bohemian shabbiness of the room.

And when the translation agency, with whom Kate had signed on, turned out to provide less than a steady flow of assignments, Beatrice put her in touch with an antiques firm, who offered intermittent flurries of work – correspondence and catalogue-text to be put into English – and paid rather well for it.

Once in a while the three of them met up for dinner at an unpretentious but well-reviewed little bistro in the Rue de Varenne, the venue chosen by Beatrice. It was cosy and candlelit, had check tablecloths and big mirrors and served a hearty, spicy *couscous au poulet*. In Beatrice's eyes this was semi-slumming but the prices had Kate mentally re-jigging their slender budget.

Greg was impressed but not overawed by Beatrice. He treated her with a teasing flirtatiousness which she seemed to enjoy, twitting her amiably about her designer clothes and Faubourg St Honoré style, comparing it to his own student scruffiness. Beatrice laughed back at him, narrowing her long eyes – so like Odile's, Pascal's, Nelly's – and once again Kate blessed Greg's easy way with people.

But Beatrice always set limits on their intimacy. She never introduced them to David Lacoste, though he was a potent off-stage presence, his opinions quoted frequently, the ups and down of his on-going career described at length. David just hated the new Louis Malle film, adored the Latour exhibition, had a certain grudging affection for de Gaulle in spite of his politics, told Gallimard he wasn't going to be messed around . . .

There seemed little room in her life for spontaneity. You met Beatrice by appointment only. It was she who had suggested to Kate the regular Wednesday tea-date. Which presumably she must value, because she'd only ever cancelled twice.

But there was always a sense that Beatrice held herself aloof in some way, that her relationship with Kate – and Greg – was not altogether a friendship between equals. The feeling was elusive, but it was there . . . Was it a question of age – she was three years Kate's senior – or of money? Or, on the contrary, did the attitude stem from Kate herself, from the hero worship that had coloured her view of Beatrice ever since she'd first met her at the age of fourteen?

And, in fact, it wasn't quite that simple. Because, at the same time, Kate sometimes felt almost sorry for Beatrice. Her own life with Greg, and the new friends they were making, was rackety and easy-going. Beatrice always seemed so controlled. It was as if, at twenty-eight, she already belonged to an older and more formal generation.

'. . . So anyway,' Beatrice was concluding, 'All they can do is wait for the outcome of the legal proceedings and that might take years . . . And Bermann will be sweating on the top line for all that time. And his reputation isn't exactly enhanced by it . . .'

'What a swinish situation,' Kate exclaimed, although she hadn't followed the precise twists and turns of the story.

For some reason this prompted her to tell Beatrice about a tweedy American academic Greg had met at the Institut who might need a research assistant for the following year. 'Something like that would perk up our finances rather nicely.'

'Greg'll swing it if anybody can. He'd charm the spots off a leopard. Or the dollars from an academic's wad.'

'Fingers crossed.' Kate never cared for the suggestion that Greg's charm was in any way deliberate. She glanced at her watch. 'Time I was going . . . I've got to work this evening. Got a rush job on.'

Beatrice looked at the pastries. 'What am I going to do with these?'

'Eat them?'

Instinctively Beatrice glanced down at her slender body. 'I don't do cakes . . . What about Greg?'

'Need you ask?'

As Beatrice parcelled them up, Kate put on her shiny black mac. She adored it. It was short and sharp, conferring instant chic on the wearer. She kissed Beatrice goodbye and went downstairs, out into the cold, black February streets. Kate always walked home from Beatrice's. At this point in her life the winter weather could not depress her. It had been raining and the lights from the shops were reflected in the dark, wet pavements. Beatrice lived in an agreeable, unpretentious neighbourhood between the Eiffel Tower and the Invalides. Every few yards Kate was assailed by delicious food smells from some grocery or restaurant. She would stop off on the way home and buy a couple of portions of Brittany fish stew to take home for their supper.

It always struck Kate, as she started up the bare, hollow-sounding staircase of their apartment building, how she just couldn't wait to get to the top and back to the room she and Greg called home, their wonderful warm, familiar womb, the haven that made her recall her days in Maida Vale with a shudder. And yet, objectively speaking, it was just as tatty. Only its tattiness was foreign, and it was shared with her husband. Greg. Her husband. As Kate reached the top floor the timer light went off and she saw an amber strip of brightness under the door. On the dim landing she smiled to herself. He was home.

Greg must have heard her footsteps because he'd laid his book down on his lap and their eyes met the moment she opened the door. And, as always, her spirits soared at the sight of his thin, familiar, smiling features. He lounged by the electric fire in one of their uncomfortable 'easy' chairs, a cushion squashed behind him. He wore jeans and the big, black knitted jacket he pulled on over his sweatshirt when the weather was cold.

'God,' he greeted her. 'You look sexy in that mac.'

'I always look sexy.' She bent and kissed him, elated as ever by his presence in the flesh, the wiry physicality of him. 'Mmm, it's warm in here. It's a dog of a night out ... I've brought us some *cotriade* for supper ... And Beatrice sent you some cakes.'

'God bless the marquise. How was she?'

'Fine. Same as ever. Ravishing. Elegant.' She dumped the bag with the food on the table and began to unpack. 'Let's eat right away before it gets cold ... Is there any wine left?'

'No, I drank it all.'

'You ...' Kate exclaimed accusingly, then saw him laughing and grinned herself. 'You lie, dog.'

'You ask so airily, but you'd have been pissing steam if I had.'

He got up and took her in his arms, held her to him and kissed her mouth. Then he crossed to a cupboard, got out the two V-shaped glasses with twirly stems they'd bought at the flea-market, and a half-full litre bottle of red wine. He poured them both a drink.

'*Santé.*' Greg took a slug of his and refilled the glass.

Kate spooned the stew into two dishes, giving Greg the lion's share. They sat down, on opposite sides of the small table by the window, where they also worked. Kate loved eating here with, on her left, the dark shapes of wet rooftops reflecting the neon glimmer of the sky and, to her right, the cosy clutter of their room.

The stew was salty with fish, filling with potato, tangy with cloves, bayleaf and thyme. The wine was cheap and gutsy. Under the table she moved her foot to touch Greg, to be in contact with his warmth and solidity.

He looked up from his meal and grinned, rubbed his leg against hers. 'You coming to the Trestrignel later? I told Luc I'd see him there.'

'Can't. I've got to work.'

'There's always tomorrow.'

'That's when it's due back. If I finish early I'll come for a drink.'

'Nah. Give it a miss this time . . .'

She glanced at him through lowered lids. 'Get thee behind me . . .'

Kate felt no resentment at the fact of having to work. In fact it was almost a pleasure to sit warmly ensconced, with her typewriter and a coffee at their table, in their room, knowing that – if the mood took her – she could join Greg at any time.

The translation, from the agency, was an unusual and comparatively pleasant assignment, a film-treatment, and the sort of thing she could do almost as fast as reading aloud.

From time to time Kate looked up from her work, and looked about her, absently absorbing details of this private space, this room in a foreign city, where she could say with certainty – right now, not in retrospect – that she was happy.

A largish studio flat, the ceiling sloping towards the window with the pitch of the roof. The walls a weathered cream colour, the paint flaking off in places. Furnished with an ugly and mismatched selection of basics – a bed, a wardrobe, a table, shelves, and two ugly, chunky foam-rubber easy chairs upholstered in beige mock-crocodile.

Other than an electric kettle, they had no means of cooking. Kate was charmed by the feckless necessity for eating out, or bringing home bread, cheese and charcuterie, or unfamiliar ready-cooked delicacies like tonight's *cotriade*.

But what pleased her most about the room was the mingling

276

of their personal effects and possessions, hers and Greg's, setting their stamp on the neutral surroundings, bearing witness to their joint reincarnation as a married couple.

Their books were jumbled together on the shelves, their clothes in the wardrobe. The Braque reproduction Pascal had given Kate hung on one wall, and on another was Greg's Toulouse-Lautrec print of a naked woman pulling on her stockings – the acceptable face of pornography, so he claimed. Greg's Indian counterpane, with its lines of red and blue elephants, covered the bed, and beneath it was the striped blanket Kate had borrowed from her room in Plas Felix. Beatrice's Art-Deco plates paraded across the high shelf opposite the window. And above their bed the two of them had created a montage of pin-ups, family and friends. Bob Dylan and Jeanne Moreau rubbed shoulders with Greg's family – his father and one of his sisters had the exact same lively, skinny face as his own. A boyhood friend of his aimed an outsize blunderbuss at the unseen cameraman. There was a dutiful shot of Ellis, Fay and the two children, personal snaps of the Felixes, including a big coloured blow-up of Nelly and her sleeping baby, across which she'd scrawled in black pen, 'Isn't he a dead ringer for Donald Pleasance!'

With smooth momentum Kate worked on her translation, was tapping out the final page of the treatment at a furious pace when the door opened and Greg returned with their friend, Luc. The two men were tipsy and expansive.

'Look at her!' Luc paused dramatically in the doorway. 'Truly, women are the backbone of society . . . Kate, you're an angel, a studious, diligent angel . . . while we *connards* . . .'

He crossed the room and went to embrace her, but she raised a warning hand, keen to hang on to the mood of perfect concentration she'd achieved during the last two or three pages. Swiftly, and with the satisfied sense of a good job done, Kate typed the final long paragraph, rolled the page out of her typewriter and sorted it into top and two carbon copies.

She looked up. 'OK, Luc, I'm all yours.'

He took her hand, pulled her up from the chair, kissed her with playful fervour. 'I just had to come up for a taste of your enviable domesticity before slinking home to my bachelor cell.'

'By all means . . . Taste your fill.' Among their predominately single friends she and Greg were an intriguing novelty.

Luc was one of the few people they'd met who wasn't a student, though he looked like one with his hanging woolly scarf and unkempt bush of curly brown hair. He was well over six foot, and big-bodied, with a long, handsome bloodhound face that made Kate think of Oscar Wilde, and an intriguing hangdog smile. And, apparently, Luc too wrote poetry, and had it published sometimes in little magazines, but he earned his living at a job he despised – working on the house magazine of a South American bank with branches all over Europe. He presented these facts about himself with an air of rueful detachment, almost as if he were talking about somebody else.

Greg made some coffee and they sat round the fire and Luc talked about a female colleague he thought he was in love with. And Kate and Greg – with the Olympian wisdom of beings who'd retired from the hurly-burly of the chase – helped him formulate a strategy for wooing and winning the object of his desire.

Around half past twelve they hinted that Luc should leave. He was reluctant. 'Isn't there room for me in your little bed . . . I'd keep you warm . . . I hate my room. I'm going to be lonely . . .'

Amiably, Greg bundled him out. Closing the door, he turned to Kate. 'I feel like God expelling a sinner from paradise.'

Chapter Twenty-Nine

✳✳✳✳

Kate's days were filled with a kaleidoscope of small pleasures that started on waking. There were mornings when Greg had to get in early to the Sciences-Po, so he got up and made coffee and brought it to her in bed. While he showered and dressed, Kate drowsed beneath the Indian coverlet and watched him, and they chatted, sleepy and intimate. Other days the roles were reversed and it would be Greg's turn to loll in comfort, Kate's to get out and bring home the bacon. And, as Kate washed and dressed and made coffee, he would laughingly try and inveigle her back into bed, and sometimes he succeeded. The best days were when neither had any pressing reason to go anywhere and they would doze and cuddle and make love for half the morning, then go out and have coffee and croissants at one or other of the nearby cafés.

Kate no longer suffered panic attacks over her professional solitude. In her mind an invisible thread linked her to Greg, wherever he was, whatever he was doing, and she worked surrounded by their shared clutter. She couldn't help knowing that her new state of happiness showed through in her eyes and her voice and her smile, and made people like her – from neighbours and shopkeepers and waiters to Monsieur Gassier at the Agency and Laurence, his cool, quiet secretary. Even Madame Arnaud who managed the office side of Edouard Meissonier Antiques – a heavy, black-haired, black-moustached Gallic dragon with a voice like rusty iron filings – now greeted her with a gleam in her opaque sloe-eyes that verged on the benevolent.

And the friends Greg made at the Sciences-Po were welcoming too, marvelled at how good her French was, how fluent and accentless, and saw her – in her ciré mac and boots – as a specimen of the new type of English girl, like Julie Christie or the one in *The Knack*.

She became friendly with one of Greg's fellow students in particular. Juliette was a small, compact woman with short black curls and an animated, unmade-up face, highly attractive in spite of – or perhaps because of – her high-bridged, slightly hooked nose and gap teeth. They had coffee together and sometimes went to the cinema, specially to the kind of film the men didn't want to see.

But they went out as a foursome too, with Juliette and her rather rich, rather bourgeois boyfriend, Paul – his family disapproved of her, so Juliette confided to Kate. And they were friendly with another couple, Patrick and Simone, who were politically-minded and talked a lot about the American involvement in Vietnam, the wickedness of the endless bombing raids. And Kate and Greg agreed with everything they said. How could you not? The whole thing was just unspeakable. But somehow life was too full and too pleasant to do much about it. And, anyway, what could they do?

At parties, quite soon, she knew enough people to talk, dance and flirt on her own account. But all the time she would keep one eye on Greg across the room and think how attractive he was, in his sweatshirt and jeans, the way his smile seemed to well from some private store of amusement deep inside. And she would see that other women thought so too.

Then, walking home, Greg would say he'd been watching her, and she was the cutest, the nicest of all the girls there – he'd barely been able to stop himself from dragging her into the dark room where the coats were and having his wicked way with her.

'That sounds like your style.' Kate flashed him a knowing smile. 'But you can just wait till we get home – you won't get me stopping off in some shop doorway . . .'

Then, the moment they got back to their room, he pulled her astride him on one of the mock-croc easy chairs, and they had sex there and then, before Kate had even got her mac off . . .

And, when they'd done, he looked at her with a hot, laughing look in his blue eyes. 'That'll learn you . . .'

'Greg's so proud of you,' Juliette declared over coffee on the terrace of the Trestrignel, on the first really sunny day of spring. 'It's almost a bore – he's always quoting you and bringing you into the conversation.'

And the bright, raw sunshine that lit up their winter pale faces, and dazzled on the white café tablecloth, seemed to flood Kate's veins with a sudden wild happiness.

Sometimes, though, she worried a bit. Greg was surrounded by female students, and he was so sweet and engaging . . . But the worry didn't go very deep, because everything he did showed Kate how focused he was on her. Marriage was supposed to be stuffy and boring. Yet hers was anything but. She couldn't remember, ever, feeling so alive.

For some years Grand-mère had been suffering from arthritis in the hip. In spring she finally decided that she could no longer cope with the exertion of living alone. For some time she'd had her eye on a comfortable 'home' for well-heeled old ladies and, in April, Odile travelled to Lausanne to help her move in. On the way back she stopped off in Paris to spend a couple of days with Beatrice.

She paid a visit to Kate and Greg, admired the bohemian glamour of their studio flat and exclaimed over the view from the window. Odile had brought them some quality table linen that Grand-mère no longer needed, and they thanked her profusely, though they never used anything so bourgeois.

Beatrice invited them both out for a meal the following evening, at the Bistro Allard in Saint Germain, but Greg's personal tutor was hosting a small soirée that night, which it would be undiplomatic to miss, so Kate went on her own.

She arrived first and sat waiting with a bottle of Perrier. A couple of minutes later, through the frosted glass of the street door, she spied the shapes of Beatrice and her mother. Odile led the way in, and Kate saw with sudden clarity how European she was, in her simple but expensive coat with a heavy silver brooch of Grand-mère's pinned to the lapel, a boldly patterned silk scarf, her hair – markedly greyer than it used to be – swirled deftly into a womanly chignon. And, for the very first time, she glimpsed the process whereby Odile might grow into Grand-mère. And she understood, too, that Beatrice had not necessarily plucked her own refined style from the air of Paris, that she had a tradition to draw on of bourgeois chic that was in the blood.

Though Kate had polished her boots and wore a black Saint Laurent shirt Beatrice had tired of and pressed on her as a gift, she would never, ever, attain the instinctive elegance of these two.

Odile kissed her affectionately. 'How smart you look – quite the Parisian.'

When she'd taken off her coat Odile became, in Kate's eyes, more herself, in one of her familiar scoop-necked, loose-waisted dresses, this one in blue-green wool. She settled herself at the table with an air of happy expectancy. 'Isn't it a treat for us all to be here together? We're going to have a lovely meal. And I haven't cooked it and we won't have to wash up afterwards.'

'Oh, ma,' Beatrice laughed, 'don't be so housewifely.' She took charge and ordered wine for them all. 'You'll love this. David let me in on the secret, and it's not that dear . . .'

Kate didn't bother to memorize the name. However cheap Beatrice thought it, she knew it would be beyond her price-range. But it *was* delicious – red, with a softness about it, a mellow, almost buttery flavour. Nothing like the rasping stuff she drank with Greg.

The food was homely but superbly cooked. Kate chose a creamy tart with leeks, followed by a rich rabbit stew. Beatrice ordered a second bottle of the nice wine. They talked about family things – Grand-mère's move, Odile's garden, Olivier's latest job, doing up houses for some kind of entrepreneur he knew. Odile raved about her adorable grandson, and her pleasure in looking after him twice a week so that Nelly could have a little time to herself. It was cosy and companionable and nothing had to be explained. Kate was almost glad Greg hadn't been able to come.

'How's Jerome?' she asked Odile.

The casual question was greeted with a heartbeat of silence, a palpable stiffening of the atmosphere that both Odile and Beatrice understood, but Kate didn't. A wariness clouded Odile's brown eyes. Beatrice looked down at the remains of the cassoulet on her plate.

'Jerome is well,' Odile stated flatly.

Kate gazed at her, bewildered. 'You don't sound very sure.'

Odile shrugged her shoulders. The movement was defensive rather than dismissive. 'Jerome and I . . . we are in dispute.' She leaned forward to prop her chin in her hand, laid the hand across her mouth in an instinctive gesture of self-censorship.

Kate was stricken. 'What's the matter?' She checked herself. 'I don't want to pry.'

They sat there, all three of them, for a moment without speaking, round the table that had been so festive.

Then Odile addressed her daughter. 'I think I should explain to Kate.'

'Ma, are you sure?'

Odile looked at Kate, a disconcerting nakedness in her eyes. 'This is embarrassing. Only Beatrice knows this. I've never talked to the other children about it . . . But we're here and . . .' She turned to Beatrice. 'Kate has always been a sensible girl. And *sympathique* . . .'

Kate tried to reassure her. 'You don't have to tell me, whatever it is. But if you do, I'll never breathe a word to a soul.'

'I know that.'

Beatrice spoke briskly as if to dispel the atmosphere of hesitation. 'The fact is, Pa's been a bastard. He's been unfaithful. Lots and lots of times.'

'Beatrice . . .' Odile seemed to protest at the brutality of her daughter's statement.

'That's the truth.' Beatrice took her mother's hand. 'You can't get round it. Kate might as well have the facts, straight from the hip.'

Kate was struggling to take in the devastating . . .absoluteness of Beatrice's information when the round-faced young waiter came to clear away their plates.

As if at the touch of a button, Beatrice assumed an air of sprightly command. 'We may as well go the whole hog, don't you think? The prune tart is just heavenly . . . What do you say?'

Dumbly Kate and Odile acquiesced. And Beatrice passed on the order with smiling composure.

When the waiter had gone Kate turned troubled eyes on Odile. 'I don't know what to say.' In her head she held an image of Jerome and his wife on the evening of Nelly's wedding, dancing together, alone, talking and laughing with playful intimacy. A long-established couple proudly celebrating a rite of passage. She could not begin to imagine that, at the same time, Jerome . . . 'Have you known about this for long?'

'Some years . . . And then I hear nothing and I think it's all over . . . He's in London a lot . . . The women are, how shall I say it . . . ?' A grim, hurt smile. 'They're not his intellectual equals. The first I knew of was his cleaning woman.'

'And there was that stupid cow he used to be on the quiz show with,' Beatrice put in. 'What was her name? . . . Rowena Yardley.'

'Good heavens.' In her mind's eye Kate pictured baby-fine blonde hair, the kind of parody hour-glass figure that was held up as desirable back in the fifties. The woman had been ubiquitous for a time, then dropped from sight.

'She's a drunk now,' Odile stated with flat disdain.

'And then there was a make-up girl he met in the telly studios.'

'Enough, Beatrice.'

'You get the idea.' Beatrice's expression was blank, veiled.

'I'm shocked.' Kate said. 'I'm astounded.'

'And now there is a new one.' Odile fiddled with her glass. 'He's like something out of Balzac or Flaubert, with his *grisettes*. And I'm the virtuous wife who stands by and pretends to be above it all.'

'Why don't you leave him?' The question came faster than thought and, immediately, Kate regretted it.

But Odile was not offended. It was clear that she herself had considered the question. 'I think it's hard for you young women to understand. To you it must seem a terrible, cowardly compromise. But sometimes pride is less important than . . . familiarity . . . your own surroundings. There's so much that's attached to my life with Jerome. Things you wouldn't think important . . . my garden, my kitchen, my house. And there's my children . . .'

Kate reproached her. 'But you'd still have your children.'

Odile shook her head. 'But not in the same way . . . As it is now, I represent their home to them. They don't have to think about me. If I left Jerome I would be this person with no roots, someone they had to worry about . . .'

The puddings arrived. The young waiter was clearly intrigued by the intensity of the mood that had descended on the table.

But Odile waited until he was gone before continuing, 'Kate, I have explained this to Beatrice . . . I am comfortable. Jerome is not the big, big thing in my life . . . I can still be happy. I have many pleasures – like my grandson. Like this meal with you and Beatrice.'

As if in illustration, Odile took a mouthful of her tart, but seemed to chew it without enjoyment. She put her spoon down again. 'I'm not always thinking of Jerome . . . But sometimes . . . Just before I left things boiled over and I screamed at him. I attacked him. I would have liked to kill him . . .' She paused, with a bitter smile. '. . . And he is always so controlled.'

'I've told Ma she's artistic, and practical too. She can do anything she turns her hand to. She could start a business for herself. She could live an independent life . . . Open a restaurant, an interior design shop . . .' Beatrice addressed Kate, earnest, hectoring.

'Oh, Beatrice . . .' With a glimmer of black humour Odile held up her hands. 'None of this is real to me. It's as if you're telling me fairy stories . . .'

Kate had the impression that they'd had this exchange many times and reached stalemate. That they were reiterating it simply for her benefit, inviting her to plump for one side or the other.

Instinctively she found herself agreeing with Odile. But why? Why shouldn't she change? Perhaps it was simply that something inside Kate protested at the thought. She wanted and needed Odile to remain the self-effacing, but essential, linchpin of the family.

But she couldn't say that. It sounded too selfish and too discouraging. Kate played safe. 'Of course you could go into business if you wanted. I'd eat at your restaurant any day of the week . . . But it's a big decision to . . .'

'I'm tired of this conversation.' With an abrupt movement Odile drained her glass of wine. 'I came to enjoy myself . . . Kate, I want to hear all about *your* life, what you do here, how you live . . .'

She began to ask Kate questions about her work, and about Ellis and Fay, and Kate replied. It felt awkward at first, as if they were keeping a stiff upper lip against strong odds. But, later, over coffee, the conversation flowed naturally again. Kate began to describe the ploys she'd devised to slither past the Cerberus-like figure of Madame Colin, the concierge, without getting involved in one of her long, resentful diatribes, and Odile laughed with the glee of a young girl.

As Kate made her way home in the cool, damp spring night, fragments of the evening's conversation swirled inside her head and she was confounded, all over again, by what she had learned.

Jerome's cherubic face shimmered in her mind, its benevolence abruptly tinged with treachery.

He liked to treat his children, and Kate, to indulgent meals at good restaurants – 'It's one of the few pleasures left to us oldies' he claimed, with his comfortable, comforting smile. His presentation of himself as a crumbling old buffer had always amused Kate. But now she found herself confronted by his bad faith, for, on the contrary, it seemed he had pleasures galore.

She couldn't help picturing him, plumply naked, pawing and panting over young, nubile female bodies. Rowena Yardley, for God's sake, with her pneumatic, much-touted tits – how galled Odile must feel. The image was ugly but insidiously exciting. And it resurrected another, similar picture. That of her own father screwing Fay in the firelight. Though that memory had been all but superseded by the arguably more painful incarnation of Ellis as euphoric husband and father.

Another fragment of remembered conversation surfaced in her

mind. 'Nobody could understand why Odile married me,' Jerome had declared over a family meal at Plas Felix, not so long ago, two years at the most. 'She was like a lovely young princess and she could have had a handsome prince, but instead she chose the frog.'

Kate could no longer recall what had triggered the remark. He'd flashed a provocative sort of grin at his wife seated at the opposite end of the table. She'd ignored him, her face a mask of cool irony. And now, in retrospect, Kate understood an unsettling breath of malice that had seemed to hang in the air until, like smoke, it slowly thinned out and dispelled.

Chapter Thirty

❁❁❁❁❁

Beatrice sat reading by the light of her grey frosted Simpliste table lamp. She was bathed and scented, her legs freshly waxed. Her hair hung loose on her shoulders. She wore a mauve wild silk caftan and beneath it a satin bra and knickers in a deep shade of purple. No tights, no trousers, David specified, as if his rampant lust could not brook the slightest barrier. Though that was no longer true. Most times they went to bed with the unhurried equanimity of a long-married couple.

She looked at her watch. It was getting on for midnight. He'd said half past ten at the latest. This was what she hated about her relationship with David, this waiting, primped and pomaded, feeling like a *poule de luxe*. Though she never let her dissatisfaction show. When David arrived she behaved as if she'd hardly noticed the passing of time, too involved in whatever she was doing to think about it. It was beneath her dignity to make a scene.

It had not always been thus. Beatrice recalled their first months together with nostalgia, and a kind of horror at her own naïveté. Back then she'd been such a blundering, blinkered creature, with her studenty clothes and her hair hanging anyhow. She'd been so ignorant of the rules, hadn't known there *were* rules. She used to sulk and throw tantrums, had hit him once and been terrified by the speed and fury of his retaliation.

'*Never* do that to me!' He'd slapped her hard across the jaw, twice, and sent her sprawling.

And Beatrice never had done it again. Some women enjoyed courting that kind of danger but it wasn't a road that attracted her.

In those days he'd paraded her almost like an explorer might

288

bring back and show off a strange animal on a chain. His ravishing but *farouche* little English girl with her cheap clothes and hoop earrings. And she'd been confident and opinionated, in no doubt of David's passion for her – he proved it all the time.

One day he'd had a sudden windfall – a big chunk of American royalties. 'Let's go shopping, Beatrice,' he suggested. 'I'll buy you some clothes.'

He took her to a series of small, smart, terrifying boutiques recommended by a woman friend, bought her dresses and shoes and sweaters. They were like two kids on a spree. And Beatrice had discovered two things that day. The first was that she had a decided taste for the expensive things he bought her. The second, that David thought her lacking in style and sophistication.

From then on it had become her aim to perfect herself in his eyes. And, gradually, it got so that she herself could not bear to be less than perfect. Beatrice had facials, manicures, pedicures, leg-waxing, treated her long hair with henna wax and olive oil. She could no longer stand to wear badly made clothes.

David was appreciative of the change in her. 'You know, Beatrice, these days I simply can't fault your taste . . .'

But, paradoxically, now her looks were elegant and seamless – now her corners had been rubbed off – David was not more but less interested. He'd said, from the word go, that they would never live together. Yet now their lives were quite separate. Beatrice put it down to the passing of time. A cooling of passion was inevitable. And, after all, he slept with her three nights a week. And two or three times a year they went away together for long weekends. But there had been a time when David couldn't stay away, took her out all the time to parties and restaurants, introduced her to all his friends . . .

Now such things were occasional treats. And sometimes, when she let herself, Beatrice couldn't help imagining that she had been relegated, and that David had someone else, someone like she used to be – young and temperamental, excitable and spiky – and that she had become some sort of background wife figure. The thought was torture. It used to make her writhe and sweat in her bed at night.

That way madness lay. Beatrice had made herself cultivate detachment. She would accept what David offered, and not demean herself by demanding more, risking refusal. In David's company she behaved as if her life as a whole were perfectly satisfactory to her. The masquerade had become second nature.

Nobody knew, but David gave her money. Each month he paid a set amount into her account. It had started when she first came to Paris and had nothing of her own. Back then it had seemed a casual arrangement, almost in the nature of a loan.

Then later, when she found her job with the gallery, Beatrice gave him notice that his subsidy was no longer required.

'Please,' David had said. 'Allow me, little one . . . It gives me pleasure you know.' He'd spoken with a warmth in his eyes that was rare and precious and which she had never forgotten.

So the situation remained, hush-hush, sub rosa. Beatrice lived in some comfort. People must assume she was frightfully well paid. Only there were times – like now, waiting – when she felt that David had somehow bought off her right to . . . explanation, common courtesy. And she fantasized renouncing the arrangement in a brave burst of independence. But fear stayed her hand – David might take it that, in refusing his money, she was rejecting him . . .

All in all, the regular deposit paid by her lover into her account remained a tangible assurance that he still valued her. That was worth something. And anyway she'd got used to living beyond her means . . .

She heard the street door slam shut. This must be him. David had his own set of keys. Beatrice rearranged the cushions on which she was reclining, and glanced round the room, savouring its welcoming comfort and order. She assumed a position of artful languor and returned with deliberation to her book. Always her heart pounded as she listened for his key in the flat door . . .

But the eagerly awaited sound never came. It must have been someone else. Beatrice closed her eyes and took several deep breaths to compose herself, to combat the wormy niggle of disappointment, resentment.

Kate had visited earlier in the day for their regular tea-date. And, as she lounged, idle and solitary, pictures of the girl drifted into Beatrice's mind. Both as the waif she had once been and the way she was now, sharper and brighter than life.

Beatrice had always been oddly impressed by Kate's aura – the pale, gawky kid she'd been – impassive on the surface, but the hungry depth of her feelings showing through in her eyes, dark and solemn beneath the long, straight fringe of hair . . . Kate still had the same uncontrived adolescent looks – the slight body, the black elf-locks hanging to shoulder length. But nowadays her whole being was alight with exhilaration and satisfied desire. She made Beatrice feel old and jaded. She made her feel unloved.

Once or twice Beatrice had tried to imagine how it might feel to be the wife of someone like Greg. An attractive, lightweight nobody, without pretension to status or fame. But she could *not* imagine it. The public glamour embodied in David's features was like a drug. She could not entertain the thought of a life without it . . .

Beatrice jerked awake to the sound of David's key turning in the lock. Though befuddled by sleep, she glanced automatically at her watch. It was nearly two. Her book had slid to the floor. David stood in the doorway, wearing a black shirt, a light jacket. In the monochrome semi-darkness he seemed a photo in *Paris–Match*, a book-jacket portrait come to life. The tip of his cigarette flared, glowed coral, then receded back into shadow. The wrinkled young-old features were public property, but in this room they existed just for her.

'I must have dropped off,' she mused, drowsily serene. In her slumberous state it was easy to greet him without pique or rancour. Beatrice offered him a sweet, sleepy smile, held an arm out towards him. 'What's the time?'

'Late.' David came and knelt down by the sofa. He placed a soft kiss on her lips. 'Forgive me, *chérie*. I got involved. I couldn't get away . . .'

He proffered no further explanation. But at least he had apologized. David reached beneath the caftan she was wearing, stroked

291

her smooth legs with an appreciative murmur. 'You smell good. You feel soft.'

He wore a charming, wry, conciliatory smile. His presence filled her with an overwhelming sense of gratitude and relief.

In July Pascal and Sofia proposed to come to Paris for a long weekend. Kate was excited, eager to show off her new world. She and Greg offered to put them up.

'It'll be a bit primitive,' she told Pascal on the phone. 'But I'm certain we can borrow a couple of sleeping bags . . . Though if you'd rather stay with Beatrice . . .'

'Beatrice won't have us,' Pascal informed Kate drily. 'She's got a spare room, but she always books us into some pension or other. She offers to pay, but I'm too gallant to let her . . . Your floor'll be just dandy for our needs.'

They arrived a little before twelve on Friday night and all of them sat up until three, talking and drinking wine, and consuming a huge quiche Kate had bought from Petit Christophe on the Boulevard Raspail.

She and Greg were bursting with a wild new project. They had wedding present money saved and had suddenly decided to blow it on a mammoth trip to the States, paying visits to their respective parents, then taking off on their own, driving clear across America like Jack Kerouac, taking in legendary sites like Mount Rushmore and the Grand Canyon, Hollywood and the Golden Gate . . . Their flight was booked and they were leaving within the month.

'You jammy buggers.' Pascal groaned with envy.

While they talked, Kate observed her domain as if through his eyes – this little area of Parisian space that she and Greg had colonized. As she had guessed, his imagination was immediately stirred by their way of living, the picturesque shabbiness of the flat, the archetypal view from the window. And she was quietly gratified by the thought that, at this very moment, the hero of her teenage years might actually covet some aspects of her world.

But Pascal's own life had taken an upward turn. He'd been entrusted with the making of a half-hour programme – about a group of amateurs on a housing estate writing and producing a play and taking it to Edinburgh – and saw it as a huge chance. This trip was a brief escape before he plunged heart and soul into the project.

He and Sofia planned to take in as many movies as time allowed. And tomorrow evening there was a party at the flat of Patrick and Simone, who lived close by, in a side street parallel to their own.

During the morning and afternoon Kate had work to do. Sitting at the table by the window, translating descriptions of art-nouveau ink-stands and vases and lampshades, she was invaded by a sensation of queasiness, which she put down to the previous night's wine, the lack of sleep. And, in fact, halfway through the afternoon, Kate laid her head on the table in front of her and dozed. Waking, she felt unrefreshed and oddly bloated. She made a coffee to perk herself up and finished a packet of rusks that happened to be left in the cupboard. Then she lay on the bed and fell at once into a deep sleep.

She had arranged to meet the others at the party at half past nine. When she surfaced into consciousness it was already nine o'clock. Her overwhelming instinct was to stay where she was and sink back into sensuous slumber. But that would be ridiculous. She'd ached for the pleasure of showing Pascal and Sofia off to their new friends, and vice versa.

Kate made herself get out of bed. She switched on the light. Her features in the mirror looked thickened and pasty. She splashed her face with cold water, put on make-up and a red top that always had a tonic effect on her spirits. The ten-minute walk to the party made her feel somewhat brighter.

The flat where Patrick and Simone lived was situated above a sombre, tidy shop-front that advertised *Pompes Funèbres* in mirrored letters edged with black.

Simone was enchanted by the proximity. 'There's a room down there, right underneath our bedroom, where they lay out the corpses and wash them and paint their faces. I lie in bed and think about them – it's incredibly calming.'

It happened that Patrick's father owned the building. And,

though Patrick – as an aspiring revolutionary – was embarrassed by the fact, he had been unable to resist the temptation of a large, sunny first-floor room, bedroom, bathroom, kitchen and wrought-iron balcony, all at a nominal rent.

As Kate mounted the dark wooden staircase, the pulsing of the Rolling Stones grew louder with every step. The large living-room – with its Mucha posters and flea-market lamps, the big framed photograph of Che Guevara – was pleasantly full but not intolerably crowded. A few couples were already dancing. Kate spotted Simone, with her fringed, bobbed Louise Brooks hairstyle, talking to Pascal and joined them.

Simone turned her stern little-girl face to Kate. 'This man says he's your brother . . .'

'He's adopted.' Kate smiled at Pascal, pleased with his claim. 'Well, how many movies did you manage?'

'Only three. We couldn't get in at the Ursulines . . .'

'Three!' Simone was shocked. 'It's madness.'

'I intended four. Five, if it hadn't been for this party.'

'Oh, la la . . .' Simone mocked, though she was clearly taken with his quiet fanaticism.

Kate viewed Pascal for a moment as if he were a stranger, as he must look to Simone. Appealingly pale, attractively unshaven, a touch haggard from his late night and cinema marathon. A wonderful soft leather jacket worn over a dark T-shirt. Hair rumpled. Smiling a little at the force of her reaction, his eyes amused and mock-innocent. He was perfect. She was proud of him. But proud, too, of Simone, so small and taut and chic with her twenties dress and haircut. Kate tingled inside with a sharp sense of proprietary pleasure.

Patrick came, bringing a glass of red wine for newcomer Kate. Excitedly Simone related Pascal's intensive round of cinema-going. Patrick merely smiled, his warm, beautiful brown eyes twinkling appreciatively.

For all his enthusiastic participation in demos, on radical committees, there was something cosily imperturbable about Patrick. Luc referred to him as a *fils à papa*. And, with his stocky build – verging on the plump – his tweedy jacket, white shirt and tie, he did appear the well brought-up son of a comfortably-off family. Which, of course, he was. Only his soft, brown hair, curling poetically to collar-length, offered a hint of rebellion.

'Did you invite the corpses?' Greg returned from a dance with Sofia.

Mentally Kate approved her husband's foxy grin and rangy body. Sofia followed, plum-lipped and voluptuous.

'No. But it may be that they'll gate-crash.' Patrick replied in his quietly formal manner.

'And we'll all do a dance of death,' Kate put in.

'A bacchanal out of an engraving by Posada,' Pascal agreed.

'Posada!' Simone exclaimed. 'We love his cartoons, me and Patrick. We've got a book of them.'

'We saw an exhibition of his,' Sofia explained, with her wide eyes and sleepy voice.

The cultural coincidence was like a passport, admitting Pascal and Sofia on to an intimate footing with their hosts. All six stood chatting with collective, enthusiastic goodwill. Everything was just as Kate had hoped it would be.

After a while Simone crossed to the record-player and put on one of her Françoise Hardy records.

'Dance, Kate?' Pascal asked.

They took the floor. The song was somnolently slow.

'Not that you can dance to these things,' Kate grumbled. 'I can't abide these French girl pop stars with their thin voices and smug little-girl-lost . . .'

'You grouch . . . I'd do Françoise Hardy a turn any time.'

'So would Greg. That's not the point.'

'It's the only point.'

They could manage little beyond an aimless shuffle to the tiresome music. But Kate had danced with Pascal only a few times in her life and his glamour, at such close quarters, made her blood quicken.

'I can't tell you how good it is to catch up with you and Greg,' he enthused. 'You seem like fish in water here . . . You make marriage look almost tempting.'

'No one's stopping you.'

'Me and Sofia?' He shook his head. 'It'll never happen.'

With a sudden tender movement Pascal pulled her closer. 'Dear Kate. Darling Kate.'

Surprised, she looked up at him and he kissed her on the lips. She was elated yet, simultaneously, the gesture felt quite natural and her lips returned the pressure. In a subconscious flash Kate grasped that the kiss had many layers. There was the pleasure of being with someone deeply familiar in an unlikely setting, the sudden sharp awareness of their having grown up together. But there was also the flaring of a subtle, yet undeniable, erotic charge, which startled her by its mere existence.

Simone was standing nearby. She caught Kate's eye and raised an eyebrow, her smile amiable-malicious.

'*Vive l'inceste*,' she murmured. Kate was just close enough to hear.

Kate stared down into the murky bowl of the lavatory she and Greg shared with their neighbour, Roland. She retched convulsively, dribbled out a thin stream of bile, then vomited in earnest, bringing up red wine, the small, salty biscuits she'd nibbled at the party, even the rusks eaten hours earlier.

Afterwards Kate closed her eyes with a sensation of relief, a sort of ebbing away. She stood up. Her knees felt weak. She reached for the dangling, knotted chain and flushed the toilet.

Stepping out on to the landing, she encountered Sofia in the bilious light. With her elongated eyes and avid lips, she seemed a caricature, her smile greedily intrusive.

Expressively Sofia lowered her eyes to Kate's flat belly. 'You going to be a mama, Kate?' she mocked.

'Don't say that.' Kate was irritated by her clumsy familiarity.

She re-entered the room, where Pascal and Greg sat slumped in the crocodile chairs, Pascal smoking a last cigarette.

'You look like a ghost,' he greeted her.

'I've been sick. I must have overdone . . . something or other.'

It was nearly four in the morning.

Sofia returned from the lavatory and repeated her witticism. 'I reckon Kate's going to be a mama.'

'Leave off,' Kate protested. 'I've been sick just once, right?'

'Come here, baby.' Greg pulled her down on his knee, stroked her cheek, half tender, half satirical. An excitement, a hint of sexual vanity showed through in his smile. 'You'd make a sweet mama.'

Kate was exasperated. Pascal and Sofia seemed taken with the idea and played with it, as if the imagined pregnancy belonged to all of them. Kate let them talk. She leaned back against Greg's shoulder, closing her eyes.

But Sofia's smart-alec prediction turned out to be justified. From that weekend on Kate threw up each evening, felt nauseous on and off all day, couldn't stand the smell of cigarettes or food shops or alcohol, could hardly bear to eat anything much beyond plain white bread and butter.

The wonderful American trip loomed. The open road. Blue skies. Mountains. Canyons. But all Kate could think of was herself hunched over a sick-bag as the car bowled towards these dream horizons.

'Jesus, Katie, there's no way we can go while you're like this,' Greg repeated helplessly, maddeningly, day after day.

The doctor confirmed what had become obvious. When Kate knew for sure that she was pregnant a small flame of wonder and pride flickered inside her, but was subsumed by the relentless advance of their departure date, her endless nausea.

'We'll have to cancel,' Greg said, as if hearing the threat might make Kate pull herself together.

Kate wondered if it might too. The thought of cancelling was like the door to paradise slamming in her face. But then she caught a whiff of some cold pasta salad Greg had bought for his dinner and ran across the landing to be sick.

Chapter Thirty-One
1967

❦❦❦❦

It was like admitting chaos to her well-ordered apartment, Beatrice thought. But she still looked forward to Kate's visits. In a funny way she thought of them as keeping her in touch with real life. She'd even bought some terry nappies and bibs and babygros, as Kate called them, and kept them at the flat, so Kate didn't have to lug quite so much paraphernalia with her.

'Is there something you've forgotten to tell me?' David teased.

The drawer-full of baby bits and pieces amused him, provoking what Beatrice thought of as his real smile – quick and natural. He was actually quite touched by her affection for little Jack. It was so unlike his idea of her. She played up to the fond aunt persona, and it seemed to amuse him.

But Beatrice found she really *was* rather fascinated by four-month-old Jack, who had the alert blue eyes of Greg, his father, but staring unnervingly out from under a white woolly cap. She'd always thought of babies as mere organisms – shitting and puking machines – and would run a mile rather than be asked to cuddle one. But she could see how Jack might grow into a real human being and felt absurdly pleased to be on the receiving end of one of his unfocused but oddly genial smiles.

At work, though Beatrice usually left her private life behind her at the door, she allowed herself to refer casually to 'my nephew' and talk about the faces he made and how it wouldn't be long before he was on the move, his chubby little legs were raring to go . . . Jean-Pierre, one of her colleagues, had a little one about the same age and they showed each other photographs on the quiet, as if sharing a secret vice. She loved to shop for the kind of expensive baby outfits Kate could never afford. Jack looked so sweet in them.

The door bell rang and Beatrice hurried to open it. Kate stood there, looking hot and bothered in jeans and a crumpled broderie anglaise blouse. In her left arm she held a zip bag, a folded push-chair. From under her right arm Jack's round face peered out at the world.

Immediately Beatrice focused on the baby. He was as engaging as she remembered. She offered him a wide smile. 'Hello, Jack. Come to visit your auntie, have you?'

'Can *I* come in too?' Kate asked pointedly.

Beatrice took the push-chair and stowed it in the hall, led Kate through to the living-room. She'd laid a clean blue blanket on the floor, ready for Jack to kick on. This visit was one of the chief pleasures of her week. She could not have borne for Kate to understand just how much it meant to her.

'Was the Métro awful?'

'Bloody awful. Though a nice Algerian carried the push-chair for me.'

'Sit down. Relax.'

'Jack needs feeding.'

'Be my guest.'

Beatrice retreated to the kitchen to make tea. When Kate took out her swollen breasts she, Beatrice, found it impossible to behave naturally. The breasts, the child's suckling mouth – like some tenacious sea creature – drew the eye inexorably. Yet it felt prurient to stare. On the other hand, avoiding looking risked making one appear prudish, disapproving.

In the early months of her marriage Kate had burned as if with a fierce inner flame. Now she seemed more earthbound, less lit up inside, with a cut-the-crap edginess to her that probably stemmed from lack of sleep. Beatrice could not remember when she'd last seen Kate wearing make-up. And her hair hadn't been cut in almost a year – it hung, carelessly brushed, halfway down her back. And her stomach showed no signs of returning to its former, almost concave spareness.

The perfectionist in Beatrice was bothered by these details. Yet, at the same time, it was as if Kate had entered a new state of being, a world in which such considerations must seem petty and irrelevant. As Beatrice arranged the white bone china teapot and cups on a tray, sliced a pale lemon cake, she felt, by contrast, spinsterish and fussy.

But Kate did appreciate the care she took. 'Gosh, that looks so civilized,' she sighed as Beatrice re-entered the living-room. Beatrice didn't miss the breath of mockery in her tone. But it was incidental to a heartfelt warmth.

Later, Beatrice produced a smart red carrier bag from alongside her chair.

'I got this for Jack.'

'Beatrice!' Kate protested.

'Don't say anything. I couldn't resist it.'

Kate unwrapped a tiny, stretchy, dark blue all-in-one garment with short trousers and a sailor collar. Her smile held a mixture of pleasure and scepticism.

'You're incorrigible,' she said. 'Thanks.'

'Put it on him when you change his nappy.'

Kate cast her a withering glance.

'Go on.' Beatrice grinned. 'Indulge me.'

'You should get a doll to play with.'

'It wouldn't be as good.'

In the mini sailor suit, propped against a cushion, Jack looked as droll and compact and oblivious as Beatrice had known he would. Kate looked on forbearingly as she got her camera and took several snapshots of the child.

Suddenly a key turned in the apartment door and Beatrice's insides lurched, almost guiltily, even before her conscious mind had sussed that it must be David. Disconcerted, she turned towards the door. He almost never nowadays came unannounced.

He grinned as he entered the living-room. 'You look as if I'd come to haunt you.'

David glowed with bronzed wellbeing. He'd been to some sort of literary seminar in Avignon, which all concerned – so he claimed – regarded as an occasion for living high at the expense of the organizers.

'You're back early,' Beatrice said.

'You sound like a wife caught *in flagrante* . . . I got bored, that's all.'

He turned to Kate, gazing at her with an approving warmth. 'Kate! What a pleasure . . . It's been years. Look at you. A *maman* . . . filled out and simply blooming . . .'

He spread his arms expansively, crossed and kissed her on both cheeks, held her to him for a long, fervent moment. Kate's face gave nothing away.

Then David turned his attention to Jack, who was staring at him with rapt, round eyes. 'You too, *mon brave*. What a beautiful boy . . . Just as your auntie described you . . .'

He took hold of Jack's little feet and waggled them. Beatrice watched dubiously but, right on cue, a vague, jolly grin spread across the child's face and David crowed with satisfaction.

He bent down and felt the side of the teapot. 'This doesn't feel very hot.'

'It's some time since we drank it,' Beatrice replied.

'I wouldn't mind some fresh.'

'No sooner said than done.' She whisked the tray away with an appearance of good humour but, with Kate as witness, felt dismissed. From the kitchen she could hear the animated rumble of David's voice – clearly he'd set out to charm Kate.

It came to her that he'd had some kind of a fling with the girl, that hot summer, just before she came on the scene. But, dazzled as she was at the time with the bright glare of her own happiness, she'd barely given it a thought, and even Kate's presence in Paris had not resurrected the half-buried memory.

Now, seeing them together, it occurred to Beatrice to wonder what Kate felt about the episode. She almost fancied she'd glimpsed a certain stiffness in Kate, a certain resistance to David's casually imperious embrace. But maybe it was her imagination.

When she re-entered the living-room David was ensconced on the sofa with Kate and the baby, and relating the saga of his dispute with his British publishers – Beatrice knew the tale backwards.

As she poured the tea, adding the slice of lemon David preferred, and cut him a triangle of cake, he continued with his narrative without so much as glancing in Beatrice's direction.

'Thank you,' he said briefly, as she placed them on a low table at his elbow.

His manner, though not precisely rude, took Beatrice for granted as if, rather than lovers, they were a long-married husband and wife. With Kate present she could have wished him to demonstrate a little more vivacity and affection towards her.

'. . . Then I met the translator,' David continued earnestly, 'and he was a real little *pantouflard* . . . Only twenty-five or so, but a fat little eunuch . . . What on earth could a creature like that understand about the emotions I describe?'

'It's largely a question of translating words,' Kate demurred. Her attitude to David, Beatrice thought, was cool, resistant. She showed no signs of being softened by his charm.

'Ideally a translator should be a reader – someone who's enthused by your book and wants to do his very best for it. That young man would have been better suited to handbooks . . . accountancy . . . quantity surveying . . . whatever . . .'

'I do all sorts of things,' Kate countered. 'Antiques catalogues, for instance, though I've no special feeling for antiques . . .'

'Now you're the sort of person . . .' David butted in. He gave a reminiscent smile. 'I remember when you were just a kid – not more than eighteen – that you talked with passion about my books. They'd meant something to you . . . I was so touched . . .'

Kate shrugged, as if the memory was not perhaps so dear to her as it was to him, but there was a brightness to her eyes, a flush to her skin. A long slick of hair had tumbled forward and hung down to her breasts.

'I'm not bullshitting.' His smile was flirtatious, his voice consciously seductive. 'I'd be ecstatic if I felt I had a translator who'd read my books for pleasure at the age of sixteen.'

Stubbornly Kate stuck to her guns. 'I'm really not at all convinced that it makes a difference.'

David felt in his pocket for cigarettes and a lighter. He offered one to Kate, who refused. Beatrice accepted. Absentmindedly he proffered the lighter, then lit his own. Unhurriedly he settled back on the sofa and puffed contemplatively for a while, his eyes resting on Kate.

'I've had a thought,' he announced, then took another drag on his Gauloise, seeming to savour the enquiring silence that followed his words. 'I have to tell you, Kate, that Beatrice speaks very highly of your abilities . . .'

'She's a damn good translator.' By way of gaining a toe-hold in the conversation, Beatrice endorsed his statement with energy.

David ignored her. 'Kate, I have a proposition . . . Supposing *you* were to translate my next novel . . . I should have it ready by Christmas at the latest . . .'

Kate looked surprised but, before she could comment, David gave an amused smile. 'I can just see you sitting at your typewriter with this little fellow' – he ogled baby Jack – 'playing round your feet, while you transform my Gallic prose into graceful but pungent English. It's a charming image . . . What do you say, Kate?'

She looked doubtful. 'I can't quite believe you're serious.'

'I was never more serious in my life.'

'Don't be hasty, David,' Beatrice urged. 'There are clauses in your contract . . .'

'To hell with them.' He was vehement, hostile. 'It's a sign, Kate being here this afternoon . . . I've found my English translator. It's a gut-feeling. I've never been more certain about anything. I'll happily fight . . . Those *connards* need me more than I need them.'

Beatrice knew from experience that, when David got the bit between his teeth like this, it was not advisable to urge moderation. This whim would no doubt die the death when he realized all it entailed. After he left she would have a private word with Kate not to get her hopes up.

'*En principe*, Kate, you wouldn't be against the idea,' David persisted.

She gave a dry smile. 'If you sent me a contract and some money I'd translate the telephone directory.'

He was amused by her scepticism. 'You think I'm jerking off. But you'll get your contract, you'll see.'

He turned to Beatrice. 'I'll be off, *ma chérie*. I'm meeting Georges . . . I was just passing by.' He smiled at Kate. 'But what a piece of luck! And what pleasure to see you again. And your little Jack . . .' He waggled his head at the baby, but this time Jack merely stared, blank-eyed and wondering.

David embraced Kate again, twinkling anew at her *jeune maman* status, her bonny, fecund looks.

Before leaving he gave Beatrice a cool peck on the cheek. '*Ciao*, baby,' he said, like a character in a film. 'Till tomorrow night.'

He left in a high good humour. And, all in all, Beatrice was not displeased with his visit. He had, after all, called in of his own accord, just to see her . . .

'How's the little chipmunk?' Juliette asked. 'And his *maman*? I've only seen Kate once since . . . Though I've talked to her a few times on the phone.'

'She's fine,' Greg said. 'Busy though . . . And she gets tired. And, of course, she feels rather out of the way in Buttes-Chaumont.'

Both of them missed living in the centre of things the way they used to. But, with the baby on the way, they'd been forced to move out to the suburbs where they could afford to rent something a bit larger.

It was a hot July evening. A sexy, Turkish bath sort of summer night. As Greg strolled past the terrace of the Café de Flore, his friends, Juliette and Paul, caught sight of him and called him over to join them for a drink.

'I thought you'd be home by now, bathing the sprog and changing nappies.' Juliette took a sip of her Scotch. There was laughter in her eyes, and she looked tanned and summery in an inviting white dress that zipped all the way down the front.

'I've been to one of Patrick's anti-Vietnam meetings,' Greg said righteously. 'I'm on my way home now.'

A waiter brought the Scotch Paul had ordered for him. Greg didn't usually patronize the Flore or drink Scotch, but it was a pleasure sitting here in the soft, warm air, in the fluorescent pool of artificial light – the whisper of a breeze in the roots of his hair –

watching the cars, watching the girls in their miniskirts, laying aside for a moment his fatherhood, his husband-hood. Feeling young in a foreign city.

'Give Kate my love,' Juliette said. 'I miss our trips to the cinema.'

'I'll tell her,' he promised automatically.

Though right now thoughts of his wife trailed a dull ache of displeasure. Last night they'd ended up screaming at one another in a way that scared Jack and made him cry.

'I'm so bored I could scream,' Kate had blurted last night. 'If I'm not at my typewriter I'm feeding Jack, or burping him, or changing him . . . Then it's back to the typewriter again – there has to be more to life . . .'

'Pity you didn't think of that,' Greg snapped, 'before playing Russian roulette with your diaphragm.'

'You fucking hypocrite!' He'd been unprepared for the slit-eyed, savage fury that invaded her. 'You went along with it! Maybe it would've helped if you hadn't always had to have sex hanging from the chandeliers like some bloody stupid acrobat –'

'Well that's not a problem now,' he'd retorted, stung to the quick. 'With you looking like something the dog dug up in the backyard.'

He said it to wound her, and it did. But he'd been lying. Since Kate had the baby she'd changed, it was true. It was like having a new woman around the house. Shirt pulling across her big milky breasts, long drapes of black hair, soft rounded belly. Something slatternly about her that turned him on, constantly. But she wasn't open, the way she used to be, to his casual urgency. It seemed to irritate her. And she was punctilious now about breaking off, stopping to insert her diaphragm. And by the time she had, the moment had passed . . .

'What's this sudden enthusiasm for politics?' Paul's Colgate-white teeth contrasted photogenically with the brown of his skin. 'I had you down for a card-carrying hedonist.'

'Like Patrick says, it's weird how politically apathetic a lot of the Sciences-Po students are . . .' Mildly riled by Paul's comment,

Greg got in an answering dig. 'It's as if politics was an academic subject. They pore over their set texts and, meanwhile –' he spread his hands – 'in the real world all sorts of stuff is going on.'

If Greg were honest, he'd started attending meetings to avoid going home. Though Jack, with his vague, jolly smiles, was the cutest thing he'd ever seen. Though he loved Kate in great, erratic surges of tenderness. If he spent any length of time in the too-small, too-square set of rooms they rented in Buttes-Chaumont, Greg became stir-crazy. Staying in town to go to the movies just looked selfish. But a protest-meeting had a worthy ring to it. No one would go simply for pleasure.

'I plead guilty to apathy.' Paul drained his glass with affected languor.

Greg was getting sucked into the atmosphere of excitement and righteous anger. His former careless disapproval of the Vietnam campaign had sharpened up, become honed and informed. At meetings he was something of a trophy, almost an American, yet ready as anyone to vilify and condemn. This evening he'd had a long, intense discussion with Dany, a friend of Simone's, whose olive skin and bitchy expression had always attracted him. She'd sat elbow to elbow with him and for a moment her distracting, red T-shirted breasts had brushed against his arm . . . On Saturday both of them planned to take part in a peaceful demo outside the American embassy.

'We're going to a late-night movie show,' Juliette said suddenly. '*Bonnie and Clyde*. Want to come?'

He'd read about the film, and it sounded very much to his taste. Greg had a sudden longing for the freedom to say yes, to make a spur-of-the-moment decision.

'Can't really . . . Kate's on her own.'

'Of course,' Juliette agreed respectfully.

Within the space of a few months, Greg mused, Kate had metamorphosed from playmate to martyr, whose isolation it was his duty to share.

Chapter Thirty-Two
1967–8

✺✺✺✺

Mellow autumn sunshine entered the consulting room via a window high above the row of grey filing cabinets. It illuminated a trailing cobweb that hung from a corner of the ceiling, drifting in an imperceptible breeze. Lying on the brown leatherette couch, her bottom on a piece of scuffed tissue paper, Kate watched its dreamy movement, trying to relax, as instructed, while the doctor's long knobbly fingers probed her vagina, the neck of her womb. Simultaneously she wondered about Jack, who hadn't been at all happy at being left with her neighbour Gisèle.

The doctor must be in his sixties. He wore a brown pin-striped suit and a nubbly oatmeal tie. He had a long, narrow skull, a coarse reddish complexion. His expression was blank, as if his brain engaged solely with whatever it was he felt with his fingertips.

Eventually he withdrew them. '*C'est ça. Couvrez-vous.*'

She was vaguely disgruntled by the instruction, as if she had been shamelessly, gratuitously exposing herself. While the doctor shed his rubber gloves and ran his hands under the tap, Kate thankfully resumed her knickers and jeans.

Dr Roux sat down behind his brown polished desk and waited, head inclined. Kate took her place opposite him. He remained silent, as if contemplating the message he was about to deliver. His deliberation provoked her. Nowadays she was easily irritated.

'What do you think?' she asked bluntly.

Given his age and his professional gravitas, the doctor was not a man you addressed in tones of equality. His manner anticipated a certain obliqueness of approach, a certain deference. In these circumstances Kate's forthright question constituted a lack of courtesy. They both sensed it.

'Eh bah.' Roux spread his hands, countering with his own brusqueness. 'It's simple. You're pregnant.'

'It's not possible,' she protested. Though, incredulously, unwillingly, she'd known it all along. Since Jack was born she'd had just one period. And now she felt a weird, indefinable . . . rawness, a dragging in the pit of her stomach, nothing you could quite pin down . . .

'And why is it not possible?' the doctor jeered.

'My baby's only just seven months old . . . And I've been so careful.'

A smile compressed his lips, drawing their corners down rather than up. 'Nature has her own ways, madame. We delude ourselves if we think we're in control.'

The thought appeared to give him a grim pleasure. He was probably a good catholic and father of six.

'Oh, God,' Kate wailed, raising her hands to her head in a gesture of half-humorous anguish. Only too aware of the serious anguish that waited to ambush her just as soon as she was on her own.

Roux kept his counsel, observing her drama as if it were commonplace, as if he'd seen it all a thousand times before.

During the winter months Kate went to ground. Apart from her weekly visit to Beatrice, she left the flat only to buy food. She felt slow and lethargic. During the day Jack hardly slept at all now. But each lunch-time Kate dozed on the low divan in their small, square living-room while Jack, through the bars of his playpen, gazed at the flickering screen of the television perched on a corner shelf.

To her surprise David Lacoste had followed through on his impulse and made whatever arrangements, entered into whatever disputes were necessary for Kate to be offered a contract to translate a motley, extensive assemblage of short stories. His new novel would not now be ready until February at the earliest, but the assumption seemed to be that Kate would undertake that too.

The work meshed well with her hibernating instincts – a dense and continuous task to plod on with through the grey, wet months of November, December, January, seated at the table by the window that overlooked a windswept car park. During this time Lacoste's abrasive characters and diverse locations took the place, for Kate, of real life.

Even Greg seemed distant. There had been a time when she felt intimately connected to his comings and goings. She used to visualize a cord of fine elastic attached to her own heart and to his, binding them together whatever they did. Now, when he disappeared, it was into a vague haze of activity that had nothing whatsoever to do with her.

In February he was out more than usual and on the phone a lot, talking earnestly to Patrick and others about the Tet Offensive. Kate heard the phrase all the time on the radio and television and it meant little more to her than the rest of the specialized, remote vocabulary relating to Vietnam.

Ensconced as she was in the small world of Jack and her work and the new baby growing inside her, Kate could not believe Greg's new political fervour to be sincere. He used to be like her – deploring the Vietnam shambles, but with a resigned shrug of the shoulders. She could not imagine any motive for his activism beyond the desire to escape from the stuffy confinement of their jerry-built flat.

To begin with Kate had been envious of his freedom to disappear into a life where she, too, had once felt at home. But now such envy was beyond her. The parties and cinema-trips and casual friends that once spiced her days had become increasingly unreal to her. She no longer even felt frustrated by the narrowness of her world. Her comforting routine was precious to her and she shunned anything that threatened to disrupt it.

Conjuring up the sexual euphoria of the first year of their marriage was like telling herself a story. Kate could not imagine that she had ever been that miniskirted sexpot, Greg's equal partner in impromptu lust. Had they really fondled one another so shamelessly and so publicly and laughed together at their own rude daring?

Nowadays his advances affronted her. They were all about him, not her. Perhaps they always had been, but she'd been too elated to see or care. One evening Greg lost his temper and that night they talked. 'I wish you didn't have to be so bloody macho all the time,' she'd told him. 'I wish you'd just hold me, in bed, take time, go gently, as if it was *me* you wanted to make love to.' But as she spoke even that desire seemed to her to belong to the past. For a time Greg had made an effort. But to Kate it seemed just that. Effort. She imagined a glum diligence in his lovemaking, like that of a child buckling down to his thank you letters.

From the word go, from back in March when they decided to take it, both Kate and Greg disliked the apartment in Buttes-Chaumont. But Jack had been due within the month and the rent was low. At first Kate had made a half-hearted attempt to liven it up, covering one wall of the living-room with the jaunty montage of photographs and magazine-cuttings they'd had in their Boulevard Raspail attic.

But the new apartment was damp and the edges of the cuttings began to curl, and by then Kate had lost interest beyond keeping the three rooms acceptably tidy. This winter, though, she no longer seemed to have the energy even to dislike the place. It was her refuge, her lair, her bolthole, and she accepted it just as it was.

Tall, shambling Luc was the only person who occasionally braved the Métro journey to come and see her. They would sit for two hours or so in the heavy, slate-grey, electric-lit winter afternoons, chatting desultorily, playing with Jack, drinking coffee into which Luc tipped a couple of nips of brandy from his hip flask. With the detached curiosity of a sociologist, Luc informed Kate that she was suffering from 'sarcellitis' – a disease of alienation peculiar to post-war housewives and named after the huge, soulless housing estate of Sarcelles.

'Thanks.' She grinned dubiously. 'It's consoling to know I represent some kind of a phenomenon.'

One drizzly morning in February, Greg brought a letter up from downstairs addressed to Kate in her father's hand. Though the two of them wrote dutifully three or four times a year, and every Christmas Ellis enclosed a generous cheque, she hadn't seen him for . . . how long was it? Six or seven years.

They'd had their fabulous American trip all planned the summer before last. But then Kate fell pregnant with Jack, and she felt like death all summer. And anyway the money was needed to buy prams and cots and things, and they had to cancel. And neither of them had ever quite forgiven the other for that . . .

'It seems your old dad has achieved desirable academic status,' Ellis wrote perkily. 'This spring I'll be dipping my toe into the European lecture circuit.'

In late March he would be giving lectures in Brussels and Louvain, and proposed taking the train to Paris, staying twenty-four hours – sadly he could spare no longer – and flying home from there. 'It's a heaven-sent opportunity for me finally to get acquainted with my son-in-law, and to admire my new grandson, quite apart from catching up with my prodigal daughter . . .'

Kate read the letter while she gave Jack his breakfast bottle, still in her nightdress, with a milky coffee and a croissant at her elbow. It was one of the private, pleasurable moments that marked the predictable progress of her day.

She reacted to Ellis's letter without pleasure, with a sinking of the heart, as if at a bothersome chore. The flat would have to be brought up to scratch, a spare bed arranged, shopping done. Kate had no idea where she would find the energy and initiative for such an effort.

As far as Beatrice could recall she'd met Kate's father only a couple of times, ages ago, and she hadn't taken much notice back then. But this evening she couldn't help but admire the impression he created of being . . . a happy man. Professionally fulfilled. At ease with himself and with society in general.

Where she and Kate and Greg were pasty and winter-pale, Ellis had a discreet winter-sport tan. His hair was thick and well-cut and pleasingly peppered with grey. His sherry-coloured eyes were clear and direct, his smile frank and friendly, but not too much so.

His clothes were informal – a chunky grey-blue sweater worn over a checked shirt, navy corduroys, sporty brogues – all new-looking and of excellent quality. Ellis was the sort of man who would look right in a wood-panelled ski-lodge, or in the foyer of an international hotel. But, in this mean little room in this mean little flat, he appeared decidedly out of place.

Just as she must do, Beatrice supposed.

Kate had roused herself to make preparations. 'I've lost three whole days' work,' she'd confided ruefully to Beatrice, 'what with trying to make this place look like something, taking blankets to the launderette, poring over cook-books, buying ingredients, transforming them into proper French cuisine . . .'

She and Greg had moved the table away from the window, pulled out the leaf at each end, and now it all but filled the room. It was laid with one of Grand-mère's good linen cloths, embellished with embroidery and drawn-thread-work, white on white, looking incongruous against the cheap patterned carpet, Jack's plastic high chair and the scruffy montage of photos and yellowing magazine-cuttings. A bunch of anemones in a white jug stood in the middle of the table and the clear, bright colours of the flowers toned with the Art-Deco plates Beatrice had given them and off which they ate.

This evening Kate looked nervy and somehow pissed-off. It was as if she resented her role as hostess, but couldn't leave it alone – hovering, offering things, refilling wine-glasses, face set. Kate wore a dear little maternity top Beatrice hadn't been able to resist buying her. Black, with a sweetheart neckline and adorable little glass buttons like tiny mauve pansies, echoing the mauve piping at the neck and on the sleeves. But its charm was cancelled out by the washed-out jeans she'd teamed it with, and by her carelessly scraped-back hair.

The more she saw of Kate, the more Beatrice became convinced that the girl was in the grip of some kind of depression. During last week's visit the urge to put it to Kate, to press her to seek some kind of help, had been almost overwhelming.

But the fact was she shied away from that kind of intimate conversation, suspecting that, in her turn, Kate saw into Beatrice's own life, perceiving things about her that she would prefer not to acknowledge. In her heart Beatrice admitted that her existence was dedicated to remaining available to David – her fear was that, if he called on her and she wasn't there, he would become impatient, look for, and find, consolation elsewhere. Such vigilance left no room for the pursuit of friendships. Apart from the occasional drink or meal with colleagues from the gallery, Kate was the only person she saw.

Yet, as long as her loneliness and dependency remained unexpressed, Beatrice was able tacitly to deny them. Her public persona proclaimed emphatically that all was well with her world. She saw without surprise that Ellis was impressed with her, that he thought her chic and clever, very much in control of her own life. Everyone thought that about her, at first.

But at present Greg held the floor, bubbling over with an account of some student meeting Patrick had been to the night before. As he sat at table he dandled his baby son on his knee – the child lolled, comically content. Almost unwillingly Beatrice was charmed by Greg's rangy body and impish-amused expression. He seemed full of beans and she wondered whether he was blind to Kate's moroseness or whether he was simply used to it. Or whether, with his show of vivacity, he was deliberately compensating.

Both Beatrice and Ellis questioned him eagerly. During the week there had been a series of fracas outside American banks and American airline offices on the Right Bank. Windows had been smashed. Clearly the gestures had been aimed at the war in Vietnam and the police made arbitrary arrests of known student activists. Their comrades called a meeting to protest against the high-handed action. The demo had taken place out at Nanterre, the university annexe. The venue was not accidental.

'Nanterre's like a big cell-block in the middle of nowhere,' Greg explained to Ellis. 'There's always trouble there – disputes, campaigns – far more than at the Sorbonne . . . And that's down to the simple fact that it's a shithole, whereas the Quartier Latin is an awfully pleasant place to hang out . . .'

'I could be supremely happy there,' Ellis concurred with smooth affability.

Last night's manifestation had apparently begun like any other.

313

Angrily the students demanded the release of their fellows. But after the speeches were done, it somehow hadn't seemed enough. They'd wanted some kind of satisfaction, Patrick said, some kind of real action. They stampeded into the big tower block and up the stairs, bust their way into the administrative offices, staged a debate and formed themselves into a student council. They'd been told time and time again that politics didn't belong on campus. And the defiance felt good.

Ellis smiled, cagily indulgent. Earlier on he'd described himself wryly as a pinko–liberal–dove, or Greg would not have been so outspoken. As a college faculty head, Ellis could hardly condone the students' action, but clearly he was entertained by his son-in-law's eager account.

Beatrice noticed that he'd pushed half his boeuf bourguignon carelessly to one side of his plate and had apparently finished eating. Kate had laboured over the dish and would be vexed.

'More mashed potato?' She addressed her father with a breath of acerbity.

'No thanks, Kate. I'm fine.' He made no move to praise the casserole or excuse himself for neglecting it.

'Patrick always says that demos are just theatre. Just mime. Sort of symbolic. But last night for the first time he felt a *frisson* . . . as if he was part of something that could make a difference.'

Beatrice was sceptical. 'Debates. Councils. It sounds mighty abstract to me.'

Greg shrugged. 'I'm only repeating what Patrick told me. He's no wild–eyed *enragé*. And he's no fool.'

'I can understand the feeling.' Ellis came to his defence. 'For ages in America it seemed as if it was only lone voices, fringe voices denouncing the war . . . And now suddenly it's as if there's this whole anti-war movement. You must have read about the New Hampshire Primary a couple of weeks ago – the dove, McCarthy, taking on the President and almost beating him . . . In six months' time, who knows . . .'

'You wonder how many people will be killed meanwhile.' Kate's voice sounded husky and she cleared her throat. She spoke as if musing aloud, rather than participating in the discussion. It was as if she deliberately chose to remain outside the conversation.

Ellis glanced at her but seemed at a loss. Between father and daughter there was almost no communication. Beatrice sensed in both a bleak longing to connect. But it was as if they were separated by a thicket of anger, misunderstanding, betrayal, through which they could find no path. It was easier for Ellis to concentrate on extrovert Greg, for Kate to fall back on empty phrases and gestures of hospitality.

'How's the translation going?' Beatrice asked, to draw Kate into the conversation.

'Steadily.' She was less than communicative.

'What are you working on?' Ellis enquired.

'A set of short stories by Lacoste. I've nearly finished.'

'David Lacoste?' Ellis was clearly taken by surprise.

Kate gave a quick, sardonic smile. 'The very same.'

She hadn't told him. Beatrice was baffled by Kate's attitude. She would have expected her to be delighted with the assignment, proud at being chosen. At the very least it must be better than the dreary stuff she used to churn out for the agency.

'How interesting,' Ellis enthused. 'I've read some of his stuff. Wrings the withers. He's damn good.' He smiled at Beatrice with a hint of gallantry. 'Saving your blushes, Beatrice.'

'It's just a job,' Kate maintained coolly.

As soon as Ellis had departed for the airport the following day, Greg rushed off to meet up with Patrick and catch up on all the excitement he'd missed.

Before leaving, Ellis took seven or eight photographs of Kate, Greg and Jack in various permutations. Kate's smile felt to her like a pair of cartoon lips stuck on a stone statue. When her father was gone she made herself a sandwich and sat by the open window. The sky was a tender blue, the air soft. A tree in the corner of the car park below blazed with white blossom.

Next to it a billboard showed a group of young men and women smoking together and smiling. Kate stared at them. Clearly their lives left nothing to be desired.

Jack was tired after the disruption of Ellis's visit. He laid his head against her belly and dozed. Next month he would be a year old. The movements of the new baby thumped and rippled inside her. They were company, comfort, these two. Hers. Her flesh. Warm.

Kate thought of her father's visit without emotion. She'd expected nothing of it, she told herself. Their relationship would never be any good.

But subversive thoughts nibbled like fish. She could have allowed Ellis his surprised pleasure in her work for David Lacoste, could have shared in it a little. She didn't have to douse it with such cold finality. And what a pity it was he hadn't visited two years ago, when she and Greg were so happy.

Chapter Thirty-Three
1968

❧❧❧❧

Early May. A breezy day, not quite warm. Knots of students were gathering on the Boulevard Saint Michel. As Greg turned off towards the Sorbonne he thought he heard a kind of ragged jeering. He seemed to sense something intangible in the air. A *frisson* – he liked that word – of urgency, potential disorder, though he could not have said quite why. Then he almost collided with the broad-shouldered bulk of a cop, speaking tersely into a hand-held radio. The man looked like something out of Cocteau's *Orphée* – all in black, helmeted and goggled, startling, bigger than life, clearly unaware of Greg's sidestep to avoid him. Beads of sweat stood out on the man's nose and cheeks.

Something must be happening down there. Greg was late for the protest meeting. If he were honest he was less than happy at the way, in the last month, everyone's focus had shifted away from Vietnam to the anarchic diversionary tactics of the Nanterre rebels.

Not that he'd ever say so out loud, but their gambits struck him as infantile. Wryly, Greg acknowledged that deep down he probably had a small-town boy's respect for law and order. Sure, the university system needed a good shake-up, but he felt no sympathy for the brattish manoeuvring of the Nanterre *enragés*. No wonder the authorities had closed the place down. What did they expect? Red-haired Cohn-Bendit, the leader, reminded him uncomfortably of beefy little Len Costa who lived down the street from him as a kid and stole a new pair of sneakers that belonged to Greg, though no one had ever been able to prove it.

New shouts rang out, louder now he was closer, and simultaneously a dark police van – lights flashing, klaxon whooping – turned the corner towards him. Greg stared. The windows of the vehicle

317

were grilled, but he could see that it was full. Of protesters. Must be.

As he approached the Rue de la Sorbonne a scuffle of students enveloped him. And beyond them, with a startled chill of awe, he glimpsed a gang of cops, all uniformed in black, with shields and truncheons. Faceless behind helmets, visors. The almost clichéd embodiment of state repression. At the sight of them Greg was invaded by a sharp rush of adrenalin.

Outside the university building a huge mêlée of students swarmed, confused, shouting. Another police van inched slowly away from the gate. The cries of the students became a rhythmic, derisive chant. A group of them rushed forward and began to pound on the vehicle's metal flanks. A young girl with black hair who looked like Kate screamed wildly, beside herself, tears streaming down her cheeks.

Passionately she appealed to her companions. 'They've taken him! They've taken Charles! For no reason . . .' Her voice resonating with innocent outrage.

Slowly the van tried to force a way through the surging, clamouring students. From somewhere a stone hurtled, then another, shattering the windscreen of the van. With a shock Greg saw the driver's face streaming blood. A bunch of male students heaved and rocked a parked car, straining to push it into the path of the van, to block its progress.

A green Citroën – nothing to do with either students or police – was trapped in the throng. Through the side-window Greg glimpsed a pork-pie hat, dark glasses, a mouth open in consternation. A long-legged kid with cropped hair, a striped shirt, scrambled on to the bonnet, yelling encouragement to his companions.

Simultaneously came the exploding thud of a gas grenade. Then another. Clouds of acrid smoke swirled and spread. Greg felt his eyes smart unbearably. He turned his head away, and saw the girl he'd noticed a couple of minutes earlier. She was sobbing in great panting gasps, tears coursing from her reddened eyes. His own were weeping, copiously, painfully. He grabbed her hand and retreated in the direction of the Boulevard Saint Michel.

*   *   *

Flames from a burning black Peugeot – unceremoniously upended – licked shockingly into the deep blue May night. Greg drank in the lawless beauty of the tableau. Alongside it lay another car, all four wheels in the air, a jumble of hoardings, traffic signs, iron gratings from round the trees that lined the boulevard, the detritus forming a kind of barricade between students and cops. Dispersing clouds of tear-gas hung in the air, yellowish, suffocating.

Though he could barely breathe, Greg felt light and elated, his body insubstantial. His thoughts no longer came in words. It was as if, in all his life, he'd never been so truly himself. All evening, alongside others, he'd baited and taunted and dodged the police all up and down the boulevard. With righteous anger, he'd hurled cobblestones, torn up from the road, at the forces of law and order. The cops were like animals, giving the impression they'd waited years for an opportunity like this – the licence to club and beat and kick spoilt brats of students.

Greg had seen a girl who looked no more than sixteen dragged and jerked by the hair. He'd seen a tall policeman snatch the glasses off the face of a pale, scared-looking boy and trample them underfoot. But it wasn't just students. A crowd of what appeared to be office workers – mid-thirties if they were a day – had emerged cautiously from a café. Clearly they had nothing to do with the *bagarre*. They'd been jostled, had protested. A dark-faced cop had lashed out, catching one of the men a blow above the eye. He'd staggered back, almost comically outraged, blood splashing in great bright blotches on to his white shirt and yellow tie.

The savagery of the police had abruptly snuffed Greg's doubts and hesitations. Whatever the students' cause, it was now his. Any society that used brutes like these to do its dirty work was worth rebelling against.

'We'd done nothing,' the girl kept insisting earlier. She'd been at the initial protest meeting at the Sorbonne. Her black hair and elegant straight brows were so much like Kate's. 'We did nothing wrong. Then out of nowhere these Martians appeared and forced us out and started loading us into trucks . . .'

Her boyfriend Charles was diabetic, so she said. He'd get ill cooped up without medication or food. She left to go to the Santé prison, where she assumed he would be held, a wild-eyed waif preparing to pit herself against hostile authority.

There was a momentary lull in the action, students and cops facing one another warily from their respective positions on either side of the makeshift barrier. The police consulted tensely among themselves. A young kid, drunk on the turmoil, shouted imaginative insults at them, capering like a jester, crowing like a cock.

Greg had run into Jules and Jean-Claude, a couple of acquaintances from Patrick's anti-Vietnam group. With others they prised up cobbles from the road and piled them up ready for use. Greg's arms and shoulders had endless, tireless strength.

Another police-van arrived and parked, waiting. Any moment the cops would charge again.

The phone rang just before six in the morning. Kate came awake the same moment as her arm reached clumsily for the receiver. Even in sleep it was a reflex not to leave it ring in case Jack was disturbed.

'Hello?' Semi-conscious, she mumbled into the mouthpiece, dragging her pregnant bulk higher up the bed.

'Kate . . . Did I wake you?' It was Greg.

'Mmm.' She was confused. What was Greg's voice doing on the far end of a telephone line? Then, in the half-light, she saw that his side of the bed was smooth and empty.

'I'm at Patrick's . . . He's been arrested. I just managed to escape . . . Simone was upset so I stayed to keep her company.'

His voice was overwrought. His words made no sense.

'What? Greg. What are you talking about?'

'Didn't you hear about the protest? The riots?'

'No.'

'It's too complicated to explain. Turn the radio on. You'll hear all about it . . . I just rang to let you know where I was and say I'm not sure when I'll be home.'

'But you were going to take Jack to the park today so's I could work in peace . . .'

320

'I have to stay with Simone. I really do.' He sounded scratchy and over-excited. 'Kate, she needs moral support.'

Still struggling for comprehension, Kate was provoked by his self-important airs. 'I've been relying on you . . .'

'Listen. Things are upside down right now. Believe me. Turn the radio on. You'll understand.' She heard the click of the receiver his end.

Greg put down the phone and went to check on Simone. She was still sleeping on the chaise-longue in the living-room, beneath a framed photograph of Che Guevara.

Last night he'd been touched by her dismay at Patrick's arrest. He'd always found Simone rather cool and stern. But yesterday, wrapped in Patrick's towelling robe, with her square-cut schoolgirl hairstyle, she'd looked like a tired, scared kid. He'd poured her a brandy and she accepted it with a wan smile.

'I'm glad you're here, Greg.'

Her waif-like gratitude added to the sense he had of being powerful and alive. He himself had barely escaped from a cop who had it in for him. Greg had dodged down a side street. He was faster than the cop and managed to give him the slip. Then he made his way to the apartment above the funeral parlour where Patrick and Simone lived, bursting to tell his tale.

He and Simone talked into the small hours. Then he urged her, 'Try to get some sleep. I'll sit here with you.'

She dozed off almost at once, her head on an embroidered cushion. But Greg was still buzzing with adrenalin. He sat by the window, pictures of the night's mayhem filling his head, his body tense and wakeful. He watched Simone sleep, curled up small on the chaise-longue. Fleetingly, betweentimes, he imagined himself picking her up and carrying her into the bedroom, straddling her small naked body and plunging himself deep into her, thrusting hard, hard until he came. If he could just do that Greg knew he'd be able to sleep. But it was an idle fantasy. Patrick was his friend, and Simone was faithful, and Greg was a knight in shining armour.

*   *   *

By Monday, two days later, Greg had not come home. And, though Kate listened to the official news bulletins, they went nowhere towards explaining his absence. There'd been a commotion, a few arrests. The Sorbonne had been closed down. It seemed a mere matter of campus politics, the sort of thing Greg had never had much time for. What the hell was he doing dancing attendance on Simone when his own wife was two weeks away from giving birth? Her stomach curdled with resentful bile.

Kate could forget her anger only by losing herself in work. She'd embarked by now on David's new novel, a sort of intellectual who-dunit. She upped her daily quota, leaving Jack to be entertained by the television for as long as he would put up with it, making brisk excursions to the park with the focused aim of tiring him out and so buying extra time at her typewriter. She worked for half the night.

Late on Monday evening, with Jack asleep, Kate paused to cook herself a couple of fried eggs. In the kitchen she switched on the radio, turning the dial idly to Radio Luxembourg, to be greeted by a muffled roar of voices, the crackle of explosions, terse shouts, a wailing scream. Against this background reporters were giving a blow-by-blow commentary, sounding breathless and shaken. On the Boulevard Saint Germain barricades had been set, forcing back the riot police. Demonstrators threw stones, braved the onslaught of fire-hoses. Under the reporters' eyes a group of policemen clubbed a young black protester until he lay senseless. Kate stood listening, mesmerized, as her eggs sizzled in the pan. Nothing like this had been mentioned on the official French radio and television channels.

She carried her plate and the radio into the living-room, sat in the semi-dark, eating and listening to the sounds of a running battle taking place just a Métro ride away.

Greg came back next morning for a change of clothes. His sweatshirt and jeans looked as if he'd been mending roads in them and his narrow jawline sprouted a three-day growth of beard. But his blue eyes shone with a deep, exhausted happiness. For all the hours she'd spent cursing him, Kate warmed to the flesh and blood magnetism of his presence.

He stood in the hallway, looking cautious and contrite.

'Where the hell have you been?'

'I'm sorry, baby. What can I say?' He gave a helpless shrug acknowledging his guilt, but there was an absence, an exaltation in his eyes. 'Only . . . I've been living through history in the making.' A silence. He looked at her with wary defiance. 'And it's not over yet. I have to go back.'

'For God's sake, Greg.' She was outraged.

He shrugged again.

'They don't need you!'

He said nothing, pulled his grey sweatshirt over his head, made as if to open the bathroom door.

'But I do. I need you!'

'You can get by without me . . .' His tone was dismissive.

'I can't believe what you said . . .'

'. . . For a day or two.'

'And if I go into labour?' But that was a manoeuvre. Jack had been ten days late. They'd agreed the same pattern was likely this time.

The look on his face called her bluff. 'Come on – you've got a couple of weeks yet.'

He pushed open the bathroom door. Kate heard him showering. In the kitchen she gave Jack his breakfast. It all felt quite normal. Why wasn't she angrier? When Greg was dressed she made him coffee and toast, questioned him about what was going on.

Patrick had been released. Simone was fine. The cops were bastards – you just wouldn't believe . . .

'I thought you despised all this student capering, this Nanterre stuff.'

Lying full-length on the divan, propped on one elbow, Greg gave a wry smile, acknowledging the contradiction.

'This is just a whole lot more than that. I can't explain it in any way that doesn't sound stupid. If I hadn't been there I'd be cynical like you . . . It's as if the university stuff is getting to be a side-issue and people are fighting against, I don't know . . . conformity. Power structures. De Gaulle. Just the straitjacket way we're all processed by society . . .' He waved his arms in vague, self-mocking arabesques. 'It's like a force of nature. It's the most amazing thing I've ever been part of . . . I can see you're not convinced, but you'd feel differently if you'd been there.'

'How could I be there?' She spoke savagely. 'Someone has to mind the baby.'

Kate felt excluded and bleakly envious of this mass exhilaration, this romanticism. This folly. Envious even if it were that.

She went shopping, leaving Jack with Greg. When she returned Greg was crawling on the floor, snuffling like a pig, while Jack hiccuped with wild laughter. A jealous anger swept through her at her husband's winning way with the child, at Jack's rapturous adoration. And, in a few minutes, Greg would have vanished out the door, free as air. And she and Jack would be left to share their stale captivity.

'He's like a hobby for you,' Kate said, as if stating a cold fact. 'To pick up and put down as the mood takes you.'

'I'm a shit,' he agreed blandly.

A muffled misery rose up in her throat, suffocating her.

This evening the demo was festive and good-humoured. The Sorbonne was barred and bolted. The *flics* occupied the Latin Quarter. So the march straggled gaily round the Grands Boulevards, tens of thousands strong, picturesque beneath hundreds of fluttering flags. Red for socialism. Black for anarchy.

Greg was intoxicated by the joy of it. The word solidarity resonated in his head and for the first time he understood, really understood, what it could mean. He had niggles, sure – Vietnam was his cause – but now all doubt seemed petty. It was as if tonight everyone suddenly saw just how the confused and ragged skirmishing of the previous days had coalesced into something huge and powerful.

He marched with Patrick and Simone, Juliette, Paul. And the

alluring Dany. They chanted slogans, mocking the mandarins who viewed the unrest as the work of a handful of extremist cliques. *Groupuscules* as they'd dismissively termed them.

'*Nous sommes un groupuscule*!' the students jeered. Thousands and thousands of them.

As they walked, Dany suddenly linked her slim, cool arm through his. When she turned her face towards him he saw her eyes were brimming with tears.

'I feel so happy.' She had to shout above the hubbub to be heard. 'I wish I could hold on to tonight forever.'

Greg was thrown off balance by her attention. He cupped her bare arm with his free hand. 'Live for the moment, kid,' he responded inanely, in English.

But he was touched by the passionate candour of her words. His image of Dany was dark, sultry, bitchy. It was an image that attracted him. And for months she'd signalled subtly that she knew he thought of her in a sexual way.

'Ooh. Your hand's so warm.' The look on her face turned to one of provocation, a look he associated more readily with her.

'This is like Carnival,' he shouted to her later, when they'd crossed the river and reached the Champs Elysées. 'Like Mardi Gras. Like you could do anything and get away with it.'

'Oh, yes, Greg? What *do* you want to do?' Her smile now was blatantly sexual.

Greg felt his mouth dry, his breathing shallow. He was invaded by an insidious excitement, intimate, liquid and golden. Dany was available to him, he was suddenly certain. It was a part of all this chaos. He contemplated the thought with something like a mental whistle, low and gloating. Kate's face hung briefly in his consciousness, wearing a look of bewildered reproach. But she was a ghost, without power. His betrayal of her was inevitable. Wild times like these came once in a lifetime – less – and he was going take anything that was on offer.

Chapter Thirty-Four

❧❧❧❧

Early Wednesday morning, barefoot, still in her white Swiss cotton nightshirt, Beatrice took a yoghurt and half a grapefruit from the fridge, sat down at the kitchen table to eat breakfast. Strong coffee gurgled in the shiny percolator. She switched on the radio, tuned to Europe No 1.

'. . . The most creative, the most spontaneous, but also the most vehement manifestation of energy to erupt in this country since . . . since 1848, since 1871, and I make no apology for the comparison . . .'

It was David's voice. For a disorientated moment Beatrice had the impression that she'd conjured it up herself, that the sound was inside her head.

This seemed to be some kind of ad hoc forum, hosted by an overwrought young reporter. Beatrice thought David sounded edgy. His fame and media experience were proving no match for the exuberant, loutish arrogance of a pair of student spokesmen, representing a couple of the political *groupuscules* who'd set the whole ball rolling. No one she'd heard of – not Jacques Sauvageot or Danny le Rouge – but bumptious none the less, and full of themselves.

Beatrice listened as she ate her austere fruit and yoghurt, followed by her voluptuous dark coffee and cigarette. Poor David was having a rough ride. While he praised and endorsed their enterprise, the two students patronized him, sent him up a little. One of them addressed him as Uncle David. Beatrice could hear in his voice how pissed off he was. But there wasn't much he could do. To lose his temper would be to sabotage his own role as their advocate. She felt sorry for him and rather sad. David sounded middle-aged and out of touch. She'd never seen him in that light before.

On Thursday, pushing Jack back from his daily romp in the park, Kate felt the muscles of her belly clench and lengthen, as if its football roundness were straining towards a rugby oval. There was no pain. In fact the sensation was not unpleasant.

That evening, after she'd put Jack to bed and sat at the table by the window working on David's book, the process repeated itself, once, twice, then a third time. Her supper lay heavy on her stomach. Later, in the bathroom, she vomited up the bread, cheese and tomatoes eaten two hours earlier.

Kate came awake in the small hours and lay for a long time, passive, fascinated, while her belly flexed and tautened as if experimentally. But nagged too by apprehension like a faint toothache. Was this it? She had no real frame of reference. With Jack her labour had been induced. Where the hell was Greg? He'd promised to phone each day. She'd heard nothing since Tuesday midday when he left.

At seven o'clock she rang Patrick and Simone's number, let the telephone ring and ring, but there was no reply. Later she might try calling the Sciences-Po and leave a message. But the way things were it seemed hardly likely that Greg was clocking on each day for study.

At seven thirty, as she lifted Jack from his cot, her waters broke, flooding warm and yukky down her legs on to the brick red linoleum floor.

'Ugh.' She was disgusted, then scared.

Her nightdress soaked, water seeping between her thighs, Kate carried Jack through to the bedroom and dialled Beatrice's number, praying to God she hadn't yet left for work.

'Hard labour. That's what I'd give them. Make them sort out the shambles they've made. Spoiled brats, don't know they're born.'

The taxi-driver groused about the detour he was forced to make in order to bypass the ravaged boulevards.

'Where will it all end?' Beatrice responded, tongue in cheek.

Trouble was, she was inclined to agree with the man. Ten years earlier, she knew, she would have revelled in the chaos. But having – to her own incredulity and consternation – just turned thirty, she'd probably reached an age when personal convenience loomed larger than the romantic longing for a more perfect world. Sad that. Beatrice wished the students well, but saw them as headless chickens, feverish young posers.

Beatrice wasn't sure how she felt about Kate's SOS. It was a damn nuisance, she did know. She had letters to write, lots of them, to potential customers in the States. And she had a meeting that afternoon with Véronique Taillandier to talk about hanging her odd, irregularly shaped paintings. Beatrice hated to relinquish that little plum to Jean-Pierre.

She prided herself on being absolutely reliable. It was the reason she'd progressed from being a pretty protégée of David's – taken on as a favour – to a mainstay of the gallery. It went horribly against the grain to let them down.

Beatrice was scared stiff at the thought of taking sole charge of Jack. What on earth did you do with a baby all day? And where the hell was Greg?

But, in a perverse way, she'd liked phoning the gallery, telling snooty Alice, 'My best friend's about to drop her kid. She needs me to look after the toddler . . .' It sounded airily out of character. And Beatrice felt oddly pleased by Kate's appeal, flattered, challenged. As if she'd been summoned to plunge her hands into real life, whatever that entailed.

'My God, you look like something out of *Vogue*,' Kate wailed when she opened the door to be confronted by Beatrice in her African print shift and bronze bracelets.

'I was on my way to work, for Christ's sake.' Beatrice held out her Pierre Cardin holdall. 'Don't throw a fit. I've brought jeans and stuff.'

Jack opened his mouth, a cagey, dazed look on his face. Slowly he ate all of the scrambled egg Beatrice fed him, turning the yellow curds round and around in his mouth. Beatrice experienced the warmth of something like satisfaction.

It had been a different story earlier on, after she'd delivered Kate to the hospital and took the kid back to the empty flat. She'd tried to console him, amuse him, made funny faces and waggled toys at him.

'Look, Jack, quack quack. Here comes Mister Duck . . .' Her voice thin and self-conscious in the silence. Thank the lord no one could see her.

Jack just howled, his little face crumpled and red, his whole body shaking, while Beatrice, dismayed by his distress, attempted to comfort him.

Later she stopped trying, turned the telly on, wrote letters to Odile and Nelly, ignoring the child. He seemed to recover, toddled here and there with a little truck full of odds and ends, absorbed in a private game. Beatrice kept quiet, terrified of ruffling his fragile contentment.

But after lunch she'd had to change a pooey nappy and that set the cat among the pigeons again. Jack squirmed and wriggled and the stinking ooze went everywhere. Beatrice gagged and ran a bath and dumped him in it, still bawling. She managed to get a new nappy on him somehow. It hung like an unravelling loincloth, but she trapped the flapping ends inside his plastic pants.

At bedtime he wailed, but half-heartedly, Beatrice thought, and not for long. He fell asleep and she felt as if she'd swum the Channel or wrestled a boa-constrictor and survived. She poured herself a glass of Greg's cheap red wine and telephoned the hospital. Kate had just been delivered of a baby girl.

The bleach-haired teenager in the next bed was having an awful time trying to get her baby on the breast. There was something to be said for experience, Kate thought, as Stella – she and Greg had agreed on the name weeks back, if it was a girl – suckled calm and steady as an angel. But, that small note of satisfaction apart, Kate's mood was one of growing anxiety and disbelief. She had the message that Beatrice had rung, but from Greg not a word.

'Hold your nipple like this –' an olive-skinned nurse with a slight moustache demonstrated graphically to the agitated girl – 'so's it really stands out.'

But the nurses were far more involved in exclaiming over the latest exploits of the students. Last night, apparently, had topped everything, the running battle between students and police reaching a size and a fury more destructive than anything yet seen.

'Nearly two hundred cars smashed or gone up in flames,' the incoming ward sister reported with relish. Her voice was rich and authoritative, with a slight wheeze like a concertina. 'Five hundred arrests. Four hundred injured . . . They've gone too far!'

Negotiations between the two sides had been broadcast live on Luxembourg, so she said. The authorities had climbed down, offered to reopen the Sorbonne the following day, but too late. 'The kids have got the bit between their teeth now. They told them where they could stick their offers.'

At visiting time Beatrice arrived carrying Jack and a bunch of lilies of the valley. She wore one of Greg's sweatshirts over a pair of jeans. Her hair hung loose and rather tangled on her shoulders. Jack had his trousers on back-to-front, Kate noticed, with wan amusement, and beneath them the nappy looked bunched and wadded.

Beatrice glanced dutifully at Stella, asleep in the crib next to the bed. 'She's beautiful.'

'I know.'

Jack reached his arms out to Kate and grizzled. Beatrice set him down on the bed. Fervently Kate enfolded his familiar little body, inhaled the scent of his wispy hair.

'How's it been?' she asked Beatrice.

'In a few years I'll look back and laugh.' But Beatrice seemed happy and pleased with herself.

A pause. Then, humiliated, Kate asked, 'Nothing from Greg?'

''Fraid not.' Beatrice's expression was guardedly neutral. 'But last night was the worst ever on the riot front.' She sat down heavily on the white cotton coverlet of Kate's bed, was reprimanded in ringing tones by the ward sister, got languidly to her feet again, wearing a look of mute, ostentatious disdain.

'I guess we'd have heard if he'd been hurt. Or arrested,' Kate mused. She shook her head, pulling down the corners of her mouth. 'Thanks for everything,' she said. 'Thanks a million times over . . .' She tried to smile. 'The Felix family to the rescue . . . Story of my life.'

Passing the Gare de l'Est on his way home, Greg thought how weirdly normal everything looked away from the scene of the riots. He felt spaced out, as if he were still living in a place of darkness, smoke and urgency, and this sunlit normality had nothing to do with him. He had no money left, was walking home, hadn't wanted to taint his farewell to Dany with a mundane request for a loan. Greg felt like a hobo, penniless and unshaven, his hair and clothes clotted with grit and smoke and sweat.

He was like a hobo with a hangover. His head ached dully with an overload of sensation. His mind teemed with pictures and sounds and smells. Last night. The dark red neon sky, flames and black smoke, the stifling stink of tear gas and burning rubber, the crazed shimmer of broken glass, cheers, cursing, jeering. Running hand in hand with Dany alongside a thudding mêlée of comrades, choking on gas, a mad joy in his throat.

The cop who jammed him up against a wall, baton in his chest. The man's dog-like, panting breath, the depth of his hatred . . . Until Dany kicked him in the knee, rammed him with the heavy torch she was carrying and they vanished into the anonymous welter of bodies.

Then Dany's room just before daybreak. Dany with her T-shirt up and jeans down, brazen eyes, pale brown nipples, hand down between his legs, face twisted in shivery elation, body filled with an electric intensity.

He was supposed to have exams today. But they'd been cancelled. Finally the snobby Sciences-Po had got itself involved. Greg recalled how he'd dreaded the ordeal of the terrifying oral. It seemed in another life. An occupation was mooted. Patrick was raring to go, his soft, clever face transfigured by energy. The professional revolutionary come into his own. Greg was just exhausted. All he wanted was to stagger home.

Though he was dubious of his welcome. He'd sworn to phone and never had. The promise had loomed over him like a tedious chore, ever present, increasingly impossible . . . He was otherwise engaged, body and soul. Once or twice, when he had leisure, Greg had been gripped by a chill of fear. What if Kate . . . ? But he couldn't stop himself taking the chance. It was only a small chance, after all. He longed now for his home and his kid and his wife, ached to cuddle them and spoil them and be spoiled in return.

As he walked along the Rue Botzaris, alongside the park, Greg's thoughts returned to Dany.

'This is it,' he'd told her. 'We can't meet again. Because of Kate, you know . . .'

'I know.' Dany had nodded, with solemn eyes but a sweet-malicious smile. 'I wondered when you'd remember.'

Greg felt like someone in a cool French movie. They'd kissed, embraced, sentimental, teasing and tough. He made his exit, felt good about himself. It was easy. Though some kid deep inside him had yearned to cling to her and weep and tell her that these few days would be the most amazing memory of his life.

Beatrice was playing peep-bo with Jack when she heard the key in the lock. A moment later Greg walked in, looking like a sleep-walker. He was gratifyingly startled to see her. His face fell, and the thoughts racing through his mind were clearly, almost laughably legible.

'Where's Kate?'

'In hospital.' She was coolly terse.

'So the kid . . . Hey . . . Oh my God . . . She's had it.'

Beatrice let him flounder.

'Has she?'

'Yesterday.'

'Oh my God.'

He stood and stared.

'Look, Greg, I need to go. I've got a date. I've been here for two days . . . I'm all packed and ready.'

He said nothing. Jack was sitting on the floor, his eyes round and large. Suddenly she hated to leave him.

'Goodbye, darling.' She knelt to give him a kiss. How sweet he was. 'Bye bye.' She waved her hand. Jack gazed at her blank-faced, then a small smile broke through and he flexed his tiny fingers.

'It's a girl, by the way,' she told Greg as she went to fetch her Cardin holdall. Passing through the hall, she stuck her head round the door again. 'You're a shit, you know. A *shit*.'

'Yeah.'

Around half past four, a couple of hours before visiting-time, Kate was jerked from a semi-sleep by the sound of two voices raised in argument. One of them was Greg's. He wanted to be let in but the ward sister would not permit it before the patients' early supper had been served and the babies had had their six o'clock feed. Kate stayed put, drowsing, listening to the dispute as if it barely concerned her.

Her bed was diagonally opposite the doorway. Later she saw Greg walk in, appearing slight and subdued among the eager groups of smiling relatives. He trailed a bunch of blood-red, long-stemmed, floristy-looking roses and Jack was sitting up in his arms. Greg looked thin, Kate thought. Their eyes locked from a distance, warily, expressing no emotion. He came and stood at the end of the bed, glanced into the crib and back at Kate.

'I'm a shit,' he said.

The contrition on his face, and in the set of his body, was gawkily appealing, making her think fleetingly of Steve McQueen. But his remorse was somehow irrelevant and connected in no way with the wet, red wound she hid inside her, along with the despairing thought that in some unsuspected way she deserved his treatment.

'I'm sorry, Kate. God, I'm sorry.'

Kate had wondered what angry words would spill from her mouth when Greg finally put in his appearance. But she wasn't angry, she was empty, and almost embarrassed by her lack of a response. It was a relief when Greg put Jack down beside her and he curled up, leaning his head against her new flat, loose belly.

'Say something,' Greg urged, with a kind of pleading exasperation.

'I don't know what to say. I don't know what I feel.'

He shrugged and turned away, bent over the crib with eager eyes, mouth relaxing into a smile. He contemplated his daughter for a moment, then reached in and lifted the little body in a movement full of easy tenderness.

He looked into the baby's eyes. 'Hi, Stella. Hi, sweetie. It's your dad.'

He was nice with kids, Kate thought. But that didn't mean anything. Nothing meant anything.

When she got home Kate went back to work immediately. Stella was fed and changed at all the right intervals, then laid back in her cot while Kate returned to her typewriter. She wasn't blind to her daughter's beauty – her eyes blue like Greg's, the soft pale skin, the surprising energy of her tiny limbs – but saw her in a hasty, harassed, foggy way.

Finishing this translation was the most pressing thing in her life, an obsession almost. It was like a labour she just had to complete before she could shake her mind free of nameless worries, vivid, disturbing dreams, an unspecified sense of anxiety that hung about her all the time.

'For God's sake,' Greg urged, 'ease off. You look all in.' She had all the time in the world. The deadline was months away.

He was home a lot and in a biddable mood, taking care of Jack nearly all of the time to give his wife a break. They were polite and amicable with one another, Greg because he felt guilty, Kate because it saved energy.

Sometimes he came up behind her as she sat at the typewriter, massaged her shoulders, kissed the back of her neck, told her she was tense and to loosen up. She lost time and concentration when he did that, was offended by his fingers kneading insistently into her muscles, but sat still and let him. It was easier that way.

It was a singular time. Huge sections of the working population were inspired by the students' example. Factories were occupied. As the month of May progressed France became enmeshed in the tentacles of hundreds of interlocking strikes. Everyone wanted to be in on the action – not just workers but schoolkids, film-makers, musicians, even footballers . . . And, in Paris, against the ironic backdrop of all this conflict, the Americans and the North Vietnamese met to talk about peace.

Greg was very much a part-time revolutionary now. Once or twice he took Jack out for the day in his push-chair, walked all the way into town to visit the occupied Sorbonne and the Sciences-Po. Patrick was in his element, joyously involved in study-groups, plans for curriculum reform, even cleaning rotas. For him the situation was a dream come true and he was disappointed by Greg's apathy. With perfect sincerity Greg pleaded family commitments, but in fact he had little taste for this rapturous self-organization. The best had been the first spontaneous eruption of wild defiance.

For Kate the turbulence of the times felt almost personal, a mirror image of the uncertainty inside her. At the back of everything was a kind of shivery awe that, for a few crucial days, Greg had stepped outside the rules, done just exactly what he wanted and hadn't given a damn about her. He could do it again. She'd been powerless, and the feeling had an echo to it, harking back to something she couldn't place. But then it came to her. She'd felt like this watching Ellis home in on Fay, greedy for his own happiness whether his daughter liked it or not. Kate saw a callous honesty in both actions and maybe that was what life was all about.

One afternoon, when Greg was in town, Juliette cycled out to see the new baby. She looked terrific, wearing cut-off jeans, hair cropped even shorter than usual and curling close to her healthy tanned face. Juliette raved about the joys of cycling, with traffic reduced by the petrol shortage.

'Look at the muscles in my thighs!' It was great for the figure too. Kate admired her shapely brown legs.

But it turned out her friend had a hidden agenda. As they sat drinking iced water in the small living-room – with the windows open and the curtains shifting in the breeze, the sound of vehicles and voices from the car park below, with Stella lying kicking on a rug on the floor – Juliette claimed that, during the days Greg

335

had been incommunicado, he'd been fucking a girl called Dany, a friend of Patrick and Simone's. Her sultana-brown eyes stared obliquely into Kate's as she made the revelation.

Her words conjured up pictures of bodies, pale and headless, like the set of blurry porno-photos Greg had showed her once. They promised new and excruciating depths of pain, but she wouldn't look at them, not yet, not now, under Juliette's subtly expectant gaze.

'So that's the reason you cycled out to see me.'

Juliette looked offended. 'I thought you'd want to know . . . I would, in your place.'

When Greg got home she told him about Juliette's visit and what she'd said, and saw his cute, bright face disintegrate in front of her.

'So it's true,' she said.

He nodded, seeming too overcome for speech. By what he'd done? Or by the shock of its becoming known?

'You're white as a corpse,' Kate marvelled.

She was impressed by his horror, the nakedness of it. Greg's disarray made her feel calm and powerful.

Later, when he'd put Jack to bed, she saw that there were tears in his eyes. 'I'm sorry, baby,' he kept saying. 'It didn't mean anything . . . She was just there and everything around us was so crazy . . .'

He tried to embrace her, his cheeks wet and blubbered. She had the impression he wanted her to sob in his arms, to weep with him, for them to achieve together some sort of release and reconciliation. But the thought of such emotion seemed messy and self-indulgent. She just couldn't summon up the energy.

Greg began to talk about going back to Canada, all of them, and getting started on their real life. Though he had commitments, notably an index for tweedy Doctor Lazell from Berkeley, who'd been in Paris on and off for years, working on a huge history of the French Revolution. The proofs would be ready in October. Greg reckoned he could get the job done by Christmas.

Kate got on with her own work and let him plan. Only her imagination began to play with the daring thought that she didn't have to stay married if she didn't want to and, just as soon as this translation was finished, she'd be free to think about that too. But it was just an idea.

At night, while drifting into sleep, she would picture herself at Plas Felix with Jack and Stella, eating breakfast on the terrace while horses grazed in the field. Greg wasn't with them. She saw Jack toddling across the grass between Odile and Jerome, herself and Nelly on the beach below the house, splashing with their children in the shallow waves, early evening sun sparkling on the sea. The pictures made her happy, but they were only dreams and didn't commit her to anything.

During the day she lived in David Lacoste's world, hunched over his manuscript, head filled with his sardonic characters, with their jazz, their scotch and their cruel, casual adulteries. In David's books infidelity was integral, viewed without drama. Processing the detached prose, hour after hour, day after day, Kate could almost see Greg's unfaithfulness with the same cool eye. Just another plot-strand.

But then, first thing one morning, fresh from bed, she walked in on Greg playing with Jack in the living-room.

'Who's Daddy's best boy?' Greg held him high in the air, made popping noises with his lips against the child's bare belly, while Jack screamed in near hysterical delight.

The room was so small and cramped that father and son seemed to fill it. Greg's head was flung back and he was grinning, his profile lean and full of life. And his laughing tenderness conjured up a vivid sense of the first precious winter of their marriage. At the same time her mind flashed an image of Greg lying beside this woman, this Dany, in a half-lit room, touching her, teasing her with lazy sexual intimacy.

She closed her eyes and was ambushed by a sense of betrayal so powerful it made her head spin, the room spin, made her legs feel like rubber. She felt sick, sweaty, held on to the door jamb for support.

337

'Say hi to Mommy.' Even as Greg turned, smiling, to include her Kate fled.

In the bedroom she was confronted by the framed photograph of the two of them, a few weeks after they'd met, sitting on the floor in Pascal's flat, flanked by a gonk in a flat cap, a present from Sofia to Pascal. Greg had his arm round her shoulder and together they smiled into the camera like good, happy children.

The public disorder simmered on, with labour disputes and political manoeuvring and periodic outbursts of violence like a boil coming to a head. For a time it seemed clear that, at the very least, De Gaulle was done for. But then the tide appeared to turn. People got restive and hankered after order. The student movement was running out of steam. There was talk of squalor at the Sorbonne, rats in the cellars, whores and drug-dealers muscling in. The *groupuscules* squabbled among themselves while the Right closed ranks. New air was pumped into de Gaulle's collapsed balloon, which grew larger and more buoyant by the day. Elections were declared and, at the end of June, he was returned to power with a triumphant majority.

The following week Kate came to the end of her translation. That evening the manuscript, lying on the hall table ready to be posted, compact in its brown paper parcel, seemed invested with a tactile, symbolic quality like a talisman. Greg bought a bottle of cheap champagne to celebrate. He was fed up to the back teeth with her everlasting working.

She'd counted on the event to usher in a feeling of clear-headedness, a time for taking stock. But no such epiphany occurred. She remained locked in the muddy truce with Greg that was becoming habit and could go on for ever if she let it. The weather was hot. The flat felt small and stifling. If anything she missed the anaesthetizing sense of purpose her work had provided.

Kate took snaps of Jack and Stella, using up a roll of film that had been in her camera since last winter. When they were developed she chose the two best to stick in her album.

Flipping through the pages, Kate was confronted by faces she

loved. Nelly and Odile and Olivier, their sweet guilelessness contrasting with the treachery she now saw in the smiling portrait of
Greg that used to take her breath away. And again she thought
longingly of being at Plas Felix. A day's journey and she could
be home.

Greg seemed to have forgotten he had anything to atone for,
was back to his cheerful self. At the height of the heat-wave he
got the decorating bug. He decided to paint the living-room, get
rid of the tatty collage, make it simple and streamlined.

'We could make this place a lot more liveable,' he mused, as if the
living-room were only the start of it. 'I could build shelves . . .'

Everything would have to be stacked in the hallway and climbed
over for God knows how long. Kate couldn't face the upheaval. To
her his new enterprise seemed perverse posturing, as if he were
willing himself into a domestic role.

But Greg was adamant. 'I want you to choose the colour,' he told
Kate in a warm, encouraging voice, as if inviting her to enthuse over
an unwanted gift.

He persisted, so she picked out a clear yellow that she thought
would look cool in summer, cheerful in winter.

Full of his project, Greg began to strip the cuttings off the wall.
In places the drawing pins had chipped the plaster, and there were
long cracks above the window, although the building could not be
more than five years old.

'I'll have to fill these in before I can get started.'

Next day Kate took the kids to see Beatrice, whom she hadn't
visited since Stella was born. In her orderly flat it was cool and
civilized. She'd made iced tea with mint leaves in it, bought chocolate milk for Jack and expensive little Italian animal biscuits. She
cuddled Stella with cautious goodwill, played on the floor with Jack
in her cream linen trousers. Being with Beatrice reminded Kate of
how valiantly she'd stepped in to help. It brought Greg's monstrous
neglect to the front of her mind.

The Métro home was hideously hot and crowded. Stella began to
cry and that set Jack off. Kate felt the sweat running down between
her shoulder blades. A sour-faced woman shouted at her because

she tripped over the folded push-chair and Kate shouted back. She could feel a headache coming on.

When they arrived home Greg had filled the cracks in the walls and he was sitting by the open window in the empty room, with a cold beer and a cigarette.

'Hi, folks.' He greeted them chirpily, relaxed and pleased with his day's work. 'How was the marquise?'

'OK,' Kate replied tersely. Today his breezy reference to Beatrice offended her. Beatrice had been loyal, Greg false. She couldn't bear his self-satisfaction.

Kate went to get a drink of water for herself and Jack. In the kitchen, on the draining-board, stood a plate with the hardening remains of Polyfilla. An abrupt flame of anger leapt inside her. He'd mixed it on one of Beatrice's Art-Deco plates. She could not believe such crass indifference, such barbarism.

Kate stood and stared at the plate. She found herself trembling. There were tears in her eyes. She felt crazy, as if she'd been crazy for a long time without knowing it. There was a crawling sensation on her skin like prickly heat but worse than that. As though she'd kept the lid down on a jarful of maggots, but now they'd boiled up, forced the lid off, eager to spread their seething loathsomeness over everything.

She carried the plate into the next room and shoved it under Greg's nose. 'Look what you've done, you bastard. You smug bastard! Look at it!'

Kate dashed the plate to the floor and began to hit out at Greg, beyond caring that Jack could see and looked scared.

'Hey, hold on . . .' There was a hint of tolerant laughter in Greg's voice that maddened her, and she hit him harder, harder, harder, so he would know it wasn't a joke.

PART 3

✖✖✖

The Seventies

Chapter Thirty-Five
1975

❧❧❧❧

For over a month now Olivier's stuff had been occupying an increasingly large and sprawling space in the small Hertfordshire cottage where Kate now lived alone with Jack and Stella. His personal effects arrived, a few at a time, on successive visits. Kate had promised to drive him and his boxes up to Oxford in her Morris. Olivier was on the move once more. This time to a narrowboat moored on the Oxford canal.

'I have to say, I'll be glad to get rid of this lot,' she told him as they set out, 'and be able to pull the curtains again without risking falling flat on my face into a mess of glasses and crockery.'

It was the summer holidays and the children came along, squashed uncomfortably with the boxes in the back of her estate car. It was hot and Oxford was packed with tourists.

They had to park the car on a bit of stony ground by a bridge then carry all of Olivier's things to the boat. The children were tickled by the idea of straggling along the towpath with his exotic bits and pieces – the green and red glass lamp with the oily bubbles in it, his fifties fan-heater, the portrait in crude acrylic blues and mauves done by one of his girlfriends seven or eight years back, the patchwork quilt sewn by another – then walking the plank and dumping them any old how in the bare, damp-smelling cabin.

'I feel as if I've got lost on my way to the station,' Kate laughed, as she lugged the battered suitcase that contained his clothes. It seemed more incongruous to be carrying that alongside the weeds and nettles that bordered the path than the open cardboard boxes of books and records, pots and pans.

'Thirty-two years old and all your worldly goods fit into a Morris

Traveller,' she mocked, as they arrived at the gang-plank for a second time.

Olivier took the suitcase from her and hoisted it on to his shoulder. He gave her a sardonic glance from beneath his long lashes. 'And that's the way I like it.'

As he stowed case and boxes in the cabin Kate mused on the sparsity of his possessions. Did it signify an admirable lack of materialism, or a stubborn refusal of responsibility? In fact most of what he *had* got seemed to have been given him by a miscellaneous succession of women and girls.

As Olivier emerged from the cabin, seven-year-old Stella approached, half-buried beneath a huge plum-coloured velvet floor cushion. On her head was Olivier's floppy, multi-coloured cap, a present from Caz with whom he'd briefly lived last winter.

She looked adorable, Kate thought, in the outsized headgear, lanky, toothy, all eyes and straggly fair hair. In her blue dungarees Stella made her think of an American farm kid out of some thirties photograph, skinny, freckled and uningratiating. She panted and puffed elaborately as she drew near, then screwed her face into a wry, protesting smile as she saw Olivier and her mother watching.

'Like the hat, chipmunk,' Olivier teased.

It was a family joke that Stella hated the nickname. She tore the cap from her head and threw it at him, dropping the cushion in the process.

'Watch it!' Olivier just managed to save the hat from plopping into the canal.

'Ooh.' Stella watched with suspended dismay, followed by a pop-eyed look of relief.

Kate laughed, and noticed a red-haired woman staring from the next-but-one boat. Gazing at Olivier in particular, naturally, so striking and lithe and colourful. The shoulder-length dark blond hair that always hung just right. Chic, piratical Zapata moustache. Washed-out jeans – patched and customized, of course, by some girl he knew – resting on narrow hips. Wiry brown arms emerging from a batik T-shirt in shades of orange, red and gold.

344

He stood smiling as eight-year-old Jack approached, some way behind his sister, cradling Olivier's guitar as if it were something rare and precious.

'Get your skates on, Jimi Hendrix.' Olivier's voice was gentle. Jack's earnestness had that effect on adults.

The boy's face lit up. Olivier had taught him a few chords and the nickname was their private property.

Kate stood waiting. Jack never hurried. There was something angelic about him, in his pale blue jeans and T-shirt. He was dark like her, with the same straight, fine hair which was cut in a page-boy style, framing his serious face. She loved his self-contained gravity, but sometimes it caught and wrung her heart as if she'd done him some huge wrong.

It took one more trip to transfer the rest of Olivier's belongings to the boat. There was some gas left in the cylinder in the galley-kitchen and the water-tank had been filled. Olivier put the kettle on for tea. They spread cushions and his patchwork quilt on the floor. The children lounged ostentatiously, diverted by the prospect of an impromptu picnic. They swigged at the remains of a bottle of warm Coke. There were hotdogs bought from a van in a lay-by on the way up. Olivier had leanings towards vegetarianism, but the sizzling sausages had undermined his resolve.

When he'd eaten, Olivier lit a joint. Kate didn't mind him smoking in front of the kids. To them a cigarette was a cigarette. But she made him roll them in private. It was too intriguing a performance.

'Are you really going to live here?' Stella gazed round the chaotic cabin, half sceptical, half envious.

'Next time you come there'll be plastic roses and a telly and a three-piece suite,' Olivier promised with the fuzzy, mildly stoned smile Kate knew well.

'What's a three-piece suite?'

'Wait and see.'

'We'll be able to come here on holiday,' Jack said hopefully.

'Lots of times,' Olivier agreed.

345

Kate could not relax for long. 'I hate to leave you in this mess. But I've got to go. Work to do, as ever was.'

'I'm just mighty obliged to you, Katie, for bringing my stuff up. You're a friend indeed.'

Olivier walked them to the car. It was a humid, overcast August day. The trees looked heavy green and sullen, the canal milky brown.

'Three weeks time, I mean it,' he told the kids as he kissed them goodbye, lifting Stella up to straddle his waist.

'Three weeks is too long,' Jack complained.

Kate unlocked the car, then reached up to give him a hug. 'Hope it all works out,' she said, with a breath of anxiety. 'Don't forget to phone.'

Kate's thin, lively face, framed by the new Afro hairstyle, grinned at him from the window of her car. The kids made monkey gestures. Olivier waved until the Morris was out of sight.

Kate had joked to him, a couple of weeks back, that Afro frizzes were like some science-fiction curse that claimed its victims one by one.

'Every time I go out someone else in the village has been possessed. I just know it's going to get me one of these days.'

She looked brilliant, Olivier thought, at the wheel of her stylish old banger with its wood trim. Like one of those new women you saw in adverts nowadays and on the telly. Bright and independent. In charge of their own lives, as the cliché ran.

He was proud of her. What good friends they'd become since she split with Greg. Yes, Kate was probably his best friend. And how he adored the kids. And they him. Without vanity, Olivier knew that. Kate had told him so enough times. And, anyway, they showed it.

It was like having a family. Only he didn't have to be married and get a proper job and a mortgage – all the things that were as incomprehensible to him as living on the moon.

Olivier turned and retraced his steps towards the emptiness and the jumble and the damp, rooty smell of his new home. They filled

346

him with the kind of pleasure another man might experience in response to the polished order of an expensive hotel. Olivier was never happier than when starting from scratch.

He began to sort things out, tidy them away. Tomorrow he would try and lay hands on a table of sorts, a chair or two, a bookcase, a portable telly. As much as anything he wanted to surprise the kids next time they came by the transformation. They looked to him for excitement and he was eager to supply it.

The boat, named *Creeping Jenny*, belonged to Blackie, whom he'd known for years – an unlikely entrepreneur, a classics graduate with a nervous giggle, who earned his living buying houses, renovating them top to bottom, and selling them on for a profit. Almost to his surprise, in the brisk market of the early seventies, Blackie had got rich. Now, half dazed with success, he owned a six-bedroomed house in a Cotswold village called Filkins, had a wife and two babies.

Blackie had lived on the narrowboat for two years in the sixties and he kept it on as a sort of bolthole, out of the superstitious fear that one day the bubble would burst, his wealth and his marriage would collapse about his ears and he would return to zero.

Olivier had helped Blackie out many times over the years. They worked well together, could transform a rubble-strewn yard into a lawn and shrubbery in the space of a day, had spent whole nights, fuelled by amphetamines, decorating vast bare rooms under harsh, unshaded bulbs, falling into their sleeping bags at dawn for a few hours' rest before starting all over again.

'Why don't you join me? You're the only bugger I trust.' Three years ago Blackie had invited Olivier to go into partnership with him.

But Olivier refused. The offer sounded too much like responsibility. And he could only stomach hard labour if he could see a definite end to it.

For much of the time Blackie let the *Creeping Jenny* out to friends but, with the best will in the world, it often stood empty. In spring he'd had squatters and had to pay them to get out. Now he offered Olivier a retainer to live there, to act as a sort

347

of caretaker and make sure the boat stayed in a decent state of repair.

'Why don't you just cut your losses and sell it?' Olivier had felt honour-bound to suggest.

'Never.' Blackie had shaken his head, given that self-mocking, self-deprecating look of his. 'The *Creeping Jenny*'s my "Rosebud". I'll probably croak out her name on my death bed . . .'

He'd sorted out a job for Olivier too, if he wanted it. In a newly opened tourist hotel Blackie had some kind of an interest in. If he agreed, Olivier could work as barman there four nights a week. What's more, the hotel offered minibus tours of the dreaming spires. Amiable and personable as he was, Olivier would be ideal as a guide.

'There's bound to be tips,' Blackie coaxed. A shy man himself, he was ruefully envious of Olivier's winning way with people. 'You'll charm the pants off all the rich old ladies . . .'

'I'd want extra for that.'

But the time was right. The health-food shop Caz ran with her friend, Tina, had gone stale on him. He'd had a brief affair with Caz that seemed to end amicably. But since then there'd been an atmosphere in the shop, though he tried to ignore it. Then one day, out of the blue, Caz screamed at him that his wry smiles and his endless niceness were driving her up the wall.

Afterwards she said sorry, that she had PMT, and to take no notice. He gave her a forgiving cuddle. But when Blackie came up with his offer it seemed the perfect opportunity for Olivier to get out, move on, re-invent himself.

He squatted down to spread out his sleeping-bag on the floor of the cabin. And on top of it he draped the eagle quilt Serena had pieced together out of the big sack of rags she kept in her cluttered fairy-tale flat overlooking the canal in Paddington.

Outside the gang-plank creaked. A woman's face peered in the doorway. She had long, frizzy red hair, parted in the middle.

'Hi, I'm Carol. Your neighbour.' Her eyes took in his bed-roll, cushions, guitar. 'This looks cosy.'

* * *

By the time they got to Aylesbury, Stella was asleep, curled up small on the back seat, head cradled in her arms. Car journeys always had that effect on her, leaving Kate and Jack to a sort of adult intimacy.

'I wish we could've slept there,' he said, leaning into the space between the two front seats.

'We will. We'll take our sleeping bags up . . . But we've got to give poor Olivier time to get straight first. And anyway I've got work to do.'

'You always have.'

'That's right.' She turned to flash him a look of mock-severity. He grinned. It was a bone of contention between them so familiar it had become a joke. Most of the time.

A silence. Then Jack said, 'Anyway, Olivier likes having us around.'

'Yes he does. But not every moment of every day.'

Of the four Felix siblings, Kate was closest to Olivier at this point in her life. He came by at least one weekend in three, spreading his own brand of *joie de vivre*.

Families were more fragmented nowadays. That was a fact – Kate read it everywhere. But the trend hadn't spread to the village where she, Jack and Stella had their home. Here the nuclear family ruled OK, and the kids often felt the lack of a father.

Though he never forgot Christmas, or their birthdays, Greg had never visited his children. He pleaded poverty and the excuse rang true. He was back in Canada now, had remained a student until '73 when he ran out of foundations to fund him. He'd borrowed money from his parents for the divorce settlement . . . Kate had mixed feelings about his defection. She personally had no desire to see him. Things were tidy as they were. A visit might have stirred the kids up, raised emotions and expectations that could never be fulfilled. And yet . . . He *should* have come, should have moved heaven and earth to stay in physical touch with his children.

Instead they had Olivier, a young uncle, whose presence was less constant but far more dashing than any of the fathers they knew. He was handsome and modern, took them swimming in summer, tobogganing in snowy weather on old fertilizer sacks, taught Jack guitar, brought tubes of grown-up looking paints for Stella, told them jokes, gave them aeroplane spins, cooked huge pizzas in Kate's big roasting tray.

Kate recalled an evening when the kids were in bed and she and Olivier were lounging on the floor with a litre bottle of nasty red wine watching the news on television. Olivier had laughed that he wouldn't recognize an interest rate if it bit him on the bum.

Kate was abruptly irritated by the complacent fecklessness of the remark. 'You always say what an air-head you are,' she accused. 'But you're not like that with the kids. You never let them down. You really take your uncleship seriously . . .'

'It's the only thing I do take seriously,' he'd replied mildly, leaving Kate puzzled as to why she'd snapped at him in the first place.

But the exchange somehow encapsulated her attitude towards him. Much as she loved Olivier and cherished the sheer fun he brought to their lives, her feelings for him were shot through with an inescapable thread of impatience.

'Look –' Jack pointed suddenly – 'there's the house with all the gnomes in the garden. Olivier says he's going to buy you some for Christmas . . .'

'He'd better not.'

For the children's sake, Kate had resolved to keep the village a sex-free zone. She'd had a couple of short-lived affairs, but conducted them well away from her home ground, and they'd petered out for lack of any kind of a real-life setting. Yet oddly, though Olivier was strikingly handsome and Kate starved of physical contact, there was almost no sexual tension between them. Though he visited constantly and often stayed the night, it was taken for granted that he would sleep on the sagging Put-U-Up in the living-room. People talked anyway, Kate knew that, speculating about her and the children's intriguing uncle.

Her neighbour, Allie, claimed to have stuck up for her. 'I told them, why shouldn't Kate have a bit of fun . . . She deserves a break if anyone does.'

'But I don't *have* a bit of fun,' Kate protested. 'Olivier's no more than a brother.'

Whatever verdict was reached on their relationship, Olivier was liked in the village. People were disarmed by the unassuming friendliness that belied his charismatic looks. If she were honest, that was another reservation Kate harboured as regards Olivier.

With strangers she saw a smoothness to his charm, a mechanical quality in the warmth of his voice, in his understanding chuckle, in the particular amiability with which he laughed at their anecdotes, endorsed their opinions.

'Oh, right,' he would say, a smile in his voice. 'Absolutely!' In Kate's eyes the phrases had become seductive tics with no thought or feeling behind them.

She was more sanguine about his use of soft drugs. Olivier smoked grass every day, and dealt in a small way among friends. For a time she used to join him, welcoming the relaxing, mellowing effects of the cannabis, the moments of anarchic gaiety. For eighteen months or so she and Olivier had relished their private stoned evenings.

But after a while the effects seemed to change. When Kate smoked she began to feel exposed, guilty, paranoid. She seemed to see with a sharply heightened lucidity what a mess her life was, how she wasn't getting any younger, how she never had enough time for the kids, not really, her mind always half on her work. The money worries never stopped and, out of selfish pride, she'd deprived her children of a perfectly adequate father.

And gradually Kate began to refuse the joints Olivier offered. The last thing she needed during her precious off-duty hours was to be wrestling with unpalatable truths.

Chapter Thirty-Six

❧❧❧

'This must be the least picturesque village in England,' Olivier had marvelled back in January '71, the first time he came to see them in the little house in Downridge, East Herts, Kate had bought with the 'once-and-for-all' settlement she and Greg had agreed on during their divorce proceedings.

'It's not on a railway line either,' Kate pointed out, 'which is why I can afford a place here. And you'll find the night-life closes down at seven o'clock sharp.'

Downridge consisted of a strip of dusty High Street bordered by small, largely terraced houses, a pub, a newsagent cum post office and a Wavy Line self-service grocery. Four side streets and a car park branched off the main artery. At one end of the village stood a church, at the other a pleasant, red-brick Georgian-style farmhouse and just along from it St John's primary school, also in red brick, with a tarmac playground in front of it – the back gave on to open fields. There were a number of small outlying hamlets and a couple more farms in the vicinity.

Kate's house was in Wilbert Close, in the side-road nearest the church end of the village. On Thursday evenings the bell-ringers practised their rapturous-monotonous carillons, falling silent on the dot of eight thirty.

Her cottage was one of a terraced row of five, built in 1898 – a plaque on the central house proclaimed the date – for workers from the nearby gravel quarry, long since disused. Each had its gabled dormer window, tiled porch like a tiny roof over the door, and long straight front garden. Kate's house was on one end of the terrace, so her garden was a little wider and had a passage through to the small backyard.

It had been an ecstatic relief to move into her own place after renting the top floor in the house of a couple in Wood Green, friends of Jess's, who argued all the time and each tried to rope Kate in as an ally. She hated it there and Stella got whiny and clingy. Wood Green seemed gloomy and amorphous and Kate latched on to the idea that she wanted to bring her children up in the country.

'You're mad,' Jess told her. 'You'll be so isolated. You'll find yourself in some incestuous inbred community where the only pastime is buggering sheep.'

'I'll be able to watch then, won't I.'

If anything Jess's opposition merely hardened her resolve. Her friend was head of history now at the school where she taught and seemed to think she knew what was best for everyone.

The cottage wasn't beautiful and the rooms were almost as small as the ones in the nightmare flat in Buttes-Chaumont. But Kate loved it just because it was hers. Downstairs were a living-room and kitchen, upstairs two bedrooms and a tiny bathroom conversion. Which ruined the line of the roof, so a woman in the newspaper shop who Kate didn't know from Adam had complained the very week she moved in.

In the early days, with Olivier's help, Kate had painted the rooms white throughout but, since then, she never seemed to have the time to think about décor. Her furniture was secondhand and nothing went with anything else. Olivier brought her presents sometimes, purchased from one or other of his arty friends – a hanging plant pot in a macramé holder, patchwork cushions, a batik 'throw' – and these added haphazard touches of ornamentation to her mismatched interior.

The first spring she and Olivier laid the long front garden down to turf so the children would have somewhere to play. Her neighbours, George and Allie, disapproved. The fashion was for rows of brussels sprouts and fat leeks and dark green leathery cabbages.

As they worked George stood watching over the waist-high fence, still and sceptical in his tweed jacket, tweed cap and muffler.

'You can't eat grass,' he commented flatly, after several minutes of silent contemplation.

'We're townies,' Kate answered. 'We buy our food.'

Her reply had tickled his inexcitable countryman's funny-bone to the extent that he'd quoted it back to her times without number over the years.

Kate saw, almost from the moment they moved in, that the children had a sense of coming home, seemed to know they had a place now where they belonged and would continue to belong. Stella stopped her whining as if at the press of a button. Jack radiated a sort of solemn contentment as he pottered back and forth in the garden between the secondhand tricycle and the climbing frame bought from a small-ad in the local paper. The change in them was miraculous and she couldn't help knowing that most of it stemmed from her own sudden sense of relaxation and relief.

The children's new and demonstrable happiness was a comfort to Kate, a solid satisfaction to be relished at the end of the day, like a job well done, vastly outweighing any reservations she might harbour on her own account.

Because, in a sense, Jess had been right. For all its wholesomeness the life here had a limited, parochial quality. There were days, walking down the same grey strip of High Street – in drizzle, dusty sun or freezing rain – to meet the kids from school, after six hours spent at her typewriter and the prospect of at least four more before bedtime, when Kate mused dourly that a spot of sheep-shagging might actually liven the place up a bit.

The summer Olivier moved to the boat Kate was deeply involved in translating a book called *Le Gros Rouge* by a Belgian writer named Ghislaine Poswick whom David Lacoste had met at some writer's do in Chicago. The novel was long and the deadline tight and Kate was afraid she'd be unable to manage the usual fortnight she spent each August with the children at Plas Felix.

'Come for a week anyway,' Odile urged over the phone. 'Bring your dictionaries and things. You can work in the mornings while I take charge of Jack and Stella.'

'I shouldn't . . .'

But Kate knew she would. Plas Felix was her villa, her *dacha*.

The summer would be featureless and incomplete if they didn't go. And it gave her a warm pleasure to see how much the children loved the place, how they regarded Nelly's kids and Odile and Jerome as family – cousins, grandparents, like their friends at school had. Odile and Jerome were the family elders now. In 1970 both Grand-mère and Jerome's mother had died within a few weeks of one another.

Kate hadn't seen Ellis since that stilted evening in Paris, when she and Greg were still together, Jack was a baby, and she was resentfully pregnant with Stella. Nowadays father and daughter rarely even bothered to write. Though Ellis and Fay had taken to sending out a duplicated letter with their Christmas cards, documenting the achievements of each member of the family.

Olivier adored the bulletins and made Kate save them each year for him to read.

Kate despised the whole smug tradition. 'They never say anything that doesn't redound to their credit – no kids caught cheating in exams, wife having it off with the boss, husband sobbing in a rainy car-park wondering what's the point of it all . . .'

But she loathed Ellis's offerings with a particular venomous passion. Their impersonality. The atmosphere they gave off of healthy success and buoyant togetherness. On the other hand he sent them out good and early and always enclosed a generous cheque that financed their Christmas in fine style.

When she drove to Wales Kate set out around four or five in the morning, so as to be well on her way before the traffic got heavy. For Jack and Stella the early start was part of the fun – setting off in the dark, snuggling in their sleeping bags in the back of the car. Somewhere beyond Shrewsbury they would stop in a lay-by for a breakfast time picnic.

'Be sure you arrive in time for lunch,' Odile had ordered. 'I'll invite Nelly and Robert and the children. Jerome has a new passion for the barbecue.'

It was just after one when Kate turned off the road down the lane towards the house. Five minutes back they'd passed the bend in the road where the children craned their necks, eagle-eyed, competing to be the first to shout, 'I can see the sea!'

The house came into view, solid and foursquare, the oaken door standing half-open. Kate drew up in the small courtyard. She got out, stretched her arms and sniffed the air, spicy with sun on the bracken that grew up the hillside above. She could hear voices from the terrace.

'Go round the side. Surprise them,' she told Stella and Jack.

For herself she wanted to go inside first, to where the broad staircase led up from the hall, to breathe in the particular warm, polished odour of the house. Walking in like that always brought a ghostly awareness of past arrivals. The day she'd come from France with the two babies – not quite believing the decision she'd made, nervy and running with sweat after a long, horrendous journey with both kids bawling – to Odile's practical, unjudgmental welcome and Jerome's imperturbable smile, the moisture-beaded bottle of Gewürztraminer he'd put in the fridge against her arrival . . .

Kate heard footsteps. It was Odile coming from the kitchen, thinking herself alone. Seeing Kate she stopped short, startled, then gave a pleased, surprised grin.

'Kate – I didn't hear you . . . We're all out on the terrace.' Her eyes took in Kate's new hairstyle, but she made no comment.

'I sent the children round.'

Odile was carrying a pottery bowl of tomato salad. Kate embraced her as best she could.

'I'm so glad you came. You work too hard.' Odile gazed critically at her. 'You must get some rest. Do some swimming. You look tired.'

'I've been up since four o'clock . . . Can I bring something from the kitchen?'

'No. Come out and show yourself.'

Following Odile, Kate reflected with a pang of protective tenderness how grey she'd become, how her body in the striped summer dress had thickened. The thought was no longer new. But, coming home from France, Kate had been shocked by the difference in

356

her adoptive mother, as though a queen had metamorphosed quite suddenly into a peasant.

Up until then the memory of that night with Beatrice – when Odile had told the secret of Jerome's unfaithfulness – had never seemed quite real to her. Their conversation had had the effect of a flash of sheet lightning, illuminating but soon done with. It had not had the force to supplant in Kate's mind the benign image of Jerome – of he and Odile as a couple – that she'd carried with her from the age of fourteen.

Coming home, Kate had seen quite clearly that things were different. The change in Odile showed through not just in her looks, but in her whole way of being. She used to be the elegant, creative châtelaine of her own small world. But, with Jerome's attritional infidelity, with the departure of her children, that role had gradually dissipated. Odile had been diminished. Now she needed her children more than they her, she needed to make herself useful. And Kate noticed that she had a new ritual. At six o'clock each evening she would open a bottle of wine and begin to drink, not festively but with a kind of relief, as if another day were taken care of.

The terrace was hot and bright after the cool of the house. In a flash Kate refreshed her memory of field, sea and sky, the view she knew by heart. All faces turned towards her.

'Here she is!' Nelly called.

'Kate! You made it then.' Her husband, Robert, stood with Jerome by the new barbecue.

'Aha. The wandering daughter.' Robert's greeting was drowned out by Jerome's richer tones.

The children, Kate saw, were already down in the field, playing in and out of a tent someone had pitched.

'Wow, like the hair!' Vivid, corporeal, Nelly bounced up to Kate, threw her arms round her, lifted her exuberantly off her feet. Kate caught a waft of some dry, piercing scent. For a moment she was crushed to Nelly's warm flesh, face to face with her hot, narrow eyes and avid smile. Then Nelly set her down. 'You don't get any fatter, you cow . . . Look at my thighs. They wobble . . . Ugh.' She shook them to demonstrate. 'And there's no space between the tops of my legs.'

Kate laughed at her self-denunciation. 'How can you live with yourself?'

Nelly's despair was playful, paraded for public consumption. She looked terrific and must know it. Her skin glowed with health. Her honey-streaked hair was thick and full of bounce. She wore a formidable pair of high-heeled wooden clogs that drew attention to her tanned legs. She was plump, certainly. But, in white shorts and a folksy cheesecloth blouse that emphasized the soft, sliding weight of her breasts, Nelly looked to be in her sexual prime.

There was always a particular pleasure to her reunions with the woman whose animated features were so much a part of her growing up. They would never be as close again, but seeing her was like recalling a poignant love affair.

Strolling towards them, Robert said drily, 'Nelly reckons if she talks enough about dieting she won't actually have to do it.'

'It's your fault! You bugger my motivation by keep telling me I'm not fat, just cuddly, just voluptuous.'

They exchanged a glance that combined humour, friendship and sexual complicity, causing Kate a momentary stab of envy, nostalgia.

'Hi, kid.' Robert stooped to give her a kiss on the cheek, a quick squeeze. 'Good to see you.'

His fringe fell slantwise across his forehead the way it used to, but the face beneath it was leaner, older.

'You're beginning to look like Robert Redford playing a lawyer,' Kate said.

'Don't tell him that,' Nelly ordered. 'It's exactly what he thinks himself.'

But their former schoolmate did cut an impressive figure. Robert had not changed so much as stripped away the aspects of himself he didn't need. Things like puppy fat, diffidence, the youthful need to strain for effect. In the process he seemed to have become more essentially and economically himself, exuding an air of unassuming strength that contrasted intriguingly with Nelly's effervescence.

Robert was a partner in a firm of solicitors in Criccieth, doing mainly probate work and conveyancing. He was patient and understanding with clients either freshly bereaved or struggling with the frustrations of the housing market. His quiet competence – coupled with the fact that he was a local boy – caused people to trust him and attracted business via word-of-mouth recommendation.

Kate crossed now to where Jerome, in baggy shorts and a stripey apron, was peering at his glowing charcoal.

'Don't lose your eyebrows.'

'I'm no novice, I assure you.'

He enclosed her in a warm bear-hug and Kate's spirits rose. Though her mental picture of Jerome was less cosy than it used to be, she always felt better for the sight of his canny baby-face.

'He has cooked two barbecues,' Odile confided, turning from the trestle table that had been set up on the terrace. 'The first we had to throw away. The second was perfect.'

'You see?' He grinned and gestured with his small, plump hands. 'Praise indeed from a cook like my wife.'

Their exchange seemed absolutely amicable. Odile appeared not to want anyone to take sides against her husband. Kate wondered how they were in private. She didn't understand how Odile could . . . when by now all the children knew about Jerome's exploits. Yet, when she herself had left Greg and come here, Odile seemed to applaud her, to feel she'd done something brave and right . . .

Paradoxically, Kate felt a certain sadness for Jerome. His professional fortunes had declined considerably since the palmy days of the mid sixties. It was generally felt that he had spread his presence too widely and too thin. He'd become a tired joke, an over-exposed and rather irritating media-hack.

A fellow academic, reviewing his latest book in the *Sunday Times*, had included a bitchy portrait of Jerome, comparing him to the capering coxcomb in *Death in Venice*, with his dyed hair and cheap false teeth, his charmless, relentless compulsion to gambol, jest and entertain.

The lampoon was cruel. Unfair – Jerome's hair and teeth were as nature had provided. But the parallel had a certain damning resonance. With jaunty defiance Jerome cut the review out and tacked it to the notice board in his study, but Odile revealed that he had considered the man a friend, was wounded and shocked.

From the kitchen Odile fetched an enormous dish of chicken joints, marinaded in yoghurt and Indian spices.

'They're hot,' she warned Kate, 'but not fiery. Will the children eat them, do you think?'

'You bet they will.'

With careful concentration Jerome laid chunks of meat on the rack over the smouldering coals. They sizzled and a hot, aromatic smoke rose into the bright air. He prodded at them gently with a pair of tongs, making fussy minor adjustments. Odile caught Kate's eyes, smiling at his involvement with the task.

'They smell divine,' Kate said.

'There's wine,' Odile told her. 'Or beer. Help yourself. Nelly has already started.'

'It won't take me long to catch up.' Kate crossed to the table, poured herself a glass of chilled white, sat down and turned her face up to the sun. It was blissful to be so spoiled. With the first slug of wine she could feel the work-anxiety that never really left her recede into the middle distance.

As they ate Jerome bustled between table and barbecue keeping up a supply of freshly cooked chicken, which he served with theatrical professionalism.

'Pa, this chicken is finger-lickin' good,' Nelly mocked. 'How *do* you do it?'

'Last of the great philosopher-cooks,' Kate confirmed.

Mellow and semi-pissed, they twitted Jerome for his flamboyant role-play, when everyone knew the specialness of the chicken was down to Odile's preparation, that it was she who'd produced the whole of the rest of the meal – salads, bread, pilau rice.

'We must buy him a tall white hat for Christmas.' Odile warmed to the girls' teasing.

Robert speared another drumstick for himself. 'Ready for his jacket photo on *Jerome's Barbecue Cookbook*.'

360

'Too kind.' Jerome countered their jibes with his habitual good humour.

It was a perfect summer day. The humidity of the last two weeks had moved on, leaving a a lazy blue and gold afternoon with a small breeze that ruffled the white table-cloth. The adults sat, torpid and satiated.

'Mmm,' Kate purred. 'I'd rather be here than anywhere else in the world.'

'We want more chicken and more bread.' Stella was struggling up the steps to the terrace carrying Odile's big old wooden tray. The children had taken their food down to the tent in the field.

'They sent *you* did they?' Odile teased.

What a perky little figure she looked, Kate thought, in her red shorts and yellow rubber flip-flops.

'Rhys sent me,' the child chirped. Almost ten, Rhys was the elder of Nelly's two sons.

'He's a sly one,' Nelly told her. She lounged in the sun, nursing the remains of her wine, feet with their heavy clogs propped on a nearby chair. 'He knows we won't say no to a nice little girl like you.'

Stella smiled, not sure what to say.

'Do you want some more salad too?' Odile asked.

'No thank you,' Stella replied politely.

'It's good for you,' Odile persisted.

Stella smiled again, lifting her skinny shoulders.

'You liked my chicken?' Jerome asked, to provoke the others.

She nodded shyly.

Odile refilled the children's plates.

'Be careful now.' Handing the loaded tray back to Stella. 'Leave room for some ice-cream,' she called, as the child made her cautious way back towards the steps.

'Have the children heard from their father recently?' Odile asked.

'He remembered both their birthdays. He always does ... Though he never seems to have the money to come and see them. And last month he sent them a Mickey Mouse card out of the blue. Just saying "Hi kids Daddy loves you" in big red loopy writing.'

'Oh God.' Nelly pulled a derisive face.

In the eyes of the Felix family Greg was a bad thing. Untrustworthy. Unfaithful. He'd let Kate down. She was grateful for their collective, protective solidarity. It made everything seem simple.

Because there were nights when she lay in bed awake and the whole situation between her and Greg seemed turned on its head. And she remembered his tenderness with Stella, pictured him on the floor with Jack, growling like a bear, making his son squeal with ecstatic fear. She recalled a night in Paris, early on, when she had bad period pains. They were in bed and Greg got up and got dressed, went downstairs and out into the street, looking for a shop where he could buy her a miniature of brandy. He returned triumphant and, when she'd drunk the liqueur and its warmth was seeping through her veins, he held her in his arms, kissed her and stroked her hair until she drifted into sleep. At times like this it seemed to Kate that she'd judged Greg's whole life by one mistake, by one single lapse from grace.

But, for all that, Kate had never for a moment been tempted to go back, though there had been a time when Greg would have taken her. 'I'm never going to live with a man again,' she'd vowed to Jess.

Kate looked back in horror on those days in Buttes-Chaumont, viewed herself then, with trippy distortion, as some kind of monster, her body out of control, deformed by her own biology, with leaking balloon breasts or a belly grotesquely swollen and distended, navel jutting like a blank eye. Her face peering from a mangy mane of tangled hair which she had neither the time nor the vitality to get fixed. Wallowing in shit and vomit and urine, the waft of bodily functions forever in her nostrils, however continuously she seemed to clean them away. And alongside this her work like a never-ending treadmill. She'd been sunk then in a sort of pit, too far down to claw her way out and renegotiate the baffling contract that gave Greg the right to come and go, free as the wind, while she remained like a troll marooned in her cave. The days of her marriage were shameful to Kate, like weakness.

'So, Kate.' Jerome sat down at the table with the rest of them, lit one of his cheroots, poured himself a brandy. 'Tell us what you're working on just now.'

'A book by a Belgian writer – the usual thing I suppose . . .' She grinned. 'One woman's struggle to take control of her own life . . . But it's rather well done.'

'Sounds like the story of your life,' Nelly teased.

'I read a whole slew of reviews a couple of months back,' Jerome said, 'of David's new book. The consensus seemed to be hate the novel, love the translation . . .'

'Pa's a groupie,' Nelly giggled. 'Forever waving cuttings at us.'

'Because we're proud of Kate,' Odile reproached.

'Kate's like something out of Germaine Greer or Kate Millet,' Nelly said. She pouted in an amused, aggrieved fashion. 'It's old hat to be married nowadays.'

Kate took a composed sip of wine to cover the pleased embarrassment that flared inside her. Visiting the Felixes put her life in a different perspective, laid the doubts and demons that tormented her when she was alone. They saw her as courageous, coping, even successful, and when Kate was with them she could see it too.

Later, when they'd had the ice-cream, Odile and Jerome retired to the kitchen to do the washing-up and refused all offers of help. Nelly began to tell the story of the rugby-club dance, four years ago, when she and half the team – not Robert, she emphasized – had got so drunk that at midnight they climbed the great big sycamore tree at the far end of the ground. Kate had already heard the story more than once, but each time Nelly told it with the same elated sense of discovery as the first.

'I was wearing this yellow lace dress Robert paid a fortune for . . . Thank God I had the sense to take it off or it would've been *ruined*. I started climbing in my bra and knickers and the lads . . .' – she smiled at her own ironic use of the word – '. . . took their lead from me. So there we all were, eight of us . . .'

'Five,' Robert put in. 'There were five of you.'

'. . . in our undies, pissed as newts, swinging from the branches like chimpanzees . . .'

Flushed and excited, Nelly sat with her elbows on the table, hair wild, face propped in her hands.

'We went up and up, just kept climbing, on and on, till we got as high as anyone could . . . I looked down and there was this huge drop and I didn't bat an eyelid . . . If I'd been sober I would've been petrified. D'you remember Donald, Kate? He pissed down from the very top of the tree . . . He had on this amazing pair of pants with a skull and crossbones and his willy came out of the skull's mouth . . . The sky was just full of stars and we sat up there singing rugby songs . . .'

Kate was uncomfortable with Nelly's bubbling narrative, found it hard to smile and exclaim in the right places, but wasn't sure why she felt so ill at ease. Though she'd heard it a good few times, the story amused her rather, seeming typical of the Nelly she had adored back when the two of them were inseparable . . . Only then Nelly had been a teenager.

But age wasn't the problem. Kate approved rather than otherwise the idea that Nelly, in her thirties, would still pull a stunt like that. Why shouldn't she?

Most likely it was her attitude that put Kate off. Nelly related the story with a sort of laughing boastfulness, a dizzy straining after the way she used to be. Offering her wildness with an overwrought complacency for their applause and admiration.

Robert said little, but was clearly out of sympathy with the anecdote. It showed in the set of his body, an eloquent stillness.

'Time we got going, missis,' he said, when finally she drew breath. 'I've got work to catch up on . . . I'll go and round up the boys.'

'Robert doesn't like me telling that story,' Nelly confided, flashing Kate a wide, blind smile. 'You know, whenever I see Donald we laugh about that night. He says his wife's never forgiven me.' She appeared elated at the thought.

Chapter Thirty-Seven

❧❧❧❧

The blank black November night showed at the boat's windows. Inside all was cosy lamplight, patterned furnishings, brightly painted wood. Kate, Olivier and Olivier's neighbour Carol lounged on an assortment of cushions watching Olivier's black-and-white portable television. On screen, Marya Arnold, Pascal's actress wife, was being insulted by another woman. She bore the tongue-lashing with eyes demurely downcast.

Carol stated the obvious. 'She's sickeningly beautiful.'

'Mmmm.'

Kate and Olivier responded without enthusiasm. Among the Felixes Pascal's wife was regarded with more than a certain wariness. Though only Nelly said out loud that Marya was a stuck-up bitch whose stranglehold on her husband led him to neglect his real family shamefully.

The boat's living-space was temporarily divided by a fabric screen decorated with a hand-printed design in blue and shades of orange. Behind it Jack and Stella lay in their sleeping-bags with an array of books and comics. Intermittently Kate heard them murmur, giggle. On weekend visits to the boat they positively welcomed bed-time.

As they watched the screen Olivier and Carol passed a limp, damp spliff between them. Kate made do with the remains of some whisky from a bottle standing alongside bleach and Fairy Liquid in the cupboard under the sink. Burrowed into a big velvet floor cushion, she felt warm and lazy.

'I have to admit I didn't expect to discover such a nondescript little being,' the second actress taunted in an amused and brittle fashion. Marya stared dumbly back at her.

The play was a half hour two-hander, a confrontation between wife and mistress, the twist being that the wife was vividly attractive, the mistress shrinking, dun-coloured. But the paradox was fatally undermined by the fact that the wife was played by a conventional blonde while, as the mistress, Marya radiated a fierce, subversive allure.

'I know which one I'd rather shag,' Olivier muttered.

'I didn't ask you to come here,' Marya was protesting. Her voice was thin and without resonance, had a certain intriguing primness to it.

'The play's pretty dire,' Carol commented. 'Have they got any kids, this woman and your brother?'

'Just the one.' Olivier passed her the mangled spliff. 'A little girl. She's four now . . .Jocasta.'

Carol raised her eyebrows. 'Ooh, I say.'

'The wedding was bizarre,' Kate put in. 'Pascal and Marya had a blazing row the night before and were still hardly on speaking terms . . . And Marya certainly wasn't on speaking terms with any of us.'

Carol grinned. 'Sounds a barrel of laughs.'

Kate recalled the reception, in Marya's parents' big, comfortable thirties house and immaculate garden across from the sea just outside Bournemouth. A day alternating thin, brilliant sunshine and squally showers. Marya, hugely pregnant, but nevertheless in white – a floaty dress with frills on the shoulders – her hair, released from its overnight plaits, a crinkly pre-Raphaelite cloud. Her beautiful face had been closed and tight, though occasionally she favoured someone in her own 'camp' – the atmosphere made you think in those terms – with a luminous, troubled smile. Jerome got drunk and giggly with the tension. Pascal seemed at a loss, trying to appease everyone.

'I've never met her since,' Kate said.

'Have you, Olivier?'

'A couple of times up in London . . . She can be very sweet when she wants . . . It's just that she doesn't very often want.'

'She gets a lot of work these days,' Kate said.

Olivier said mildly. 'Being married to Pascal must be a boost for her.'

366

Carol glanced away from the television. 'Hubby pulling strings what?'

'Not really that . . .'

Olivier was unfailingly charitable as regards his sister-in-law. Odile and Jerome kept their counsel. But Nelly always declared outright that Marya had married Pascal purely and simply for the entrée he provided into his own desirable world. In the current decade the elder of the Felix sons was prospering, had progressed from camera-work to making his own programmes, was known for his sharp yet sympathetic profiles of contemporary figures, usually but not always in the realm of the arts.

'The wife . . .' Olivier mused suddenly. 'In that spotty blouse, with her hair like that and her tits . . . She's like something off a naughty postcard . . .'

Carol considered for a moment. 'You're right, you know.'

They giggled at the discovery with foolish stoned hilarity. Kate laughed with them, infected by their bubbling merriment. Now, as the wife postured, gave her arch smile, half closed her eyes, the picture of actressy sophistication, they saw her through fresh and irreverent eyes, the dialogue lost in a barrage of infantile ribaldry.

'Ooh, what a lovely pair, missis.'

'Carrying all before you.'

'Shipshape and Bristol fashion.'

The joke struck them as irresistible and, as they jeered, Marya too was tainted by their mockery. Her pallor, her tragic eyes seemed suddenly to invite exasperation.

'Talk about a dying duck in a thunderstorm.'

At the climax of the play the two women clung together in a rush of sisterhood. It was too ludicrous. The three of them greeted the embrace with a crescendo of derisive laughter.

As the credits rolled, Carol said reluctantly, 'I must be getting back to my old man . . . Only popped in to give Olivier his Nescafé back . . .' There was always a fluttery quality in the way she spoke.

Surging to her feet in a swish of floor-length Indian cotton, blue boots, a sweater hand-knitted in multi-coloured stripes. She was tall, thirtyish, her hair brightly hennaed. A heavy but pleasant face,

367

always emphatically made up – thick foundation, green eye-shadow, a wide red smile.

Carol lived with her boyfriend, Mickey, on the boat two along, formed part of the easy-going community Olivier had acquired along with his tenancy of the boat, into which he fitted snug as hand in glove. She'd helped him kit out the *Creeping Jenny* with secondhand finds, helped him paint his furniture in bright, unlikely colours.

She'd also knitted him a sweater, stripey, just like hers. For Kate the pattern of the relationship rang familiar bells.

'Are you two having an affair?' she'd asked Olivier.

He'd smiled and shaken his head. 'Mickey's a nice chap . . . I wouldn't want to do the dirty on him.'

It had crossed her mind then how Olivier always gave the impression that sex to him was an easy, take-it-or-leave-it matter, nothing to agonize about.

'Nightcap?' he offered when Carol had gone, holding up the couple of inches left in the whisky bottle.

'I'll go halves,' Kate said. She peered round the screen. The children lay breathing peacefully in a mess of comics. Olivier looked too and smiled, his eyes glazed with the cannabis.

'Those two would sleep through a hurricane,' he marvelled. 'I forgot all about them there, roaring with laughter at the box . . .'

It was cosy sharing this tenderness with him. A domestic pleasure but without the chains and antagonisms of marriage. Olivier extinguished all but a single oil lamp. They flopped down on the cushions to drink their whisky.

'What would Pascal make of that play?' Kate wondered.

'Oh.' Olivier shrugged. 'He'd defend it against rhyme and reason. Far as he's concerned the sun shines out of Marya's arse.'

'Have you been watching his new series?'

He shook his head. 'No I haven't,' he confessed. 'I work some evenings . . . But that apart . . .' He paused, as if embarrassed, then continued in a rush. 'I get uptight. I never used to care but suddenly I find myself knotted up. Pascal's so . . . Suddenly I feel something I never thought myself capable of. Envy. Gut-twisting envy.'

'Of his work?'

'Everything . . . His work. His good work. His beautiful wife. His pretty child. All that makes me feel . . .' Olivier's eyes were glittery, naked, intense.

'Olivier,' Kate soothed, 'don't get things out of proportion, you know . . . You've always said that kind of set-up wasn't for you.'

'It isn't.' He made a deprecating gesture, stoned, a little drunk. 'It isn't. I couldn't do it. Sustain it. But just once in a while I wish I could.'

Almost as much as the children Kate enjoyed sleeping on the boat, rolled in her thick, padded sleeping bag among the faded cushions. Olivier, nearby, was a sweet sleeper, loose and calm. The communal warmth felt like camping out, as if she and Olivier were simply the big kids, on the same footing as Stella and Jack.

Usually she dropped almost at once into deep, refreshing sleep. But tonight, in spite of the whisky she'd drunk, Kate was wakeful, unsettled no doubt by Olivier's surprising display of self-doubt – from a child he'd always embodied a sweet and sunny contentment that attracted people to him, put everyone at their ease.

He was sleeping now. She could hear his breathing, steady and quiet. And, paradoxically, it was thoughts of Pascal that filled her head. Because of the play they'd watched maybe or, more likely, due to Olivier's wry confession of jealousy.

She hadn't seen him for at least two years, so the image that glimmered in the dark of her mind was Pascal the way he looked at the start of *Profiles*, his programme, introducing that week's celebrity.

'Tonight I'll be turning the searchlight on a most singular painter . . .' '. . . a political maverick . . .' '. . . a highly individual writer . . .'

Each time he sat at the same desk, in a dark sweater, books behind him, radiating a sort of laid-back earnestness. He looked older, in a way Olivier – with his footloose lifestyle – did not. Pascal's hairline was beginning to recede. He wore wire-rimmed spectacles – the look of a media intellectual, a look that hardened at times into something more austere, some bookish revolutionary, perhaps, out of *Doctor Zhivago*.

369

But – in the way he lifted his head, in the long, narrowed eyes, the quick private smile – Kate could still glimpse the sixteen-year-old who'd so captivated her when she first knew him, twenty years ago. The timbre of his voice was so familiar that, watching him, she tensed, like a mother at a school play, as if he might fluff his lines.

In fact Pascal and Marya lived quite close – two villages away from her. A big old half-timbered house – Odile had showed her photographs. Kate had never been there. She was hurt that he'd never asked her round, not even for Sunday lunch, not even for coffee. More hurt than she cared to admit. But, then again, none of them saw much of him nowadays.

Jerome and Odile had opted to put a brave face on the situation, to excuse Pascal, plead his success, the demands of his work.

'He's a busy man.'

'Pascal is under so much pressure.'

They had visited his home just three times, said how pretty the little grand-daughter was, how appealing and original, how Pascal doted on her. They chose to speak of Marya with cool tact, but implicit, always, was the unstated opinion that their daughter-in-law was a calculating snob who had Pascal exactly where she wanted him, a cold woman, interested only in the furthering of her mediocre career . . .

Kate turned on her side, pushed the big floor cushion away from her, reached for something smaller and squashier, curled into a ball, inexorably wakeful. Shadows of Pascal dissolved, fresh images drifting in to take their place . . . A couple of weeks ago Kate had been confronted with a ghost from the past. The 'highly individual' writer Pascal featured on *Profiles* had been no other than her old boyfriend, Duncan Mitchell.

His reserve, his slight gawkiness, had worked surprisingly well on camera. *Profiles* made a point of presenting its subjects in everyday surroundings, gave the impression of allowing them to speak for themselves, though presumably questions were put to prompt the flow of opinion, explanation, anecdote. Duncan had looked embarrassed at times, self-mocking, rather amused at the situation in which he found himself, but he'd had plenty to say and came across as a thoughtful and genuine man.

It had been disconcerting to see on her small screen the strongly moulded features she used to know so well. He was filmed much of the time in chiaroscuro, giving full value to the sculptural quality of his face – the broad cheekbones, deep-set eyes, the thick but cleanly etched lips. Duncan's light hair rose back from his forehead in the way she remembered, though, following fashion, he wore it longer at the back than before. He looked better now, Kate thought, as if he'd grown into his looks. Essentially Duncan seemed at peace with himself. A private man but gratified that his consuming purpose, his particular brand of fantasy cum satire, had found its own appreciative audience.

There were glimpses of a pleasant-looking wife, twins – a boy and a girl – a new baby. Apparently Duncan had returned to Norfolk where he'd been raised. His house was square and modest, seemingly quite isolated. The programme showed him sawing wood to make shelves, playing football with the twins, walking in the flat Norfolk countryside, brewing tea, his life apparently congenial, unexceptional.

When it was over Nelly rang her up. 'He's so dishy,' she gushed. 'You should've hung on to him!'

'You reckon?'

An irony in her tone. Because – though Nelly didn't know it – Kate had sacrificed Duncan in favour of the Felix family. He hadn't fitted smoothly enough into the jigsaw of her relationship with them. He hadn't clicked, so she'd dumped him, without putting up the smallest struggle. What power they had wielded, her adoptive family. Carelessly. Unconsciously. And here was Nelly now burbling that she should never have let him go.

'He did seem awfully nice, Kate. Didn't you think?'

'He seemed OK.'

'Cagey bugger.'

Would she do the same again now, Kate wondered. Twelve years on. Years of discretion . . . Who could say?

A couple of years after her return from France Kate found, in a secondhand bookshop, a dog-eared paperback copy of a collection of short stories by Duncan Mitchell, published four years earlier.

One of the tales, only six pages long, was called 'Mating Rites' and, reading it, Kate recognized a surreal and painful account of Nelly's wedding.

The setting was transplanted to a green, mythical Shangri-La, the day presented as a ritual where all involved knew and played their parts. The Felix family members were caricatured with cruel accuracy. Kate herself was shown as a desirable, inscrutable elfin figure, watching and judging.

But Duncan reserved his deepest scorn for the protagonist. Himself. A primitive, snarling Yeti-like creature, to whom the ceremony is incomprehensible. The creature is ignored, kept at bay and, out of vengeful pride, tramples and destroys the trappings of the feast, while nursing a wounded yearning for acceptance and approval, for the elf to take him by the hand, lead him away from the alien rites, throw in her lot with his. Kate was shaken by the harsh passion of the writing and saw how much she must have hurt him.

Just before dawn Kate drifted into sleep. When she opened her eyes it was light. The gas heater was on. Olivier's mattress lay vacated, his quilt rumpled. The door was open. Jack peeped in, still wearing his pyjamas.

He complained, 'Stella must've gone out with Olivier while I was asleep.'

Kate put on a sweater, went outside to join him, breathing in the misty air, the damp, peaty, organic smell of the canal. Some way off down the towpath, Olivier was cycling towards them. Wearing her red jacket and Olivier's floppy cap, Stella was perched on his crossbar, leaning into the curve of his torso, snug as a fledgling in the nest.

'We got croissants,' she called. 'They're warm.'

They drew close, elated, flushed with the cold. Kate could see no trace in Olivier of the previous night's angst.

'There's a new bakery in Walton Street,' he told her. 'Me and Stella've been down to buy us all breakfast.'

Stella whooped as Olivier brought the bike to a showy, skidding halt, for all the world like a child himself.

Chapter Thirty-Eight
1976

❈❈❈❈❈

Half past six. Saturday. A blustery March morning dawning dimly round the margins of the curtains. The chirruping Trimfone by the bed dragging her up from sensuous depths of sleep. The air cold on her arm and shoulder as they emerged from the enfolding warmth of the blankets.

'Hello?' Her eyes still closed.

'Kate. *C'est toi?*'

She mumbled assent.

'*Écoute. Je suis dans la merde.*'

'*Qu'est-ce qu'il y a?*' Switching automatically to French even before her conscious mind had framed the identity of the caller.

It was David Lacoste. Begging a favour. On his knees. Voice husky with persuasive seduction. Though he offered no apology for rousing her from precious sleep.

Apparently he'd become involved in a project initiated by an international writers' group. A volume was being compiled with the aim of focusing attention on the use of torture in regimes worldwide. The book was to be published simultaneously in French, English and Spanish, the proceeds to go to Amnesty. David had promised an original short story. He claimed to have mistaken the deadline.

'It's due this Thursday. Or else. I'm so late I have to provide translations myself . . . If I don't deliver my credibility will simply evaporate – pouf – in a little cloud of malodorous smoke . . .' An attempt at jocularity which seemed underscored with a very real anxiety. 'To be honest, Kate, without your help I'm fucked.'

His suggestion was that Kate fly to Paris on Monday, at his expense, for three days. He would book her a hotel room. They

373

would work together, Kate translating each page as it rolled from the typewriter.

'It could be quite interesting,' he reflected. 'Quite entertaining . . . Writing at close quarters like that. Under that kind of pressure . . . In public, so to speak . . .' Clearly David assumed that Kate must share his anticipation. 'Don't worry about the Spanish version,' he stressed. 'I've found a woman who'll do the work overnight . . . Though I've no idea how good she is.'

He omitted to enquire whether Kate had any pressing commitments, or what she planned to do about the children.

Kate hesitated. The project was inconvenient, no two ways about it, coming out of the blue like that. In the normal way she knew that Allie, her neighbour, would be willing to have the kids. But at such short notice? And she would have liked more time to get the children used to the idea. Yet, impossible to deny it, she was intrigued.

'Kate . . . Are you still there?' A sharp disquiet in his tone.

'I'm thinking . . . It's not that easy.'

'I beg you. I kiss your feet. I wish you could see me. My forehead's touching the floor.'

David's flat was in the Boulevard Raspail, near the Montparnasse cemetery, somewhat south but not that far from where she and Greg had spent the first eighteen months of their marriage.

His flat was almost perversely bare and studenty, smelled acridly of strong tobacco. He showed her round.

'It's just a base,' he emphasized. 'I hardly feel I live here. I spend nights with friends. I travel . . . All I need is a bed and a table to work on.'

Though in his bedroom, at least, the spartan effect was undermined by the gaping door of a fitted wardrobe that ran the width of the room, revealing hanger upon hanger of expensive-looking suits. He closed it with a smooth, unobtrusive gesture.

David himself wore a charcoal-coloured sweater in a wool that seemed fine and soft – cashmere or something of the sort – toning slacks and backless shoes in supple leather.

374

'I bought them in Madrid,' he explained, when he saw Kate looking at them. 'Everyone should own a pair. Putting them on is like sliding your feet between the thighs of a dimpled whore.' He smiled, a little self-conscious, and his eyes flicked to see her reaction. Kate guessed he'd used the phrase many times.

'I can't comment. I've no basis for comparison.'

David's smile widened to a grin, in which she glimpsed, for a second, as if from the corner of her eye, a ghost of the irreverent young man she and Nelly used to rave about as adolescents. It seemed to Kate that, even then, alongside the easy grace of youth, there had existed the near-invisible spores of complacency, mushrooming slow and quiet until, in middle age, the growth had almost overwhelmed the powerful natural charm he'd once possessed.

At present David must be somewhere in his early to mid-fifties. He was heavier than he used to be, the monkey liveliness of his features modified by an added – not excessive – layer of flesh. Physically he seemed in reasonable shape, though his midriff had a new solidity to it which, by comparison, made his legs appear too thin. All this was to be expected, simply the wear and tear of life. From Kate's personal perspective it was the palpable, yet thin-skinned self-satisfaction he exuded that killed his attraction for her.

'Kate, *ma chère*.' He gestured helplessly, like a dreamer forced to focus on practical matters. 'I've nothing yet for you to work on . . . Please go out for an hour or two. Do some shopping. Have lunch. Drink champagne . . . I assure you, the expense is immaterial . . . while I get something down on paper. I'm counting on the pressure of your impending return to quicken the constipated state of my imagination.'

In the thin March sunshine Kate walked northwards on the Boulevard Raspail, rediscovering with a quiet, active pleasure the particular greyish-champagne colour of the tall buildings, their wrought-iron window-screens. The knobbly, etiolated, black-boughed trees. The pungent waft of harsh tobacco. From restaurants the smell of garlic and sizzling meat. Among passers-by, so it seemed

375

to her, an unabashed energy in gesture, movement, the pitch of voices. A familiarity, the sense that this, for a while, had been her neighbourhood. A feeling of freedom. The ability, for now, to see her time with Greg in perspective, with its balance of pleasure and pain.

On her return David opened the door to her, seeming animated and expansive. 'I'm on the move.'

He worked in his living-room, which was bare and rather dark, sitting on a kitchen chair at a large table of ginger-brown wood, beneath a bulb shaded by a round paper lantern. His typewriter was a modest fifties Olivetti portable.

From somewhere he'd unearthed another for Kate, an upright affair that looked as if it dated back to the thirties. She tried it. The keys clacked loudly and the ribbon was smudgy and black.

David returned to his place. Two pages lay ready for Kate to work on. She read them through.

The story was set in the time of the Algerian War, when David had been young and probably more passionate than now about the wrongs of the world. As she read a buried memory resurfaced in her mind. David, back then, haranguing a much younger Odile in the kitchen of Plas Felix, seductive in his vehemence. At the time Kate had understood nothing bar the one word *Algérie*.

The narrative offered the thoughts of a nondescript French soldier, a sanguine, unimaginative man, pondering with puzzled lethargy on his comrades' jeering attitude to the Algerians. The style was deliberately flat and colloquial. David used specific army slang terms he must recall from previous research. A couple of times Kate had to ask him what they meant.

Quite soon she became sucked into the always-fascinating conundrum of rendering the flavour of French prose in her own tongue. In the deep, suspended silence of concentration the sporadic clatter of their typewriters no longer seemed an irritant. David completed a third, then a fourth page. Kate took them in hand. There was something agreeably purposeful in the collaboration. Kate sensed that David felt it too. How oddly natural it seemed, this shared undertaking, though she'd begun the day in another life. In her own country, her own village, her bed, feeding and organizing her own children.

They worked until half past eight. Then David sat back in his chair, stretched his arms slowly above his head, closed his eyes, as if recouping strength in the wake of Herculean effort.

'That's it for today. I have to leave you, little Kate . . . The social round . . .' He got to his feet and began to collect up the carbon pages of his story thus far, ready to drop off at the flat of the Spanish woman.

Glancing up from his task to flash, with calculated charm, a look of melting gratitude. 'I can't tell you how appreciative . . . When you've finished those pages, I beg you, Kate, *please*, go pig yourself on caviare and truffles at my expense. Come back tomorrow at ten o'clock sharp. I'll have another chunk ready . . . It's going well, don't you think?'

They continued the following day. In David's story the soldier-narrator stood guard over an Algerian prisoner, thought him handsome. They talked and smoked a cigarette together. Then he was ordered to assist in the man's torture. The scene was long and graphic. Kate found herself translating it with effortless precision, a focused, horrified fluency, as if some outside power had charge of her mind. The story ended in telling banality, with the man going off-duty, having a drink with a pal, considering a visit to the cinema.

'Phew.' Just after nine Kate finished. No work would after all be required the next morning. She felt drained, exhausted. David poured them both a whisky. They clinked, silent, eyes glazed, still under the spell of the narrative.

David laid his empty glass on the table. 'Let's go dine.'

Kate washed and brushed her hair, applied the lipstick, the almost depleted mascara she'd stuffed into her tote-bag. She wore working clothes, a black shirt and jeans, hoped he wasn't planning to take her anywhere posh.

'I'm not dressed for Maxim's.'

David pooh-poohed her doubts. 'What could be more simple and elegant?'

But he took the hint. They went to an unpretentious bistro not far away. David was all attention, ordering a good Burgundy, pouring her a hefty glass.

'To my heroine.' He took a slug. 'You've saved my reputation. The relief . . . I can't tell you.'

She was struck. 'Was it so important?'

'Without going into detail, yes, it was.'

Kate found herself liking his wry confidentiality, the lowering of his guard. Disarmed herself, no doubt, by the two days of comradely co-operation.

'It wasn't too painful was it, the whole experience?' His flattering concern was exaggerated, no doubt, but she was beguiled none the less.

'I've enjoyed it.'

She glimpsed in his eyes a darting of genuine pleasure, saw the gratification as human, endearing, rather than the vanity of a fêted man of letters.

He followed up. 'Did you like the story?'

'Like's the wrong word. I was disturbed by it. I learned something. It's very powerful.'

He smiled. 'I value your opinions. You tell the truth.'

Kate reflected that her own particular vice was a tendency to be suspicious of compliments. All the same she was warmed by his remark.

The bistro was dimly lit, with dark wooden tables. Candles in heavy glass holders cast soft, quivery, intimate pools of light.

'This chiaroscuro makes it damned difficult to see the menu.' Wearing reading glasses, David peered at the card. 'Tell me what it says, Kate. Your eyes are still young enough to read by candle-light.'

Amused, she did so. They ordered from a shy young waiter, whose name David knew. 'He's the son of the proprietor,' he explained. 'I've seen him here since he was a little kid. It makes me feel old.'

He enquired after Kate's children, remembered Jack's name, recalled meeting him as a baby, tried to guess how old he was now, marvelled at the passing of time. Was Stella as dark and lithe as Kate, he asked, but, halfway through her reply, she saw that his attention had switched off and understood that his hearty interest had been feigned.

When their *civet de lièvre* arrived the conversation turned to Beatrice. Since Kate now had the following day free she planned to lunch with her before flying home.

On the subject of his mistress – something about David made one think in such terms – he assumed an Olympian, man-of-the-world detachment Kate thought of as 'Latin', but maybe it was more of a generation thing. He discussed her with a sort of pained concern, as if he and Kate had a monopoly on balance and detachment, while Beatrice was odd and excessive.

'To be honest, Kate, she's centred her life round me, and it's done her no good. And I never asked for such . . . such veneration. Though of course –' a rueful smirk – 'it's flattering. Not to say convenient . . .'

As he talked the sympathy Kate had felt for him moments earlier ebbed swiftly away.

'But, Kate, Beatrice is nearing forty. Of course she still looks marvellous. But I wonder . . . She's fond of your Jack. Of both your children. And I'm certain – not that she'd ever admit it – that Beatrice is feeling that, as far as that's concerned, she's missed the boat . . . I've always made it quite clear that, for me, children are out of the question . . .'

Everything he said was, quite probably, true yet Kate felt the need to push against his male certainty.

'I admire Beatrice,' she asserted stoutly. 'I don't think you should make the mistake of seeing her life solely in terms of love and sex and procreation. She's clever. She's efficient. She more or less runs that gallery . . .' Kate spoke with a manufactured conviction that matched David's own. 'Everyone's life consists of choices and I'm sure Beatrice has weighed up the pros and cons of hers.'

Actually, she doubted it, but he made her feel argumentative. In her capacity as his translator, Kate had dined with David in London four or five times over the years and on each occasion they'd had some version of this same conversation.

David ordered a second bottle of wine and they proceeded to another topic that he raised with the same inevitability. Kate's sex life. Or the lack of it.

'And you, Kate? What about love?' He smiled at her with teasing warmth.

'You don't want to know.'

'Nothing?'

'Nothing.'

He made sympathetic Gallic noises of shock and horror. 'How long is it since the economist?'

'Three years,' Kate stated through teeth mentally clenched. She would have liked to announce an embargo on the subject but that would give the impression that she found it too painful to mention.

'Poor Kate.' A sleazy smile.

'I cope.' She sounded, Kate thought, like a Frenchman's stereo-type of the frigid Englishwoman.

A silence. David gazed at her across the table, by the pale light of the candle.

'For a woman like you,' he finally declared, 'life should be a box of pralines from which to pick and choose.'

Kate shrugged. The image was an annoying simplification. She had no desire to explain to a man with David's outlook that she'd made her own austere rules. That she refused to allow the children to become attached to any man who might subsequently vanish from their lives. That she would not risk embarrassing them by causing saucy gossip in the village. And Kate had stuck to these principles. Though she'd never been quite certain in her mind how necessary they were, whether she wasn't simply, pointlessly punishing herself.

The economist had been someone she met through her friend, Jess. He was a lecturer. Attractive. Bushy-haired. Divorced. Rather abrasive. Good in bed. She used to visit him in his flat in London, leaving the kids with Jess, or sometimes Olivier. They would eat –

a Chinese or Italian takeaway – drink wine and Kate would stay the night. It was a glorious, hedonistic break in her round of duty. But she couldn't impose on Jess – or Olivier – too often and, anyway, she didn't want to dump the kids every Saturday night. A few times she got Allie to babysit for an evening, took the train to London and they ate out or went to the cinema. The relationship wasn't going anywhere but that was fine by Kate. Only Gerry – that was his name – wanted more. He got insistent. But Kate, knowing the affair would end some day, refused to bring him home, make him one of the family. It did end. Sooner than she wanted. A couple of years before that there had been Alun, a copywriter, and the pattern had been the same.

'It's sad,' David said.

'David,' she laughed, provoked by his pity, 'I cope.'

He lit a post-prandial cigarette, took a pleasurable drag, leaned forward, elbows on the table, as if settling to the main business of the evening.

'You'd be surprised,' he mused, eyeing her with expansive affection. 'How often it comes back to me. The memory of that beach in Wales . . . You were so young. And you knew all my books. Remembered them better than I did myself. And a virgin . . . I get a *frisson* thinking about it now.'

Each time she dined with him he reminisced in this same way. His voice rumbled sensuously like an actor's. If her experience of him had been different, how easily she could have been charmed.

As it was, Kate gave him a look she hoped was enigmatic. She could have retorted that the day after this idyll he'd dropped her flat, left her annihilated. That for more than a year afterwards she could not hear or read his name without a special bleak anguish constricting her heart . . .

But she was living in the real world. A great deal of the work she did came from David. It was work she liked and which gave her a certain status, paid adequately if she kept at it. He valued her, recommended her to other writers.

'Don't look so cynical,' he chided, amused. 'You can't be that indifferent. After all, it was your first time.'

381

'I'm sure I'm just as sentimental as you where my memories are concerned.'

He grinned at her evasion. Then came the suggestion he made each time. 'You'll come home with me won't you, Kate? For old times' sake?'

In London they lunched. It was easy to get away. The children were her abiding and genuine excuse.

Tonight, in Paris, in this cosy anonymous bistro, with this freedom she had from everyday responsibility, with the wine glowing in her veins, Kate could be tempted. For all her ambiguity, her moments of dislike, she was not unaffected by David's famous face, his inviting smile. The alcohol, the circumstances, made her feel sexy, made her long for the touch of another body, the warmth, the lewd complicity. And all she had to do was say yes.

Only there was an obstacle. Beatrice . . . Not so much Beatrice as a friend – though she'd stood by Kate when it mattered, had been unfailingly, unobtrusively kind, and Kate loved her for it. But just now, in this state of torpid lust, Kate knew she was more than capable of two-timing a friend.

No, her loyalty to Beatrice was as one of the Felixes. A member of the family who'd rescued and cherished her, to whom she owed everything. She would not betray one of them. The taboo was absolute. Even if David never pushed another page of translation her way.

'I can't,' she said. 'Beatrice is . . . She's my sister. I just can't.'

A gesture of impatience. 'She doesn't have to know. *I* won't tell her, you can be sure.' A cut-the-crap smile. 'Don't tell me you're not tempted.'

'Of course I am.' She'd allow him that. 'But I won't. That's final . . . Even if you never push another page of translation my way.'

A silence. Kate held her breath for his reaction. It was a long time coming, as if demons and angels were wrestling inside him.

Finally David shrugged. 'You're a perverse animal.' He reached across and touched her cheek with indulgent exasperation, as if she were eighteen again.

*   *   *

382

It was a surprise late winter day of heartening sunlight. Warm enough, in her Saint Laurent coat, for Beatrice to sit out on the terrace of the Adelphi Restaurant in the Place de la Bastille. She was early and ordered a coffee, waiting for Kate in a mood of unhurried anticipation. Meeting a friend for lunch. It made her life sound normal, sociable.

But, of course, there was Charlie now. The thought of him bolstered her contentment still further. She hadn't know him long, yet had a deep confidence that they would always be friends, that he would never let her down. Only he was a secret. A secret comfort. She wasn't ready to talk about him, not even to Kate.

Here she came. Beatrice observed her approach along the Rue Saint Antoine, admiring her freedom from Beatrice's own abiding involvement with physical and fashionable perfection, cosmetics, designer clothes.

Exuberantly she got to her feet and waved. 'Yoo-hoo! Over here.' Throwing her arms round Kate and kissing her on each pale cheek. 'This is such a bonus . . . It feels like old times seeing you in Paris.'

Kate gave the come-off-it grin Beatrice recalled. 'With the small difference of no babies in tow.'

'David's been on the phone to me already, raving about your professionalism . . . Sit yourself down. We're going through the menu and damn the consequences. My treat.'

For once, Beatrice decided, she was going to eat herself silly.

On the plane Kate relaxed as best she could in the tight space allotted. Closed her eyes and unfastened the waistband of her jeans. She'd eaten far more than she wanted – specially after the meal with David last night – but Beatrice had been hell-bent on offering a blow-out. It seemed important to her, and Kate had not had the heart to refuse. All through the meal Beatrice had gloated over their gluttony as if they were two schoolgirls sharing a midnight feast.

Seeing her today had been a shock. In the harsh sunshine Beatrice looked as dramatically chic as ever, sporting dark glasses, hair pulled tightly back, and wearing a beautiful black coat. But – was it her imagination, after all she'd seen her in Wales over Christmas – for a scary second Kate had the impression of sitting down to dine with a supremely elegant skeleton. Beatrice made her think of the Duchess of Windsor, every detail under control, the effect strangely alienating. At one point – while she was laughing actually – Beatrice had pushed her sunglasses up and on to the top of her head, and Kate was painfully struck by the lines of strain round her eyes.

But she seemed in pretty good spirits, chatting brightly, hinting at some new relationship, then clamming up as if thinking better of it. What bliss if she were to dump the august David. If she were Nelly, Kate knew, she would have badgered Beatrice, given her no peace until she'd prodded the details out of her. But Kate had remained typically and tastefully discreet and so was none the wiser.

Chapter Thirty-Nine

❈❈❈❈❈

June was hot, wonderfully hot. As July continued in the same vein people saw that this summer was something special. It felt like living in Spain or Italy, waking each morning to the certainty of blue sky and baking heat. All day Kate kept the windows open, the curtains closed, in an attempt to make the cottage a little cooler. The contrast between the radiant furnace outside and the quiet twilight of the house added its own particular flavour to the summer.

She began to get up around five thirty each morning to fit in a couple of hours' work during the cool of the day. For the children, who stayed up late and slept fitfully, those two hours were the time of their deepest sleep. At half past seven Kate had to drag them from their beds, fractious and unrefreshed. But, as soon as they got out into the hot, dusty street, the brightness of the air lifted their spirits, restoring their energy. Kate viewed the heat-wave with a mixture of weariness and exultation. She was frequently ambushed by drifting echoes of that fierce summer when she was eighteen, returning to Plas Felix after her years in exile.

The third weekend in July, Jack and Stella went with the school on an end-of-term camping trip to an outdoor centre in Norfolk. At the last minute Kate took advantage of their absence for impromptu visit to Olivier in Oxford.

The parched towpath had crackled into crazy patterns, scored through by deep crevasses. The canal was low, the water faintly, persistently malodorous, but sparkling gaily with sunny reflections. With the continuous summer Olivier's small community of narrowboat dwellers were in their element, like beachcombers on some holiday island.

When Kate arrived Olivier was sitting on deck with Carol and

Mickey and a woman called Trish. He wore nothing but a pair of shorts and his hair was tied back in a ponytail. The four of them were drinking beer and they greeted Kate casually, cordially, as a frequent visitor.

It was refreshing to leave her own preoccupations behind and get sucked into the undemanding gossip of Olivier's small circle.

'So you're up here on the razzle, without the nippers then, Kate?'

Mickey, Carol's boyfriend, was a Londoner, a chunky man in his late thirties, curly shoulder-length hair springing from round a balding dome. His slanting tartar eyes lent the most innocuous comments a suggestive sub-text.

'Absolutely. I'm planning to cram all the decadence I can into twenty-four hours.' Kate had never warmed to him.

'Let me know if I can help.'

She was bland. 'OK.'

As evening approached the hard sunshine gave way to a mellower light, took on a soft, enchanted bloom. The neighbours drifted back to their own concerns. Olivier went inside and began to strum idly on his guitar. Kate stayed where she was, savouring the leisure, the warm air on her skin, Olivier's familiar proximity. Birds twittered and trilled. A boat passed, rocking her with its wash. The occupants raised their glasses to her and Kate waved lazily back. With touchy dignity a pair of swans glided by. From the cabin came the soft strains of 'Guantanamera', a tune she knew so well it bored her, but seeming suddenly to reveal a fresh and heartbreaking beauty. Kate looked up at the sky through a lacy screen of leaves, one corner burnt away, pierced by the dazzling rays of the sinking sun.

Later, stooping, Olivier re-emerged through the low doorway. 'I'm famished. What do you say to a spot of pizza?'

'Suits me. Though I could lie here forever and contemplate the joys of idleness.'

They walked together along the towpath, Olivier in shorts and an open shirt, Kate in a singlet and cut-off jeans, a pair of rubber flip-flops like Stella's. She had a vivid sense of physical wellbeing.

Her legs were slim and brown, as they'd been the summer she was eighteen. They crossed the bridge to look out over the bleached expanse of Port Meadow. Above it hung the wide evening sky, extravagantly streaked with vermilion, pink, apricot, slate-blue and silver-yellow. In town a baked heat still rose from the paving stones. They sat outside a pub and had a drink. Inside, the juke-box played 'A Little Bit More' by Dr Hook.

'Carol never stops singing this,' Olivier said.

'It's the kind of song that makes me wish I had a handy feller to take to bed.' She could say that to Olivier. They knew where they stood with one another.

Afterwards they bought a huge pizza from a small Italian restaurant in Ship Street, took it home and shared it, sitting outside in the blue luminous night, surrounded by the black shapes of trees and boats, the air still sensuously warm. Olivier's hurricane lamp cast a cosy wash of amber light. A faint breeze stirred the muted, silvery chinking of Carol's wind-chimes. They broached Olivier's whisky.

'You know, it's odd,' she mused, 'how, whenever I come here, this bottle's always just one-third full . . .'

'It's self-replenishing.'

They clinked glasses. Kate took a slug. A tickling warmth meandered through her body.

'I'm happy,' she said.

'I'm glad.' Olivier lounged on his big floor cushion. 'What you need in your life is greater unproductivity.'

He rolled a first joint and, for once, Kate did not refuse. Feeling safe tonight from the snaking tentacles of paranoia.

Around midnight they went inside, Olivier bringing the hurricane lamp and hanging it on the hook he used. As he reached up, his profile and raised arms were outlined momentarily by the soft, warm light. It was, Kate thought, like a frame from a film. Turning, he came face to face with her, watching, and with perfect simplicity he bent to kiss her on the lips.

Kate slipped her arms round his body and held him close. It seemed to her that the embrace was not sexual, but rather an expression of comfort and solidarity. They were just two human beings on their imperfect journeys through life, who found in one another continuity and shelter. Most of the time they were only dimly aware of the need. But just now, in this mood – so it seemed to her – of stoned wisdom, Kate understood perfectly what she and Olivier were to one another.

She felt obscurely that there should be some new way to celebrate this insight. But what was there beyond sinking down on Olivier's eagle quilt, slipping out of their few clothes, lying close and naked in one another's arms. Luxuriously Kate recalled the warmth of flesh on flesh, the resilience of muscle, the exquisite sensitivity of skin. How perfect their bodies were in the low, golden light. The door stood open. The love they made was simple and tender, a part of the summer night, the moon and the still water, the whisper of the trees.

Kate always laughed that she couldn't smoke dope. When she did her demons would get her. But tonight she lay burrowed beneath the quilt, breathing quiet and gentle as a kid. On the contrary, Olivier thought, it was he who felt edgy. He'd come out here in the dark, naked, with the dank smell of the water, the creaking of the boats, to try and relax himself with yet another joint.

Not that he begrudged Kate her rest. God knows she deserved it. To him her life seemed full of headaches, work always on her mind, thinking ahead to how she was going to pay for the children's clothes and shoes, the rates, electricity, car-insurance, whatever . . . The kids themselves were conscious of money in a way Olivier had never needed to be, which probably explained a lot. About him.

In a funny way he'd come almost to feel jealous of Kate with her worries, her juggling with work, her planning. Things that would once have been anathema to him. Recently, to his bemusement, Olivier often caught himself envying other people. Like Pascal. Like Blackie, with the novelty of wife and kids, and money leaping at him from all directions . . . Only Olivier could not begin to understand the way they lived. Their lives were as opaque to him as the lives of Zulus or Eskimos.

388

Raising the cigarette to his lips, he could smell Kate on his hands, still taste her on his tongue. She was special. He thought of her with an ache of tenderness, and yet . . .

'You're hardly a demon lover,' a girl called Annie had told him once. Years ago, but he'd never forgotten it. And Olivier knew it was true. He could perform acceptably in bed but his lust had never had the focused fever of Pascal's . . . Or Robert, who had pursued Nelly like the Holy Grail through thick and thin, across years.

When it came down to it, Olivier reflected, he had the life he'd chosen. Work he could do with his eyes shut, sufficient money for his needs, the freedom to up sticks if the fancy took him. A desultory affair with Barbara who worked with him in the bar. At the hotel he felt popular. But sometimes, on the boat, on his own, in the early morning or late at night, Olivier had the scary feeling that he didn't exist. He felt wispy and insubstantial, like the thin, dry skin round garlic.

Since forever he had taken it for granted that friends and family were admiringly amused by his footloose progress through life. Those who weren't he dismissed as straights and breadheads. Now, incomprehensibly, it seemed as if the rules were changing.

Sometimes his mother questioned him cautiously about some woman he might have mentioned, as if she were wistfully eager to marry him off. Kate looked crossways at him when he boasted that he'd never heard of the International Monetary Fund. When he first arrived in Oxford, Carol had the hots for him, but recently her attitude was one of impatient affection.

'You just don't live in the real world, Olivier,' she would chuckle, shaking her head. Which was rich from her with her crystals and her herbal medicines.

He lived in the world he'd always lived in. It was everyone else who was changing.

One morning, a little while ago, after an evening spent with Blackie drinking some posh whisky that tasted to Olivier of soap, he'd got up and glanced in the small mirror Trish had given him last Christmas, the frame decorated with a mosaic of broken pottery shards. Instead of the cheerful young man's face he took for granted,

389

Olivier had seemed to see a sort of grey-complexioned young-old stranger. A mask, with his hair, his moustache, and through which his puzzled eyes gazed out.

Crouched solitary in the dark cockpit, while all around him people slept, Olivier experienced a familiar, rising panic. He was thirty-three. Young. Just. But time would move on. He would be thirty-five. He would be forty. Who was he? If he wasn't young, who was he?

Kate surfaced from sleep, sun in her eyes, dozed for a while, semi-conscious, beneath the eagle quilt. Remembered last night. A sweet experience, but tinged this morning with the stirrings of apprehension. Raising herself on to one elbow, pushing the hair from her eyes . . .

There was no sign of Olivier. Kate pulled on her shorts and vest, saw his bike was gone, guessed he'd cycled down to buy rolls for breakfast from the café in Walton Street. She put water on for coffee, vague, entranced, still beguiled by the lingering magic of the night, the scent of her own body, its secret sensuous glow, recaptured after so long.

But the trance was ruffled by a nagging doubt, the idea that she'd maybe been a fool to succumb to the combined charms of a summer night, a loving friendship, booze, dope . . . that she'd maybe disrupted the status quo and perhaps it wasn't such a good idea . . . Between herself and Olivier she wanted nothing to change. Kate hoped he felt the same.

'Hi!' she greeted him when he cycled up. 'I thought you'd left me to rot here on the *Marie Céleste*.' Setting a breezy tone.

'They were doing bread pudding down the caff. It smelled divine. Hope that's OK with you.' His smile was as open as ever. He'd brought the usual *Observer* for her, *News of the World* for himself.

They settled in the sun with coffee, bread pudding and the papers. Trish walked past in an ankle-length print dress like something out of *Oklahoma*. She was with a man. They said a casual hello. All seemed as it always had been, except that Kate was watching Olivier. For signs. Clues. There were none that she could see. He sat – long legs stretched out, trunk half-turned, with the adolescent grace he'd never lost – reading her droll snippets from the *News of the World*. Maybe last night really had changed nothing, would merely remain a sweet, fading memory, like the other time, in Wales, all those years ago.

'I slept like a log with insomnia,' Olivier said. 'I soul-searched.' A faint smile. 'I rummaged in my soul.'

'Did you find anything interesting?'

'Just the usual . . . Heartbreak. Angst.'

A sceptical look. 'What, you?'

His answering smile was quick and adorable. 'Maybe I'm not as shallow as you think.'

Kate returned to her *Observer*. The sun burned pleasurably on her bare limbs. Later they would walk to the Trout Inn, have a drink and a ploughman's on the terrace by the river. Then she would return to her real life, restored, refreshed.

With a glint of amusement Olivier observed, 'You slept the sleep of the just last night.'

'The sleep of the satiated.' She met his eyes, half-mocking, half-earnest. 'It was a magic night. It's been a long time . . .' Striving subtly to convey that the experience, though treasured, had not opened a new door.

'We're good mates. We have the best times together. With the kids too.'

'Absolutely.' Kate was ravished that he still saw things precisely as she did.

A pause. Then Olivier said. 'I wish you'd marry me, Kate. Then it could always be like this.'

His eyes, in the sun, were very light, an anxious boldness in their depths. She saw now that the skin beneath them was no longer as taut and smooth, had collected a network of small wrinkles that she had never noticed. Kate felt bemused, wrongfooted – she'd jumped so ecstatically to the wrong conclusion.

The confusion must be plain on her face. Olivier gave a sheepish grin. 'Hey, just a suggestion.'

'I don't know what to . . . Like you say, we're mates.'

He gave a brief, protesting laugh. 'But the fact's not cast in bronze.' Then, parodying a snatch of song, 'Mates can sometimes be lovers too . . .'

He grinned at her with the dark humour she found attractive. And Kate could not deny a certain incredulous, insidious gratification. The Felix boy and poor, orphaned Kate . . . It smacked of Mills and Boon.

Only her life was, not a grind exactly, but something she had to work at. She had plenty on her plate. Kate had the abrupt conviction that marrying Olivier would be like having a third child to organize and chivvy . . . A vivid flashback to the blinding anger she used to feel against Greg, and never needed to feel now.

Seeing Olivier was like a holiday. It was always fun. But you couldn't *live* on holiday.

Kate shrugged, embarrassed. 'I love you, baby. I really do. But I don't think it would work . . . I'm a boring swot. I have to be. And you . . .'

'No hassle.' A broad, dismissive gesture as if already he'd detached himself from the proposal. 'Nothing heavy. It's OK . . . really. You're probably right.'

Chapter Forty

❧❧❧

The dawning sun shone brilliantly on Odile's kitchen garden, gilding the tall, dried-out seed-heads of dock, cow parsley, teasel, looped round with yellowing trails of bindweed, whose bright white flowers associated gorgeously with the rose-pink spires of willow herb. Odile stood in her dressing-gown, nursing a mug of strong coffee and contemplating the chaos with a hard satisfaction.

For nearly thirty years she had worked this patch of ground, keeping the earth clean, friable and productive. And then, one day, she had simply decided that she was bored with the effort involved in nurturing the rows of lettuce, tomatoes, beans, potatoes, and she didn't have to struggle on if she didn't want to. Almost immediately the wilderness had reasserted its claim.

Odile didn't think she would ever cultivate this plot again. How easy the renunciation had been. When for years she had been under the impression that her tidy, flourishing kitchen garden was somehow tied in with the person she was. Now, quick as turning over a page, she had come to view it as a punishing discipline she had imposed quite pointlessly on herself.

The shift of perception had opened her eyes. What peace there was in letting go. Why not take it further? Odile sat down on the bench by her overgrown, un-netted raspberry canes, turned her face up to the sun and made her plans.

'Nelly got a real bee in her bonnet. Come February she was mad for a swimming pool, whether we could afford it or not. Had to have it installed before the summer months. Course, as it happens, it's been the hottest summer this century and she's crowing . . . Won't let me hear the last of it, as if she knew all along.' Robert spoke in the earnest, Welsh-voluble and apparently uncritical tone he used when relating his wife's excesses. Beneath the film-star sweep of hair his face, so it seemed to Kate, became ever thinner, graver, ever better looking. 'Personally I can't see the point of a pool when you got the sea five minutes away.'

Kate thought the same, but opted for tact. 'Well, the kids seem to think they've died and gone to heaven.'

The pool, with its bright turquoise liner, took up half the Williams's back garden. Much of the rest was occupied by a menagerie of inflatable sea-creatures that had caught Nelly's fancy – a dolphin, a shark, a seal, a sea-horse, a giant octopus.

'I couldn't resist those manic grins they've got,' she enthused. 'I just had to buy the whole lot.'

Skinny and suntanned, their hair slick with water, the four children played in and out of the pool. Rhys led them in a wild game of follow-my-leader, round the garden, in and out of the house, back again to the glinting Hockney water. Passing by the plastic creatures, grouped at one end of the pool with their mad, frozen smiles, he aimed a kick at the shark's belly, and the others did likewise. Nelly shrieked with laughter.

There was a fourth adult present, a man called Nick, a newcomer to Robert's firm of solicitors. His wife, apparently, was in New Zealand, visiting her parents. He looked to be in his late twenties, had a shy smile, wore heavy black spectacles and black Speedo bathing trunks which revealed a long, slim, unmuscled body.

'We're looking after Nick,' Nelly explained, ruffling his hair. 'Keeping him on the straight and narrow.'

Nick smiled in a nervous fashion. He, Kate and Robert lazed on what remained of the lawn. But Nelly – in a ruched white one-piece swimsuit, like something Lana Turner might have worn – was restless, pacing up and down, calling to the children, sitting down on the edge of the pool and splashing her legs in a short-lived frenzy.

'This swimsuit cost a bomb,' she said to no one in particular. 'It's a Cap Ferrat.'

Nelly seemed to Kate to be off in her own world, odd and erratic, not quite connecting with the rest of them. She picked up the inflatable octopus, flourished it briefly at Stella, then came over to where Nick was sitting.

'Hi, Nick,' she said in a squeaky American accent. 'Wanna shake hands?'

With a weak smile he grasped one of the creature's pink arms. But Nelly had already lost interest. She sat down with them on the grass, and eyed her tanned legs with impersonal approval.

'I'm hungry,' she said. 'Hey, Rob, isn't it about time you started a-peeling and a-chopping . . . ? Rob's doing the honours today,' she explained. 'He's a lovely little cook.'

To Kate it was as if the wayward, whimsical girl she used to idolize had been replaced by a loud and charmless counterfeit. But the alarm she felt was not a new emotion, merely an intensification of the vague unease she now experienced each time she was in Nelly's company.

Kate turned to Robert. 'I'll help you chop and peel.'

'Done.'

'Away the two of you and turn the spit.' In her strange Hollywood swimsuit Nelly lay back on the checkered car rug. 'Nick and I will entertain ourselves famously.'

The Williamses lived in a comfortable, four-bedroomed, thirties style house just outside Criccieth. It was whitewashed and had a rounded porch flanked by the showy hydrangea bushes that bloomed identically in all the neighbouring front gardens.

Inside the walls were painted with strong, off-beat colours, the furniture Habitat-simple, though spiced with the occasional amusing heirloom – a wall of sepia family photographs in antiqued gilt frames, a pair of green china cats, positioned one each end of the living-room mantelpiece. Nelly had domestic help twice a week and, beneath a comfortable layer of family clutter, the house was pleasantly clean.

The kitchen was spacious and sunny with a red-tiled floor. Robert had made his preparations in advance. He considered what was still to be done, a frown of concentration on his handsome, decent face.

'I'm not ambitious. It's just cold chicken and a big plate of salad. Only, Nelly . . .' He let the sentence drop. 'Could you slice these big tomatoes, Kate. I've got feta, olives, French bread – quite classy for Criccieth . . .

395

'How does Nelly seem to you?' he asked, as he arranged the ingredients on a big pottery plate.

'Full of beans . . . A bit overwrought maybe.'

Robert stopped what he was doing and turned to face her. 'I'll tell you something, Kate. If you'd seen her the way I . . . Look, last autumn Nelly had this black depression. I can't tell you what it was like. She wanted to die. She *seemed* dead, through and through. And nothing I could do or say made it better. Not holding her in my arms. Not making love. Nothing broke through the absolute despair . . .'

He looked haunted, remembering. Kate listened, unbelieving, knife in one hand, a section of tomato in the other.

'She was like it once before, when you were in France, only not so bad. So when I see her, like today, smiling and teasing, I tell you, it feels like a miracle. Even if she *is* overwrought. That's why I went along with the swimming pool thing, though God knows we can't afford it. I was just so happy she could work up the interest.' A dark smile. 'I'll even forgive her those sodding inflatable animals.'

'Poor Nelly. I'm . . . Poor Nelly. She's just simply the last person I can imagine being depressed.'

'Nelly's like a kite. The wind can blow her here there, up down. And it's as if there's nothing she can do about it.'

Kate was struck by Robert's total, unselfconscious involvement in his wife's situation. He spoke of her quite without blame or condescension, with an old-fashioned chivalry you came across rarely. Kate understood that, for all the inconvenient complexities of the outcome, Robert still saw Nelly as the prize he had won for himself through passion and persistence. She was moved.

'One thing though, Kate. Don't tell Nelly I told you. She's mortally ashamed. Though I tell her that's crap. She shouldn't be.'

'What about Odile and Jerome. Do they know?'

'I think they saw she wasn't one hundred per cent. But in public, for a short time, she has this ability to pull herself up by her bootstraps.'

'I saw her at Christmas and I'd never have guessed.'

Though she'd experienced the familiar unease, as Nelly aped the person she used to be. Kate recalled her dancing to an old Elvis

396

record, heavily parodying the movements she used to make with such lightness of spirit. And now so much of what had worried and puzzled her fell into place . . .

A while later they carried trays of food into the garden.

'Thank God,' Nelly hailed them. 'We're all starving to death out here. Aren't we, kids?' She gave a chuckle, actressy-wicked. 'I'm finding out loads about Nick! D'you know this pillar of the community is heavily into whips and leather!'

Nick looked dazed. 'Not really,' he said quickly.

The week Kate and the children spent in Wales, Jerome was absent at some conference in Minnesota. Two days before they were due to leave Kate remembered Jack's holiday homework. He was supposed to do a project on some place of interest, but the obligation had got lost in the traditional round of familiar holiday pleasures. If they didn't do something quickly it was going to be too late.

'There's the iron-age fort,' Odile said. 'We can go there today. But be warned, it's quite a climb.'

'You look like some spunky female travel writer,' Kate exclaimed admiringly, when Odile appeared in corduroys and hiking boots, the grey sweep of her long hair an uncompromising contrast to her suntan and wrinkles. Momentarily viewing the erosion of the older woman's quiet elegance in terms of gain rather than loss.

To her chagrin Kate found the long, steep path quite a challenge. Apparently she had passed the stage in life when you could have a sedentary job and still count on fitness. If anything Odile took the climb more effortlessly in her stride. The children rushed up and down, back and forth, frisky as puppies, investigating the dry, cracked sheep-tracks that crossed and paralleled the path, covering at least twice the basic distance.

The effort was worth it. High up on the mountainside, isolated, bone-white against the russet of late summer bracken, stood the almost undamaged walls of a whole villageful of interlinked pre-historic huts. Jack was enchanted by the find. Kate lent him her camera. She and Odile sat down for a breather.

Kate watched her children explore, examine, calling to one

397

another, clambering on to the walls, their faces bright and curious, bodies supple in their shorts and T-shirts. Stella's mouse-blonde elf-locks and coltish legs. Jack's dark bob. Eager blue eyes, like Greg's. The heartbreaking gravity with which he knelt and positioned the camera, pondering each angle and viewpoint.

'You should be proud of them, Kate.'

'I am.'

'They are as special and important to me as Nelly's children . . .' Odile's mouth twisted. 'How I wish I saw more of Jocasta. She'll never know me the way your children do.' Kate had never heard her lament openly over Pascal's estrangement.

She rushed to soothe. 'Things might change. And who knows. There's still Olivier and Beatrice . . .' Immediately regretting the facile reassurance which could likely do more harm than good.

But Odile met Kate's eye with a glitter of irony. 'I'm not counting on them.'

'Mum! Odile!' Stella waved wildly from the top of a wall, a small, capering figure against the flat blue of the sky.

They waved back. 'She's like a little monkey,' Odile mused. 'And Jack is so thoughtful and serious.'

Then, impulsively, she caught Kate's arm. 'There's something I want to tell you. Something big. I've spoken to no one about it yet. Only Jerome.'

'Sounds mysterious.'

'I'm not sure if you will like it . . . Kate, I've decided I want to sell the house.'

'Goodness.' Kate was caught off-guard. Almost before her mind made sense of the information, it had a physical effect. She felt her legs lose their strength, the blood drain from her face.

The idea was a bolt from the blue. To her Plas Felix was quite simply the family seat. The notion of it as property, to be put on the market and disposed of, had never ever occurred to her. It was like selling Hampton Court or 10 Downing Street.

'I want to simplify my life,' Odile continued. 'I've had enough of romanticism. What I would like now is a nice big flat in London with every convenience.'

398

'Phew.' Kate shook her head. 'I just can't imagine you living anywhere else.' Though that was just one among the turmoil of thoughts and emotions that swirled and pitched inside her head.

'No one can.' A steely tone entering her voice. 'And it's probably my own fault. I've put my whole heart into the place. But it doesn't have to go on forever.'

A sidestep. 'What does Jerome think?'

'He thinks he knows what is good for me. That I'm forever this domestic creature who loves her home and her garden and that I must never be anything else. He likes me tucked away here pouring my soul into a home he lives in only half of the year . . .' Odile turned to Kate as if to gauge the effect of her harsh words. 'But his fantasy rests on my co-operation and if I refuse it . . . In any case he has done me wrong. He owes me reparation.'

'Because of his affairs?'

'Precisely.'

'Are they still going on?'

'Kate, I don't know and I don't care. I don't go looking.' She wrinkled her nose, turned down her mouth. 'If you don't turn over stones you don't have to see the slimy creatures beneath . . . But I do have this huge, righteous sense of what he owes me.'

'Jack!' Kate called. 'Stay away from the edge.' He was approaching a sort of rampart that had once formed part of the village wall.

He turned protestingly. 'I want to take a photo of the view.'

'Wait till I come.'

All around, far below the thick rough wall, a parched landscape lay spread beneath the sun, its undulating contours cut through by roads and snaking stone walls, boundaried in the distance by the shining sea. The children gazed, impressed. Jack took his photograph. Odile pointed out the landmarks they knew from ground level.

Kate stood wrapped in private incredulity, dawning dismay. Plas Felix, with its sprawling silhouette, the sweep of field and cliffside down to the beach, was enshrined in her heart. Her whole existence was warmed and stabilized by the certainty of welcome, refuge, the moment she set foot inside. Plas Felix in the hands of strangers. She couldn't bear it.

399

Chapter Forty-One
1977

❧❧❧

Kate decamped to the kitchen with her typewriter, sweeping the mugs and cereal bowls to one end of the table, leaving the living-room to Olivier and the children. She had been up since six, determined to finish the chapter she was on before she, Olivier and the children embarked on a five-mile hike to the ford at Foxtree Farm.

Kate had promised Jack and Stella that they could wade across in their wellies. Olivier too. If they were lucky a Range Rover might trundle through the wash or, better still, a tractor.

'Hooray for simple pleasures,' Olivier mocked.

'There might be some lambs by now.' Kate dangled a further temptation. She'd been shocked by her lack of fitness last summer and tried to induce them all to go walking as often as possible.

Through the open door to the living-room she could hear the three of them bickering gently. Jack and Stella were playing their current favourite game, that of proposing new, far-fetched careers for Olivier. The ritual was that each suggestion must be countered by an appropriate feeble objection.

'You could be an astronaut,' Stella was saying.

'No thanks. I'm not into wearing nappies.'

The children giggled.

'What about a quantity surveyor.' Kate knew Jack had been saving that one up.

'I wouldn't know what quantities to survey.'

'You could *learn*.'

'Would *you* want to learn how to survey quantities?'

Listening – as she raced without difficulty through the laconic love scene she was translating – Kate smiled sceptically to herself.

The game being played seemed to mirror *ad absurdum* the way Olivier was in real life. It had indeed been inspired by events . . .

Last November Olivier had come up with the sudden fancy that it was time he really did something with his life. Kate had taken him seriously. Together they enumerated his skills. He played guitar reasonably and could draw tolerably well. He could cook without panic for large groups of people. He had experience in decorating, bricklaying, gardening . . . Olivier had been encouraged by this polymath image.

They talked for most of one night, in the warmth and flickering light of Olivier's little gas fire, with the children sleeping behind the rough screen and the rain drumming on the roof of the boat, sitting up in their respective sleeping bags, eager, inspired. Maybe Olivier could set up his own business. Decorator. Landscape gardener. Kate would sort out her own finances, see how much she could afford to lend him. Jerome would surely help too. Kate promised to send off for bumph about vocational courses, small business schemes . . . Or maybe now was the time to take Blackie up on his offer of a partnership.

He'd actually done something about that. Phoned Blackie and said he wanted a serious talk. But timing, it seemed, was everything.

'If only you'd come to me five years ago . . .'

Blackie had moved on. Far as he was concerned, there would always be a job for Olivier. Like the bar-work, the guided tours he did now. But partnership was no longer an option. Blackie's world, the whole way he operated, were different now.

The dose of reality had the effect of a large bucket of water emptied over the small, tentative flames of Olivier's ambition. He clammed up. His interest drained away. All the helpful literature Kate had obtained for him remained, unread, in a stack of fading brown envelopes.

'Quite honestly, Kate, the idea of me turning into this hardworking entrepreneur is just a fantasy. It's like picturing myself as a Hollywood movie star . . . In fact, of the two, I'm more likely to become the movie star.'

'You don't get to be anything all in one go. You take one step at a time. And no one step is difficult. Enrol on this carpentry course, for instance. You're good at that sort of thing. It leads to a City and Guilds . . .'

The expression on his face was polite but bored. The way Stella looked when Kate lectured her about making an effort to keep her side of the bedroom tidy. Yet it was clear that Olivier was no longer happy with his old, footloose life. For weeks on end, each time Kate saw him, she would argue, urge. Between times she did the same over the phone. The kids couldn't help overhearing. Hence the game . . .

'President of the world,' she heard Stella squeak.

'Aha, chipmunk, now you're talking.'

Eventually Kate stopped nagging. The whole impasse began to bore her. Only nothing was quite the same as it had been before. Olivier had voiced his dissatisfaction and the words could not be unsaid.

His proposal of marriage, Kate saw as another aspect of the same malaise. Presumably, she and the children represented for him a kind of accessible, unthreatening stability. If they belonged to him his life would have a framework. But this, too, was a passing fancy which had not survived the first flicker of discouragement. Olivier had backed off with palpable relief.

'What you want,' Kate accused, before she opted out of the whole farrago, 'is someone to wave a magic wand over your life and make everything come right.'

He'd grinned at her with frank self-mockery. 'You know someone who could do that for me?'

Monday evening. Ten past eight. Mid March. The bar was deserted. Rivulets of rain ran down the dark windowpanes. Disconsolate, Olivier surveyed the flat acreage of green and gold carpet, punctuated with identical round polished tables, each with its quota of four ladder-back chairs, positioned just so. Unless it was crowded this place had all the atmosphere of a tarted-up barn.

There were periods when the bar lifted his spirits. Summer was a busy time. From late May through September. December too.

Then, from early on, there was a good-humoured buzz to the place, and Olivier came into his own. He was in his element, deft, good-looking, friendly but not familiar, a whizz with cocktails, dazzling customers with his ability to memorize long lists of orders and add up, niftily and accurately, in his head. At the end of the evening Olivier would have the satisfied sense that he'd done something well. However trivial. Each to his own. He was a good barman.

The hotel kept Barbara on stand-by, to be called in when required. It suited her. She had a child and was studying with the Open University and they paid her cash in hand. He pictured her in the dark dress and black tights she wore for work, baby-fine blonde hair hanging limply on her shoulders. He and she worked well together. Like a two-headed octopus, Barbara joked. They remained calm and unflustered, however great the rush. Olivier never fancied her so much as when, at busy times, she skirted neatly round him, back and forth, back and forth – focused but flirtatiously aware of him – in the process of filling great trays with a miscellany of assorted drinks. He liked her then, so much, the way he used to at times, before their affair became something they didn't quite know what to do with, but hadn't the heart to break off.

Tonight, though, the job seemed part and parcel of the aim-lessness he perceived in his life. Olivier poured himself a double whisky. The hotel was strictly a dope-free zone. He stood the glass on a shelf below the level of the bar, sipped it occasionally as he polished glasses and realigned bottles. It was important to look busy and chipper. Olivier topped the whisky up, his spirits bolstered by its tingling warmth.

Around nine o'clock two young women entered the room and sat up on two of the tall stools next to the bar. They spoke French and were sniggering over the hotpot they had just eaten in the hotel restaurant. Repeatedly the word 'hotpot', in English, gurgled out of the flow of French. Olivier listened for a moment, amused.

Turning to serve them, he saw that they were very young. Sixteen or so. Here, presumably, with parents or relatives. In any case they ordered Cokes. He was touched by their jaunty femininity. One was short and stocky with black curly hair, like one of those thirties Parisiennes photographed by Brassaï. The other was Pascal's type, slim, olive-skinned, her thick chestnut hair hanging with classic simplicity to shoulder length. They were dressed alike in short mohair sweaters, flared jeans, high-heeled boots. Once he would have seen them as prey, but nowadays Olivier practised self-censorship. The girls' features struck him as only marginally more mature than those of eight-year-old Stella.

'You're here as tourists?' He spoke French. It was his practice to proffer a scrap of conversation. If customers were not feeling chatty he would tactfully withdraw.

'We're looking at language schools,' the dark one said. 'Your French is very good,' she added, sounding surprised.

On her fluffy black sweater the girl wore a badge that said in English, 'I may not be perfect but parts of me are excellent'. The message pleased Olivier. He asked where she got it.

'In California,' she replied casually.

'You've seen the sights of Oxford?' He was supposed to push the hotel's tours, but couldn't be bothered.

They'd seen colleges. A church. They seemed unimpressed.

'We saw punks,' the slim girl said, rolling her eyes expressively. 'How hideous they are. Why do they want to look like that?'

Olivier felt the urge to explain. The punk movement both attracted and repelled him with its iconoclasm, its cult of ugliness. He was too old for it, but he wished the youngsters well. He had a sort of theory which he began to explain, about life, about the contradictions and polarizations it encompassed, the way society was forever pulled in opposing directions – left–right, cruel–kind, rigid–flexible. And from the constant struggle some kind of middle way emerged. In recent years the world had gone too far on a flabby peace and love spree. And the punks were there as a healthy corrective. He'd talked about this very thing two nights ago, over a spliff, with Carol and Mickey . . .

But almost at once it dawned on Olivier what an idiot he was to imagine he could explain all this to these two little foreign girls. The other night his thoughts had seemed to possess the freshness of truth. This evening they sounded rambling and strange. And anyway his French wasn't up to it. He got bogged down. He ploughed on. The girls looked confused, and then they began to giggle.

He saw the black-haired kid wave one hand covertly in front of her nose, as if signalling to the other girl that she was repelled by his whisky breath. How could she think he wouldn't see? The pretty one rolled her eyes, inclining her head just slightly, to draw her companion's attention to his hands, which he'd laid on the bar. This morning Olivier had helped Mickey shift a load of muddy logs. His fingernails were black. He hadn't noticed until now. The girls shuddered with little eddies of snorting laughter.

Olivier felt himself flush. He felt a sudden lurch in his stomach, in his bowels. Humiliated, devastated, he turned away, retreating to the lavatory a few yards along the corridor. Leaning against the tiled wall, he closed his eyes, shivering, yet drenched in sweat. Routed by the shallow ridicule of a pair of rude kids.

Yet it wasn't them he loathed but himself. With a pitiless inner eye Olivier saw himself as they must see him. As a dirty, incoherent drunk, with long hair and old eyes. A lecher. A child-molester.

'Bloody golden boy,' Blackie used to say with rueful envy.

'Peter Pan,' Carol called him now, ruffling his hair.

He was slipping down in a way he couldn't understand and felt powerless to change.

Chapter Forty-Two

❈❈❈❈❈

Just before Easter Odile put Plas Felix on the market. 'Selling it won't be easy,' she told Kate on the phone. 'The estate agent thinks that it might take years . . . It's too big for any normal family, he says. And too isolated for a business.'

'You can't be the only weird people in the world.' Kate tried to reassure her. 'There must be other romantics. And compared to prices in this part of the country Plas Felix is dirt cheap.'

She herself was unsure whether she wanted the house to sell quickly or linger on. There was something to be said for a short, sharp shock. Going to stay would never be the same anyway with an axe hanging over their heads. But sometimes Kate had the feeling that she craved access to the house on any terms, even as a slowly deteriorating white elephant, even with 'the end' written across it like the final frame of a film.

Olivier took the news harder than Kate herself. Subconsciously he remained what he'd been as a boy. The sweet baby of the family, adored, indulged. He could not quite believe that Odile had tired of her own role. That of patient priestess to the Felix family temple.

He was bemused. 'She's always loved the place. I can't imagine her anywhere else.'

'But *you've* all left. It must be hard to carry on loving an empty house.'

'When it's gone the *Creeping Jenny* will be the only place I've got to call home.'

'And here with us, don't forget,' Jack put in.

He and Stella were intrigued by the adults' disarray. They loved to go to Plas Felix, but change was exciting.

'You're a brick, young Jack.' Olivier grinned, but Kate saw that his eyes shone with sudden tears.

Such moments of brimming emotion alternated with a mood of listlessness, as if his brief burst of ambition had numbed and exhausted him. Though he fell in with any plans Kate made, Olivier no longer took any initiative in their weekend activities. He wasn't gloomy exactly, but indefinably distant, as if smiling at Kate and the children through frosted glass.

So now, instead of urging him to dream, Kate attempted to make Olivier feel better about the life he had. She saw that the interior of the *Creeping Jenny* had a grimy look she'd never noticed before. The eagle quilt was torn and dirty. She bought him a woven black and orange Welsh blanket. Carol washed his curtains for him and repainted a chair with good luck symbols. The alliance between the two women felt distressingly like a sister and a neighbour combining to force an elderly widower to pull up his socks.

At short notice Jess invited Kate and the children to spend the Easter weekend with her and her son, Cal – short for Caleb – in a holiday cottage in Norfolk. Bill, her husband, had turned bolshy, claiming she'd made the arrangements over his head, and Jess wanted to prove she wasn't taking any crap from him.

'It'll be perfect,' she enthused. 'Showing the kids a good time all day, then you and me getting smashed every night. We haven't *talked* for ages.'

In the event it rained most of the time and keeping the kids happy meant doing all the incomplete cardboard jigsaw puzzles that were stacked in the damp-smelling sideboard, and playing endless games of snakes and ladders. Jess overheard Stella telling Jack that she'd seen Cal's willy through the gap in his pyjamas. Stella was mortified when, gleefully, Jess repeated the confidence to Kate.

Kate had forgotten how bossy Jess could be. Her friend made a point of assigning chores to each of the children and overseeing them in a fashion that struck Kate as hectoring rather than jolly.

'Honestly, Kate, you let your kids get away with murder.'

'Yes, I probably do.' As ever Kate found herself both amused and riled by Jess's outspokenness.

'I wish it was Olivier here instead of Cal and Jess,' Stella whispered.

Cal was tall and beefy like his father, Bill. He was two months older than Jack, round-eyed, with a look on his face Kate saw as querulous, middle-aged, though it seemed an unkind thought to have about a child. He and Stella clashed constantly. Irresistibly Kate saw their conflict in terms of a wildlife documentary. Cal as some massive, slow-moving buffalo-like creature. Stella as a small, nippy, yappy wild dog. She felt constantly impelled to call Stella off, though Cal, with his stolidity, was built to go the distance.

When the children were in bed Jess and Kate would pour themselves wine and add more coal to the small, smoking fire. Huddled in a big, brown acrylic cardigan that matched the colour of her short, rough hair, Jess would sit cross-legged on the gritty mulberry-coloured hearthrug with its flattened pile. Kate would stretch out full-length on the sofa whose lumpy springs bristled beneath a thin layer of balding moquette. And they would talk.

Talking consisted mainly of Jess complaining about her husband. According to her Bill was slobbish and lazy, and he'd never got over the fact that she'd been made Head of Department over him. Rather than work under his wife he'd gone to another school. He undermined her constantly, quietly sabotaging all her initiatives and efforts at organization – witness his opting out of this holiday. She was considering having an affair with a colleague – a 'curly-haired lad' who taught music – was sick to death of Bill's wham-bam-thank-you-ma'am approach to sex.

'What about you?' She fixed Kate with a hard, speculative eye. 'Are you really as celibate as you seem?'

''Fraid so.'

'Why, for God's sake? That Gerry really liked you.'

'I'm devoting my life to the kids and earning money.' Kate's tone was ironic but the statement, in itself, was not.

The truth was that she was getting ever better at finding reasons for avoiding the complication of sex. Last month she'd had the two downstairs rooms decorated by a local handyman called Lol Tyler – Kate could hardly believe such a name existed outside *Cider with*

Rosie. He was younger than she, well-built, with mean, hot eyes. As he worked and she worked, the two of them alone in the house all day, the sexual tension between them was heavy and oppressive as a gathering storm. Why not, Kate thought. Why not? But, for all the fever in her blood, she chose to focus on the fact that Lol was marked down in the village as a tightfist, known in the pub for ducking out of his round whenever he could. The absurdity of that thought was like a bollard to which she clung and so avoided being swept into the swirling sea of sexual intimacy.

'You'll get old and grey and find you've never lived,' Jess said.

'Jess. There's no need to write my epitaph just yet.'

What she hadn't yet told Jess was that Greg had written just before they came away, to tell her that he'd met someone new, someone wonderful, and they planned to marry. Kate had marvelled at his tone of buoyant optimism as if at something strange and rare, but would not, would not, allow herself to feel envy.

The break in Norfolk was not an unqualified success and, when she arrived home, Kate found herself bathed in a sort of elegiac melancholy. She could point to no one overriding cause, but there were niggles a-plenty. The imminent disappearance of Plas Felix from her life. Olivier's apathy. Jess's gloomy and all too convincing pronouncement as regards Kate's future.

She had a new Lacoste novel to translate. It would take her most of the summer. She looked forward to losing herself in the minute, absorbing process.

Olivier opened his eyes. The light, filtered by the thin Indian cotton scarves he used as curtains, was watery and pale. Another so-so day. It was May and he craved brightness. What time was it? With an effort he withdrew his right arm from beneath Kate's warm, Welsh blanket, squinted at his watch. Almost one. He turned and punched the pillow into fresh billowy-ness, farted, lay back again, closing his eyes. He found it hard nowadays to drag himself from bed. Knowing when he did get up it would be to . . . not squalor precisely, but a certain disorder, a certain rancidity.

He used to pride himself on using just one mug, one plate, one set of cutlery, washing them up the moment he'd used them. Now such economical logic was beyond him. Washing-up seemed a mountainous chore. He used all the crockery he had and, if he was lucky, Carol would do it for him, exasperated by the mess. He'd got lazy in his day-to-day life, though, if Kate and the kids were expected, Olivier would have a big clean-up. He didn't want to put them off.

A brisk double knock at the door. Olivier groaned inwardly. It would be Carol, on her everlasting mission to spruce and organize him. Last week she'd taken a bundle of his clothes to the launderette and dragged him along to have his hair trimmed. Olivier had the feeling he was a sort of hobby for her.

'He's a very clean old man,' Mickey joshed that evening.

'A positive Beau Brummell,' Carol agreed.

His pride protested against their patronizing manner. But they accepted him, cared about him, and Olivier knew he couldn't afford to quarrel with them.

The knock came again.

'OK!'

In his mauve underpants Olivier hauled himself from the bed, slipped the bolt, opened the door. Experienced a moment of total disorientation. Instead of Carol, with her coarse skin and bright, messy hair, Olivier was confronted by the tall, handsome figure of his brother, Pascal.

They stared at one another for a long moment, absorbing details, impressions.

Pascal laughed. 'You don't look overjoyed to see me, little bruv.'

'I'm knocked all of a heap.' Managing to inject a spark of satire into his voice to disguise the dizzy sinking of his heart.

'Can I come in?'

'You'll have to take me as you find me.' Sounding like a char in a forties movie. Oddly embarrassed that he was still in bed at lunch-time, though once he would have found it a source of bohemian pride. Sneakingly aware of the fusty air, the smell of farts, the jumble of dirty plates and cups on the draining board, a couple of foil trays from the Chinese takeaway, their congealed, queasy contents adding their own perfume to the atmosphere. Himself in washed-out, bobbly nylon underpants with a three-day growth of beard.

Pascal, a well-groomed stranger. Cool, with his round metal spectacles, high forehead and well-cut hair, neither too long nor too short. A tang of lemony aftershave. Dark button-down shirt, corduroy jacket and trousers, a chic Fair Isle slipover in heathery shades, clearly not found in a charity shop.

Both of them used to wake up to this kind of mess and make no bones about it. But Pascal had moved on. In a vivid mental flash Olivier imagined a sumptuous-austere bedroom, dark chambray sheets and duvet, the nymph-like nakedness of his beautiful wife. With what distaste Pascal must view his brother's present surroundings.

'You might have warned me you were dropping by.'

'How? By carrier pigeon? I came on the off-chance. I was up here to meet Frank Castle.' He mentioned a young academic who'd made a name for himself on television through sheer bullish rudeness. 'I was thinking of doing a programme on him. But I decided I couldn't stand the bastard . . .'

'So you came to see me instead . . . I'm out of milk and sugar . . .' Olivier picked up the Nescafé jar. 'And pretty well out of coffee . . .' He pulled up and zipped his jeans, put on his stripey sweater.

'I thought we could go for a drink.'

As they strolled along the tow-path and through the streets of Oxford, Olivier questioned Pascal about his work and about the well-known people he'd met. It was like making conversation with a stranger at a cocktail party. Pascal talked easily, amiably, rather as he might chat to a new young employee who needed putting at ease.

They went to a place Pascal favoured. It was brown and cramped, oozing history. They found two seats at a rustic-looking table. Pascal bought beer and beef sandwiches.

Most of their fellow drinkers were formally dressed, as though this lunchtime conviviality was a mere break in the purposeful thrust of their various days. In his youth – only a short time ago –

Olivier would confidently have dismissed them as braying wankers. Today, on the contrary, he was uneasily aware of the stubble on his chin, the unravelling neck of his hippie home-knit. He looked what he felt he was. The family wastrel being briefly acknowledged by his successful sibling. When, how had this reversal in his vision come about?

There were questions he longed to put to Pascal. Why had he cut himself off so from his family? Did he realize how much his attitude hurt Odile? How did he feel about seeing his childhood home up for sale? But there was something bland yet edgy in Pascal's manner that held him at bay. Olivier dared not compound his unappetizing appearance with any kind of emotional appeal. They chatted of politics, prospects for the Ashes, wandered somehow into a discussion as to the best Avengers girl, the best Doctor Who.

Help me, he yearned to say. I'm sinking. I'm lost. I want to change but I can't. You see how I live . . . The words resonated in his head, drowning out their perfunctory conversation.

'How's the family?' Olivier asked.

'Fine.' Pascal opened his wallet and took out a snap. Marya, long-haired and lissom in a bikini, laughing, her eyes narrowed, feline. On her knee an angelic naked child. Two Arcadian nymphs.

'Beautiful,' Olivier said.

'You've never been tempted by bourgeois wedlock, father-hood?' Pascal's breezy manner anticipated a conventional response. Nothing messy.

Olivier obliged. 'They're not my thing . . . But I see a lot of Kate's two.'

'How old are they now?'

'Jack's ten. Stella's about to be nine. They're great kids.'

Pascal looked at his watch. 'God, is that the time? I have to be going . . . It's been good to see you.' To Olivier's ears the statement resounded with blatant insincerity.

Outside the pub Pascal embraced him. 'Look after yourself.' As he stood back Olivier read a nebulous anxiety in his brother's eyes.

'You too.'

Pascal gave a laconic salute, set off in the direction of the High. Olivier watched him go. It seemed to him that Pascal took long, fast strides as if trying to place as much distance as quickly as possible between himself and his shameful sibling.

Chapter Forty-Three

⚭⚭⚭

Towards the end of May, Carol telephoned Kate to say that Olivier no longer seemed to be going into work.

'I don't know if he's got the sack or if he can't be bothered. I daren't ask him. He thinks I'm an interfering old busybody as it is . . .'

'He's coming down this weekend. I'll see what I can find out.'

'For God's sake don't tell him I phoned you.'

When he arrived Olivier seemed withdrawn . . . damped down, the way he did nowadays. But he looked well. He'd shaved off his moustache and seemed to have lost a little weight, not that he needed to. His skin was smooth, his eyes luminous.

Over coffee Kate asked casually how work was going and he said they were busy in the bar. Summer was getting under way.

'How's Barbara?'

'Fine, I think. Frantically studying. I haven't seen much of her all this month . . .'

He said he'd been sleeping badly and had been to the doctor for pills.

'Did they work?'

'The first lot didn't. I got some others. They're better . . . I feel better.'

At his request they did the walk to Foxtree Ford. Then Olivier and the children watched television while Kate cooked spaghetti. He rolled no joints, drank just one glass of wine after the kids had gone to bed.

It seemed to make him want to communicate, as if he'd discovered a new insight into life and wished to share it. But Kate could not grasp what he was trying to say.

'Does anyone live they way they want to?' he asked with an odd lack of emphasis, as if musing aloud. 'Did my parents? Do Robert and Nelly? Pascal? Do you?'

'I'm not sure I know what you mean. I live the way I have to.'

'That's it. It's self-perpetuating. And your kids will do the same. How does anything ever get to change?'

'What are you saying, Olivier?'

He shrugged, seemed to lose interest, switched the television on again. They watched the final half-hour of a documentary on the Northern Ireland impasse.

'See?' Olivier commented. 'Self-perpetuating.'

She was disconcerted by his incoherent insistence, as if Olivier were viewing the affairs of the world through some obscure lens of his own.

Around lunch-time on Sunday he got ready to hitch back to Oxford.

'Come on kids,' he called. 'Give your old uncle a hug.'

Laughing, they clung to his waist. With a sort of fierceness he gathered them to him. Kate saw his face was twisted, as if with strong emotion.

'You're OK?' she asked as he came to embrace her. Normally she avoided all such anxious queries like the plague.

'Sure.' A half-smile, familiar to her since forever.

'Ring any time. *Any* time. Or come down.'

'I know.' He kissed her forehead, held her for a moment tight against him. Then left with a lift of the hand. Kate was saddened by the hollow jauntiness of the gesture.

It was the year of the Queen's Silver Jubilee. Celebrations were to take place in June. The village of Downridge planned street parties and communal sports on the school field. For a fortnight beforehand the teachers of St John's Primary strove to whip the children into a frenzy of patriotism. Jack and Stella brought home shiny gold cutout crowns, Union Jacks hand-coloured in felt-tip, rampant lions stuck all over with little wads of brown tissue paper. All these were hung up in the downstairs front window.

Across the road old Pat Parrish painted his garage door red, white and blue.

When the post arrived on the Saturday after Jubilee Day, Kate was in the kitchen, grilling fifty small sausages and making ham sandwiches for the Wilbert Close party that afternoon. She yelled at Jack to put the letters on her desk and to bring the milk in, and find out what Stella was doing upstairs.

'I'm trying to work out what to wear,' Stella shouted. All the children had been instructed to appear in red, white and blue. 'Jenny's got this white dress with little flags all over it. All I've got is my blue school skirt and . . .'

'A-a-ah . . . Never mind, Cinders. At least you get to go to the ball.' However she might sympathize with the children's covetousness, Kate's policy was to give it short shrift. She'd explained many times that most of their friends had two parents in work. Jack and Stella couldn't hope to match them in terms of toys and clothes. 'I need you both to help carry this food across to Annie Parrish.'

With gusto the Parrishes had assumed responsibility for the Wilbert Close celebrations. Annie was co-ordinating food. Outside, her husband Pat supervised the setting up of trestle tables. Their house swarmed with hyperactive life. Kate delivered her contribution, then fled, promising to be back later to help with the leg-work.

Back home, she made eggs on toast for the three of them, chatted inconclusively to Stella about her party outfit, decided she could fit in three hours' work before any action was required from her as regards the party. The kids went out to watch the goings-on. Sitting down at her desk with a cup of strong coffee, Kate noticed the post Jack had left there.

On top was a postcard which showed a gorgeously distressed doorway, framed by faded curtains and flanked by a collection of terracotta pots bright with geraniums. She turned it over. It was from Beatrice, from Provence.

'Down here with a mate', it said. 'Hedonism. *Douceur de vivre*. Love you. B.'

How intriguing. Beatrice with a 'mate' – even the terminology sounded incongruous. Then Kate recalled the vague hints Beatrice had dropped last time she saw her, God, over a year ago . . . But the card explained nothing.

There was a new cheque book and, underneath, a blue-grey envelope addressed to her in Olivier's hand. How strange. He never wrote. Kate ripped it open. Inside was a single matching sheet of Basildon Bond. The stationery struck her as peculiarly smart and co-ordinated for Olivier. The paper was covered in a headlong ballpoint scrawl.

'Darling Kate,' she read. 'I can't quite believe what I'm writing here. I feel like someone in a book. Because this is a goodbye note . . .' She frowned, puzzled.

'. . . I'm sending it to you because you've been my dearest friend. I really do love you and the kids. Only, Kate, I can't go on . . .'

She turned cold. Her stomach lurched. Did this mean what it seemed to?

'. . . I'm living in a world where I just don't seem to fit. I'm not young any more and I don't know how to grow old. I feel weak and despised. I'm turning into a joke, some kind of Peter Pan or Holy Fool and it can only get worse. I see you worrying about me. I see Carol trying to jolly me along and I can't stand it. I'm ashamed. I can't live with myself. I don't know how this all happened but I want out. Say sorry to Jack and Stella for me. The worst thing I can imagine is them getting to think of me as an embarrassment, a pain in the arse. Say sorry to Ma and Pa. I've let you all down . . .'

The world stood still. Light voices echoed from the street. They seemed to float to her from another planet.

'. . . This isn't a cry for help. By the time you get it I'll be dead. Carol and Mickey are away for a few days. That's why I've chosen now to do it. Forgive me, dearest Kate.'

She closed her eyes. Clamped one hand hard across her mouth. Then read the letter again, searching for a sign that would reveal it as some kind of a practical joke. Surely, surely, it must be a joke. She heard a ragged burst of ironic cheering from the street outside.

* * *

417

In every town and village she passed through were flags and streamers, T-shirts and funny hats, grinning faces, brightened, heightened like a disturbed dream. How bizarre it was, this royalist jubilation, when the purpose of her journey was to verify that Olivier was dead. At the back of her mind lurked the shadowy image of a half-remembered painting – the poet Chatterton, dead or dying, a beautiful youth, deathly pale, draped across his bed in an attitude of voluptuous abandon. She was stuck here in limbo, in the little tin box of her car, its progress screamingly slow . . . She recalled now his mention of sleeping pills. Her thoughts ran ahead. She ached with the desire to arrive, to know. Yet, somehow, she made herself drive punctiliously, observe the speed limit, raised her eyes frequently to the rear-view mirror, overtook only under perfect conditions.

She'd been on the point of phoning the Oxford police, had got their number from Directory Enquiries. But, at the moment of dialling, Kate replaced the receiver. Alive or dead, a couple of hours would make no difference. But if Olivier were floating somewhere between the two, she did not want to imagine his being jerked back into the world by accusing, intrusive officials. She'd told the children Olivier was ill, and left them in Allie's care. Jack wanted to come with her. 'I don't care about the party,' he kept insisting, and it had been hard to put him off.

The big half-timbered pub that, for Kate, signalled her arrival in Oxford, was hung with a Union Jack the size of a bedspread. Along the Woodstock Road the houses fluttered with pennants. Down side streets she glimpsed tables set up, briefly caught the rhythmic ripple of a steel band. The festivity was relentless. Even the bridge by the bit of ground where she parked sported its own royal coat of arms and swagged streamers.

Kate stared down the towpath. Here the air of celebration was less ecstatic. None the less, as on every Saturday afternoon, small gatherings of friends sat together, some drinking and smoking, others merely chatting, either on board or spilling over on to the path. Fervently Kate wished she could be transported somehow seamlessly to the deck of the *Creeping Jenny*, without running the gauntlet of these sociable groups, which would undoubtedly contain people she knew.

Sure enough. 'Hiya, Kate,' a man named Ozzy called, almost the moment she set foot on the dirt path.

'Seen Olivier?' she asked, guarded, casual.

'I think he's away. His boat's all locked up.'

Kate lumbered on – refusing to speculate, her head giddily vacant – through the sunlit normality of the scene. Drawing near the *Creeping Jenny*, she saw that the curtains were drawn, the door closed. She boarded and felt for the spare key Olivier kept under the blue and white pot with its brittle remains of a rosemary plant.

Before setting the key into the lock, Kate stood for a moment in the cockpit, bracing herself against the door frame, steeling her whole being against the dread of what she was about to discover. She had never in her life seen a dead body and understood now that she *expected* to find Olivier dead. Though, alongside that expectation – with a die-hard shimmer of hope – she could envisage the ecstasy, the crazy relief of discovering that he was not.

Clumsily she fitted key to lock, took a breath, turned it, pushed cautiously at the door and, at once, her senses were assaulted by a throat-gripping stench of shit and whisky. To begin with she could see nothing but the dimness of the interior. She took a step inside, then another, past the stove and sink, her eyes beginning to adapt to the half-light.

Then, heart beating, breath held, she peered into the central cabin where Olivier lived and slept. Her eyes seeking out the mattress below the window on the right. And, with sinking inevitability, Kate saw what she had expected to find though, in semi-darkness, it was hard to make sense of the humped, foreshortened shape lying on the dark Welsh blanket. She made out jeans, a black T-shirt, the paleness of feet and arms . . . And, horribly, a grey plastic bag where she would have thought to see his head. The gagging stench told her that Olivier had soiled himself. On the floor beside his mattress were an empty glass, an overturned whisky bottle, its pungent contents still dampening the bedside rug. There was to the crumpled form an utter, utter stillness that Kate knew at once as the stillness of death. She stood in the doorway, frozen, awed. Seized with a superstitious dread of approaching or touching the body. It had become, not Olivier, but something alien, something taboo. She would call in the authorities to deal with it.

The policeman with the slicked-back hair reckoned he'd been dead for less than twelve hours. Olivier must have carried out the ritual of his suicide in the small hours of that morning. Kate had proffered his letter, and it had been taken from her.

'I'll get it back, won't I?' she'd asked in a sort of rising panic and been assured that she would, eventually. Some time next week she would be required to attend an inquest.

As she drove, now, along dark country roads, making her way home, Kate's headlights picked out a succession of bleached, ghostly trees. It amazed her that she could admire their beauty, and produce the skills needed for handling the car, while, at the back of her mind, there shimmered the hazed and troubling image of Olivier's lifeless face. She made herself contemplate it, dwell on it, as if, through familiarity, she could somehow neutralize its power to ambush and haunt.

She had not, after all, been able to evade closer contact with the corpse, had been called on by the police to identify the body before its removal to the morgue. Briefly, reluctantly, she had stared into the face of a stranger, with white lips and sunken cheeks. Inanimate, waxen – except that it seemed to be made from some substance more inert than wax.

'That's him,' she had confirmed, 'Olivier Felix.' Only, if he'd been elsewhere, in neutral surroundings, if he'd worn different clothes, Kate suspected that she would not have known him.

From the police station, in the early evening, she had rung her neighbour, Allie, to say she would not be home until late. Then, unable to face breaking the news to Odile, she had telephoned Jerome in London. He'd reacted with a long, uncomprehending silence. When at last he could speak, it was in a voice broken and hoarse, punctuated with long, gasping silences, a voice which broke her heart. Attempting to answer his questions in the small, airless, windowless room, with a young policewoman seated discreetly in one corner, Kate closed her eyes, imagining his pain, hot tears welling from beneath her lids. Later Jerome seemed somehow to collect himself, became terse and practical, as if the situation were a challenge he must rise to. He would phone Pascal and Beatrice, drive down to break the news to Odile and Nelly, return to Oxford the following day . . .

'You're a good kid, Kate,' he said, just before he hung up, and set her almost-dried tears flowing again.

The policewoman brought her a mug of tea, spoke gently to her, called her Kate, touched her shoulder briefly in sympathy. Later she asked a lot of questions, but in a routine fashion, as if she had been through this sort of thing many times before. Afterwards, when she was allowed to go, Kate bought fish and chips from a van parked in St Giles and ate them sitting in her car, staring out at the darkening sky, exhausted and drained of all emotion.

Chapter Forty-Four

◈◈◈

After a couple of half-hearted hymns, an evasive five-minute ramble, during which he barely mentioned the deceased – who was in any case unknown to him – the duty vicar discreetly pressed a concealed button, causing the coffin to glide slowly through an aperture into the putative flames which would consume Olivier's earthly remains.

Kate could not bear it. For two weeks now she had lived on a frontierland of tears, slipping easily from one side to another, without transition, almost without noticing, and now they came again, coursing hot and effortless down her face. Pascal reached out and grasped her hand, both offering and seeking comfort. Her own hand gripped his, returning the pressure.

For years she had harboured anger against Pascal for his neglect of his family and, more particularly, for his ignoring of her, when they lived a mere fifteen minutes' drive away from one another. But, here and now, she could not hold on to her resentment. His grief was so palpable, his face so white and haggard, his eyes, behind the chic John Lennon spectacles, shocked, bruised. Clearly he suffered and, for that, she could forgive him.

As the curtains closed, screening the coffin from view, taped recessional music filled the white chapel of the crematorium. The vicar blessed them, his lowered eyelids forming pious half-moons against the freshness of his round cheeks. Then he made his way matter-of-factly to the back of the room in order to admit the next consignment of mourners, leaving the present flock to shuffle out of the side door opened for the purpose.

'God, what was the point of that?' Pascal muttered. 'The whole thing's just a question of logistics, like shifting passengers on and off the cross-channel ferry.'

The ceremony, Kate acknowledged to herself, had been entirely unsatisfying. But – unless the Church occupied the centre of your life, and you lived in the same place for years and years, left your mark on the community, and hundreds of people came to your funeral – wasn't that inevitable?

Outside it was warm and overcast. The small group of mourners gathered round a modest collection of wreaths and flowers dedicated to Olivier.

As she approached Kate saw that Odile, supported by Beatrice, was weeping wildly, her face contorted in an agonizing, clown-like rictus.

'Maman, don't . . .' Beatrice tried to enfold her mother in a calming embrace. With her sunglasses and dark dress she looked as abstract and streamlined as a drawing by Aubrey Beardsley.

But Odile's grief could not be checked. Shoulders hunched, she rocked her body back and forth, seeming near to collapse, though her wracking sobs remained voiceless as if in passionate mime.

'Let's find the car. Let's sit down for a while.' Beatrice half dragged, half carried Odile away.

'Well, thank God the funeral farce is over,' Jerome greeted Kate and Pascal. How small and shrunken he looked. For all his sixty-five years Jerome had until now retained a youthful, plumped-up quality. Today he seemed wizened like a deflated balloon. 'Now all we have to do is hang on and get through the rest of our lives.' He faltered, stared ahead of him, as if combating tears. Pascal threw his arms round his father, holding him close and patting his shoulder. Kate saw that he was weeping too.

'No Marya?' Jerome asked when, after a long while, they pulled apart.

Pascal shook his head. 'She couldn't face it.'

Odile had wanted family only at the funeral. So far none of the Felixes had attempted to contact the motley string of friends and acquaintances Olivier had gathered on his vagabond progress through life. But Carol and Mickey, Olivier's ex-lover Barbara, his mate Blackie, all knew of his death and had invited themselves. As a group they approached Jerome to pay their respects. Kate watched, touched, as he accepted their tributes to his son. A little old man he seemed – crushed, frail, but with, even now, the ghost of his subversive smile.

Robert and Nelly came to join them. Robert had his arm tight round Nelly's waist. Kate had caught a glimpse of her before the service and been disconcerted by her appearance.

She had assumed at once that Nelly was sedated in some way – her face appeared heavy and waxen, eyes hammocked in swollen flesh. Yet her toilette was oddly studied, too studied for a funeral. Nelly's shoulder-length hair had been set in luxuriant Lana Turner curls. She wore a wide-shouldered forties-style dress with panels of gold embroidery on the bodice, black seamed stockings, high open-work shoes in patent leather. Worn exuberantly to a party, the outfit might have been seen as amusingly flamboyant. But, combined with Nelly's dull, glassy stare, a slash of smudged burgundy lipstick, the effect today was bizarre.

Robert, on the other hand – tall and serious in his dark suit – looked, more than any of them, in control of the situation. And, indeed, Kate remembered Nelly telling her once that, in the course of his legal duties, her husband was called upon to attend many funerals. Today he seemed Nelly's minder, grave and protective, never leaving her side, daring anyone to disrespect her eccentric appearance.

The five of them lingered on for a while attempting to converse. But the brutal, bald fact of Olivier's suicide hung over them, combining with the heavy sultriness of the day, rendering anything they could say petty and fatuous. Nelly seemed dazed and spoke not at all.

Eventually Jerome threw in the towel. 'I'm going to the car to see how Odile is . . . I think we'll be getting along . . . What about you two?' He addressed Robert.

'No reason to hang around.'

Their farewells were subdued, lacked the sentimental expansiveness that could uplift even the saddest occasion. It was as if an unspoken sense of shame or guilt hung about them, chilling their mutual affection, as though they were all complicit in an unnamed crime.

As Kate took Nelly by the shoulders to kiss her goodbye she glimpsed a fleeting animation in her long eyes, the ghost of a smile, giving the unnerving impression that the real woman was somehow trapped inside this alien carapace.

Pascal promised to return to Oxford at the end of the week to pick up Olivier's ashes. They would be buried beneath a plaque in the small, overgrown churchyard near Plas Felix.

Finally he and Kate were left standing alone.

'What are you doing now?' he asked.

'Just going home. I came by train. Left the kids and my car with a friend. Jess, you remember? She's taking them and her boy to see *Bugsy Malone*.'

'Do you fancy a drink before you go?'

They took a taxi to the Bear in Alfred Street. Kate stared out at the passing townscape. Pascal observed her covertly. He hadn't been alone with her for years and years, hadn't *seen* her since . . . his wedding? He could not remember. Though he was vaguely aware that she lived not far from him and Marya. He'd been inclined to take Greg's side in their marriage break-up, felt vaguely pissed off at Kate for what he perceived as her flightiness. He'd had a letter from Greg soon after the split saying he would've kept the marriage going given the choice . . .

In the wake of Olivier's suicide she'd stepped abruptly back into the limelight of his consciousness. His brother had sent his final living words to this woman. She'd found his body. Set out to find it.

'How did you feel,' he asked suddenly, 'when you got Olivier's letter?'

'I couldn't take it in.' She glanced at him. Pascal sensed a flicker of hostility in her gaze. 'Not until I actually knew he was dead. Not even then really . . .'

She seemed unwilling to elaborate. Pascal eyed her, mentally condemning the cheap and nasty canvas wedgie shoes she wore. Marya would shudder. Kate had on a grey cotton dress, a graceful enough garment, though creased by now. The neck and arms emerging from it were almost as slim and taut as he could wish. Her mid-length hair was slippery and flat, as if she'd washed it in

425

haste that morning but lacked the time or expertise to do anything with it . . . Even in the wake of his brother's funeral Pascal could not help mentally rejigging and refining her image, figuring how he would light her . . .

She spoke again suddenly. 'On the table just near his body I saw a writing pad and envelopes. A matching set . . . Olivier never had anything so . . . well, bourgeois. He must have gone to a shop and bought them specially to write his suicide note . . .' Her voice faltered and she looked at him, as if to solicit a reaction. He squeezed her hand briefly, comfortingly, though in his view the detail added little to the enormity of the whole situation.

In the dim, brown anonymity of the pub Pascal bought them both double whiskies. As an afterthought he asked for a packet of cigarettes. They had Gitanes. Today he would indulge himself. Marya hated him to smoke and he rarely did. But his body still craved that first drag like a meeting with a louche old lover.

Kate had bagged a quiet corner seat. The place was half empty. It was early yet.

Pascal sat down opposite her. 'Do you mind if I smoke?'

She made a casual 'feel free' sort of gesture then, raising her glass to him briefly, took a large slug of her scotch, let out a gusty sigh. 'I've never needed anything so much.'

Pascal held the cigarette pack out to her. She shook her head. He took one for himself, lit it, inhaled deeply. And at once it was as if all his ragged nerve-endings were coated in finest gossamer. He sipped his whisky, savouring its fiery anaesthesia.

'God, that's better.' Taking another drag on his Gitane, another swallow of scotch. 'That funeral was ghastly.'

'I can't imagine how your ma is ever going to get over this.' She fixed him with a gaze he saw as judgmental. Rightly or wrongly.

They fell silent. Kate finished her drink. Pascal finished his.

'D'you want another of these?' she asked.

'Do you?'

'Yes.'

He liked the way she said that. Pascal watched her as she crossed to the bar. He'd fallen into the habit of comparing all women with

426

Marya, but there were other yardsticks. He saw a man on the opposite side of the room following her progress with his eyes. The dress she wore was loose and reached to mid-calf, was in no way provocative. But the body inside it was slight and youthful. Ordering the drinks, she grinned at something the barman said, answered him back with some remark that made him smile too, shrugged her shoulders, quick and amused. He wondered if there had been anything sexual between her and Olivier.

But that thought activated the particular desolate ache, the self-hatred that lay in wait for him now at all times of the day and night. This thing had happened while he, Pascal, was otherwise engaged. He'd ignored Olivier for years, and then, when he *had* seen him . . .

'There.' Kate placed the two drinks on the table between them. 'Oblivion in a glass.'

When she sat down Pascal asked guardedly, 'How've you been coping?' He had the sudden desire to compare notes.

'I'm not sure I have.' Kate looked at him levelly, as she lifted the glass to her lips and took a sip. 'I've felt like a bit of driftwood, tossed this way and that by the tide.'

A lot of the time, Kate told Pascal, she was riddled with guilt. She'd known Olivier was down but had never dreamed he was as desperate as that, kept thinking and thinking what more she could have done . . . At other moments she was invaded by a tide of anger at his lack of guts, just the ordinary guts everyone needed to live their lives. He'd let her children down. They loved him and took it for granted that he would always be around . . . Then, again, she would be shaken top to bottom by an overwhelming sense of pity. Olivier was the least . . . harmful person she had ever known. She would never understand why he'd lost faith in himself the way he did . . .

'I saw him last month . . .' Pascal said.

'Did you?' She seemed truly amazed. 'He never told me.'

'I had a few hours to spare. I dropped by on the off-chance.'

Pascal recalled the scruffy, smelly interior of the boat, littered with dirty cups and plates, trays of half-eaten Chinese food. It had offended him. He'd been disconcerted too by the fact that at lunchtime Olivier was still in bed. He could no longer imagine such aimlessness . . . But none of that would really have mattered if Olivier himself had not seemed so shamefaced.

'We went to the pub and made polite conversation . . . I did notice that he seemed out of sorts, but I bent over backwards to gloss over any awkwardness. I acted as if everything was fine. I didn't want to embarrass him . . .'

He had the impression that Kate was listening with an acute and very personal attention.

'I think now that if I'd been less tactful, if I'd probed a bit, I might have got some truth out of him. I might've been able to help him somehow . . . But I had a thousand things to do that day and I chose to let sleeping dogs lie. And now the thought of it keeps coming back to me. As if Olivier was dangling off the edge of a cliff and I just left him to hang there.' His eyes appealed to hers. 'Maybe I could have saved him.'

Kate's expression remained impassive, though it seemed to Pascal that, in some intangible way, her attitude towards him had softened. 'Maybe.' Her tone was gently sceptical. She shrugged her shoulders. 'But I doubt it.'

Pascal was supposed to be taking a taxi out to Charlbury where Marya and Jocasta were staying with the actor, Leon Callan, and Judy, his wife. They were going to eat together, along with another theatrical couple. And get rat-arsed, Leon had promised.

'It'll be a lovely treat after your gruelling family wake,' Marya had enthused.

Pascal had asked her to come to the funeral, though without much conviction. He knew how much Jerome and Odile would have appreciated the gesture. But Marya had winced at the very thought.

'You're kidding. I hardly knew your brother. I can't be expected to run the gauntlet of your collective family misery . . .'

She'd been standing by the basin in the bathroom when he made the request, naked, smoothing a lotion into her belly and breasts that smelt sickly-delicious of vanilla. He could see her now, looking over her shoulder at him, her body slim and white, her hair falling in

428

childish elf-locks halfway down her back, eyes dark, black-lashed, in the composed pallor of her face. Quite perfect. And Pascal had seen the world through her eyes for so long that he was unable to feel – let alone express – anger at her refusal.

Just now, Pascal reflected, he was not in the mood to spend an evening with bloody posturing Leon, with his low, amused voice, the contrived sexy-wolfish grin he plastered across his face at the slightest provocation, the way he belittled his own wife. Leon had eyes for Marya – made a point of parading the fact – and she basked subtly, sensuously in the brash sunshine of his lust, was always randy after an evening spent with the Callans in a way that drove Pascal wild and simultaneously broke his heart. Under normal circumstances Pascal felt impelled to keep a watchful eye on their meetings.

But this evening, just suddenly, he could not be bothered. He needed to be with someone who knew Olivier. He was half-cut and it was comforting sitting here with Kate. He had the abrupt conviction that she was the only person in the world to whom he could confess how he felt about his brother's death, the only person who could possibly understand. She was almost family but not quite, possessing both intimate knowledge and a degree of perspective.

'Have you got to rush off?' he asked her.

'Not really.'

'Will you stay for a bit? Are you free?'

'Yes. Jess isn't expecting me at any particular time.'

'Hang on for a moment. I'll make a phone call.'

Judy answered the phone. She liked him. Between the two of them there existed a sort of unspoken solidarity. He said something had come up, to go ahead and eat without him. He would arrive as soon as he possibly could.

'I'll tell Marya.'

The very neutrality of Judy's tone signalled her anticipation of fireworks. Just now Pascal thought to hell with it. Tomorrow, no doubt, he would be made to see the error of his ways, but he'd face that when he had to.

'I've cancelled,' he told Kate.

429

'What were you supposed to be doing?'

'Eating and getting pissed with Leon Callan.'

'What, *the* Leon Callan?'

'The very same.'

'Instead you're getting pissed with me. I'm honoured.'

''Nother li'l drink?' He parodied a music-hall drunk.

'I shouldn't, but I will.'

It was around eight o'clock. Pascal returned to their table bearing fresh glasses. The place was filling up. The encircling presence of self-engrossed groups and couples made their corner space feel all the more private. He lit another cigarette.

Kate lifted her third large whisky with a wry 'here goes' look on her face that recalled to Pascal the way she'd been as a girl.

'Olivier was incredibly envious of you,' she announced, challenging, rather drunk.

Pascal was sceptical. 'I would have thought I had just exactly the kind of life he didn't want.'

'He changed. As time passed he seemed to lose faith in his philosophy of life . . . He came to be envious of your success, your child, your marriage . . .'

For a second Pascal contemplated this neat encapsulation of his world. Viewed from the inside, his hold on these elements appeared tenuous to say the least.

'I'm not sure I feel enviable.'

She smiled crookedly. 'You look it from here.'

'If I say otherwise I'll sound ungrateful. Whingeing. I'm basically doing the kind of work I want. Only it involves compromises, always. Always. The final product's never what I want it to be . . .' He could see her listening, respectful but sceptical. 'I won't bore you . . . But an awful lot of the time the struggles, the in-fighting outweigh the satisfactions . . .'

'And Marya?' A diffident murmur, as if she might be pushing her luck. She clearly saw – all of them must see – that this wasn't your average common or garden marriage. There was a discreet honesty in the query that appealed to the honesty in him. He was drunk. His guard was down.

'You know me from way back. I'm a beauty junkie. I always was. Beauty has always been what I looked for in a woman. It sounds shallow, I know, but it doesn't feel like that. It feels as if I'm tapping into some kind of magic . . .' He shrugged. 'That's just how it is . . .'

'Go on.'

'Well, for me, Marya is the embodiment of that enchantment. The ultimate embodiment. I wouldn't even say that what I feel for her is primarily sexual.' He smiled defensively. 'It's just that I'm addicted to her. Slavishly so.'

He paused, looking into Kate's eyes, reading no trace of mockery or embarrassment. She was rapt as if at a story.

'I don't expect our marriage to last. Sometimes I almost will it to end, because I know it will, and I want to get the pain over and done with . . .' A grin. 'Do I sound enviable?'

'I'm not sure. Since Greg I've done everything to avoid that kind of pain.'

They lapsed into silence. Pascal became conscious of the chatter and laughter that surrounded them. He had no real picture of Kate's life and lacked the energy to probe, to imagine. It was enough tonight to be in her presence, to escape the loneliness of his brooding over Olivier.

'Your family miss seeing you,' Kate said suddenly.

Pascal fielded the implicit reproach. He was clear-eyed as to the situation. 'All my time and energy go on Marya and Jocasta and my work. It's a shame, I know, but I can't imagine it changing forseeably. Marya isn't a family person . . . Sometimes I see wives who like and mix with their in-laws and I'm boggled by them.'

'You're lucky. You can take your family for granted. They'll never give up on you.'

He was struck by something in her tone. Not a bitterness exactly – more a wistfulness. And he was reminded of the initial circumstance that bound them together. Kate's estrangement from her father, her embracing of his own family. Time and adulthood glossed over such convulsions, but the scars must of course remain.

'You think I'm a neglectful bastard.'

431

A deprecating gesture. 'I'm not trying to lay a guilt-trip on you.' She leaned her elbows on the table, propped her chin in her hands. Just now, Pascal thought, she made an appealing picture, black hair framing her pensive face. Her lips were alluring to him, swollen and softened, alcohol-sexy.

She began to speak, low and serious. 'You know, Pascal, I can't ever convey to you what your family's meant to me . . . You came into my life, all of you, like a gift from the gods . . .' Glancing cagily across at him as if anticipating mockery. 'You welcomed me, accepted me, made me feel I belonged, and I've loved you ever since. Your family's been, well, my fortress against the cruel world . . .'

'Steady on,' he teased.

Kate smiled along with him at her own earnestness. 'I'm drunk,' she said. 'Indulge me.'

A brief pause, then she picked up the thread of her reflection. 'When I was a kid I saw all of you as so special . . .' A half-embarrassed grin. 'Almost mythical, in fact. So much so that I'd do almost anything to make you like me, and shut my eyes to anything that might make any of you seem flawed or fallible . . .'

Kate shrugged, but her eyes swam with unshed tears. 'But now . . . with Olivier . . . Well, something's happened that's cruel enough to force me to wake up and finally admit to myself that you . . . the wonderful Felix family . . . well, you *don't* possess charmed lives. You're not immune to the horrors of the world. You're only flesh and blood, just like anybody else. And my fantasy's been ripped away from me. And without it life seems more ordinary somehow . . . Sadder. Colder.'

She sat back, stuck a flopping lock of hair behind her ears, smiled crookedly at him, giving him licence to laugh at her intensity. But he was infected by her tipsy volubility and almost sad that his family could not live up to her ideal.

All that summer Kate went about as if with in-drawn breath, as if walking on eggshells, as if carrying inside her a fragile container brimming with grief that would stay intact just so long as it wasn't jostled or jogged. But if she were to grow careless for even one minute she knew it would burst, and the contents rush everywhere – messy, overwhelming and quite beyond her control.

Covertly, closely, she observed the children. Throughout July Stella seemed whiney, the way she used to as a young child, when her world was in flux, before they settled in Downridge. Jack was always more self-contained but there were times when Kate glimpsed a confusion in his young eyes that broke her heart.

Constantly they quoted the dead man. 'Abba aren't crap,' Stella protested to Jack. 'Olivier says.'

'Olivier was going to teach me to play "Guantanamera",' Jack remarked one evening, as he took himself off to bed.

Kate found the invocation of his opinions and promises almost more than she could bear. Repeatedly she burned with rage towards Olivier for his betrayal of their trust.

Socially, too, his absence left a hole like a jagged tooth socket in the fabric of their lives. At weekends Kate found herself thinking up expensive distractions – visits to the seaside, to Longleat, to the theatre – to divert their attention from the lack of Olivier. The summer holidays loomed. Kate spoke to Odile often on the phone. She sounded hazy and muddled with grief. It would be impossible to take the children on their usual August visit to Plas Felix. Kate decided that, by hook or by crook, her money would stretch to a fortnight abroad. Both the anticipation and the holiday itself would keep the children's minds occupied.

A couple of years ago, she recalled, Jess and family had been to a campsite in the Pyrenees and had raved about the scenery and all the amenities available to them – luxurious tents, a huge swimming pool with fancy slides and a wave-machine, horse-riding, a cable car . . . She telephoned Jess to ask for the details.

'Fabulous idea! You don't mind if Cal and I come too . . .'

Kate was wrongfooted by her cheek, indignant, dubious – Cal and her own children did nothing but squabble. Then again, she reflected, it might be good to have another adult along. And if Jack and Stella were fighting with Cal, they certainly wouldn't be brooding over Olivier.

Five days before they were due to leave Kate had a phone call from Robert. He sounded dreadful, a hoarse, cracked quality to his voice. 'Nelly's in hospital. She's been admitted to the mental ward in Bangor.'

Kate exclaimed in distress, conflicting images flashing into her mind. Nelly at the funeral – garish, remote – alongside the laughing girl she used to be. The contrast was too painful.

'To be perfectly honest, Kate, it's a relief. She's been through a bad spell. She's been like a dead person. This thing with Olivier has really got to her . . . But it's put the shits up her too. She *wants* to do something about her highs and lows, these mad mood swings . . . Maybe going into hospital is the best thing that could've happened . . .' He spoke headlong, his Welsh accent intensified by emotion. 'Only why I really rang was to ask a huge favour. I'm spending half my life at the hospital and I've got a big case on. My ma's bad with her breathing, and I wondered if you could come down . . .' He sounded abashed at his own effrontery, his need. 'Bring your typewriter, bring your work, just be here with the kids . . . Maybe we could take shifts . . .'

'Oh, gosh, Robert, I'm booked to go to France.'

'OK. I see.' He sounded crushed.

But at once Kate was deeply unhappy with her reply. She owed the Felixes more than she could ever repay. Chances to reciprocate came rarely. She knew she would never forgive herself if she let one go.

'Listen, Robert,' she heard herself saying. 'This needn't be a problem. What if I take Rhys and Aled with me? A change of scenery might be the best thing of all. If you put them on the train, I can meet them this end . . .'

Kate was startled by the words emerging from her own mouth, but even as she spoke they gained in feasibility. Why shouldn't they come? She had Jess, who was bossy enough for two. Together they could marshal five kids. She was filled with a sly amusement at the thought of confronting her friend with the *fait accompli*.

'Would you do that? It's a fantastic idea. You're a saint.' Robert's voice shook with relief and gratitude.

PART 4

✧✧✧✧

The Eighties

Chapter Forty-Five
1982

◄►◄►◄►

Fourteen-year-old Stella peered out of the car window at the little flurry of passengers emerging from the station. Commuters all of them, as far as she could see, the numbers thinning out as they joined the bus queue or ambled towards the car park.

'Don't say he's missed the train.' Kate tapped anxiously on the dashboard.

Stella gazed avidly in the direction of the station exit, eager to be the one to spot him. It had been she who'd initially picked up the phone two hours ago when out of the blue Rick Stephens, her mother's half-brother, called to ask if he could come and see them.

'There he is!'

The figure of a young man emerged from the glass door. Right away Stella knew it was him, because of the enormous backpack that dwarfed his slight figure. She rolled down the window, called yoo-hoo and waved. He grinned and began to walk towards them.

'Oh God, he's got hippie hair,' Stella groaned. It waved across his forehead, hopelessly seventies.

In the flesh he didn't look as healthy and all-American as she had expected. He wore a black top, khaki chinos, trainers. As he drew closer she began to place the features familiar from the smiley family photos her mother hated and always hid away in her desk drawer. Actually his face was quite nice, quite interesting.

Kate got out and greeted him and helped him stow his backpack in the boot of the car. Then he took his place in the passenger seat next to her. As her mother made boring, necessary conversation with the young American, Stella examined him covertly from behind and, when she could, in one or other of the driving mirrors. He had very nice brown eyes. She remembered Kate saying once that her father's eyes were the colour of some drink – brandy or sherry or something. Stella had imagined that he would be very suntanned and have big, white teeth. But, in fact, his complexion had an almost English grey-whiteness to it, there was stubble on his chin and, when he wasn't smiling, his face had a slightly worried look. He seemed altogether more ordinary and human than she had expected.

He told Kate that he was on his way to meet up with a couple of friends in Paris. They were going to spend a month backpacking in France, Italy, Greece and the Greek islands. He had just one night's stopover in London and, on an impulse, had decided to try and make contact with this sister he had in England and couldn't even remember meeting, though Dad said he had as a little boy. He'd been real nervous dialling her number, almost put the phone down, but felt better as soon as he heard Stella's voice. He flashed her a crooked smile over his shoulder. Stella found herself charmed by his accent, his diffident but friendly manner, and quietly elated by the fact that this agreeable stranger was in fact a blood relative.

Stella could recall the way Olivier used to read out Kate's father's yearly Christmas letter in a suave, smarmy American accent. Nowadays she and Jack did the same and Kate never minded. For as long as Stella could remember Kate had spoken of her father with a disparaging twitch of the lips.

'My God!' she'd exclaimed earlier, putting the receiver down after agreeing to meet her half-brother at Harlow station, raising both hands to her head in mock-horror. 'My God!'

So it was amusing now to watch her mother conversing with Rick as if butter wouldn't melt in her mouth. Stella would tease her about that later.

'We wondered if you'd like to come out for a meal with us. If you're not too jet-lagged that is. There's a new bistro opened in the village.'

'Sounds great.'

Stella grinned to herself in the back of the car. Bottles Bistro great? Boy was he in for a disappointment.

*   *   *

Bottles, Kate reflected, was not known for the liveliness of its ambience. The self-styled bistro had opened up the previous year in Downridge High Street, in premises that had, according to Allie, housed a draper's shop until the mid sixties. The main room had low beams and leaded windows in abundance, along with red-checked table cloths, red-shaded lamps, green plants cascading from an antique whatnot in the corner. But the effect remained dispiriting unless the place was chock-full of semi-drunken customers, which happened just once a week, from half past eight to eleven o'clock on a Saturday night.

This evening only one other table was occupied, by a pair of elderly women, comparing notes on aspects of marital tedium, so Kate gathered from overheard snippets. But the very dreariness of the place lent a certain half-hysterical liveliness to their own little corner. Deirdre was serving, one of an army of nieces and nephews claimed by George and Allie, Kate's next-door neighbours. Rick was clearly taken by her black-rimmed eyes and spiked black hair, she by Rick's engaging foreignness.

In a confidential whisper she warned them off the chilli-con-carne and the flabby baked potatoes. After a brief consultation all four of them settled for the garlic bread starter, followed by chicken Kiev and chips.

'And may I recommend the garlic ice-cream for afters,' Stella quipped, laying claim to an old family joke and offering it up to Rick, new-minted.

'My favourite,' he grinned.

'The old jokes are the best ones,' Jack jibed.

'Better an old joke than no joke at all.' Stella narrowed her eyes scornfully, like Trisha Yates in *Grange Hill*.

It was intriguing for them to hear information gleaned from Ellis's impersonal Christmas bulletins quirkily relayed by a live human being. Kate knew, for instance, that her father had retired but was amused to learn that he'd taken up cooking as a hobby. Fay was still working and, for several nights on the go, had returned home to find an ambitious three-course banquet waiting for her.

'Mom's always watching her weight and, in any case, she'd

just as soon have a sandwich. The situation got a little tense at times.'

He spoke of his parents, Kate noticed, with easy affection. His sister, Justine, was the smart one, Rick told them. He wasn't into studying. Sometimes he felt a disappointment to his mother and father. Ellis particularly . . . He'd mooched around for several years not knowing what he wanted to do with himself. Then, out of interest, he and a friend started making furniture, using reclaimed wood, teaching themselves as they went along from books, some modern, some really old. They started to sell some of the things they produced and began to see the pastime as a possible business.

'Trouble is,' Rick sighed, 'I'm a perfectionist. I have to speed up or I'll never get anywhere . . .'

Ellis had been sceptical at first, but was coming round. He and Fay had ordered a store-cupboard for the kitchen. Rick was twenty-four now. This trip was his final fling before he got down to being serious . . .

As the four of them talked and ate, Kate was intensely aware of the children eyeing the young American, drinking him in – a real live relative.

Stella's curiosity bubbled close to the surface, constantly visible in the brightness of her eyes, the quick toothy smile she gave whenever Rick said something of which she approved. Jack was more inscrutable and less trusting. Already, at fifteen, he knew how to veil his blue eyes and hide what he was feeling. He and his friends made a habit of jeering at American films and pop music as schmaltzy and mainstream. He could be surly with visitors. But tonight Kate seemed to sense a suspension of his ruthless teenage critical faculties. She guessed he was drawn to Rick in spite of himself.

And so, it seemed, was she. Kate found herself touched by his goodwill in seeking them out. This well-meaning young half-brother struck her as thoroughly likeable. She felt rather ashamed of the mocking, semi-hostile attitude she had foisted, by example, on her children as regards her father's transatlantic family. Rick's open friendliness made it clear that no such scepticism had been cultivated on their side.

'This is the bit I like,' Deirdre confided later, after she'd wheeled the laden sweet trolley across the dimly lit restaurant to their table. 'It makes me feel like a fairy godmother, ladling out the goodies at a christening.'

Kate was stuffed, but Jack and Stella regarded profiteroles as the height of luxury and sophistication. They ordered a plateful each and urged Rick to do the same. But he took his time choosing, questioning Deirdre about every item on the trolley, both of them clearly entertained by the quiz.

'Bakewell tart,' he repeated, when she pointed out that delicacy. 'Now that's one of the things about England that Dad says he misses . . . Maybe I'll give that a try.'

'No, it's boring.' Again the children pressed the claims of the profiteroles, or at least the chocolate mousse, but Rick was adamant.

Later they asked him what he thought of it.

'Good. Solid. Chewy. Nothing fancy about it.' A sly, amused grin. 'A bit like Dad himself.'

By the time they got home Rick was beginning to droop with jet-lag. Jack offered to give up his room to the surprise guest. He slept now in a small extension Kate had had built four years or so ago on the ground floor at the back. Rick followed her into the room to help change the bedclothes.

He looked about him with curiosity. 'An English kid's bedroom.'

Compared to Stella, Jack was tidy, liked his records and books organized in rows, on shelves. Rick examined his Madness and Specials posters, his Spurs pennant, the guitar propped in the corner, which Jack had inherited from Olivier.

As she stripped the bed, Kate explained the history of the instrument. Rick recalled the bare bones of the story from one of the scrawled annual messages on Kate's Christmas card.

'Olivier taught him all the rudiments,' Kate explained. 'When he was small the guitar lessons made Jack feel special.'

'He must miss him.'

'They both do. Or did. They missed him for a long time.'

'It must have been hard on them.'

'It was.'

In the years following his death both children changed. Stella was more emotional, angry at times, wept sometimes out of sheer anger. Jack became remote, rude, surly. It was easy to lay the blame at Olivier's door but who could tell? Maybe the developments would have surfaced anyway as they entered adolescence.

'I like them. They're smart kids.'

'Thank you.' She unfolded the fresh duvet cover. It featured a life-sized image of Superman. 'Sorry about this. Jack's disowned it. But it's the only one I've got clean.'

'I'm not proud.'

Rick held out the duvet while she fitted the cover round it. As she tugged and tweaked he said suddenly, 'There's something I want to tell you. I don't want to leave here without telling you.'

'Oh?' She drew the cover cleanly up and began to snap the fasteners at the top.

'It's about Dad.'

Kate laid the duvet roughly on the bed, sat down herself. 'I'm listening.'

Rick stood leaning against Jack's chest of drawers. He looked serious, perhaps a little embarrassed. 'Well, Dad doesn't talk about his feelings much. But there was this one night when Mom and Justine had gone to stay with Mom's parents and I came home late . . . Dad was watching a football match. I sat down with him and we had a couple of beers and, when the match was done, we got talking . . .'

Rick hesitated. He looked tired and disorientated, ready for sleep, but doggedly determined to finish what he had to say.

'Look, I'm not trying to influence you . . . I just want you to know that he said how bad he felt about losing touch with you. That he thought you were angry with him and he felt it was justified. That he'd been a bad father to you and the Felixes had been wonderful and he guessed you didn't want him in your life. That the situation was his fault and he didn't know how to change it . . . Kate, I'm not asking you to do anything. I just want you to know.'

He said no more. Kate sat silent, his words turning in her mind. She was touched by Rick's goodwill, but it was too soon for her to make anything of his message. She got up off the bed and began to pull the duvet into place. 'I'm pleased you told me. I'm not sure yet what difference it'll make.' She straightened up, crossed to where he was standing and placed a swift kiss on his cheek. 'I'm glad you came. I'll leave you now. Curl up with Superman and get some sleep.'

They dropped him off at the station first thing next morning, before Kate drove the children to school. Their farewells had a heightened quality as if, on both sides, a delightful discovery had been made. Rick promised to keep in touch, to sends cards from all corners of Europe.

'He's basically a good guy, you know, our dad,' he murmured to Kate as he kissed her goodbye.

For a split second he gazed at her, intently, as if searching for something in her eyes. She smiled, but cagily, not ready to commit herself to anything.

Affectionately they watched him head towards the station entrance, towards a month of studenty freedom. There was a poignancy to the way his hippie curls hung in his eyes, to the stoop of his slim figure beneath the size and weight of his backpack.

'He was OK,' Jack said. The laconic verdict was his highest form of praise.

'He was cute,' Stella agreed. 'Even with that droopy hair. Did you like him, Mum?'

'Very much.' Hoping they wouldn't, at this point, call into question the cynicism of her wider attitude towards Ellis's family.

Kate had a fight with Jack that evening – about homework as ever. Their confrontation followed its time-worn pattern, with Kate losing her rag while Jack flaunted a patronizing cool.

Later, when both children were in bed, Kate made herself a mug of tea and flopped down in the living-room, flicked on the radio, sat listening to voices discussing the on-going hostilities in the Falklands. What you heard on the radio was franker and less edited than the TV footage. It was odd, though, how remote and unreal the fighting seemed, like a campaign between toy soldiers in some never-never land. In shops, bumping into friends in the village, the subject was barely mentioned, could almost be overlooked. But, alone at night, it was impossible not to be sucked in. However much you hated the flag-waving coverage, the xenophobia of the tabloids, the war itself, a knee-jerk patriotism remained. It was us and them, and you wanted us to win.

As Kate sipped her tea, the voices from the radio mingled in her head with the more immediate concerns of her daily life. She was still rattled by her row with Jack and wondered dully, inconclusively, whether things were different in two-parent families . . .

At the same time her brain played with a couple of teasers thrown up by her day's work. She'd embarked just this week on rather an amusing Parisian detective novel. Over time her reputation as a translator had consolidated. She got work from all over, almost more than she could manage, but it went against the grain to turn anything down. In the last three years her income, though never lavish, had risen appreciably. But, then again, so had the children's needs. Money counted. Kate knew that now, with her gut as well as her head.

With a wholly personal logic she saw Olivier's death as a watershed. The division between before and after.

The time before he died Kate conjured up as a golden age, a fool's paradise. The children young, unspoilt, biddable. Herself similar in many ways. Thinking back to that weekend spent with Olivier on his boat, in the tawny heat of a perfect summer, she saw the two of them as dreamers, superannuated kids, still believing somehow in safe places, the protective power of good parents.

Afterwards that dream was shattered. Kate understood – as Olivier must have done – that the world was cold and offered no guarantees, no protection. She loved her surrogate family but their existence could save her from nothing. They could not even protect themselves from the cruelties of chance.

She saw now that what there was, what remained, were moments of warmth. Times when you shared warmth with someone else and the coldness receded. The way it had been with Rick last night. With a flicker of fondness she recalled his young face. Something rueful about it, whether smiling or serious. The residual pleasure of their encounter still warming her. She remembered, too, the eagerness in Stella's eyes. Jack allowing his macho severity to slip, laughing fit to bust at one of Rick's wry jokes, offering his bed to this congenial relative, unasked.

'He's basically a good guy, our dad.'

The statement pleased her with its unassuming tact, shamed her with its quiet generosity, made her see the grudge she'd born against Ellis for so long as the wounded pique of a child, nursed, nurtured. Never re-examined. Rick was the catalyst. She owed it to her children, if not to herself and Ellis, to try and put things right.

She found her address book and looked up the number but was seized by a kind of stage-fright. How easy it would be to let the moment pass. She turned on the television, sat for a while, channel-hopping, watching fragments that made no sense. It was just after one here. She counted back. That would make it seven, eight o'clock in Vermont? Kate made a resolution. On the dot of half past one she would pick up the receiver and dial. The big hand on her watch crept inexorably forward. There were butterflies in her stomach.

The time came. Kate stood up and switched the television off, crossed to the small table in the corner where the telephone stood, switched on the standard lamp. She had a mental picture of herself under the spreading beam of light, darkness all round her, as she dialled her father's number. Hearing the muted ring, she almost put the phone down, remembered Rick saying the same thing . . . If her little brother could stick with it, so could she. Kate closed her eyes, waited.

445

The receiver was lifted the other end. 'Hello? Fay Stephens here.' Kate had hoped to reach her father direct.

'Fay . . . It's Kate.' After how long – fourteen years – she sensed an explanation might be needed. 'Ellis's daughter. From England.'

'Oh my!'

Kate smiled to herself. Fay used to say that years ago and even then it had struck her as endearingly old-fashioned.

'Ellis!' Fay was calling. 'Ellis, turn that thing off!' Kate became aware of floaty television tones, abruptly silenced. The rumble of a querying male voice. She pictured the light and comfort of a home thousands of miles away. 'It's Kate . . . Your daughter, Kate!' Resuming her telephone pitch, a trifle anxious. 'Nothing's wrong?'

'Everything's fine,' Kate soothed. 'How are you?' But Fay had surrendered the receiver to her husband.

'Kate?' He sounded unbelieving, cautious.

'Yes. It's me. Your long-lost daughter . . . Rick came to see us last night and . . .'

'Rick visited you?' So he hadn't known. The visit had been purely Rick's initiative. But the gladness in her father's voice was unmistakable.

'Yes. Out of the blue. We all went out for a meal. I liked him so much. The kids did too . . . And I thought I'd phone and tell you so.'

There was silence at the end of the phone and then, incredibly, a sort of gasp. As if Ellis were catching his breath, mastering strong emotion . . .

'Kate . . . This is marvellous . . .' He clearly had difficulty in speaking. 'It's so good . . . so good . . . to hear your voice.'

Chapter Forty-Six

❧❧❧

Early one morning, in the aftermath of the Falklands victory, when the media still seemed hell-bent on squeezing every last drop of gung-ho triumphalism from the situation, Kate stood in the kitchen, half-awake, listening to the news on the radio and collating the children's packed lunches. The cadenced voice of the news-reader reached her through the fog of her own thoughts, so there was a second or two of delay before Kate registered that the death had been announced of French novelist David Lacoste, at the age of fifty-nine.

'Good God!'

And yet she knew from Beatrice that he'd had lung cancer for . . . must be a year . . . more.

'What's up?' Stella entered the kitchen, dressed but barefoot, ready to make herself toast.

'David Lacoste's died.'

Stella pulled a lugubrious face. 'Your meal ticket.'

'Watch your mouth, girl. He *did* get me started, but I've learned to walk since then.'

Kate was concerned for Beatrice and tried to telephone her, but could get no answer. That evening, on the television news, there was a quick, cursory appreciation of the writer. It showed a clip from a late fifties interview. Kate was startled by how young and irreverent and downright fanciable he had been. She'd forgotten.

'He wasn't bad once.' Stella was grudgingly impressed.

The clip was followed by footage of David addressing a writer's conference, just over nine months ago. What an old man he looked, frail and emaciated.

Kate was left pensive, a little saddened. She'd seen him only once since the mid-seventies, but as recently as last Christmas he'd sent her an affectionate and cheerful letter. She despised sentimentality and yet . . . There was no denying it, death lent a certain indulgence to one's judgement.

In the event, Beatrice rang her. She sounded calm, said she'd been expecting the end for a month or more.

'Won't you come to the funeral?' she asked. 'I could do with the moral support.'

At the airport Kate rearranged the Duncan Mitchell novels from spine to face out. Whenever she was in a bookshop she gave him a small helping hand. Not that he needed it. She also bought a *Paris-Match* with David's face on the cover.

On the plane she leafed through the magazine. It featured a eulogy to the dead novelist along with several pages of appetizing photographs. David with André Malraux, with Jean-Luc Godard, with John Updike. A small snap of him with Beatrice – she wore dark glasses, looked inscrutable, elegantly emaciated, less than happy – a larger one of David with a pretty, short-haired actress. Kate closed the magazine, closed her eyes. She'd been up ridiculously early to catch this plane, planned to stay over with Beatrice and fly home tomorrow. For the first time ever she had been invited to sleep in Beatrice's spare room. Kate wondered whether the offer had anything to do with the fact of David's death.

Jerome had toyed with the idea of accompanying her, but cried off when the date of the funeral was announced.

'Can't do it I'm afraid. That's a Survivors' day.'

Survivors was a support group Jerome had founded in the wake of Olivier's death, specifically for parents whose children had committed suicide. To keep it functioning was his first priority, with monthly meetings, fund-raising, a rota of long-standing members constantly available to listen to and comfort the freshly bereaved. To him the claims of this brainchild were sacrosanct.

He'd retired now and dabbled with book reviews and occasional television appearances. After his years in the wilderness the media now treated him gently. His public persona had changed. Jerome seemed sadder and wiser, his manner almost childishly direct. Though more recently he had regained a little of his old bounce.

He and Odile lived in Hampstead now, in a modest, convenient ground-floor flat with a tiny garden. They had finally sold Plas Felix in 1978, the year after Olivier had died. For a couple of years the purchasers had run the house as a hotel, but the enterprise had failed.

Odile revelled in the smallness and convenience of her new habitat, looked back on the never-ending effort involved in running Plas Felix with a kind of horror. The flat in Frognal was a comforting womb, cushioning and protecting her. Here she could order her life to please herself.

She had not recovered – and never would – from the death of her youngest and most vulnerable child, would take no part in Jerome's self-help bustling. But Odile had regained a certain equilibrium. She soldiered on with her quiet life, pottered in her tiny garden, enjoying the play of the seasons in this private, manageable enclosure, walked a little on the Heath, visited the Everyman Cinema some afternoons on her own. Once a year she went to stay with Beatrice in Paris for a week. She shopped in Hampstead High Street, amazed by the marvellous convenience foods you could get nowadays. She no longer sewed her own clothes.

Odile had lost the peasanty spread of middle age, seemed shrunken in both body and mind. She was thin and elegant, splashed out on good clothes for herself, austere costume jewellery, thick wool coats, well-made shoes, which she took an age to select – Kate had accompanied her once on a shopping expedition.

'Why not treat myself?' she had enquired of no one in particular. 'Even if I do look like a walking corpse in them.' Odile had a habit now of saying honest, disconcerting things.

Kate's thoughts turned to the funeral that lay ahead.

'Throw a single white rose into the grave for me,' Nelly had instructed whimsically on the telephone the previous evening.

The two of them spoke often, and were closer than they'd been for some years. Nelly had a therapist called Sybil, whose opinions she quoted frequently, too frequently sometimes for Kate's taste.

One of Sybil's primary articles of faith was in the therapeutic importance of family and friends.

'It's me doing my homework again,' Nelly would joke, when Kate picked up the phone.

But Kate, in her turn, found Nelly easier and more approachable than for a long time. She was on a medication which tempered the highs and lows of the manic-depressive illness from which she had been diagnosed as suffering.

Her recovery had been a long, slow process, the regime involving both drugs and therapy. The latter Nelly adored. It spoke to her, seemed to her to make sense out of the chaos that had been her natural element. But she hated her medication. She felt slowed by it, damped down, missed her own exhilarating flights of zany fancy. She was clumsy, nauseous at times, loose-bowelled, her hands trembled. She felt condemned to the middle range of emotion, the appropriate, the mediocre.

'I feel as if I'm living in a bowl of tepid dishwater,' she'd complained once to Kate. 'Some days I think, why don't I just throw my pills away . . .'

Olivier's suicide was the spectre that kept Nelly to the straight and narrow. Though there was absolutely no evidence that he'd suffered from the same condition as she, his death was the crushing and final answer to her temptations, her vacillations.

For a couple of years now she'd been working as a doctor's receptionist. Nelly was inordinately proud of her job, seeing it as a triumph, not merely over her illness, but also her innate fickleness, the chequered history of her working life.

Her physical appearance had changed to suit. For ease of maintenance her exuberant hair was kept simple and short. Nelly had filled out so that, in her sensible work clothes, she looked more matronly than Kate would ever have believed possible. Rejecting the Hollywood fancy dress of her middle period, Nelly found an outlet for fantasy in the Fair Isle sweaters she collected, sprinkled naïvely with gambolling sheep, or ladybirds, or round, pink pigs.

There seemed a touching irony in the fact that Nelly – so dizzily promiscuous in her youth – should have ended up with perhaps the most rock-solid marriage Kate had ever come across. Through thick and thin she and Robert came through, seemingly without pretence or compromise. Where Robert had once adored her wayward sexuality, now his tenderness was for her courage, her new workaday willingness to submit to the discipline of life.

To him and to her doctors – to her children no doubt – Nelly was a success story. But, treacherously, Kate found herself distressed by a dazed look her friend had sometimes, a sort of carefulness . . . She couldn't deny a painful mourning for the vivid girl she'd once known.

'The funeral's out of my hands, thank God,' Beatrice said in the taxi taking them to the flat in the Boulevard Pasteur – home to David's brother Paul and Renée, his wife – from where the funeral cortège was to set out. 'The family's made all the arrangements.'

Kate looked unusually ladylike, Beatrice thought, in a loose two-piece of sombrely striped cotton, little ankle boots in punched leather, her shoulder-length hair sprayed and blow-dried. Apparently Stella had got up at the crack of dawn to do it for her.

But it was her own appearance that chiefly concerned her. She had bought herself a draped charcoal dress by Sonia Rykiel. It had cost a bomb and she would probably wear it only once. Beatrice saw this funeral as her final performance in the role she had played for more than twenty years now, that of discreet, self-effacing mistress – no other word would do – to the writer David Lacoste, and she couldn't wait to relinquish the part.

'How are you doing?' Kate asked sympathetically, squeezing her hand.

'OK.' Beatrice smiled at her. 'Really.'

There would be a memorial ceremony at some future date, so Beatrice had told her. The funeral was only for family and friends. All the same, Kate thought, among the mourners gathered in the Lacostes' spacious living-room there was a fair sprinkling of famous names and faces. She recognized the actor Daniel d'Agoult talking to Henri Danillac, whose most recent book Kate had translated, though this was hardly the time to introduce herself. She noticed the red-haired film-actress Natalie Servin and the gamine Anna Stern, whose photograph, alongside David, she had seen earlier that day in *Paris-Match*.

'All sorts of women are crawling out of the woodwork,' Beatrice had remarked dryly in the taxi. To Kate's surprise she appeared genuinely untroubled by the thought. And it was clear that, in the family's eyes, Beatrice was the woman in David's life.

'They're OK, Paul and Renée. I've come to quite like them,' Beatrice had said, when Kate asked about David's relatives. 'I've only got to know them in the last year or so . . . They're grateful to me.' She'd flashed Kate a wry, sidelong look. 'I've taken most of the load off their shoulders.'

During the last months of David's life Beatrice had liaised with his family and a couple of his close friends to devise a system that would permit David to stay in his own flat for as long as possible. He had a certain amount of nursing care, along with a pre-arranged rota of friends and family members checking up on him, spending time with him. Of all of them Beatrice had been by far the most constant presence.

The Lacostes' large first-floor flat was light, white-painted, filled with African artefacts, a souvenir of the couple's years in the Congo. Paul and Renée looked old to Kate, and rich and bourgeois. They greeted Beatrice with grave, funereal kisses. There was a ritual quality to their movements, which seemed to Kate either bred in the bone, or learned from decades of similar ceremonies – a kind of funebrial ballet, in which Beatrice participated to the manner born. And again Kate was amazed and impressed by her composure.

All along the Boulevard Montparnasse strangers stood respectfully to watch the cortège pass. A crowd of well-wishers followed gravely on foot. What a shame, Beatrice thought, that David was not here to see it. A waste, too, that she, who would once have been so thrilled and excited by these marks of recognition, now regarded the mourning with detachment, like a crowd scene in a play.

'This is fairly amazing.' Kate had clearly not imagined anything so public.

'David was an internationally known writer.' Beatrice's serenity was ruffled just slightly by Kate's surprise. 'And in France they value their intellectuals.'

As the car glided slowly towards the cemetery she sat upright, serious, widowly, consciously playing her part, although none of this was anything to do with her.

She'd said her goodbyes to David. Their relationship had been a mixed blessing to say the least. Nowadays Beatrice was able to admit that to herself. Now it was as if a timer were ticking off the seconds until the moment when she could lay down her mask, resume contact with an autonomy, a spontaneity she could barely recall, barely conceive. That moment couldn't come fast enough for Beatrice.

'*Hé, madame*!'

'Beatrice!'

There came a frantic knocking on the window of the car. Beatrice turned to face a pair of photographers, avid, jostling, thrusting their cameras against the glass, snapping her where she sat. As the cortège neared Montparnasse Cemetery there were more of them. Beatrice remained calm. This was the last time she would have to bother about the way she looked. She lifted her chin, sucked her cheeks in a little. Already she could imagine the blurred photos in tomorrow's newspapers, the weekly magazines. Beatrice wanted to do herself justice. The French admired looks and style in a woman above anything else.

Following David's instructions, the ceremony was short, simple and entirely secular. Afterwards Renée handed Beatrice a long-stemmed white rose – Kate thought of Nelly's flippant words – and she let it fall into the fresh, deep hole, on to David's coffin. And, for the first time, Beatrice appeared to lose a little of the cool control that had sustained her thus far. She closed her eyes, swayed for a moment as if she might lose her balance and topple into the grave, was steadied by Henri Danillac.

But the moment was brief, unobtrusive. A spitting rain began to fall. In pairs and small groups the graveside mourners began to drift away. Kate saw Beatrice kiss Paul, Renée and Henri Danillac as if in leave-taking.

'We can go now.' She came to join Kate. 'It's all over. Let's walk, stretch our legs.'

'It's raining. What about your dress?'

'Who cares.'

As they departed on foot the cemetery gates were opened to admit the public.

Arriving back at her flat after an invigorating walk in the summer rain, Beatrice dried her hair, pulled on jeans, opened a bottle of Médoc, poured a glass for herself and Kate, lit a cigarette, pulled the cushions off all the chairs and sat down on the living-room floor. She was filled with an intoxicating lightness of heart.

'Cheers, darling Kate. You're an angel for coming.' She raised her glass, took a slug of wine. 'Here's to the beginning of the rest of my life . . . God . . .' She lay back on the cushions with a sigh of pleasure. 'Thank Christ that funeral's over and done with . . . I feel as if I could float, way up to the ceiling.'

Kate was smiling. Startled. Rather pleased. 'I've never heard you talk like this before.'

'No. Probably not.' It still surprised Beatrice how sanguine she had become, almost without conscious effort. 'For an awful long time I was brainwashed.'

'By David you mean.'

'I was living in his web like a trapped fly.' Beatrice spoke the words with relish. Once they would have been unsayable. Unthinkable.

'So do you regret the time you spent with him?'

'Yes and no.' Beatrice shrugged. 'There's not much point in regretting.' She nodded towards the wine-bottle on the table. 'Help yourself to a top-up.'

She had no desire to pick over the bones of her relationship with David. It was what it was. Mentally she'd come to terms with it as far as one ever came to terms with anything. The previous eighteen months or so had, in any case, altered the balance between them, so that she could look back on the last twenty-three years, not as one big swindle – the way she had for a time – but as something evolving, imperfect, but not altogether without value.

Two things had happened to effect the change. Firstly she'd made a new friend. Charlie had come into her life back in the seventies. They'd clicked at once, though they were wildly mismatched. Being with Charlie was always warm and easy, entirely free from anxiety. It made her see how absolutely *wrong* her relationship with David had become.

The other thing was that David got ill. He needed her and, for the first time, it was he who had to fit in with the demands of *her* life – her job, the evenings she spent with Charlie. At the same time she had more than done her duty by him. Keeping him company, jollying and bullying him out of his depressive moods. Towards the end she'd sat with him through frightened, sleepless nights, read to him, administered his medication, even cleaned up after his bouts of incontinence . . . His grateful family had made the collective decision to view her as a saint.

'You're my wife, Beatrice,' David had whispered to her, just a fortnight ago, in the bleak, dragging hours of an insomniac night. 'And I've taken you for granted like a wife . . . But, believe me, I see and love your endurance.'

Once upon a time the words would have filled her with rapture. But, in her weary, bleary state she'd merely seen them as her due. It had been years since she was starry-eyed about David. If he hadn't become ill she would probably have left him by now. But Beatrice was glad she'd stayed and seen things through. It had deepened what there was between them.

At the end there was a bruised and battered affection, and there was equality. They were enough to restore a measure of her self-esteem. And there would be money. With the approval of his family he'd willed her a gratifying sum. She'd lost her youth of course. But everyone did, in one way or another.

'There's a new little restaurant opened down on the corner,' Beatrice said, crossing to the table to refill her own glass. 'The food's heavy, but damnably tasty. What d'you reckon?'

*   *   *

'I do hope you like Charlie,' Beatrice was saying, as she wolfed a large bowl of cassoulet, while making frequent forays to the bread basket in the centre of the table. 'You and he are my very best friends . . .' She stopped to take a gulp of wine. 'I've never introduced him to Ma when she's been to stay. He's gay, you see, and while she's fine about that in theory, I'm not actually sure what she'd make of him in relation to her little girl . . .'

'Where did you meet him?' Kate asked.

'One day he delivered some paintings to the gallery – a set of Norwich School landscapes, I remember. He's a one-man transportation firm, specializing in antiques. We got talking and straight away we got on. We went out for a meal that night and we've been friends ever since. He stops by whenever he's within any kind of feasible distance, and we've been on holiday a few times . . .'

Across the table from her Beatrice looked flushed and animated, dressed down, in jeans and a white T-shirt, long hair hanging loose for once, glowing with wine and a simple happiness Kate had not seen in her for years.

'He's been in Bruges today. He's driving down just to meet you. I tell you, Kate, he saved my life. You see he just came out of the blue, and we didn't know a thing about each other – he'd never met David or any of you – and right away we could tell each other anything . . .'

The restaurant was small and cosy, done out in earth tones, the walls a sort of smudgy terra-cotta, the table-cloths burnt umber. The tables were too close for real comfort, but the atmosphere of the place inspired indulgent goodwill.

'When he was young,' Beatrice continued, 'Charlie had an affair a bit like mine – with an old gangster . . . Don't look like that, it was aeons ago . . . So he could understand exactly what was happening in my life . . . *Merci!*' She flashed a smile at the waiter who came to refill their glasses with the last of the wine.

'What did David make of him?'

'At first he was amused and rather dismissive. Talked about my *pédé* friend with a sort of silly grin. Then he got pissed off. He was used to me dropping everything the moment he called, but if I'd

456

arranged to see Charlie I just wouldn't. In the end . . .' Beatrice shrugged '. . . he just sort of accepted him. They only met once and it wasn't too successful.'

'I can't wait to clap eyes on this mystery man . . .' Kate pushed her plate away. 'Gosh, that cassoulet was delicious . . . Shall we have coffee here or back at your place?'

What Charlie usually did, Beatrice explained, as they walked back to her flat through the cool, damp, neon-lit summer evening, was to leave his van in this great big supervised car-park some fifteen minutes' walk away, spend the evening with her, snatch two or three hours' sleep, fully clothed, then let himself out around four in the morning to resume his journey home.

He arrived half an hour or so after they got back. Beatrice went to open the front door, then ushered him into the living-room with a sound like a flourish of trumpets. Drunk, exhilarated, she offered Charlie for Kate's approval.

In Beatrice's chic living-room he cut an incongruous figure, tall and big-boned, taking up far too much room, his skin too coarse and sun-burned. He looked to be in his forties, had the body of an athlete running to seed – long legs, a solid, prominent abdomen. His eyes were markedly blue, his hair a greying crew-cut. He wore a broad grin that struck her as both brash and innocent.

'Kate, Charlie. Charlie, Kate,' Beatrice said, stretching an arm out to each of them as if to draw them together.

'Good to meet you,' Kate said. 'Beatrice has been talking about you all evening.'

He shook her hand, rather formal. 'Yeah,' he said. 'Don't tell me. She does run on a bit.' His voice surprised her, softer and shyer than she would have expected, his accent richly London. 'How was the funeral?' He addressed the question to Kate.

'The ceremony was short and to the point. But there were crowds . . . And we got snapped by the paparazzi.'

'How you coping, Bea?' He placed a large hand in the nape of her neck.

457

'Tonight I feel euphoric, just euphoric. There's bound to be a reaction. Tomorrow or the next day I'll feel like shit.'

'Yeah, probably. But you won't feel like shit forever.'

'You must be hungry.' Beatrice changed the subject.

'I'm famished.'

'I've got some of that onion tart you like.'

'Great stuff. And if you could see your way clear to making a pot of vile dark brown tea . . .' This was clearly a private joke.

'If you insist . . . There's some wine left.'

'I got my licence to think of. I don't have the option of getting rat-arsed like you whenever the mood takes me.'

Kate was intrigued by their affectionate give and take. She could not remember seeing Beatrice so . . . cosy with anyone, not even way back in the early days of Plas Felix. There seemed an element of flirtation in their dialogue, Charlie's homosexuality notwithstanding. The two of them appeared charmed with their relationship, and to want to demonstrate the fact to Kate.

While Beatrice was out of the room brewing Charlie's evil tea, he confided how stressed and exhausted she had been during David's last months – his manner made it clear that he thought the writer undeserving of such dedication. He hoped now that she would take some time off, take it easy for a bit, not rush into the next phase of her life.

'She's leaving the gallery then?'

'Maybe.'

'You think she'll come home then? To Britain, I mean.'

He shrugged, apparently unwilling to speak on Beatrice's behalf.

When Beatrice returned with the tray for Charlie, she cast an unexpected light on the subject.

'Ever since we've known each other,' she told Kate, 'we've joked about retiring to a cottage in the country with roses round the door, and opening up a little antique shop together.'

Charlie glanced up at her, hands laced behind his head. 'We were joking, were we?'

They grinned at one another, amused, intimate.

'Maybe we'll find out one of these days,' Beatrice said.

Chapter Forty-Seven

❁❁❁❁

In the wet November night Pascal drove along the dark, deserted ribbon of the A414 towards home. The desolate beauty of the lashing rain and stark, passing trees meshed with his mood of clenched misery. He was going home to nothing – to the emptiness of that whole big house. Just him, with that vast, blank space around him, divided up into a network of meaningless rooms.

At seven thirty that morning, when he left, there had been a journalist and a couple of photographers waiting at the gate. When he got home there might be more. Maybe they'd been asking the neighbours about him and Marya. Perhaps they would waylay him as he walked from the car to the house, with their flashlights and their sneering questions. Or wait outside all night as he lay sleepless and alone, look in the windows, ring the bell. And all because his wife had finally left him for a family friend who'd been seducing her with his eyes ever since they'd known him. A man who happened to have struck lucky in Hollywood.

On the outskirts of one of the indistinguishable villages bordering his route Pascal drove past a roadside telephone box, braked violently, and backed the Volvo up level with it. The idea had abruptly entered his head to phone Kate. It was nearly twelve, but he knew she was a nightbird. He had the sudden desire to be in her unjudgmental, unhysterical company.

In his diary – he refused to carry a Filofax – he found her number. The phone box smelt of piss, but at least it was in working order. He dialled.

'Hello? Kate Stephens here.'

It was heartening to hear her voice. He released his coin into the slot.

'Hi, Kate. It's me . . . Pascal. Look, I know it's late. But I'm about ten minutes away. I wondered if I could look in for a coffee . . . Or cocoa, maybe, at this time of night.'

'OK.' A bemusement in her tone. There always was when he phoned. But she was game. 'I'll leave the front door on the latch. Don't ring the bell.'

He got back into the car and drove on, the tension inside him alleviated by a flicker of anticipatory warmth. Since Olivier's funeral Kate lingered at the back of his mind, an accepting, down-to-earth presence, someone he could count on if needed, whose welcome didn't have to be earned, other than by keeping in minimal touch. During the last five years he'd phoned her perhaps once every three or four months. One December, just before Christmas – discovering both would be in London on the same day – they'd met up for a drink. And there had been that Sunday morning last year, when Marya was away in the States and he'd dropped by with Jocasta, stayed for an impromptu lunch with Kate and her teenaged kids. He'd taken some nice photographs that day, but never got round to sending them to Kate. And meanwhile, under the bright, hot California sun, Marya and Leon Callan must have been exploring the enchanted early stages of their long-delayed affair . . .

'I'll phone you when I'm settled.'

Those had been Marya's banal final words to him. Two days ago. Standing on the doorstep in her long, black coat, a taxi waiting. Hair on her shoulders, touchingly lank. Her eyes dark and innocent as a child's. That callous innocence he adored, though there were times when her absolute freedom from guilt seemed inhuman to him . . . verged on the psychopathic.

Jocasta standing just behind her. Marya's familiar. A carbon copy of her mother in miniature. Same eyes, same straggly hair. And loved by him with the same helpless, hopeless passion.

Pascal turned off the main road towards the dreary-looking village where Kate lived. His own hamlet was up-market, photogenic, property prices forever inching higher and higher.

Today he had been working up near Leicester, filming a crime novelist doing real-life off-duty things – hanging a picture, cooking

460

spaghetti, sweeping up leaves, stroking his lean, vicious tabby. Pascal had interacted with the touchy, tetchy author and with his own camera crew – issuing instructions, arguing, vetoing, soothing ruffled feathers – offering a precarious impersonation of a functioning human being. And, seemingly, the counterfeit had been accepted, though Pascal himself had felt as hollow and mechanical as the Tin Man from the *Wizard of Oz*.

He drew up outside Kate's house in the deserted close, got out and closed the car door as quietly as he could. Walking up the long path to her front door he saw she'd left an outside light on for him. He was struck by the smallness of the house, yet an impression it gave of being packed with the energy of the three lives lived inside it. His own house was handsome and roomy, yet it seemed to Pascal that there had always been a chilliness to it, as if he, Marya and Jocasta had never quite succeeded in colonizing all that space.

Kate must have heard him coming because she was waiting in the hall, wearing a black tracksuit, looking tired, her hair clumped and tangled. His instinct protested at her lack of vanity.

'So this is how I get fitted into your busy schedule,' she laughed, kissing him on the cheek.

'I know it's hideously late. Only I was driving home and I thought of you . . .'

'No, no –' a smiling, dismissive gesture – 'if it was a problem I'd have given you your marching orders . . . Do you really want cocoa? I actually have some drinking chocolate. Stella's got a craze on it.'

'Why not? Haven't had it for years.'

He stood in the small, harshly lit kitchen while she boiled the kettle, mixed the powder with milk in the bottom of the mugs.

'Well? How's life?' she asked.

'Pretty awful. Marya's left me.'

'Oh, Pascal.' She turned to him full of concern. 'When?'

'Day before yesterday. She's flown out to be with Leon Callan. She's taken Jocasta.'

'Oh God . . . You must be devastated.'

'That's about what I am . . . I don't want to talk about it. I just wanted to be with someone . . . You more than anyone.' It was true, though he doubted she'd believe him.

Kate did not reply. She filled the mugs and stirred them briskly, nodded her head towards the living-room. 'Let's go in there. We're less likely to disturb Jack.'

He looked in shock, Kate thought, as she observed Pascal hunched on the chair next to the gas fire, elbows on knees, cradling the mug between his fingers. There was a sort of vacancy about him, as if the images that filled his head were far more compelling than any conversation they could possibly have.

The flicker of the fire and the dim corner lamp provided the only lighting in the room. Partly, Kate admitted to herself, to camouflage the homeliness of her clothes and hair. After Pascal's phone call there would have been time to pull on jeans and a decent sweater, at the very least, and do something with her hair. But a perverseness in her refused to make even the most minimal fuss over his sudden arrival. God knows, he was casual enough as regards *her*. All the same she was not indifferent to the thought that in distress he'd had the urge to come and see her.

'I thought it might be my father on the phone,' Kate said, simply for the sake of conversation. Pascal had said he didn't want to discuss Marya and the effort of talking about anything else seemed beyond him. 'Dad usually rings at the dead of night . . . We've been in contact recently, for the first time in years . . .'

'Really . . . That's good.'

'We speak about once a fortnight, we take turns to ring . . .' Kate ploughed on with her soliloquy. 'We just talk about ordinary things. Nothing deep. But I'm so happy we're back in touch . . . You're not listening to me.'

'I am. Honest.'

In his quick smile Kate caught a glimpse of the old Pascal, the youth she barely recalled.

He appeared to rouse himself, telling her about the job he'd been engaged on that day, laughing about the touchy vanity of the author he'd been filming, with his brush-over hairstyle that got dislodged

462

by the November winds while he was sweeping up leaves for the camera, so he'd gone inside and rooted about for a sixties-style denim cap. 'It altered his whole self-image. With that cap on he saw himself as this cool young dude sweeping up leaves in 1964.'

Paradoxically Pascal's telling of the light-hearted anecdote revealed all the more clearly the strain he was under. There was a defence-lessness to his eyes, a rustiness in his voice that struck her to the heart. She'd always seen Pascal as sure and self-sufficient, but his presence in this darkened room made her think of a wounded animal gone to ground.

But she was moved too by other things, physical things – the curve of his long fingers round the mug, the crouched curve of his body, the sudden sardonic grin breaking through his grief like wintry sun – stirring echoes of the way she'd felt about him as a kid.

Back then she had censored all sexual thoughts of Pascal. He'd always seemed beyond her reach, too much in love with a certain kind of beauty. But, here and now, Kate acknowledged a voluptuous longing to comfort him, to put her arms round his body, to take him into her bed as she might an unhappy child, to hold him against her in a healing, sheltering embrace.

Nothing could touch the undigested store of bile, bitterness and yearning that lodged like a stone in his guts, and yet Pascal felt his nerves soothed by the warm flicker of the fire, the milky sweetness of his drink, the intimacy of Kate's company in this homely room. As they chatted companionably of this and that, he watched her reclining sideways on the sofa, propped on a pile of cushions, her body still graceful beneath the unflattering tracksuit. The lamplight warmed her skin tones, the reflected amber of her face contrasting pleasingly with the darkness of her clothes and hair.

Alongside their conversation his imagination was ambushed by a parallel scenario. Himself following Kate upstairs into the dark, mysterious privacy of her bed, the two of them making blind, urgent love – not the heightened act of worship sex was with Marya, but something more ruttish and primeval – and then he would lie in her arms, warm and torpid, and sleep, sleep . . .

But Pascal knew that he would make no such move. His spirit was frozen, his initiative dead. And, in any case, how crude and crass Kate would find his imagined advances. Her sympathy misconstrued, her kindness presumed on . . .

'I ought to go,' he said.

'Stay if you need to. I can imagine how awful you feel.'

'There were a couple of photographers outside my house this morning. I hope to God they're gone . . .'

'No!' She was disgusted. 'God they make me sick, those vultures . . . Look, if you want, you can sleep on the Put-U-Up for tonight. If you don't want to run the gauntlet . . .'

'I don't, but it's not just that . . .' Pascal checked himself. If he launched into some self-pitying diatribe they'd be here all night. Wistfully his mind flashed a new and graphic image of Kate's nakedness . . . But even the Put-U-Up would be better than going home alone.

When Kate came downstairs the following morning Pascal was gone, the Put-U-Up folded back in place, the bedclothes in a tidy pile. On the chalk board in the hallway where the family left messages he'd scrawled, 'Ta! Cheers! Love You!'

Jack and Stella were intrigued by his flying visit and annoyed to have missed out on the ripple of excitement. They were indignant on Pascal's behalf, but titillated by the connection with Leon Callan. Four or five years ago the actor had starred in a Sunday afternoon serialization of *A Tale of Two Cities* – Stella had fallen in love with him – and since then all of them had had a proprietary interest in the progress of his career. From Shakespeare at Stratford coupled with a brisk television career, Callan had suddenly entered the ranks of British character actors exported to Hollywood to play interesting villains.

'Trust Marya to jump on the bandwagon now Leon's a superstar,' Stella commented with sour satisfaction. She had never met Pascal's wife but had absorbed the Felix family's opprobrium – both implicit and expressed – for as long as she could remember.

After her morning's work Kate sauntered down to the newsagent cum post office to cash her family allowance. The air was damp and unseasonably mild. She felt both dull and light-headed. She hadn't got much sleep. And a dreamily pervasive sensual awareness of Pascal still lingered in her bloodstream.

Outside the newsagents samples of the daily papers were displayed in wire racks. Kate's eye was drawn at once to the *Sun*. Dwarfing a perfunctory headline about the decline of the pound stood a striking photograph of Leon Callan cuddling Marya, with the caption 'Leon's New Squeeze'.

The picture must presumably have been beamed from California because Leon wore an open shirt and Marya a top with spaghetti straps. Leon appeared wolfishly triumphant, Marya demure, desired. You could read a calculating satisfaction in the muted gleam of her eyes, the curve of her mouth. But it was the sort of face into which you could read anything you wanted.

Kate stared at the photograph, as if through Pascal's eyes, and could not begin to imagine his pain and humiliation. Inside the shop she bought a copy of the paper to show the kids. Tonight she would phone him, listen if he felt like talking, maybe invite him for the weekend if he wanted.

Chapter Forty-Eight

❈❈❈

For the first time since Olivier's death all of them were going to spend Christmas together. Pascal had invited everyone to his big, empty house in the attractive commuter village of Lydon.

'It's an act of contrition,' he joked wryly to Kate. For so many years he had neglected his family.

'I feel enthusiastic about Christmas for the first time in years,' Nelly told her on the phone. Then, invoking her therapist, 'Sybil's chuffed to bits that we're all getting together again . . .'

There was a feeling in the air of regroupment. As if a period of disarray might be drawing to a close. Olivier could never be replaced, but Pascal was reaching out and everyone was keen to rally round him. Beatrice was back in England too. Perhaps this Christmas would see the beginning of some kind of positive new pattern that might in time supersede the bittersweet memories of those far-off festivities at Plas Felix, when the world was young.

'Oo-o-h. Posh,' Allie had said with sarcastic mock-admiration, when Kate told her she would be spending Christmas in Lydon. According to Downridge lore the neighbouring village had fallen into the hands of snobs and, more recently, yuppies – an even more damning concept.

Pascal's house was a mellow, well-proportioned Georgian affair, hard by the village green. Kate and the kids arrived late morning on Christmas Eve. Opposite – in a field flanked by a medieval barn and a large lone willow arching its graceful, bare gold branches to the ground – a pair of farm horses cantered through mist tinged with the glare of a cold midday sun, their breath steaming in the frosty air. And Kate could sympathize with Allie's cynicism at the

466

thought that the whole timelessly beautiful ambience was available to anyone with enough cash to buy it.

Since Marya's departure Pascal had begun to phone her regularly and she knew that he was apprehensive about this gathering of the clan, and worried that Laurel House, as it was called, would seem cold and unwelcoming to his family.

'Marya and I were always buzzing about – working, visiting people. We had the place done up but, even with Jocasta, it was really only a pied-à-terre.'

Kate had driven past Pascal's front door many times, but she'd never been inside. When they arrived Pascal was alone. He welcomed them and began to show them round, rather as if he were merely the keeper of this large, deserted house. Everything was clean and tidy – a woman came in twice a week to keep everything up to scratch – but it seemed to Kate that there *was* a lifelessness to the place, a feeling that the air of the rooms and corridors was rarely disturbed.

'As far as atmosphere goes, I've thrown money at the problem,' he told them drily. 'It's about the best I can do.'

Proof of his expenditure lay in the eight-foot Christmas tree in the living-room, shining with tinsel and lights. A cupboard full of expensive-looking booze and groceries. A home-computer in Jocasta's old play-room with a stack of games, on to which Jack and Stella fell with cries of delight. A number of mattress-y things he called futons to solve the sleeping arrangements.

'I want it to be good,' he said to Kate. 'To make up for all the lost years . . .'

Harsh winter sun streamed through the windows in the top hall that gave on to three of the five bedrooms, one of the two bathrooms. In its shrill light Pascal looked young-old, pale and worn-down, his long brown eyes clear but without vivacity. He looked shell-shocked, humbled. She hated to see it.

'It's going to be fine,' she assured him. 'You can't imagine how everyone's looking forward to it.'

The front door bell rang. 'That's probably Beatrice.' Pascal turned and ran downstairs to answer it. But Kate heard the voice of a strange woman, full of warm, voluble good cheer. Pascal's side of the conversation reached her as a low rumble.

'No, no,' she heard the woman protest. 'It's sweet of you, but I've got a thousand and one chores still to do . . . I just wanted to wish you and your family a Happy Christmas.'

Another rumble from Pascal. The door closed. When Kate joined him in the front hall he was holding a clingfilm-covered dish of home-made mince pies, looking surprised but rather touched.

'I can't get over it. Now I'm on my own everyone's coming over all neighbourly – people who for years I've only ever exchanged two words with . . . Marya would run a mile.'

As he stood by the grill making cheese on toast for everyone, it occurred to Pascal how crowded it felt in the kitchen, how convivial. Kate and Beatrice and Jack and Stella, all seated round the big, rough-hewn, distressed-looking table he and Marya had bought in the Cotswolds – during a visit to the Callans, he recalled.

It seemed to him that it was the first time the kitchen had contained anything approaching a family group. In his imagination this room was a transitional space, populated by sprites – Marya in one of her long Victorian nightdresses, Jocasta in the antique white broderie anglaise petticoat he'd bought her in a Parisian flea-market. Both of them living on tiny snacks – pots of yoghurt, grapes, melon slices, rice cakes. Hardly ever a real meal. Though, to be fair, he, Pascal, was rarely home in time for a shared supper.

'Jack, here you go, mate.' Handing the boy two doorsteps of bread, smeared with ketchup, oozing thick, golden, melted cheese. Dainty Stella was chomping her way through a similar snack.

'Great stuff.' Jack looked up from the *NME* crossword, thin-faced, crop-haired, the watchful air of his mother. 'Mum, you're stingy. You should take lessons from Pascal. He really knows how to make a good, solid –'

'Artery-blocker.' Wryly Kate eyed the snack.

Pascal was moved by Kate's kids, glimpsing in them the tough-innocent sweetness he loved in Jocasta. The habitual anguish contracting his heart, the anguish that crouched behind everything he did, behind actions as banal as grilling toast.

'Same for me, but only one of them. Mayonnaise instead of ketchup, though. Plenty of cheese. A couple of turns of the pepper-mill on top.' Beatrice sipped a glass of the excellent Beaujolais Pascal had purchased for them to tipple over Christmas.

Her arrival, twenty minutes earlier, had stirred up eddies of shock, bemusement, admiration. For his sister had cut her hair. Instead of the long silky tresses that had been her trademark since forever – worn loose as a girl, centrally parted and tied back as a woman, neat and unaltering as the painted hair of a Dutch doll – Beatrice sported what Pascal thought of as a crew-cut. Spiky, half an inch all over.

'Don't say anything,' she'd instructed, entering the front hall, self-conscious and rather defensive. 'I don't care what anyone thinks. I love it.'

'I love it too,' Stella had piped up.

Beatrice blew her a flamboyant kiss. 'Best mate of mine.'

At first Pascal had viewed the change as nothing short of mutilation. He had always had a sentimental preference for long hair in women. But already his sister's new look was growing on him. She had the natural elegance to carry it off, the right kind of fine-boned face. And it was impossible not to see the dramatic transformation as a sign of Beatrice's emancipation from her years of bondage to David Lacoste.

At the same time she exuded an air of balance, of good nature, as if Beatrice had emerged into her quasi-widowhood with a new appreciation of the homely joys of life. Pascal found himself warming to his elder sister as never before. Her seeming resilience offered a glimmering of hope for his own future.

'There you are. Mayonnaise. Twist of pepper.' He handed her the delicacy on a small plate.

She raised her glass to him. 'You'll be able to add short-order cook to your cv.'

'Kate?'

'Just one slice. With mustard. I like sesame seeds on top. Have you got any?'

469

'Fresh out, I'm afraid.'

'Well, a sprinkling of those Italian herbs I can see in your spice rack.'

'God knows how old they are.'

'I'll take a chance.'

Kate flashed him one of those special, ironic smiles of hers. In the last few weeks she had become his best friend, his mainstay, the way she must have been for Olivier until his will to fight ran out. What Pascal saw in her now was an unassuming strength that, once upon a time, he would neither have noticed nor valued.

Yet again he experienced a wave of thankfulness for the presence of his family, at their readiness to insinuate themselves like soothing balm into the jagged void left by Marya. Without them he could not have carried on. At the same time there was the chastening sense of returning to an earlier incarnation, as if he'd neglected them heedlessly to chase a dream, and the dream had died, and here he was, aged forty-three, crawling back into the fold.

'What's your place like?' Kate was asking Beatrice as he held out her bubbling cheese on toast. She looked up at him and grinned. 'Cheers.'

'Comfortable. Highly civilized.' Beatrice was flat-sitting in Belsize Park for friends of Jerome and Odile. 'And all I have to do is water their plants. Long may they continue to amuse themselves in Australia.'

'So what about this antique shop with roses round the door?'

'Me and Charlie are still talking about it. Looking too, in a vague sort of way. If we're not careful we'll have to go through with it.'

'Bottles Bistro in the High Street is closing down after Christmas . . . But, trade-wise, Downridge is a dead-and-alive sort of hole . . .'

'Everywise,' Stella put in perkily.

She made Pascal think of a cartoon chipmunk. But a chipmunk dressed in a droll sports outfit – grey sweatshirt with the neck and arms cut out, a short frilly skirt in the same material, basketball boots.

Turning to Pascal, Beatrice changed the subject. 'How did you cope with all the work-related Christmas bacchanalia?'

'I opted out. Couldn't face anything like that. I was able to take some leave. Got a new project going in January.'

'Oh, what?'

'*Profiles*. Roughly the same format. But profiles of nobodies. Contemporary stereotypes. The unemployed. The beleaguered small businessman. The thrusting little city sharpster . . . But shown in all their vulnerable individuality . . .' Pascal heard an inappropriate note of jeering irony in his voice.

'Sounds really good.' Jack glanced up from his *NME* again. And Pascal was warmed by the kid's casual partisanship, a generosity he had done nothing to earn.

Subtly he fostered the impression that this was a bright new departure in the wake of his split with his wife. But in fact the project had been mooted a good six months ago, and in response to a challenge of Marya's . . . At a colleague's dinner party in Islington she'd derided his programmes as trite and formulaic, fawning on the famous, animated *Vogue*.

'Pascal's lost touch with real life, buzzing around with cameras, making complete strutting wankers look warm and wacky and cuddly and profound, in some total dream world.' She was drunk on slivovitz and the admiration of the men.

He'd pleaded guilty, treating her accusations with dry amusement. Though in fact they'd really hurt him, and privately he thought her criticism a bit rich, coming from a woman whose aspirations clustered round the very wankers she was presently denouncing.

Marya went on to talk about Janey, her cleaning woman – though for current purposes she claimed her as a 'friend' – who certainly had her share of misfortune, an autistic daughter, a depressive mother, but who soldiered on 'womanfully', Marya said, with her rocky life . . . At the candlelit table Marya held the company riveted with her deep, luminous eyes, the low passion of her voice, her whole being burning with a white flame of intensity, achingly desirable. Pascal watched her performance with a kind of bruised pride.

'Now Janey's the sort of person who *deserves* to be celebrated,'

Marya had concluded with a provocative glance across the table at her husband.

'I'd be perfectly happy to make Janey look warm and wacky and profound if there was any call for it.' Pascal was flippant, hiding both his hurt and his adoration.

The up and coming project was like a message he was sending Marya. A valentine. For her sake, Pascal knew, he would do the work with passion and love, he would fight for what he wanted all of the way. No shrugging of shoulders, no compromises for the sake of a quiet life. Hungrily he hugged the prospect to him, with its precious, secret connection to his wife.

'I suppose,' Beatrice had said to her brother after lunch, 'this is going to be one of those Christmases where, to get a smoke, you have to go outside and lurk behind the bike-sheds.'

''Fraid so.'

'Traitor. Turncoat.' Nostalgically Beatrice recalled the careless days when Pascal used to puff complacently on tar-enriched French cigarettes.

He shrugged, semi-apologetic. 'Marya never let anyone smoke in her presence. If I filled the house with nicotine now, I'd feel as if I was defiling her shrine.'

Beatrice was in a mellow, accepting mood. Pascal's garden was a secret enclosure, screened by trees and rampant ivy, a large delicious lichen-mottled nude stone nymph dominating the leaf-strewn lawn. Her statuesque presence and the cold, elegiac silence became part of the pleasure of smoking.

That evening – after her parents had arrived, and Nelly and family, and between them all they'd managed to serve up a spaghetti supper for eleven, washed down with liberal quantities of wine – she invited her brother outside for a self-indulgent cigarette.

'Moral flabbiness likes company,' she urged.

'I'm tempted,' Pascal admitted.

As they lingered with their cigarettes by the guardian-nymph, Beatrice experienced the scene in a wider, cosmic sense. Here they stood, she and Pascal – the family achievers – older, eroded in some way by life, with lowered expectations, wordlessly comforted by an awareness of the parallels between them. Pascal, she sensed, was not ready to understand the beauty of sheer survival. But Beatrice was filled with a happiness that soared and spread like golden rain.

It made Nelly smile inside, the selfish way her mother had now, sitting in Pascal's living-room like Lady Muck, in one of his big, black leather chairs, watching Christmas morning television while she, Kate and Beatrice ran themselves ragged, cooking a brace of ducks and all the trimmings. Odile was dressed to kill in a brown cashmere sweater – a huge amber and silver brooch adorning the shoulder – smart tweed skirt, legs elegant in smooth dark tights and stack-heeled brogues, hair mauve-rinsed like Grand-mère's used to be, and twisted into an impeccable chignon.

'I am not doing the cooking,' she'd announced yesterday on arrival. 'I've finished with all that. It's someone else's turn.'

Though she'd brought her offering in an insulated bag – a large container of special festive ice-cream, with port and nuts and dried fruit in it.

'It's home-made,' she explained. 'But not by me. I bought it in Bürgi's delicatessen in Swiss Cottage. It's good and very expensive.' It was clear that, with this gift, Odile considered her obligation to the festivities discharged.

This morning, she sat with her legs propped on a footstool, while Pascal brought her cups of tea and coffee, and Stella looked for her reading glasses and Aled fetched her magazine from upstairs. As Nelly walked through the living-room Odile was watching a pair of stags lock antlers by a lake.

'Stand up to the bully,' she addressed the loser in conversational tones. 'Don't let him have it his own way . . .' And it seemed to Nelly that the on-screen world was more absorbing to Odile than the real-life presence of her children and grand-children.

Meanwhile, in Pascal's study, Jerome – a white-bearded, almost saintly figure – had already spent an intense and earnest hour on the phone in his role as chairman of Survivors, and was still offering comfort and advice to a distraught policeman in Braintree, Essex, whose daughter had taken an overdose.

'Funny isn't it,' Nelly mused to Kate, as the two of them sat at Pascal's kitchen table peeling potatoes, 'how Ma and Pa have swapped roles. Ma's the one we all pander to nowadays, while Pa's become the very soul of altruism.'

Kate looked up with a grin from her bowl of spuds. 'I'd never have thought it possible, but Odile's turning into Grand-mère.'

'And it's our turn to be dogsbodies . . .' Beatrice stood by the stove. Willowy and enviably elegant, Nelly thought, for all her cropped hair and lack of make-up, wearing jeans and a sweater of Pascal's, stirring a saucepanful of rich gravy concocted from duck fat, stock cubes, a selection of Pascal's superannuated herbs and spices, along with vast amounts of his Beaujolais.

All of them amused, but also, Nelly suspected, more disconcerted than they cared to admit, by Odile's new intransigence.

'But at least there's three of us. Ma was always on her own.' Beatrice poured another slurp of wine into the pan. 'This gravy's almost pure alcohol.'

In a sudden small sliver of silence Nelly heard strange oscillating, chirruping electronic sounds issuing from Jocasta's playroom, followed by curses and shouts of triumph. Aled and Rhys, along with Kate's two, were spending nearly all their time in there with the games – exclusive, competitive and thoroughly happy.

'It's the best Christmas ever,' Rhys had told her with unusual graciousness.

Beatrice tasted her brew. 'Not bad . . . Good gravy's the thing to lift a meal into the Rolls-Royce class.'

Kate gave a little ha of indignation. 'Not to mention perfectly cooked duck and beezer roast potatoes.'

From the living-room came a series of scrapings and thumpings as Pascal and Robert attempted to set up a trestle-table Pascal had stored in the garage. For all its size, the rustic kitchen table had not seated all eleven of them satisfactorily, and anyway Pascal had developed qualms about eating among the dirty pots and pans. As if in competition Odile turned up the volume on the television set.

474

Nelly heard Pascal object and Odile counter-protest, but after a moment the sound dwindled down to a normal level.

Jerome appeared in the kitchen doorway. Seeing him rarely nowadays, Nelly was still shocked by the evidence of his ageing. The whiteness of his hair and beard, the thinning and desiccation of his body – once he'd had a certain . . . greasiness, for lack of a better word. Since forever her life had been hedged about by his robust, smiling, confident, selfish personality. And those qualities had made her feel safe in his presence. Now, when she hugged him, his shrunken figure made her feel the protector.

He looked dazed and rather shattered in the wake of his session with the bereaved parent. 'Poor bugger . . . I could do with a drink.'

Beatrice clasped the wine-bottle to her chest. 'Stay away from the cooking sherry.'

'I had something a bit stronger in mind.' He opened Pascal's well-stocked larder and chose a malt whisky, poured himself a chunky glass.

'Bottoms up, Pa,' Nelly said.

A ghost of his old grin. 'Here's looking at you, kid.'

Consciously Nelly savoured the very ordinariness of this whole Christmas morning. Similar in so many ways, and yet terribly different from the old, taken-for-granted Christmases at Plas Felix. Olivier's suicide had changed everything forever and, one way or another, all of them were scarred. But there was a mood of 'picking up the pieces' that chimed emphatically with Nelly's own.

In her head Sybil sat watching, impassive and foursquare, just as, in life, she sat enthroned on her blue and brown sofa, listening, evaluating. A woman in her sixties with straight, square-cut hair and spectacles, with a taste for navy-blue worn head-to-foot – from her Welsh wool sweaters to her mid calf-length skirts, low-heeled court shoes and matching tights. A woman you wouldn't look twice at in the street but, within her own special realm – the cosy, cluttered consultation room – invested with mysterious power.

Her therapist possessed an unwavering belief in the value of the mundane. Sometimes, fancifully, Nelly imagined her as a medieval lady in a pointed hat and veil, for whose sake she went forth to do battle with the ordinary world, her small successes offered to Sybil like trophies. It was for Sybil that she persisted with the medication that made her hands shake, that made her feel dull and uninspired. For Sybil she stuck with her routine job, attended PTA meetings, played hostess to her husband's professional friends without an imp of mischief pushing her to talk dirty to them, or argue too vehemently, or boast about her misspent youth.

For the sake of Sybil's approval Nelly had lost touch with a self she remembered with yearning – a young and vibrant woman with the courage of her unconventionality, full-bodied, curly-haired, full of certainty and power. Times when she barely needed sleep and life raced in her veins like speed . . .

But with Sybil's help she kept at bay the other, skewed image, seen in a cracked mirror, recalled with dread. The annihilated being who saw herself as shit, less than shit, longed to disappear so her husband and children would be free from her putrefaction. Drinking alcohol to give herself courage simply to get out of bed. No roots, no anchor, floating free in terrifying space, amazed to see people laugh or smile, unable to comprehend such lightness of heart.

Pascal's kitchen was warm and safe. Nelly belonged to these people and they to her. And cooking Christmas dinner was such a normal thing to do. Sybil would be proud.

Just before lunch Stella found some long, thin candles in a drawer and stuck them in three empty wine bottles, wound them with tinsel borrowed from the tree, and stood them at intervals along the trestle table Pascal and Robert had finally succeeded in erecting.

'We must have a fancy table for Christmas.' Lighting the candles with ceremonious pomp.

How playful and self-possessed she looked, Kate thought, in a red sweater and her new Christmas dungarees, tiny enamelled Christmas puddings dangling from her ears, mousy fair hair freshly washed and blow-dried, a wild rose flush to her cheeks.

'Bravo.'

'Just the touch it needed.'

Robert and Pascal clapped, approved, and Kate experienced a fierce thankfulness that she had this world to offer her kids, for all its trauma and tragedy. Since arriving here she'd looked for signs of Olivier's aura and found none – over the last five and a half years his absence had been slowly and painfully assimilated. And yet simultaneously his influence was all-pervasive, source and catalyst for the new adjustment towards which the Felixes were fumbling their way.

'I've told you twice. Get yourselves round the table,' Nelly ordered. Then, rolling her eyes heavenward, 'It's like trying to get a lot of playschool brats to organize themselves.' Hands swathed in padded oven gloves, she carried a large dish containing two glazed, golden-brown ducks.

'Cheese, Nelly.' Pascal crouched down in front of her with his high-tech camera.

She posed, a touch impatient, while he snapped her. Full-bosomed in a sweater patterned with reindeer. Black trousers and heeled shoes to minimize her broad hips. Smoky eye shadow, coral lipstick. Short, feathery hair, curling with the steam of the kitchen. A pleasant-looking middle-aged woman. But an image that appeared more complex, more poignant, to the eyes of anyone who'd known her as a girl, or glimpsed the mental turmoil she would be fighting forever.

Jerome stood sharpening a long knife ready to carve, stepping into his old role as family head. Unobtrusive, absorbed, Pascal prowled with his camera. From girlhood Kate recalled the air he had of focused certainty, as if he saw things that others didn't.

'Hands up all those who want the red . . .' Robert circled the table holding two bottles of wine, wearing a Warhol soup-can T-shirt one of his sons had given him, the garish garment incongruous on his gravely handsome person. Kate saw him raise an eyebrow at his wife in marital shorthand.

'Half a glass,' Nelly told him. She rarely drank at all nowadays.

The teenagers were allowed their share. They'd gathered at Jerome's end of the table, sat two and two, flanking him. How tall and good-looking Nelly's two boys had become – Rhys was the spit of his father at that age. Kate loved to see Jack and Stella chatting and laughing with their 'cousins'. As a group they were giggly and irreverent, with a teenage scepticism as regards their parents' generation. Yet they treated Jerome with tolerance, even tenderness.

He sat by, beaming at their chat, interrupting now and then to ask for explanation of the slang they used, the names they dropped, clearly amused by his role as elderly ignoramus. During their childhood Odile had been the closer grandparent but, since the death of Olivier, she had lost interest in her grandchildren, as in so much else. Jerome was intrigued by their video games and had paid several long visits to the playroom to be initiated into their mysteries.

Pascal was still at work with his camera, so engrossed he seemed to have lost sight of the fact that this was a celebratory meal. He was particularly interested in Beatrice, with her newly cropped hair. At first she'd smiled and co-operated, raising her glass while he photographed her from this angle and that, but finally she lost patience.

'For God's sake, Pascal, sit down and eat!'

With a last deep focus shot of the whole long table, Pascal obeyed. The meal proceeded in a buzz of convivial conversation.

'It's like it used to be when I was little,' Kate heard Stella say to Jerome.

Sampling each ingredient with care, Odile kept up a running commentary on the quality of the food. Just as Grand-mère used to, Kate recalled.

'Beatrice, this sauce is rather too alcoholic, but I like the hint of sage . . .'

'Nelly, Kate, the duck skin could be a little crisper, but the flesh is good and moist.'

'Much obliged, Ma,' Nelly said with mock-humility.

Pascal ate in subdued near-silence. The air about him seemed still and charged. Kate noticed now that he'd lost weight, his cheekbones sharp, his cheeks hollow, a pale austerity to his presence. He took a large gulp of wine, as if for fortification rather than conviviality. It was as if his camera had been a protection and now he felt the lack of it. Kate realized how intimately aware she was of everything he did. And it was a physical awareness, a pulsing of the blood. All yesterday and again today she'd experienced moments of a vivid longing to hold and soothe him. As if, in his need, she might reach out to him in a way that had been beyond her imagining while he was riding high.

Later, over the pudding course, Odile quizzed them earnestly, as if seeking their views on the meaning of life. 'This ice-cream is good, don't you think? I find it rich but refreshing. Robert, Pascal, you can taste the port, *hein*?' She gave the neighbour's mince pies short shrift, but praised those Pascal had bought from Marks and Spencers.

They pulled crackers, compared and swapped trinkets, read out the mottoes, perched paper hats on their heads.

Then, as if moved by some inner compulsion, Jerome lurched to his feet, stood at the head of the table, smiling, a little pissed. The conversation dying away as if in anticipation.

In one hand he held a yellow slip of paper from his cracker and peered at it through half-moon reading glasses. 'We learn from the mistakes of the past how to make new ones,' he announced, then raised his eyebrows quirkishly in a way that made Stella laugh.

'My big mistake was to marry the wrong man,' Odile commented, in her disconcerting fashion.

'A common error, m'dear.'

Jerome appeared not the slightest bit put out, and the exchange seemed to typify the accommodation they had reached after forty-five years or so of more or less acerbic marriage, rubbing along in eccentric harmony, but strangely separate.

Picking up his wine-glass, Jerome proceeded to the point. 'I'd like to propose a toast. To us, all of us. Life hasn't been particularly kind these last years and, one way or another, we've all had to learn to cope. But we're still here, and this Christmas we're together . . . So let's drink to us and to better days.'

Carrying some dirty dishes to the kitchen, Kate happened on Nelly and Robert, standing by the open washing-up machine, locked in an embrace. She stood for a second, unseen, watching with affection and a certain rueful envy.

Then, with heavy emphasis, she cleared her throat. 'Can anyone join in?'

Robert stretched out an arm, pulled her into the clinch. 'Not anyone . . . But you, definitely.'

'You got a gem there, missis,' Kate said a little later, when she and Nelly sat on the stairs drinking coffee while the men clinked and chinked in the kitchen emptying the washing-up machine and putting things away.

Nelly ruffled Kate's hair with skittish friendship. 'You're the one who deserves a nice man. If anyone does, you do.'

Kate shrugged, inured to regret. 'I deserve Harrison Ford, but I'm not going to get him.'

Jocasta telephoned Pascal around five o'clock. He thought she sounded much older than her eleven years, as if these last few weeks – in a strange country, dancing attendance on her mother's new affair – had caused her to grow up. She sounded very together, her voice kind, as if it had been impressed on her that Daddy was to be pitied, gentled . . .

'We're in New York for Christmas,' Jocasta told him, 'staying with Pete and Callie McKinley' – mentioning an English thespian couple who'd settled in the States permanently. 'Their daughter's here. Camilla. She's a great laugh.'

'Kasti, I'm so glad you're having a nice time . . .' His voice hollow and dead. Pascal felt like a scorned lover, even in the eyes of his daughter. Would he have preferred Jocasta to sound broken and unhappy? Surely not.

'I've got a full house here,' Pascal told her. 'All the family. Rhys and Aled, Jack and Stella . . .'

'That's nice.'

Clearly it meant little to her. She'd met her cousins once, twice . . . They'd almost always spent Christmas abroad – somewhere sunny, or else skiing.

'It *is* nice. I'd love you to be here, darling, as part of the family . . .'
It sounded like a theme park. The Family Experience.

'I wish I could see *you*, Daddy.'

'We'll see one another soon, sweetie. Easter maybe.'

As Pascal replaced the receiver he was seized by a desolation so wild and devastating the room seemed to spin about him. He grasped the edge of his desk, breathed deeply, deeply, to hold himself together. There was no desire to weep. He was beyond such theatricals. Pascal collapsed into his chair, sat clenched, shoulders hunched, fists balled and jammed to his mouth.

Kate passed by the open doorway of his study and glanced in. She could not miss the chaos and confusion on his face.

'Hi,' he said, giving her permission to see him.

'Marya?'

'No, Jocasta.'

'Ah.' She took a step inside, hesitated.

'Oh, Christ, Kate.' The words jerking hoarsely from his anguish.

She came and stood beside him, laid a hand in the nape of his neck, massaging gently, and he found a sliver of comfort in the tenderness of the gesture.

'There's nothing I can say,' Kate murmured.

He raised one hand to cover hers, acknowledging the value of her wordless kindness. On an instinct he touched her palm to his lips. With her free hand Kate stroked his hair. He had the fierce urge to stand and cling to her like a drowning man to a rock.

The phone rang. Once, twice. He let it. But after the third ring Pascal reached reluctantly for the receiver.

'Hello?'

'This is Ellis Stephens. Kate's father. Who's speaking?'

Pascal hadn't the energy to introduce himself. He offered the receiver to Kate. 'It's for you.'

Then he rose and made discreetly for the door.

'Compliments of the season to *you*,' Kate was saying as he left.

Chapter Forty-Nine
1984

❦❦❦

Don't expect too much, Kate told herself, as the train hurtled across country from New York to White River Junction where Ellis was to meet her. She remembered the old pattern – the anticipation, the leap of joy on seeing her father. Then the grudges and grievances seeping back like fog, obscuring harmony and affection with their corrosive vapours . . . But she was an adult now. Surely, surely, she could make it different this time.

These thoughts were a repetitive counterpoint to her pleasure in the journey. The train was comfortable. It was late October and, outside the window, a bright blue sky contrasted with the golds and blazing reds of the transmuting trees.

She felt like someone else, travelling alone through this unfamiliar landscape, wearing the good new clothes she'd bought herself for the trip. Well-cut trousers, expensive short boots, a soft, dark full-length coat with a hood. She'd had her hair cut too, in a sharp, up-to-date bob, at some West End salon Beatrice recommended. All in all, contemplating her reflection in the mirror, Kate felt she looked like someone who was prospering rather than merely surviving, which was pretty well the impression she hoped to give.

Outside the window a piebald horse stood in a rustic corral, ears pricked, watching the train pass. The lush grass beneath his feet was strewn with small bright yellow leaves. There were houses now, some in white clapboard, sparkling among the gold and red and orange trees. Then came neighbourhood streets, shops and businesses. The train began to slow, drew smoothly up alongside a platform. Kate grabbed her holdall and stepped down.

Her eyes scanned the figures around her, seeking Ellis. A few yards along the platform she noticed a man of about the right age – bearded, wearing a heavy knitted jacket – who seemed to be searching too. Kate eyed him discreetly. Their eyes met. He stared dubiously, then beamed and approached. She stepped gladly towards him. He threw his arms about her.

'Kate . . . Kate . . .'

'Hi, Dad . . .'

They clung together in a rapture of recognition, clumsy in their winter clothes, the embrace seeming a symbolic finale to their years of estrangement.

Simultaneously Kate experienced a flash of memory, a vivid sense of the way she'd been the last time she saw her father. In Paris, during the years of her marriage, she'd been like a kid at a party – wildly over-excited at first, then as violently sick and disenchanted. No underlying sense of balance or proportion. But here, on this station platform, she understood how far that giddiness lay behind her. Understood – as Ellis must – the value of tolerance and compromise. There could surely be no danger of their pissing this fresh opportunity away.

Finally he held her at arms' length, shaking his head. 'I just can't tell you how happy I am to see you.' A heartfelt vehemence. The brown eyes she remembered, shining in an old man's face.

Yet, confronted at last by her father in the flesh, Kate saw how much more vigorous he looked than Jerome – his contemporary. How burly and self-assured. As if life had dealt him nothing but a succession of favourable hands. Jerome used to have that same buoyancy before he became acquainted with grief.

Ellis drove her home through further unrolling vistas of flaming trees. Kate drank in the endless beauty. She felt rested and alert, had slept last night in a hotel at the airport and seemed to have evaded jet-lag.

'This scenery is an absolute visual feast. I've been in raptures ever since I left New York.'

Her father smiled, pleased by her pleasure. 'Fay and I adore this time of year.'

Coningsburgh was very much as Kate remembered – sprucely attractive, with its Green, its white church and historical buildings, tastefully maintained. For years now Ellis and Fay had lived on desirable Bernhard Street. Their house was classically appealing with its picket fence, white clapboard frontage, barn-style roof, the street door and downstairs windows charmingly gabled. Close by stood a large tawny maple, its nodding branches casting dappled shadows across the white flank of the house and the surrounding lawn.

'This is gorgeous,' Kate exclaimed.

'Welcome to our home. To *your* home.' Ellis spread his arms expansively.

Stepping into the front hall Kate had the immediate feeling of entering a world of good taste and affluent simplicity. White walls, a honey-coloured wood floor, a hand-plaited circular rug in shades of blue and green, a bookcase, a plain, well-made side-table. A painting Kate remembered from the other house – Fay's canvas of stark fir trees in pink-tinged snow.

At once Fay emerged from the doorway ahead. What a handsome woman she'd become. Slimmer than in her youth. Hair blonded or still blonde, short, chic, freshly washed. Complexion warm, wrinkles expressing vigour, humour. Fay wore narrow russet slacks, a Fair Isle sweater that picked up the red-brown, contrasting it with cream and Prussian blue.

'Hi, honey.' Engulfing Kate in a long, strong embrace. Then, 'Oh, Kate,' she sighed, finally releasing her to arms' length. 'This visit means everything to us.' Tears welling in her eyes.

'I'm ecstatic to be here.' The statement was terse but sincere.

'I have coffee all ready to go . . . I haven't forgotten how you used to like your coffee. Come into the kitchen. Ellis, take her coat.'

A sunny, welcoming room, with windows on two walls, Mexican tiles on the floor, a big table in pale, scrubbed pine, a blue bowl of oranges, the aroma of baking, a warm waft of cinnamon.

'You've got me baking cookies, Kate, and I don't do that but once a decade . . .'

Ellis scanned the titles in the big bookcase in the hall. He was looking for the American edition of the Henri Danillac novel he'd bought by chance in the town bookstore and only then discovered the translation was by his own daughter. He could see through the doorway into the kitchen where Kate and Fay were conversing animatedly. Fay was showing Kate the fine, large cupboard Rick had made for them.

Admiringly Kate stroked the smooth finish. 'I'm green with envy.'

'We must have Rick make something for you,' Fay enthused. 'It would give us a reason to buy something more from him . . . Though he has plenty of orders to be going on with . . .'

Kate protested that her house was small, that the shipping costs would be astronomical. Unconvinced, Fay planned and persuaded.

Kate looked perfect, Ellis thought. Slender and unfussily elegant. A soft sweater with a loose roll collar in a grey-mauve that contrasted with the dark bell shape of her hair, gunmetal corduroy pants tucked into casual short grey boots, all of excellent quality. Her manner friendly, composed. Ellis felt safe, he felt relieved. He'd sensed immediately that Kate had outgrown the sulks and inexplicable grievances she'd never taken the trouble to hide, not even in her twenties. He had the grateful conviction that at last they could make their relationship work.

Watching her, he experienced the swelling of a deep, solid satisfaction. Kate was a daughter to be proud of. Blood would out. Obscurely he inferred a deficiency in the Felix family. There had always been something tacky about Jerome . . . a sort of vulgar facility. As a young man Ellis had envied it, but in middle age – with his populist omnipresence – the fellow had dug his own grave. Then there was the matter of the suicidal son, the manic-depressive girl . . . Kate was loyal to them all, but Ellis was of the opinion that his own daughter was worth the lot of them put together. And his reunion with her would add the final felicitous touch to his own life, like the missing piece of a jigsaw slotting quietly into place . . .

It was good to meet up with Rick again. He lived and worked in a village several miles outside Coningsburgh, came by to visit his parents once or twice a week. He seemed tickled to death by Kate's visit, as if he'd masterminded the whole thing.

'If it weren't for young Rick setting the ball rolling . . .' It clearly pleased Ellis to acknowledge his son's initiative. 'I owe you, son, I owe you.'

Rick came for a meal the second evening, bringing Janice his girlfriend, a chubby, smiley young woman, hair wound round her head in plaits, who earned a modest living stripping down old pieces of furniture and painting them to look distressed and folksy. She wore a long antique dress in floral cotton found in one of the junkyards she combed in search of suitable pieces to customize.

The following day Rick drove Kate out to the village where he lived in a large rented barn, whose space was divided into a workshop and two separate sets of living quarters – one for himself and Janice, the other for Jim, his partner, and his companion of the moment.

The furniture they made was classic and beautifully finished, had acquired a reputation for desirability in the surrounding area. But each piece took time, was unbelievably labour-intensive. Kate was charmed and intrigued by the set-up. There was something in the way they lived that made her think of Olivier in his younger days, before he'd begun to doubt himself.

Rick enjoyed his life but was fatalistic. 'As long as we earn enough to pay the rent, the rest is a bonus.'

He, Jim and Janice were throwbacks, he reckoned, to the seventies or earlier, didn't belong in Reagan's America. Ellis wanted them to organize themselves, take on apprentices and train them, make the whole project bigger and more businesslike.

'Maybe we'll do it some day.' But he and Jim liked the fact that they were responsible only for themselves.

Rick asked after Jack and Stella with genuine interest and affection. Kate was charmed all over again by her young half-brother, found her relationship with him easy and unforced, almost as if they'd spent the last two decades in regular communication.

Justine was more problematic. A pale, pensive, fine-boned

woman around twenty-five, with rough, blondish hair, grey eyes that seemed to evade, then became, all at once, piercingly direct. She had inherited Ellis's love of history, had opted for an academic career, was battling her way towards 'tenure' in Pittsburgh, from where she travelled up for a night – at her parents' urging rather than voluntarily, Kate suspected – to spend a little time with her long-lost sibling.

'Justine's smarter and quieter than the rest of us. And she's always been a little shy.' Fay's words held the breath of a caution.

If it hadn't been for her stepmother's warning Kate might have been tempted to view her half-sister as arrogant and aloof. It was hard to say quite why, for the self-contained woman in black sweater and jeans was perfectly polite, greeted her with a measured kiss, quizzed her with intelligence and seeming interest on her work.

Perhaps it was just that, after a few days in America, you became so accustomed to warmth, even effusiveness, that mere courtesy had the effect of a cold shower.

That evening they all went out to the Dutchman's Kitchen, apparently Justine's favourite eating-place since earliest childhood. Kate remembered it from her own months in Coningsburgh, though in those days it had been a homely, family-run restaurant special-izing in chunky burgers, milkshakes and cherry pie. Now both cooking and décor had become up-market traditional – chowders and pot-roasts, glazed hams, Boston beans, sweet potatoes, pecan pies and apple cake.

The restaurant clearly provided employment for half the middle-class kids of the town – both Rick and Justine had worked there in their time. The Ellis family were acquainted with all of the staff and introduced Kate with pride. Kate was intrigued to notice that, even with these near-contemporaries, Justine's manner retained its elusive touch of hauteur.

'My two smart, beautiful daughters.'

Ellis was elated to have them both at the same table here in this cosily familiar environment where, from way back, the family had celebrated the birthdays and anniversaries and personal triumphs of its members. Over the delicious corn chowder Ellis raved about their cleverness, his own pleasure in their respective achievements. To Kate it was odd to hear the job she'd done for so long in a scrabbling, hand-to-mouth fashion – always pressed, always beset by money worries, no sense of security or real continuity – elevated thus to a body of work.

She had mixed feelings about his pride. Ellis had, after all, small hand in what she'd become. Once she would have said as much, paraded her scepticism. But she'd vowed herself to forbearance and allowed him his vanity.

'The first time Justine came here was on her fifth birthday. The waiters gathered round our table to sing Happy Birthday. Justine was so embarrassed she sat facing the wall throughout . . .' Ellis smiled at the funny-tender memory.

Justine raised her eyes to the ceiling, half exasperated by the anecdote, which had clearly been told countless times down the years. She glanced sideways at Kate as if to say 'parents . . .'

The grimace made her seem more human. At the same time it occurred to Kate that she could not remember Ellis ever recounting anything of the sort about her own childhood. It was as if – along with recollections of his first wife – Kate's infancy had been expunged from his memory, as belonging to a period he preferred to forget. But the pain no longer gnawed. It was buried deep beneath layers of scar-tissue.

'I'm glad you came,' Justine said the following day as she took her leave. 'It's made Dad's *century*.'

Kate fancied she saw a gleam of genuine friendliness pierce the seamless skin of her half-sister's formality.

'Remember, if you're ever in England . . .' she began.

'Don't say anything rash. I just might take you up on it.' Justine gave a sudden broad smile that, from one so reserved, felt like an impromptu gift.

Mornings started with breakfast in the Stephens' warm, bright kitchen, with Fay and Kate ensconced at the table drinking coffee while Ellis, with his late-flowering enthusiasm for cooking, rustled up corned beef hash or Mexican scrambled eggs, baked his own cinnamon rolls or banana bread. Kate was touched by this homely, hospitable side to her exacting parent, and the leisurely breakfast routine was one of the best parts of her day. It was also a wonderful opportunity to catch up on everything that had happened on both sides of the Atlantic during their years apart.

One particular morning it was Kate's turn to talk about her life in England, her children, the Felixes.

Ellis — standing by the stove in a blue checked flannel shirt, stirring eggs — mused aloud, 'It's hard to see where Jerome and Odile went wrong . . .'

'What d'you mean?' Kate kept a neutral tone.

'It's just that . . . What with Olivier's tragedy and Nelly's problems . . .'

Kate pounced. 'You mean if Jerome and Odile had been better parents . . .'

'I don't think Ellis does mean that,' Fay put in decisively, her voice holding a firm warning for both of them. 'I think he simply expressed himself clumsily.'

Kate took her point and so, apparently, did Ellis. The moment passed and soon all three of them were on easy terms again. Fay's down-to-earth charm smoothed the abrasions that would always exist between Kate and Ellis. She had a sideways, laughing look — secretly amused yet also merciful — that took the sting out of Ellis's less sensitive pronouncements.

One morning Ellis was absent from breakfast and Fay explained that he'd gone out early to appear as character-witness for a former student of his who'd come to court on charges of car-theft.

'The kid had a lousy background and some nasty friends. But there's always been something about him that showed he could do better. Ellis is convinced that this prosecution will be enough of a warning. Whereas prison could damn him forever.'

'I admire the life you have here,' Kate told Fay. 'The continuity of it, the involvement . . . You and Dad, you've become pillars of the community.'

Fay pulled a face. 'If you live anywhere long enough I guess you get to be a pillar of the community. You might also get to be smug,

489

blinkered, conformist . . . And small towns have their own petty rivalries . . . This is one way of living, but you shouldn't necessarily see it as admirable. It's like . . .' she grinned '. . . those letters people send out at Christmas – Ellis always does one – presenting their lives as one big roster of success . . .'

A wry twitch at the back of Kate's mind, as if, by some mysterious means, Fay might have knowledge of the jeering derision she had always poured on her father's seasonal messages.

Fay continued as if, in her husband's absence, there were things she wanted to make clear. 'And, Kate, don't be fooled into thinking that Ellis and I are the perfect couple. There's no such thing. As a family we've had our bad times. The kids too. There was a year in the early seventies when Ellis and I came close to divorce. Your father can be real pig-headed. You know? And at that particular time I felt stifled. But basically he's a good man. I decided to stay on and fight, and I'm glad I did . . . I made my point and we're both stronger for it.'

A pause while she positioned toast under the grill, reached plates down from a high shelf in Rick's cupboard.

'Kate, I know you have resentments against Ellis. I see them snaking to the surface, oh, lots of times, and I don't blame you for them. All the same I really, deeply believe that this getting together is a hundred times better than all the years of nothingness.'

'Try some of Kate's seafood curry,' Ellis was urging all and sundry as they jostled round the buffet table.

'He's so proud of you,' Marjorie beamed.

At least, Kate thought her name was Marjorie, but she'd become confused in the welter of introductions. Bill and Genevieve. Larry and Anna. Richard. Candice. Bernice. Local worthies. All charming and personable. All prosperous.

'This curry is gorgeous,' Larry called over Marjorie's shoulder.

It was Kate's pet recipe, torn out of an evening paper someone had left on the train back from London. Easy. Impressive. She'd done it to death in England. But Coningsburgh was virgin territory.

'You really must give me the recipe.'

Candice? Bernice?

'Everyone's raving about your curry,' Ellis corroborated, appearing at her shoulder, flushed, blooming with the joy of the evening. His estranged daughter so publicly and unequivocally returned to the fold. Friends and neighbours under his roof. Each bearing witness to the other. 'You're going to have to leave us the recipe. It seems we're going to have to make copies for everyone we know . . .'

Kate warmed to his exhilaration. And, mentally, once more, she paid tribute to the rewarding, deeply rooted life her father had coveted and carved out for himself with the help of his splendid second wife. It could never have been like this with Rose, Kate recognized. Her own mother had been a retiring person who saw socializing as a threat.

Frequently, throughout her stay, Kate had been ambushed by waves of a real tenderness for Ellis. And yet that remark he'd nearly made, the other morning at breakfast, about the Felixes lingered in her mind, rankled like toothache.

Ellis inhabited his own agreeable world of thriving certainty. He felt he deserved his happiness – God knows he'd worked hard enough for it over the years – and life had brought him nothing to contradict that conviction. It was clear to Kate that, obscurely, her father suspected that the Felix family's ill-fortune stemmed from some failure on their part, was somehow of their own making.

There were moments when, vengefully, Kate longed for some misfortune to befall Ellis – wished for one of his children to fail or to go to the bad – so that her father might entertain the thought that disaster could befall the undeserving, might strike even those who had spent their lives striving and playing to the rules.

With a special smile Ellis laid a hand on Kate's shoulder. 'Saving your blushes, daughter, I intend to propose a toast to you. I want everyone here to drink your health. Bear with me, kid. Brace yourself.' One arm around her waist, Ellis called, 'Quiet everyone!' He barely needed to raise his voice.

Chapter Fifty

❧❧❧

'Make your way to Washington Square, then follow my map,' Pascal had said.

Here in Greenwich Village the streets had names rather than numbers. It was a clear, cold night. Hallowe'en. A bearded young man crossed Kate's path wearing transparent houri trousers, a beaded bolero, bare torso shining white in the neon light. She registered the sight without surprise. Flitting like a shadow through this marvellous urban anonymity, her expectations were a blank canvas.

She peered at the scrawled map. Left here. The restaurant should be down there on the right. And it was. Quigley's. A row of pumpkin masks grinning from the darkened window.

'It's nothing fancy,' Pascal had said, when they first made the arrangement, months back, to meet up here. 'But I always eat there at least once when I'm in New York. It's a piece of nostalgia I've imposed on myself, and it'll be even better if you're there too.'

Kate entered the glazed door. The interior was homely, dimly lit, candles on the tables in orange glass containers painted with witchy faces. She looked about her. It seemed almost too much to hope that the casual idea – conceived one hot, lazy afternoon in August – was about to come into being.

'Kate.' A dim figure rising to his feet.

'Phew. You're here. I somehow couldn't quite believe you would be.'

'Of all the gin joints in all the world . . .' He bent to kiss her. 'You look great. You look like the cat that's had the cream.'

'I feel great. Everyone should run away from home once in a while.' She sat down opposite him.

'Drink?'

'I'm a bit hungover. But what the hell. Campari and soda.'

'That's a new one for you.'

'Fay drinks it. I'll probably never touch it again once I get home.' She would always associate its bitter taste with this journey of reconciliation.

They smiled at one another. A sense of wonder to this sudden encounter with familiarity in a far-flung setting, among the conversational buzz of strangers.

The waitress wore a mask, a curly tail and horns in her hair. Pascal ordered the Campari and a Jack Daniels for himself. There was a sort of disjointed liveliness about him, as no doubt there was to her. As if in a foreign country you became more emphatically yourself. He looked a touch haggard and as if he might have lost weight. The fatigue suited his existentialist-intellectual style, features photogenically gaunt behind his wire-rimmed spectacles.

'So tell me about the trip,' Kate said.

Pascal was in America to promote a series of his – entitled *Dramatis Personae* – which had been sold to various educational channels. He'd been aiming to cover ten cities in as many days, as well as fitting in a weekend with Jocasta.

He gave a sardonic grin, attractive, contagious. A glint of black humour in his eyes. 'The promotional bit was just about what I expected. No one knowing who I was and caring less . . . One interviewer accused me of being a Red, someone else introduced me as a die-hard Thatcherite . . .' He shrugged. 'Well, I've done my duty. Humoured the powers that be, for what it's worth.'

Pascal's series profiled eight British characters, each of whom in some way typified the eighties, presenting them – in Kate's opinion – with delicate irony but enormous sympathy. She'd loved the programmes and they had been critically acclaimed, garnered awards.

The waitress brought their drinks. Pascal raised his glass. 'Bottoms up. It's wonderful to see you.'

'Likewise.'

'You know, I couldn't care less about those programmes now,'

Pascal mused. 'I made them to impress Marya – arsehole that I was . . . as if she gave a shit.'

'Did you see her?'

'Briefly. In neutral surroundings. If I'd gone to their – quote – "bohemian home in the Hollywood Hills" I'd have lost my rag, sure as fate, and trashed the place.'

'How was she?'

'Very calm. She seems happy . . . I'm over her. Don't get me wrong, I don't want her back. But I do nurse a vile, secret hunger to see her suffering. I'd love for Leon to quit her for some young bimbo.' A dour smile. 'He shows no sign of it whatsoever.'

'And Jocasta?'

'Growing up . . . Very intelligent, very composed. But hard work. We've got very little in common any more . . . It's actually easier when I have her to myself in the school holidays. But she has less and less interest in coming to England.'

'Take heart. It's never too late. I'm the living proof. My Pa and I are the best of friends after two-thirds of a lifetime's enmity.'

'That's supposed to cheer me up?'

'Yes. In the long run.' Kate grinned sympathetically at his dismay. 'When Jocasta's in her twenties you might become this total mentor to her . . . Who knows? Relationships change. They have their seasons. I'm learning that.'

They both had chilli – a homely dish, but excellent here. Pascal recommended Mexican beer swigged from the bottle. The days of pointless travelling were behind him. Sleeping alone in a succession of hotel rooms, always different yet always the same. Eating alone. Repeating the same tired litany to interviewers with eyes that looked past you. It had added up to a fairly dispiriting few days. And then Jocasta, so self-sufficient, so thoroughly at home in her new world, making Pascal feel stale and redundant.

But, at first sight of Kate, looking so chipper, a gaiety had seized him, and as they ate and talked he was filled with a new harmony, a sense of relaxation.

After her stay in Coningsburgh, Kate appeared renewed, as if

494

in the wake of a heartening experience. There was colour in her cheeks, laughter in her eyes. Her mood was playful, thoroughly delightful.

Her presence sparked one of those spasms of reflection, when he wondered how it would have been if – rather than becoming the eager slave to a self-obsessed femme fatale – he had married a woman of more earthy disposition, with a sense of give and take, a willingness to pay her dues.

Kate was bubbling with impressions of her time in Vermont, full of enthusiasm for her American stepmother and siblings, and happy at having at long last achieved a reconciliation with her father, though she remained clear-eyed as to their differences.

'A part of me is touched that he's so proud of me. He's very sweet and open about that . . . But at the back of my mind there's always the suspicion that his love has to be earned . . . I mean, I think I'd stick by my kids, whatever happened. If they were junkies, murderers, whatever. But I'm not sure that's true of Dad . . .'

Pascal was amused. 'That's OK . . . Just make sure you stick to the straight and narrow.'

'I mean if I'd gone to Coningsburgh, unemployed, with ratty hair and a drink problem, I rather think he'd have slammed the door in my face . . .' A pause. 'Fay wouldn't . . . But Dad's got a certain idea of the way his life should look.'

A smile. Wry. Whimsical. She took a swig of her beer. Pascal observed her, liking the bleak honesty of her indictment.

'Don't worry, Kate. I'd always take you in.'

She looked levelly at him, loose, a little drunk. 'That's why I love you. Love your whole Goddam family. Always have. Always will.'

Wanting to prolong the cosy tête-à-tête, Pascal persuaded Kate to join him in a brandy. Over the shared nightcap she began to quiz him, rather tipsily, on the women he was seeing.

'What about that Nicola you brought to the party at Beatrice and Charlie's?'

'We've split up.'

'Why? I thought she was nice.'

'Our friendship just outlived its allotted span.'

A sceptical look. 'And Stephanie? The one you told me about. Whose brother has a cottage in the Loire.'

'We still see each other.'

'You sound a bit lukewarm.'

'There's no one serious.'

He made quite sure there wasn't. Somewhat to his surprise – he was forty-five and had been out of circulation for a long time – Pascal had no trouble in finding young or youngish, intelligent, attractive women to go out with, to sleep with. In fact, with his professional success, he was seen as something of a prize. He'd overheard a young production assistant describing him as dishy – it was a word he despised, but he had no quarrel with the sentiment.

Only he never approached any woman who might trouble or obsess him. And his instincts were sure. He had never met anyone who disturbed and enchanted him as Marya had. But there were women who exuded a certain indefinable quality that touched him on the raw. He avoided them like the plague. Pascal had made the decision that he would never lose control again.

'Anyway, what about you?' He turned the tables on Kate. 'Isn't it about bloody time you got off the fence?'

'Touché.' Her smile jaunty but with an edge of defensiveness. 'Don't you start. I get the same from Jess, Nelly, Beatrice . . . Even the kids, and they used to be my excuse . . . Quite apart from the fact that I'm not exactly inundated with offers, I reckon I'm terrified of losing control. And the older I get the more scared I become.'

He had the sudden absurd feeling that she had read his mind.

The brandy was making him feel vaguely debauched. And, at this moment, he fancied Kate far more than he had ever fancied Nicola, say, or Stephanie . . . Quite why, he wasn't sure. Pascal visualized the appeal of the two younger women as direct and upfront. What you saw was what your got. He imagined Kate's sensuality as diffuse, intriguing, arousing a weasel curiosity spiced with the tantalizing aura of incest.

Two years ago, when Marya had left, there'd been a palpable sense of sexual possibility between the two of them. But their lives had moved on and the atmosphere had dissipated. But tonight, alone together in New York . . .

He pointed to her empty glass. 'Another of those?'

Avenue of the Americas. Kate savoured the resonance of the name. To her there seemed a hallucinatory quality to the night, the dark narrow sky above the tall buildings, the neon-lit canyon beneath, the car lights undulating ahead like a long, twinkly caterpillar. And the Hallowe'en costumes. A huge man in a shiny red devil's outfit. His girlfriend, platinum blonde and palely powdered, dressed like a French maid in apron and puffy mini-skirt, suspenders and sheer black nylons, indifferent seemingly to the bite of the cold. From a semi-illuminated shop window a figure in witch's garb, a jutting false nose, cursed the passers-by in menacing dumb-show. And, rising high above the surrounding roof-tops, the Empire State Building gleamed against the dark blood colour of the sky. Brandy glowing in their veins, she and Pascal shared the exoticism of the street.

'This is one of those moments . . .' She turned impulsively towards him '. . . when you really grasp how amazing it is to be alive.'

'Babes in New York . . .' He flung an arm round her shoulder, amused, flirtatious. Pale and handsome in the livid light. Black scarf and thick overcoat. Depositing a quick, teasing kiss in her wind-blown hair. She was touched, pleased, but acknowledged – through her tipsy euphoria – a stirring of unease.

Two years ago Pascal had been in need and she'd tried to comfort him. That, if ever, would have been the time . . . He'd bounced back since then, had plenty of women. Her instinct rebelled at the thought that he might wish to add her to his casual bill of fare.

Pascal had booked them into two rooms at the Chelsea Hotel, where he stayed whenever he was in New York, out of a vague, romantic attachment to its associations with turbulent bohemia. Dylan Thomas, the Beats, Sid Vicious – Jack would be impressed. Kate had checked in earlier and been intrigued by the take-it-or-leave-it mystique of the place. Their rooms were on the first floor and they tottered a little unsteadily up the grimly majestic staircase hung with flamboyant paintings.

They reached Kate's door first. Stupidly, she could feel her heart pounding. Her fingers trembled as she fitted the key to the lock.

She was tense with the crouched and feral conviction that she had only to give a sign and the thing – so intensely desired in childhood that she had declared all thought of it taboo, the fantasy she'd never really outgrown – would come to pass. She would lie with her desired sibling, skin to skin, touch, caress, make love.

But she turned towards him with a false, bland smile. 'I've had such a good time.'

In the dim and empty corridor he raised one hand to the nape of her neck, bent to give her a slow, sweet, sexual kiss, rich with suggestion, invitation. It was as if he were laying some simple and tender gift at her feet, a gift it would be churlish not to take up. The temptation was dizzying, overwhelming. And yet, if she did accept, Kate surmised wildly, she would lose her head, she would drown.

Gently she withdrew. Shrugged apologetically. 'It's better not . . . It might complicate things . . . with you and with your family.' How lame her words sounded. She was humiliated.

For a moment Pascal stood silent. When he spoke his smile, his tone of voice were ironic but – to her relief – amicable. 'I'm sure what you say is perfectly right and reasonable.' He bestowed another kiss – light, affectionate, exonerating. 'I'll just drag my inebriated carcass further down the corridor.' He turned away from her, casually, but with finality.

Kate let herself into her own room. All was as it had been. She was off the hook. The status quo had not been disturbed. Yet she mourned, mourned for the risk and danger, the intensity she had refused. So amazing to be alive, she'd gushed earlier. What an idiot. What a coward.

Chapter Fifty-One
1985

❧❧❧❧

'Why would I want a husband?' Beatrice used to demand belligerently in the early days, given the slightest provocation. 'It's too late for kids. And I'm used to living on my own. I like it . . . Far as sex is concerned I'll take it if I find it, no strings attached. All I need is company. And Charlie's the best.'

But, Kate reflected, she never bothered to say these things any more. Her close – yet ostentatiously separate – relationship with her gay best friend had become a *fait accompli*. Even Odile pretty well accepted it.

With the money inherited from David Lacoste's estate she had bought outright a sturdy, unremarkable whitewashed house in the village of Lydon where Pascal lived. Already, Beatrice gloated, it had risen in value by at least twenty thousand. The place had been converted into a pair of flats, each with its own kitchen and bathroom. Beatrice herself lived in the upstairs apartment, renting the ground-floor rooms to Charlie because of his passion for gardening.

The first thing he'd done after they moved in was to plant a red and a white rambling rose, one each side of the front door, thus realizing the roses-round-the-door pipe-dream they'd laughed about for years. Already the bushes reached as high as the lintel.

The other part of the dream – the antique shop – had also come into being. A greengrocer's in the village High Street had closed down and Beatrice and Charlie leapt in with an offer to rent it, along with the flat above the shop, which would be invaluable for storage, and the concreted yard out back where Charlie parked his van.

There were mixed feelings about their arrival in the village, plenty of people who grumbled that all the useful shops were closing down, so you had to drive several miles to Sainsbury's or Tesco just to buy a pound of potatoes . . . And there was a sense that they didn't add up, this svelte, elegant woman and her big cockney partner – not married, not lovers, they made that quite clear – but living in the same house, incongruous, unclassifiable.

Charlie treasured the memory of a couple who'd come timidly into the shop the day they opened ˙. . . He and Beatrice made a big fuss of them, tried to put them at their ease, but found it hard going. The couple just stared with mistrustful eyes, rigid faces, before beating a premature retreat. And before the door closed behind them Charlie heard the man observe loudly, 'I reckon he's a poof.'

He was not averse to the small ripple of titillation caused by his presence in the village, but he'd encountered little outright hostility. Though there had been a week or two last summer when it was fashionable among the fourteen-year-old boys to pick up handfuls of gravel from a neighbour's drive and throw them at Charlie's front door, along with taunting cries of 'Woofter'. In fact the owner of the vanishing gravel had been more indignant than Charlie. He called in the village copper and quickly scotched the trend.

Generally speaking, however, the advent of Felix and Marsh Antiques was welcomed, specially among commuters and those who considered themselves village aristocracy – the two categories often overlapped.

'An asset to the village,' was the well-worn phrase and, by and large, the approval extended to the shop's oddly matched proprietors as well.

On Saturday mornings, particularly, when the commuters donned their Barbours and patronized the dwindling number of shops in the High Street, Felix and Marsh – with its colourful, attentive proprietors – was an attractive stopping-off point, a place to browse and be seen in, where you ran into friends and where there was always the possibility of an attractive 'find'.

Beatrice and Charlie kept the shop well stocked with small impulse buys for the locals to dither over. But Lydon was an affluent community and modest beginnings often led to more considerable sales, along with an insight into who was interested in what, requests for the two entrepreneurs to keep an eye out for certain collectors' items on their travels.

All this was fun, but Kate gathered that most of the real money came from unobtrusive dealer-to-dealer transactions. And both retained their links with Europe, though Charlie went there far less often than he used to. For much of the week they paid a woman to mind the shop while they went to sales and auctions, house clearances. Both of them adored the excitement of the chase.

'I can't believe what a lovely life I have,' Beatrice sighed sometimes to Kate. But then she would cross her long faintly yellowed fingers – she was an unrepentant smoker – and murmur, 'Touch wood.'

Never, for a moment, did she take her happiness for granted. In France for years her life had been cagey and uptight. Now she was open, easy, casually dressed, though still stylish with her cropped hair and streamlined figure. She almost never mentioned David Lacoste, the man to whom she had devoted half her life. She rarely spoke about that time. It was as if she had been born, fully formed, into the contentment of the here and now.

The previous summer Kate had translated David Lacoste's last work – a novella about a dying man. The publication of the original had been delayed by legal problems. Libel, Kate gathered, but she was not sufficiently familiar with the ins and outs of David's world to interpret the clues contained in the text. And Beatrice's reticence on the subject discouraged questioning.

Confined within his own four walls the invalid reflected on his past life, passages of reminiscence alternating with the pain and hopelessness of the present. Above all the story was a cry of disbelief at his own ageing, his imminent death, as if somehow a trick had been played on him. The dying man contemplated photographs of his younger self and felt more affinity for the smiling figure in the snaps, taking the pleasures of life in his stride, than for the strained, grey face that looked back at him from the mirror.

At other times he summoned up random memories of former friendships and love affairs. Moments, however inconsequential, that lingered in his mind. The invalid's retrospective eye was harsh and pitiless. There was no fuzzy sentiment clinging to his pictures of the past. And he was frank about his own manipulative motives, his lifelong selfishness.

David's rapture was reserved for an impression of his hero the day his first novel was published. The stack of virgin books on a table, bearing his name. A walk in the sunny Parisian streets. A drink in a café. An amused and tender portrait of a callow youth – dressed Frank Sinatra style in snap-brimmed hat, sports jacket – living the most perfectly happy hours of his life.

In his illness he was tended by a middle-aged woman. She didn't particularly want to be there but was incapable of turning her back on him. He resented his own dependency on her. The woman was described without sentimentality. She was tired-looking, too thin, past her prime. They were two flawed human beings tied together less by inclination than by convention. Necessity. Because everyone had to have someone.

Then, as a parallel to the portrait of the youthful novelist, there was a delicate evocation of a young woman, a lover. Sitting in the sun, eyes closed, dress pulled up to show long, downy young legs. Then turning towards him and laughing, her movements spiky and immature, face like a flower. Then lying across a bed, torpid, satiated, the play of sun and blue shadow across her tender skin.

David went on to make it clear that the young girl and the middle-aged woman were one and the same. She was his life's companion – consistently undervalued, yet awakening in him now a belated tenderness and recognition. If they had their lives to live again he would doubtless treat her no better. She had been a butterfly and he had slowly rubbed the iridescent powder from her wings . . . Kate wondered what Beatrice had made of the book.

Odile's wellbeing had been boosted immeasurably by her elder daughter's return to England. Beatrice was scrupulous about see-ing her often and doing things her mother enjoyed – shopping, a film, lunch at some interesting restaurant. But her presence in Lydon had similarly enhanced Pascal's world, Kate's world. Beatrice valued family and friends as never before, as if she were greedily, joyously compensating for the loneliness of her years in Paris.

Sunday afternoons, particularly, they often met up in the big master-bedroom Beatrice had turned into her comfortable living-room, with a view over Charlie's bushy, flourishing garden. Thirties design was her particular speciality and her flat served partly to house and display pieces which might well later be sold. The décor was fluid and changing. But there was nothing of a showroom feel to her apartment. It had its own casual, racy chic. She was as fascinated by cheap everyday things as by potential heirlooms. Her shelves were full of early Penguins, her walls – painted a subtle but absolutely contemporary sunflower colour – were hung with framed thirties posters and advertisements, the ephemera cheek by jowl with a painting by Eric Ravilious, a Moorcroft coffee set, a limed oak sideboard by Geoffrey Dunn, all of which waited on the right buyer.

One doomsday dark afternoon in February Kate sat with Beatrice drinking tea and reading the Sunday papers – Beatrice took them all. Down below the window Charlie was digging a deep hole into which he planned to plant a mauve lilac bush – in years to come it would perfume Beatrice's living-room, his own kitchen. Kate was touched by their buoyant faith in a shared future.

Framed by purple-grey clouds Charlie waved up at Kate, looking healthy and happy. He wasn't always here at weekends. Some weeks, after he and Beatrice had closed the shop on Saturday afternoon, he would vanish until late Sunday night.

'Visiting friends. And lovers,' Beatrice reported serenely. She made a point of emphasizing that Charlie's life was his own. 'He's a free man' was a phrase she used with a certain frequency. Rightly or wrongly, Kate saw in it a reaction to the constraint of her years with David.

Beatrice edged a dish towards her with one foot. 'For God's sake, eat some more of this gingerbread.'

Kate had a vivid sense of déjà-vu, a mental flash back to similar tea-times twenty years ago in Paris. She shook her head. 'I wish I had room. I've had three slices already.'

Beatrice bought cake and Italian bread from Ruby who ran a fancy bakery three doors along from the antique shop. The tradespeople of Lydon made a point of supporting one another. The more shops there were in the village the better for all of the businesses. Ruby was into pretty china and Beatrice saved her cheap bits and pieces from job lots.

Kate threw the paper down. 'I ought to stop reading the Sundays . . . All they do is leave me with a vague feeling of spleen and alienation.'

She was dully pissed off by the habitual bill of fare. Unemployment. The miners' strike fizzling out like a cheap firework. Some feisty, self-congratulatory industrial boss owning up with complacent remorse to his own aggression and short temper. Little black dresses that cost more than she earned in a month . . .

The front doorbell rang.

'That's probably Pascal.' Beatrice jumped to her feet, lithe in corduroys and a Fair Isle sweater. She bounded down the stairs. Kate heard a jumble of voices. By the sound of it Pascal had a woman with him. Stephanie probably.

'They're nauseatingly smug. They've been for a long, strenuous walk,' Beatrice announced, re-entering the room.

Pascal and Stephanie brought with them a cold breath of the outdoor. Both wore thick, speckled socks, having left their muddy boots downstairs in the porch. Their cheeks glowed with ruddy virtue.

'Hi,' Kate said. 'Come and join the drones.'

'It was all Stephanie's idea.' Pascal bent over Kate's chair, kissed her on the cheek.

'That's right. Make me sound like a bossy schoolma'am.'

Which was more or less what she was. Stephanie taught in an inner city comprehensive, was in fact Head of Integrated Studies (whatever that was). She was thirtyish and down to earth, emphatically not Pascal's 'type'. She wore her short brown hair roughly spiked, had an easy smile, prominent front teeth, her movements brusque and somehow boyish.

Beatrice had confided that Stephanie's unpretentious presence always made her feel futile – a woman with a pleasant, poncey job, no use at all in the real world.

'Kids doing their own thing?' Pascal asked Kate.

'As ever.'

'You'll be wanting tea,' Beatrice said.

'It was only the thought of it that kept me going across all those dreary fields.' Pascal brightened. 'Is that one of Ruby's ginger cakes?'

'Dig in. I don't want it hanging around making me fat.' Beatrice had lost the skeletal look she'd had towards the end of her time in Paris, but an ingrained self-discipline remained.

Pascal knocked at the window, making tea-swilling motions to Charlie down below.

'Be with you in a minute,' Charlie called.

While Beatrice brewed tea, Kate, Pascal and Stephanie chatted among themselves. There was no awkwardness between Kate and Pascal in the wake of their evening in New York. The next day they had breakfasted together, shopped for presents before flying home, each of them assiduous to impress on the other that everything was cool, nothing had changed between them. In the following months Kate's regrets had faded. The brief intoxication of that evening had come to seem a remote anomaly.

Later, as Beatrice poured the fresh tea, Stephanie urged, 'Come on, Pascal, break the news to Beatrice . . . You've been dying to.'

Beatrice looked up with a questioning smile. 'What news?'

'I've been given the go-ahead to make a two-hour special on David Lacoste,' Pascal announced with quiet satisfaction.

'Wow,' Kate said. Then, after a brief pause for thought: 'Are there still that many people interested?'

'The powers-that-be seem to think so . . . So, big sister, you're about to become a star.'

'Oh, no I'm not.' Beatrice spoke with full-blooded finality. She stared at her brother in a challenging fashion. He looked back, blank and nonplussed.

'I won't be in your programme.'

'Oh, come on, Beatrice. You knew him better than anyone.' Pascal's tone was mild, reasonable. Kate found herself sympathizing with him. He wasn't a presumptuous man.

At that moment Charlie entered, shoeless, outdoorsy with his greying crew-cut and check shirt, blunt features radiating easy good nature. As ever he gave the impression of a man at peace with himself. His large bulk altered the dynamic of the room.

'Hi, folks.' Then, sensing the atmosphere, 'What goes on?'

'Pascal's making a programme about David. I'm just telling him I won't be in it.'

'That's fair enough.'

For all the mildness of Charlie's words, his manner was trenchantly certain. As if he knew more than any of them about Beatrice's emotions, Beatrice's past. And, Kate acknowledged, he probably did.

'But why on earth not?' Pascal was genuinely puzzled.

'Because, Pascal, I'm out from under. I like my life. I'm a different person. There's no way you're getting me to pick over those old bones on film.'

Kate saw that both he and Stephanie were confused by the vehemence of Beatrice's protest, like finding jagged, spiny rocks beneath the placid surface of a lake.

The following Friday, Kate walked down Piccadilly, ducking her head against the driving rain. The Luna Gallery was down one of these side streets. What a dog of a night. A cosy image of her own fireside flickered in Kate's head. She had accepted this invitation a few weeks back by way of 'making an effort' – she had become lazy about this sort of professional do.

Drinks. Then a private screening of a French film based on a novel she had worked on three years ago now. Not the usual minutely dissected relationship thing the French never seemed to get enough of, but a sort of fantasy set in a grim future, shades of *Blade Runner*.

'Shit.'

Turning the corner, Kate was splattered with muddy water from under the wheels of a long silver car. Arriving at the gallery, she felt disgruntled, damp and wind-blown and made for the Ladies to repair the damage.

Her hair was decidedly the worse for wear but, since she'd started going to Beatrice's pricey hairdresser, a certain stylishness could generally be salvaged. With a tissue she wiped the muddy spatters off her trousers and shoes, then examined the final effect in the mirror. Her anonymous black top and trousers were accessorized with a wide-shouldered jacket, cut like a man's, but in some dark red silky fabric. A few years back she would have giggled at the gangster-type shoulders but out of the blue they'd become the height – or breadth – of fashion, and the flamboyant garment seemed to lend her appearance a kind of swagger.

The drinks room was an austere and pared down art gallery. The walls were painted the silken off-white of flower petals. The floor had a rubbery, industrial texture in a grey that was almost black. Grey-white light was diffused from behind panels in the ceiling. A succession of small, scribbly line-drawings were framed on the walls. A set of stackable black and chrome tables, pushed together at one end of the room, served as a bar.

Earlier on the ambience must have been chilly but Kate had taken care to come a little late and the room buzzed with conversation. All the same, entering an animated party had always felt to Kate like the moment of taking the plunge into water that was too cold for comfort. But she was spotted before she had even had time to scan the guests for familiar faces.

'Thank God, someone I know!' It was Piers Pelissier, a fellow translator she'd conversed with around half a dozen times over the last ten years, always on occasions like this when you latched on to anyone you recognized. Tonight she even merited a kiss.

'Piers, I vaguely wondered if you'd be here.'

'Actually I was surprised to get an invite. I had bugger all to do with the book.'

He was short and round with a plump, unlined face and a high-pitched voice that was exaggeratedly something . . . Not quite posh. Vaguely Welsh. Kate respected him as a translator.

'I imagine that, like me, you were on the Ballards' all-purpose guest list.'

'May we . . . ?' Piers summoned a young woman with a tray of champagne glasses, gestured Kate to take one, replaced his own empty glass on the tray and helped himself to another.

'Actually,' Kate confessed, 'I'm hungry more than anything . . . Haven't eaten since eleven o'clock.'

'You won't get a square meal here, I warn you. The food's themed. It's all black – olives, stuffed vine leaves, something or other wrapped in seaweed . . .'

'Doesn't sound very filling . . . Have you spotted anyone famous yet?'

'I've fallen in love. With Anna Stern . . . She's in the film apparently.'

'Oh, yes? She had an affair with David Lacoste once upon a time. She was at his funeral.'

'Look. Over there.' Discreetly Piers directed Kate's attention to the appropriate quarter.

How pretty and perfect the actress was. Well into her thirties and yet, with her short hair and student-expensive clothes, still exuding a sort of adolescent allure – something of Marya in that.

Kate noticed, halfway across the room, the long, interesting face of Daniel d'Agoult, who apparently played a supporting role in the film. He was locked in conversation with Don Kemble, managing director of Ballards.

'D'Agoult was at David's funeral too,' she told Piers. Then, 'Pathetic, isn't it, the way we stand round covertly gawping at anyone remotely well-known.'

From the corner of her eye, through the press of guests, Kate noticed a tall man with a head of light hair worn *en brosse*, and with it came a faint, unspecified impression of familiarity, but her attention was claimed by Piers.

'Look at Don brown-nosing there,' he scoffed.

The managing director was laughing with unnatural heartiness at something Daniel D'Agoult had said. The actor's expression was enigmatic.

'Don't jeer. In his place we'd be doing exactly the same.'

From a circulating waitress Kate managed to snatch a handful of assorted small black morsels. She was starving.

*   *   *

508

An earnest woman from the film distribution company was con-fiding to Kate and Piers what a long-shot this offbeat French movie was, but all of them were right behind it, sometimes you just had to go with your instincts and have faith in the ability of the public to recognize a flawed masterpiece when they saw one.

By then Kate had drunk three glasses of champagne. She felt detached and, rather than concentrating on what the woman was saying, she found her attention wandering vacantly towards the various living vignettes visible over her mauve jersey shoulder-pads. Anna Stern looked bored. An editor Kate had met once or twice seemed pretty pissed, highly flirtatious. And again that flash of pale hair, the almost subliminal drift of recognition.

Piers' vivacity had flagged too, as the woman drew comparisons with other risky ventures that had turned to gold. Kate felt her stomach rumble.

Suddenly a hand descended on her shoulder. 'It *is* you, isn't it? Kate?'

She jumped, looked up, found herself face to face with the owner of the light hair glimpsed across the room. And, yes, the features were familiar . . . For a second Kate puzzled, then it came to her. 'Duncan!'

He grinned. 'Thank God you recognized me. I had a horrible feeling you wouldn't.'

'I'm gobsmacked.'

'I was just leaving and I noticed you as I walked across the room.'

'Not staying for the film?'

He pulled a half-guilty face. 'To be honest, I'm too hungry. I'm off to get something to eat . . . Are you committed to the movie?'

'Not desperately . . .'

'You don't fancy some kind of meal?'

'Don't I just.'

'I can't tell you how good it is to see you.' In the Indian Restaurant

509

in Soho Duncan sat, arms crossed, gazing at her across the table with frank pleasure.

'Me too. I can't get over it.'

In a daze Kate chose basic chicken tikka. She could not begin to concentrate on the menu. Duncan ordered some kind of biriani.

'I thought you only ate ham sandwiches,' she teased him.

'I've become marginally less hidebound over the years.'

'It's been *so* long.' The obvious struck her as marvellous, seemed eminently worth stating. 'What were you doing at the party anyway? I didn't know you had a French connection.'

'I met Laurent' – he used the author's Christian name – 'at a sort of fantasy convention a few months ago. He's a nice guy. Doesn't take himself too seriously. He asked for me to be invited tonight . . . I was up in town anyway, so I thought I'd look in, but blow me the author wasn't there . . .'

Something lingering and deliberate in the gaze of his deepset eyes, Kate remembered, as if from a dream.

'How come you were at the party?' Duncan asked.

'I translated the book.'

'That would explain it.' A wryly chastened smile she found charming.

With appraising eyes Kate studied her former lover. It had been a shock to see that, though thick as ever, his light hair was now grey-white rather than fair. It grew the way it used to, springing upward from his forehead but, like her own, more expertly cut. She remembered what a hard time she used to give him back then, when the local barber used to scalp him – such things had seemed desperately important when she was young.

Duncan had the kind of strongly moulded bone structure that held up well against the ravages of time. It seemed to her that his style was much as it had been, but that over the years he'd grown into it, wore it with greater authority. He looked good.

'I met your . . . whatever he is . . . foster brother,' Duncan said. 'Oh, about ten years ago. He said you were going great guns in the literary genre. When I knew you it was patent specifications and such like.'

'Pascal.' She recalled the programme he'd made on Duncan. 'What else did he say?'

'That you were divorced with two kids. Working yourself into the ground, but tough as old boots.'

Kate considered the statement. Was that how she looked? A dry smile. In those days she hardly ever saw Pascal.

'I watched the programme,' she said. 'You seem to have a nice life.'

He appeared to hesitate. Then the food arrived and they got sidetracked as to who had ordered what.

After they'd served themselves Kate remarked, 'You went back to Norfolk then, back to your roots.'

'To bring up the kids.'

'Happily ever after.' Did she sound bitter? Sarcastic?

'Not really . . . My wife died three years ago. Breast cancer.'

'God. I'm sorry.'

'Don't be. You didn't know.'

They began to eat, subdued.

'How are you coping?' Kate asked.

'The first two years were hell . . . in retrospect. At the time I was too busy trying to keep the kids in some sort of state of normality . . . In the last year I'm beginning to feel like a person again.'

He began to talk, haltingly at first, about the course of his wife's illness. She listened, fascinated. After a while Kate found herself telling Duncan about Olivier's death and the particular effects it had had on her own children and on each individual member of the Felix family. Duncan drew parallels from his own experience. The conversation had a momentum, a denseness of its own. Kate forgot her surroundings, the passing of time, everything except the absorption of comparing notes. Between them there was an immediate assumption of familiarity, as if their youthful intimacy did away with the necessity for social manoeuvring.

'What do you miss most about Frances?' Kate asked.

'I miss taking her for granted. After all this time it seems a miracle that I had this beautiful, loving woman to live with . . . That we belonged together. And yet once it seemed so absolutely unre-markable . . . I want to tell her things all the time. More than anything

I want to talk over everything to do with the children. I find it bloody lonely being the sole parent . . . But you must think that too.'

Kate gave a rueful smile. 'I have a different attitude. I thank the lord there's no one to interfere. I don't have to explain myself to anyone, be jealous of anyone . . . I imagine that simply reflects our different experiences of marriage.'

He thought about that. 'To be honest I have to resist the tendency to picture Frances as some kind of saint. She wasn't and I wasn't. We had plenty of differences, plenty of rows. Grudges even.'

'For a time I used to think of Greg as the Prince of Darkness. Then my outlook got a bit more mellow . . . Now I hardly think of him at all.'

'I miss sex,' Duncan said. 'And someone to cuddle in bed.'

'Has there been anyone since Frances? *Is* there anyone?'

'Once or twice I've . . .' He hesitated. 'I was going to say made the effort. But it did feel like effort. It felt like something I was doing for the good of my soul. Like going to evening classes or something.' A crooked grin. 'To tell the truth I'd probably have got more honest-to-goodness fun out of it if I'd actually been cheating on Frances . . .'

They had a coffee and talked some more. They had a second coffee. Their waiter brought the bill without being asked and all at once it occurred to them that they were the only people left in the restaurant.

'Hey.' Kate looked at her watch. 'I must rush or I'm going to miss the last train.'

'My car's only a few streets away, on a meter. I could drive you to the station.'

'Right. Just ahead. Oh, God, it's one way . . .'

'Don't panic, Kate. I swear I'll get you there on time.'

When they did arrive, Duncan thought, she was going to have to rush away . . . He had to make certain things clear.

'It's like a miracle that I've run into you again . . . I just can't tell you . . .' Simultaneously he peered out at the traffic signs along Moorgate. 'I'd so much like to see you again. Assuming you feel the same way.' Was that the turning? No. Further on. Through his preoccupation with the road Duncan thought he heard sounds of encouragement from Kate. 'I really hope we can keep in touch,' he continued, 'Only . . .' Hastily he changed lanes.

'Only? Talk about suspense.' A dry hint of offence.

'Only I'm going away. Until September . . . My sister lives in Australia now and . . . The twins've finished school. They'll be taking a year out. And Evie, my youngest, will go to school out there . . . I'm planning to do some exploring, by way of research, and get a book written.'

'It sounds an absolutely wonderful idea.' Kate sounded delighted for him. Duncan could have preferred a trace of disappointment.

'Please, Kate, before we get to the station, write your address on something or other.' His urgency was absurdly belated, Duncan thought, as he spotted the turn. Why on earth hadn't he sorted all this out back at the restaurant?

Kate rustled in the tote bag she carried. Found some paper. Scrabbled some more. 'Shit, I can't seem to find a pen . . . I know I've got one somewhere . . .'

'There's one in my inside pocket.' He needed both hands for the turn. After a moment he reached into his jacket. Handed the pen clumsily to Kate.

She dropped it and cursed. Rooted around by her feet. Found it apparently. Began to scribble, resting the paper on her knee. 'I hope to God you can read this.' A short laugh. 'Absolutely can't see what I'm doing . . . The train leaves in five minutes, less . . .'

'The station's just down there. But it's one-way again.'

'I'll get out and run.'

She shoved the pen back at him, along with a crumpled sheet of paper. Swooped towards him and planted an uncoordinated kiss on his cheek. 'It's been great . . . Enjoy Australia. I really mean it. Keep in touch!'

Then she was gone. In the white glare of the street lights he watched her running, leaving him behind. Duncan cursed himself. What an unholy balls-up he'd made of their parting. At this moment the desire to see Kate again consumed him, more urgent by far than his desire for the Australian trip that – up to this evening – had seemed his salvation.

Chapter Fifty-Two

❈❈❈

At Eastertime that year Jack and Stella flew to America to make the acquaintance of the American branch of the family.

It was Ellis who had badgered Kate to allow them to come, had offered to pay all expenses – 'Fares, entertainment, spending money . . . everything. I'm in a hurry to get to know my grandchildren.'

Stella was ecstatic at the opportunity, Jack less so. In his mind the years of Kate's consistently dismissive references to her father could not so easily be swept away. And he remained resistant to American films and music, viewed with the righteous, uncompromised eyes of an adolescent the American cultural colonization of the world.

On the other hand, he liked Rick and, in spite of everything, had always nursed a romantic hankering after the tough, multi-cultural glamour of New York. The plan as finally formulated was that Rick would meet them at the airport and the three of them would spend a couple of days exploring the Big Apple before driving up to spend time in Coningsburgh. With this appetiser in the offing, Jack's enthusiasm soared.

While accepting Ellis's offer of the fares, Kate had insisted on providing the children's spending money, paying their hotel bill in New York. On the Wednesday before Easter she saw them off at Heathrow. As they passed through the barrier, beyond her reach, she gazed after them with a kind of anguished pride.

'Don't forget now, no wild parties,' Jack ordered, turning to give her a reassuring wave. A few days off his eighteenth birthday – so young – the familiar rueful-tough smile, prickly Action Man hair, scruffy rucksack dangling from his negligent fingers.

'Can't get me now,' Stella taunted, a grinning, capering figure in dungarees and trainers. 'Right here's where I start behaving like a brat.'

Kate seemed to see a nakedness in both their eyes as if, like her, they were not altogether blasé about the parting. Driving home, she felt raw inside, though the whole idea of the journey, the prospect of her children discovering a new family, a whole new world, filled her with a deeply personal pleasure. And in any case she had entertainment of her own to look forward to.

'What are *you* doing at Easter? D'you fancy some walking?' Pascal had suggested a couple of weeks ago.

'Possibly.' Kate hadn't been sure she could afford anything Pascal might suggest.

'Remember Bôn-y-maen?' He'd grinned.

'How could I forget?'

It was the name of a hotel on the Bangor Road that Jerome used to mock when they were kids. 'The rumour is you have to show your birth certificate before they take your booking,' he used to claim. 'No one under eighty ever sets foot across the threshold.'

'It's had a make-over, apparently. They're advertising cheap packages for the Easter weekend. A sort of loss leader. D'you fancy taking a chance?'

'Why not? But only if the package is cheap enough . . . I've splashed out money I haven't got on the kids' jaunt, and all to prove to my Pa that I'm a woman of substance.'

In the event Kate decided that she could afford it and Pascal booked two rooms.

'Stephanie going away for Easter?'

'Not as far as I know.' He gave her an old-fashioned look. For all that he saw Stephanie three weekends out of four, Pascal was scrupulous to deny any commitment.

They drove down in Pascal's Volvo. All that had ever been visible of Bôn-y-maen from the road was a dusty, impenetrable hedge of rhododendrons and an off-putting notice-board in black and gold, reminiscent of an undertaker's sign, which included the stern declaration 'No children. No animals.' Today the hedge was still there but the sign had been repainted in upbeat red and white, the offending announcement done away with.

Behind the hedge – studded at this time of the year with pale mauve blossoms – lay a horseshoe-shaped sweep of gravel drive, a well-tended lawn, mature trees. The hotel itself was a big, graceless, grey building, tucked at the foot of a rocky hillside. Inside everything was bright and fresh, the air redolent of paint and new carpeting. The staff on the desk were intensely pleasant, full of solicitous queries that seemed designed to impress on Kate and Pascal the hotel's new user-friendliness.

Their rooms were done out with Laura Ashley-style soft furnishings, sprigged curtains, flounced cushions, small dishes of pot-pourri on the television and windowsill. Cramped, irregularly shaped spaces had been sectioned off and ingeniously adapted to accommodate a basin, a shower and a lavatory, so justifying the tag 'en suite'. Pascal and Kate opened cupboards and drawers, examined the little packets of soap and shampoo and moisturizer, made a cup of complimentary coffee, drank a sneaky whisky from their tooth-glasses, then drove off to find a beach to walk on.

The following day they tackled a long, strenuous, circular walk across the Sychnant Pass. The first uphill pull was hard going but, after that, Kate got her second wind. It was a damp April day of subdued colours, the misty clouds seeming to hug the high rolling acres of springy glaucous green turf and tawny dried bracken. The air was thin and fresh. She and Pascal were ants trudging by slow degrees across the rugged but accessible landscape.

The combination of physical activity, the open air, the company of Pascal, the wide dramatic scenery was soothing to Kate's soul. And these pleasures were enhanced by her awareness of Jack and Stella, on the other side of the Atlantic, being entertained by Rick and Ellis and Fay, their presence deepening and consolidating her own reunion with her family. As she walked Kate had the comforting illusion her life had a shape to it, a wholeness, rather than consisting of a random collection of ill-fitting parts.

The feeling was obscurely reinforced by her chance meeting with

Duncan a few weeks back. With him, too, there had always been that sense of unfinished business and it pleased her that the two of them were once more on a friendly footing – never mind that he'd removed to the other side of the world.

Amazingly, the address she had scrawled sight unseen on the back of a Tesco's receipt had turned out to be legible. He'd sent her a postcard of an Aboriginal rock painting. It had stated simply, 'We're here. Jet-lagged and culture-shocked. *Great* meeting you. I just wanted to say you grew up very nice.'

She recognized the final sentence as a quote – give or take – from Marlon Brando in *On the Waterfront*. The card brought back a memory of their watching it together on her small TV in Maida Vale. There was a danger, on running into an ex, of being horrified by your own bad taste. With Duncan, on the contrary, Kate acknowledged to herself that she'd undervalued him, frantic as she was at the time to cut a dash in the eyes of the Felixes.

As ever, Pascal had brought a camera. And every so often they had to stop and Kate had to hang around while he focused on lichened rocks, or tree-bark, or even puddles. Which seemed mad to Kate when all around them the view was so sublime. She said as much.

'You reckon I could capture the infinite on black and white 35-mil?' he scoffed. 'It's the specific I have to focus on. Grainy textures. Craggy shapes.'

They sat down below a waterfall to eat their lunch. Kate leaned her back against a rock. There was crumbly white Caerphilly cheese in her sandwiches and the black coffee in her flask was strong and hot. The exercise had induced a mood of wellbeing, combined with a heightened calm. She felt wonderful.

Pascal ate his ham-and-tomato, swigged from a can of lager. He looked young and wind-blown in a high-necked tweedy sweater. Then he packed the garbage away in his rucksack and lit a cigarette. Post Marya he was in a constant state of wavering, never quite allowing himself to embrace smoking full-time. With the cigarette between his fingers trailing blue smoke, he picked up his camera, focusing it idly on the waterfall above them. Kate heard the shutter snap a couple of times while Pascal cursed the greyness of the day. Then he turned the viewfinder on Kate.

Sometimes she felt vaguely threatened when faced with a camera-lens, patting her hair and lifting her chin. But just now – with the pleasure of the day – Pascal's smiling attention, his angling and focusing, seemed a matter of amusing indifference. She stared at him with a quizzical smile. He snapped her, snapped her again, came closer, altering the camera's focus dial. She gazed at him sardonically, then looked past him at the receding valleys and peaks, the broad slatey sweep of the sky. Pascal persisted, intent and assiduous, until he ran out of film.

'These'll be great,' he said.

In the evening they bathed and got smartened up and went down to the hotel dining-room with its stencilled walls and pale swagged curtains, toning table linen. They ate the five courses the brochure promised – everything served on beds of radicchio, or fanned chicory leaves, or black noodles – and shared a bottle of wine. A wonderful righteous, sensuous languor lay upon them from the exertions of the day.

Though the hotel's image had changed the clientele proved remarkably tenacious. In their mid forties, Pascal and Kate were regarded as the young folk, accounts of their fifteen-mile hike marvelled over, vicariously relived.

'The old couple behind us keep looking our way and whispering,' Pascal muttered.

'It's like being honeymooners,' Kate grinned.

The atmosphere made them giggly and skittish, cheeks glowing from the fresh air and the alcohol. Afterwards they went upstairs, collapsed on to the twin beds in Kate's room, drank whisky and channel-hopped, before turning in at a blamelessly early hour.

The following day they drove over towards the Lleyn, planning to do the old, well-trodden walk up to the Iron Age village.

Afterwards, Kate and Pascal agreed, they would go and sneak a look at Plas Felix.

The scramble up to Tre'r-Ceiri was pleasantly nostalgic, though today the panoramic view from the top was obscured by low grey clouds. Pascal snapped the photogenic ruins. Kate remembered Jack, as a child, solemnly doing the same.

'I was up here with your ma,' Kate recalled, 'in the hot summer of seventy-six. It was here she first told me she was selling Plas Felix . . . I was devastated. I didn't think I could live without that sanctuary in my life. My haven . . . But you do. You get used to it.'

In retrospect how young and strong and full of life Odile seemed that day. The summer before Olivier died.

On the way down the mountain a palpable apprehension hung over them. Neither of them had set eyes on the house since it was first sold in seventy-eight. Nelly never went there either. She couldn't bear to. After it had failed as a hotel, there had been talk of its being turned into a health farm, but Nelly had heard that the entrepreneurs ran out of cash.

'I feel nervous,' Kate said.

'I know what you mean.'

'It meant so damn much to me as a kid . . . Maybe Nelly's right to stay away.'

'I'm not backing out now I'm here,' Pascal said. 'If you want to you can wait in the car.'

The lane was overgrown in a way it never had been in the days when regular toing and froing kept the encroaching vegetation at bay. Even this early in the year the slow progress of Pascal's Volvo was hampered by nettles and ivy, vigorous self-seeds of mountain ash. Near the bottom someone had erected a barrier and there was a notice saying that the building was unsafe and that trespassers entered at their own risk.

'Sounds like an invitation,' Kate said.

Now she'd arrived it was absolutely clear to her that, for better or worse, her curiosity was stronger than her dread.

With difficulty Pascal backed the car on to a patch of rough greensward. They got out and scrambled over the barrier, turned the corner into the courtyard.

'Good grief!'

They had walked into a scene of advanced dereliction. The courtyard sprouted nettles and dock. The house was encased in a framework of scaffolding. Up above, roof timbers were visible through displaced slates.

'My God.' Kate peered closer. 'I don't think a single window has been left intact.'

They stood and stared, their first reaction shock and surprise rather than any more reflective emotion. Shredded fabric wafted at the shattered windows. Kate recognized the faded russet of Odile's kitchen curtains.

They walked round to the back of the house. Both doors, back and front, were barred, along with the big French windows. Gingerly Pascal tested one of the broken sash windows. It wouldn't budge. With a plank he stove in the jagged glass that remained in the lower pane, then climbed cautiously through into the kitchen. Kate followed, catching the ball of her thumb on a broken shard. A dark drop of blood welled up. She sucked it away.

The kitchen floor was covered with splintered glass. A catering-sized cooker that must date from the hotel phase was thick in dust and rubble. The air was filled with the raw, sour smell of damp and demolition.

Pascal wore his camera on a strap round his neck. He began to peer through the viewfinder at the mutilated room.

'Good God, Pascal!' Kate protested, half laughing, half angry at his obsession, his looking to turn this wreckage into . . . what? Art?

She left the kitchen, wandered along to the big entry hall that always used to smell warmly of polish, of familiarity, of home. Now the stench in the air was of stale urine. Odile's green carpet was disrespectfully strewn with builders' rubble, beer and coke cans. A broken WC lay on its side. The skirting boards had been stripped away and lay in a mess of broken plaster. By the back door Kate saw empty bottles of lemonade, cream soda, vodka, gin. Some kids must have broken in and had a party, a destructive orgy . . . She took it all in with avid, empty eyes, too disorientated for feeling.

Kate set foot on the bottom stair, one hand on the knob of the balustrade. She crunched plaster underfoot. On the wall alongside someone had written 'Fuck You Paul' in big, uneven red letters. Four or five brass rods were strewn across the stairs, as if they'd been hurled down, then left to lie. Halfway up she encountered a dead bird, one wing outstretched, the other close, wispy and desiccated, as if the creature had become exhausted and starved, then faded rather than rotted, frail as a moth.

Upstairs, in Nelly's room, the shelves had been ripped down and lay pell-mell, their skewed fittings protruding from long, rusty nails. Further drink cans littered the bare floor and, on one wall, someone had drawn the life-sized image of a naked woman, the breasts and genitals crudely emphasized. Kate's own room was similarly vandalized. Among the detritus she noticed the pale crumple of a pair of condoms. The curtains and their fittings lay in a rumpled heap, crowned with a large, dried-out human turd.

She had seen enough. Kate left the room and walked back to the top of the stairs. In the hall below Pascal stood, focusing his camera through the banisters at the Fuck You legend that adorned the walls.

A breathless anger swept through her at the sight of him blandly, blankly photographing the wreckage of his own home. At the clichéd crouch of his body, his straight-faced absorption in the act of reducing this desecration to a set of chic and artful photographs. It seemed to Kate that he'd done this since forever, viewed life as a series of aesthetic images. He'd even seen his own marriage that way . . .

'For God's sake, Pascal,' she screamed. 'Look at it with your own eyes for once! With your own bare eyes!'

Startled, he lowered his camera, looked up at her. Stared up, saying nothing. His silence had an active quality, seemed to Kate unnaturally suspended.

'Mind your own business, Kate,' Pascal said finally, mildly. 'Each

521

to his own.' And, with emphatic calm, he returned to framing up the shot.

Kate went outside and sat down on the edge of the terrace. The stone seemed imbued with all the cold and damp and neglect of the past winter. She gazed at the sloping field, the wan sea and the sky, the sight so ineradicably imprinted on her memory that it figured in her dreams. She began to sob, convulsive, dry-eyed, in an attempt to give release to the shock and pain inside her. But her body held back. She couldn't cry, but sat staring dully out at the empty field.

After a while Pascal came up behind her and laid a hand on her shoulder.

'Are you ready to go?' His voice was gentle, conciliatory.

They were quiet in the car, each sunk in his own thoughts. Although thoughts was too coherent a word for the confused fragments that filled Kate's head. It was as if, with each breath, she resurrected the elusive atmosphere of Plas Felix, the way it used to be, saw little pieces of it, misty and disembodied. Jerome at the head of the table, refilling his own wine-glass, the gesture rich with indulgence – for himself and others – before his life became complicated by rejection and death. An ironic, tender look Odile used to have when Kate first knew her. Nelly, wild-haired, jiving with Robert in one of the bare rooms on the second floor. Doomed Olivier with his innocent eyes and sweet, sunny smile. The long communal dining table and the open French windows. The horses grazing in the field outside. The happiness of those days seemed far off, like the blue and gold haze of a child's story, imbuing the whole house with its enchantment. Kate had never really allowed herself to contemplate how the loss of Plas Felix, of that whole world, had impoverished her. But it had.

Just past Caernarfon Pascal suddenly pulled into a lay-by, where a white van stood parked.

'I'm going to get some fish and chips,' he announced. 'How's about you?'

'What about supper?' Kate protested.

'I'm not in the mood,' Pascal said, 'to sit in that cutesy dining-room with all the old buffers, eating sodding nouvelle cuisine off pretty plates.'

'I see what you mean.'

Back at the hotel Pascal poured each of them a whisky that came two-thirds of the way up their Duralex tooth beakers. They sat on the floor of his room with the television on, eating fish and chips from the paper, the pervasive greasy, vinegary fumes vulgarly at odds with the floral swags and flounces of the décor. A hard despondency hung in the air between them.

'I'm sorry I screamed at you.' Kate understood that Pascal's antics with the camera had stemmed from anything but indifference.

His answering shrug was dismissive, unemphatic. Clearly her anger was the last thing on his mind. He looked shell-shocked as if, like Kate, he found the barbaric defilement of their home too bitter to be expressed in words.

Pascal had another bottle of scotch in his luggage and they broached it recklessly, its sharply pungent aroma joining that of the fried food they had eaten earlier, and overwhelming the spurious flower scents of the pot-pourri. They lounged, shoes off, floppy as ragdolls, Pascal on the floor, Kate on the pretty, quilted double bed. There was an understanding between them that this was serious boozing, and that they were drinking out of mourning for Plas Felix.

Whisky brought your pain to the surface. Kate had shed the tears that wouldn't come earlier. For a long time they welled hot on her cheeks, effortless, cleansing. Whisky lent a kind of poetry to your pain, made you see it romantically as part of the human condition, and crying was not without its own passionate pleasure. Pascal held her hand, stroked her back, but let her cry.

The tears had stilled now, dried on her cheeks. She felt drained and relieved. In the twin rectangles of window the sky had turned blue-black. Pascal sat on the floor, leaning against a floral armchair. His glass dangled loosely from between his fingers. His head was tipped backward. His eyes looked heavy and dark.

'Thank God,' he said, 'that Ma wasn't there to see the house.'

Flat on her back on the bed, one arm across her eyes – glass on the floor by her side, just within reach of her dangling fingers – Kate considered his words. She thought Pascal had the sentimental view of his mother that Odile had always repudiated. As a wholly domesticated woman devoted to serving her husband and children, devoted to tending her realm of home and garden.

'Actually I think Odile would've coped better than either of us. It was we kids, and Jerome, who adored Plas Felix. For her, in the end, it simply came to represent a hell of a lot of work . . . I can imagine her saying something utterly practical and anticlimactic: "Thank God I don't have to clear up all this mess . . ."' Kate mimicked Odile's down-to-earth French tones. Pascal gave a short bark of laughter.

'Odile's coped with the death of a child. That's something a thousand times worse than either of us have suffered.' The whisky she'd drunk rendered the thought fresh and enlightening. 'I mean a friend . . . even a brother . . . It's just not the same.' Kate turned on her side, looked at Pascal through groggy, half-closed eyes. 'Think of it, Pascal, a child. And she's still walking around, still living . . .'

Pascal didn't move. He didn't acknowledge her words. And Kate didn't care. For a while they said nothing.

Then Pascal mused slowly, 'For me Olivier's dying was all mixed up with the beginnings of losing Marya. And, for me, all the stuff to do with Marya was much worse, much more important. Shameful, isn't it? My little brother kills himself and I was far more cut up by my shoddy relationship with that bitch.'

'I hate you calling her a bitch. It doesn't sound like you.'

'And it's not what I think. I love her. I worship her. I think she's a goddess . . . She's shat on me, destroyed me, killed me . . .' His voice had a drunken detachment, a musical equanimity. 'I walk around like a robot, pretending I'm not dead, pretending I give a shit about my mediocre life . . .'

His head was tipped backward, his eyes shut. Kate saw tears welling from beneath the lids.

'You're pissed.'

'That's the only time you let yourself look at things the way they really are.'

Kate lay propped on one elbow, staring with a private drunken fixity at Pascal, half envying his despair. At least he was feeling something. Ever since Greg she herself had nursed a dread of any relationship that could lead to that kind of pain.

Then, with no conscious decision on her part, she rolled off the bed, kneeled on the carpet next to Pascal, put an arm round his neck.

'What you're feeling is only part of the truth,' she said. 'It's only one side of it . . . The things you feel when you're sober are just as true . . .'

He grinned wanly at that and ruffled her hair. Then he kissed her, setting his mouth gently to hers. In an almost experimental mode she savoured the pressure, the mobility of his lips, and for once had no thought of consequences, implications . . .

Pascal pulled her down to a lying position. Full-length on the floor they clung together as if uniting against all the cruelty of the world, the disappointment of love, the callous wreckage of their home . . .

'Hold me tight,' he whispered.

She pulled him closer, pressed her body to his in a blind, protective instinct. Gently he kissed her again, then moved one hand to her breast, the gesture unequivocally sexual. A touch that all her life she'd seen as taboo, but seeming now – with the anaesthesia of the whisky – merely natural, sensual. In a brief drift of perception she regretted the diminution.

She shivered as a breath of chill air wafted under the door.

'This room's none too . . .' she began. Then, 'Let's get into bed.' And again, what had once been unthinkable appeared, at that moment, perfectly simple. It was mutual comfort rather than lust that made them strain together, embracing the secret cold-hot intimacy of flesh on flesh.

'I'm too pissed . . .' he began.

'Me too.'

They lay curled spoon-wise, Pascal's body enfolding hers, one arm circling her waist, one hand cupping her breast, drowsing. Like sibling puppies in a basket, Kate thought. Babes in the wood. A strip of light showed under the door. There were footsteps in the corridor, and voices. They lay in the warm, sightless safety of bed, silent, breathing quiet and deep, as if waiting for the angel of death to pass them by.

Kate surfaced into deepest darkness, becoming foggily aware of Pascal's erection pressing against her buttocks. She lay still for a while testing the sensation, unsure whether she was sleeping or awake. Then, with drowsy instinct, she turned towards him, spanning the sinewy thickness of his penis with one hand, rubbing herself against it.

Pascal was awake, or came awake, with a low growl of pleasure. He moved, burrowing down the bed, spreading Kate on her back. She felt his tongue licking at her clitoris, rough and wet, as if in an erotic dream. She had the confused fantasy that the two of them were in a tunnel under the black earth. Ecstatically she spread her thighs wider, arched to meet the hot tongue rooting at her core, the hot insistent tongue making her bloom with melting, electric sensations, the orgasm coming far too soon, a deep delicious convulsive overflowing, making her twist and writhe and tangle her fingers in his hair.

Then the thick blunt penis entered her, sliding in without resistance and beginning its deep, visceral, sightless probing. As Pascal kissed her she could smell her own juices on his skin. Eyes closed in the dark, his animal rooting filling her whole being. Pushing, pushing against her raw, intimate parts, causing ripples of pleasure and pain. He moved faster. She grabbed his buttocks and thrust up against him until, with a cry, with a hard convulsion, Pascal came.

'Christ, that was good.' He lay beside her, spent and torpid, kissed her neck and shoulder softly, repeatedly. Kate raised one hand to touch his face. He took her fingers in his mouth. A languor between them as if in some way a nightmare had been exorcised.

Chapter Fifty-Three

✠✠✠✠

'You look like a painting of a Victorian lady reading a love letter,' Jess taunted Kate. 'With a smug little smile on your face. All you need is a linnet in a cage beside you.'

'It's not a love letter. It's a letter.' Jess always riled her a little.

Her friend flashed a sidelong look. 'I'm not so sure.'

The letter was from Duncan. He and Kate had quite a correspondence going. Jess had the annoying habit of inferring that he was wooing her from afar.

With a show of indifference Kate refolded the two sheets of airmail paper and placed them next to her on the garden bench, along with the bill for car repairs. She would read it later, when Jess wasn't around.

It was a sunny August, late morning, early in the school holidays. Jess had rung first thing to say she fancied a drive out and could she stop by for lunch. She'd bring some bread and cheese from the Italian deli near her. Kate had plenty to do, but it was easy to give in. Pleasant to sit here in her small backyard, on the slatted bench and drink tea with her oldest – and most cussed – friend, squinting at the sunshine and mentally admiring the potted geraniums George next door always grew for her, and which seemed to flourish in spite of the fact that Kate was too lazy to keep them watered properly.

When Jess arrived she moaned and groaned, acting as if she was in the last stages of nervous debilitation. The school year had been hell, she was absolutely stressed out. She hated her job more and more, the way more and more obligations got piled on you, the way so many people had a say in it, felt themselves competent to judge, the way government types who'd shit their pants faced with the kids she had to teach kept telling the world what a shiftless, useless

527

lot teachers were, so every little nerd of a parent felt qualified to pass comment . . . Just as soon as Cal had finished college she was taking early retirement, leaving the whole bloody mess behind . . .

Kate had heard the diatribe many times. And she sympathized. Jess made her think that the solitude of her own job had something going for it, though a lot of the time it drove her crazy.

'Cal feeling confident about his A-Levels, is he?' Kate asked, not really caring. The boy would do well enough, for sure, to earn his allotted place on this computer-cum-work-placement thing Jess had explained to her at least twice, though she'd forgotten the details.

'I think so . . .' A sharp look. 'How's about Jack?'

'Come off it.'

Jack and Kate and all of Jack's teachers expected him to do fairly dismally. Between Jess and Kate their children were pretty much a no-go area. Kate privately saw Cal as stodgy and prematurely middle-aged. Jess thought Kate's kids showed the lack of a father's hand. Though her own husband, Bill, was a lazy oaf – Jess made no secret of that – who left all the discipline to her.

'You don't sound too worried.'

Kate smiled grimly. 'It's too late. What's done is done. I'm only too glad to have the aggro behind me. And next year's going to be the best ever for him.'

The children's trip to the States last Easter had been more successful than Kate could have dared imagine. To her pleasure – and private amazement – Ellis and Jack hit it off right away, instinctively adopting a jokey, antagonistic stance to one another, conducting an endless argument on all things English and American, each of them stimulated, so it seemed, by the prejudices of the other. Stella came home doing a spot-on imitation of Fay's cooing-yet-decided tones. Both of them had a wonderful time with Rick in New York, and were enchanted by the way he lived, the big barn workshop, Janice with her junk furniture and antique clothes – she'd given Stella a floaty twenties dress that she wore jauntily over footless tights.

It was Fay who, over a meal in the Dutchman's Kitchen, came up with the notion of each of the kids spending a year in America once they'd finished school. Immediately all of them began to play with the idea, and Rick suggested that Jack could work with him – unofficially because of the visa situation – as odd-job boy and maybe all of them could do some trips together to parts of the country they'd never got round to visiting . . .

'Jammy little bugger,' Jess said dourly, clearly considering that ne'er-do-well Jack had an unfair advantage over her deserving Cal.

Kate gave a dry smile. 'Maybe they'll manage to instil the work-ethic in him.'

The blossoming relationship with her American family bred a satisfaction that ambushed her constantly with waves of private pleasure. Ellis and Fay phoned every fortnight and all of them took turns to speak. Kate treasured Ellis's reaching out to her children and found the hard knots of resentment against him, that still clustered grittily like gallstones, beginning to soften and erode.

'I'm famished,' Jess announced. 'What about you? What say we go and unpack the bread and cheese?'

'I'm game.'

They cut themselves large slices of the gorgeous olive oil and rosemary bread you could get in London – sliced and wrapped white was all Downridge ran to, Kate drove to Lydon to buy her bread – along with a crumbly blue cheese Jess couldn't remember the name of and the great big misshapen tomatoes Odile used to grow. Then they sat outside and gossiped about their nearest and dearest. As she chatted and ate Jess turned her indoor-pale face up to the sun, a dumpy, indomitable figure in long shorts, dressy sandals, a yellow T-shirt with built-in shoulder pads.

Cal had a girlfriend who, Jess claimed tight-lipped, had him just where she wanted him. Bill was off to Alsace in October with his sodding wine-club. Jess had harangued him to go out and find an interest . . .

'Trust him to come up with the most expensive hobby this side of brothel frequenting.'

Pascal was about to spend a week with Stephanie at her brother's house in the Loire. He'd been back and forth to France most of the summer, filming his special on David Lacoste. Kate had done an interview to be chopped up and slotted into the final programme.

'What, telling all?' Jess mocked.

'You know me. I'm much too discreet. Though I do mention what a crush I had on him as a kid . . . and the amusing anecdote as to how I came to be his translator.'

Pascal had begged and cajoled Beatrice to take part, but she was adamant. Pascal was pissed off. Her side of the story would have deepened the whole thing . . . Henri Danillac was good value. And Anna Stern was ravishing, but frustratingly secretive . . .

Nelly had her medication reduced but hadn't coped and the higher dose had been reinstated. Odile complained that Jerome devoted all the hours God gave to his support group . . . He was tiring himself out, and had become a complete mono-maniac. Naturally he took not the slightest notice.

Kate glanced at her watch. 'Time I chucked you out . . . We don't all get six week summer holidays.'

'Holiday! If you could see the pile in my figurative in-tray . . .'

'You wanted to borrow that bumf about the Amstrad.' Hastily Kate headed off Jess's tirade on the behind-the-scenes exploitation of the teaching profession.

In her study Kate riffled through her desk drawers, looking for the information. Jess waited, peering at the bookshelves, examining a fossil Kate had found on the beach in Wales. Then she flipped vaguely through some folders stacked against the end wall.

'Nosy devil,' Kate commented.

'What's this?' Jess picked on a big brown envelope, torn down one side, from which a photograph protruded. Pulling out a sheaf of black and white enlargements. 'Ooh . . . glam.' Laying them out on the desk.

Various versions of Kate stared up at them, tousled and wind-blown against a rocky background. The photographs Pascal had taken at Easter time. Kate hadn't looked at them for some months and it was like seeing pictures of someone else, a stranger who appeared stronger and more self-possessed, more attractive, than Kate felt inside.

A note fluttered on to the desk-top in Pascal's writing. 'Mean, moody and magnificent . . . Will they make the White Album?'

'What does that mean?'

'Oh, just a book of photos I've had since I was a kid.'

After waving Jess off, Kate went back to pack the photographs away. Before picking up the glossy, narcissistic enlargements, she stood and looked at them for a moment. They aroused a drift of sensation, the breath of a particular atmosphere. In an instant her mind superimposed a kaleidoscope of images. A rolling expanse of mountain, a low sky. The obscene desecration of Plas Felix. The blind, black urgency of the nights making love with Pascal. The pair of them, on the final day, sitting in a pub that looked out on a sea sparkling and dancing in the shrill April sun, both suffused with a light-headed exhaustion, drained beyond pretence, as if up to then they had been wearing masks and now they were naked. The pictures were specific and complete in themselves. There had been and would be no sequel. Between them the habit of friendship was deeply ingrained, Pascal's enduring obsession with Marya a fait accompli. But for a time they had shared a raw intimacy and the memory of it remained.

Kate's correspondence with Duncan was gaining in momentum. They'd started with cards and breezy one-liners before graduating to full-scale letters which became increasingly frequent so that, by now, a kind of dialogue had been established. The arrival, around eleven in the morning – the post seemed to get later and later – of a stripey-bordered airmail envelope was currently one of the pleasures of life.

Kate switched on the word processor in her study, then sauntered through into the garden again, to sit in the sun for five minutes, luxuriously alone, and enjoy her letter.

Duncan's black handwriting was forward-sloping and looked rushed, giving the impression that his thoughts came faster than his pen could keep pace. She had a vivid sense of him sitting writing – at the kitchen table, he told her, because Evie, his eleven-year-old was in the living-room watching some schlock TV show.

From past letters Kate knew that he was renting the house of a pair of well-heeled pensioners, acquaintances of his sister's, who'd gone to Europe for a whole year. A suburb called Hunter's Hill, very agreeable, quite plush in fact – his sister was green with envy. The house was roomy and tastefully furnished, with Aboriginal paintings on the walls and views from the windows of blue sea and white yachts. The only drawback was that he had to keep after the kids all the time to treat the furniture and the immaculate wood-block floors with respect.

He had finished the book he was working on. Since he last wrote, Duncan told her, he'd got even more heavily into researching the early history of Sydney, which was fascinating on its own account, but was also stirring definite ripples in his head. The hardships and conflicts, the whole atmosphere could form the starting point for the sort of fantasy novel he specialized in writing . . .

The twins – Paula and Jamie – were away for the weekend with mates. They didn't want to come back to England yet. Evie, on the other hand, couldn't wait to return to her home and friends. Duncan himself had mixed feelings. He liked Sydney and could spend months more researching given the chance. But he certainly wasn't indifferent to the tug of the old world.

'I'll come straight out and admit that the thought of maybe seeing more of you is one of the things that attracts me to coming home. I don't even know how free you are. You haven't mentioned anyone, but you might be in some cosy long-term relationship. Whether you are or you aren't, I'd like us to be friends again. You probably wouldn't believe how gutted I felt back in February seeing you rushing out of my life just a few short hours after the incredible fortune of finding you.'

Kate read the paragraph with a quickening of gratification, of quiet elation, automatically quashed. The reflex was immediate and effective. How expert she had become over time at dousing any pleasurable anticipation for fear it might trail disappointment in its wake.

Kate heard footsteps, voices. It was Stella back from swimming, with Daisy, her friend. Perky and nubile in their T-shirts and jeans, hair in rats' tails. It did your heart good to see them. Why was it that adults in general lost this quality of sheer light-heartedness?

'You missed Jess,' Kate said.

'Ooh, tragic.' A mocking smile. 'Can we have the rest of that bread and cheese?'

'If you promise not to drop the crumbs everywhere.'

Stella nodded towards the two sheets of flimsy blue paper Kate was holding. ''Nother letter from that ex of yours? He's a bit keen isn't he?'

Chapter Fifty-Four

❁❁❁❁❁

Deep blue-grey clouds above the A11 were backlit by a luminous primrose sky that flooded the fields on either side with a weird, intense green, made the yellowing leaves alongside the road stand out like splashes of bright paint. It was Saturday tea-time in early October and Kate was en route to her reunion with Duncan at his home in the Norfolk village of Netteshall. She was in an alert and receptive frame of mind, sharply alive to the colours, the beauty that sped past.

But her mood was not without an elegiac undercurrent. Two weeks ago Jack had left for Coningsburgh. The house seemed quiet without him. And, pleased though she was by the timely opportunity – unemployment was rife among village teenagers – Kate found her heart clenched at times by an attack of something like fear. Jack was grown-up and gone, pretty well, and it wouldn't be long before Stella was the same. And she, Kate, would be someone different, no longer the mainstay of a family unit.

Stella had Daisy to stay the night. She'd left the two of them settling in with videos, a big Marks and Spencers' pizza to heat up, a tub of posh ice-cream, a can each of sparkling Lambrusco chilling in the fridge, instructions not to move on to the bottle of Johnny Walker in the larder.

'You look great,' Stella said as Kate left. Then, with a saucy smile, 'He'll love you.'

Kate threw her daughter a withering glance, but the casual compliment made her smile inside.

'No wild parties now,' she cautioned before starting the car. A family catchphrase.

Like Downridge, Netteshall was not a picturesque village. At first sight it appeared spread out and featureless, with several unassimilated blocks of new yellow-brick houses that stood out like a sore thumb. There was a deserted feel to the semi-dark streets, a thin waft of slurry in the air. Driving through the heart of the village towards the far edge where Duncan lived, Kate had a sudden sense of momentousness, of fate, which was clearly rubbish she told herself.

By the time she reached the isolated phone box that featured as a landmark in Duncan's instructions, the houses had become spaced out, the surroundings more rural. A hundred yards later, opposite a field where cows grazed, she drew up outside what must be his cottage.

The house had an air of squareness and solidity, with four symmetrical windows and a central door. The roof was pantiled, the façade decorated with a geometric pattern of brick and flints. The windows arched slightly and were embellished with unobtrusive, ornamental brickwork flourishes. The front door was roofed and porched. A knee-high stone wall divided the garden – mostly lawn – from the road, but beyond the house Kate had an impression of open vistas.

Duncan had said to park on the concrete drive in front of the garage. As she pulled in a tall figure appeared round the side of the cottage and flicked a switch in the porch. A light came on that bathed the area in front of the house with yellow light, made everything beyond it appear suddenly darker. Kate saw that Duncan was carrying a hatchet.

She rolled the car window down. 'I'm early, I'm sorry . . .' Then, switching off the engine, 'I didn't expect to be met by a mad axe-man.'

He bent to her level, his hair very pale in the wash of artificial light. 'I thought we could have a fire. I was splitting logs.'

The prospect pleased her with its implications of warmth and welcome. His presence filled her with a journey's end sort of satisfaction. Here they were, face to face, not by chance but by design. He opened the car door and she got out. He bent to kiss her. She was heartened by his flesh and blood solidity, the chill of his lips and cheek overlaying a robust heat.

Inside the light and warmth were cheering. The house seemed empty. She knew his twins were away at university. 'Where's Evie?'

'Staying with a friend. The invitation came out of the blue. Otherwise I might have engineered one ... I wanted our first meeting to be without distractions.'

Kate had the impression that Duncan too had the feeling she'd denied to herself – that the occasion held an unspecified significance.

'Tea?'

'Yes please.'

The kitchen was straight ahead, a sizeable room, shabby but cheerful, with blue-painted walls, a big, scuffed dresser filled with multicoloured plates and mugs, a large table, six classic, but unmatching, wooden chairs, a deep stone sink, a gas cooker. Duncan filled the kettle and placed it on a hob, reached down a brown teapot, two blue and white striped mugs.

'Those aren't the ones you used to have in Maida Vale?'

He grinned, amused at her remembering. 'One of them just might be ... But if they break I replace them. They're what I like to drink tea out of.'

Kate was drawn to Duncan's casual domesticity. He wore a navy ribbed sweater and jeans. She recalled the width of his shoulders, the bony thickness of his wrists.

'This feels amazingly natural,' he said as he handed her a mug of tea with a slightly embarrassed smile that she found charming.

'I've made up the bed in Paula's room,' he told her.

On the way to stow her overnight bag he showed her the living-room, his own smallish study. It was cluttered and book-lined, a bit dark, the walls – where visible – painted grey-green. The surface of his desk was strewn with papers covered in the black hasty handwriting she knew well. His computer hummed, the cursor flickering. He switched it off.

There were photographs. Kate stared. A succession of oval-framed school portraits. A recent one of the twins and Evie in shorts in the sun, a stretch of water behind them. Smiling, attractive children. 'Jamie's the image of you.'

'So everyone says.'

Kate picked up a large framed photograph of a woman. 'Frances?' He nodded.

She was lying on grass, propped on her elbows, looking art-lessly up at the camera, wearing a striped T-shirt, her mid-length red-brown hair tucked behind one ear. Freckles. A semi-smile. A certain dreaminess in her eyes.

'It's a nice picture.'

Duncan nodded, his expression opaque.

Something about the house reminded Kate of her own. A sense of function predominating over décor and style. A tangible feeling of family intimacy that could not be tidied away.

Paula's room was small and irregularly shaped. A yellow Nelson Mandela poster on the wall, the one Jack had. Another, like Stella's, denouncing acid rain. A photograph of Lauren Bacall wearing a beret and smoking a cigarette, a lazy, sultry look in her eyes. On the bookshelves Enid Blyton, Stephen King, Maya Angelou, a history of the Russian revolution.

'The bathroom's just next door,' Duncan told her. 'Have a wash if you want . . . whatever, then come downstairs and have a drink.'

'I've planned for us to eat in, if that's OK by you,' Duncan had said. 'You have to go miles here to find a restaurant, and then it's so-so, and you can't drink because you're driving . . .'

'I'd *like* to eat in. Now I'm here I assure you I haven't the faintest desire to move.'

Outside the windows the world looked dark and cold. Inside the kitchen glowed with colour and warm light. Kate sat at the table with a glass of red wine while Duncan chopped vegetables for a stir-fry. Red peppers, fennel, broccoli. The steamy, grainy scent of rice cooking. A sense of ease and rediscovery. The inevitable opposing prick of caution warning her not to be lulled.

'Stir fries are my speciality,' he explained. 'They're quick, and the only way I can get Evie to eat her vegetables.'

She was amused by his parental complicity. 'When I knew *you* you never touched a veg if you could help it.'

'I got old and sensible. And brainwashed by my wife.'

He spread a cloth intricately patterned in gold, dark red, deep brown. An Aboriginal design, he told her. He placed a tall candle in the middle of the table and lit it, glancing across at her with a questioning smile. 'Too corny?'

'Nothing wrong with corny.'

Smoothly Duncan chopped pork into thin slivers, set out the ingredients separate and to hand like a TV cook, found a large wok in one of the cupboards.

'Here's where I dazzle you with my controlled but flamboyant expertise.'

She *was* impressed by the practised way in which he marshalled the ingredients, shook the wok over a leaping flame with no visible sign of fluster, adding ginger, chilli, and rice wine he'd had to drive to Norwich to obtain.

'Very Ken Hom.'

'He's my guru.'

The result was delicious, fresh and sharp, with the starchy, comforting contrast of the rice. As they ate they chatted about Duncan's time in Australia, Kate's reunion with her father, how it felt when your children began to leave home, the conversation as open and effortless as if they had never lost touch. Across the table Kate found herself seduced by the slow burn of his blue eyes, the half-smile on his lips that caught light in his eyes whenever she said something that particularly engaged him.

Clearing the plates, Duncan said fervently, 'It's so *good* to see you . . .' He shrugged, a hint of self-mockery in his eyes. 'It feels as if I've been stumbling around in this bleak rocky moorland and suddenly I've come across this cottage with a fire and lights in the windows . . . No, Christ, this is premature . . . I don't want to scare you off.'

What he said expressed exactly her own unarticulated feeling.

Deliberately Kate summoned up the self-preserving scepticism that never left her for long . . . It was too good to be true. There would be a catch in it somewhere.

When they'd eaten, Duncan laid a fire in the living-room grate. He crouched, encouraging the flames to catch paper, kindling, and the logs he had been splitting when she arrived. Kate watched him, covertly appreciating the strong length of his braced thighs, the forward hunch of his broad shoulders, his blank concentration on the task in hand.

Facing the fire was a sofa draped with a striped blanket. On either side an easy chair, at right-angles. When Duncan was satisfied that the blaze was self-supporting he slumped on the sofa next to her, stretching his long legs out towards the hearth. A low table between them held mugs of coffee. The flickering flames, augmented by a discreet corner lamp, cast a cosy light.

Above the mantelpiece hung a painting in an aluminium frame. Kate recognized it as the art-work to one of his books. A spreading tree, a house viewed between branches, the neutral scene rendered menacing by some trick of the painter – an angularity in the draughtsmanship, something sulphurous in the colours.

'I always spread your books out, turn them face out to give you a good display. In shops or at the airport,' she told him. 'For years . . . ever since I came back from France.'

'I'm honoured . . .' An amused, wryly gratified look.

'Think nothing of it.' She reached forward for her coffee. 'Ages ago I read that story you wrote . . . The one about Nelly's wedding. Do you remember?'

'God, yes.'

'Why God?'

'I'm embarrassed to read it now. The vengeful whingings of this pretentious little brat . . . There are things you try to forget.'

Vehemence brought out a homely Norfolk inflection that was latent in his speech, and which she found appealing.

'I thought you were kind to me in the story. I deserved worse.'

'You were young. We both were. And devilish callow.'

'I was so dazzled by the Felixes back then. Desperate to belong at any price.'

'And now?'

'Now I know I do belong. And they don't dazzle me. They're just ordinary people, coping. Like me. Like everyone. But they're *my* ordinary people . . .'

'They awed me in those days. They seemed to me like invincible rivals. I hated them . . . They made me feel pathetically inadequate . . . Then years later Pascal came and filmed me and he was a perfectly nice chap . . . I saw Jerome on the box a little while ago and he seemed this sweet and kindly little old man . . . And yet he really used to get up my nose.'

'They certainly came between us back then . . .'

'But we've got another chance.' The statement hung in the air, rich with implication.

But the conversation veered off at a tangent after that, to Laurent Raisner, the French writer Duncan knew and Kate had translated. Duncan had met and liked him at a Fantasy Convention out in Denver, an amiable, eccentric figure, rather out on a limb. Kate had only his letters to go by, written in a round, earnest hand in fractured English, like communications from a childhood pen-friend. His French too was so simple it was almost infantile, so easy to translate you could have given it to a sixth-former. 'Easiest month's work I ever did.'

They laughed. Duncan touched her hand. A sense of flirtation in the air that set Kate's mind racing in the old cautious groove . . . She must make sure she knew exactly what it was she wanted, must not give out the wrong signals . . . But almost immediately the stale, time-worn reflex was overridden by the sheer pleasure of Duncan's company. He offered her a brandy and she accepted. The insinuating glow of the liqueur mingled with the flicker of the flames. She was cocooned in a bubble of comfort and hedonism, loose as a ragdoll.

'I feel as if nothing bad can reach me tonight. No anxieties or disappointments, no worries over things I haven't done . . .'

'Me too.'

Duncan leaned towards her, kissed her with the warm, full lips whose shape and feel she recalled from long ago. It was like resuming something that her body had never unlearned. There was an inevitability to the kiss. Kate realized that she had been waiting for him to approach her all evening . . . Biding her time in fact – though she refused to admit it even to herself – from the very night they had run into one another again, getting ratty with Stella, with Jess, because, in some indefinable way, they sensed it too. She pulled him closer, kissed him back.

Kate remembered Duncan telling her – over that Indian meal the first evening of their re-encounter – how for a year after his wife's death he had slept in the marital bed, as if in so doing he could retain some breath, some residue of the years through which they had shared it. The bed had been secondhand when they got it, from his sister when she left for Australia. With the wear and tear of the Mitchells' family life, the springs had begun to sag, the paint to chip . . . One day, in a burst of exasperation with his own grief, Duncan had made the decision to replace it, recognizing that, even in his own mind, any lingering afterglow of Frances' presence had long since evaporated.

The new bed was a five footer. Clearly, even then, Duncan had hoped not to sleep alone forever. That first time he and Kate lay together beneath the chequered duvet there seemed to her something almost connubial about it, surrounded as they were by a room, a whole house suffused with the atmosphere and artefacts of Duncan's family life.

At once he enfolded her, the way he used to, with his long wiry body. She could feel the strong beating of his heart. From his throat came a low, lustful growl as if he were taking possession of something desirable beyond words. She was moved. It seemed years since she had thought of herself that way.

There was a lack of prevarication about him, a homespun quality which, as a young woman, she used to compare unfavourably with the style and savoir-faire of Pascal and Olivier, but which even then had spoken to her on some wordless sexual level. As time passed, and Kate came to know herself and the world better, she had gradually reached the conclusion that no lover before or since had satisfied her in quite the same uncomplicated way.

His body in her arms was alive and animal, his cock stiffening obediently beneath her hand, familiar, unfamiliar, reminding her of a power she still possessed. She recalled the particular scent of his flesh, the healthy acridity of his hair. His caresses, knowing and insistent, were like the touch of flame to dry grass, bringing her to life. She was flooded with wonder and fierce tenderness as they twined and turned, accomplices, hard-breathing, narrow-eyed. She was weightless, she was transported, holding on, holding back until she could finally no longer resist the waves of pleasure deepening and deepening inside her.

Later they lay spent, damp skin warmly fused, in one another's arms in the quiet and dark of the room. From time to time a car passed, the sound of its engine, the flash of headlamps, advancing and receding, leaving silence and night behind again. How good her body felt, torpid and used. The calm, miraculous sense of something beginning.

'If I'm dreaming,' Duncan murmured, 'don't let me wake up.'

She smiled lazily, eyes closed, kissed his shoulder, drifting towards sleep, letting go, no longer struggling against a weightless optimism that enveloped her as lightly and softly as a quilt.

Chapter Fifty-Five
1986

❧❧❧

'We haven't seen you for ages,' Jerome said over the phone. 'Too busy gallivanting with this man of yours.' An amused satisfaction in the reproach.

'I'll come for tea on Sunday,' Kate decided.

'You're on.'

In the background Odile shouted something inaudible.

'My wife says to tell you she'll buy a cinnamon streusel cake from Bürgi's.'

Kate grinned to herself at this confirmation of Odile's perennial preoccupation with food, dedicated cook turned discriminating shopper. 'Tell her she's made me an offer I can't refuse.'

A thick, misty, slushy February afternoon. The gas fire burning silently, cheerily in the Felixes high-ceilinged Hampstead flat. A wall of books. On the floor a patchwork of good, faded rugs. Sentimental memorabilia on the mantelpiece and crowded on to the shelves with the books. Kate's eye always sought out and found the clay statuette of Jerome she'd made as a teenager, with its half-moon spectacles and co-respondent's shoes.

Jerome was reading Ruth Rendell by the fire when she arrived, a white-bearded codger wearing a heavy-knit Fair Isle cardigan. He greeted her with a kiss, and a smile like a saucy cherub's. 'You look blooming, Kate. And in the dreary depths of Feb. Ain't love grand . . . Remind me to try it some time.'

'You already tried it more than enough,' Odile remarked dourly.

She was elegant and shrunken in a sage-green sweater, dark trousers tucked into patchwork suede boots, over which Kate exclaimed admiringly. On one twiggy wrist she wore a heavy pewter bangle that toned with the colour of her upswept hair. Her reading glasses lay on the arm of a chair along with a tattered French cookbook she appeared to be reading like a novel.

'Good plot?' Kate teased.

'Plots don't interest me. I'd rather sit and plan meals I'll never have to cook.'

Straightaway she disappeared into the kitchen to brew tea – refusing as ever Kate's token offer of help – as if the task were an itch she had to scratch before allowing herself to relax. Kate understood the form. She and the Felix children laughed with affectionate mockery over their elders' increasing stock of small eccentricities.

Kate sat down across from Jerome.

'Heard from Jack recently?' he asked.

'He's not the world's greatest letter-writer. I talked to him last week . . . He seems pretty happy. Learning a lot from Rick. Made a coffee table with a tiled top for Ellis and Fay . . . Still no idea what he wants to do with his life.'

'He's terribly young,' Jerome soothed with a grandfather's unhurried perspective. 'How does he get on with Ellis?'

'Mixed. He's fond of him. The two of them love to argue with each other. Ellis is proud as punch of Jack. To the extent that Jack finds it a bit of a liability . . . My grandson this, my grandson that . . . The way he is with me, rather belatedly.' Against her will the old rancour surfacing in Kate's voice. 'Jack's got a girlfriend. Lori's her name. The two of them plus Rick and Janice are off to Fay's cabin in Virginia for Easter . . .'

It was no coincidence that Ellis was mentioned while Odile was out of the room. One day last spring, shortly after Jack and Stella got back from their initial visit to Coningsburgh, Odile's composure had cracked, and she'd railed savagely against Kate's father, reaping the joys of fatherhood, of grandfatherhood, he'd done nothing to earn . . . While she and Jerome, who'd done his job for him, lived every day of their lives eaten up with the private cancer of their son's suicide. The outburst had been as short-lived as it was vehement, but neither Kate nor Jerome wanted to provoke another. When Odile returned with the Darjeeling and the promised cake the subject was quickly dropped.

'You've heard about Robert and Nelly.' It was a statement rather than a question, as Odile poured the tea. The look on her face a droll mixture of disapproval and indulgence.

Kate grinned. 'You bet. *So* romantic.'

The whole family was agog with the news. Apparently Nelly and Robert had been watching a travelogue on television one night not so long ago, and Nelly had suddenly become enthused with the idea of the two of them maybe visiting the Taj Mahal one day. A week later Robert had come home with tickets for a trip to India in September. An anniversary present, so he said.

'Nelly is bubbling with joy.' A dry tenderness in Odile's expression, an inward smile. 'Robert loves her so much.'

'Just as well,' Jerome put in. 'Our little Nelly's become a bonny fighter, but she's got a lifelong struggle on her hands . . . so it's a good thing she's got someone rock-solid on her side . . .' He seemed to muse for a second, then turned to focus on Kate. 'But it's *you* we want to hear about . . . Come on, give us the lowdown.'

Kate shrugged and smiled. 'It's hard to know quite what to say . . . Out of the blue we're back together, Duncan and I, and we're terribly happy. Everything seems to be going beautifully . . .'

The whole thing was both miraculous and banal. Kate was half embarrassed by her own irresistible smileyness – smugness even – though no one, not even Jess, seemed to hold her good fortune against her.

'I remember that young man quite clearly. He was gauche then, but seemed genuine . . . It was unfortunate that we were all too occupied with the wedding to pay him much attention.' In a nutshell Odile summed up one of the turning points of Kate's life.

'Of course even now it's not absolutely all smooth sailing.' Kate was eager to lay claim to the odd teething trouble. 'I've had moments when I felt jealous of his first wife. We had a row about that one evening, then a long talk, and I think we've straightened it out. Then there's our kids, of course. Evie, Duncan's eleven-year-old, seems to like me, thank goodness. Jamie too. But Paula's more wary . . .

Then again she's pretty well left home. Stella likes Duncan a lot. She reckons she won't have to worry about me being lonely when she leaves home . . . Jack's an unknown quantity . . .' Kate rattled on in similar style for some time, before exclaiming, 'What a self-centred bimbo I sound. For goodness sake let's change the subject. Tell me what you've been doing.'

'Nothing happens to us any more.'

Odile had acquired the habit of disconcerting asides. Conversation-stoppers as Charlie called them.

'Speak for yourself.' Jerome remained sanguine. 'I'm organizing a nationwide Survivors weekend retreat for early May . . .'

'All those professional victims,' Odile jeered.

Her jibes made no impression on the smooth surface of his composure. 'Should be a nice couple of days. A country house in Yorkshire. Long walks and mutual comfort. Good food. I make sure we spoil ourselves a little.'

Privately Kate could sympathize with Odile's point of view. It sounded a touch ghoulish to her. But what did she know? Jerome's involvement with his support group clearly gave him a purpose, a mission, even a *joie de vivre* . . .

When the time came for her to leave Odile pressed the remains of the cake on her. Kate said no. Odile insisted. Kate relented, sensing that in some obscure way it was important to her.

While Odile wrapped her food-parcel Kate gave Jerome a good-bye hug. The big cardigan lent him bulk, but even so he seemed a shadow of the selfish, genial giant she recalled. At the same time, he still radiated a certain bouncy egotism that always left her feeling warmed and uplifted.

Odile came back with a greaseproof bundle. 'Ask Stella what she thinks of it and remember to tell me.'

'She's like some old peasant crone,' Jerome said.

Odile glanced sideways at him from her long eyes, seeming gratified as if at a compliment. 'He thinks the only thing in life is giving pep-talks to sad people on the end of a phone.'

Kate embraced Odile's frail bird-bones. Jerome winked at her conspiratorially from behind his wife's back. Kate laughed out loud.

Their bickering was familiar and endearing. In an odd way it made her feel safe. Who was she to judge them? They'd come through a hell of a lot together.

When she thought about – rather than merely experiencing – the almost scary joy of her resumed affair with Duncan, Kate always felt like touching wood. Surely, she reflected superstitiously, love was never meant to be this painless.

Mentally she would enumerate Duncan's many perfections. A man combining the old-fashioned virtues of decency and loyalty with those that addressed the senses – he was sexy, well-built, easy on the eye. She liked his voice, his hands, the deepset eyes that lingered on her face when they talked. She liked the way he joked with his kids, his weakness for bad movies, a certain private smile he gave when he'd said something to make her laugh, a lost look he wore when he'd been writing and someone jerked him back into the real world. The way he reached for her on waking, pulled her to him with a movement that was both imperious and languorous. An attractive man who didn't know how attractive he was. And who thought her gorgeous to boot.

'He's everything I want,' she confided to Nelly on the phone. 'But it's all been too easy. I haven't suffered enough.'

'That's crap. Don't be such a wimp. And anyway, think of all the years you've spent like a lonely galley-slave, chained to your typewriter . . . If you take "time served" into account you've suffered plenty.'

For Kate 'time served' had a different significance. She was convinced that, if they'd both been twenty again, she and Duncan would not have lasted five minutes. Back then he'd had a class-conscious touchiness, she'd been deeply unsure of her place in the world. It made her defensive and jittery, determined to strike the first blow. She had managed to be happy with Greg for a short time in Paris but it seemed to her that – even before he betrayed her – she had willed down disaster on their marriage, expected it, courted it . . . Almost as if, in some mysterious way, she were frightened of happiness.

Never again, Kate had sworn. Now the vow struck her as some kind of protective spell designed to ward off further pain and disappointment. Over the years she had not so much conquered as learned to live with her demons. Nowadays Duncan talked obliquely of marriage and Kate did not dismiss the idea out of hand. She was insidiously tempted.

The approval of the Felixes had long since ceased to be the be-all and end-all of her life, none the less, as winter progressed it pleased Kate to see Duncan getting to know and like Beatrice and Pascal, the two family members closest at hand.

Both Duncan and Beatrice had a certain native reserve. They were drawn to one another but shy at first. The ice was broken when Beatrice drove up to Norfolk one day in February to take a look at some thirties china left by an aunt of Duncan's who'd recently died. It wasn't treasure trove, but there was some highly saleable Eric Slater china and pottery, along with a couple of Rackham illustrated books in excellent condition, for which Beatrice had a customer in mind.

Afterwards the two of them had lunch together in a pub. Over scampi and chips they fell to talking about Kate. Beatrice filled him in on Greg, the years in Paris, from her point of view. Duncan was fascinated. He had work to do and Beatrice had to get back to the shop. But they sat, cosily locked in conversation, by the log-look gas fire in the pub until the afternoon sky began to darken and close in.

'You take good care of her now –' as she left Beatrice rolled down the car window – 'or I'll come and duff you up.'

'I will if she lets me,' Duncan replied.

With Charlie, Duncan had a head start. Beatrice's partner had read his books for years and was a fan. Furthermore the two of them shared an enthusiasm for the works of Ed McBain and Elmore Leonard, and filled in the gaps in one another's collections.

Pascal and Duncan had acquaintances in common. A fellow writer Pascal had 'done' in his *Profiles* series. A couple of actors who'd appeared in a dramatization of one of Duncan's short stories some years ago. At that time he'd also encountered the legendary

Marya, so Duncan confided to Kate. She'd been visiting a friend on set and he'd been dazzled by her luminous beauty, but his hackles were raised by an air she gave off of hungry narcissism. He thought commonsense Stephanie the salt of the earth, but subscribed to the received wisdom that Pascal, in a self-preserving gut reflex, had lurched from one extreme to the other.

A couple of times Kate and Duncan, Pascal and Stephanie sent out for a Chinese takeaway and sat up late into the night, watching gems from Pascal's extensive video collection, in the handsome house in Lydon, where he still lived as if camping out.

Then, one Saturday afternoon in March, they stopped by at Pascal's before driving up to Norfolk. February had been grim, but suddenly spring was making itself felt. They stood out in the secluded garden with mugs of coffee. Kate marvelled at the softness of the air, the tender green of the furled leaves, the daffodils surrounding the stoic, lichen-encrusted nymph who stood guard in fair weather or foul.

'It always makes me think of a monastery garden,' she said. 'Even with this shameless hussy baring her all.'

'Make the most of it,' Pascal said. 'I'm selling up.'

'No!' Kate protested. She'd grown used to having him close by.

'Steph and I are moving in together. And London suits us better. Steph's pregnant.'

Pascal put his arm round Stephanie, and she let him, though she had an aversion to demonstrations of possessiveness. They stood side by side. Pascal with his high forehead and steel-rimmed spectacles, his pleasing Dr Zhivago gauntness. Stephanie in plaid shirt, jeans and Doc Martens, showing rabbitty teeth in a wide smile.

'That's wonderful! Congratulations!' Kate enthused. Though simultaneously it occurred to her that, until this very moment, Pascal had persistently, consistently denied the slightest whisper of commitment. She guessed that, in choosing Stephanie, he had deliberately compromised, opted for someone 'safe' who could neither move nor harm him in the way Marya had done.

'We're pleased as punch,' Pascal said.

'Apart from me throwing up morning and night.' It was in Stephanie's nature to mistrust jubilation. 'And the prospect of turning into a waddling melon.'

'You won't have any trouble selling this place,' Duncan claimed expansively. 'For two pins I'd buy it myself, for me and Kate.'

In the car later Kate objected mildly that he'd taken her name in vain. He admitted as much. He'd got carried away.

'But it's a nice fantasy,' Kate confessed.

'It doesn't have to be a fantasy. Not if we sold our own houses.'

She made no reply to that but, as they bowled along the increasingly familiar route between their respective homes, her mind began to play with the idea, imagining Duncan and herself as a couple. In a community. The notion seeming unfamiliar, exotic, and yet undeniably tempting.

Her thoughts ran ahead of her, conjuring up Pascal's house, assigning the rooms to their various purposes. There was plenty of space for all five of their children . . .

Here was a chance to recreate the richness of Plas Felix. Kate pictured family gatherings. Pascal, Stephanie and the child dropping in for the weekend. Nelly and Robert basing themselves in Lydon when they visited. Christmases when she would at last have room to entertain the Felix clan. Or Duncan's parents. Or Ellis and Fay, Rick, Justine . . . She would be surrounded then by layer on layer of belonging. Might finally, finally, satisfy a hunger that had been with her since childhood.

'D'you realize,' Duncan said, 'that you haven't said a word since we left Lydon?'

'I'm thinking. Imagining us getting old and grey together.'

'I thought we were old and grey.'

'You know,' Kate said, 'Jerome and Odile are dying to meet you again . . . Nelly's coming up in May. Perhaps we could all get together.'

An assenting grin. 'Why not?'

'I wonder what you'll make of the aged P's . . . They've become quite a double act.' She pictured them for a second, with a drift of affection. Then raised one hand to stroke the nape of Duncan's neck.

'I've been daydreaming,' she told him, 'about us living in Pascal's house. Married.'

He glanced at her with that steady, lingering look he had, and smiled. 'Sounds good to me.'

The words were spoken, almost casually, and in a split second her whole future shifted and became something quite different. Slightly dazed, Kate contemplated the delightful ease, the rightness of the decision they had made, while simultaneously admiring the fiery red sunset that spread wide over the flat blue fields alongside the road.

The May get-together never took place. Towards the end of April – as Kate listened to the first confused and tentative radio reports on what seemed to be a cataclysmic nuclear incident in the Ukraine – the telephone rang. It was Beatrice with the message that her father had collapsed and been taken to hospital. She was there with Odile, waiting.

Kate sat for a while, stunned, staring out at the warm spring rain – which seemed suddenly sinister and polluted – while at the back of her mind Jerome's foxy smile shimmered, disembodied, like the Cheshire cat's.

Later Beatrice phoned again to say that he had died. A massive stroke, she informed Kate. The conversation was terse and sober. An awareness that it was up to them to play the adult role. Odile was the child now, to be protected and supported.

Afterwards Kate crossed to her bookshelves and picked up a framed snap of Jerome in the sixties, smoking a cheroot in the sun on the terrace at Plas Felix, leaning back in his chair, crossed legs supported on a kitchen stool, his grin, the whole set of his body, expressing an easy satisfaction with life. For sure, Jerome had his faults, and plenty of them, but just looking at that photo made her smile.

Epilogue
May 1986

❂❂❂❂

Above them reared the barred and bolted façade of Plas Felix. Since Kate and Pascal had been here last year the security shutters had been reinforced and now access to the interior of the house was impossible. A whole jagged area to the right side of the roof had been stripped of tiles. Weathered timbers showed through like ribs. On the courtyard below grey-mauve shards of slate lay jumbled among the weeds. No one seemed to know what was going to happen to the place, though there were plenty of rumours. It was getting harder to remember the house as it used to be, just a place where people lived, worked and slept and ate, quarrelled and laughed. Ordinary. Magical.

Kate stood on the cracked terrace with Nelly, Beatrice and Pascal. A fresh, blue, blustery day after a week of rain. Way below them the cold-looking sea tossed with small, foamy waves. In one hand Nelly gripped the plastic container that held Jerome's ashes.

'Make sure you stand upwind,' Beatrice cautioned.

'Gosh,' Nelly mocked. 'I never would have thought of that.'

Taking the top off the cylinder, she shook some of the ashes free. They soared and drifted across the terrace to the field beyond. Pascal moved hastily out of range. Nelly passed the container to Beatrice who sent more of the grey dust swirling dreamily against the fragile blue of the sky. Kate went next, then Pascal.

'It's still half-full.' He shook the container more vigorously and the ashes lurched out, dropping in clumps at their feet before the wind stirred them up into small eddies, like smoke, and carried them away.

'Goodbye, Pa,' Nelly said as the ashes thinned out and dispersed.

552

Beatrice and Pascal stood dry-eyed and silent, but there were tears on Nelly's cheeks.

Kate stared as the last of the dust hung in the air. A sort of horror at the thought that Jerome's irreverent spirit, his cheery egoism could be reduced like this to nothingness. She shivered and, at that moment, could not deny the infantile sense of being abandoned in a world made a little colder by his loss.